The
Isles of Penicia©

Copyright 1999 & 2010
Rev: 2011-15H

By: Jim Keely

Thanks To: The best Lady in the World, my Wife. Thank you for all your support,
understanding and ongoing prayers while I finished this book.

In Loving Memory: Those loved ones we lost in 2008 - 2009:
Geraldine
Joan
Judy
Bill
May they find peace in the arms of Jesus.

AuthorHouse™
1663 Liberty Drive
Bloomington, IN 47403
www.authorhouse.com
Phone: 1-800-839-8640

First published by AuthorHouse 8/2/2011

ISBN: 978-1-4520-9746-6 (e)
ISBN: 978-1-4520-9745-9 (sc)

Library of Congress Control Number: 2011900148

Printed in the United States of America

This book is printed on acid-free paper.

Certain stock imagery © Thinkstock.

authorHOUSE®

TABLE OF CONTENTS

INTRODUCTION

This will explain the aspects of a Role-Playing Game (or RPG) and give you a brief background of the imaginary world you are about to enter.

The particulars we will discuss are:
1) What is a Role-Playing Game?
2) Who "runs" the game and who plays?
3) How to play a Role-Playing Game?
4) What materials are needed to play?
5) Suggestions for making the game better.
6) A brief background of the "world".

1)   What is a Role-Playing Game?

Whenever I introduce this game to a group of my friends, they say, "Ok, break out the board." I then have to expand their minds and explain that a Role-Playing game is not bound by a static board. I continue to explain that the game is held within the arena of their imagination!! The game is like an imaginary movie playing in your head; only you get to participate as one of the characters instead of just watching.

2)   Who "runs" the game and who plays?

One of the first things you will do as a new group of players is to pick a referee {Ref}, so next let's describe the difference between the players and the Ref.

The participants in a Role-Playing Game [the players] initially need to generate their "characters." A player uses his or her character to interact with the imaginary world they will soon be entering.

The players will start to "generate" their characters on character sheets (See Appendix B). The character sheet will COMPLETELY describe your character and will include a name, occupation and all ability scores for him or her. As you progress in the game your character will gain experience, levels and abilities.

The Referee {Ref.} is the person who describes in detail the surroundings and encounters that your characters will be involved in. As a situation unfurls, it will be the characters who will make decisions and choose the situation's outcome. The characters will grow, live or die by their decisions. A character may live a long eventful life, or a short one; but either way, all action and intrigue will occur within your limitless imagination.

The Ref. is the director of the game. He will have the final say in all situations and will even rule if what you attempt to do is possible, but all outcomes should be determined by a <u>random roll!</u> The Ref. should be impartial – it is very frustrating, if the Ref. happens to be in a bad mood, so he kills the entire party (or group of companions).

I consider it a personal challenge, when I Ref., to bring an individual character or the entire party to the extent of their abilities – **WITHOUT** eliminating them. You must understand that if a character makes a huge mistake, that character may die – but the Ref. should not put the party in a situation that cannot be resolved. The Ref. is responsible for challenging the party at their current level of experience. What I mean is, if the characters in the party are all around first level (this is the lowest level), the Ref. better not challenge the party with a Vampire or a Troll, unless he expects the companions to flee for their lives.

3)   How to play a Role-Playing Game?

First, you must pick a Ref. The Ref is the person who sets up the situations and surroundings of where the players are located. The Ref. will lead the game, basically telling a story and giving the players certain options and alternatives. The players will consider all their options in light of their current situation and surroundings and then make their choices accordingly. The game will proceed and the present will be laid to the past. This may not seem eventful at first, but as you play, you will be required to roll dice to find the outcome of most situations. The random outcome of the roll can greatly effect the current situation, as you soon will learn. As your story continues, your characters will gain experience, levels and abilities.

4)   What materials are needed to play?

        In order to play, you will need the following basic items:
                a) paper   b) pencil   c) dice or a random number generator

        You will find there are many situations that will require you to generate a random number. The most common method is to roll dice.
        A Role-Playing Game usually uses many unusual types of dice. These dice are distinguished by the number of sides they have. The dice that are required are:
                a) 4 – sided   b) 6 – sided   c) 8 – sided   d) 10 – sided   e) 12 – sided   f) 20 – sided
        You will need at least one of each, but I suggest you get *at least* two 10 – sided die. This may sound like a lot, but dice tubes are sold in many locations where Role-Playing Games (RPG's) are sold and they have the minimum number of dice needed to play the game. (a dice tube has two 10 sided die and one of each of the others.)

        You may be asking yourself, "If I don't have any of these weird dice, can I still play the game?" Don't fret, worthy reader – any time I refer to 'rolling dice', you only have to generate a random number.

        Some other ways to generate a random number are:
(a) Use a Random Number Generator set to the correct number of sides the die has.
(b) Numbers in a grab bag.
(c) Download a Free App for your Smartphone.
(d) The Ref. can make a random decision.

Percentages:
    Regardless of the method used to acquire them, percentages are used to determine success or failure of an action that a character is attempting to accomplish. You will need to roll a percentage which is **lower** than or equal to some stated value in order to accomplish the task in question. The lower the roll, the better you've accomplished the task. The maximum percentage is 100% (a roll of '0' on both 10 – sided dice **[00]**). This percentage is considered as a **complete** success – you couldn't have done any better. This leaves us with 99% which is always a complete failure. Here are some examples of using Dice to generate a Percentage:

Roll: one 10 – sided die twice: The first number rolled is considered in the 10's place and the second number rolled is in the one's place. If the first roll = 4 and second roll = 2, then the percentage is 42%.

With two ten sided die, each die must be a different color or one die must have the ten's place clearly marked on it. If different colors, you must call which is 'high' or which one will equal the ten's place.
I.e. – Darla rolls a purple ten sided die and an orange ten sided die. She calls purple as "high" and when the
        dice stop rolling there is an eight on the purple die and a five on the orange die, so the percentage
        would read – 85%.

5)   Suggestions for making the game better:

        When I first decided to write this section, I thought I could do it in just three words: IMAGINATION, IMAGINATION, IMAGINATION!!!! Actually, this is inadequate, because as the game progresses, it will become more complex.

    There are aids that can help you:
a)   Maps and Pictures – The Ref. Should make up - either before the game or on the fly - maps, sketches, pictures, etc. to give the players a sense of where they are and where they are going. If you mark your map off with grids or draw your map on graph paper, you will be able to keep track of the movement of the players easily. There is a section called Traveling Rates that explains this.

b)   Figures and Place holders – There are many places where you can buy small lead figurines which can be painted to represent a particular character. These are very useful in some situations. They can be used to show the parties marching order (the order in which the characters are assembled while they explore new areas), the location of characters in a room or the placement of characters as they sleep, etc.

Unfortunately, these figurines are usually too large to be used on a piece of graph paper, so this is where you can utilize place holders to help you keep track of everyone or you may use specialized gaming pads with large squares on them.

NOTE: The Ref. will also find it helpful to use figurines and / or place holders to indicate unfriendliness.

6)   A Brief background on the "World":

You will be entering a highly enchanted world where only your imagination is the limit. The rules and guidelines are provided for your convenience; it's understood by this writer that you may need to enhance and / or modify some of them to fit your personal campaign.

This world's name is Penicia and it has three different playable Races: Humans, Krill and Hemar. These races have known about each other and have gotten along with each other for about 200 years. The races are located on 3 continents or isles, one primary race per continent. Friendship and trade agreements allow free travel of anyone of any race to any continent. There is a map of the three continents provided in Appendix D. Anyone from any race may live, work or own land on any of the three isles.

Summary

In conclusion, I have briefly explained about a Role-Playing Game and about the "world" you are soon to enter.   Some things to keep in mind are:

1) A Role-Playing Game is not limited to a board. Your Imagination is the boundless amphitheater in which the game will unfurl.
2) The flow of the game is controlled by the Ref., but the Players make decisions concerning their particular characters. Remember the game is bombarded with Randomness - this is what gives it a splash of excitement.
3) The Ref. runs the game, but is more or less impartial to the goings on. The Players control their own characters and work together to accomplish the adventures and story lines set down by the Ref.
4) The materials needed to undertake a Role-Playing Game are simple and mostly common. Please remember how to make a Percentage Roll.
5) Use your Imagination and common aids to help you visualize what is happening to your character. Always keep an eye open in all directions and focus on what is transpiring around your character.
6) Have fun with this world. It's set here to grow with your characters and your campaigns.

I hope you have as much fun discovering Penicia as I had creating it !!!!!!!!!!!!!!!!!!!!!
****

NOTE

Dice Notation: **10   +   2   d   12**
                          (a)   (b)   (c)

(a)   Sometimes a **base number** is used with a dice roll.   The **base number** is **added** to the roll.
(b)   This number represents the number of dice rolled.   i.e.:   2 dice are rolled.
(c)   This is the number of Sides the rolled die has.   i.e.:   12 – sided die used.

The notation is read just like it is shown: "Ten plus   Two 'D' Twelve."

The notation means to roll two 12 – sided dice and add 10 to the outcome of the roll.   This combination may yield a number between 12 & 34.

ABILITIES

There are certain criteria used to describe your character. I prefer to refer to these basic criteria as abilities. Each ability is given a number from 1 to 20. This number is referred to as your ability score. A high ability score will give your character bonuses to certain activities and a low ability score may prevent your character from learning certain skills or doing certain things.

Step #1)   Write the abilities on a sheet of paper in the order listed below or use a character sheet provided in Appendix B.
You need to randomly generate the first 5 abilities and the last one, WILL, is determined differently.

Step #2)   Use one of the methods listed below to generate each of your character's ability scores:

Method #1) Roll one 20-sided die three times and record the highest number you rolled under your character's Endurance ability. Repeat this for the next four abilities.

Method #2) Roll a 20-sided die 6 times and then place the highest 5 scores, one at a time, under each ability until all of your character's ability scores are filled.

Method #3) Instead of rolling dice you may also use a total of 75 points to distribute among the first 5 abilities, your Will score is determined another way. Every ability must have a final score between a minimum of 3 and a maximum of 20.

NOTE: All high scores to start with are very unrealistic, besides you can always Increase an Ability Score by learning a Survival Skill – worthy reader, please continue assimilating or go to page 126.

Once you have recorded all ability scores, you can record any special bonuses or restrictions the ability score gives you. You don't have to do this, because these are included in this book for reference. The ability scores that you must generate for your character are:

Endurance
Agility
Strength
Intellect
Wisdom
Will

The ability of **Will** is calculated from different aspects of your character. It is a composite of your character's level and certain other ability scores.

The ability scores numerically describe your character and his or her abilities. Below is a description of each ability and the bonuses or restrictions that each score provides your character.

ENDURANCE

END Score - is the measure of your ability to "last" in any activity or to resist pain. Your Endurance score directly pertains to how many **starting** Endurance Points (EP) your character rates. You multiply your Endurance Score by 2 and add your Occupation's bonus to find your initial Endurance Point total.
Every time your character gains a new level, you roll a specified die and add the number rolled to your EP total. (This die roll is your "Occupation's bonus" mentioned in the previous sentence).

i.e.   A Warrior will have this many Endurance Points: (End Score x 2 + 1d8/Level).
He will add a 1d8 roll to his total EP every time he achieves a new level.

Spies/Assassins and Ninja gain 1d6 points per level, so their EP total = End Score*2 + 1d6/Level.

Enchanters, Alchemists, Elementalists, and Mentalists gain 1d4 points per level,
so their EP total = End Score x 2 + 1d4/Level.

Additional information relating to Endurance Points (EP):

NOTE: You lose EP as you get wounded. As you rest or if you are Magically Healed, you gain them back, but you may never exceed your total maximum EP.
One Full Night of resting (equal to 8 hours) allows your body to heal 1d10 EP.

NOTE2: If you fall to zero Endurance Points, your character will lose consciousness, unless you make an Ability Check with Will score, to remain Conscious (an Ability Check is a percentage, it is equal to your Will score x 3; please read on for more details). If you remain Conscious and your wounds permit, you may still use Trigger Words, Potions, Pills, etc; but you can't concentrate well enough to cast a spell, to strike with a weapon or use an Occupational Ability. Your character will only survive, until he falls to a negative number of Endurance Points equal to his Endurance Score.

(ie. If your End Score = 14 and you fail your Ability Check with Will (which would be a 42% [14*3]), you will remain unconscious – but alive – until you reach a -14 EP total through loss of blood due to your wounds!! The Ref. will determine how quickly you lose these points by the severity of your wounds.)

NOTE3: If you are Magically Healed, all unobstructed open wounds are closed and sealed.

NOTE4: You must also spend some of these precious Endurance Points (EP) in order to cast a spell.
Spend = 1 EP per 10 Spell Points used for casting a spell.
-- See Enchanters Section for Complete Details.

AGILITY

AGL Score - is the ease or quickness of movement. The Agility Score gives your character a bonus to your Percentage to Evade (PTE) a physical attack from an opponent. To find the percentage your Agility Score adds to your PTE, divide your Agility Score by 2 and round up. i.e.: if you have an Agility Score of 15, you get a +8% bonus to your PTE. You may have a maximum of +10%, if you have an astounding Agility Score of 19 or 20.

STRENGTH

STR Score - is the measure of your physical brawn, durability, toughness and relates to how much you can lift with your legs or arms - also most weapons have a minimum Strength score necessary to use them. If your STR Score is high enough, you get a STR bonus to the amount of damage you do with a Melee Weapon or with a punch or kick. The last thing your STR Score will tell you is the percentage you have to break a 2" piece of oak or to bend a 1" rod of iron.

To break a Piece of Oak, you must make a successful Ability Check with Strength. (Ability Checks are discussed in detail in the Survival Skill section.) To Bend a 1" rod of Iron, your percentage equals ½ of your Ability Check with Strength. The table below summarizes these values:

Strength Score	Damage Bonus	Bench Press (LBS)	Leg Press (LBS)
1	-4	-50	-10*
2-4	-3	-25	BW
5-7	-2	-10	+10
8-9	-1	BW	+25
10-12	0	+25	+50
13-14	+1	+50	+100
15-16	+2	+100	+200
17-18	+3	+150	+300
19-20	+4	+200	+400

BW - Body Weight - This is the full body weight of your character - either Human, Krill, or Hemar.
The asterisk (*) signifies that the character is not strong enough to walk.

NOTE5: A Hemar always receives a +1 to the Damage Bonus listed if they are using a Melee weapon.
Their bonuses go from -3 to +5 !

INTELLECT

__INT__ Score - is the ability to reason, understand and learn. Your INT Score represents how many languages you can speak, read or write (S/R/W). It also describes other skills your character is able to learn, depending on your occupation.

If you are an Enchanter, Elementalist or Alchemist, it represents how many spells you may learn at each level and reflects the total spell points you rate per level. You gain more Spell Points as your Level increases.

If you are a Warrior, Spy/Assassin or Mentalist, it will tell __if__ you are able to cast spells, how many __TOTAL__ spells you may learn and reflects the total Spell Points you rate. You pick these Class (A) spells from the Enchanter / Alchemist spell list.

(At first level a Warrior, Spy/Assassin or Mentalist learns ½ the number of spells stated below and learns the other ½ while training for second level.)

Score	Language	Spells		Spy / Assassin	
				Formal training	Informal training
1	Can't learn to speak				
2					
3	Speak National (Nat'l)				
4	Language			1/L	1/L
5					
6	Speak / Read & Write				
7	Nat'l Lang. and				
8	Speak the				
9	Traders Language	I	II		
10					
11	Speak / Read & Write	A	1		
12	1) National Language	B	2		
13	2) Traders Lang.		3	2/L	2/L
14		C	4		
15	Speak / Read & Write		5		
16	1) National Language	D	6		
17	2) Traders Lang. and		7		
18	3) ONE extra Lang.	E	8	3/L	2/L
19			9		
20	Speak / Read & Write		10		
	1) National Language				
	2) Traders Lang.				
	3) TWO extra. Lang.				
Score	Language	Spells		Spy / Assassin	
				Number of "Slots" rated per level	

__I__ = This is the minimum INT required to cast spells with a classification of (A), (B), (C), (D) or (E).
   __NOTE:__ You must have at least an INT Score of 11 to learn or cast any spell.
__II__ = This is the number of spells you can learn at __each__ level if you are an Enchanter, Elementalist, or Alchemist. If you are a Warrior, Spy/Assassin or Mentalist this is the maximum number of class (A) spells you may learn.

__NOTE2:__ Your character's national language is the language that your race speaks.
__NOTE3:__ The Trader's language is primarily used for trade and communication between the races.
   The Trader's language is not as descriptive or complete as a Race's National Language.

Enchanter, Alchemist or Elementalist

(Please don't let these equations bum you out, 'cause there is a complete table of these values in Appendix M)

SPELL POINTS (SP)   **= INT Score**   **+ { (INTellect Score / 2) * (Level-1)} = Spell Points**

At 1st Level,	INT = 18:	18	+ {	(18 / 2)	*	(1-1) } = **18 SP.**
At 5th Level,	INT = 19:	19	+ {	(19 / 2)	*	(5-1) } = **57 SP.**
At 11th Level,	INT = 17:	17	+ {	(17 / 2)	*	(11-1) } = **102 SP.**

NOTE: If you're an Enchanter, Alchemist or Elementalist, and if you're Intellect Score increases, the number of spell slots you rate may increase.

(i.e. if your Intellect score increases do to an increase from a Survival Skill Slot, ect., you must re-figure your SP score and the number of spells you may learn.

Example: If your Intellect Score rises from 16 to 17 at 5th level, you rate :

3 additional Spell Points   and

5 more spell slots   )

Hint: It's always a good idea to walk around with an empty spell slot or two; there may be a new spell somewhere to copy down, or you may want to create a new one yourself.

Regeneration of Spell Points: Everyone gains back 1 SP per 1 Attack (5 seconds) when activated. This can be done ONCE per day per every 2 levels of the character.
(i.e.: 1st-2nd Level=1/day; 3rd-4th Level=2/day; 5th-6th Level=3/day; 7th-8th =4/day; 9th-10th =5/day; 17-18th=9/day)

Warrior, Spy, Assassin or Mentalist

Spell Points = Intellect Score + 1 spell point per level

NOTE2: If a Warrior, Spy/Assassin or Mentalist's INT Score increases, then he rates **ONE** extra Class (A) spell per additional point. Even though the total spell points score rises as you advances in level (+1 SP per level), you may only learn Class (A) spells from the Ench./Al. spell list.

NOTE3: In order for anyone to learn a new spell, your character must have more Total Spell Points then the number stated under the Spell's Point Cost (SPC) for the spell in question.

WISDOM

<u>WIS</u> Score - is the quality of having or showing good judgment or shrewdness.
Your Wisdom Score has three main purposes :
1) It may give you a bonus to your Detect Ambush total percentage.
2) You may add ½ of your WIS score to your Resist Enchantment Roll (RER) verses any type of Illusion.

Score	Detect Ambush Bonus	Wisdom Bonus vs. Illusions
1 - 2	- 5%	1%
3 - 5	- 3%	2 - 3%
6 - 14	0	3 - 7%
15 - 18	+3%	8 - 9%
19 - 20	+5%	10%

3) If you are a Ninja, it will determine the amount of KI Points you rate per level.

Ninja

(There is a complete table of these values in Appendix M)

KI POINTS [KP]	**= WIS Score**	**+ [(WIS / 4)**	*** (L - 1)]**	**(round up)**
At 1st level, WIS=16 :	16	+ [(16/4)	* (1-1)]	= **16 K.P.**
At 5th level, WIS=18 :	18	+ [(18/4)	* (5-1)]	= **36 K.P.**

Regeneration of Ki Points: This can be done ONCE per day per every 2 levels of the character when activated. The Ninja gains back 1 KP per 1 Attack (5 seconds).
(i.e.: 1st-2nd Level = 1/day; 5th-6th Level = 3/day; 9th-10th Level = 5/day)

WILL

WILL Score - is the power of making a choice or of controlling one's own actions. This is the only Ability that is not determined randomly. Your Will score is a combination of Intellect, Wisdom, and that which is purely you. To attain your Will Score, simply add up all of the bonuses you rate stated on the table below.

    The Will Score is used to modify your RER verses certain Enchantments or Spells and it is used to determine success when you use certain Survival Skills. I also use this Ability Check percentage to see if the character can stay conscious while close to death (see End Score for details) – it can be used in many other ways also.

Level	Bonus	Ability Score	Intellect Bonus	Wisdom Bonus	Endurance Bonus
1st - 4th	+ 4	1 – 6	+ 0	+ 0	+ 0
5th - 9th	+ 6	7 – 11	+ 1	+ 1	+ 0
10th - 14th	+ 8	12 – 15	+ 2	+ 2	+ 1
15th on up	+ 10	16 – 18	+ 3	+ 3	+ 1
		19 – 20	+ 4	+ 4	+ 2

Example :

Character's Stats	:	Intellect Score	+	Wisdom Score	+	Endurance Score	+	LEVEL
	:	15		16		17		1st
Bonuses	:	2	+	3	+	1	+	4

WILL SCORE = (2 + 3 + 1 + 4) = 10

Mentalist

Mental Point total = { (Will score / 2) * Level }.
(There is a complete table of these values in Appendix M)

Regeneration of Mental Points: This can be done ONCE per day per every 2 levels when activated. Mentalists gain back 1 MP per 1 Attack (5 seconds).
(i.e.: 1st-2nd Level = 1/day; 5th-6th Level = 3/day; 9th-10th Level = 5/day)

CHARM

CHA Score - is the quality that attracts or delights. I believe that this skill, like beauty, does not need to be rolled. This is where you bring the personality of the character into play.

    You may want your character to be charming and in charge of all situations - a natural leader. Or, you may see her as being cautious and shy. Either way, I feel all characters change and grow through the experiences of life. If you have a set score, your character's personality cannot change much. Your Ref will make his or her own decision. You can roll it if you want.

BEAUTY

BTY Score - I think there is no reason to roll this ability either. I believe you should be able to decide exactly what your character will look like, but this will be up to your Ref.

    You may want your female human character to have beautiful long flowing red hair, green eyes and weigh 107 lbs, or you may picture your male human character to have short brown hair, hazel eyes and a scar on his left shoulder.

RACES

There are 3 types of playable races residing upon Penicia.   These races are:
1) Humans   2) Hemar   and   3) Krill. Anyone from any race may learn any Occupation, as long as they are able to find a Teacher to instruct them. Each race initially gains a bonus to a certain Ability Score, i.e. most Hemar gain both a +1 to their STR Score and a +1 to all melee damage they do.   Humans gain +1 to their initial Intellect score and Krill gain +1 to their initial Agility score.

The Humans govern the center continent, which is primarily made up of planes, forests and deserts. The Krill Race governs the mountainous northern continent where common plants grow to huge size. The Hemar race governs the southern continent, which is the location of a great jungle.

Unrestricted travel and friendship has abounded between the Races for many years now. This is primarily due to the game known as IronBall. This game was wisely constructed so that a team made up of 1 Human, 2 Hemars, and 2 Krill are virtually undefeatable when faced by a team made up of all one race. The IronBall game is explained in full after the Combat Section.

Basic's that are True for all Races:

Falling: Any Falling character will take 1 point of damage for every foot they plunge. This height must be greater than 10' and for any height greater then 50' the character may make an Ability Check with Agility to take ½ Damage.

Fist Damage: All damage done by someone's fist is equal to : 1d6 Endurance Points (EP) damage + your Strength damage bonus regardless of race or sex.

Maximum Time a Character may Engage in Consecutive Melee Combat: 30 seconds per End point.
   Example 1: End Score=20 **SO** 600 seconds **OR** 10 minutes.
   Example 2: End Score=15 **SO** 450 seconds **OR** 7.5 minutes.

Maximum Time a Character may stay awake while standing a post: Characters that are trying to stay awake and are sitting, standing or lying in the same place must make an Ability Check with Endurance at midnight and another check every hour after that at a -5% until after the Column Sun dawns. The dawning of the Column Sun occurs at 6am during the Summer, at 7am during the Spring and Fall and at 8am during the Winter.
   Example 1: End Score=20 **SO** 60% @ 12pm, 55% @ 1am, 50% @ 2am, 45% @ 3am, …ect to stay awake.
   Example 2: End Score=15 **SO** 45% @ 12pm, 40% @ 1am, 35% @ 2am, 30% @ 3am, …ect to stay awake.

Characters Regain All of their Spell, Ki or Mental points after the Rising of the Column Sun each day:
   The dawning of the Column Sun occurs at 6am during the Summer, at 7am during the Spring and Fall and at 8am during the Winter. A character's Elevation or Depth Underground or Under the Sea does NOT inhibit the rehabilitating effects of the Column Sun.
Note: All Characters may regenerate their particular Points at a rate of **1** point per 1 Attack (5 seconds).
   This can be done ONCE per day per every 2 levels of the character.
   (i.e.: 1st-2nd Level = 1/day; 3rd-4th Level = 2/day;   5th-6th Level = 3/day;   17th-18th Level = 9/day)

Holding your Breath: (End Score + Will Score + 1d10) * 5 = (Total number of Seconds) **OR**
                                                             (Total Seconds/60) Minutes.
   Example 1: End+Will+10= 50: **so** 250 sec **OR** 4.16 min **OR** approximately 4 min and 10 seconds.
   Example 2: End+Will+1 = 41: **so** 205 sec **OR** 3.41 min **OR** approximately 3 min and 25 seconds.
   Example 3: End+Will+5 = 35: **so** 175 sec **OR** 2.92 min **OR** approximately 2 min and 55 seconds.

Realize that your Pocket is being Picked: Regular Characters have a percentage equal to 2% per level to realize they are having their pocket picked.

Escape from Ropes or Chains: Regular Characters get a percentage chance equal to their Intellect Score to escape from Ropes and a percentage chance equal to ½ their Intellect Score to escape from Chains; that's a 1% - 10% chance (HA, HA, Good Luck).

Total Darkness or Deep Shadows: While anyone is encased in total darkness they gain a +40% to their PTE total and while anyone is shrouded in deep shadows they gain a +30% to their PTE total.

HUMAN, MALE, YELLOW

HEMAR, MALE, MUSTANG

KRILL, MALE, EAGLE

HUMAN

Description: As you can guess, Humans are bipedal beings with two arms and a head. They may vary in skin color from white to brown (including reddish, yellowish and tan). There are even rumors of humans with unique skin colorings such as bluish or green.

Bonuses	:	All Humans gain a +1 to their initial Intellect Ability Score.		
		Speak +1 additional Racial Language.		

Age	: Morning = 1 - 20 yrs.	Noon = 21 - 130 yrs.	Night = 130 - 150 yrs.
Height	: Female = 5.0 - 6.5 ft.	Male = 6.0 - 8.0 ft.	
Weight	: Female = 90 - 180 lbs.	Male = 150 - 350 lbs.	
Standing Leap	: 15 ft.		
Running Leap	: 30 ft.		
Charging Rates	: Minimum = 15 ft/sec; Maximum = 30 ft/sec	CRM: Min = 3; Max = 6.	
Types	: Skin colors are Red, Yellow, Brown, Blue, Green and White.		

Real Life: Humans are ruled by a Government that they elect. This Government presides over a collection of City States that reside on the Human Isle. These City States are governed by elected councils that manage the affairs of their areas and relay pertinent information back to the ruling Government council. The elections for Government and City State councils are held every ten years and anyone that can read and is at least 20 years old can vote or become a candidate. Elected officials are expected to reside within the jurisdiction they're elected to.

Continent Description: Most of the continent is comprised of planes and wooded areas, but also has the largest known desert. This Great Desert is located in the center of the continent on a plateau. There is also a large undersea ridge that surrounds the entire continent. This undersea ridge holds a very diverse array of sea life and is probably the best fishing in the world.

Legends: The oldest Human Legend is that of the formation of the Great Desert. The story tellers say that the Dragons, which are fabled to guard and protect the world of Penicia, knocked invaders from the sky and the tremendous impact and resulting explosion desolated the plateau located in the center of the continent. It is also told that the Dragons created the undersea ridge that surrounds the central continent as compensation. But no one, thus far, has ever spoken to one of these colossal beasts and lived to tell the tale.

HEMAR

Description: The beings of this race have the torso (on up) of a Human; this includes stomach, chest, shoulders, arms, neck and head - but have the Body and FOUR legs of a Horse. They are very strong and may gallop for half a day and not feel winded. In addition to their fists, they can kick with their back legs or buck at an opponent (they must be facing away from their target) and they do 1d20 EP damage plus their Strength damage Bonus to their victim - they may only use their buck once every Attack. All Hemar are able to climb stairs and mountainous terrain with ease.

Bonuses   :   +1 on initial Strength Ability Score.   (Shetlands = +1 Wisdom, not Strength)
                               +1 to all melee Damage rolls.
                               Speak with particular Horse type at will.

Age	: Morning = 1 - 40 yrs. Noon = 41 - 160 yrs. Night = 160 - 200 yrs.
Height	: Female = 6.0 - 8.0 ft. Male = 7.5 - 9.0 ft.
Weight	: Female = 800 - 1500 lbs. Male = 1100 - 1700 lbs.
Standing Leap	: 25 ft.
Running Leap	: 45 ft.
Charging Rates	: Minimum = 20 ft/sec; Maximum = 35 ft/sec CRM: Min = 4; Max = 7.
Types	: Clydesdale, Mustang, Appaloosa and Shetland.

Real Life: Hemars tend to be very civilized and well mannered - no prob. hang'en at court. They all sit at tables to eat or study and they sleep lying down. The Hemar race is governed by a council of three, which any Hemar may rise to. The three council members hold the titles: Chief of Strength, Chief of Wisdom, and Chief of Cunning. The council members **WIN** their respective positions at a Tourney held once every 50 years. Hemars also love to travel and are the greatest ship builders known.

Shetlands are "wee" Hemars. They are between 3 - 4 foot tall and weigh between 250 - 500 lbs. They have made their home in the trees of the vast jungles that thrive on the southern continent. Shetlands are granted respect because a Shetland has held the Title: Chief of Cunning for 8 consecutive generations. Also, instead of +1 Strength they receive a +1 to their initial Wisdom Score.

Currently : the Chief of Strength is Charger ThunderHoof, the Chief of Wisdom is Blossom BrightEye, and the Chief of Cunning is Razz LimbJumper.

Continent Description: The southern continent has two major terrain features. The vast bay, which is located in the northern center of the Isle, is known as EverDeep Bay. The other notable feature is a deep jungle that covers most of the rest of the continent. Hemars use the great trees that grow in their jungle to fashion ships. There are numerous shipyards located along the shores of EverDeep Bay.

Legends: The most mysterious legend among Hemars is the tale of Horis the Seer who was a renowned Seer and Sailor. His predictions always came true from warnings of the Great Tsunami of 320 to the time when then Chief of Strength: Mantle's hair turned purple. Horis had a recurring dream of a humongous continent so far away that it could not be reached by any Hemar ship. The dream went on to show a terrible menace allying themselves with the Goblins and planning an invasion that will attack all three of the races.

Another legend is considered to be fact by at least 25% of all Hemars. Many peoples Grandfathers or Aunts claim to have actually spied the Beast of EverDeep. This Beast is said to be 700 feet long from it's lizard type snout to the tip of it's tail. It is a grayish color, has a long neck, a huge body with four feet shaped like flippers and an immense tail. The last time it was reported was 10 years ago in almost the exact center of EverDeep Bay.

NOTE: If a Hemar is consistently walking over cobblestone, rocks or brick streets, he should probably protect
         his hooves by getting some horseshoes put on him. This is painless and is done much the
         same way for Hemar's as for horses. Shetlands do hate to wear horseshoes however,
         because when worn, horseshoes give the wearer a -10% to all climbing checks.

KRILL

Description: Krill are slightly shorter and slimmer than humans, but have functional wings on their backs. Their wings are completely independent of their arms and can be moved with the same precision of any appendage. With a head wind, they can glide or hover for virtually an unlimited amount of time; if they are unencumbered and uninjured.

Bonuses : +1 on initial Agility Ability Score.
+25% on PTE total while flying or gliding - not hovering. ***
Speak with particular Bird type at will.

Age	: Morning = 1-10 yrs.	Noon = 11-110 yrs.	Night = 111 - 130 yrs.
Height	: Female = 4.5 - 6.0 ft.	Male = 5.5 - 7.0 ft.	
Weight	: Female = 70 - 140 lbs.	Male = 140 - 200 lbs.	
Standing Leap	: 10 ft.		
Running Leap	: 15 ft.		
Charging Rates **	: Minimum = 20 ft/sec; Maximum = 35 ft/sec	CRM: Min = 4; Max = 7.	
Types	: Eagle, Vulture, Owl, and Hawk.		

Real Life: Krill are ruled by a King and Queen of the Eagle type. The StormWing family, has ruled their race for as long as any of their kind can remember. Their society is run in a loose feudal system. Those of the Eagle type are usually Leaders and Artists, the Hawk type are Fighters and Scouts, The Owl type are Guardsmen and Messengers. The Vulture type is primarily made up of problem solvers and eliminators. This is not to say that anyone of any type may not aspire to any occupation, but these seem to suit the types of Krill which have long ago excelled in them. Krill are expert in the use of a Wrist Crossbow (or WristBow) and when they use this weapon they receive a -10% on their SPT roll. Their mortal enemies are giant mutant bats who inhabit caves on lower elevations of the mountains on their Island. They have great respect for the Giants that dwell on their Isle whose average height is about 300' tall. Currently Queen Aurora and King Stratus StormWing rule the kingdom of the Krill.

Continent Description: This continent is comprised of enormous mountains. The Krill historically made their homes on the upper regions of these mountains but have recently needed to protect the coves and trails to promote trade. Most of the plants when located on the Krill Isle are of a gigantic size, which is strange because when these same plants are located on either of the other continents, they only grow to "normal" size. The Krill have always known of and defended themselves from the gargantuan Giants that inhabit their continent. When of a mature age, these horrendous creatures range from 300 to 350 feet in height. The Giants have always been hostile to all other races even when peace, trade or negotiating parties have been dispatched to speak with them. Thankfully these great foes are not very intelligent, numerous or located on any other continent.

Legends: The Krill have many legends but none are more known then the story of how the giant mutant bats became their mortal enemies. One afternoon the eldest daughter of King Apex StormWing, Princess Arial, was exploring some mountain caves with her entourage. The party was ambushed by a horde of giant mutant bats. The bats overwhelmed the princess's guards and caused the cave entrance to collapse. That night a ransom note arrived with proof of the capture: the princess's signet ring and her severed finger. These mysteriously appeared in the King's chambers. Everyone was amazed by this cruelty and that the mutant bats had acquired the ability to read and write the Krill Language. The ransom demands where meet and delivered to the specified place, but the princess was never returned. The entire Krill race went to war at this insult. Although many bat caves were discovered and cleansed, the princess was never found. The closest a raiding party ever came was after long months of searching and combat. This raiding party had gone deeper into the cavernous mountains then any before. They caught a glimpse of some retreating bats carrying a statue that resembled their princess. Unfortunately these warriors were ambushed and the encumbered bats escaped. At the end of that terrible year, King Apex declared the mutant bats to be the mortal enemy of the Krill race. This ghastly event occurred over 300 years ago.

Note: ** A Krill's Maximum CRM while on the ground is 3 or a Charging Rate of 15 ft/sec.
Note2: *** Krill only receive their +25% PTE Flying Bonus if they are flying for more than 1 Attack. This means they do not get the bonus on take-off or landing.

OCCUPATIONS

WARRIOR

INTRODUCTION

A Warrior is a "person-at-arms", solder, fighter, guard, etc. All Warriors are taught to use melee and projectile weapons to their fullest extent. They are also able to specialize in the use of weapons sooner then anyone else.

INFORMATION & FACTS

A Warrior is taught a new Combat Skill every level. Low level Warriors are taught basic skills, but during higher levels, the warrior has a choice between several skills. You will notice there are more skills than there are levels available to learn them, so ever Warrior will be unique. The Warrior skills you choose are the ones you will have to live and die with, so choose wisely.

If a Warrior, Spy/Assassin (S/A) or Mentalist has an Intellect score of 11 or higher they may learn how to cast some minor magic spells! You must give up learning, at the start of the game, either 2 Survival Skills or 1 weapon in order to learn spells. They may learn a **total number of spells** equal to what is listed next to their Intellect score on the Intellect table. The spells you may learn are those spells listed on the Enchanter / Alchemist spell list and have a Classification of (A). You will learn 1/2 of the number of spells stated on the Intellect table before 1st level and you will learn the rest while you are training for 2nd level.
(ex. Roge has an Int score of 16 and he gave up (didn't learn) 1 of his weapons.
    Now he rates 6 Class (A) spells. He will learn 3 before 1st level and the last 3 when he is training for 2nd level.)

NOTE: Spell Point (SP) totals for Warriors, S/A and Mentalists = Intellect score + 1 spell point per character's level.

This table describes how many Actions per Attack (5 second period) the Warrior gains per Level :

Level	Strikes	Parries	Total Actions	
1st - 4th	1	1	2	(A)
5th - 9th	1	2	3	(B)
10th - 14th	2	2	4	(C)
15th - 19th	3	2	5	(D)

(A)   May make 1 Strike with a weapon and may make 1 Parry with the same weapon.
        May Strike with a weapon and Parry with a Shield.
        Paired Weapons = Strike with a short sword in your Right hand and Parry with a dagger in your
            Left hand.

(B)   Strike with a weapon and Parry 1 strike from 2 different opponents with your shield.
        Strike with a weapon and deflect 2 strikes from 1 Opponent, one with a shield and the other with your
            Parry skill.
        Strike with weapon and Benefit from BOTH your Parry skill and a Shield vs. 1 Opponent's strike.
        Paired Weapons = Strike with a short sword and Double Parry one Opponent with both a dagger and
            a short sword.

(C)   Strike twice with one weapon and parry twice with one weapon.
        Paired Weapons = Strike with both dagger and short sword and Double Parry one strike with both your
            dagger and short sword.

(D)   Strike thrice with your weapon and parry 1 Strike from 1st Opponent and employ your shield against
            Your 2nd Opp.
        Strike three times with your weapon and use your weapon to Parry 1 Strike from 2 Opponents.
        Strike thrice with a two-handed weapon and Parry the first two strikes from 1 Opponent.
        Strike twice with one weapon & parry 1 strike from 3 Opponents (substitute 1 Strike for 1 Parry)

SPECIAL ABILITIES

LEVEL		WARRIOR COMBAT SKILLS
1st		Parry & Shield Use
2nd		Feign Strike
3rd		Improve Firing Rate
4th		Accuracy Training
5th		Specialize in a Melee **OR** a Projectile Weapon

Pick 1 per level :

	/	1) Disarm
6th	/	2) Power Strike
7th	/	3) Thrust
8th	<	4) Fight for Extended Periods of Time
9th	\	5) "Dirty Trick" (Knight = Specialize with the Lance)
	\	6) Relearn 3rd level (Improve Firing Rate) with another projectile weapon
	\	7) Learn another Weapon **or** 2 Survival Skills.

7th		Specialize with Other Weapon Type (Melee or Projectile)
10th		Specialize in Fighting an Occupation.

Pick 1 per level :

	/	1) Called Strike
	/	2) "Bob and Weave"
11th	/	3) Fancy Footwork
12th	/	4) Specialize with Disarm
13th	<	5) Specialize with Parry
14th	\	6) Lunge (Specialize with Thrust)
	\	7) Specialize in Fighting for Extended Periods of Time
	\	8) Relearn 4th level (Accuracy Training) with another projectile weapon
	\	9) Learn any skill you missed between 6 - 9 levels

15th		Specialize in Fighting 1 Type of Enchanted Creature

A CHARGING HEMAR

NOTE: Charging = add an extra 1d6 Damage to your strike per CRM above CRM: 2.

I.e.: You must be charging at least 15 ft/sec or a CRM of 3 to gain the bonus.

At a CRM of 3, you would gain an extra 1d6 EP of Damage.

At a CRM of 5, you would gain an extra 3d6 EP of Damage.

WARRIOR COMBAT SKILLS

Shield Use   1st Level

    All Warriors are automatically taught the Shield Use <u>Survival Skill</u> at 1st Level. Anytime you employ a shield – either against a Projectile or Melee weapon – you get to add the percentage bonus for that particular shield to your PTE total – this only costs you any one of your Parry Actions. You must still specialize in the Shield Use Survival Skill using some of your skill slots to gain the additional abilities listed under that skill.

Parry   1st Level

    This basic skill allows the Warrior to add a bonus to his PTE total when fighting someone while using a weapon. The bonus added to your PTE total is equal to your Agility score / 2 or a maximum of +10%. Using this skill costs you **ONE Parry Action** for every weapon's strike you employ it against. If you have 2 Parry slots you may use your weapon to parry 1 melee strike from 2 different Opponents or parry 2 melee strikes from 1 Opponent. You may only employ the Parry skill verses other weapons, not verses claws, teeth, fists, ect.   Some restrictions to your parrying skill are :

1) A dagger (12") can not parry a weapon over Short Sword in length (3 foot).
2) Your Strength Score must be at least 3 "points" greater then your Opponent's Strength Score to parry his two-handed attack with your one handed weapon.
3) You may never parry a rope, chain weapon or net (lasso, Ninja Shogee, etc.)
4) If you parry an edged weapon with a Staff, etc., it has a 1 percent chance per damage point of splitting.

Attempts: You may use this skill every attack, but must state this before your Opponent Strikes.
NOTE: If you're going to use it all of the time, just call it at the beginning of the battle.
NOTE2: If you are using the 'Paired Weapons' skill, you may 'Double Parry' a single Opponent's strike.
    When using a Double Parry, you gain your normal (Parry Bonus x2). The maximum bonus would be your ((Agl score/2)x2) or a max of +20% bonus to your PTE total verses <u>that</u> Attack.

Feign Strike   2nd Level

    This deceptive skill teaches the Warrior to "fake" a strike at an area of your Opponent's body and then at the last moment switch your strike to the intended area.
Attempts: 1) Must call before you strike.
                      2) May not have parried last Attack.
Opponent suffers: Receives no Agility bonus to his PTE total during <u>that</u> Attack.

Improve one Projectile's Firing Rate   3rd Level

    The Warrior learns how to add <u>one</u> to the regular firing rate of a projectile weapon she already has had formal training in. Understand that you may only learn to shoot or throw 1 extra projectile per Attack from ONE type of weapon.
NOTE3: A regular character of 3rd level may fire or throw **2** projectiles per Attack.
        (One Strike & One Parry Act.)
NOTE4: Now, a Warrior of 3rd level may fire or throw a total of **3** projectiles per Attack.

Accuracy Training   4th Level

    The Warrior learns how to shoot or throw more accurately with the weapon he picked at 3rd level. You must "take your time" and only fire or throw only one projectile per Attack, instead of three. If you do wish to shot or throw only one <u>accurate</u> projectile, these are the bonuses you receive and the negatives your Opponent receives:

<u>Any type of a Bow or Thrown weapon</u>		
1)	Opponents receive	: - 10% to his PTE total.
2)	You receive	: - 5% on your SPT roll.

NOTE5: This uses ALL of your Actions for the Attack you shot or throw one <u>accurate</u> projectile.

Specialize in a Melee <u>or</u> a Projectile Weapon   5th Level

    The Warrior may specialize in any <u>one</u> melee <u>or</u> projectile weapon he has already had formal training in. When you specialize you become very familiar with the weapon you choose. You learn some of the weaknesses and advantages of using said weapon. If you specialize in a melee weapon your benefits are:

	Melee Weapon	
Opponent receives	:	- 20% to his PTE total.
You receive	:	- 10% on your SPT roll.

Otherwise you may choose a Projectile Weapon. You also gain the ability to fire 1 extra Projectile per Attack :

Projectile Weapon

		shoot / throw **"slow"**	shoot / throw **"fast"**
Opponent receives	:	- 20% to his PTE total	- 5% to his PTE total
You receive	:	- 10% on your SPT roll	+ 0% on your SPT roll
		Shoot only 1 Proj. / Attack	Shoot +1 extra Proj. / Attack

NOTE: "Slow" : always refers to you taking your time and shooting or throwing only one accurate projectile per Attack.

"Fast" : refers to putting all five projectiles down range as quickly as possible.

The maximum number of Projectiles a Warrior could put down range

= (Total Actions)+(1 for 3rd level ability)+(1 for Specialization)

so at 5th level the max = 3+1+1 or 5 projectiles per Attack.

Your Opponent gets a PTE roll verses <u>each</u> arrow shot at him.

Disarm   6th - 9th Levels

This powerful skill enables the Warrior to disarm her Opponent by quickly spinning her wrist in a circular motion. There are a few restrictions to this skill, but most of them are simply common sense.

To Disarm an Opponent you must :
1) Have parried your opponent's last strike.   (Unless you are using a whip.)
2) Have won the Initiative.
3) Use 1 Strike action.
4) Only use any sword, pole arm, staff, or whip to disarm your Opponent.

You may never Disarm:
1) Any bow, crossbow, lasso, whip, etc.
2) Any weapon dagger length or shorter.
3) Any spear, pole arm, or staff that your Opponent is holding with both hands.
4) Any Shield.
5) Any Opponent that is charging.

The weapons that you may Disarm according to your Level are :
1) Level that you take the Disarm skill: you may disarm any weapon that is the same length (or shorter) and handed as the weapon you are using.
2) 2 Levels after you take the Disarm skill: Any two-handed sword as long as your using a weapon that is 4 foot or longer.
3) You may at this time use any special weapon made specifically for disarming.

Attempt: You have a percentage equal to your Agility score plus 3% every additional level you have this ability.

(If you take this skill at 6th level your percentage is equal to your Agility Score +3%. At 7th level it would equal your Agility score plus 6%.)

NOTE2: Anyone that has this skill has a chance to stop being disarmed equal to 1/2 your Agility score plus 3% per level, so at 6th level the maximum percentage you could have is 13%.

NOTE3: Flying Weapons : All disarmed weapons "fly" (5' + ((your Strength Damage bonus) * 2)), so the maximum distance you can "throw" your Opponent's weapon is 13 feet, if you have the amazing Strength of 19 or 20 and you are not a Hemar whose maximum would be 15'.

NOTE4: Strength Bonuses are:

	Strength Score	Bonus
(Hemars Gain a +1	13 - 14	+ 1
to this Chart.)	15 - 16	+ 2
	17 - 18	+ 3
	19 - 20	+ 4

Power Strike
                                          6th - 9th Levels

This Combat Skill lets the Warrior put "all of himself" into a strike. This can do more damage and even knock your Opponent off his feet, if you're using certain weapon types. If you're using an Edged or Club type weapon, you get to add double your Strength Damage Bonus to your regular damage. If you're using a Staff or any type of a Pole Arm, you receive a percentage chance to knock your opponent off his feet. The percentage is based on where you strike your opponent :

Opponent's head	=	10% chance
body	=	30% chance
Leg	=	60% chance

Attempts: 1) Must have both hands on the weapon. If you are using a one-handed weapon, you must clasp one hand over the another.
2) Can't do if parried opponent's last strike.
3) May only use Power Strike every other strike.

Thrust
                                          6th - 9th Levels

This is an excellent technique to use against anyone skilled in the art of shield use or parrying. This skill will teach you how to make a straight thrust with your weapon quickly enough to avoid a counter parry or shield block from your opponent.
Attempt: 1) You must be using an edged melee weapon. (Including spear, rapier, etc.)
2) Must have initiative.
3) May only use the Thrust every other strike.
4) Subtract a -10% from your SPT roll.
Opponent Suffers: Your opponent may not add his parry or shield bonus to his PTE total verses that attack.

Fight for Extended Periods of Time
                                          6th - 9th Level

This skill will condition the Warrior's body so that he may fight in melee combat in full armor longer than anyone in any other Occupation. Regularly a person, <u>before this level or studying another Occupation</u>, can only fight for **30 seconds per Endurance point in melee combat**. If you are forced to fight for a longer amount of time, you must subtract 5% from your PTE total for every 6 Attacks (30 seconds) you continue to fight.

With this skill the Warrior may fight for an extended amount of time depending on the level that he learned it. The amount of time you may fight for according to your level:
1) Level in which you learn it: 1 minute per Endurance point.   Ref. Note: Max= 20 min.
2) 2 Levels after you learn it: 1 1/2 minutes per Endurance point.   Ref. Note: Max= 30 min.
NOTE: If forced to fight longer than this, you must still subtract -5% from your PTE total per 6 Attacks you are forced to stay in melee combat.

Dirty Tricks
                                          6th - 9th Levels

This skill gives the Warrior extra pseudo-strikes that can distract, blind, do minor damage, or even "sweep" your opponent off his feet. There are 3 types of "tricks" the Warrior may use :
A) The grab and toss: The Warrior may grab a small object, chair, etc. and toss it at his opponent.
    a) 1 small object does minor damage. An empty beer mug would do 1d4 Endurance Points Damage (no Str bonus.), a chair would do 1d6 EP Damage, if it strikes your opponent.
    b) 1 small handful of sand, sawdust, etc. may possibly blind your opponent. You receive a -20% on your SPT roll for any "handful" and if you hit your opponent's head you automatically blind him for 2 Actions.
B) Leg Swipe: As stated in Ninja section.
C) Quick Jab: If the Warrior has learned boxing in the past and has nothing in his off-hand, he may throw a Quick Jab. The jab does 1d6 End Points damage but you get no Strength Damage Bonus.
Attempt: 1) Warrior can't be using a shield or two-handed weapon to do (A) or (C).
        2) Can't do if parried last round and your Opponent always gets a PTE roll.
NOTE2: A **Knight** may **NOT** learn this skill so they have the choice to learn this next skill instead:

Specialize with the Lance
                                          6th - 9th Level

Only a Knight may specialize in three weapons - a melee, a projectile, and the Lance. This gives all the bonuses of any other specialized melee weapon, see the description listed at 5th level.

Relearn 3rd Level Skill with another Projectile Weapon   6th - 9th Level

You can learn to shoot or throw one extra projectile from another weapon you already have Formal Training in. You <u>may not</u> try to learn to shoot or throw more projectiles from the weapon you previously learned at 3rd level !

Learn one more Weapon or two Survival Skills   6th - 9th Level

Lastly, if you can't find any skill above that peeks your interest, you may choose to be taught the use of any new weapon or any two Survival Skills.

Specialize with Other Weapon Type   7th Level

This level is a busy one for the Warrior who can learn this skill and pick one from above. The Warrior gets to specialize in the weapon type that she **didn't** pick at 5th level (either Projectile or Melee). Rules stated at 5th level.

Specialize in Fighting an Occupation   10th Level

At this level the Warrior learns a particular Occupation's vulnerabilities that can be capitalized on in combat. The Warrior can pick whichever Occupation he wants. When you fight someone of that Occupation in combat, your opponent receives a -10% on his PTE total and you receive -10% on your SPT roll. If you pick the Warrior's Occupation, you gain these bonuses when fighting anyone of the Warrior, Knight (True or Black) or Savage Occupations.

Called Strike   11th - 14th Level

This skill allows the Warrior to "call" an area of his opponent's body he wants to strike. You may call a general area or a specific area, <u>but your Opponent does get his regular PTE roll</u>. When using this skill, you follow the rules stated below, instead of making your regular SPT roll.

1) <u>Call General Area</u> (Head, Body, Arm, ect.) : The Warrior has a percentage chance equal to her Agility score + 1% per level to strike the area she called. If you rate any rolls from the SPT, make them according to where you hit your Opponent, as usual.
      Ref Note: Max= 31% at 11th; 39% at 19th.

2) <u>Call Specific Area</u> (Eyes, Spine, Chest, Neck, ect.) : The Warrior has a chance equal to 1% per level to automatically strike the specific area she called. Again, if you rate any rolls from the SPT, make them as usual.
      Ref Note: Max= 11% at 11th; 19% at 19th.

Attempt: 1) Can't do if parried last strike.
        2) If opponent successfully evades, then your roll is disregarded.
        3) Can only do once per Attack.
        4) Use in place of regular SPT roll.

"Bob and Weave"   11th - 14th Level

This skill teaches the Warrior to "Bob and Weave" with his body to cause his opponent to strike a body area that is not so vital. It may also be used to protect a wounded area of your body. When you use this skill, your opponent must add a +25% to <u>his</u> SPT roll **OR** you gain a +10% to <u>your</u> PTE total – You must pick one **or** the other at the beginning of each Attack you want to use this skill in.
Attempt:
      1) You must say you intend to use this skill and you must specify when you want to stop using it.
      2) Fight for ½ regular time. This skill reduces the amount of time you may fight in melee
            combat by ½ with no penalties.
NOTE: You may use this skill in conjunction with your parry skill or a shield.
NOTE2: This skill <u>cancels</u> the Called Strike skill; If both opponents use these converse skills, then run
            combat as normal.

Fancy Footwork   11th - 14th Levels
     When you learn this skill, you get a bonus of +1/2 of your Agility score to your PTE total when you don't use your Parry. This skill is useful when you can't use your Parry skill, like when you are boxing, using a weapon that you can't parry with, fighting a Creature or when utilizing a Warrior Skill that does not allow you to parry.
Attempts: 1) May use it every Attack.
              2) Can't use in conjunction with your Parry skill.
              3) When you use this skill it reduces the amount of time you may fight in melee combat with
                    no penalties by ½.

NOTE: To Specialize in a Warrior Combat Skill, you must have already taken that skill previously. You must still follow all rules stated under the original skill, unless stated differently in the specialized skill's description.

Specialize with Disarm   11th - 14th Level
     When you specialize with the Disarm Combat Skill, you receive these bonuses:
1) Gives you a +10% to your Disarm percentage and +10% to your "stop being disarmed" percentage.
2) Lets you throw your opponents weapon +10 feet.   Ref note: Max= 23'/25'.
3) Lets you Disarm any Two-Handed sword, battle axe, battle hammer, bardiche, mace, etc, if using a
          weapon 3' or longer.

Specialize with Parry   11th - 14th Levels
     When the Warrior specializes with the Parry skill, you receive these bonuses:
1) Lets you add your entire Agility score to your PTE total instead of 1/2 of it.
2) You may parry any one-handed weapon with a dagger.

Lunge (Specialize with Thrust)   11th - 14th Level
     When this specialized skill is used correctly, your weapon's thrust is so straight and fast that your opponent looses his shield, Parry and Agility bonuses that are usually added to his PTE total.
Attempts :   1) Same as stated in Thrust.
              2) Can't use if used Power Strike last Attack.
              3) -20% on SPT to hit a General Area.

Specialize in Fighting for Extended Periods of Time   11th - 14th Level
     When the Warrior specializes in this skill, he is put through even more intense conditioning then the first time he took it. This conditioning will give the Warrior these bonuses:
1) Lets you fight in melee combat for 2 minutes per Endurance point.   Ref note: Max= 40 min.
2) If you are forced to fight longer then what you rate, you only have to subtract 2% from your
     PTE total every 6 Attacks (30 seconds).

Relearn 4th Level skill with another Projectile Weapon   11th - 14th Level
     If you have learned to shoot or throw an extra projectile with a second weapon during
6th - 9th levels, you may now learn Accuracy Training with that weapon. Follow all rules stated at 4th Level.

Learn Any Skill You Missed   11th - 14th Level
     If you want, you may learn any 6th - 9th level skill that you didn't "pick-up" during those levels.

Specialize in Fighting 1 Type of Enchanted Creature   15th Level
     This Combat Skill is much like the one you learned at 10th level, except that you learn the vulnerabilities of a specific type of Enchanted Creature. When you fight that specific type of Enchanted Creature in combat it receives a -10% penalty on its PTE total and you receive -10% on your SPT roll. If you pick Vampires, you gain the bonuses verses all types of Vampires. This is the same for Goblins, ect.

     There are some Occupations that take the Warrior Occupation one step further. These Occupations are very specialized and are usually harder to play then regular Warriors. They have special abilities and purposes, but they can use all of the Warrior Combat Skills at the levels stated in the Warrior Section - unless specifically stated below. These Occupations are the **Knight** and the **Savage**.

KNIGHT

The Knight is a special type of Warrior. They may only be trained by other Knights, must meet certain obligations and criteria, and most importantly, must take a special oath to live and die by :
The Knight's Code of Honor.

To become a Knight you must first find a Knight of 10-12th level and become his or her Page. She or he will start your training and teach you about the Rank Structure and how to follow the Knight's Code of Honor. (It is quite obvious that even a brave and well-rounded Knight can't know everything. So, if you wish to learn a weapon or Survival Skill which is not known to your Sire - he will enroll you into a Warrior's school long enough for them to teach you and even pay for it out of the his own pocket.)

When you have fought some battles and done some good deeds, the Knight will promote you to Squire (2nd level). The Knight promotes you when SHE thinks you are ready, which can be anywhere between **20 & 40** Experience Points. At 3rd level (again picked by your Knight, usually right after you have performed a good deed - between **60 & 80** XPO), you must take an oath to live by: the Knight's Code of Honor. After you recite the oath, you are knighted and receive your first set of Shoulder Rank Insignia. After you've taken the oath, you must live by it and you may never let your Morality Rating (MR) drop below **15**! If it does, you become a "Dark Knight" - you loose all Knightly abilities and may be shunned by all other Knights - shunned only, not sought out. You must raise your MR back to 15 and then you will gain back all abilities, also while your MR is below 15 you loss your Agility bonus for your PTE total and you gain **NO** XPO.

NOTE: If you ever drop below a Morality Rating of **10**, you will become a Black Knight
- new abilities and problems which are discussed at the end of this Section.

Listed next are 5 sections that deal with: Knightly bonuses, restrictions, the Knight's Code of Honor, the Rank Structure you follow and the Black Knight rules. We'll start with the good news first :

True Knight's Bonuses Per Level

Auto Horsemanship & Starting Weapons & Skills   1st Level
a) You learn the Horsemanship Survival Skill during your initial training. You are highly encouraged to Specialize in this skill because Knights *gain ALL Specialization bonuses* by Specializing just once!
b) The other Survival Skills Knights are taught are Boxing, Shield Use and 2 extras of your choice. You will also be taught how to use 1 Bow, 1 Sword, the Lance, and 1 extra weapon of your choice.

See "Dark and Black Knights"   3rd Level
As soon as you are Knighted you will be able to "See" if anyone you look at is a Dark or Black Knight.
A hood of "sparkling shadow", known by Knights as the 'Malady', will hang over any
Dark Knight's face and a "Hood of Shadows" will shroud any Black Knight's features.
When you look upon a Dark Knight, the 'Malady' appears as a veil of shade sparsely covered by
shimmering spots covering his or her head. All knights, True and Black, pay close attention to
knights afflicted with the 'Malady', as those afflicted could follow *either* path. You will usually
try to help any Dark Knights to again attain the path of Righteousness, but you will always
challenge a Black Knight to battle on sight.
True Knights may identify a Black Knight even if his "Hood of Shadows" is invisible to everyone else.
If the Black Knight invokes his Hood of Shadows before you first look at him, you will NOT be
able to identify him or her personally, you will only be able to tell that he or she is a
Black Knight.

Ladies' Favor   Anytime after 3rd level

This Bonus is broken into 2 sets of different circumstances:

a) The first is when you are at a Tournament (Tourney) or on a Quest. Before you step on to the field of honor or start a grand Quest, you may accept a Lady's Favor. She will lay her scarf on the tip of your Lance or give you a personal item. Take this item and put it somewhere in which it won't be stained - usually up the sleeve of the arm you hold your Lance with. As long as you hold it during **this** Tourney or Quest, you will receive a - 5% on your SPT rolls and a +5% on your PTE total. When the Tourney or Quest is over you must return the Ladies' Favor and thank her properly.

b) The second circumstance is when (and if) you are appointed a Ladies' Champion. This means you must protect that Ladies Honor in all battles and conflicts. If someone speaks wrongly about her or if she is accused of a crime, you must fight whoever spoke out against her. If you win she is considered innocent - for truth always prevails over evil. When you fight <u>for her Honor</u>, you will receive a +10% on your PTE total and you may Double your Str Dam bonus while <u>in this combat</u>. If you know the Warrior's ability: Power Strike and use it, you gain a Strength Damage bonus of x4.

NOTE: You only get these bonuses when you are directly fighting for the Ladies' honor!

Mount Horse in Full Metal Armor   5th Level

Every one else, and you before this level, must always use something to help you into the saddle (a person, stool, stairs, etc) when wearing any type of full metal armor. Now as a 5th level Knight, you may mount any horse easily and gracefully while in full armor.

Specialize in the Lance   6th - 9th Levels

Because you're a Knight you may not use the Combat Skill: Dirty Tricks; the Combat Skill: "Specialize in the Lance" is your number 5 selection on the Warrior Combat Table for these levels. The Lance is a melee weapon, so if you Specialize in it, make sure you follow the <u>Melee</u> Specialization rules. Every Knight may Specialize in 1 projectile weapon, 1 melee weapon, and the Lance!

Enchantments :   4th, 5th, 7th, 10th, 12th, 15th

Through the power of the Knight's Oath, the Knight is granted the ability to learn **ONE** Spell at the levels listed above. The spells a Knight may learn at these levels are listed at the end of this section. You may cast each of the spells you will learn at 4th level and beyond **once per day** at NO Spell Point Cost, but you still must spend the EP necessary or 1 EP / 10 SP stated under the Spell's Point Cost. You may pick ONE spell from the list per level.

You may still learn and cast the Class (A) spells that are listed on the Knight's Spell list. To use <u>these</u> Class (A) spells keep track of your Spell Points according to the rules listed under the Warrior section: your maximum SP total is <u>20 SP + one spell point per level</u>. These Spell Points are used for the Class (A) spells, NOT the spells you learn at 4th, 5th, 7th, 10th, 12th, or 15th levels. True Knights are only able to learn <u>certain</u> Class (A) spells, so please check the Knight's Spell list at the end of this Section to see which ones you may learn.

Knight's Restrictions

Morality   3rd Level and above

Your Morality Rating (MR) must always stay above 15 (after 3rd level). If it ever drops below 15 for any reason, you become a Dark Knight. If you ever drop below a MR of 10, you will become a Black Knight – the rules Black Knights must follow are at the end of this section, where the refuse belongs.

Follow the Knight's Code of Honor   3rd Level and above

If a Knight ever breaks any rule of the code, his MR will drop. The amount your MR is affected is listed on the Knight's Code of Honor table.

Never use Paired Weapons   Always

This is considered dishonorable by all True Knights - you should be able to overcome any evil without using such practices.

Take a Page   10th Level

You must take a Page at 10th level and you don't receive any additional experience until you do. You must train him or her in the Knightly pursuits and pay for all of his or her food, shelter, and extra training (although Warrior Schools usually only charge you a reduced rate, because you are a Great and Brave Knight.) You must also buy and fully outfit the Page with a horse, weapons and provisions necessary to survive the harsh world, once she or he reaches 3rd level. You may also be asked to train another Page during your 12th and / or 14th levels - for some reason Knights seem to die off rather quickly and good live teachers are always in demand.

Marry   15th Level

You must Marry someone that you are in TRUE LOVE with, before 15th Level or you only gain 1/2 regular XPO from then on. It CANNOT be a marriage of convenience or one just so you can collect full XPO. The marriage must be an honorable one which is consented to and wanted by both parties - yes she has to TRULY LOVE you also - good luck – HA, HA, HA!

It has be told 'The Luckiest one on Penicia, is the one who finds True Love'.
There for: the Married Knight gains a +/-10% on all rolls. This includes PTE, Ability Checks, SPT and RER rolls.

KNIGHT'S CODE OF HONOR

	Minus to MR
1) Always be kind and courteous - give help whenever it's needed and always when it's asked.	-1
(When your are able - even the greatest of Knights can't feed all the world's hungry.)	
2) Follow orders of any higher ranked Knight or any good and high-ranking Officials	-2
(King, President, etc.). The Knighthood has many Deeds to be done!	
3) Defend the Just and the Righteous and Always speak the Truth.	-3
4) Come to the aid of any GOOD out-numbered force and battle evil wherever it is found!	-3
5) Always be Generous - only keep enough moneys to feed and care for your Lands, Wife, Pages, etc.	-1
At low and high levels, you had better be giving most of your wealth to the poor, homeless, etc.	
6) Be Courageous - Never decline a battle from any Warrior type and always issue a gallant battle	-3
challenge to any retched Black Knights you find skulking about the country side.	
7) Always keep your word. If you give your word to ANYONE, you must TRULY keep it.	-4
8) Be Humble - the greatest teachers always teach by example.	-2

NOTE: All Knights are awesome! but a pompous Knight will always have a MR of 18 or less.
NOTE2: If a Knight breaks one of the aspects of the Code, she or he incurs a negative to his or her Morality Rating. These are listed in the right column above and are usually tallied when the Knight goes up in level.

Rank Structure

Knights consider themselves to be in one tremendous Corp - Regardless of where you were born, where you first learned the Knight's Code of Honor, or what Race you are! All Knights consider themselves to be brothers and sisters in arms, fighting to uphold the laws of the land and insure the peace between the Races continues.

Whoever is senior to you in Rank may give you an order, which you must follow to the best of your ability. No True Knight will **ever** give an unlawful order **or** a frivolous one. You don't have to follow any orders given by a Dark Knight - but you may to honor him and help him bring himself back up into good standing. You NEVER follow an order of a Black Knight (if you do this of sound mind and body (not Mesmerized, ect.) you will automatically become a Dark Knight (MR = 12))! Any orders you give to your lessors had better be lawful and <u>necessary</u> - Knights just don't run around giving each other orders to get their jollies!

The Rank structure and the Shoulder Insignia you rate at each level are listed below. You will NOT receive a promotion at every level, just at the ones listed in the table below. Seniority within a particular rank is determined by Level. A ninth (9th) level Major is senior to a seventh (7th) level Major.

Each Shoulder Insignia has a special design that is described below. They can be fastened on the shoulders straps of any type of armor.

LEVEL	RANK	SHOULDER INSIGNIA
1st	Page	None
2nd	Squire	None
3rd	2nd Lieutenant	1 Gold Bar
4th	1st Lieutenant	1 Silver Bar
5th	Captain	2 Silver Bars *
7th	Major	1 Gold Oak Leaf
10th	Lieutenant Colonel	1 Silver Oak Leaf
12th	Colonel	1 Silver Eagle
14th	Brigadier General	1 Silver Star
16th	Major General	2 Silver Stars
18th	Lieutenant General	3 Silver Stars
19th	General	4 Silver Stars

* These 2 Silver Bars are linked by small pieces of Silver and the Insignia looks like train tracks.

NOTE: For large battles the highest ranking General in the area will temporarily be promoted to Admiral. The promotion lasts only as long as the battle and the Shoulder Insignia is 5 Americanium stars in a circle.

BLACK KNIGHT

To "become" a Black Knight you must once have been a Knight of good standing, but now, for personal reasons, you have chosen a path of shadows. By following this path you will be granted certain abilities and restrictions. Note: You must have been at least a 3rd level True Knight and have taken and broken the Knight's Code of Honor. It has been said that "every Black Knight has a pitch black story to tell".

Abilities:
1) You gain all Physical Abilities at the same levels your Knightly counterparts do.

Mount Horse in Full Metal Armor	5th Level
Specialize in the Lance	7th Level

3rd Level

2) You are now able to "See" True Knights – (A gossamer glow will enhance their facial features.) When you look upon a Dark Knight the 'Malady' appears as a veil of shade sparsely covered by shimmering spots covering his or her head.

5th Level

3) You will be able to detect any True Knights with your mind's eye. You will automatically sense any True Knight within 10' per level of your position.

You may also make your "Hood of Shadows" visible at will. While it is visible, no one can detect your true identity using enchantment, Ninja Ability, sight or smell – Your voice even changes to a raspy hollow tone. It also causes the Cause Fear – One Spell (see Violet Spells) in any Regular Creature you confront.

4) Enchantments: You will gain the ability to cast certain spells at certain levels. The only place you will be able to learn these particular spells is from the hand of a higher level Black Knight. You must follow the rules stated in the Knight's Section. This means you must spend EP for the spells you cast at and above 4th level and you may only cast these spells Once Per Day. In regards to Class (A) spells, you must spend SP and EP, plus you must **relearn** these spells - you can only choose those listed spells listed under the Black Knight's spell list heading at the end of this Section.

6th Level

5) You may choose to gain the Paired Weapons Survival Skill at 6th level or beyond.

7th Level

6) A Black Knight is granted the ability to use the <u>Hand of Judgment</u>. If the Black Knight can gain access to the naked brow of a True Knight, the Ref. must add up ANY infringements of the Knight's Code of Honor that have been done by the Knight at Hand!!!!! If this tally is numerous it will force the MR of the Knight downward. This could instantly transform the True Knight into a Dark or Black Knight.

RESTRICTIONS AND PENALTIES

A) Matters of Honor are STILL matters of Honor – If you give your word, you will follow through on the specific Pledge given. What gets on your nerves is other people's weakness and serious lack of conviction.
B) You are now a "Purely Evil" Creature - you are affected by enchanted Sunlight and you disdain regular sunlight.
C) At 10th level: You don't get the Warriors Ability: Specialize in Fighting an Occupation, instead you gain the another Specialty Ability:

'Specialize in Fighting a Dark Knight' – you gain the same bonuses: -10% PTE & -10% SPT.
The first time you use this ability, the Black Knight has the chance to gain a Shadow Medal.
i) If you defeat the **1st** Dark Knight you engage in combat, you receive the honor to wear the Shadow Medal of Dark Defeat and gain +100 XPO.
ii) If you fail to defeat the **1st** Dark Knight you challenge (you're a Looser), you loose 100 XPO and you never rate the honor of wearing the Shadow Medal of Dark Defeat.
D) At 15th level: You can't 'Specialize in Fighting an Enchanted Creature', but instead you,

'Specialize in Fighting True Knights' – you gain the same bonuses stated in the skill: -10% PTE & -10% SPT.
i) If you defeat the **1st** True Knight you engage in combat, you receive the honor to wear the Shadow Medal of Light Defeat and you gain +500 XPO.
ii) If you fail to defeat the **1st** True Knight you challenge (you're a Huge Looooser), you loose 500 XPO and you never rate the honor of wearing the Shadow Medal of Light Defeat.

KNIGHTS AND SPELLS

True Knight's Class (A) spell choices			Black Knights Must Change Class (A) spells to:	
Find North	Opq		Glowing Hand	R
Light 1	Y		Cloud Part	B
Ice Walk	Cl		Find North	Opq
Purify Water	Cl		Sparking Fingers	R
Conv. with Animal / Bird	I		Breeze	B
See Enchantment 1	Y		Midnight Wall	Bl
Shield - Proj. (10%)	O		Shield - Proj. (10%)	O
StingRay	Y		Midnight Cube	Bl
Stone Move 1	Br		Reveal Weapon Quality	Opq
Reveal Weapon Quality	Opq		Bridge, 15'	B
Shield - Melee (10%)	O		Shield - Melee (10%)	O
Daze - One	I		Illusion 1	V
Water Bolt 1	Cl		Float	B
Blind - one	Y		Wind Bolt 1	B
Heal Wounds	G	ALL Knight's MUST Learn	Heal Wounds	G
Para. Animal or Bird	Br		Acid Pool, Mild	Bl
			Flame Bolt 1	R

The total number of Class (A) spells a Knight may learn is stated on the Intellect table.

NOTE: You must learn the spell Heal Wounds regardless if you are a True or Black Knight.

NOTE2: The total number of Spell Points (SP) a True or Black Knight rates is: Int Score + 1 SP / Level.

	True Knight's possible spells per level **		**Black Knight's possible spells per level ****	
4th	"Bunch" = See Truth, See Life, and		"Bunch" = See Truth, See Life, and	
	See Enchantment	- 2	See Enchantment	- 2
	Water Adaptation	- 3	Death Trance	- 2
	Wall Walk	- 3	Cause Fear, one	- 3
5th	Create Food and Water	- 5	Enchant Skeletons	- 4
	Sun Light	- 4	Acid Pool, Medium	- 4
	Empathy	- 3	Disguise	- 3
7th	Return Item Spell	- 4	Silence - Area	- 4
	Shield, Melee +30%	- 5	Acid Spray, Medium	- 5
	Resist Black	- 4	Resist Yellow	- 4
10th	Heal Disease	- 6	Enchant Zombies	- 6
	Invisibility	- 5	Illusion 4	- 5
	Sun Light Beam	- 8	Poisonous Mist	- 8
12th	Earth Globe	- 13	Polymorph 2	- 11
	Mesmerize Ench. Creature	- 14	In Sight Teleport	- 9
	Shield, Melee +50%	- 10	Fly 2	- 10

15th Summon Battle Mount / Companion Sky Panther: Summon Battle Mount / Companion Fire Steed:

EP: 150   PTE: 50% (Fly 85%)   EP: 150   PTE: 50% (Fly 85%)

Strikes: Paw/Bite   Damage: 1d10+5/1d12+5   Strikes: Bite/Buck   Damage: 1d10+5/1d20+5

2/day : Lightning Bolt 2 = 22+2d10 EP Dam.   2/day : Flame Bolt 3 = 22+1d20 EP Dam.

A Knight may Summon / Dismiss his or her Mount at Will unless it is brought to 0 EP, then it may not be re-summoned for 60 min. Once per day the Knight may cause his Mount to shrink to the size of a wolf. The wolf sized mount has the same EP&PTE, but the Paw damage is only 1d8+2. This adjustment of the Mount's size may last a maximum of 1 hour per level of the Knight.

** You may only pick one spell listed per level. You may cast them ONCE Per Day without a Spell Point Cost, but you must still spend the equivalent EPs – see the Enchanter Spell section for details.

NOTE3: At 4th Level, you may pick a "bunch" of 3 spells, each of which you may cast Once Per Day. Remember the EPs must be met for each spell, even though you don't spend Spell Points.

SAVAGE

Unlike other Occupations in which a Master can teach the pupil certain skills at certain levels, the major "skill" that sets the Savage apart, can not be taught. This "skill" is brought about by a great tragedy in the early life of the child. The tragedy should occur before the character reaches a certain age:

Race	Maximum Age
Human	15
Hemar	30
Krill	7

This tragedy must directly involve the child and must be something that would cause an extreme psychological imbalance (or psychotic episodes). The character that is overwhelmed by the Savage Occupation will follow the rules in the Warrior section unless stated differently below.

As a result of the tragedy, the child's Morality Rating drops to 9 and must never rise above it. His intellect can't rise above 15 and wisdom cannot rise above 16. Also, the seed of the Savage "skill" is planted in the child's brain, making the person fairly unstable and he will be "set off" easily throughout his life.

The "skill" brought on by the tragedy is called a Blood Frenzy. The Blood Frenzy is dormant while the person progresses through levels 1-4 and he is almost the same as any other Warrior, except for his "short temper". At 5th level the person "acquires" the "skill" of the Blood Frenzy. The Frenzy may assert itself any time the person sees or smells Blood! This could be in combat or just occur by accident - you know how clumsy some people can be. During the Frenzy, the Savage gains certain combat bonuses and certain penalties. The bonuses, while in Blood Frenzy, increase as the Savage goes up in Level. As the character gains levels, the affects of the Blood Frenzy increase, but the person has a harder and harder time distinguishing who is friend and who is foe. As the Savage increases in level, he has a greater chance of attacking a friend and a lesser chance of immediately "coming out" of the Frenzy when all the enemies are actually defeated. This doesn't mean that the character becomes less playable as he rises in level, it just means that when the character engages in melee combat he "becomes" a very formidable opponent, sometimes even to his friends.

The special rules for a Savage are :
1) Can't Specialize in a projectile weapon, but may Specialize in **two** melee weapons
   - one at 5th and one at 7th level.
2) Upon reaching 5th level, you gain the Blood Frenzy "skill" and you no longer receive Experience for anything except combat related activities! If you "Survive in REAL Combat" you gain double the amount of XPO listed. (You still gain full XPO for all 'First Time' Experience bonuses.)
3) You can't ever cast spells. You may use Enchanted Items, but you will forget the Trigger Words when you fall into the Blood Frenzy.
4) You must always have a Morality Rating below 9. If it ever rises above 9 :
   (a) You lose the Blood Frenzy "skill".
   (b) You don't receive ANY Experience for anything.
   (c) You develop a terrible migraine headache that causes all rolls on your SPT to be rolled at +10%.
   (d) You loose your Agility Bonus on your PTE total.

The Penalties you incur when entering a Blood Frenzy :
1) The savage may only retain bonuses from the "passive" Warrior Skills he knows – Kill'en is like that. The list of "passive" skills are:
   (a) Specialize with a Melee Weapon
   (b) Fight for Extended Periods of Time
   (c) Specialize in Fighting an Occupation
   (d) Bob and Weave
   (e) Fancy Footwork
   (f) Specialize in Fighting for Extended Periods of Time
   (g) Specialize in Fighting One Type of Enchanted Creature
2) Will engage in melee combat only. (period)
3) Will scream, rant, and rave while you dispatch your enemies.

NOTE : You may use any and all bonuses & skills UNTIL you go into the Blood Frenzy.

Bonuses you receive while overcome with the 'Blood Frenzy':

1)   You receive bonuses to your regular Strength Damage Bonus during melee combat while in a Blood Frenzy. With these increases, you also receive increases in the percentages to Kill or Stun someone, if you hit your opponent in the specific area of the heart, stomach, throat, spine, etc. You **increase** all effects to your opponent rolled on the SPT! The increase is stated on the table below: According to the table below, if you are 10th level, you gain x3 your Strength Damage Bonus and if you succeed in making a critical strike percentage listed on the SPT, the effects are multiplied by a x3.

2)   Bonus to your **Total** Strikes per Attack. You may only benefit from the use of 'Passive' Warrior skills, so you simply hack and slash until your enemies are defeated.

3)   You have a Chance to come out of the Blood Frenzy immediately after all your enemies have been destroyed. If you don't come out of the Frenzy, roll a 1d20 to see how many Actions you will continue to Frenzy after all your enemies are dead and a percentage to compare to the table below.

ROLL	ACTION
01 - 25%	Keep chopping at lifeless enemy forms (MR= -1).
26 - 50%	Attack closest moving thing to you. ^^
51 - 75%	Attack Companion closest to you.
76 - 99%	Attack all Companions.
100%	go Unconscious for 1d6 Attacks.

^^ The closest moving thing to you could be a bush flowing in the wind, a rat, etc.

4)   At some levels you have a small chance to avoid going into a Blood Frenzy, if you wish.

5)   You can keep fighting even after you drop to ZERO EP! How long you keep fighting depends on your End Score and your level. The percentage reflects the amount of extra damage you may incur before going unconscious. Once you do reach the stated amount of Endurance Points, you go unconscious and will die after one full Attack has passed.

6)   Negatives to Opponent's PTE total.

LEVEL	1	2	3	4	5	6
1 - 4th	---	-----	------	----	100% of End Score	0%
5 - 9th	x 2	3 **	100%	30%	150% of End Score	-5%
10 - 14th	x 3	4 ***	50%	10%	200% of End Score	-10%
15 - 19th	x 4	5 ****	10%	0%	300% of End Score	-15%

**   You gain 3 Strikes per Attack, but you don't get any Parry Actions.
***   You gain 4 Strikes per Attack, but you don't get any Parry Actions.
****   You gain 5 Strikes per Attack, but you don't get any Parry Actions.

---

7)   This next ability is very special and **is not included on the table above**:
        While in Blood Frenzy, you have a chance to track a bleeding Opponent by scent! You must successfully roll an Ability Check with your Wisdom. [i.e. - If your Wisdom is 10, then you must roll below a 30% to stay on the trail (10 * 3).] While tracking you will not attack anyone or make a single sound, until you find your victim and then you will attack him relentlessly. If the circumstances allow the Savage to track an opponent, this ability will supercede the #3 ability listed above.

NOT TO BE PUBLISHED
        The child is hiding in the bushes and the invader brings his parents outside and makes them kneel. As the monstrous man decapitates his mother, the child bursts out of hiding to aid his parents. Just then the Brute decapitates the child's father; unfortunately the child is so close to his father, that his blood stains the child's arms and hands. The Brute looks at the boy standing in front of him, smiles, kicks the boy to the ground and rides away laughing. - you get the picture!
        After this, the Savage "Occupation" slowly sinks into the child's being and a black hole of insanity and psychotic episodes abounds throughout his life.

SPY / ASSASSIN

INTRODUCTION

Almost every Government, Nation and City State sponsors this Occupation. Special officials may teach certain individuals the arts of infiltration, information gathering and settling personal conflicts. The differences between the titles are the morals of the Officials and the methods taught to the individuals. These individuals and the Officials must both have the same morals - this game's equivalent is your character's Morality Rating [MR]. Those Governments and people with Morality Ratings of 10 and above are considered Spies and those with Morality Ratings of 9 and below are considered Assassins. Anyone under the instruction of any Organization can learn any skill; the difference is in how the skills are used.

INFORMATION & FACTS

There are two ways you can learn these skills, Informally and Formally. The Informal way is in the "school of hard knocks." A "street wise" individual is someone who has picked-up certain skills and may have gotten some good pointers to survive from a mentor. To partake in Formal instruction, you must be accepted to a sponsored school. Most people that get accepted to a sponsored school, from the very start of their carrier, probably have well renowned or rich parents - there's politics everywhere! Most "street urchins" don't have a prayer of a Formal education unless they make a name for themselves. You may get noticed, if you obtain an object from a rival Government, borrow an item from your Government or obtain some type of vital information. You may trade one of these commodities - information being the most precious of commodities - to the Government in question for a place in one of their schools. You may ask "Why would I want to join a stuffy old school?" The answer is because there are certain skills that you can't learn unless you join a Government school. (If you progress past 5th level and do not join a Government, you earn the title: "Thief".)

No matter how you receive your initial education, you receive all of the General Skills. However, there are differences in some of the percentages, depending on which "school" you start out in. There are also differences in how many Individual skills you receive depending on which "school" you start out in, but the main factor on how many Individual skills you initially learn is your Intellect score.

If you begin with **Informal training**, these are how many Individual skills slots you initially receive:

$$1 - 4 \text{ Intellect points} = 1 \text{ skill slot}$$
$$5 - 14 \text{ Intellect points} = 2 \text{ skill slots}$$
$$15 - 20 \text{ Intellect points} = 2 \text{ skill slots}$$

If you begin with **Formal training**, these are how many Individual skills slots you initially receive:

$$1 - 4 \text{ Intellect points} = 1 \text{ skill slot}$$
$$5 - 14 \text{ Intellect points} = 2 \text{ skill slots}$$
$$15 - 20 \text{ Intellect points} = 3 \text{ skill slots}$$

As soon as you are "accepted" into a Government sponsored school, you may begin using the Individual skill slots per your Intellect score stated under Formal training at your next level.

The Spy / Assassin gains percentage increases on his or her **General skills** at every level.

You receive additional **Skill Slots** at these levels: **1st, 3rd, 5th, 7th, 10th, 13th, 16th and 19th.**

These **Skill Slots** can be used for :
1) Learning a New Individual skill.
2) Specializing in a General or an Individual skill, that you have previously learned.

To Recap: All Spies / Assassins starts out with all General skills. The number of Individual skills you initially rate depends on your Intellect score and if you have Informal or Formal training.

When you reach certain levels, you may select a new Individual skill OR you may specialize in a skill you've already learned. You must use one of the "slots" you rate and put it back into the skill you want to specialize in. When you specialize, you get whatever bonus is listed under that particular skill. You may specialize in any skill that you have already learned, either General and Individual. You may only Specialize in any skill TWICE. i.e. Use a total of 3 Slots in one skill: 1 slot to learn it and 2 slots for Specialization.

Some skills are performed successfully only if you succeed in rolling an Ability Check with one of your Abilities. An Ability Check is a percentage roll you need to make to successfully perform the skill in question. To find any Ability Check percentage, multiply your Ability Score, that is stated in the description of the skill, by 3. Roll any percentage below or equal to that number and you have successfully performed the skill. (Remember, you roll a percentage by using two ten sided dice and calling one the ten's place.)

Some Individual skills are also included as Survival skills and the Spy / Assassin may take these skills from either section, but not from both. If you pick a skill from one section and you want to specialize in it, you must specialize within that same section.

Governments are very cautious about accepting anyone to one of their schools, if they've already studied another Occupation. They feel that if you are 'bouncing' between Occupations, you don't have the dedication needed - it's very expensive to train someone. They also don't let people "out" of their service very often. You must get expressed permission to get a "leave of absence" to study another Occupation. If you don't, you could have some Spies or Assassins coming after you! For all this training, the Government you are associated with, will want you to do some work for them. Sometimes they will ask you to do an expressed mission: Watch someone, appropriate something, or they might ask you to "cancel" the earning power of a specific individual. Most often the Government will just let you "wander" about on your own, as long as you keep your eyes and ears open and apprise them of any bit of information you think they will need.

NOTE: It may be possible for a Spy / Assassin to cast certain spells, if they have a high enough Intellect.
Your total Spell Points equal your intellect score + 1 point per level.
Please, see the Warrior Section for details.

This table describes how many Actions the Spy / Assassin gains per Level.

Level	Strikes	Parries	Total Actions
1st - 4th	1	1	2
5th - 9th	1	2	3
10th - 14th	1	3	4
15th - 19th	2	3	5

NOTE2: When you attain 7th level in the S/A Occupation, you gain the ability to
Specialize in a Projectile Weapon. (See the Specialization with Weapons section for details.)

SPECIAL ABILITIES

GENERAL SKILLS TABLE	1	2
Item Appropriation	+ 10%	Agl
Conceal Object	- 5%	Agl
Conceal Self	--	Agl
Fall	--	----
Pick Locks	- 5%	Int
Running Jump	--	----
Scale Walls	--	----
Soundless Travel (Leaves NO trail)	--	----

Headings for both General and Individual Skill Tables:
1: Informal Education - If you <u>started</u> your career with an Informal "education", some skills get a bonus
percentage and some skills receive a negative percentage.
2: Dependent Ability - Some Skills have an ability they are dependent on. Roll a percentage less than
your Ability Check with the Dependent Ability, plus any level or other bonuses,
and you successfully complete the skill.
An Ability Check is a percentage equal to you Ability Score * 3.
3: Skill Bonus - When you learn some Individual Skills, you will receive a bonus to another specific skill.
These are listed in the skill descriptions and may be a General, Individual or
Survival Skill.
4: Can't Specialize - Some Individual Skills can't be specialized in.

NOTE3: S/A means Spy / Assassin.
NOTE4: 'Sp' means Specialize - You may learn a Skill **Once** and Specialize in it **Twice**, using a total of
3 slots.
NOTE5: Some Individual Skills let you add +1/2 of your Ability score to your percentage total when you
specialize.
Some skills have this listed at the end of it: (Sp : Add +1/2 Agility score to percentage). This means
if you have an Agility Score of 16, your percentage before you specialize is (16*3) = 48%.
After your 1st specialization your percentage is (16*3) +8 = 56%.
After your 2nd and last specialization your percentage is (16*3) +8 +8 = 64%.

INDIVIDUAL SKILLS TABLE	1	2	3	4
Disguise Self		Int		
Disguise Voice		Int		
Escape and Tie		Int		
Find Concealed Areas		Int	Detect Ambush (+5-15%)	
Flying Jump Kick				can't
Judo Throw				can't
Juggle		Agl		
Lie				
Measure Distance by Sound		Int	Disguise Voice (+10-20%)	can't
Read Lips				
Remove and Set Traps		Int		
Roll and Evade		Agl	Fall (+10-20 foot fall)	
Slight-of-Hand	+ 5%	Agl	Conceal Object (+10-20%)	
Squeeze	+ 10%	Agl	Conceal Self (+10-20%)	
Spy Fingers				can't
Stay Awake		End		
Trained Observer		Int	See through a Disguise (+10-20%)	can't
Unseen Attack				
Walk "Tight-Rope"		Agl		

GENERAL SKILLS

Item Appropriation :

This is the most basic skill and what "pops" into mind when you speak of Thieves. You may try to steal something from outside a persons tunic or clothes (a purse on a belt, a dagger, etc.) or from inside his tunic, pants, robes or worn on the skin. The percentage for stealing something from outside a person's tunic is: your Agility score + 4% per level. [The percentage for stealing a belt purse at 1st level is equal to (your personal Agility score) + 4% and the percentage for stealing a belt purse at 3rd level is (your personal Agility score) + 12%, etc.]

If you attempt to steal something from within a persons tunic or directly on his person such as a ring, necklace, bracelet, ect; then you must decrease your percentage by a -20%.

Every Spy / Assassin has a percentage of <u>4%</u> per level to realize if someone is trying to "pick their pocket." (Sp : Add ½ Agility score to percentage.)
[NOTE: You receive a bonus of +10%, if you had Informal Training.]

NOTE2: Regular people have a percentage equal to <u>2%</u> per level to realize they are having their pocket picked.
NOTE3: If you exceed your percentage by more than 50%, you're automatically caught.
     If you exceed it by more than 25%, your victim's percentage to realize your attempt is doubled. (That is: 4% per level for a regular person and 8% per level for another S/A.)
NOTE4: If you need to "Plant" something on someone the attempt is made at ½ your regular Item App. percentage.

Conceal Object :

This skill teaches the S/A how and where to hide small objects and to keep them hidden, even during everything but a VERY precise search. The S/A may hide the object in their palm, hair, under an arm, under your foot in a boot, etc. When you are searched, you only need to roll a percentage less than (your Agility score) + 3% per level to hide an object from your searchers. (Willamina is 3rd Level and has an Agility of 17, so she has a 26% to continue to conceal one item that is less than 6 inches long.)
The number and size of the objects you may hide are listed below:

Level	Max Size	Number of Items
1 - 4	6 inches	1
5 - 9	6 inches	2
10 -14	8 inches	3
15 -19	8 inches	4

(Sp : Add +1/2 Agility score to percentage, +2 inches added to the Max size and +1 item each specialization.)
[NOTE5: You receive a -5% to your percentage <u>total</u>, if you had Informal Training.]

Conceal Self :

This skill allows you to remain hidden from sight using natural surroundings (a dark room, starlit alleyway or just outside the campfire's light, etc.) You must crouch down and breathe quietly. Doing this correctly is enough to conceal yourself. After a successful percentage check, you may move at ¼ your CR and stay concealed. Anytime you venture within 10' of an Opponent, you must make an additional percentage check. If you fail your check, your opponent gets a Detect Ambush roll at a +25% to notice you (either see or hear you, depending on the circumstances.) The Ref. may adjust your percentage depending on the situation. The percentage to conceal yourself is: (your Agility score) + 4% per level.
(Sp :   +1/2 Agility score to your percentage total.)

Fall :

This life saving skill teaches the S/A how to partially twist in the air, go limp and roll to receive NO damage from a fall. You must be conscious, not falling "with" someone and the height of your fall must be at least 10 feet off the ground. The maximum height you may fall from and receive NO damage increases as you reach certain levels:

Level	Safe Distance
1 - 2	30 feet
3 - 4	45 feet
5 - 9	60 feet
10 - 14	75 feet
15 - 19	100 feet

(Sp :   add 20' to the distance stated above each time you specialize.)

Pick Locks :

This wonderful skill allows the S/A to open any locked device with the use of a few simple tools. The percentage for "picking" a lock is (your Intellect score) + 3% per level. You successfully pick the lock by rolling a percentage lower then the one you rate. You may attempt to pick the lock as many times as it takes to open it, but it takes at least 6 Attacks (30 seconds) per try. Complicated locks give you negatives on your percentage total and take more time per try to open. Also, there are certain special Lock Pick Tools that give you bonuses to your total.
(Sp :   Add +1/2 Intellect score to percentage and -2 Attacks / Specialization to attempt to Open a Lock.)
[NOTE: You receive a -5% to your total, if you had Informal Training.]

Running Jump :

This seemingly simple skill will allow the S/A to leap farther and higher as she progresses in level. There are stats for Humans, Hemars, and Krill. You must be carrying no more than what is stated on the Strength Table, under the "Bench Press" column, in order to get these Running Jump bonuses. You need at least ¼ of the stated distance for a running start. A S/A may attain a maximum height of ½ the stated distance during the leap.
(ex. A 5th level human S/A may attain a height of 20' at the middle of his jump, but needs a 10' running start.)

The distances are:

Level	Human	Hemar	Krill
1 - 2	25'	40'	15'
3 - 4	30'	45'	20'
5 - 9	40'	55'	25'
10 - 14	50'	65'	35'
15 - 19	60'	75'	45'

NOTE2: Regular people are able to accomplish a Running Jump at the 1st Level Range.
NOTE3: I haven't made any distinction between men and women in these Ranges, don't think there should
     be.

Scale Walls :

This skill allows the S/A to ascend or descend any non-smooth vertical surface without the use of equipment. There are rates stated below and the S/A may move at these rates at will and without making any type of roll! The S/A may, for various reasons, may want to exceed these stated rates. This is possible but you incur a 40% chance of falling for every 1 CRM per Attack you increase your rate. This means that a 3rd level Spy can move up to 15 feet per Attack but incurs a 80% chance of falling. If the surface is slippery it slows the climb by ½ the stated rate and gives you a 20% chance of falling per Minute. You may never scale a wall with more weight than is reflected by your Bench Press Weight on the Strength Table. The rates that you may scale a wall at will are as follows :

Level	Rate per Attack	Charging Rate Multiple
1 - 4	5 feet	1
5 - 9	10 feet	2
10 -14	15 feet	3
15 -19	20 feet	4

Soundless Travel :

This learned skill enables the S/A to travel at the stated rate without making any sound. The S/A may do this for as often as he likes without making any type of a percentage roll! Listed below are the rates that the S/A may travel at, notice that they increase as your level goes up. You may want to increase your rate of Soundless Travel in certain circumstances; if you do, you have a chance of making a sound.

These are the rates, you may travel without making a sound, and without making Any type of a roll:

Level	CRM	Charging Rate (CR)	Feet / Second
1 - 4	½	2.5 feet / Attack	.5'
5 - 9	1	5	1'
10 -14	1.5	7.5	1.5'
15 -19	2	10	2'

NOTE: If a S/A makes NO sound, she leaves NO trail - she may be tracked by scent though.

OPTIONAL RULES :

This table shows the percentage chance of making a sound, based on the rate at which the S/A chooses to travel. The "Stated Rate" is the rate at which the S/A may move per level listed on the table above. "x2 Rate" or "x3 Rate" are all figured from the table above according to the S/A level. Notice that there are different percentages depending on what environment the S/A is trying to travel through.

	City Streets	Fields	Forest
Stated Rate	0% / min	2% / min	5% / min
x2 Rate	15%	25%	35%
x3 Rate	55%	75%	95%

INDIVIDUAL SKILLS

Disguise Self :

This permits the S/A to conceal his or her identity. The S/A may make it look as if she or he is a different sex, may appear 50 pounds heavier or 20 pounds slimmer, and may seem 1 foot shorter or 6 inches taller. The S/A rolls an Ability Check with Intellect and the lower the roll the better the disguise. If the S/A rolls over his stated percentage, the Disguise is so pathetic that anyone could tell something is wrong (you would look like Inspector Clouseau!) Also this skill provides you the ability to tell if someone else is "sporting" a disguise. If you suspect someone is not what she seems, roll your percentage, if it is lower than her's was (when she disguised herself) you will be able to tell if she is disguised.

(Sp : +1/2 Int score added to percentage & seem 10 more pounds heavier or slimmer, and seem 3" taller or shorter each time you specialize.

   1st: You may pick a special disguise to be an alias, someone who you become to fulfill a specific roll or a special task. You only need to make a successful Ability Check with Intellect to become this practiced personage; even at the drop of a silver piece.

   2nd: You may pick up to 3 Aliases. A successful percentage roll allows you to instantly 'become' anyone of them.)

NOTE: If you attempt to disguise someone else, your percentage is cut in half.

Disguise Voice :

This learned gift is what Sergeants the of Guard have nightmares about. The S/A learns how to duplicate someone's voice by just listening to them speak a few sentences. The S/A rolls an Ability Check with Intellect and the lower the roll the better the duplication. As always, if the roll is higher than your percentage, you don't disguise your voice at all. Any S/A with this skill may attempt to detect if someone is disguising his or her voice. If you roll lower than your Opponent's original roll, you recognize the deception.

(Sp : +1/2 Int score each specialization.)

Escape and Tie :

These techniques may allow you to escape, if you are tied or chained in some way. You will also be able to tie up others so that it is very difficult for them to escape. If you are tied up, you may make an Ability Check with Intellect to escape from the ropes. To escape from chains, your percentage is cut in half. Anytime you tie up someone, <u>their escape percentage is cut in half!</u>

(Sp : +1/2 Intellect score to percentage each specialization.)

NOTE2: Regular people get a percentage chance equal to their Intellect Score to escape from ropes and ½ their Intellect Score to escape from chains (That's a 1- 10%, Ha; Ha a Ha; Ha).

Find Concealed Areas :

This very useful skill is <u>exclusive</u> to the S/A Occupation. The S/A needs to be within 1 foot of the door, slide, etc. that gives entrance to the concealed area when she makes a successful Ability Check with Intellect. When the S/A finds the concealed area, the mechanism to open it is usually apparent, if not simply make another Ability Check with Intellect to find it. The S/A may search a 2 foot x 2 foot area in one Attack, but must make an Ability Check for every 2' x 2' area he searches. Taking this Individual Skill also gives you a +5% on your Detect Ambush total.

(Sp : +1/2 Int score each specialization and check a +1'x1' area per Attack each specialization.

   That is a 3' x 3' area for your first Specialization.

   Double specialization means you can check a 4 foot x 4 foot area in one Attack!

   Also you gain +5% on Detect Ambush total each Specialization.

      NOTE3: That's a total of +15% to your Detect Ambush total, if you Specialize twice.

      You gain these bonuses if you are Wary or UnWary)

NOTE4: This also gives the S/A the best knowledge to design a concealed area.

Flying Jump Kick :

    (As Ninja. You can either choose this skill or the Judo Throw - not both. Can't Specialize.)

Judo Throw :

    (As Ninja. You can either choose this skill or the Flying Jump Kick - not both. Can't Specialize.)

Juggle :

    This entertaining skill gives the S/A the ability to juggle a number of objects and even the ability to catch a small object that is flying at him! You may juggle up to 5 objects by making only one Ability Check with Agility (this is "strait" juggling, if you want to do anything special you have to make another Ability Check.) If a small object is flying at you, you have a percentage chance equal to ½ of your Ability Check with Agility to catch it. You may not catch arrows, quarrels, etc. that are flying at very high rates of speed; but you may attempt to catch daggers, axes, Ninja Stars, beer mugs, pool balls, etc.

(Sp : +1/2 Agl score each specialization; you are also able to juggle an additional 2 objects each specialization. The objects you are juggling may be flaming after you specialize. Also, you may attempt to catch 1 additional object each Attack that is flying at your person per Specialization. You must have enough Actions available to do this.)

Lie :

    This quality seems to be in born into some people, but when you learn this skill it will teach you how to control facial expressions, think quicker, and make your "exaggerations" seem truthful. It also teaches you to always have an alibi.

(Sp : You gain two different abilities, if you specialize in this skill.

1st Sp: You gain the ability to greatly exaggerate while you tell your tail. Some know these tall tails as 'Fish Stories'.

2nd Sp: You gain the ability to become a Great Storyteller. You can hold an audience spell bound by your elaborate yarns. This person would make a great Ref.)

Measure Distance by Sound :

    This skill seems to be something that would hardly ever be used and a skill that would only waste one of your "slots." This is an excellent skill to possess if you want to know how close someone around a corner is getting to you. Roll an Ability Check with Intellect and the lower the percentage the more accurate your estimation is. If you roll over your percentage, you have no idea how close or far the noises are. This also gives you a +10% to your Disguise Voice skill.

(Sp : +1/2 Int score to percentage and +5% to Disguise Voice each Specialization.)

Read Lips :

    This ability allows you to understand what is being said from a distance without being close enough to hear the person speaking. However, you must be within a reasonable distance (unless you're using a telescope, ect.) and under circumstances to actually see the persons' lips. You must also speak the language being used.

(Sp : Can't)

Remove and Set Traps :

    When you or one of your companions find a trap, you have the ability to <u>disarm</u> it with this skill. After you are aware of the trap, you must make one successful Ability Check with Intellect to disarm the device. The roll is used to determine if you can disarm it without mishap. If the trap is especially complicated, the S/A will incur some sort of negative to his or her percentage total specified by the Ref.

(Sp : +1/2 Int score to percentage and +5% to remove a trap from a lock, or small area, etc. each specialization.)

NOTE : If you miss one of your rolls by 30% or more you will spring the trap.

        When you select this skill, you also learn the basic knowledge needed to **Set** a trap and <u>still use the area</u>.

When you initially learn the skill, the traps are 'simple traps' such as Pits, Snares and such.

(Set Traps   1st Specialization :   Falling, Sliding and moving traps of all kinds.

                2nd Specialization: Smaller traps - Needles, spring, and weight traps.)

NOTE2: If any one of your traps ever becomes Deadly for <u>any</u> reason, your Morality Rating instantly falls to a 5.

Roll and Evade :
This skill allows the S/A to roll, tumble or twirl out of the way of an attack. You can also use this skill if you're thrown by a Judo Throw and it gives you a bonus to the amount of distance you can Fall and not take damage. To evade an attack you must state you're using this skill before your Opponent attacks you and it takes 2 of your Actions. When you use this ability, you may add 5% plus your whole Agility score to your current PTE total! i.e. When you Roll and Evade: your PTE total equals your armor, any magical bonuses, your regular Agility Bonus <u>+ 5% plus your full Agility score!</u> This would give you a maximum Agility bonus total of +35% to your PTE total – instead of the regular +10%; i.e. your Regular PTE + 25%, if you have the astounding Agility score of 20!

If you double Specialize the percentage rises to +55%, including your regular PTE Agility bonus; i.e. your normal Armor, magical, ect bonuses PLUS 55% (+10% regular Agl Bonus; +25% regular Roll and Evade bonus; +20% for double Specialization).

If you are thrown by a S/A or Ninja, you will not be stunned and receive only ½ damage. You also may fall an extra 10 feet and receive NO damage.
(Sp : +1/2 Agility score to your PTE bonuses each specialization, fall an additional 5 feet & S/A may do
   1 handspring per 5 levels.)   (Note: A Krill may of course use this ability while flying.)

Slight-of-Hand :
After a S/A learns this skill, he may manipulate a small object into and out of an observer's sight. This can be used very well with the Conceal Object General Skill and gives you a bonus of +10% to that skill when you use it. You need to make a successful Ability Check with Agility to cause an object to "disappear and appear." The number of objects and their size depends on your level and are the same as stated on the Conceal Objects Table.
(Sp : +1/2 Agl score to percentage and +5% bonus to Conceal Object each specialization.)
[NOTE2: You receive a bonus of +5% to your percentage total, if you had Informal Training.]

Squeeze :
This skill teaches the S/A to squeeze into or out of small areas that he normally would have no chance to pass. You are taught to shift your torso, shoulders, wings, etc. in such a way so you can squeeze into or out of a "tight fit" or down a small tunnel. Roll a successful Ability Check with Agility if you want to use this skill. In certain situations, if you use this skill successfully, it will give you a bonus to your Conceal Self percentage (+10% bonus when applicable, like flattening your body against a wall).
(Sp : +1/2 Agl score on percentage and +5% bonus to Conceal Self each specialization.)
[NOTE3: You receive a bonus of +10% to your percentage total, if you had Informal Training.]

Spy Fingers :
This secretive skill may only be learned by a S/A that is at least 5th level and is in an 'Institutions' employ. This skill is actually a type of sign language, that when used correctly, anyone without the skill has no idea that there is any conversation going on. This "language" is a complex series of body and finger movements - even the blinking of an eye at the correct time! Every "language" is different, so you may only understand those people affiliated with your Organization. If you do suspect two or more others are engaging in "conversation" in a language not of your Organization, you may make a Ability Check with Intellect. If you are successful, you will know that they are "discussing" something, but you will have no idea what they are "saying." You may "speak" to anyone within your organization as long as you can see their entire body (usually within 40').   (Sp : Can't)

Stay Awake :
A S/A sometimes must watch a building or window all night, so this may be an important skill. Regular people that are trying to stay awake and are sitting, standing or lying in the same place must make an Ability Check with Endurance at mid-night and another every hour after that at a -5% each hour until the Column Sun dawns. By learning this skill, you train yourself to stay awake while on a stakeout. The S/A only needs to make an Ability Check with Endurance at midnight and every 2 hours after that until Sunrise. You receive NO minuses to your percentage roll for each consecutive hour you are required to stand your post.
Example: your End=18, so your character has a 54% to stay awake, but he must succeed in this roll at
   12pm, 2am, 4am, 6am & 8am, while the winter snows fall.
(Sp : +1/2 End score added to your rolls and make your check every +1 hours after midnight each
   specialization.)
[Example: Willamina is a Spy with an Endurance of 16 and she is double specialized in this skill, so she has
   a **64** ((16 * 3) + 8 + 8) **percent** chance to stay awake at midnight and she only has to roll a check at
   4am and 8am during the winter.]

Trained Observer :

When a S/A learns this skill, she is taught to expand on those innate qualities she already possesses. It teaches the S/A to recognize people, objects, and situations that seem "out of place." It also teaches her how to remember an object or person in great detail even after only seeing it for a split second. The S/A makes an Ability Check with Intellect and the lower the roll the more the S/A "sees" or remembers. This skill also gives a +10% to see "through" a Disguise.

(Sp : +1/2 Int score to percentage and +5% to Detect to see through a disguised each specialization.)

Unseen Attack :

This deadly skill enables the S/A to do great harm to his victim. The S/A must be unseen and unheard by the victim. This means that the S/A usually must use the skill Soundless Travel and be concealed at the time of the strike. When the S/A uses this skill, he gets these bonuses :

    1) A -20% on his Strike Placement Table (SPT) roll.

    2) All Critical Strikes effects on the SPT are doubled.

    3) Add an extra +1 EP damage per your level – if you use a weapon other than a Blackjack or Garrote.

NOTE: Your victim never receives his Agility Bonus on his PTE total anytime the attack is unseen.

NOTE2: An unsuspected victim, standing still, wearing no helmet and that is totally unaware of the S/A gets automatically hit.

If you use a Blackjack and you hit your Opponent's unarmored head, the S/A will stun the victim for 1d10 Attacks and has a 5% chance per Strength point of knocking out the victim for 2d10 Attacks.

If you use a Garrote and strike your Opponent's throat, he can't make any noise and will choke to death in 6 Attacks, if he can't break free.

(Sp : You get these bonuses every time you specialize, while using a <u>Blackjack or Garrote</u>:

    1) Extra -10% on you SPT roll.

    2a) Blackjack = Stun victim for +2 Attacks and victim will stay knocked out for +2 Attacks.

    2b) Garrote = Strangle victim in -1 Attacks.

You get these bonuses every time you specialize, while using any <u>Other Weapon</u> than a Black Jack or Garrote:

    1) Extra -10% on you SPT roll.

    2) 1st Specialization = Weapon Damage +2 EP damage per level.

    3) 2nd Specialization = Weapon Damage +3 EP damage per level.)

A SPY PREPAIRING TO KNOCK OUT A GUARD WITH A BLACKJACK

Walk "Tight-Rope" :

Teaches you to transverse any rope, beam, etc. that is anchored at both ends. To move across a "tight-rope" you must make a successful Ability Check with Agility every 30 feet. You receive a -10% for every 5 degrees beyond 30 degrees the rope angles. The Rate at which you may cross the rope is ½ your Charging Rate. A large Hemar (Not a Shetland) may only use this skill if he transverses a ledge, beam, etc of at least 1 foot in width.

(Sp : +1/2 Agility score to percentage each time you specialize.)

NINJA

INTRODUCTION

STORY

Warriors and Assassins where adventuring out and butchering Enchanters, Alchemists, and Elementalists for their Enchanted Items. These Enchanters started to hire other Warriors to protect them, but usually when the thieves surrounded them and the "Guards" were promised first pick of the loot, the "Guards" would turn on their employers. These "guards" were also sometimes in league with the thieves from the start and would lead their employers into ambushes. The Enchanters, Alchemists, and Elementalists then started to call conferences to talk to one another and try to discover some way to protect themselves from these fiendish attacks. One Enchanter brought a man named King So, a human, to such a conference.

King So was an expert with weapons and to the amazement of the gathering also with his hands and feet. This was not what impressed them the most though, because King So had survived in solitude on the vast mountain ranges of the Krill Island. He had developed amazing abilities and when he sat a certain way and concentrated, a glow would form between his palms. No Enchanter could "See" any Enchantment, but when one brilliant Alchemist drank a See Life potion, she was almost blinded! King So could consolidate and amplify his Life Force! He called this his Ki (the essence of himself and therefore the essence of his name.)

The gathering persuaded King So to accept 13 pupils and teach them all he knew. King So and his pupils where sealed up in a special Training Camp for 20 years. This wasn't exactly kept secret, so many Spies and Assassins attempted to gain entry. Most of them awakened outside the Camp the next day telling of how "spirits" came at them and knocked them out. Some never told stories, being dead and this discouraged most others.

When the pupils emerged, 12 where Masters, 1 was not present (it was told that he broke his **Oath** and death came to him.) King So was gone – and has not been seen since. Now all Ninja must take a Vow at 4th level to attain 5th. At 5th level all Ninja must become the Guardian of an Enchanter or Alchemist and take an **Oath** to protect them onto death.

There is a down side to this story, Enchanters and Alchemists had no trouble bonding with the Ninja. But when an Elementalist did, they found that no Elemental would answer the call of a spinning Ring or Disk.

How someone becomes a Ninja:

All parents that wish to have their children become Ninja must deliver the child to a training Camp in the dead of night. The child must be left outside the gate without any type of identification! Yes, a Ninja will never know who his or her parents where. The child must be left during their per-school years; between these ages: Humans = 4 - 6 yrs; Hemar = 8 - 10 yrs; Krill = 2 - 3 yrs.

As the child grows, he will be taught some of the basics of being a Ninja. This will include training in the Staff and one other weapon of the child's choice. Also he will learn the Survival Skill of Improved Charging Rate and 2 others of his choice. He will be educated in his native language and any others that he has the Intellect to learn. The child will also start to make his belt.

When the children have spent 20 years at their camp, they will be asked if they wish to continue training and attempt to become a Ninja. If they answer "No", the gates will be opened for them and they may go to lead their lives in peace. If they reply "Yes!", they will be given an Ascension Test to see if they are worthy (details follow). If they survive the test, they will attend a ceremony in which they will consolidate their Ki for the FIRST time. When they do, their personally made belts will be tied around their waist. When the ceremony ends, the belt will automatically become "linked" to the Ninja's Ki. The belt may never be taken off. Now the Ninja, of 1st level, is ready to go out into the world and seek her fortune.

The 1st level Ninja will leave the Training Camp with two Gee (+15% PTE), a Standard Adventure's Pack (SAP), one Staff, 10 Silver Pieces, a map of the general area around your Training Camp, and 2 Enchanted items:

(1st) 1 measure of Enchanted Smoke Bomb Alchemist's Dust in a small pouch. (See Violet Spell Section)
(2nd) 1 Potion - Ref's choice, but usually an Enchanted Potion of Healing for 50 EP.

These Enchanted Items are gifts from the camp's current High Alchemist for completing the Ascension Test.

Training Camp Personnel (of note) :
1) Master Teacher: Minimum of 15th level - Head Ninja of the Training Camp.
2) High Alchemist: Minimum of 10th level - Head Medic of the Training Camp.
3) Executioner: Minimum of 12th level - ready to take orders from elders and take care of any problems, etc.

The Ascension Test can be a specific test the character must overcome before he becomes a Ninja or could just be part of the story the Ref. is telling. Either way it should be held in a special building with many rooms and paths but only one correct way out. The character must dodge and think his way though the maze or be lost and confounded. Upon successfully conquering the test, the new Ninja can begin the ceremony and consolidate their Ki for the first time.

INFORMATION & FACTS :

Ninja Requirements:

1) A Ninja must always have a Morality Rating (MR) between 5 and 15. If these MR are ever exceeded, then the Ninja's belt will turn Dull Gray and he will loss all **Ki abilities** (even the ability to consolidate Ki and to withstand a Stun Strike).

   If the Ninja's MR is not between 5 -15, he will not gain any experience until he gets his MR back between 5 -15, at which time his belt will resume its regular color and he will regain his abilities.

2) A Ninja must successfully take and complete a Vow at 4th level.

3) A Ninja must become the Guardian of an Enchanter or Alchemist at 5th level.

4) A Ninja can't wear any Armor, he can only wear his Gee which provides a +15% PTE bonus.

5) A Ninja is the only Occupation that can consolidate Ki, and for this reason they are the only Occupation that CAN'T gain access to any Spell Points.

   A Ninja may NEVER learn ANY spells!

   He can use Potions, Dusts, Pills, and Enchanted Items, Scrolls, Rings, Disks, Wands, ect. if he knows the Trigger Word.

The Belt :

A Ninja's belt is a direct reflection of his Ki. It is linked with their Life force, a link that can only be severed by death. The belt must be made by the Ninja's own hand before he reaches 1st level. You will be taught how to do this by your elders using very thick white cloth and heavy white thread. When you pass your Ascension Test, a ceremony will be performed that will link your belt to your Life-force, or Ki.

The belt's color will change or grow darker every level - including at 2nd when it will go from pure white to a pale white - and as you rise above 15th level it will grow blacker every level; by 19th level it will be as dark as midnight. When you accumulate enough Experience Points to attain the next level, your belt will immediately change color or grow visibly darker. After this happens, the next time you Meditate, which takes 8 hours, you will automatically be granted the additional Ki Points you rate and will completely understand your next Ki Ability.

The belt will reflect all aspects of your Ki. Because of this, when you take your Vow at 4th level your belt will show a wide GOLDEN line down the center and the tips of your belt will change to a particular color that describes your Vow.

All Ninja must keep there Morality Ratings (MR) between 5 - 15. If you ever go beyond these limits your belt will immediately turn a Dull Gray.

If a Ninja ever breaks his Oath, his belt will immediately change to a bright, almost glowing Red.

If your belt's color ever becomes Dull Gray or Red, you immediately loss your ability to consolidate your Ki and so can't use any Ki Abilities. This signifies that you are no longer a Ninja and you can now even be affected by the Stun Strike of another Ninja. You may ask why I can't just take off your Belt. I'll answer this question:

A Ninja may NEVER take off his belt, because it is linked to his Life force and to break that link would mean death. Because this is true, your belt can never be harmed in any way! It can't be cut, burnt, torn, untied, etc. and it can't even become dirty - just change color. The only time a belt will ever "let go" is when you die. If you are killed and your belt is Red, your body will crumble to dust and your executioner may return your Red belt to your "charge".

Below is a list of the colors your belt takes on as you progress in levels. It will never become a different color unless you rise in level, start your Vow level, violate the MR restrictions or break your Oath.

Level	Belt Color
1st - 2nd	White
3rd - 4th	Yellow
5th - 9th	Green
10th - 14th	Brown
15th - 19th	Black

Vow Level :

When all Ninja reach 4th level, they must take a Vow and keep it throughout the full level to prove that they are worthy of the upcoming honor: Guardianship. There are different Vows you may choose from. Each Vow will cause the tips of your belt to turn a different color and you will gain some type of benefit, if you successfully reach 5th level. Once you take a Vow, you must complete it – there is no other way out!

If you ever break your Vow during your struggle to reach 5th level, your belt will immediately turn a Dull Gray. If your belt becomes Dull Gray, you loss the ability to consolidate your Ki and all of your Ki Abilities. You also must subtract all Experience Points (XPO) you've attained in that level and start the level over. If you start over, you must complete 4th level without the benefits of ANY Ki Abilities and with your belt a Dull Gray showing your disgrace!!

To take your Vow, you must travel back to the Training Camp where you were raised and tell one of your Masters which Vow you want to undertake. There will be a short ceremony after which you will recite your Vow. Now your belt will show a wide Golden line down the whole length and the tips will take on a specific color that describes your Vow. When you attain 5th level, you gain any bonuses that are listed in the Vow's description, but not until then!

VOW'S NAME	TIP COLOR	ABILITY BONUS
Silence	Black	Soundless Travel ability.
Hunger & Thirst	Blue	Double duration of the 2nd level Ki ability.
Truthfulness	Indigo	+2 added to your Wisdom score.
Absence of Ki	Silver	+10 KP [yes, Ki Points!]

Vow Descriptions

Silence :

This Vow requires that you not communicate with anyone or anything during your Vow level. If you attempt to communicate in any way with anything, your belt turns Dull Gray. This includes speaking, whistling, or signaling in anyway! If you are terribly wounded, etc. and scream as a result of this, your belt will not change color, as long as your scream is not a word or a signal.
Bonus = Ability to use the Soundless Travel skill as described in the Spy / Assassin Section.

Hunger & Thirst :

This vow requires that you do not eat, drink or sleep for the entire Vow level. It's possible to sustain yourself through the use of your 2nd level Ki Ability, as long as you use it every day.
Bonus = You are able to go 2 days without food, water or sleep for every time you use your 2nd level Ki
        Ability after 4th level.

Truthfulness :

This simple Vow requires you to tell the **complete and total truth** to any person you choose to answer. This means you must not mislead your questioner in ANY way and you are required to volunteer any additional information that you even suspect your questioner may need. You may choose not to answer ONE person per day; all others you must answer truthfully and completely.
Bonus = Add TWO points to your Wisdom Score.   (Remember to adjust your Will Score if necessary.)

Absence of Ki :

This Vow requires you to not use any of your Ki Abilities for the entire Vow level. You can do nothing that requires or relates to the use of your Ki! This includes no consolidation (for an emergency, for example), meditation, healing instead of sleep, Ice walking, etc.
Bonus = +10 KP.

Note: You may take any Vow you wish but you must complete ONE or be stuck in a relentless "loop".

Ref Note: It is the Referees duty to try and get the Ninja to break his Vow! This has to be a test and if it isn't then the Vow level is worthless. Some ideas are:
1) If you player has taken the Vow of Silence, you could put him in a situation in which he must yell to save a friend from danger.
2) If your player has taken the Vow of Truthfulness, put him in a situation in which if he reveals his companions hiding place they will all be in grave danger.
3) Put the Ninja who has taken the Absence of Ki Vow in a situation where he must go into a Death Trance or be caught.   *I'm sure you get the picture!*

Guardianship :

When a Ninja reaches 5th level, he must become a Guardian for an Enchanter or Alchemist. The Ninja may either pick the person or have one appointed to him. Either way you can't progress beyond the start of 5th level unless you become a Guardian (You don't receive any Experience Points toward 6th level until you do.)

Be warned that once you've picked a "charge" (I use the word "charge" to refer to the person the Ninja becomes Guardian of) and have taken the Oath, you must protect him or her with your life for the rest of your years. The reason that the Occupation of Ninja came about is so an Enchanter or Alchemist could have someone they could trust and depend upon to defend them no matter what.

Once you've picked (or had appointed) the person you are going to be Guardian of, you must take him or her to the Training Camp where you graduated from. When you get there simply inform the Head Master that you wish to take the Oath. The arrangements are simple so you should, in most cases, be able to take the Oath within a couple of days of your request.

The ceremony of the Oath is very short but requires you and you "charge" to be present. You will be asked to consolidate ALL of your Ki and your "charge" will also, have to have, ALL of his or her Spell Points available. A special spell called the Oath Spell will be cast on both of you or you will both have to drink 1/2 of a special potion that contains this spell. As soon as the Ninja quaffs his portion of the potion, he must recite the Oath:

"I (your full name) promise to Guard and Protect ("charge's" full name) with all of my ability and Life-force. I swear I will sacrifice my life to Protect (him/her). I swear never to deceive my "charge" or never willfully bring danger upon (him/her). If my abilities are not enough and my Guardianship fails, I swear to avenge my "charge's" death. I swear this by my free will. Let our link never be tarnished and only be severed by the hand of death."

The spell will drain All or your Ki Points and all of your "charges" Spell Points for that day, but will link you both together in a way that can only be broken by death. The bonuses that this "link" will bestow on BOTH you and your charge are:

1) Tell exact location of the other person as long as you are within 2 feet per 1 Maximum Ki Point of the Ninja - If you are 5th level and have a Wisdom of 19 (ie. 38 KP), then you will know each others exact location within 76 feet of one another.
2) Know if the other is in great danger, such as fighting for his or her life, etc. regardless of the distance separating the two of you.
3) Matches your Life spans - both living the longest life span.

NOTE: The Enchanter or Alchemist is expected to give the Ninja a gift of some Enchanted Item - to thank him for the years of service to come.

By taking the Oath you DO NOT become some sort of slave or servant, on the contrary. Because you are responsible for your "charges" health and life, your decision should be final on all matters dealing with the security of your "charge". This includes what route to take, when and where to sleep or rest, etc.

As you see there are many responsibilities that the Ninja has to the Enchanter or Alchemist, there also are some things that the protected are responsible for. The "charge" must assure that the Ninja has sufficient tools for the job of protection. The "charge" should make sure the Ninja has about the same number of Enchanted Items as she does. The question of food, housing, equipment, etc. can be handled in many ways. If the bounty from the adventures are to be split evenly then the Ninja should take care of his own necessities. This is the most common way. In the question of housing, the "charge" is always responsible for it while in a town, city, etc. - this includes a room or small dwelling for the Ninja when the pair is not adventuring. When "out-and-about" the Ninja will pick the areas to set up camp and when to rest.

As you can imagine there is a great demand for these Guardians, so the fee to attain one is very high. The cost is usually not handled in cash. There are more valuable things than that: Information, Items, or Promises – Yes, many Quest slots to be filled!

This table describes how many Actions the Ninja gains per Level.

Level	Strikes	Parries	Total Actions	Examples
1st - 4th	1	1	2	(A)
5th - 9th	1	2	3	(B)
10th - 14th	2	2	4	(C)
15th - 19th	3	2	5	

(A)   May make 1 Strike with a weapon and may make 1 Parry with the same weapon.
       May Strike with a weapon and Parry with a Shield.
       Paired Weapons = Strike with 1st Sai and Parry with 2nd Sai.

(B)   Strike with a weapon and Parry one strike from 2 different opponents.
       Strike with a weapon and Parry 2 Strikes from 1 attacker.
       Strike with a weapon and Benefit from BOTH your Parry skill and a Shield verses one attack.
       Paired Weapons = Strike with 1st Sai and Double Parry one opponent with both Sias.

(C)   Strike 1 Opponent two times with your weapon and parry the 1st two strikes from that Opponent.
       Paired Weapons = Strike once with 1st Sai and once with 2nd, then Double Parry 1st Strike from one Opponent.

The Ninja may Specialize in a projectile type weapon at 7th level or in a melee weapon at 9th level.

SPECIAL ABILITIES

NINJA LEVEL ABILITIES *

LEVEL	ABILITIES		
1st	1) Front or Circle Kick	**AND**	Leg Sweep
	2) Block or Catch Projectile		
	3) Disguise	**OR**	Conceal Self
	4) Automatic Improve Charging Rate		
	5) Fist or Kick = Base Damage (Fist=1d6) + x1 Strength Damage Bonus		
2nd	1) Parry		
	2) Walk Tightrope	**OR**	Scale Walls
3rd	1) Back Kick	**OR**	Wrist Lock
	2) Soundless Travel	**OR**	Pick Locks
4th	Vow Level		
5th	1) Guardianship Level		
	2) Flying Kick	**OR**	Judo Throw
	3) Fist or Kick = Base Damage + x2 Strength Damage Bonus		
6th	Percentage MINUSES on Strike Placement Table		
7th	May Specialize in One Projectile Weapon	**OR**	wait until 9th level.
8th	Disarm		
9th	May Specialize in One Melee Weapon (**If** you did not Specialize at 7th level.)		
10th	Fist or Kick = Base Damage + x3 Strength Damage Bonus		
15th	Fist or Kick = Base Damage + x4 Strength Damage Bonus		

* All Ninja Level Abilities are supplemented by Ninja Ki Abilities (see the next section).

NINJA ABILITIES DESCRIPTIONS

Kicks: 1st, 3rd, 5th Levels
    All kicks are Melee attacks and take a Strike Action to use. All kicks do more damage than your open hand, but if you miss your Opponent, you will suffer certain penalties.
1st Level: *Front or Circle Kick -*
        Hit = 2d6 + Strength Damage bonus.
        Miss = Roll Ability Check with Agility or loss your Agility Bonus on your next PTE total.
3rd Level: *Back and Side Kicks (Hemar excluded- Remember they already have their Buck=1d20+Str Dam) -*
        Hit = 3d6 + Strength Damage bonus. Opponent must be directly behind or to the side of you.
        Miss = Make Ability Check with Agility at a negative 10% or loss Agility Bonus on your next
            PTE roll.
5th Level: *Flying Kick -*
        Hit = 4d6 + Strength Damage bonus and 2% chance per point of damage done to Stun
            Opponent for 1d6 Actions. You are required a Running Start of a minimum of 10 feet
            to use a Flying Kick.
        Miss = loss <u>one</u> of your next Parry Actions and your Agility Bonus on your next PTE roll.

Judo Moves: 1st, 3rd, 5th Levels
    All Judo moves are Melee attacks and take a Strike Action to use. You may learn both the Leg Sweep **and** the Front Kick at 1st Level, but at 3rd and 5th Levels you only learn the **ONE** of your choice.
1st Level: *Leg Sweep –*
      Hit = Your opponent gets no ARMOR Bonus on her PTE roll. If your Opponent fails this special PTE
          roll, she will fall to the ground (Hemar excluded.) [Getting up costs 1 Parry Action].
      Miss = Roll Ability Check with Agility or loss your Agility bonus on your PTE roll on the next Attack.
3rd Level: *Wrist Lock –* You must have the Initiative and your Opponent gets no Armor Bonus on his PTE roll.
        If your Opponent misses his special PTE roll, you caught his wrist which causes Pain, does
            1d6 damage and he has a 50% chance that he drops whatever he is holding.
            NOTE: The Ninja doesn't need to make a SPT roll – you are trained to strike the wrist.
      Hit = Opponent losses <u>one</u> of his next Strike Actions and you may put him to his knees or Leg Sweep,
         etc.
      Miss = You must go dead last on the next Initiative, even if your party wins.

5th Level: *Judo Throw* – You must have Initiative and your Opponent gets no Armor Bonus on his PTE Roll. If Opponent misses his special PTE roll, you grabbed his arm and threw him.

Hit = Opponent is thrown an amount of feet equal to x2 your Strength Dam Bonus, plus takes 1 point Damage per foot he flew and has a 50% to be stunned for 1d6 Actions.

(example: Ninja with Strength = 17, throws Opponent 6 feet. Opponent takes 6 EP Damage and has a 50% chance to be stunned.)

If your Opponent CHARGES and the Ninja is successful, your Opponent flies a distance equal to x4 your Str Dam Bonus in Feet and receives 2 points of EP Damage per foot flown.

(example: Ninja with Strength = 17, so you throw your charging Opponent 12 feet and he takes 24 pts EP Damage and has a 50% chance to be stunned.)

Miss = You go dead last on the next Initiative and lose your Agility Bonus on your PTE roll for next Attack.

NOTE: The Ninja must have a Strength of at least 13 to throw any victim.

NOTE2: Your Opponent must not weigh more than 500 lbs over your maximum Bench Press Lift weight. This includes the weight of their Armor as well.

Block or Catch Projectiles: 1st Level

You may attempt to Block or Catch certain objects that are speeding toward you or one of your companions, if you are aware of the projectiles. If the projectile is flying at **you**, you may either block or catch it - but if it is flying at one of your companions you may only attempt to catch it. You may attempt to block or catch a number of projectiles equal to 1/2 of your total levels (1st level = 1, 3rd = 2, 5th = 3, etc.) or until you miss one, which ever comes first. The percentage to Block a projectile is your Ability Check with Agility and your percentage to Catch one is 1/2 your Blocking percentage. This takes your Entire Attack to accomplish, but you may actually block any number of objects equal to ½ of your total levels, ie. A 15th Level Ninja could block 8 objects, but this would be all he could do that Attack. Ie. If the number of projectiles you attempt to block exceeds your number of Actions / Attack, you can still Block them but that is all you can do this Attack.

NOTE3: You must be aware of the projectile - the 5th level, Sense Enemies abilities may work with this ability, if the circumstances are right.

Automatic Improve Charging Rate: 1st Level

You get an automatic upgrade in your Charging Rate when you attain 1st level Ninja. Your new rates are listed below.

Human	= 20 ft/sec - CRM = 4
Krill & Hemar	= 25 ft/sec - CRM = 5

Disguise Self OR Conceal Self: 1st Level

When you reach 1st level, you may pick ONE of these skills to learn. These skill descriptions can be found under Spy / Assassin skills, use them the same way with the same restrictions, bonuses and percentages.

Fist or Kick Damage: 1st Level

As you attain certain levels, you learn how to Strike more effectively to cause additional damage with your fist or foot. Your Strength Damage Bonus for a hand or foot strike is increased at 5th, 10th, and 15th levels. At 1st level your Strength Dam Bonus is regular.

Parry: 2nd Level

You are taught how to Parry an opponent's Strike. This is the same as the 1st level Warrior Combat Ability. You may use a Ninja Sword, Sais, Tonfa, Kama, Staff, or any other weapon listed in the Warrior section to Parry a Strike.

Walk Tightrope OR Scale Walls: 2nd Level

You may pick <u>one</u> of these skills when you attain 2nd level. Follow all rules as stated under Spy / Assassin Section.

Back Kick OR Wrist Lock: 3rd Level

Follow rules stated above.

Travel Soundlessly OR Pick Locks: 3rd Level

Pick <u>one</u> of these Spy / Assassin Skills to learn.

Vow Level: 4th Level

      Remember that EVERY Ninja must take a Vow and keep it through the entire level or **never** reach 5th level.

Guardian Level: 5th Level

      Every Ninja must take an Enchanter or Alchemist to be their charge at 5th level.

Flying Kick OR Judo Throw: 5th Level

      Follow rules stated above.

Fist or Kick Damage: 5th Level

      At this level you learn how to put more force behind you punches or kicks, so you do Double your regular Strength Dam Bonus when you use your fist or foot to strike an opponent.
Fist Damage = 1d6 + x2 Strength Damage Multiple. Remember to add this bonus to your normal Kick Damage as well.

Percentage Pluses on Strike Placement Table (SPT):   6th Level

      When you use any type of Weapon (including fist, foot, sword or bow) you receive a Percentage bonus on your SPT rolls from this level on. The Percentage bonus is equal to your personal (Wisdom/2)+1%/Level, so if your Wisdom is 20, your Percentage bonus is 16% at 6th level. These bonuses will get you to a General Area of the body and are always subtracted from your SPT roll. If you have a Wisdom Score of 18 and are 10th Level, you have a 19% bonus on your SPT roll. If you Strike someone and roll a 15% on the SPT, which normally would hit the Body, when you subtract your percentage you get something less than zero, but you still only hit your opponent in the GENERAL Area of the Head. To hit your Opponent in the Eyes or Neck you still have to ROLL (with no bonuses) a natural 01 or a 10 respectively - this includes strikes to the Heart, Spine, etc.

Specialize in a Projectile Weapon: 7th Level

      You may either Specialize in a Projectile Weapon at this level **OR** wait until 9th Level and Specialize in a Melee Weapon. Follow all rules stated in the Weapon Specialization Section. Remember to add all bonuses, including firing rates, Opponent's PTE reduction, and Damage Bonuses where applicable. See the Weapon Specialization Section for the weapons you may Specialize in.

Disarm: 8th Level

      You learn the Disarm Warrior Combat Skill at this level. The Ninja may use his hands, Sias, Kama, any Ninja weapon made for disarming or any weapon listed in the Warrior's section under the Disarm skill.

Specialize in a Melee Weapon: 9th Level

      If you didn't Specialize at 7th with a Projectile Weapon, you may now specialize with a Melee weapon. Please see the Weapon Specialization Section for details.

Fist or Kick Damage: 10th Level

      At this level your Fist Damage does 1d6 + x3 your Strength Dam Bonus. Remember to add this bonus to your normal Kick Damage as well.

Fist or Kick Damage: 15th Level

      At this level your Fist Damage does 1d6 + x4 your Strength Dam Bonus. Remember to add this bonus to your normal Kick Damage as well.

NINJA KI ABILITIES

NINJA KI TABLE

LEVEL :	KP :	ABILITY
1st :	12 :	(1) Death Trance *
:	:	(2) Consolidate Ki * # @
:	:	(3) Heal x2 Rate (Meditation) * # @
2nd :	14 :	(1) Go without Food, Drink and Sleep
:	:	(A) Walk Over Un-solid Surfaces (W.O.U.S.): Ice type
3rd :	16 :	(1) Minds Eye
4th :	18 :	(1) Stun Strike
:	:	(A) W.O.U.S.: Mud type
5th :	25 :	(1) Since "Enemies" Presence
:	:	(2) Consolidate Ki on Move @
6th :	27 :	(1) Silent Step or Touch
:	:	(A) W.O.U.S.: Quicksand type
7th :	30 :	(1) Ninja Jump
8th :	35 :	(1) Fire Walk
:	:	(2) Pass
:	:	(A) W.O.U.S.: Sticky type
9th :	40 :	(1) Levitate
10th :	45 :	(1) Heal Self or Charge
:	:	(2) Transfer (+20 KP)
:	:	(3) Resist Mesmerize and Illusion
:	:	(A) W.O.U.S.: Water - Calm type and through Tree Tops & Limbs
11th :	50 :	(1) Vibration Punch - only Inanimate objects
12th :	55 :	(1) Power Punch - 1d20/(1 for every 4 completed levels) or 3d20 at 12th
:	:	(A) W.O.U.S.: Water - Wavy type
13th :	60 :	(1) Shadow Step
14th :	65 :	(1) Block Enchantment #
:	:	(A) W.O.U.S.: Water – Stormy
15th :	70 :	(1) Pass Through Solid Objects
16th :	75 :	(A) W.O.U.S.: Air - Only Strait, NOT up or down

*   Means you can't move or fly - only for 1st level abilities.

\#   Special Ki Positions - (A) "Ki Seat" (B) "Ki Stance".

@   Takes no KPs to use.

(A)   All abilities that are designated by an (A) have to do with Walking Over some type of Un-solid Surface, and they are all explained at the end of the Ninja Ki Abilities descriptions.

NOTE: A Ki Point Example – These values are summarized in Appendix M.

> A **5th** level Ninja with an **18** Wisdom has Ki Points (KP) = 36

$$KP = (Wisdom) + [(L-1) * (Wisdom / 4)]$$

$$Total = (18) + [(5-1) * (18/4)] = 18 + [4 * 5] = 36$$

NOTE2: Most Ninja Ki Abilities require your character to spend a certain number of Ki Points (KP). The total number of Ki Points required to use each Ki ability are listed on the table above. The descriptions of the skills are listed below:

NINJA KI ABILITY DESCRIPTIONS

Consolidate Ki = No KP cost   1st Level

    At low levels, Ninja must assume a Ki Position (A or B) and then concentrate to consolidate his/her Ki Points. While doing this the area between your palms will begin to glow. You can Consolidate one KP per Attack, but must stay in a Ki Position and not move while you do. You may Consolidate your Ki once per day per 2 levels of experience. (i.e.: 1st & 2nd Levels = 1/day; 3rd & 4th = 2/day; ect.)

Ki Seat   (position A):   Sitting cross legged with feet turned upwards and Palms facing each other.
Ki Stance (position B):   Heels together, back straight, shoulders back and Palms facing each other.

Death Trance = 12 KP   1st Level   D: 30 min/Level

    When you spend the indicated Ki Points and call on this ability, you go into a trance like state in which all vital signs stop - breathing, heart rate, pulse, even bleeding etc. While in the Death Trance you can't feel pain or even drown! You can still hear, and see if your eyes are open. You can "wake" up at any time before the Duration ends and take action. If you let the Duration run out, you automatically "wake" up.

Heal x2 Rate (Meditation) = No KP cost   1st Level   D: Takes 8 hrs.

    You may cause your body to Double its natural Healing Rate, but it takes 8 hours and replaces sleep. This doesn't cost any Ki Points, but you can't be disturbed for the entire Duration or you heal the Endurance Points normally. After a night of Meditation, you feel refreshed, just like 8 hours of sleep. Using this ability allows the Ninja to gain back 2d10 EP damage from an eight hour Meditation. If you have been bandaged by someone with First Aid, double those bonuses as well. You also must Meditate for 8 hours to gain your new Ki ability when you go up in level.

Go Without Food, Drink and Sleep = 14 KP   2nd Level   D: 1 Full Day

    Once you activate this ability, you can function without any penalties when you have no sleep or food or water for the entire day. You don't need food, water, or sleep to maintain optimum performance.

Minds Eye = 16 KP   3rd Level   R: 5 ft/L   D: 1 hour/L

    This ability will allow the Ninja to see normally to the front if she is blinded in any way. This includes blindness caused through darkness, eyes wounded by normal or enchanted attack, or even if you were born blind. You are able to see to a distance of 5 ft/Level to the front. You can't see colors, but this is the only difference from regular sight. In normal darkness you receive normal day vision.

Stun Strike = 18 KP   4th Level   D: 1 Strike only

    This outstanding ability allows the Ninja to Stun most opponents by simply striking them. As long as you have the Ki Points already Consolidated, you only need hit your opponent with your BARE HAND and spend the correct amount of Ki Points. The length of time your opponent is stunned is equal to the level of the Ninja +1d4 Actions. When an opponent is successfully struck, he must make a <u>Special</u> Ability Check with Will. Your Opponent's Will check is modified by subtracting your level from his Will Score and then multiplying by 3! If your Victim fails his roll, he becomes Stunned, but if he is successful, he only takes normal damage and you don't loss your Ki Points. You can affect all creatures except:

                (1) other Ninja
                (2) Enchanted Creatures that are NOT affected by spells held by an Indigo gem.

i.e. You have successfully struck someone, are a 4th level Ninja and:
        Your Opponent's Will Score = 15.
        Your Opponents percentage to NOT be Stunned is 33% [(15 - 4) x 3 = 33%].
        If your Opponent is stunned, he will be affected for 4+1d4 Actions.

<u>STUNNED</u>: If your Opponent is stunned, he will suffer these penalties :
              (1) Loss Agility Bonus to his PTE total while stunned.
              (2) Can't make any loud warning sounds.
              (3) He may not Strike with a weapon or begin the Concentration Time for any spell.

<u>NOTE</u>: A Stunned or Dazed victim may always use Potions, Pills, Dusts, or any Enchanted Item activated by a Trigger Word.

Sense "Enemies" = 25 KP   5th Level   R: 50 Feet/L   D: 10 min/L

This ability will let you Sense any "Enemy" that is within Range. An enemy is anyone or thing that willingly, instinctively, or randomly wishes your or your charge harm. This includes "arch-enemies", guards, or even hungry predators. While this is "activated" you won't be able to stop another Ninja from sensing you, the only means of bypassing this ability is the 8th level Ninja Ability **Pass** or a Black Knight with his Hood of Shadows invoked. Once you Sense an enemy, you get a very vague direction and distance (like behind you close or to the right and at your ranges extent). You will Sense all enemies until the duration ends.

NOTE: Everyone "sensed" has a different "feel", so you can learn the "feel" of a particular enemy over time.

NOTE2: This doesn't work against Zombies, Skeletons, etc. that don't have thoughts of their own, but you could always Sense the controller of these types of creatures, if he is within Range.

Consolidate Ki "on the move"   5th Level

When you reach this level, you may Consolidate your Ki Points as you walk, ride, or jog (1/2 CR max). You may never Consolidate Ki while in combat or in a "high stress" situation. The Ki consolidated regenerates at 1 KP per 1 Attack (5 second period) and can be done Once per day per two levels of experience.

Silent Step or Touch = 27 KP   6th Level   D: 30 min.

This amazing ability will cause your steps and anything you touch to make absolutely no sound. This means your footfalls, even over a creaky floor, will make no sound. Also, if you open a creaky door it will be silent from your touch, the same applies to the normal ringing sound of metal on metal, sword on sword, and even your mount's hoof falls will cause no sound! You may speak normally.

Ninja Jump = 30 KP   7th Level   D: 30 min.

When you learn this ability, you will be able to Jump strait up to a height of 40'+1'/L and/or Jump forward to a distance of 20'+1'/L at a 45° angle. You will always land perfectly so this is also invaluable if you happen to fall from a high place. While falling, if you wait until you are 40'+1'/L off the ground and spend the stated Ki Points, you will be able to land with no adverse affects. You are allowed to make as many jumps as you like as long as you do not enter a combat situation. If you enter combat, you may take only a number of jumps equal to your level and then the Duration Ends. Also, you are able to do one complete flip in mid-air for ever 5 levels you've attain. The Ninja may make only 1 Jump / Attack.

Fire Walk = 35 KP   8th Level   D: 30 min.

This impressive ability will allow you to walk over hot coals, open flames, or even lava. You will receive no damage whatsoever from walking across these burning surfaces. You also receive a +25% on your FIRST RER verses any Enchanted flame, fire, heat or lava that you do not walk on. Once the RER is used the ability stops, but if you don't encounter any of these Enchantments, the Fire Walk ability will last until the Duration ends.
NOTE3: If the Ninja is walking across Enchanted lava or flames, he will NOT have to roll a RER, he will be totally unaffected by the hot surface and the effects of the Fire Walk ability will continue.

Pass = 35 KP   8th Level   D: 6 hours

This ability will enable you to pass over any type of ground and leave no trace. This includes all types of sand, snow and even thin ice. This ability will prevent you from making noise - you can't break twigs or rustle leaves, etc. This does give you another interesting immunity - no Regular or Mutated Creature will attack you while the Duration lasts as long as you don't violently provoke it. Trained guard dogs will let you pass and you could even share a den with a panther or mutated bear, as long as the Duration lasts and you don't provoke the animal. You also can't be tracked by smell, while using this ability. These last benefits may be the best because Pass is the only Ninja ability that will cancel the 5th level "Sense" Enemies ability and you can't be detected by a See Life spell.

Levitate = 40 KP   9th Level   D: 30 min.

This ability will enable you to travel strait up, strait down or stay at one elevation for the Duration. The Rate you move is 15'/Attack (CRM= 3) either up of down. You may Strike, either with melee or projectile weapons, with no penalties. This ability will also stop you from falling. This ability can be done automatically with NO Ki Points spent, if you assume your Ki Seat.

Heal Self or Charge = 45 KP   10th Level   D: Inst.

       This allows you to either Heal yourself or your charge of <u>wounds</u>. In order to Heal yourself, you must assume one of the Ki positions for 1 Action. To Heal your charge, you must grasp at least one of his or her palms in yours for 1 Action. This ability will Heal 1 Endurance Point (EP) for every 1 Ki Point you spend. This means you automatically Heal at least 45 EP, to yourself <u>or</u> your charge, when you use this ability. You may heal as many EP as you have KP to either your charge or yourself by using this skill and spending more Ki Points.

Transfer = + 20 KP   10th Level   D: Stated under abilities

       This astounding ability lets you "Transfer" all benefits from an ability you are using, to your charge. You must add an extra +20 Ki Points to the regular cost of the ability in question, if you want to Transfer the ability to your charge. Your Charge must be touched, while you are activating the ability in question, in order to affect the transfer. The Duration of the ability is not affected and you <u>both</u> get all benefits listed under the ability. You can do this with any KI ability you can use, except those types of abilities that deal with punching or striking.

NOTE: By using Heal Self or Charge and Transfer, you can Heal yourself <u>and</u> your charge of 45 EP each for
           only a KP cost of 65. (You must follow all rules in both skills.)

Resist Mesmerize or Illusion = 45 KP   10th Level   D: Special

       This unique ability will protect you from being Mesmerized or from believing any type of an Illusion. This ability is handled differently from the others, so please read it carefully. Once you have sufficient Ki Points Consolidated (45 KP) this is <u>automatically "ON"</u>. This means that if you encounter either of these types of enchantments, either Mesmerize or an Illusion, the Ki Points will **AUTOMATICALLY** be subtracted from your total consolidated KP to protect you from the enchantment. Some Ninja think that this is a drawback, but it is the way this ability works - and yes all Ninja MUST learn and master this ability! You receive a +25% on any RER verses either of these enchantments types.

Vibration Punch = 50 KP   11th Level   D: 1 Punch

       This ability manifests itself in your fist, and enables you to "crumble" an inanimate object when you strike it. This includes sections of walls and doors made out of rock, stone or wood. The affected area is exactly stated by you and has a maximum of 10'x5'x2' (100 ft^3 or any combination that doesn't exceed that amount of material.) The material affected can not be living matter, this includes people, creatures, living plants, etc. The Vibration Punch does NOT crumble metal, but if it is used against someone in full armor it will vibrate the metal and stun the individual wearing it for 2+1d6 Actions - if victim misses an Ability Check with Will. If the wall you strike is Enchanted, it will only "crumble" the stated section if you roll lower than the <u>caster's</u> Ability Check with Will.

"Power" Punch = 55 KP   12th Level   D: 1 Punch

       This awesome ability also manifests itself in your fist, but it enables you to cause substantial damage to the creature that you strike. Your hand becomes encased in a ball of Lightning which will ignite flammable substances 25% of the time as well as cause great damage. The damage it does is a 1d20 per 4 of your completed levels.   i.e. 3d20 at 12th, 4d20 at 16th.

The stipulations are:

    (1) You must make a successful strike to use the Power Punch.

    (2) The Creature must be living, it doesn't work against Zombies, ect.

    (3) Ref Note: I allow my Ninja to also add their Strength Damage Bonus: Ie. 3d20+(Str Dam x 3).

Shadow Step = 60 KP   13th Level   D: 12 hours or 30 min.

       This prized ability will allow you to actually "step" into a shadow and become part of it for the Duration. The difference in Duration depends on if you attempt to MOVE while you are "in" the shadow. If you don't move you could stay "in the shadow" for up to 12 hours. If you attempt to move, this ability only lasts for 30 minutes. You may only move at a walk (5'/Att) and only through connecting shadows. If the shadow disappears for ANY reason, you will be "rooted" to the spot, but will be invisible for the rest of the Duration. You may only see and hear from "within" the shadow; you can't speak, make noise, blah, blah, blah. You can not be found by a See Enchantment spell, but another Ninja using Sense Enemies may be able to sense you and if a See Life spell is being used, the shadow in which you are concealed will glow. You can't be harmed by any type of enchantment or weapon while concealed "within" the shadow. The shadow you choose must have a minimum area of 6 inches square and it must initially be <u>stationary.</u>

Block Enchantment = 65 KP 14th Level D: 1 Spell

As the name indicates, this amazing ability will allow you to actually Block one Enchantment or spell. You can step in front of the spell to protect your charge or yourself. You must have initiative to invoke the ability, this is the 1st Action. The ability will "protect" you until the end of the Attack from the 1st Enchantment that strikes you. You can't Block any spells that directly affects the mind or an Area. You can also use this ability to pass through certain types of Barriers or Globes and take NO EP damage. The types of Barriers or Globes you may pass through are: Fire, Smoke, Air, Fog, and Water.

Pass Through Solid Objects = 70 KP 15th Level D: 20 min.

This is the pinnacle of all the Ki abilities. It allows you to Pass directly through any Solid Object and much more. You may Pass through any non-enchanted objects, but you must walk (5'/Att) [CRM: 1]. This also allows you to cause yourself to sink through a floor, but you will fall to the next floor once you pass through. You can even sink down into the ground, travel forward at 5'/Att, and rise back up at a rate of 5'/Att, as long as you don't exceed the Duration. The consequences of getting caught while passing through any solid object is <u>death.</u> Your using your Ki, or Life force, to do this, so if the Duration runs out and you are still passing through a substance your Life force, as well as you, gets crushed and you immediately die.

Walk Over Un-solid Surfaces D: 30 min. / level

Once you acquire the stated levels, you may walk, run or waltz over the indicated substances for up to 30 min per level. You only need to spend 1/2 the Ki Points (rounded up) <u>stated at that level</u> to transverse the surface indicated. You may also transverse any surfaces "lower" on the table than the one you spent for. This means: when you are 10th Level and you spend 23 KP, you may walk over clam water, quicksand or mud, etc. for the Duration. All Levels, Surfaces and Costs are listed below:

Level	KP Cost for Un-Solid Surface	Surface Type
2	7	Ice (Slippery)
4	9	Mud
6	19	Quicksand
8	18	Sticky
10	23	Water - Calm and Tree Tops/Limbs
12	28	Water - Wavy
14	33	Water - Stormy
16	38	Air *

* When you use this ability to walk across Air, you can only walk strait out - not up or down. Of course you could always walk strait off a cliff, stand there and then walk back as long as the Duration lasts. Also some clever Ninja, use the 9th level Levitate ability with this one and then virtually fly through the air.

ENCHANTER

INTRODUCTION

Enchanters are able to cast the most diverse amount of spells with the least amount of restrictions. Enchanters are also able to enchant many different types of materials as they increase in level. Any Enchanter may construct their own personal staff, make wands, scrolls, and may make a companion - they may also Enchant Items and gems. You may learn any spell on the Enchanter / Alchemist spell list as long as you have enough Spell Points to cast it. Your Spell Point total is dependent on your Intellect score and your level. The more powerful the spell, the more Spell Points and Endurance Points you must spend to cast that spell.

The amount of Spell Points your rate per level is a reflection of your Intellect and your "inner self." Your Spell Points increase as you go up in level. This happens NOT because you gain more inner self - that's impossible. You gain more Spell Points as you rise in level because you learn how to "ration" your inner self more wisely. To cast any spell you must spend Spell Points and Endurance Points. For every 10 Spell Points you use, you must spend 1 Endurance point. (This means if you want to cast a StingRay 1, you need to spend 10 Spell Points and 1 Endurance point. If you want to cast the Light 2 spell, you must give up 22 Spell Points and 3 Endurance points.)

Some of your first questions might be, what is magic and how do I, as an Enchanter, cast a spell? The answer to the first question is: Magic is a force which has the ability to manipulate and control matter, energy and living creatures or inanimate objects in many different ways.

To cast a spell, you must first learn it. To learn a spell you must go to a school, mentor, etc. and copy down the very long and precise description of the particular spell you want to learn into your "spell book." The spells are usually copied in the Enchanter's native language, but sometimes the descriptions are written in the Traders language. While copying the spell, you'll notice that the last line of the description is a Trigger Phrase. The Trigger Phrase is never no more than 5 words long and is what you actually say when you cast the spell. After you've finished copying the spell's description into your spell book, you must rehearse the entire wording over and over until you know every minute aspect of it by heart. Once you've totally memorized the spells' entire description, you may cast it. When you are ready to cast the spell, you have to concentrate for the time specified under the Concentration Time which is listed in the spell's description. As you Concentrate, you review the entire spell's description while gathering your inner self, then you say the Trigger Word or Phrase in a loud, boisterous voice, and spend the Spell Points and Endurance Points necessary. The spell is cast and affects the environment or opponents in a particular way.

The Trigger Word or Phrase for some spells are the same, so you may ask how you cast one and not the other, if you know them both. You distinguish between them while you are concentrating. The Trigger Word for Flame Bolt 1 and Flame Bolt 2 are the same: "Flash!" If you want to cast Flame Bolt 2, you concentrate on it's specific description for its Concentration Time (CT) and then spend its unique Spell Points and corresponding Endurance points (It will take longer then concentrating on Flame Bolt 1's description.)

(ex. As you concentrate and visualize the words of the spell, magic swells about you. As you say the Trigger Phrase - you mold your Spell Points as a vessel to house the magic - giving it shape and substance. Then, with what it is that keeps you alive, you seal and launch the force outwards to fulfill the spell.)

NOTE: Please remember, you may only learn spells that you have enough Spell Points to cast.

Concentration Time is based on Actions. It will cost you **One** Action for every number listed under the Concentration Time of a spell and then **One** Action so say the Trigger Word to cast that spell.

In order to say a Trigger Word that activates an Enchanted Item, it will cost you ONE Action.

Actions / Attack	vs.	Level
2		1
3		5
4		10
5		15

Enchanters may only make ONE Strike per Attack. They may not learn to use the Warrior's Parry skill, but may learn the Survival Skill: Shield Use and benefit from a shield's PTE bonus. Remember, you must use one of your Parry Actions to employ a Shield vs. an Opponent's single attack.

The total number of Spell Points an Enchanter, Alchemist or Elementalist rates per level depends on their Intellect Score: (See the table in Appendix M for a complete list.)

Total Spell Points   :   **INT Score + ((INT Score / 2) * (L - 1))**

1st level with INT : 16 $16 + ((16/2) * (1-1)) = 16$ SP

5th level with INT : 19 $19 + ((19/2) * (5-1)) = 57$ SP

8th level with INT : 20 $20 + ((20/2) * (8-1)) = 90$ SP

NOTE: If your INT score goes up for any reason you must re-figure your Spell Points.

NOTE2: A complete list of Spell Points, depending on your Level and Intellect score is listed in Appendix M.

NOTE3: All Enchanters at first level gain the spell See Enchantment 1 in ADDITION to what is stated on the Intellect table.

NOTE4: You may only cast ONE Offensive spell per Attack.

ENCHANTING AN ITEM

The Enchanter is able to enchant items by casting spells directly into them. The item must either be made completely by the Enchanter or made by "Weavers" with strands of Mithral or Americanium throughout the item. An Enchanted Gem (see the Enchanted Gem section for a complete description) may even be set into a clasp and attached to the Americanium or Mithral strands running throughout the item. An item <u>without</u> an Enchanted Gem set into it may only hold **1** single spell, but an item with an Enchanted Gem set in it may hold as many spells as reflected by the Gem's Perfection Rating (GPR).

When you cast a spell into an item to enchant it, you must include a Trigger Word or Phrase. The Trigger can be any word or short phrase and when said loudly and forcefully (it can't be set off in normal conversation) it will cause the spell to be cast. (To say any Trigger Word or Phrase will cost you one full Action - you must "mean" it.)

The types of materials you may enchant are totally dependent on your level and are listed on the table below. You may only cast spells with certain spell types into an item at certain levels. The dependent spell types are: Defensive, Attack, and Miscellaneous.

LEVEL	MATERIALS	LEVEL OF SPELL & MAGIC TYPE
1st	Rope, Cloth, Sting	1st ----- Defensive, Misc. and Attack **
2nd	Wood, Glass	2nd ----- Defensive
		3rd ----- Misc.
		4th ----- Attack
5th	Leather, Silver	5th ----- Defensive
	Iron	6th ----- Misc.
		7th ----- Attack
10th	Mithral,	10th ----- Defensive
	Ransium	11th ----- Misc.
		12th ----- Attack
15th	Americanium,	15th ----- Defensive
	Langor	16th ----- Misc.
		17th ----- Attack

** Only a lasso, snare, etc (or any type of offensive type object) can hold an attack type spell.
   Ie. You cant cast an Attack spell into a shield, ect.

NOTE: Items with Mithral incorporated into them may only hold Class (A), (B), or (C) spells.
        Items with Americanium incorporated into them may hold any
           Spell Classification: (A), (B), (C), (D), or (E).

NOTE2: Weavers are Enchanters that have followed a particular path. They may weave Americanium or
           Mithral though out any cloth item and they may enchant items at TWO spots better than stated
           above with respect to Materials and Magic Type only. (i.e. 1st Level Weaver may enchant any
           material up to Leather or Iron. At 2nd level she may enchant all materials up to and including
           Mithral and Ransium.) {See the end of the Survival Skills section for Prices}

NOTE3: Enchanted Items may be broken up into 3 separate forms and the 'See Enchantment' spells
           distinguish them by "hi-lighting" them differently as shown below:

Type	Glow under 'See Enchantment' spell	Example
1) Spell cast into item:	Main Part of item / weapon will Glow.	Dagger's Blade glows.
2) Enchanted Gem set into item:	The Enchanted Gem will Glow.	Gem at clasp of cloak glows.
3) Raw Spell Points pumped into item:	Whole Item Glows with same Intensity	Whole Door Glows.

   3a) This form of Item Enchantment is explained at the end of the Enchanted Items Section (pg. 230).

COMPANIONS

An Enchanter or Alchemist may cast the Companion spell. The spell makes and then links you and the companion by an invisible "line" of enchantment. Once the Enchanter or Alchemist enchants their companion, he or she gains certain abilities and bonuses :

1) An enchanted telepathic link is established between you and your Companion. You are able to "speak" telepathically with your companion at will while you are within a distance of one mile per Level of each other. The enchanted link is detectable only when you are actually telepathically "speaking" to your companion; it may be detected by someone using a See Enchantment spell.

2) Your companion will follow your directions, never trying to twist them, and because these directions are issued Telepathically, the entire content of what you want done is understood. Your companion will perform in any way it's capable - it will be your spy, forward or rear guard, night watch, etc. It will even protect you, if your life is in danger - but there are heavy penalties if your companion is destroyed or killed.

3) The Companion will be affected by all spells that affect the Enchanter. This means that they are affected by all Indigo spells and by a Paralyze Person spell **NOT** by any paralyze creature spells.

4) Your Companion always has the same RER that you do, so if you cast a Resist Fire spell on yourself, your companion will also receive that bonus as long as it is within one mile per level of you and the spell's duration lasts. Example: If you've cast a Resist Fire spell on yourself and your Companion is affected by a Flame Bolt 1, it gains the +25% bonus to it's **RER** and then the spell's duration ends!

5) Regardless of it's form (Statue, Mobile or Giant), the Companion is always aware of it's surroundings. It may act according to your instructions in any circumstance.

6) The CRM of the Companion is always the same as the Character, if you increase yours so does it.

7) When a Companion is in its small mobile (regular) form, it has certain stats:
   EP: varies (see below)   PTE: 15% (+50%Fly)   Actions/Att: 1 Strike & 1 Parry   Damage: 1d4 / Att.

8) Survival Skills: The Companion will have Survival Skills based on the what the Character knows. If a Character has learned and / or specialized in any of the below listed skills the Companion may use them:
   ID Plants (or other objects), Locate Traps, Tracking, Hunting, Fishing, Detect Ambush, Attack Unseen Enemy, Measure Distance by Sight or Sound.

NOTE: The Ref may award certain specific skills to certain Companions based on their type:
   I.e. a Goat may gain Mountain Climbing, a Fox may gain Tracking, or
       a Cheetah may gain a permanent +1 CRM or maybe the ability to produce a burst of
       speed up to CRM: 10 twice per day, ect.

Penalties and Restrictions :

1)   The Telepathic link and all bonuses only work if you and your companion are within ONE mile per level of each other.

2)   You may only enlist the aid of one companion at a time. The only way you can create another companion, is if the original one is destroyed or killed.
   A) A second companion must have a different form then your first companion.
   B) If your companion is destroyed (taken to Zero EP) the enchanted link will pull *you* towards death and these are the penalties:
   B1) Permanently loose the Endurance Points that were granted to the Companion.

   B2a) Roll below your Endurance score on percentage dice or fall unconscious for 1d4 hours.
   B2b) If you don't go unconscious:
       i) You will be Dazed for 1d20 minutes.
       ii) 25% chance of acquiring an insanity – Ref's choice.

COMPANION STUFF:

1) Steps for making a Companion:
    a) Obtain an amount of Mud, Stone, Wood, ect. that you will form your Companion from.
    b) Unroll and read the Companion scroll.   (15th level spell)
    c) Form a complete picture of your Companion in your mind.   (See step #2)
    d) Use at least 5 EP, multiply them by 2 and the total will become your Companion's starting EP.
        These EP are given to the Companion and are 'lost' from the Enchanter's (Alchemist's) total.
    e) Your Companion must have at least 10 EP, but may never have more than twice your Original
        EP total.
    f) You may add to or take back your Companion's EP only at the Levels listed below.
        5th, 10th, 15th   Change amount of Companion's EP.   Minimum = 10 EP.
        5th, 10th, 15th   Set or Replace an Enchanted Gem.   (See step #6).

2) Form a COMPLETE picture of your Companion in your mind: including it's color, fur or hide consistency,
        size of wings or appendages, etc.

May definitely use :

1 Cat	2 Bat	3 Dog
4 Hawk	5 Eagle	6 Wolf
7 Horse	8 Tiger	9 Elephant
10 Snake	11 Miniature Dragon.	

The Companion will gain all physical abilities of the creature imagined. A bird could fly, a cat would
        have claws and an elephant would have a prehensile nose, ect.

3) Size Increase: Your Companion may increase it's size **ONCE PER DAY** for a maximum of **20 min.**
        The change takes ONE full Attack [5 sec.] to complete.
        With each increase in size, your Companion gains EP, a better PTE and Damage capability.

Level	PTE	Damage	Strength Dam. Bonus	Height or Length		EP Bonus
1st	+15%	1d6	+1	2 foot	=	+ 10
2nd	+20%	1d8	+2	4 feet	=	+ 20
5th	+25%	1d10	+3	6 feet	=	+ 30
10th	+30%	1d12	+4	8 feet	=	+ 40
15th	+35%	2d8	+5	10 feet	=	+ 50

NOTE: Your Companion's ALWAYS gets only 1 Strike and 1 Parry Action / Attack.

4) Once you have Created and Enchanted your Companion, it can change between these forms:
        a) Original Statue form.   - at will
        b) Mobile form – the form you imagined (if a cat, it will have fur, paws, etc.)   - at will
        c) Giant form.   - once per day

5) At certain levels (5th, 10th, 15th), you may grant your Companion more EP and / or cause a Gem to
        become part of it's statue. You also may only replace an Enchanted Gem at these levels.

Level	Maximum Gem Perfection Rating (GPR)	Spell Classification Note
5th - 9th	VSI2	9(A) or 3(B) or 1(C)
10th - 14th	VVSI2	10(A) or 9(B) or 3(C) or 1 (D)
15th - 19th	VVSI1	10(B) or 6(C) or 2(D) or 1(E)

6) Gem qualifications and abilities:
        You only need a Gem if you want your Companion to hold and cast spells. The companion may cast
            the spells stored within the Gem when you instruct it to or when it is in danger.
        a) Companion gains the ability to hold and cast the types of spells the Enchantment Gem is associated
            with.
        b) Gem location: You may implant it in the Forehead, the Chest, in place of an Eye, etc.
                1) Not inside mouth, ect - 'cause Enchanted Gems must always be <u>showing.</u>
                2) May implant ONE Gem only.

X) Example :
        A 2nd level Enchanter is given a Companion Scroll, finds a nice sized chunk of marble, and after reciting
the scroll, he calls to his mind the form of a falcon, and uses 10 EP. His newly made Companion has 20 EP
and immediately gains all "Natural" abilities of the majestic falcon.
        At 5th level he adds a Rose Quartz (GPR=SI2) to his Companion in place of it's left eye. Now he can
cast the appropriate number of spells into the Enchanted Gem and the companion may cast them when it
chooses too. This Enchanter has decided to cast one (1) Flame Jet into his Companion's Gem.

SCROLLS

A scroll is simply a piece of parchment with a spell written on it in such a way so that anyone holding the parchment may cast that spell just by saying a short Trigger Phrase.

To make a scroll, you first must learn the Scroll spell and you may only put a spell on a scroll that you already know and are able to cast. Next you must acquire the main ingredient for the "ink" to write the spell in. To make enough ink to write one spell, you need ¼ karat of Enchanted Gem dust from an Enchanted Gem that could "hold" the spell you want to put on your scroll. If you want to put more then one spell on a scroll, you will need more Enchanted Gem dust. You may only put spells that can be held by the same colored gem on one scroll and you can't put more than 3 spells on any one scroll. Now that you have the parchment, Enchanted Gem dust and have learned the Scroll spell, you only need a small vial filled with ordinary water and a quill to write with.

This is a unique spell in that it is cast in two parts. You cast the first part of the spell on the mixture of Enchanted Dust and water, this will make a smooth colored ink that is easy to write with. You now must write out the entire description of the spell in the special ink. You must write the Trigger Word or Phrase of the spell in very bold and dark print and then cast that spell on to the scroll. Most Enchanters (and Alchemists) write the spell's description and Trigger Phrases in their native language, but some scrolls are copied in the Traders Language. It will take you about three hours (one hour per spell classification) to copy a Class (C) spell - you must not make any mistakes at all! When your are finished copying the spell or spells, you cast the end of the Scroll spell on to the parchment and this dries and sets the ink. To activate a spell written on any scroll, all you need to do unfurl the scroll and read aloud the Trigger Word or Phrase, this costs you One of your Actions. When you say the Trigger Phrase aloud, the spell "springs" off the parchment and travels to the recipient. If the recipient rates a RER, they make it normally.

NOTE: ANYONE of any class that can read the language that the Scroll is printed in (and Knows to read only the Trigger Word or Phrase aloud) can cast a spell from a Scroll.

NOTE2: You must use your 1st set of Spell Points, the ones you received directly from the dawning Column Sun – not any you rate from regeneration – if you want to put multiple spells on your scroll. You must have enough Spell Points, from your 1st set, to cast the Scroll Spell and ALL other spells you want to copy onto this scroll. If you don't complete the scroll in ONE sitting before the next rising of the Column Sun, all your work will be canceled and you will have to start over with new ink.

Example: If you wish to put the Flame Bolt 1 spell and the Flame Jet spell on the same scroll, you'll need 112 SP – these all must be original Spell Points, not regenerated ones.

NAME	SP
Flame Bolt 1	18
Flame Jet	44
Scroll Spell	50
Total	112 SP

CONSTRUCTING A STAFF

When an Enchanter reaches 5th level, she or he may want to construct a Staff. When you attain 5th level, a scroll with the Staff Link spell on it will be presented to you by your Master. After you have this scroll, you can start your quest for the staff's wood and components.

The only wood that may be used to construct a staff is Zonith Wood - you actually use a root from that tree. (After your done reading this, you can find a complete description of the Zonith Wood tree and how you go about retrieving a root from that tree by referring to the Zonith Wood description in the Creature Section.) There are two different types of these trees: the Golden and the Red Zonith Wood. Enchanters with a Morality Rating of 10 and above must use a root from the Golden Zonith Wood tree and Enchanters with a Morality Rating of 9 and below must use a root from a Red Zonith Wood. All roots are perfectly straight and you will receive one that is exactly 25 inches longer than you are tall. All roots will be 3 inches in diameter. Once you have received the correct type of root, you must strip off all the bark, cut it so that it is 1 foot taller than you are, and dip the ends in Americanium. Each end must be dipped in Americanium to 6 inches from the tips. Once the staff has been debarked and dipped, you may carve the staff in anyway you wish or affix some symbol on the top with Americanium. To affix something on top of your staff, melt Americanium on the bottom of the object and more on the top of your staff and then melt them together. Once the staff is constructed, you are ready to cast the spell.

Even though the spell is on a scroll it is very long and complicated; it will take the better part of a day to completely cast. You must spend 10 Endurance Points when reading the scroll to "link" the staff to yourself - the Endurance Points spent are not permanently lost, they will return with normal healing. Once the spell is finished and the staff is "linked" to you, you will receive all bonuses and abilities that the staff bestows. You may only cast this spell once in your life and you must always stay either at a Morality Rating of 10 or above, if you hold a Golden Zonith Wood staff; or 9 and below, if you hold a Red Zonith Wood staff. If the holder of a staff ever exceeds these boundaries, the staff will "shatter."

(To cover 6 inches of both ends of your staff (or the "heels" – top and bottom), it takes 1 ounce of Americanium. 1 coin Americanium = ½ oz   so   2 coins (1 oz) = 200 silver pieces.)

NOTE: Because of this GREAT expense, your mentor or school will usually provide you with enough Americanium to complete your staff. The Americanium will usually be given to you when you produce the Zonith Wood to your elders.

Bonuses granted to the Enchanter after the Staff is made:

1)   The primary function of an Enchanter's staff is to lesson the amount of Endurance points the Enchanter must spend to cast a spell. It DOES NOT affect the amount of Spell Points the Enchanter needs to spend to cast a spell, only the Endurance Points. The staff will reduce the Endurance points the Enchanter must spend by HALF. The staff must be held by the Enchanter and must be in the "open" position for this function to work (see below for details.) i.e. When casting the Flame Bolt 2 spell you usually need to spend 53 SP and 6 EP, but when you are holding your staff in the "open" position you only need to spend 3 EP – the 53 SP cost remains unchanged.

2)   You may store spells in your staff depending on your level.

Level	Maximum number of Spells Held within your Staff
5 - 9	2
10 - 14	3
15 - 19	4

Although you may store any spell in the "slots" you rate according to your level, your staff will "amplify" certain spells depending on what type of staff you wield. If you hold a Golden Zonith Wood staff, it will DOUBLE the Range and Duration of all spells stored within it which can be held by a Yellow, Indigo, Brown, or Crystal gem. A Red Zonith Wood staff will DOUBLE the Range and Duration of all spells that are stored in it which can be held by a Red, Blue, Violet, or Black gem. All spells that are stored in the staff are cast by uttering a Trigger Word or Phrase.

3)   Do to the link between you and your staff, you may control it though telekinesis. This means you may move it with nothing more than your thoughts as long as you concentrate. It must be within 30'+2'/L and the rate it travels at is a CRM of 2 (10 ft/sec).

4)   You are able to make your staff shrink in length to a size of 1 foot long - where the Americanium "heels" touch. This is referred to as the "closed" position. The width stays the same but any symbols on it's top will shrink proportionately. On command, the staff will "spring" to the "open" position with a strength equal to your own. The staff can change size in 1 Action. (This function uses a mental command.)

5)   Because of the link between you and YOUR staff (not just any staff), you may use your Zonith Wood staff as a weapon without taking any formal training. Your opponent does not receive any of the usual PTE bonuses that he would regularly get, if you attacked him with a weapon you have not had training to wield.

6)   All Zonith Wood trees are immune to any type of fire. For this reason, when the staff is in the "open position" and is held by the Enchanter, it will give him a +10% to his RER verses fire.

7)   After the Staff Link spell is cast on the staff, it becomes totally immune to all forms of enchantment and is unbreakable. You could throw your staff into a pool of acid and it would not be affected in any way! Even though the staff is unbreakable, it will bend under great pressure. If you happen to be caught in a room with it's walls closing in on you and you try to brace the walls with your staff, it will work for a while but then the staff may start to bend.

8)   I've said in the Constructing Staff section that your staff can "shatter". There are only two ways your staff may **EVER** "shatter" or break, or be damaged in any way, for that matter:

   A) If you exceed the Morality Ratings of your Zonith wood staff:
        An Enchanter wielding a Golden Zonith wood staff falls below a Morality Rating of 10 OR
        An Enchanter wielding a Red Zonith wood staff rises above a Morality Rating of 9.

   B) An Enchanter may consciously choose to cause his staff to "shatter" with a mental command.

      These are the only two conditions which your staff can break or be harmed in anyway. If the staff ever "shatters" it will cause a Blinding Flash and a Thunderous Boom that will Blind and Daze everyone (including you) within an area equal to 10' + 1 foot for every 5 Spell Points that were stored in the staff. This effect lasts for 10+1d10 Attacks and there is NO RER allowed.

ENCHANTER HOLDING A CROSSBOW AND CASTING A STINGRAY (AREA) SPELL FROM HIS STAFF

WANDS

An Enchanter may learn the Wand Preparation Spell and cast it on an appropriate length of Zonith Wood. To construct a wand you need at least 12" of Zonith Wood. Any Enchanter with any Moral Rating may make and use either type of Zonith Wood wand. Once you have attained the length of root, you can either "whittle" it's diameter down or keep it at the 3 inch width. You then must dip 6 inches of the wand into either Mithral or Americanium and this becomes it's tip, where the spells will be "emitted" from. Once you have gotten the wand to this stage, cast the Wand Preparation Spell on it. After this spell is cast onto your wand, it is ready to hold spells. Next, you must write the Trigger Word of the spell you intend to put into the wand on the wooden end or the "Handle". You must use Mithral or Americanium as the "ink" when you scribe the Trigger Word on the handle of the Wand. Now you just cast the intended spell into it and you have yourself a wand.

NOTE: If Mithral is used to coat and scribe the wand, then it may only hold Class (A), (B), or (C) spells, but if Americanium is used, the wand may hold any spell classification: (A), (B), (C), (D) or (E).

Here are the benefits and restrictions of a wand: (A wand may only be used once per Attack).

1) You may cast any spell you wish into any type of wand (Golden or Red) and these spells will be "held" until used. All spells "held" in the wand are cast by saying the Trigger Word inscribed on the handle.

2) The number of spells that may be held within your Wand is dependent on your level.

Level	Maximum number of Spells Held within your Wand
5 - 9	2
10 - 14	3
15 - 19	4

3) A wand made of Golden Zonith Wood will automatically duplicate any spell cast into it that can be held by a Yellow, Indigo, Brown, or Crystal gem. A wand of Red Zonith Wood will automatically duplicate any spell cast into it that can be held by a Red, Blue, Violet, or Black gem. NOTE2: The maximum number of spells which can be held by the wand does not change, though.

   (i.e. A 5th level Enchanter has a Red Zonith Wood wand and casts a Flame Bolt 2 spell into it. The Flame Bolt 2 spell can be held by a Red gem, so this spell is automatically duplicated by the wand. Now the Enchanter may cast TWO Flame Bolt 2 spells out of the wand.

   If a 10th level Enchanter did the same, she would be able to cast one more Flame Bolt 2 spell into the wand, but it would not be duplicated, because the wand would be full; ie 3 spells are held in it.)

4) You may only cast the SAME spell into any wand at any one time. All spells must be **exactly** the same: (2) Lighting Bolt 1's or (3) Flame Bolt 3's, or (4) Shield, Melee, 20%'s, etc.
   NOTE3: All spells must have exactly the same Range, Duration, Area Of Effect (AOE), etc.

5) If you want to change the spells held in the wand, you must first totally "empty" it, then scrape or melt off the old Trigger Word or Phrase. Now you may make up another Trigger Word, scribe it into the handle using Mithral or Americanium and cast a different spell into it. Now the wand is ready to use with brand new spells.

6) If you empty your wand of spells, want to cast the same spells back in to it again and you want to use the same Trigger Word, just cast that spell back into the wand and it is ready to go.

AN ENCHANTER'S STAFF AND A WAND

NEW SPELL CREATION RULES

Any Enchanter, Alchemist or Elementalist of at least 5th level may attempt to create a new spell. At the outset, let me stress that this is a dangerous process! The first step is to describe the spell fully in writing - and make up a Trigger Word / Phrase. You must state EXACTLY what you want the spell to do or affect - and in some cases even what you don't want it to do or affect. You must state exactly what the Range, Duration, and Area Of Effect of the spell is. Second, when you get this done you must go to a place where you will not be disturbed. If your concentration is broken for any reason then go directly to the New Spell Creation Table and roll the percentage with a +50% penalty. If the spell is to affect something or someone, you must have the recipient of the spell there the first time you try to cast it. The Ref. must decide on his or her own and <u>in secret</u>, how many Spell Points it will take to cast the spell. The player must have NO IDEA of how many Spell Points the spell will actually take to cast - I told you it would be dangerous!

Now the caster, must attempt to learn this spell in the regular way. Once you have rehearsed the spell a few hundred times or so, simply go someplace where you won't be disturbed. Concentrate on the entire description, say the Trigger Phrase, and let the spell "come to life." As the spell starts to work, it will automatically "suck" Spell Points from the caster and this can't be stopped until all the points are spent or the caster reaches negative Spell Points, which ever comes first. This can very easily and often has harmed many an Enchanter, Alchemist and Elementalist that thought they could handle a new spell. Now you understand why the player can't know how many Spell Points the spell will take to actually cast.

If the spell takes all of your Spell Points and "sucks you dry", the spell creation fails and you must go to the Overcast Table and roll on it! If you have enough Spell Points to cast the spell, go to the New Spell Creation Table below, roll a percentage, and compare your roll to the table. If the spell doesn't work and you are still able to cast magic, you may not have described the spell well enough or may have slipped in your concentration so re-do these and you may try again. Each additional time the Enchanter, etc. tries to create the same spell, she gets to deduct a -10% from her next percentage roll on the New Spell Creation Table.

NOTE: You may only make a new spell if you have an open spell "Slot".

NOTE2: Any time you spend Spell Points, you must also spend Endurance Points: 1 EP / 10 SP.

NEW SPELL CREATION TABLE

Percentage	Results	
01 - 50 %	Spell Works	- No Penalties.
51 - 75 %	Spell Works	- But practiced so much that you forget 1 random spell or lose one empty slot.
76 - 85 %	Spell Not Work	- And Reduces you Intellect Score by 1 point for 10 days.
86 - 95 %	Spell Not Work	- And Reduces you Intellect Score by 2 points for 20 days.
96 - 97 %	Spell Not Work	- And Reduces you Intellect Score by 3 points for 30 days.
98 %	Spell Not Work	- And Reduces you Intellect Score by 4 points for 40 days.
99 %	Spell Not Work	- And Reduces you Intellect Score by 5 points for 50 days.
100 %	Spell Works	- Your newly created spell requires 1 Spell Point / Level less then initially rated by the Ref.

OVERCAST TABLE

If you ever spend more Spell Points than your current Spell Point Total, you must make a percentage roll and follow the rules stated below. You may fall to exactly ZERO Spell Points without any penalty. Only if you take your Spell Point total below zero (or into the negatives), do you have to roll on the Overcast Table.

Percentage	Results	
01 – 50 %	Stunned	- For 3+1d6 Actions.
51 – 75 %	Dazed	- For 4+1d8 Actions.
76 – 95 %	Unconscious	- For 5+1d10 Actions.
96 – 98 %	Unconscious	- For 6+1d12 Attacks.
99 %	Coma	- For 2+1d4 Hours.
100 %	Stunned	- For 3 Actions

DAZED: The victim becomes disoriented. This disorientation will cause:
    (1) The victim's Opponents gain a +25% to their PTE totals. (2) Stop Charging Hemar / Krill must Land.
    (3) Victim can't use any Occ. Skills or start Concentrating. (4) Victim looses Agility bonus to his PTE roll.

STUNNED: If your Opponent is stunned, he will suffer these penalties :
    (1) Loss Agility Bonus to his PTE while stunned.
    (2) Can't make any loud warning sounds.
    (3) He may not Strike with a weapon or begin the Concentration Time for any spell.

NOTE: A Stunned or Dazed victim may always use Potions, Pills, or any Enchanted Item activated by a Trigger Word.

ENCHANTER OCCUPATIONAL SPELLS

Most of the next set of spells deal with what are known as Enchanted Links. An Enchanted Link is initiated by a spell and usually lasts for the entire life of the character. Each Link grants the recipient or recipients certain abilities and sometimes certain penalties. Any person is only able to have a maximum of THREE (3) Links on him or her at any one time.

All of the Casting Times are listed at 1 Day. The spells don't actually take the full day to cast, but they all call for some type of personal sacrifice so it is expected that the recipients rest for the remainder of the day.

Staff Link spell (D)   R: T   AOE: 1 staff
SPC: 100 - M   D: Permanent   CT: 1 day

This spell is cast to link a newly constructed Zonith Wood staff to a 5th level Enchanter - this makes the Staff truly yours. You now receive all of the bonuses stated in the Enchanter Section, including: storing spells into the particular Staff and being able to spend ½ normal EP when casting a spell. Now you are also able to use THIS Staff as a Weapon without formal training – your Opponent doesn't gain a Percentage bonus to his PTE total. Your teacher will present you with a Scroll with this spell written on it (and hopefully the Americanium required) in recognition for your dedication in reaching 5th level.
This creates an Enchanted Link.

Oath spell (E)   R: T   AOE: 2 recipients
SPC: 150 - M   D: Permanent   CT: 1 day

This spell is cast on a 5th level Enchanter and a 5th level Ninja or a 5th level Alchemist and a 5th level Ninja. The Spell will link the Ninja and the Enchanter or Alchemist for life. It provides special abilities and bonuses to both of the recipients. Here are the particulars: The Oath Spell will be cast on both the Guardian and the Charge or you will both have to drink 1/2 of a special potion that contains this spell. As soon as you quaff your portion of the potion, the Ninja will recite the Oath. The spell will drain all or the Ninja's Ki Points and all of your Spell Points for that day, but will link the both of you together in a way that can only be broken by death. The bonuses that this Enchanted Link will bestow on <u>BOTH</u> of you are:

1) Tell the exact location of the other person as long as you are within 2 feet / 1 Maximum Ki Point of the Ninja.
If the Ninja is 5th level and has a Wisdom of 19 (ie. 38 SP), then you will know each others exact location within 76 feet of one another.
2) Know if the other is in great danger, such as fighting for his or her life, etc. regardless of the distance separating the two of you.
3) Matches your Life spans - both living the longest life span.

NOTE: The Enchanter or Alchemists is expected to give the Ninja a gift of some Enchanted Item, to thank him for the years of service to come.
This creates an Enchanted Link.

Companion Spell (D)   R: T   AOE: 1 recipient
SPC: 100 - M   D: Permanent   CT: 1 day

To become a Master (Teacher) of other Enchanters, you must be at least 10th level and you must learn this spell. The complete description of all the Bonuses, Penalties and steps for creating a Companion are listed in the Enchanter's Section. This creates an Enchanted Link.

Wand Preparation Spell (C)   R: T   AOE: 1 recipient
SPC: 50 - M   D: Permanent   CT: 1 day

This spell enables an Enchanter to prepare a wand for use. You must first appropriate a 12" piece of Zonith Wood and 1 ounce of Mithral or Americanium. You then carve the rod into whatever diameter you wish, but the length must remain at least 12". Dip the tip into the melted Mithral / Americanium to 6", write the Trigger Word on the shaft and cast the spell. If Mithral is used, the wand may hold Class (A), (B) & (C) spells. If Americanium is used the wand may hold any classification of spell: (A), (B), (C), (D), or (E).
See Enchanter Section for details.
NOTE2: No Enchanted Link is created when you make a wand.

Scroll Spell (C)   R: T   AOE: 1 recipient
SPC: 50 - M   D: Permanent until used   CT: 1 day

A scroll is a parchment with a spell or spells cast on it. These are ready to cast but may only be used by anyone who can read it. To make a scroll, you first need to obtain the parchment and Ink. The Ink is made of ordinary water and ¼ karat of Enchanted Dust per spell. The Enchanted Dust must be same color as the spells to be put on the scroll. Red is for Fire, Orange for Shield, ect. You cast 25 SP into the Ink mixture at the beginning of the spell. You then copy the COMPLETE spell's description onto the scroll, cast that spell onto the scroll and then cast the remaining 25 SP of the scroll spell onto the parchment to 'Dry' the Ink. If more than one spell is to be put on a scroll, you must have enough Ink and Spell Points. All spells must be written, cast and the Ink must be 'Dry' by using only your 1st set of Spell Points, not from any regenerations. You can never put more than 3 spells on any one scroll and all the spells must be of the same color.
NOTE: No Enchanted Link is created when you make a Scroll and Alchemists may also cast this spell.

Marriage Spell (E)   R: T   AOE: 2 recipients
SPC: 150 - M   D: Permanent   CT: 1 day

This spell is cast on the momentous day when two people decide to publicly declare their True Love for one another. The couple is required to exchange 20 Endurance Points with each other. This is done through the enchantment of the spell and all observing this glorious occasion see a lustrous pure silver light passing between the couple. Because each participant <u>exchanges</u> the same number of EP neither is harmed, but they are Linked to each other in the most intimate way. This is a Life Long commitment! Once this is cast, it can never be severed or obstructed by any physical, mental or enchanted means. The only thing that can disrupt this Link is Death itself.

Like all other spells that link their recipients for life, this spell grants certain abilities to the new Lovers. These abilities are listed hereafter and are granted to each spouse:

1) Project Thought & ESP with other at will.   R: 100 miles / Year of Marriage
2) Loan Endurance Points once per week.   R: 1000 miles / Year of Marriage
   Maximum Loan = x4 your Endurance Score (80 EP Max.)
   It takes 1 Action from the 1st spouse to Loan the EP and 1 Action from the other spouse to accept the EP.
3) Teleport to your Spouses side. ONCE per YEAR, you may actually Teleport to your Spouses side regardless of the distance separating you. This is not "bankable", if you don't use it by the end of the year, you loose it. The couple gets 6 hours together and then the spouse is Teleported back.
4) Automatically know if your spouse is affected by a Mind Altering enchantment, regardless of the distance separating you. Examples: Order Spell, Mesmerize Person, Vampire's Poison, etc.
5) Automatically know if your spouse is in mortal danger or fighting for his / her life regardless of the distance separating you.

NOTE2: I always set these few guidelines when dealing with marriage in my campaigns.
I've listed these in order of importance:

A) The couple must be in TRUE LOVE with each other – NO marriages of convenience.
B) Both people must be at least of an Age listed as NOON in the Race Section and must be of opposite sex or the spell does not function at all.
C) Interracial marriages are possible, but these couples will <u>NEVER</u> have children.
   - the genetic codes are incompatible, conception can NEVER even begin.

NOTE3: Enchanters in the past have taught Alchemists to cast the Oath, Marriage, Companion and Scroll Spells. These spells are listed here for connivance and because this is where I explain about Links. This creates an Enchanted Link.

IronBall Field Spell (D or E)   R: **   AOE: **
SPC: 100 or 150 - M   D: **   CT: **

The IronBall Field spell creates the field, the entire canopy, the IronBall, standard catchers (enough for both teams), and "bleachers" for the spectators. See the IronBall section for details.
100 SP = Creates an IronBall Playing Field for Two 3 player teams: 6 Catchers.
150 SP = Creates an IronBall Playing Field for Two 5 player teams: 10 Catchers.
Enchanters have taught this spell to Alchemists and they usually make enchanted Dusts to use the spell.

NOTE4: See the Enchanter / Alchemist Spell Section for the other spells an Enchanter can learn.

ALCHEMIST

INTRODUCTION

Alchemists are able to cast spells, make enchanted Potions, Alchemist's Dusts, or Pills, and they are able to gain a Companion (see the Enchanter section for details). The Alchemist also is the only Occupation that doesn't need to give up Endurance Points to heal someone with a Heal Wounds Spell, so they are able to heal themselves!

You can't take up Alchemy at just any time in your life. If you want to become an Alchemist, you must become an apprentice to an Alchemist of 10th level or higher before a certain age.

Human: 13 - 15 years   Hemar: 26 - 30 years   Krill: 6 - 7 years

When you reach the age group stated above you must drink a "full shot" of Life Tree liquid. Yes, this is the liquid that mutates anything that drinks it, and causes insanity to men and woman who do – sounds like a bummer to start with, hey? Your Mentor Alchemist will tell you to drink the liquid and when you do she will cast a special spell that will "curb" the mutation and change you into an Alchemist. This mutation will allow you some benefits and will mark you for life!

The benefits are: : 1st level :
1) Learn any spell listed in the Enchanter / Alchemist spell section and those spells listed only on the Alchemist Occupational Spell List located at the end of this section.
2) Heal yourself and others by spending Spell Points instead of Endurance Points.
3) Converse with Plants (3/day, 10 min ea.)
4) Converse telepathically with Life Trees at will. (Please, see the Life Tree section for a complete description.)
5) Enchant potions: This is an ability not a spell. The Alchemist only needs to acquire the ingredients.

: 5th level :
1) Plant Growth (1/day, as spell).
2) Immune to all types of non-enchanted venoms and natural poisons. +25% RER vs. all Enchanted Poisons.
3) Convert a Potion to an Alchemist Dust: This is done by casting a spell on an Enchanted Potion.
4) Convert an Alchemist Dust to an Enchanted Pill: This is done by casting a spell on a portion of Alchemist Dust.

: 10th level :
1) Immune to all non-enchanted disease.
2) Immune to all types of Enchanted venoms and poisons.
3) EP Drain Touch - may use your Spell Points to cause a drain of Endurance Points (EP) from your Victim to yourself, to someone else or no one at all.
    You must use 1 Spell Point (SP) for every Endurance Point (EP) Drained or transferred.

The mutation caused from becoming an Alchemist will either effect your eyes or hair, your may choose. If the eyes are selected, it will cause the irises of your eyes to permanently become either a very intense emerald green or a very bright orange. If hair was picked, all the hair on your body will be permanently changed to either an emerald green or a very bright orange.

The other drawback of drinking the liquid of the Life Tree is: you may only cast certain spells directly into the environment: onto a person, animal, or object. These spells are those that are held by a Green gem, an Orange gem, those spells listed on the Alchemist Occupational Spell list or those spells with a Spell Classification of (A).

All other spells learned by the Alchemist must be used to enchant a Potion and then may be converted to an Alchemist's Dust and then to an Enchanted Pill.

ALCHEMIST'S POTIONS, DUSTS AND PILLS

INFORMATION & FACTS

The Alchemist is able to cast only certain spells into the environment, most of the spells they learn must be cast directly into a potion. Once you have enchanted a potion, you may change its form, to make Alchemist's Dusts or Pills. The main ingredients common to all potions are :
1) Enchanted Gem dust from any Enchanted Gem - an Enchanted Gem has a specific
   Gem Perfection Rating (GPR).
2) The liquid from the coconut-like fruit of the Life Tree. (1 ounce required per potion and 4 ounces / nut.)

The gem dust used in making a potion must come from a gem that has already been enchanted – it has a GPR. Once you obtain an Enchanted Gem and know its Gem Perfection Rating (GPR), it may be changed to Enchanted Dust by casting the 'Gem To Dust' spell. (This spell is listed in the Alchemist Occupational Spell section.)

The Enchanted Dust now has the same GPR as the Enchanted Gem it was disseminated from.

NOTES

A) Concentration Time is based on Actions. It will cost you **One** Action for every number listed under the Concentration Time of a spell and then **One** Action to say the Trigger Word and cast that spell.

Actions / Attack	vs.	Level
2		1
3		5
4		10
5		15

B) 1 Attack = 5 seconds: 12 Attacks = 60 seconds = 1 minute.
C) Alchemists may only make ONE Strike per Attack regardless of level. They may not use the Parry skill, but may learn the Survival Skill: Shield Use. You must use one of your Parry Actions to employ a Shield vs. an Opponent's single attack.

D)

Spell Classification	Minimum Gem Perfection Rating usable *
(A)	I2
(B)	SI2
(C)	VSI2
(D)	VVSI2
(E)	VVSI1

* Please see the Gem Section for more info.

ALCHEMIST HEALING HER WING   ALCHEMIST CASTING FLAME JET SPELL FROM A DUST AND DROPPING A VIOLET ALCHEMIST DUST FOR NEXT SPELL

PREPARING THE INGREDIENTS FOR A POTION

To make and enchant a potion the Alchemist must first obtain the "coconut" fruit of the Life Tree and an Enchanted Gem. Now you must change the gem to dust (or have it done for you, if you're not a high enough level) and then extract the liquid from the nut. When you cast the "Change Gem to Dust spell" it will convert an *Enchanted Gem* to dust. The amount of dust you need to mix into the potion is what is produced by a ¼ karat stone - so the amount of dust produced from a 1 karat stone can by used to make 4 different potions. The amount of liquid you need to mix into your potion is 1 ounce. There is always 4 ounces of liquid in the center of every Life Tree "nut."

ENCHANTING A POTION

Once you've blended the appropriate amount of Enchanted Dust and Life Tree liquid in a small glass potion vial, you're ready to enchant the potion. The type of dust you blend into the liquid depends on what spell you wish to cast into the potion. The dust used for the potion must be of the same color as the spell you want to cast into it (ie. the spell will be listed under a particular gem color on the Ench/Al spell list.) To cast a Shield spell into a potion, you must have the dust from an enchanted Topaz or Orange Quartz and if you want to make a Heal potion you must have the dust from an enchanted Emerald or Green Quartz. Next you need to blend the Enchanted Dust with the Liquid of Life. Now you need to only cast the spell directly into the blend of dust and liquid. To gain the benefits from the enchanted potion, all you need to do is drink it (of course the potion can be used by anyone.)

The only potions that can benefit someone are those that hold spells which can be directly cast on people; all Defensive spells and some Miscellaneous ones. Some examples of usable potions are those of Healing, Shielding, Resist Enchantment, Invisibility, Flying, Polymorph, Conversing, ESP, Telekinesis, etc. If you want to be able to use Attack and other Misc. spells, you must convert your potion to an Alchemist Dust or a Pill. This costs you extra Spell Points and the conversions *must done using your ORIGINAL Spell Points* (not regenerated Spell Points). This transformation must occur before the rising of the Column Sun or you may NEVER convert this potion into an Alchemist Dust and from an Alchemist Dust to a Pill.

MAKING DUSTS AND PILLS

To be able to use spells like Flame Bolt, Paralyzation, Bridge, Enchanted Barriers, etc. you must convert your potions to Alchemist Dusts or Pills. All conversions between forms are done by special spells and must take place within one minute of each other using only your 1st set of Spell Points - so if you do the nasty math, you must have 50 SP to make a StingRay Pill (StingRay spell = 10 SP, Convert Potion to Dust spell = 20 SP, and Convert Dust to Pill spell = 20 SP).

After you have enchanted a potion and you want to change it to an Alchemist Dust, simply cast the "Change Potion to Dust" spell, (SPC: 20 SP), on the potion and make up a Trigger Word or Phrase (see Enchanter section for details). In order to use the Alchemist Dust just sprinkle it or throw it outward and say the Trigger Word.

When you have a measure of enchanted Alchemist Dust, you can convert it to a Pill by simply casting the "Change Dust to Pill" spell (SPC: 20 SP) and use the same Trigger Word or Phrase. The size of the Pill depends on what type of spell is held in it. If the spell is Defensive or Miscellaneous to be used on your person, the pill is 1\4 inch in diameter and all attack Pills are 2 inches in diameter. To use an attack Pill (or some Misc. Pills) simply throw it and say the Trigger Word. All Defensive and personal Miscellaneous Pills that directly benefit a person are taken internally.

Example: Flame Bolt 1 Spell (18 SP) + Dust Spell (20 SP) + Pill Spell (20 SP)
         = 58 SP to make a Flame Bolt 1 Pill.

NOTE: All Potions, Dusts, and Pills will take on the Color of the Gem used to make it. The deeper the color the more powerful the enchantment - a Class (B) Flame Bolt 2 pill will be a deeper color red then a Class (A) Flame Bolt 1 pill.

NOTE2: A question that always comes up is: At 10th level, is an Alchemist immune to the enchanted poisons of Goblins and Vampire. Answer = Yes!

USING POTIONS, DUSTS AND PILLS

It will take one Action to drink a Potion, to throw a measure of Alchemist Dust or Pill and say it's Trigger Word. The Trigger Word or Phrase for the same types of Alchemist Dusts or Pills may be the same.

All measures of Dust can be thrown 5' and all attack Pills can be thrown 1' per Level. These thrown distances are *ADDED* to the Range of the stated spells. Now you can start to understand why an Alchemist can be so deadly in a combat situation. Although, they do need time to prepare their arsenal. When they do hit the road and get into a scuffle, they only need sprinkle some measures of different colored Alchemist Dusts at their feet and hold some pills in their hands. When the scoundrels and madmen come a callin' - because you wouldn't do anything wrong, being the great and pure-hearted Alchemist - you just hold out your palm and start calling off Trigger Words and watch the "fireworks" begin. When a Trigger Word linked to a measure of Alchemist Dust is forcefully and loudly spoken, that amount of Alchemist Dust flies off the ground to just in front of your open palm and then the spell will take on its form and speed toward your vile opponent. The Alchemist must be careful because Dusts can be blown away by a strong wind.

NOTE: You must say a Trigger Word for each measure of Alchemist Dust or individual Pill to activated it - even if they have the same Trigger Word. So if you have 3 Alchemist Dusts with the same Trigger Word, you must say the Trigger Word 3 times, which takes 3 Actions.

NOTE2: You may only cast ONE Offensive spell per Attack.

Alchemist Dusts of Healing are preferred over Pills by most Alchemists, because you just need to sprinkle a measure on a companion in battle, says the Trigger Word and your companion will be healed. If you make a Pill, you must get your companion to take the Pill internally, so you see the problem while you are in a battle situation.

HOW LONG DO POTIONS, DUSTS AND PILLS LAST?

A Potion will last 50 days + 2 days per Level of the Alchemist who made it. After this the potion will separate and the enchanted gem dust settles to the bottom of the Liquid of Life. (These separated Potions are sometimes found in deserted castles or on long dead travelers.) Alchemist Dusts or Pills will never separate or become unenchanted. Anyone may transform a Pill back into a Dust or a Dust to a Potion by casting a Cancel Enchantment spell on it. You must have it in your posession and not be in combat. With one more Cancel Enchantment, you may then separate the potion back into Enchanted Gem Dust and Life Tree liquid, known as the "Liquid of Life." Then these may be used as ingredients to cast another spell and make a different potion.

NOTE3: If the Trigger Word is known, all Alchemist Dusts and Attack Pills can be used by anyone.

NOTE4: There are no Trigger Words for potions or Pills which are intended for consumption, just "tilt your head back and empty the cup" -- or swallow the Pill.

OTHER ALCHEMIST STUFF

An Alchemist can make a Scroll by simply following the rules that are stated in the Enchanter Section. Enchanters and Alchemists create Scrolls in exactly in the same way and an Alchemist can put any spell she wants onto a Scroll.

At 2nd level her Mentor usually awards the young Alchemist a Companion Spell Scroll, just as with Enchanters. The Alchemist can cast this and create a companion - just follow the rules listed in the Enchanter Section.

There are some differences for an Alchemist's Companion and they are listed here:

a) When an Alchemist constructs his or her companion's base form; it doesn't have to be a statue. An Alchemist may choose his or her companion's base form to be practically anything that is physically large enough to constitute the material used. The base form could be a large necklace, large forearm band, a belt buckle, etc.

b) An Alchemist can't enchant and set a gem into their companion, so their companion may "hold" and cast these number of spells per level. The spell(s) are given to the companion by letting it drink a potion enchanted with the spell in question. The companion may "hold" the spells until used.

Levels 2 – 4	1 Class B or 3 Class A spells	
Levels 5 – 9	1 Class C or 3 Class B spells or Equivalent (see GPR table)	
Levels 10 – 14	1 Class D or 3 Class C spells or Equivalent	
Levels 15 – 19	1 Class E or 2 Class D spells or Equivalent	

The companion may be in any form to cast spells. They may do it while stalking as a sleek cat or when they are hanging about the Alchemist's neck, disguised as a medallion.

c) The Companion still forms an Enchanted Link with you and you gain all benefits listed in the Enchanter's Section.

Only Alchemist's are able to learn this next list of spells. These spells are the basis of the Alchemist Occupation and are all held by Enchanted Green Gems: Emeralds or Green Quartz.
NOTE: See the Enchanter / Alchemist Spell Section for the other spells an Alchemist may learn and cast.

COLOR = GREEN   GEM: EMERALD or GREEN QUARTZ

Revitalize Nature (A-E)   R: T   AOE: see below
SPC: * - M   D: inst.   CT: **

This astounding spell is used to Revitalize an entire natural area. All plant life, animal life, and even the soil and water in the area will be affected. Living things will be energized with new life and the water and soil in the area will be cleansed and purified. All water and soil will be totally cleansed of any impurities including all toxins, poisons or disease in the area. All plants and animals within the area at the time of casting will be cured of all diseases and poisons that might be affecting them. Plants in the area will produce fruit or flower, etc. when the spell is cast. This is true even if the plant doesn't usually bloom in the current season. If this is cast in the dead of winter, leaves and buds would have to form before the plant could bear fruit so the spell may have to be cast several times in this certain situation. The area the Alchemist is able to effect depends on the amount of Spell Points she wishes to spend:

Description		Area of Effect	Spell Point Cost *	Casting Time **
Garden	small	5' x 5'	10	1 Action
	medium	10' x 10'	25	1
Field	small	25' x 25'	50	2
	medium	50' x 50'	75	2
Glade	small	100' x 100'	100	3
	medium	250' x 250'	125	3
Forest	small	500' x 500'	150	4
	medium	1000' x 1000'	175	4 Actions

Note2:   This spell does not effect the age of the plant or animal in any way.

Heal Wounds 2 (B)   R: T   AOE: 1 recipient
SPC: 30+ - M   D: inst.   CT: 1

This is essentially like the 2nd part of the "Heal Wounds 1" spell explained in the Enchanter / Alchemist section. The Alchemist still only needs to spend Spell Points to Heal someone. This spell differs because when you cast it, you automatically heal someone 30 EP. To heal someone more than 30 EP, you may spend any amount of Spell Points up to <u>six times</u> your Endurance Score and heal the recipient an equal number of Endurance Points. This means it's possible to heal someone from 30 EP to a maximum of 120 EP, if you have an Endurance Score of 20 and enough SP to spend. You may never heal someone past their Total Original Endurance Points (TOEP).

Heal Blindness (B or C)   R: 5'+1'/L   AOE: 1 recipient
SPC: 40 or 70 - M   D: inst.   CT: 1 or 2 Actions

With the casting of this spell, the Alchemist may heal any type of blindness, magical or otherwise. The Alchemist may heal any type of blindness caused by an Enchantment – even by acid – by sacrificing 40 Spell Points. You may heal a non-magical blindness by sacrificing a total of 70 Spell points. This includes blindness caused by some ordinary accident or even blindness from birth. This spell will never affect the consequences of a Harmful Birth Gift. Oddly enough, this spell will also cure someone of an <u>Illusionary Fear</u> if 40 SP are spent when cast.

Transform Alchemist Spell (D)   R: T   AOE: 1 Potion
SPC: 100 - M   D: inst.   CT: 1

This Spells transforms an adolescent into an Alchemist. Please see above for details.

Potion to Dust Spell (B)   R: T   AOE: 1 Potion
SPC: 20 - M   D: inst.   CT: 1

This spell will convert any one enchanted Potion into a quantity of enchanted Alchemist Dust. This spell must be cast on the potion to be converted within one minute of when it was enchanted and using your 1st set of Spell Points and *must* be cast by the same Alchemist who enchanted the potion.

Dust to Pill Spell (B)   R: T   AOE: 1 Quantity of Dust
SPC: 20 - M   D: inst.   CT: 1

This spell will convert any one quantity of Alchemist Dust into an enchanted Pill. This spell must be cast on the quantity of Alchemist Dust to be converted within one minute after the enchantment and must be cast by the same Alchemist who enchanted the Dust using his 1st set of Spell Points.

Heal Poison (C)   R: T   AOE: 1 recipient
SPC: 50 - M   D: inst.   CT: 2

This spell's name is deceiving and it's one of the few spells that requires any type of ingredient to cast it properly. To be cast properly, the Alchemist must have a small sample (.1 ounce) of the poison that the recipient was inflected with or ¼ karat of Enchanted Emerald Dust. The sample of poison or Enchanted Emerald Dust is spread on the recipient's skin over the wound and the spell is then cast on him. This will totally cure the poison in question.

If an Alchemist doesn't have any Dust or the type of venom or poison, this spell will slow the quickness of the venom to 20% of the normal rate. You may cast this on a person more than once to try and "slow the poison to a crawl."

Heal Paralyzation (C)   R: 5'+1'/L   AOE: 1 recipient
SPC: 55 or 75 - M   D: inst.   CT: 2

This spell will heal all forms of Paralyzation (enchanted or natural.) Any type of magical paralyzation can be healed by spending 55 Spell Points. Any type of natural paralyzation caused by combat, birth, or a natural poison can be healed by spending 75 Spell Points.

Heal Disease (C)   R: T   AOE: 1 recipient
SPC: 60 - M   D: inst.   CT: 2

This spell will cure any type of disease. It will not cure any side affects that the disease may have caused, and the recipient of the spell will still have an equal chance of being re-infected. Strangely enough, this spell will also restore a victim from the <u>coma caused by an Illusionary Death</u>, restore two points to your beauty score obtained from Acid Damage, save a person from <u>becoming a Ghoul</u> or wake someone from a Snake <u>Vampire's Poison</u>.

Heal Wounds 3 (D)   R: T   AOE: 1 recipient
SPC: 100 - M   D: inst.   CT: 3

This follows the rules of Heal Wounds 2 and when you cast it, you automatically heal someone or yourself for 100 EP. Unlike the other heal spells, you may heal as many EP as your companion needs, as long as you have the Spell Points necessary. It does not depend on your Endurance Score so there is no limit on how many EP you can heal one person with this spell. You may never heal someone past their Total Original Endurance Points (TOEP).

Restore (E)   R: T   AOE: 1 recipient
SPC: 155 - M   D: inst.   CT: 4

This spell is the most powerful of any of the healing spells. The enchantment of this spell is so strong it can replace a limb, cure any amount of EP (same rules as Heal Wounds 3 - minimum of 155 EP) or any type of disease, blindness, paralyzation or poison (without any need for ingredients) - but it can only do one of these per spell. It will cure a major insanity 50% of the time and cure a phobia 75% of the time. This spell will also restore the victim from the coma caused by an Illusionary Death, instantly quench Illusionary Fear, wake a person from a Vampire's Poison or stop the transformation into a Ghoul. It has no effect if the person is dead, but will heal someone to one-half of their original EP if they are below zero EP, and still alive. Like all other magical healing, it will have no effect on a Harmful Birth Gift. You may never heal someone past their Total Original Endurance Points (TOEP).

Gem to Dust Spell (D) R: T AOE: 1 recipient
SPC: 100 - M D: inst. CT: 4

The Gem to Dust spell is a very controversial spell because it actually converts an Enchanted Gem into a small amount of Enchanted Dust. Some people use the term 'Destroy' instead of 'convert', because no one has every found a way to change the Enchanted Dust back into a gem. Alchemists need Enchanted Dust to make their potions, which they can convert into Alchemists Dusts or Pills. Enchanters require Enchanted Dust to make scrolls. The gem in question must first be enchanted (See Gem Section). Once you have obtained an Enchanted Gem, you must put it into a container, cast the spell and touch the gem. It will instantly be converted to an amount of Enchanted Dust. It may now be used to make either Potions, Alchemist Dusts, Pills or Scrolls. The Enchanted Dust retains the GPR of the Gem used and a one Karat stone provides 4 measures of dust. This spell is the only means known that can effect an Enchanted Gem in any way.

This spell will only affect Enchanted Gems that weigh 1 Karat or less.

Usually, an Alchemist will cast this spell for someone for 25 Silver (SP / 4), but a Master won't usually charge her students.

ELEMENTALIST

INTRODUCTION

An Elementalist manipulates the power of an Elemental Plane by "borrowing" the powers of a specific Elemental. The Elementalist may even summon that Elemental to our Plane! There are four "Primary" Elemental planes and four "Secondary" ones. The four Primary Elemental Planes are composed of and designated as: Fire, Air, Water, and Earth. The Secondary Elemental Planes are Smoke, Fog, Mud, and Lava. These Secondary Elemental Planes are more difficult to "contact" then the Primary ones, so an Elementalist must be of higher level to use their power.

In order for the Elementalist to cast any enchantments or to summon Elementals, he must be able to "bridge" the gap between our Plane and the Elemental's Plane. In most cases, to "bridge" this gap, the Elementalist must use a Ring or Disk constructed by another Elementalist or himself.

There are only 2 situations when an Elementalist does not need a Ring or Disk to bridge the gap between the planes:
1st) The Elementalist may cast any Elementalist Spell with a classification of Class (A) without a Ring / Disk.
    – these spells only require a Spell Point Cost of less than 20 SP.
2nd) The Elementalist may cast any Elementalist Spell that is related to any of the **Primary Planes**,
    if he or she spends DOUBLE the number of Spell Points listed under the spells description.

Once you have constructed or obtained a Ring or Disk, you may "pull" spells through it, from a specific Elemental. The first time the Ring or Disk is used: the first spells you "pull" through are made "Permanent" and can be used Once per day by simply saying a Trigger Word or Phrase. (I use the word "permanent" in quotes, because even though you don't have to spend Spell Points to use these spells, you can only use them 1/day.) By wielding a Ring or Disk, you can use the "permanent" spells held within it once per day and the Elementalist may bridge the gap and cast any other spells associated with that Plane simply by concentrating, saying the Trigger Phrase, and spending the required Spell Points and Endurance Points. The Ring or Disk bridges the gap for you.

INFORMATION & FACTS

The materials you construct your Ring or Disk out of will govern what spells it can actually "channel" and "hold". If Mithral or an Enchanted Quartz gem is used in the making of the Ring or Disk, then it can only "channel" Class (A), (B), and (C) types of enchantment. If Americanium and a true Enchanted Gem - a Ruby, Sapphire, Diamond, etc. - is used then the Ring or Disk can "channel" any Classification - (A), (B), (C), (D) or (E) - of enchantment. As you can guess, Mithral and Quartz Rings / Disks are more common, because these substances are not as rare or expensive.

After you have constructed a Ring or Disk, you will be ready to "pull" or "channel" certain spells through it for the first time. When you do "pull" the 1st spells through the Ring or Disk it is known as "awakening the Ring/Disk". You must of course have enough Spell Points to cast these spells and all spells must be cast from your 1st allotment of SP you gained directly from the Column Sun, not from one your regenerations during the day. When you "awaken" the Ring or Disk, by "pulling" a spell through for the first time, the Enchanted Gem set into the Ring or Disk "remembers" the patterns of the enchantment and it becomes "Permanent". You are actually borrowing a specific Elemental's power when you "awaken" the Ring or Disk and the Elemental will provide the power needed for the spell when it is used once per day. The spell patterns imprinted inside the Enchanted Gem will "shape" the Enchantment as it comes out of the Gem. You must also assign a Trigger Word or Phrase to the spells when you cast they for the first time. The next time you forcefully say the Trigger Word/Phrase - after sunrise the next morning - it will trigger a signal the specific Elemental will hear and that Elemental will give you the necessary Spell Points for that specific spell.

When wearing an Enchanted Ring or Disk, the Elementalist can "bridge" the gap between the planes without any penalty - another words, the Elementalist can cast any spell he knows that is associated with that particular plane by spending the amount of spell points stated in its description. If the Elementalist needs to cast a spell and doesn't have a Ring or Disk to "bridge" the gap associated with that particular plane, then he must spend DOUBLE the spell points stated in the spell's description. Either way, when the gap is "bridged" and you have said the Trigger Word and have spent the correct number of spell points, you use them to "shape" the essence of that particular plane which forms your spell.

NOTE: An Elementalist doesn't need any type of Ring/Disk to cast any Class (A) spell from the Primary Elemental Plains - Fire, Air, Water, and Earth! Because of this, most Elementalists will learn a wide range of Class (A) spells from all the Primary Plains. Remember, you **always** need an enchanted Ring/Disk to "pull" spells from the Secondary Elemental Planes or to summon an Elemental to our plane.

To "pull" spells from one of the Secondary Elemental Planes, you need to construct a Ring/Disk with TWO Enchanted Gems set in it. The 2 gems needed to be set together to contact these planes are listed below:

ELEMENT	COLOR			GEMS
Element of Smoke	Red and Blue	Ruby & Sapphire	or	Red & Blue Quartz = Fire & Air
Element of Fog	Blue and Clear	Sapphire & Diamond	or	Blue & Clear Quartz = Air & Water
Element of Mud	Clear and Brown	Diamond & Andalusite	or	Clear & Brown Quartz = Water & Earth
Element of Lava	Brown and Red	Andalusite & Ruby	or	Brown & Red Quartz = Earth & Fire

Notice, to contact any Secondary Plane, you need the Enchanted Gems that are associated with the Primary Planes that are on either "side" of the Secondary Plane (see "Pie" chart at the end of this section).

YOU CAN NEVER SET TWO GEMS OF THE SAME PLANE OR OF OPPOSING PLANES IN THE SAME RING/DISK . If you try this, the Ring/Disk will explode most bodaciously! In order to "Awaken" a Ring/Disk with two Enchanted Gems set in it, you must "pull" at least one spell through each respective gem - follow the rules above and the spells in question become "permanent" and castable by just speaking the Trigger Word once per day. Notice, the spells you "pull" through the Enchanted Gems when you "awaken" the Ring/Disk are associated with the Primary Elemental Planes. Now to actually cast a spell associated with a Secondary Plane, you must learn that spell and cast it by saying its Trigger Phrase and spending the required Spell Points while wearing the newly awakened Ring/Disk. No spell from a Secondary Elemental Plane can ever be made "permanent" or be cast without an Enchanted Ring/Disk.

There are TWO stipulations on how many spells you may pull through the Ring/Disk when you "awaken" it (Remember these spells will become "permanent"). The first stipulation is governed by the GPR (Gem Perfection Rating) of the Enchanted Gem you used in constructing the Ring/Disk (see the Gem section). The second consideration when "awakening" the Ring/Disk is: all spells to be made "permanent" and castable once per day must be cast or "pulled" through the ring using your 1st set of Spell Points. You must have enough Spell Points to initially cast the spell or spells you want "permanent" and castable once per day. You, or anyone else, wearing the Ring/Disk and who knows the Trigger Word, only needs to say the Trigger Word or Phrase forcefully and take an Action to activate the "permanent" spell - this just means that you can't whisper or activate it in normal conversation.

Every spell cast by YOU (not those that are permanent in a Ring/Disk) requires a certain amount of time to be cast. This required time is known as the spell's Concentration Time (CT) and is listed under the spell's description.

The Concentration Time is based on Actions. It will cost you **One** Action for every number listed under the Concentration Time of a spell and then **One** Action to say the Trigger Word to cast that spell.

To say the Trigger Word that activates an Enchanted Item will also cost you an Action.

Actions / Attack	vs.	Level
2		1
3		5
4		10
5		15

NOTE2: Elementalists may only make ONE Sword Strike per Attack. They may not learn the Warrior's Parry skill but may learn to use a Shield by learning the Survival Skill: Shield Use. Remember, you must use one of your Parry Actions to employ a Shield vs. an Opponent's single attack.

NOTE3: A 'Permanent' spell, held in a Ring/Disk, is cast in just 1 Action by saying its Trigger Word or Phrase.

NOTE4: An Elementalist may only cast ONE Offensive spell per Attack.

SPECIAL ABILITIES

To construct an Elementalist Ring, you must set an Enchanted Gem in it. To do this, the Elementalist needs to appropriate approximately ½ ounce of either Mithral or Americanium. He also needs to acquire an Enchanted Gem. The weight of the Enchanted Gem can't exceed **5** karats for a Ring - there is no limit to the size of the Enchanted Gem for a Disk. Once you have enough metal and an Enchanted Gem, you will need the equipment to make the Ring and the Survival Skill: Ring/Disk Construction. The equipment costs between 20 and 100 Silver Pieces and consists of one wax block, a small knife, a funnel, (etc. – see diagram below). First you must carve the Ring's design and its setting out of wax, make sure it's the correct size for your finger! The more complicated the design the longer it will take to carve (a simple "Mithral band" with a setting to hold the Enchanted Gem will take about 8 days to carve). When you accomplish this, you put the wax Ring in the box with clay surrounding it, then you simply pour in the molten metal using the funnel, and get it spinning. The Liquid Metal melts the wax and when it cools, you have your Ring. Now you secure the Enchanted Gem in the setting and get ready to "awaken" the Ring.

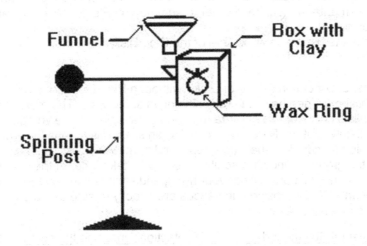

To construct a Ring with TWO gems you must be at least 5th level. You simply follow the same rules stated above. This will take at least 1 oz. of metal and 2 Enchanted Gems that are less then 5 karats in weight. The gems you use MUST be different types and CAN'T be of opposing Planes. To make a Ring, with 2 gems, follow the directions above - but you carve a setting for each Gem, so this will take more time. You must "pull" at least one spell from each respective Primary Plane to "awaken" a Ring with 2 Enchanted gems.

NOTE: You can now cast spells through the Ring from either of the Planes that are represented by Enchanted Gems PLUS any spell that you have mastered from the Secondary plane represented by the pairing of the Enchanted Gems.

To construct a Disk, you must be at least 10th level. An Enchanted Disk can be used by wearing it as a pendent and it even may be put into a weapon (A ring can only be worn on a finger). The amount of metal used for a Disk is a minimum of 2 oz in weight and you must use Enchanted Gems that weigh at least 5 Karats. You just carve out the Disk's shape from wax, but you must set the Enchanted Gem in a hole you make in the middle of the wax Disk. Put the wax Disk and Enchanted Gem in the box and pour in the metal - Remember Enchanted Gems are not affected by heat, fire, acid or lightning in any way. You "awaken" the Disk the same way you "awaken" a Ring.

To make a Disk with 2 Enchanted gems you must be at least 15th level. Follow the instructions above but put both the Enchanted gems in the middle of the Disk. Remember, you must be aware of the restrictions listed under the paragraph that explained the construction of a Ring with 2 Enchanted Gems which concerns what types of Enchanted gems may be put into the same Ring/Disk.

NOTE2: Only a Disk may be forged into a weapon. The weapon must be forged of Ransium if Mithral was used to construct the Disk. If Americanium was used to make the Disk, then the weapon must be forged from Langor. When a disk is forged into a weapon, you can not use it to summon an Elemental, but the wielder of the weapon may activate the "permanent" spells once per day by saying the Trigger Word.

As has been briefly stated before, when an Elementalist "awakens" any Ring or Disk, she actually makes "contact" with a specific Elemental and "borrows" its power. There is a consequence when you "link" a Ring/Disk with an Elemental. The consequence is that you give the Elemental the ability to roam our Plane of existence. The Elemental is able to pass into our realm 1/year on it's own in full force. You may say "So what!", but when an Elemental roams on its own, sometimes it accidentally kills innocents and destroys buildings, farm steeds, etc. without realizing it - An Elemental doesn't understand our frailties! This tends to make certain people very angry, like the ones that have lost their entire homesteads to a "curious" Fire Elemental out for a stroll. These people would be very angry and would probably try to exterminate all Elementalists, if they ever found out that: "It is your fault that my home is ablaze!" For this reason, all Elementalists are sworn to keep this secret onto death! All Elementalists have always discouraged people who want to learn another Occupation after learning this "Great Secret". For this reason, an Elementalist will never train someone who is already trained in another Occupation.

Now let us discuss the three things an Elementalist must consider in order to summon an Elemental:
  (1) What level an Elementalist must be in order to summon an Elemental? The answer is 5th level.
  (2) How to summon one.
  (3) What this does to the "permanent" powers of the Ring/Disk.

1) First, you must construct or obtain a Ring or Disk - without a Ring/Disk there is no way to summon an Elemental! The Elementalist must get the Ring/Disk spinning in some way. The method you use is purely up to you, but most Elementalists consider this an area requiring great style. Once you get the Ring or Disk spinning, you must immediately cast the Ring Spin or Disk Spin spell; this means that you must concentrate for the number of Actions listed under the spell, then "spin or flip" the Ring/Disk and immediately cast the spell before the Ring/Disk hits the ground. Once the spell is cast, it will "take hold" of the spinning Ring/Disk, keep it spinning, move it to a position within one foot of your head, and encase it in a protection enchantment specific to an Elemental Plane. The encasing substances are directly related to the Elemental Plane the Ring/Disk is "linked" to and are listed here:

Elemental Summoned	"Protection" encasing the spinning Ring/Disk
Fire	Ball of Flame
Air	Invisible Ball of Air
Water / Ice	Water Droplet / Ball of Ice
Earth	Small Stone
Smoke	Ball of Smoke
Fog	Translucent Ball of Fog
Mud	Small Clay Ball
Lava	Small Lava Ball

2) When the Ring/Disk is spinning and protected, it will send out a Beacon that will summon the Elemental. The Elemental will arrive within 2 Actions of the start of the Spin Spell and will materialize within 20' of you. The Elemental will know it's summoner by the "signature" that the specific Ring/Disk leaves on the hand or neck of the wearer (see below for details.) You get 5 hours "free" on your summoning when you cast the Ring Spin Spell, but after that you must spend 10 Spell Points per hour to keep the Elemental here. You can mentally move the spinning Ring or Disk any where within 1 ft of your head - But you can't cover the Spinner up in any way or have it spin inside a sack, pocket, cloak, etc.

3) When used for Summoning, the Ring/Disk looses the ability to cast all "Permanent" spells held within it, but the "Permanent" spells can be used again after the next Sunrise. This obviously means that if the Elementalist uses any of the "Permanent" spells held in the Ring/Disk, he can't summon an Elemental that day with that Ring/Disk. Also a particular Ring/Disk can only be used to summon an Elemental Once per Day.

NOTE: The Elemental may use its power and the patterns held in the Ring/Disk to cast the spells which are "permanent" - so it might as well use 'em now, 'cause the "Permanent" spells will be uncastable by the ring bearer until Sunrise of the next day.

Anyone, including Elementalists, can only wear 1 Enchanted Ring on each hand and only 1 Enchanted Disk around their neck. The reason is because a Ring/Disk quickly "saturates" the hand or neck of the wearer with an Enchanted signature that is totally unique. This permits the Elemental to identify its summoner even if other Elementals are being summoned by different people at the same time. The Enchanted signature left by an Elementalist's Ring/Disk will repel all other Rings or Disks from either of your hands or your neck. You can always take off and replace the SAME Ring/Disk as many times as you wish. (The only way to circumvent this is for an Elementalist to cast a special spell called "Erase Signature" or to wait until the Column Sun rises the next morning.)

NOTE: You must be wearing a Ring/Disk to use any of its permanent spells.

NOTE2: When an Elementalist completes his or her initial training and is ready to start adventuring and gaining Experience Points, your mentor usually gives you a "low level" ring before you start your adventuring.

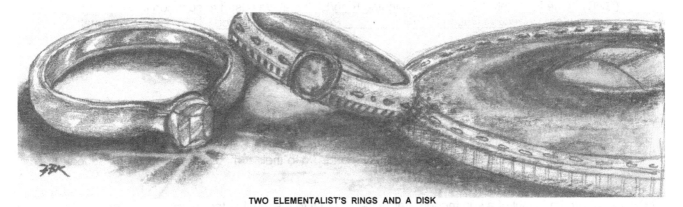

TWO ELEMENTALIST'S RINGS AND A DISK

ELEMENTALIST FLIPPING A DIAMOND RING AND IT FORMING INTO A BALL OF ICE WITH THE RING SPIN SPELL.

80

ELEMENTALS

All Elementals have an Intellect Score between 15-20. Unfortunately, they do not understand us – people - or the world we live in. They utterly don't understand the concepts of friends, enemies, male, female, family, names, pain, death, hate, love, anger or any other emotions. They do recognize their summoner, but only by the Enchanted signature left by the Ring/Disk used to summon them. Even after years of summoning, an Elemental still can't recognize it's Summoner in a crowd. Note: An Elemental can always sense the Enchanted Signature given off from the Summoner's hand or neck regardless of distance.

Elemental Specifications and Stuff :
(1) All summoned Elementals have exactly the same number of Endurance Points as that of their Summoner.

(2) The Percentage To Evade (PTE) of the summoned Elemental is based on the Gem Perfection Rating (GPR) of the Enchanted Gem in the spinning Ring/Disk that was used to summon it.

Gem Perfection Rating (GPR)	Percentage To Evade (PTE) of the Elemental
I2	25%
I1	30%
SI2	35%
SI1	40%
VSI2	45%
VSI1	50%
VVSI2	55%
VVSI1	60%

NOTE2: Some types of Elementals get a PTE bonus do to their composition which will be added to these PTE bases.

(3) The maximum height of a summoned Elemental is equal to the level of the Summoner in feet. The Elemental has the choice to assume any height it wishes between 1 foot tall and 1 foot tall per the level of the Summoner. It can grow or shrink to any height between these limits in just one Action. The height is important because it directly relates to the damage an Elemental can inflict with it's fists.

(4) The Resist Enchantment Roll (RER) of a summoned Elemental is exactly the same as the Summoners'. This is true even if the Summoner has a Resist Enchantment Spell affecting her or him. If the Elemental is effected by an enchantment that triggers the +25% RER bonus of the spell the Elemental receives the bonus and that spell ends for both the Elemental and the Summoner.

(5) When the Elemental is here it doesn't know any spells, but it can shape the Enchantment of its plane to fit the patterns held in the gem used to summon it. Each "permanent" spell can be activated by the Elemental only ONCE per day.

(6) The form the Elemental assumes is always a "human" bipedal form.

(7) The Elemental's Charging Rate Multiple is always the same as its Summoner.

(8) The Elemental's Number of Actions per Attack = 2. These are for moving and attacking while in combat.

(9) All Elementals are unaffected by all spells that can be held by an Indigo gem.

(10) Elementals gain certain Survival Skills dependant on the its type:
   a) <u>Detect Ambush</u>: ALL Types = Same as Summoner (SaS).
   b) <u>Tracking</u>: Earth & Mud = 60%; Water/Air/Fog/Smoke = SaS; Fire & Lava = None.
   c) <u>Attack Unseen Enemy</u>: The first percentage is what is added to your Opponent's PTE total while he is in total darkness, the second is added to your Opponent's PTE while he is in Deep Shadows. These bonuses are added to an Opponent's PTE, if the Elemental is attacking him, while he is in darkness or deep shadows instead of the usual +40% / +30%.

Earth = 20%/10% if Opp. on ground	Water/Ice = 20%/10% if Opp. is in water
Air = 20%/10% if Opp. is flying	Fog = 20%/10% if Opp. is in a fog bank, clouds, ect.
Smoke = 20%/10% if Opp. in smoke	Mud = 20%/10% if Opp. is in mud
Lava = 20%/10% if Opp. is on Lava	Fire = 20%/10% if Opp. is in fire (Oh, yea Right!!)

   d) <u>Find Concealed Areas</u>: Air & Fog & Smoke = Ability Check Percentage equals Summoner's Wisdom * 3.

Elementals' Fists, Damage and Automatic Abilities

An Elemental's Fists are shaped like hammers, balls or clubs depending on it's type. (When an Elemental wants to pick something up it only needs to touch it and the item is transferred to the middle of its body.) The Damage an Elemental can do is based on the shape of its Fists and on its Height at the time it strikes an opponent. All Elementals have certain Automatic abilities which are based on its type and these are listed below.

Elemental		Fist		Damage		Automatic Abilities
Fire	:	Ball	:	1d20+1/ft	:	Flaming **, Fly (CRM=8)
Air	:	Club	:	2d8 +1/ft	:	Fly (CRM=12), Invisibility
Water	:	Club	:	2d8 +1/ft	:	Water Walk, wavy *, tip boat***
Ice (5)	:	Ball	:	1d20+1/ft	:	Water Walk, wavy *, may walk on land
Earth (10)	:	Hammer	:	2d12+1/ft	:	Pass Earth @ Will, Poly into Rock
Smoke	:	Club	:	2d8 +1/ft	:	Fly (CRM=10), Poly into Smoke
Fog	:	Club	:	2d8 +1/ft	:	Fly (CRM=11), Poly into Fog
Mud (5)	:	Ball	:	1d20+1/ft	:	Pass Mud @ Will, Poly into Mud Pool
Lava (5)	:	Hammer	:	2d12+1/ft	:	Pass Lava @ Will, Poly into Lava Pool

The number in parentheses behind the Elemental's type is the PTE bonus that those Elementals receive. This bonus is added to the Elemental's PTE base granted by the GPR of the gem used in the Ring/Disk for the summoning.

*   Same as spell of the same name, but there is no Spell Point Cost and no Duration limits.

**   A Fire Elemental can "turn off" its Flaming ability if it wants to walk through a forest and not burn it down. While it is flaming it will ignite any flammables it touches 50% of the time. While not flaming it still glows brightly.

***   A Water Elemental may tip over any boat that is shorter, from bow to stern, then twice it's maximum height.

@ Will: These Elementals may Pass through the stated substance at will moving at a CRM of 4.

Poly: Polymorph into stated substance at will. The size is 1 foot in diameter per Level of the Summoner.

Elementals and Combat verses People and Creatures:

When Elementals combat people, or Regular, Mutated or Enchanted Creatures they use either their fists or spells. If in close range they will first expand to their full height, if the conditions permit, and then strike at their opponents with each fist per Attack. They will continue to do this until that opponent stops moving, at which time they will move to another Opponent, or until the Elemental is beaten to zero Endurance Points (EP) which will force them back to their home Plane. If the Elemental is not within "reach" of an opponent or they are using projectile weapons or spells, the Elemental will cast the spells that are patterned in the Ring/Disk – the "Permanent" ones. An Elemental can cast these spells anytime it wishes but it usually casts them at these times:

    (1) Attack spells   - at first chance in their first combat situation.
    (2) Defensive spells   - cast them on the Summoner either right after it's summoning or at the beginning of the first battle they are in.
    (3) Miscellaneous spells - at anytime when the spell might help either the Summoner or the Elemental.

When an Elemental needs to battle another Elemental, regardless of their perspective origins, they will simple come together and lock arms - like wrestlers do - and EP will start to cancel and drain from each of them at a rate of 20 EP per Attack. When one Elemental is completely drained, it will be sent back to its home Plane. The "winner" may go on and continue its mission or the battle.

NOTE: Elementals NEVER cast spells at <u>each</u> other, they simple get to one another as quickly as possible and lock arms! If both happen to get fully drained at the same time (they each had the same amount of EP when they locked arms), then they both will be forced back to their respective home planes at the same time.

Elementals Verses Enchantments and Spells:

An Elemental rates a Resist Enchantment Roll (RER) verses all types of enchantment just like anyone else. The RER is equal to that of the Summoner. The only exceptions are:

(1) The Elemental may not be harmed by any enchantment (or any natural force) that is the same as its composition and Plane of origin. A Fire Elemental can't be harmed by any type of Fire or Flame spell, regardless who or what casts it and may even stand right in the middle of a bonfire. An Earth Elemental can't be harmed by any spell dealing with penalization, rocks, stones, quicksand, etc. and won't even be disturbed by a natural landslide.

(2) When an elemental comes in contact with any enchantment that is composed of an opposing plane, the Elemental will suffer <u>double base damage</u> and will have it's RER is cut in half! An Air Elemental will take 28+1d12 EP Damage from a **Stone Storm 2** spell, unless it makes it's RER, which is cut in half, at which time it will receive normal damage – 14+1d12. A Lava Elemental will suffer 24+1d6 from a Fog Jet. (This is true for Enchanters and Alchemist Bolts, Jets, etc. as well as Elementalist Spells or any source of enchantments, such as Enchanted Creatures, wands, scrolls, pills, dusts, staffs, etc.)

Elemental Verse Barriers, Banks, Globes, etc.:

An Elemental is completely unaffected by any enchanted OR non-enchanted barriers that are composed of the materials of their home Plane. An Earth Elementals may walk right through an enchanted Stone Barrier or ANY non-enchanted stone walls. A Smoke Elemental can pass through a Smoke Wall unaffected and see through a Smoke Bank with no penalties.

An Elemental CANNOT pass an Enchanted Barrier, Bank, or Globe that is composed of a material of an opposing Plane. An Ice Elemental has no hope of crossing a Fire Barrier and a Lava Elemental is completely halted by a Fog Globe.

Elemental Psyche:

The Elemental considers being "whisked" away from its Plane a minor inconvenience. It will serve the Elementalist in any way he asks or instructs without trying to "twist" the instructions in any way - you just have to remember that Elementals can't understand certain basic concepts. You could ask the Elemental to recover something (as long as you give it an accurate description and location), defend you (you'll have to be very specific on who to attack and who to defend), watch over you as you sleep, be a lookout as you move, etc. You only need to give SPECIFIC instructions. All instructions are issued telepathically to the Elemental so the content is well understood as long as the Elementalist is specific.

Elemental Element Transfer:

The Elemental can be ordered to bring into our world a certain amount of the element of its plane. This material is always non-enchanted and can <u>never</u> be used for <u>any type</u> of an attack or strike while it is being brought into our world.

An Elemental from a Primary Elemental Plane (Fire, Air, Water or Earth) may produce 1 cubic foot of material per level of the caster. This can be done once per minute for every level of the caster. This can only be done once per summoning. Here is an example:

At 5th level, an Elementalist could have an Air Elemental bring in 5 cubic feet of pure air a total of 5 times over 5 minutes. This would total 25 cubic feet of pure air.

At 10th level, an Elementalist could have an Earth Elemental bring in 10 cubic feet of stone a total of 10 times over 10 minutes. This would total 100 cubic feet of stone.

An Elemental from a Secondary Elemental Plane (Fog, Smoke, Mud, Lava) may produce ½ cubic foot of material per level of the caster. This can be done once per minute for every level of the caster. This can only be done once per summoning. Here is an example:

At 5th level, an Elementalist could have a Smoke Elemental bring in 2.5 cubic feet of black smoke a total of 5 times over 5 minutes. This would total 12.5 cubic feet of black smoke that would rise into the air.

At 10th level, an Elementalist could have a Lava Elemental bring in 5 cubic feet of molten Lava a total of 10 times over 10 minutes. This would total 50 cubic feet of hot lava that would eventually cool and turn to normal stone.

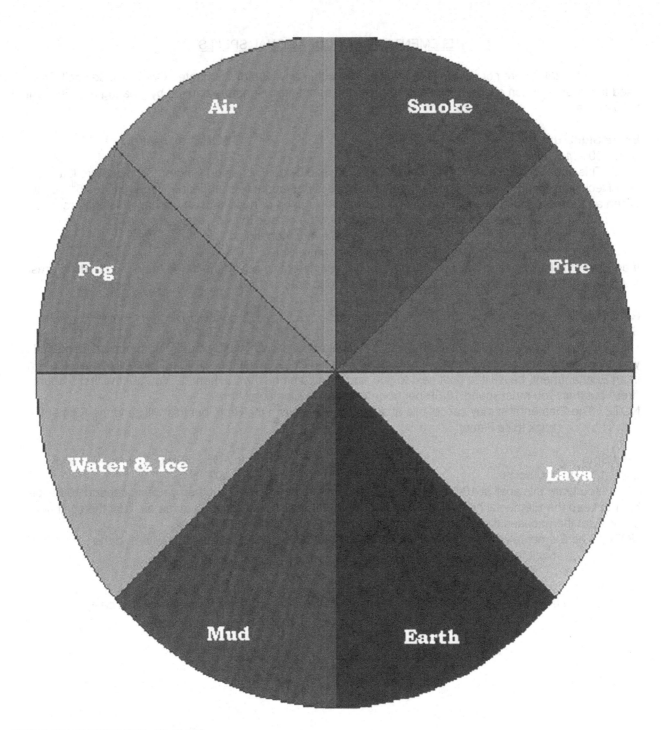

PRIMARY ELEMENTAL PLANES
> Air
> Fire
> Earth
> Water / Ice

SECONDARY ELEMENTAL PLANES

Fog	=	Water & Air
Smoke	=	Air & Fire
Lava	=	Fire & Earth
Mud	=	Earth & Water

OPPOSING PLANES

Water	vs.	Fire
Air	vs.	Earth
Fog	vs.	Lava
Smoke	vs.	Mud

ELEMENTALIST OCCUPATIONAL SPELLS

    Elementalists are not able to hold these spells within any type of Enchanted Gem. These spells are used to either summon an Elemental or to "erase" the enchanted signature caused by wearing any Enchanted Ring or Disk.

Erase Signature   R: T   AOE: 1 signature
SPC: 50 - M   D: Inst.   CT: 2

    This spell will Erase the Signature left on your Hand by an Enchanted Ring or the Signature left around your Neck when an Enchanted Disk is worn. The spell is not taught to a student until he reaches 5th Level. When an Elementalist puts on a Ring/Disk, it saturates his hand or head with an enchanted signature that repels ALL other Rings or Disks. The signature can only be erased in two ways.

#1) At Sunrise every morning.

#2) Erase Signature Spell.

If an Elementalist wishes to use two different Rings, at different times, on the same hand, he needs to erase the signature of the first one before putting on the second one.

Ring Spin   R: T (**)   AOE: 1 Ring
SPC: 50 - M   (10/hour)   D: **   CT: 2

    You are not able to learn this spell until 5th level and it allows you to actually Summon an Elemental to your side. You must get the Elementalist Ring spinning in the air, cast the spell and this will encase the Ring in an Enchantment, cause it to float next to you and then summon the Elemental. You get the first 5 hours "free" but then you must spend 10 SP per hour to keep the Elemental here.
NOTE: The Elementalist may cancel this at any time and reclaim the Ring, but this will send the Elemental back to its Plane.

Disk Spin   R: T (**)   AOE: 1 Disk
SPC: 100 - M   (10/hour)   D: **   CT: 3

    You learn this spell at 10th level. You get the first 10 hours "free" but then you must spend 10 SP per hour to keep the Elemental here. You must get the Elementalist Disk spinning in the air, cast the spell and this will set the encased disk floating next to you and then summon the Elemental.
NOTE: The Elementalist may cancel this at any time and reclaim the Disk, but this will send the Elemental back to its Plane.

NOTE2: See the Elementalist Spell Section for a list of the other spells an Elementalist can cast.

MENTALIST

INTRODUCTION:

A Mentalist is one who is taught to use the powers of their mind to affect the world around them. Through intense study and patience, you will learn how to access and use the power of your mind in many new ways. You will be initially taught to use one mental Discipline and two skills within that Discipline. The mere act of learning a mental discipline gives you certain beneficial abilities.

INFORMATION & FACTS:

To become a Mentalist, you need a lot of patience. You will be required to study a minimum of five months to acquire the abilities of a 1st level Mentalist. You are required to have a minimum Will score of 8 in order to qualify for training. You must also find a Mentalist of at least 12th level to train you and then embark on the long process of 'opening your mind'.

You learn a new mental Discipline every three levels. The 1st mental Discipline at 1st level, the 2nd Discipline at 4th level, the 3rd at 7th level. You learn the 4th Discipline at 10th level, the 5th at 13th level and you learn your 6th and final Discipline at 16th level. Each new mental Discipline will take you 1 month to study and learn completely.

Your Disciplines are supplemented by many different Skills. You learn to use a total of 2 skills each level. These are picked by you and each may be learned in any Discipline you have mastered. Each skill only takes 1 hour of meditation and practice, per Mental Point required, in order to master. Your character has a maximum number of Mental Points dependent on your Will and Level. These points are figured as follows: (see table in Appendix M for all of your totals per level)

Mental Point total = { (Will score / 2) * Level }.

You must spend a certain number of Mental Points to use any Skill. You may never attempt to learn a Skill that requires more Mental points to use then the total you have in that mental Discipline.

These points regenerate at a rate of 1 MP per 1 Attack (5 seconds). You may activate this regeneration 1 time per day per every 2 levels of experience you have. You regain your entire base of Mental Points at the rising of the Column Sunrise every morning.

These Mental Points must be divided between all of the Mental Disciplines that you have, the equation above represents the TOTAL number of Mental Points you rate. When you attain 4th level, you will learn a new mental Discipline. Now you must allocate some (or all) of the new Mental points you rate at 4th level towards the new skills in the Discipline you just learned.

I.e.   If you are a 3rd level Mentalist and have a Will score of 12, you rate a total of 18 MP. All 18 of these will be used for your first Discipline. When you attain 4th level, you rate a total of 24 MP and a new Discipline. You will have to spilt up the MP you just gained from 4th level (6 MP) between your 1st and 2nd Disciplines. Some possibilities are : 18 / 6 or 20 / 4. Jake has decided to split up his points this way: 19 / 5.

When Jake attains 5th level, he gains a bonus of +4 to his Will score, due to level and ability bonuses, bringing it to 16 which gives him a total of 40 MP. He chooses to split them up like this: 28 / 12.

If we look down the road, at 15th level, Jake's Will score would have increased to 20 giving him a total of 150 Mental Points and also he would rate five Disciplines. These 150 MP would be divided into 5 groups representing the points Jake has allotted to each Discipline. He decides to split up his Mental Points this way: 40 / 40 / 30 / 35 / 5 .

Concentration Time is based on Actions. It will cost you **One** Action for every number listed under the Concentration Time of a skill and then **One** Action so say the Trigger Word to activate that skill.

Actions / Attack	vs.	Level
2		1
3		5
4		10
5		15

NOTE: Mentalists may only make ONE Sword Strike per Attack. They may not learn the Warrior's Parry skill, but may learn to use a Shield by learning the Survival Skill: Shield Use. Remember, you must use one of your Parry Actions to gain the Shield's PTE bonus vs. an Opponent's single attack.

SPECIAL ABILITIES

Through the intense study of learning a Discipline, you automatically gain certain abilities. All of the Disciplines are listed next with an explanation of the benefits gained by the character at the completion of study in that Discipline.

MENTALIST DISIPLINES:

<u>Body Control</u> – This mental Discipline gives you the ability to know your body. You automatically know if you have been poisoned, have a cold, disease, or other aliment. You also automatically gain the
Survival Skill: First Aid or the next specialization in that Skill.

<u>Extra Sensory Perception (ESP)</u> – Studying this mental Discipline grants you a +10% bonus on all of your Detect Ambush totals.

<u>Pyrokinetics</u> – Through the study of the mental flame, you gain +10% to all RER vs. Fire.

<u>Telekinesis</u> – This Discipline grants you a very unique ability. You are able to attract a small object to your hand. The object must weigh 3 lbs. or less, but it may be either stationary or moving! This means it will work on speeding arrows or daggers flying at you or a friend. You, of course, must be aware of the object and have an Action available. Your character may only perform this 'Object Snap' two times a day per level, i.e. 2/day at 1st, 10/day at 5th. The object must be within 20' of your character, not be in someone else's possession, weigh less than 3 pounds and it takes 1 Action to complete. This costs you NO MP and you will catch the object doing NO damage to yourself.

<u>Telepathy</u> – By mastering this Discipline you gain a +10% bonus on your RER verses all spells held by an Indigo gem and all Illusions (which are held by violet gems).

<u>Embedding</u> – The Mentalist gains a higher level of concentration which grants him a +2 to his Intellect Score.

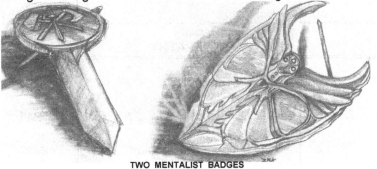

TWO MENTALIST BADGES

MENTALIST SKILLS:

Next is a list of the skills relating to all the Disciplines. Each Skill has a number listed next to it. This number is the amount of Mental points that must be spent in order to use the skill.

You will notice some of the skill costs include a '+' sign. This designates that additional Mental Points may be expended to increase the skills effectiveness. For example, the first skill listed under the Body Control Discipline is: Psychic Heal, and it's cost is '1 +'. When you read the skill's description, you'll see that for every 1 Mental Point you spend, you heal yourself or a companion 1 Endurance Point.

In some skills there is an 'A' listed; this means that the skill can be 'turned on' and it will automatically activate when a specific event occurs, if you have enough MP in that Discipline to cover the cost of the skill. If the skill is 'turned off' it won't activate, this is a good way to preserve your Mental Points, but you won't gain the benefits of the ability in question.

Abbreviations: MP = Mental Points;   EP = Endurance Points;   A = Automatic;   inst = Instantaneous
 T = Touch;   R = Range;   D = Duration;   AOE = Area of Effect

NOTE: The victim of a Mentalist Attack is entitled to a RER. If the victim is successful, she or he will take ½ the base damage of the skill. The base damage is usually equal to the Level of the Mentalist using the skill; see skill descriptions for specific base damages. If the victim fails his or her RER, they will take full damage stated in the skill's description.
(Some say that Mentalist Abilities are not an Enchantment, so they shouldn't rate a RER. I say: "Are you sure?")

MENTALIST DISCIPLINES and SKILLS

BODY CONTROL			EXTRA SENSORY PERCEPTION			PYROKINETICS		
Psychic Heal	A	1 +	Blind Sight		3	Block Flames	A	1 +
Adrenaline Control		3 +	Sense Danger	A	5	Light		2
Body Stretch		4 +	Enhanced Sense		7	Heat		3
Harden Body		5 / 1 +	Psycomitry		10 +	Searing Ray		5
Bio-Electric Shock		5	Read Karma		15	Flare		10
Vascular Control		7	Deja Vu		20	Flickering Sword		15 +
Chameleon Skin		10 +	Sense Catastrophe	A	30	Fire Trap		20
Scent Control		12	Reactive Party		40	Blinding Light		25
Alter Body		15 +				Flaming Photon		30
Ability Boost		20 +						
Body Amp		40						

TELEKINESIS			TELEPATHY			EMBEDDING		
Move Object		1 +	Detect Mentalist	A	2	Detect Embedded	A	2
Block Projectile	A	3	Detect Emotions	A	5	Detect Enchantment	A	2
Bend Object		10 +	Read Mind		10 +	Read Embedded		7
Throw Object		20 +	Mental Illusion		15 +	Embed Discipline		12
Move Self		25	Mental Communication		20 +	Embed Skill		17
Move Other		30	Massive Illusion		30 +	Embed Automatic		27
Explode Object		35 +	Multiple Illusion		40 +			

MENTALIST SKILL DESCRIPTIONS

BODY CONTROL

Psychic Heal   R: --   AOE: Self or Others
MP: 1 + - Auto   D: instant   CT: Auto

    The Mentalist may use her Mental Points to heal herself or others. It costs 1 MP to heal 1 EP of Damage. This ability can be 'Turned On' to automatically heal yourself, if you have sufficient MP available. If 'Turned On', this skill will automatically heal the first amount of damage done to the Mentalist, to the maximum MP he has in the Body Control skill.

Adrenaline Control   R: --   AOE: Self
MP: 3 +   D: 15 min / Level   CT: 1

    Your character may add 1 to his CRM for the Duration. If you wish to increase your CRM past +1, it will cost you an additional 20 MP. (23 MP = +2 CRM; 43 MP = +3 CRM.)

Body Stretch   R: --   AOE: Self
MP: 4 +   D: 5 min / L   CT: 1

    You are able to extend the length of any 1 appendage. The appendage or your neck is increased by 2' for every 4 MP used.

Harden Body   R: --   AOE: Self
MP: 5 / 1 +   D: 5 min / L   CT: 1

    This skill has two distinct bonuses: Harden Fist and Harden Skin. To harden one of your fists the cost is 5 MP and does an extra 1d4 Damage to an Opponent, so this would mean that you fist damage = 1d6+1d4. This may be increased 1d4 EP damage / 5 MP spent. You may also harden your skin which grants you a +1 PTE point for every 1 MP you spend.

Bio-Electric Shock   R: 20'   AOE: Victim
MP: 5   D: inst.   CT:1

    This mental skill allows you to quickly build up a static electric charge in one of your hands. When your victim comes within 20 feet of you, you may cause damage equal to: Your Level + 2d10. Your Opponent does rate a RER to take ½ base damage or (Your Level)/2 + 2d10.

Vascular Control   R: --   AOE: Self
MP: 7   D: 10 min / L   CT: 1

    This skill slows down your body's oxygen consumption rate and allows you to hold your breath for four times longer than you could normally hold your breath.
Ref note: Max=16 min and 40 seconds if End+Will+10=50.
    It also allows you to Engage in Consecutive Melee Combat for twice the time reflected by your Endurance Score.   Ref note: if End Score = 20, then 1,200 seconds or 20 minutes.

Chameleon Skin   R: --   AOE: Self
MP: 10 +   D: 30 min / L   CT: 1

    You may mentally manipulate the color of your skin (and clothes or armor) to match your surroundings. As long as you remain still and quite, your Opp. will receive a -50% added to their Detect Ambush total to notice you. If you are slowly moving (CRM: 1), they still receive a -25% added to their Detect Ambush total. You may increase these percentages by -1% for every extra Mental Point you spend. I.e. if you use 20 MP, then the percentages are: -60% & -35% respectfully. If you Attack or Kill someone while camouflaged (invisible) please see the Morality Table.

Scent Control   R: --   AOE: Self
MP: 12   D: 30 min / L   CT: 1

    Learning this teaches you to control the amount of scent your body gives off. You may force your body to give off absolutely no scent, which is particularly useful if you are being pursued by wolfs or a Savage in the throws of his Blood Frenzy. You may also increase your scent to four times normal, incase you want to be followed.

Alter Body   R: --   AOE: Self
MP: 15 +   D: 30 min / L   CT: 1

This skill is also known as Mental Disguise. You may make moderate alterations to your body for a cost of 15 MP. This includes: Increase or decrease height <= 6", change facial features or hair color, appear older or younger by <= 5 years, etc. For significant changes the cost increases. Your Ref. will designate the cost for your particular alteration. I charge 35 for a complete appearance change (8" height change, different face and a beard and 20 years older) and 30 for a set of wings.   Note: This can not alter the characters Str, Agl, or End scores, ect.

Ability Boost   R: --   AOE: Self
MP: 20 +   D: 1 min / L   CT: 2

You are able to increase either your Strength or Agility score for a cost of 20 MP. You increase either one of your scores by 2 points. If you spend 40 MP, you may increase either your Strength <u>or</u> Agility score by 4 points.

Body Amp   R: --   AOE: Self
MP: 40   D: 1 min / L   CT: 3

This is the ultimate skill in this discipline but it is the hardest on your body. The skill Amplifies some of your basic body functions. First, this skill increases your body size and weight by 50%, which in turn increases your EP total by 50%! Next it adds +10% to your PTE total, grants you the skill Vascular Control and increases your Strength and Agility Scores by 2 each. The drawbacks are that you require immediate rest when the Duration ends and you become extremely hungry.

EXTRA SENSORY PERCEPTION

Blind Sight R: 30' + 2' / L AOE: Self
MP: 3 D: 5 min / L CT: 1

You are able to see regularly and in color, if you are in the dark or are blinded in any way. You may see out to the stated Range.

Sense Danger R: 30' AOE: Self
MP: 5 - Auto D: 1 danger CT: Auto

You will be able to sense impending danger to <u>yourself</u> 2 Attacks (10 seconds) before it actually occurs. This ability can be 'Turned On' to automatically work if you have sufficient MP available. This skill will give you a +10% bonus to your Detect Ambush total, prevent you from springing a trap or falling into a pit.

Enhanced Sense R: -- AOE: Self
MP: 7 D: 10 min / L CT: 1

You may double the effectiveness of any one of your senses for the duration. You may increase this skill's effectiveness by increasing the MP cost. x3 sight = 14 MP; x4 hearing = 21 MP, ect.
Enhanced Sight will gain you +1% on your SPT roll per MP spent in order to hit a general area.
Enhanced Hearing will gain you +1% on your Detect Ambush roll per MP spent.
Enhanced Taste will gain you a +1% chance per MP spent to recognize a Poison in food / drink.

Psycomitry R: Touch AOE: Self
MP: 10 + D: 1 min / L CT: 1

This amazing skill allows you to know the past of an object. The MP cost increases the further you want to see into the object's past. 10 = recent past or 5 months; 25 = moderate past or up to 5 years; 40 = complete history.

Read Karma R: 5' + 1' / L AOE: 1 person
MP: 15 D: 1 min / L CT: 1

This skill allows you to tell certain things about a person. Mainly his or her approximate level, morality rating and occupation. It also informs you if the person is healthy or if they have a sickness, disease or psychosis / insanity. Also, while this ability is active, you can tell if the person is lying to you.

Deja Vu R: Touch AOE: 1 person, place or thing
MP: 20 D: 1 min / L CT: 2

This skill allows you to gain extra perception about a person, place, or thing. When you use this skill roll an Ability Check with Will. The lower the roll the more you know about the person, place or thing. This is accomplished by enhanced intuition and karmic reading. If your roll is low enough, you can learn many things about your subject or surroundings.

Noun	The lower the roll the more information you gain. The list is in order: Lowest rolls to the right.
Person	Relative Health, CR, MR, Occupation, Level, Health, EP total, First Name.
Place (50'x50')	Water/Food sources, General Floor Plan, General Location of Secret/Concealed Doors or Traps.
Thing	Owners Name, Recent Past, Who Made the Item, Complete History, Secret Use/Compartment.

Sense Catastrophe R: 30' AOE: Self or Companions
MP: 30 - Auto D: 1 Catastrophe CT: Auto

This skill is one of the best! It will alert you to impending danger that may affect you or anyone of your friends who are within 30'. It will give a whole 30 seconds (6 Attacks) of warning that your life or your companion's lives are in great danger. This ability can be 'Turned On' to automatically work if you have sufficient MP available. You gain a +15% on your Detect Ambush total and all of your companions gain a +5% to their totals; also no one will set off a Trap.

Reactive Party R: -- AOE: Your Party
MP: 40 D: 10 min / L or 7 Ini. rolls CT: 4

This ability will give your party a +3 to your next Seven Initiative rolls!! [A +3 on a 1d12, just Rocks]!

PRYOKINETICS

Block Flames   R: --   AOE: Self
MP: 1 + - Auto   D: inst.   CT: Auto

This cool skill will protect you from the damage caused by any type of flame, either mundane or enchanted. It costs 1 MP to cancel 1 EP of fire damage. This must be used in the same Attack damage occurs or may be 'Turned On' to protect you Automatically.

Light   R: Touch   AOE: 20' rad.
MP: 2   D: 1 hour / L   CT: 1

You cause an object to give off light for the Duration.

Heat   R: T   AOE: 1 Small Object
MP: 3   D: 30 min / L   CT: 1

The object that you touch immediately starts to give off soothing warmth. A 15' radius is bathed in 80° F.

Searing Ray   R: 15' + 1'/L   AOE: 1 Victim
MP: 5   D: inst.   CT: 1

You mentally ignite a point of air that cascades and speeds toward your Opponent. This does an amount of damage equal to: Your Level + 1d20. Your Opponent does gain a RER to take ½ base damage or (Your Level)/2 + 1d20.

Flare   R: 100'   AOE: 50' radius
MP: 10   D: 2 minutes or 24 Attacks   CT: 1

You are able to cause a very bright Flare to speed straight up into the sky. Once the Flare reaches a height of 100' or strikes an obstacle, it explodes into a bright ball of light for 2 minutes (24 Attacks). The ball will hang in the air and shine light down on the AOE for the Duration. The caster may end the Duration at any time. NOTE: This spell can NOT be used to cause damage, to burn anything, or even to blind anyone; only as a Flare and a temporary light source.

Flickering Sword   R: T   AOE: 1 Weapon
MP: 15 +   D: 5 min / L   CT: 1

This skill must be put on a weapon. It will not consume the weapon but will give off light, heat, and flames. The flames will do an extra 1d10 EP of fire damage on top of what the weapon normally does. This may be increased by 1d10 EP per additional 15 MP spent. {MP: 30 = Burning (2d10); MP: 45 = Searing (3d10)}.

Fire Trap   R: T   AOE: 1 object or a 2 sq. Ft. area
MP: 20   D: 10 min / L   CT: 2

Using this skill will allow you to trap one object or a 2-foot square section of wall or floor. Once the trap is set, the next person or creature that touches it will take fire damage equaling (Your Level x2) + 1d20. A common question: Can I set off my own trap. Answer: Yes, so watch your step. The Mentalist may cancel the Duration at will. Also, the area may be detected by a See Enchantment spell, or by the Detect Enchantment, Sense Danger or Sense Catastrophe Mentalist Skills.

Blinding Light   R: 50'   AOE: 1 victim
MP: 25   D: 5+1d6 Actions   CT: 2

This skill will have your enemy yelling in surprise. When you use the Blinding Light skill, your victim must make an Ability check with Will minus your Will score or be blinded for 5+1d6 Actions. A Blinded person loses his Agility Bonus on his or her PTE total and all of the Blinded victim's Opponents (you and your companions) gain a +40% on their PTE totals. A Cure Blindness spell or a Cancel Enchantment spell at 25 SP will restore the victim's sight.
Ie. If your victim has a Will Score of 10, his normal Ability check percentage would be 30%. But verse this skill, he must make a special Ability Check of 30% - your Will score or be blinded.

Flaming Photon   R: 30' + 1'/L   AOE: 15' rad.
MP: 30   D: inst.   CT: 3

This awesome skill causes a photon of pure fire to blast towards your Opponents. It will affect everyone within a fifteen foot radius of the impact point. It causes (Your Level x2) + 1d20 EP Damage. Remember, your Opponents do rate a RER to take ½ base damage or (Your Level) + 1d20.

TELEKINESIS

Move Object　　　　　　　　　R: 30' + 1' / L　　　　　　AOE: 5 lbs. / 1 MP
MP: 1 +　　　　　　　　　　　　　　D: 1 minute max.　　　　　CT: 1

The Mentalist may expend MP to move objects with only the power of his mind. The object must weigh less than 5 lb. per MP you spend. You can control the object as long as you concentrate on it to a maximum of 1 minute. The force exerted on the object is equal to your personal strength. NOTE: A dense object, like a rock, causes 1d8 damage / 25 lbs of weight.

Block Projectile　　　　　　　　R: --　　　　　　　　　　AOE: Self
MP: 3 (per Projectile blocked) - Auto　D: inst.　　　　　　CT: Auto.

This skill will literally knock projectiles out of the air that are meant for you. This ability can be 'Turned On' to automatically work if you have sufficient MP available. You do NOT have to see or even be aware of the approaching projectile, but it costs 3 MP for every projectile automatically blocked.

Bend or Break Object　　　　　R: 30' + 1' / L　　　　　　AOE: 1 Object
MP: 10 +　　　　　　　　　　　　　D: inst.　　　　　　　　　CT: 1

This skill allows the power of your mind to deform an object. The force exerted on the object is equal to your Strength score +2. For every additional 10 MP you spend, the force exerted is equal to an additional +1 Strength. {20 = Str + 3; 30 = Str + 4; 40 = Str + 5}. See Strength table for bending and breaking percentages.

Throw Object　　　　　　　　　R: 2' / 1 MP　　　　　　　AOE: 1 Object within 10'
MP: 20 +　　　　　　　　　　　　　D: inst.　　　　　　　　　CT: 2

To throw an object you must first pick it up, so the MP cost you spend is divided equally between lifting the object and then throwing it. You may pick up a weight of 1 pound per Mental Point and throw it 2 feet per Mental Point expended. By spending 20 MP, you can automatically lift an object that weighs up to 10 pounds and throw it 20 feet. To lift up heavier objects simply add 1 MP per pound. You may split up the points anyway you see fit.　　{30 MP spent = 10 lbs. @ R:40' **or** 20 lbs. @ R: 20' ;
　　　　　　　　　　　40 MP spent = 10 lbs. @ R:60' **or** 30 lbs. @ R: 20'}.
NOTE: A dense object, like a rock, causes 1d8 damage / 25 lbs of weight.

Move Self　　　　　　　　　　　R: --　　　　　　　　　　AOE: Self
MP: 25　　　　　　　　　　　　　　D: 30 min / L　　　　　　CT: 2

This skill allows you to move yourself just by the power of your mind. You may fly in any direction for the duration as long as you can concentrate – if you loose consciousness for any reason, you will plummet to the ground. You Fly at your regular CRM +1.

Move Other　　　　　　　　　　R: 30'　　　　　　　　　　AOE: 1 person
MP: 30　　　　　　　　　　　　　　D: 1 min / L　　　　　　　CT: 3

This skill actually allows you to pick up and move another person. The person must be alive and conscious for this to work – you actually use his psionic energies to help you do this. If the victim does not wish to be whisked away and to stay on the ground, the victim must make a successful RER. The person Flies at their normal CRM.

Explode Object　　　　　　　　R: 2' / Level　　　　　　　AOE: 1 Object or Area = 1' x 1' max.
MP: 35 +　　　　　　　　　　　　　D: inst.　　　　　　　　　CT: 3

This devastating skill will cause an eruption that cascades throughout an object's base material and cause it to explode. Only simple materials are affected; such as cloth, wood, iron and stone. The object can not be enchanted in any manor and must not have any Mithral or Americanium within it. The explosion completely destroys the object and causes full damage to anyone within a 5 foot radius and half damage to all within a 10' radius. The damage done is equal to the number of MP that are spent, i.e. 40 MP = 40 EP damage. The object must not be in someone's possession, but may be an open area of floor or wall with a maximum size of 1'x1'.

TELEPATHY

Detect Mentalist R: 30' + 1'/Level AOE: Self
MP: 2 - Auto D: 1 minute per Level CT: Auto

This Mentalist skill allows you to pinpoint another Mentalist. The other Mentalist does not have to be using any skills, he just has to be in Range. This ability can be 'Turned On' to automatically work if you have sufficient MP available. NOTE: All Mentalists that you designate at the start of the skill will not set off the automatic portion of this skill.

Detect Emotions R: 30' + 2'/Level AOE: Self
MP: 5 - Auto D: 5 min / L CT: 1 OR Auto

This skill is unique in that you can use it two separate ways. You can use it normally by spending the MP and actively search for any strong emotions within your range. You can also just 'Turn On' this ability to automatically search for a particular emotion, like fear, hate or Love. The ability will automatically go off and pinpoint anyone feeling that emotion within the Range. NOTE2: All similar emotions from your companions that you designate at the start of the skill will not set off the automatic portion of this skill.

Read Mind R: 5' + 1'/L & in Sight AOE: 1 person at a time
MP: 10 + D: 1 min / Level CT: 1

This skill simply allows you to read the surface thoughts of the subject. The subject must make a successful RER to block your attempt. If the subject fails his check, he has no idea anyone is probing his mind, by contrast if he makes his check, he knows someone tried to make contact. If successful, you immediately read all emotions being felt by the subject. You can then sift though the subject's surface thoughts to find out general information. The length of time it will take depends on the age and education of the subject. I make the Mentalist roll an Ability Check with Will, and the lower the roll, the quicker he finds the general information he is searching for.

Mental Illusion R: 10' + 2'/L & in Sight AOE: 1 person
MP: 15 + D: 5 min + 1 min / L CT: 1

This is a deception that affects one person. If the victim fails a RER, he will experience what you force him to see – and the worse his roll, the more he believes the fallacy. This illusion must be fairly small, usually dealing with a single object or thing. You could convince someone that an Iron Piece is a Silver Piece or if the victim severely missed his roll that a small bag of Iron pieces are Mithral pieces. You could delude him into seeing his club or shield burst into flames, ect. Note that the Ninja skill "Resist Mesmerize or Illusion" will potentially protect him from any Illusion a Mentalist may cast, ie. the Ninja gains his +25% bonus to his RER. NOTE3: The Mentalist must concentrate to facilitate the changes in ANY Illusion.

Mental Communication R: 20' / Level AOE: 1 Sentient
MP: 20 + D: 10 min + 1 min / Level CT: 2

This skill allows you to mentally speak to any sentient creature within Range for the Duration. You may communicate with 1 individual per 5 MP spent, so you get 4 people automatically. An unwilling recipient needs to roll a RER. This skill is invaluable to communicate with your companions or Generals or Lieutenants in a battle situation.

Massive Illusion R: 20' + 2'/L & in Sight AOE: 1 person
MP: 30 + D: 10 min + 1 min / L CT: 3

This skill is like Mental Illusion, but you can effect someone's entire physical situation. If the victim fails a RER, he will experience what you force him to see – and the worse his roll the more he believes the fantasy. You could delude your victim into believing that the whole room has just caught fire and is rapidly becoming an inferno. Or you may delude him into believing that instead of being just behind you on his horse while he is chasing you, he seems to be steadily loosing ground and then he sees you take the right fork but you in reality flee down the left one. Note that the Ninja skill "Resist Mesmerize or Illusion" will protect him from any Illusion a Mentalist may cast, ie. the Ninja gains his +25% bonus to his RER. NOTE4: He must concentrate on changes.

Multiple Illusion R: 20' + 2'/L & in Sight AOE: Anyone within a 40 foot radius
MP: 40 + D: 20 min + 2 min / L CT: 4

This skill allows you to effect multiple people. Anyone who enters the stationary AOE must make a RER, if they fail they will experience what you force them to see – and the worse the roll the more they believe the fantasy. The effected people will experience the illusion with the same intensity as described in Massive Illusion. Note that the Ninja skill "Resist Mesmerize or Illusion" will protect him from any Illusion a Mentalist may cast, ie. the Ninja gains his +25% bonus to his RER. NOTE5: The Mentalist must concentrate to make changes.

EMBEDING

Detect Embedded   R: 30'   AOE: Self
MP: 2 - Auto   D: 10 minute / Level   CT: Auto

    This skill allows you to tell if any item in range has been embedded with a Mentalist Discipline, Skill or Automatic. This ability can be 'Turned On' to automatically work if you have sufficient MP available.

Note: All Embedded objects that you designate at the start of the skill will not set off the automatic portion of this skill.

Detect Enchantment   R: 30'   AOE: Self
MP: 2 - Auto   D: 10 minute / Level   CT: 1 OR Auto

    The Mentalist is able to discern if any item within range has been enchanted by an Enchanter, Alchemist or Elementalist. This ability can be 'Turned On' to automatically work if you have sufficient MP available.

Note: All Enchanted objects that you designate at the start of the skill will not set off the automatic portion of this skill.

Read Embedded   R: Touch   AOE: 1 item
MP: 7   D: 1 minute / Level   CT: 1

    With this skill you may tell the exact Discipline, Skill or Automatic ability that has been Embedded into any items in your possession. You can read the Range, Duration, ect of the skill as well the number of Mental Points that have been placed in the items and their Trigger Words or Phrases.

    These next Skills all deal with the Embedding of a Discipline, Skill or Automatic ability into an object. The object, usually a pin or badge, must be worn outside any clothing – not covered in any way – to work properly.

Embed Discipline   R: Touch   AOE: 1 Object
MP: 12   D: Permanent   CT: 1 minute per Point Embedded

    All of the Embedding skills have certain things in common. You must first obtain a small object made of pure Mithral or Americanium. The object can be of any design, but Mentalists are partial to pins and badges. Mithral badges or pins can be used for Embedding Disciplines or Skills, but you must use Americanium to Embed an Automatic ability. The Discipline's, Skill's or Automatic's benefits are transferred directly into the object.

    You must have enough Mental Points in the Embedding Discipline to activate this Skill and then enough points in another Discipline to actually transfer the ability into the object.

    This skill is slightly different from the others in that you need to use 12 MP from your EMBEDED Discipline and then 10 MP from the specific Discipline you want to embed into the badge or pin. The embedded Discipline's powers are continuous and are granted to anyone wearing the badge or pin. The Badge/Pin must be worn outside all clothes/armor to work properly. The Disciplines and benefits gained are summarized here:

Body Control – Grants wearer the Survival Skill: First Aid. If you have this skill it will grant you the next specialization in that Skill.

Extra Sensory Perception (ESP) – Grants you a +10% bonus on all of your Detect Ambush rolls.

Pyrokinetics – Grants wearer a +10% to all RER vs. Fire.

Telekinesis – Your character may perform an 'Object Snap' 4 times a day. The object must be within 20' of your character, not be in someone else's possession, weigh less than 3 pounds and it takes 1 Action to complete. The object caught will do NO damage to yourself and may be stationary or moving.

Telepathy – Grants wearer a +10% bonus on your RER verses all spells held by an Indigo gem and all Illusions.

Embedding – Grants wearer a +2 to his Intellect Score. (Anything learned while wearing the badge is retained).

    The material needed is Mithral and you need 1 Mithral piece worth of material to make the badge, pin or object. This is a cost of 10 silver pieces or 100 iron pieces.

NOTE2: If he already has mastered that same Discipline, a Mentalist who wears a badge with an Embedded Discipline in it receives the bonus listed under the ability plus his natural bonuses,.
Ie. If a Mentalist wears a badge with the Pyrokinetics Discipline embedded into it and he already has mastered that Discipline, he receives a total of a +20% bonus to all RER verse enchanted fire and flames.

Embed Skill   R: Touch   AOE: 1 Object
MP: 17   D: Until MPs are used   CT: 1 minute per Point Embedded

A Mithral object may be used to embed a Skill. You must have enough Mental Points in the Embedded Discipline to activate the Embedding Skill (17 MP) and then enough points in another Discipline to actually transfer the new skill into the object. If you have more points available in the other discipline then what it costs to activate the skill in question, you may put these additional points into the object. These extra stored points can be used to activate the skill successive times.

One example is the Mentalist who wants to make a badge of Searing Ray. He has 20 MP in the Embedding Discipline and 15 MP in the Pyrokinetics Discipline and he's going to transfer all these points into the badge. While holding the object, he first establishes a link between him and the Mithral badge with the Embedding skill – this uses 17 points from his Embedding Discipline. Next, he transfers in the Searing Ray skill and the total number of points he wants available for it. The Mentalist embedded the first 5 points for the Searing Ray skill and then 10 more points for 2 additional uses of the Searing Ray skill so the wearer of the badge could cast a Searing Ray 3 times before the badge is empty. The Mentalist must make up a Trigger Word or Phrase to activate the badge.

You may only put ONE skill into any object and you may only use the embedded skill ONCE per Attack. The total number of points you may put into an object cannot exceed your personal total in that Discipline and the points must be from your FIRST set of MP you received from the Column Sun; you can't just keep pumping up an object with rejuvenated points. Once the points are used, they are gone and when all points are used the Mentalist could re-input that skill or any other one he knows into the badge. You may only embed skills that do NOT have an Automatic function.

The material needed is Mithral and you need 5 Mithral pieces worth, which is a value of 50 silver pieces.

Embed Automatics   R: Touch   AOE: 1 Object
MP: 27   D: Until MPs are used   CT: 1 minute per Point Embedded

An Americanium object must be used to transfer any Skill with an Automatic function into it. These skills include Psychic Heal, Sense Danger, Block Flames, Detect Mentalist and Detect Enchantment to name a few. Just like the Embed Skill ability, you must have enough Mental Points in the Embedded Discipline to activate the Embedded Automatic ability (27 MP) and then enough points in another Discipline to actually transfer the new skill into the object. You may put more points into the object so the automatic skill can operate many times.

Because this skill is Automatic, it is constantly 'ON', so please be careful and use the object correctly:
While it is <u>worn</u>, a Psychic Heal pin with 20 MP available will instantly heal the FIRST 20 points of damage done to the wearer.
When a Block Flames badge that has 30 MP embedded into it is <u>worn</u>, it will block the first 30 points of enchanted flame damage from any source.
While wearing a badge with 10 MP available and the Detect Mentalist skill embedded in it, the <u>wearer</u> will automatically detect the first 5 Mentalists that come within range.
The material needed is Americanium and you need 1 Americanium Piece per pin, which is a value of 100 silver pieces.

NOTE: A Mentalist may only use ONE Offensive skill per Attack.

Ref. Note: There are many Mentalist skills that can be enhanced if the Mentalist spends more Mental Points on a single usage of that skill. I set a limit of 45 MP to enhance any one usage of any one skill.

EXPERIENCE POINTS   (XPO)

During our daily lives we gain experience as we accomplish new tasks and triumph over new situations. In a Role-Playing game, your character also gains Experience as he does these things. However, during the game, we keep track of the experiences your character gains with points. These are known as Experience Points or XPO. As your character gains XPO, he rises in Level. A minimum number of Experience Points are required to reach each Level – this breakdown of XPO and Levels is listed at the end of this section. As you may guess, certain tasks and situations rate different amounts of XPO. These situations are listed below with the number of Experience Points you gain as you encounter and accomplish them. The things you gain Experience Points for are separated into different categories. Most situations will "overlap" into many categories. To determine the total number of XPO your character rates for accomplishing a complex series of tasks, simply add up all of the respective XPO bonuses.

(1)   Common Situations:

- 20 XPO   Planning and Accomplishing a Task
- 10 XPO   Accomplishing a task under Direction or under orders
- 25 XPO   Participant in the IronBall Game - Winner (25 total, whether you get into Real Combat or not.)
- 10 XPO   Participant in the IronBall Game - Looser (10 total, whether you get into Real Combat or not.)
- Varies   Loosing a Personal Challenge: 2 XPO per level of Opponent
- Varies   Winning a Personal Challenge: 10 XPO per level of Opponent
- Varies   Competitions: If you are a participant, the XPO you rate depends on the # of Contestants participating and how well you do in the Tourney.

# of Contestants	Winning XPO	2nd Place	3rd Place
2	5	3	--
5	10	5	3
10	20	10	5
25+	50	25	13

- Varies   XPO for surviving in REAL Combat **

Number of Combatants	Experience Points
1 on 1	5 XPO
5	15
10	45
100	135
1000	405
10,000	1,215

** In order to qualify for REAL Combat you must DO (a) AND EITHER (b) OR (c):
- (a) Make at least one attack (melee, projectile, or spell).
- (b) Make or fail at least one PTE roll.
- (c) Make or fail at least one RER.

(2)   One – Timers:
You gain XPO the 1st time you do certain things. The XPO you gain is a base amount plus a percentage of the total difference between your current level and your next level. This difference amount is listed in the third column of the Experience Point Table below.

XPO	One – Timer	[Players Initials: ___ ___ ___ ___ ___ ___ ___ ___]
5+10%	1st time you Plan a Task and Fail to Accomplish it.	
5+15%	1st time you get a real Hangover........................	
10+20%	1st time you knowingly Acquire a Stolen Item........	
10+25%	1st Bar Brawl you participate in..........................	
15+30%	1st Night you spend in Jail / Custody	
15+35%	1st time you are Betrayed.................................	
20+40%	1st time you give an Enemy a Warning Shot.........	
20+45%	1st time you Fall in Love...................................	
25+50%	1st Sexual Relation..	
25+55%	1st time you Save someone's Life in Combat........	
30+60%	1st time you Practice a Tradition of Penicia..........	
30+65%	1st Sea Voyage you Complete...........................	
35+70%	1st successful Prison Break you participate in.......	
35+75%	1st time you Break under Torture.......................	

(3)   Going for the ODDs:

Determine the "odds" of the given situation and reward the specified experience.

XPO		ODDS	
512	Over Coming Ridiculous Odds	100,000 to 1	(They've gone Plaid)
256	Over Coming Insurmountable Odds	10,000 to 1	
128	Over Coming Impossible Odds	1,000 to 1	
64	Over Coming Extreme Odds	100 to 1	
32	Over Coming Huge Odds	10 to 1	
16	Over Coming Steep Odds	5 to 1	
8	Over Coming Slight Odds	2 to 1	
4	Over Coming Regular Odds	1 to 1	(Even)

NOTE: If you ever have a situation in which a set of Companions overcome Odds in excess of 100,000 to 1, then the XPO amount is awarded by the Ref.

Experience Point Total for __EACH__ character = (1) + (2) + (3)

Add all bonuses together and EACH Character receives that many Experience Points!

EXPERIENCE POINT TABLE

Level	XPO Total	Diff. between current and next level	20% of Diff. **
1	0	20	4
2	20	30	6
3	50	40	8
4	90	50	10
5	140	60	12
6	200	65	13
7	265	70	14
8	335	75	15
9	410	90	18
10	500	150	30
11	650	200	40
12	850	250	50
13	1,100	300	60
14	1,400	600	120
15	2,000	1,000	200
16	3,000	2,000	400
17	5,000	4,000	800
18	9,000	6,000	1,200
19	15,000	10,000	2,000
20	25,000		

** If you ever gain more experience then is necessary to bring your character to the next level, you are able to put SOME of the extra XPO towards your new level. You may add up to 20% of what is needed for your next level to your new XPO total. This amount is listed in the 4th column above.

100

STARTING WEAPONS AND SURVIVAL SKILLS

Occupation	Number of Starting Weapons	Opp. Bonus to PTE *	Number of Starting Skills	Endurance Points Per Level
Warrior	3 **	+15 %	3 + (A)	1d8
Spy / Assassin	3	+25 %	3	1d6
Ninja	1 #	+20 %	2 + (B)	1d6
Enchanter	1	+35 %	2 + (C)	1d4
Alchemist	2	+30 %	3 + (D)	1d4
Elementalist	1	+40 %	2 + (E)	1d4
Mentalist	2	+40 %	2 + (F)	1d4

NOTE: You must pick **DIFFERENT** Weapons **and** Survival Skills when you **create** your character.

* If you ever use a Weapon that you don't have formal training in, your Opponent gets the stated percentage **added** to his PTE total verses your strikes while you are using that weapon.

** All "non-schooled" Warriors - ones that were taught by a father or uncle, etc. – Only initially learn 3 Weapons of their choice.

All "schooled" Warriors - ones that go to a special Warrior school
- learn 1 projectile Weapon and 3 other Weapons of their choice.

Knights always gain the "Schooled" Warriors Bonus & Savages always gain the "non-schooled" Warriors Bonus.

\# All Ninja automatically learn how to use a Staff and get to learn any 1 other weapon of their choice. (Remember, a Ninja can always use hand strikes, kicks or throws in addition to these initial weapons.)

(A) Warriors get 3 starting Survival Skills plus Shield Use and also learn EITHER Wrestling OR Boxing.
(B) In addition to the Ninja's 2 starting Survival Skills, he also learns Improve Charging Rate.
(C) The Enchanter learns Rope Making in addition to the 2 Survival Skills that she may pick.
(D) In order for an Alchemist to become 1st level, she must learn Plant Identification in addition to 3 other Survival Skills of her choice.
(E) An Elementalist is taught Ring Making plus 2 other Survival Skills of his choice.
(F) A Mentalist learns 2 starting Survival Skills and also gains a +2 to any one ability score except Will. He may choose Endurance, Strength, Agility, Intellect or Wisdom.

Gaining New Weapon Slots

When you reach the level stated below in ANY Occupation, you may receive formal training in an additional Weapon of your choice - as long as you meet the Strength requirements.

Level	Additional Weapon	Level	Additional Weapon
3	+ 1	6	+ 1
9	+ 1	12	+ 1
15	+ 1	18	+ 1

(slots = 6 | Max: 4 + slots = 10 = Total slots possible)

NOTE2: Warriors, Spies / Assassins, and Ninja are able to Specialize in certain Weapons at certain levels, this has <u>nothing</u> to do with when they are able to learn new weapons.

Gaining New Survival Skills Slots

When you attain the levels stated below <u>in ANY Occupation,</u> you are able to learn a new Survival Skill or Specialize in one that you already know. **Specialization** increases your Ability Check percentage total and in some cases grants you new abilities within the known Survival Skill. You must use one of the "slots" listed below when you either start learning a new Survival Skill or to Specialize in one you already have training in.

Level	Additional Skill Slots	Level	Additional Skill Slots
2	+ 1	4	+ 2
6	+ 1	8	+ 2
10	+ 1	12	+ 2
14	+ 1	16	+ 2
18	+ 1		

(slots = 13 | Max: 5 + slots = 18 = Total slots possible)

NOTE: You can substitute 2 Survival Skill slots and learn 1 weapon **OR**
You may substitute 1 weapon slot and gain 2 Survival Skill slots.

NOTE2: A Warrior, Spy / Assassin or a Mentalist may :
Substitute **2** Survival Skill Slots or **1** Weapon Slot to learn some number of Class (A) spells.
BUT,
You must do this when <u>you create your character</u> (before 1st level) and you must have at least an Intellect score of 11.
You may only learn a **TOTAL number** of spells equal to the number stated on the Intellect table.
You learn 1/2 of the spells you rate before 1st level and the rest when you train for 2nd level.

Intellect Score	**TOTAL** number of Class (A) spells a Warrior, Spy / Assassin or Mentalist is able to learn
1 - 10	-------
11	1
12	2
13	3
14	4
15	5
16	6
17	7
18	8
19	9
20	10

NOTE3: An Enchanter, Alchemist or Elementalist is able to learn this number of spells each level **!!**

STARTING EQUIPMENT AND MONEY

Everyone begins the game with certain equipment and an amount of starting money. This standard starting equipment is listed below. You'll notice that everyone starts with a SAP or a Standard Adventures Pack. Each character may opt to accept this highly useful equipment or you may take an extra 50 Silver in coin. It should be noted that the SAP is worth much more than 50 Silver because it is "standard" and many merchants carry it and therefore they can put it together for a much lower price when the components are ordered in bulk.

SAP (**S**tandard **A**dventure's **P**ack)

1	BackPack, Brown	1	Large Brown Leather Sack	1	Pouch, Leather, Brown
2 wk.	Reg. Rations (lasts 3 wk. ea.)	2 wk.	Water with Flask	50'	Rope
3	Torches	1	Skinning Knife (1d6)	1 box	Flint, Steel & Tinder
1	First Aid Kit	1	Cooking Set (travel)	1	Sanitary Kit (M or F)
1	Bedroll				

Occupation	Equipment - These items are usually supplied to new Characters of an Occ.	Starting Money
Warrior	SAP + ½ Suit of Leather Armor (+15%); Short Sword [2d6]	25 Silver
Knight	SAP + ½ Suit of Leather Armor (+15%); (2) Spears [1d12+2]; Small Wooden Shield (+5% PTE)	15 Silver
Savage	SAP + Battle Axe [2d8+2]	25 Silver
Spy / Assassin	SAP + Blackjack or Garrote; Short Bow; (20) Arrows [1d10]; (1) Quiver	25 Silver
Ninja	SAP + (2) Gee (+15%); Staff [1d10]; Area Map; (1) Enchanted Dust = Smoke Bomb (Violet); (1) Enchanted Potion = Ref's Choice	10 Silver
Enchanter	SAP + Staff [1d10]; Large Cloth Sack; 50' Rope; (2) Quills & Bottle of Ink; (1) Scroll Case; (10) Paper Sheets; (10) Candles; (1) Sewing Kit	30 Silver
Alchemist	SAP + ½ Suit of Leather Armor (+15%); Woodman's Axe [1d12+2]; Mace [1d10+1]	15 Silver
Elementalist	SAP + ½ Suit of Leather Armor (+15%); 2 Javelins [1d12]	30 Silver
Mentalist	SAP + ½ Suit of Leather Armor (+15%); Club [1d8]; (2) Throwing Daggers [1d8]	25 Silver

NOTE: The numbers in brackets [xdy+z] represent the damage done by that particular weapon.
[x == Number of Dice; y == Number of sides each Die has; z == Number added to Die roll].

AN ADVENTURER AND AN OPEN STANDARD ADVENTUER'S PACK (SAP). HIS WEAPON IS AGAINST THE TREE, IS IT TO FAR AWAY?

EQUIPMENT

WEAPONS - Regular

(Regular = Iron and mundane materials)

Weapon		Damage	Minimum Strength to Use	Length	Space	Cost for Regular ^^
Lasso $$	{25'}	**	7	50'	4' *	5 Silver
Bolo	{30'}	1d4 **	6	3-4'	3' *	5
Whip		1d6 **	5	10-15'	2' *	5
Knife (Skinning)		1d6	4	6"	--	5
Hammer, 1-Handed	{20'}	1d6 +1	6	1'	--	10
Throwing Dagger	{30'}	1d8	4	8"	1'	10
Quarrel		1d8	--	2'	--	.5 ea.
Club		1d8	8	3-5'	1-3'	0 - 3
Dagger	{20'}	1d10	4	1'	--	10
Staff $$		1d10	7	4-8'	2-3' *	0 - 5
Arrow		1d10	--	##	--	.5 ea.
Sheaf Arrow		1d10 #@	--	##*	--	2
Mace		1d10+1	9	3-5'	4-6'	12
Axe, 1-Handed	{20'}	1d12	6	1'	--	12
Javelin	{40'}	1d12	7	4'	1'	5
Rapier		1d12	8	3.5	3'	35
Sword, Short		2d6	12	3'	1'	20
Spear	{35'}	1d12+2	10	6-12'	2'	10
Scimitar		1d12+2	13	3.5'	1'	25
Woodmen's Axe $$		1d12+2	14	3'	2'	25
Battle Hammer $$		2d8	18	5'	3.5'	30
Sword, Long		2d8	14	4'	2' *	30
Trident $$		2d8 +1	10	5-9'	3-7'	30
Battle Axe $$		2d8 +2	16	5'	3.5'	35
Sword, Hand-and-a-half		1d20	16	5'	2.5' *	40
Pole Arm $$		1d20+1	15	5-8'	3-6' *	50
Bardiche $$		1d20+2	17	4'	3' *	55
Battle Sword $$		2d12	17	6'	4' *	70 Silver
Lance or Long Spear *#		2d20	16	12'	*#	30
Bow, Short $$	{50'}	--	10	4'	2'	25
Bow, Short, Compound < $$	{100'}	--	14	4'	2'	(Next Price Table)
Bow, Long $$	{100'}	--	12	6'	2'	40
Bow, Long, Compound < $$	{150'}	--	16	6.25'	2'	(Next Price Table)
Crossbow $$ (+1 dam)	{75'}	<>	10	2.5'	1'	60
Garrote		@@	8	2'	--	--
Blackjack		@@	5	6"	--	--
Blowgun & Needles (5)	{25'}	1d2	3	2-5'	2-5'	25
Star	{40'}	1d8	3	3-4"	--	5
Nunchuck (12"-5"-12") $$		1d8	6	29"	2' *	10
Tonfa $$		1d8	8	21"@	1' *	15
Kama $$		1d10	9	19"@	2' *	20
Sai $$		1d10	10	21"@	1' *	30
Ninja-to (Bladed Sword) $$		1d20	15	4.5'	2' *	50
Ninja Shogee $$!#		1d12	9	9.5'	3' *	40
Manriki Gusari $$!@	{30'}	1d8 **	7	5'	2' *	30
Kusari-Gama $$!$		1d10	9	4'	2' *	35
Ninja Hand Claws && $$		1d6	4	--	--	25
Net $$	{25'}	Tangle **	4	--	2'	5
Molintof Cocktail (Oil) *^*	{30'}	1d10	--	6"	--	5
WristBow & Quarrels (10)	{40'}	1d6+1 <>	5	6"	--	80 Silver
		Damage	Min. Strength	Length	Space	Cost

104

^^ Regular weapons are constructed from Iron and mundane materials only.
- The weapons on this table are **NOT** made from Ransium, Langor or Enchanted materials.

* Signifies that you must have the stated distance on all sides of (or all around) you to use the weapon properly.

** If your Opponent misses his PTE roll by more than 10%, you have WRAPPED the area of the his body that you rolled according to the SPT. (A Lasso automatically "wraps" if strikes.)

*# A Lance or Long Spear only delivers this damage if you are charging on a Horse or if you are a Hemar in a charge. Remember that you get additional damage when you charge:
+1d6 extra EP damage for every Charging Rate Multiple above 2 or a CR above 10 feet/sec.

An arrow for a Short Bow is 27" long and an arrow for a Long Bow is 35" long - a very short person may not be able to use a Long Bow.

##* A Sheaf Arrow can only be used with a Long Bow and is 35" long.

#@ A Sheaf Arrow also subtracts a -10% from anyone's PTE total while they are wearing Armor. This Does NOT apply to someone just using a Shield or employing a Shield Spell. You only get a -5% to the PTE total when you use it against any type of Creature with natural armor.

@ Signifies that the weapon is used in Pairs and each one is the stated length.

@@ The Damage done by these weapons is Special or None and is discussed in the Spy\Assassin Section.

^ The Damage done by Flaming Oil is 1d10 per Attack for 1d4 Attacks. The Damage is rolled every 5 seconds (or Attack) the victim is within the burning oil. The damage is always rolled 1st in any Attack.

< The only people that can use a Compound Bow (either Short or Long) are those who are specialized in a bow of that type. So this means only Warrior types, S/A and Ninja may ever use a Compound Bow.

<> Crossbows are built in such a way as to give the wielder what amounts to a Strength damage bonus. In another words, the better the Crossbow is built, the more damage it will do. A Crossbow can have a damage bonus of +1 to +5, which is added to the normal Quarrel damage.

Tangle = If your Opp. fails his PTE roll, he can't move. He can't use melee or projectile weapons, but may cast a spell or use a potion, ect. If he is charging or flying, he will come to a halt or fall from the air.

&& A Ninja may use the Ninja Claw to Parry a bladed weapon. Ie: They would gain their Parry bonus vs. a Blade.

!# A Ninja Shogee is used to stab, snare or trap Opponents. It has a 13" spear type shaft and point with a 15 foot chain that ends in a 6" diameter ring.

!@ A Manriki Gusari is a 5' chain weapon with 2 blunt ends used for clubbing and trapping. This may be thrown like a bolo.

!$ A Kusari-Gama is both a Kama and a chain weapon. The chain is 10' long with a blunt end. The blunt end is sometimes hollowed out to hold a Dust, Pills, ect. If the ninja trains with this weapon, he also learns to correctly use the Kama as a weapon.

$$ Two-Handed Weapon.

{ X' } This is the maximum distance in feet the weapon may be thrown or shot with no penalties.
Penalty for over max distance is: Opponent gains +10% to PTE total for every +10' over max.

NOTE: Only Ninja can be trained and use any Ninja weapons. This is the same for the special S/A weapons, and Krill may only learn to use a Wrist Bow.

Ransium : Hard Durable Metal [Combination of Mithral & Iron]	- Requires a 5th Level Smith to make = + 5 silver pieces. - Mixture = 1 Mithral Piece / 100 oz Iron = 100 IP = 6.25lbs. - Never Rusts. - Will Harm all Creatures. - Does not Reflect Light.

Langor : Hard, Long-Lasting and Light
  [Combo. of Americanium & Mithral & Iron]
	- Requires a 10th Level Smith to make = + 15 silver pieces.
	- Mixture = 1 Americanium Piece / 1 Mithral Piece.
	- Never Rusts or Dulls.
	- Will Harm all Creatures.
	- Requires -2 Strength Points to wield.
	  i.e. A Long Sword would only require a Strength of 12 to Wield.

ARMOR

(Regular : Iron and mundane materials)

Armor		PTE Bonus	HUMAN	HEMAR	KRILL
Half Suit Leather	*	+15 %	20 Silver	40 Silver	30 Silver
Full Suit Leather	**	+20 %	50	100	75
Half Suit Plated Leather	*	+25 %	75	150	125
Full Suit Plated Leather	**	+30 %	100	200	150
Mail Shirt	@	+35 %	125	250	200
Half Suit Iron	*	+45 %	150	300	----
Full Suit Iron	**	+55 %	300	500	----
Game Armor [Iron Ball]		+15 %	10 Silver	30	20
Gee		+15 %	10	25	15
Small Shield (Hard Wood)		+ 5 %	10 Silver		
Large Shield (" ")		+ 8 %	15		
Large Shield (Metal Plated)		+10 %	25		
Large Shield, Spiked (" ")		+ 8 %	50	Add +1d10 EP Damage to your Shield Bash total.	
Knight's Shield		+12 %	30		

Small Helm (Plated Leather)		!	10 Silver	
Large Helm (All Metal)		!!	30	
Large Helm with Visor (Metal)		!!!	60	
Dog Barding		+35 %	200 Silver	
Horse Barding		+40 %	400	

* A Half Suit of armor covers your chest, back, shoulders, belly, waist and the fronts of your thighs.

** A Full Suit of armor covers your chest, back, shoulders, belly, waist, arms to mid forearm, and legs to ankles. (A Full Suit of Iron - either regular, Ransium or Langor - always comes with metal boots as well.)

@ A Mail Shirt covers your chest, back, shoulders, belly, waist, arms to elbows, and hangs down to your mid-thigh. This armor is pulled over your head like a shirt is and is belted at your waist.

! A Small Helm gives your head the same PTE total as your body.

!! A Large Helm gives your head a +10% bonus to your PTE total.

!!! A Large Helm with Visor gives your head, face, eyes and neck a +10% bonus to your PTE total.

***** SUPER IMPORTANT *****

You may **NEVER** have a PTE total higher than 85% including all bonuses: Armor, Shield, Spells, Agility Bonus, Warrior Bonuses, Enchanted Bonuses, etc.

!! THIS INCLUDES ALL CREATURES AND PEOPLE !!

WEAPON PRICES (Silver Pieces)

[(Reg+Coin)x2,(R+M+A)x2=Weapons]&[x3=Specials]   M=10   A=100

Construction Materials :			Regular	Ransium	Langor
Lasso	[Weaved]	{25'}	5 Silver	30 Silver	230 Silver
Bolo	[Weaved]	.5 {30'}	5	20	220
Whip	[Weaved]	.5	5	20	220
Quarrel	[Tipped]	.5	.5 (ea.)	5 (ea.)	20 (ea.)
Club	[Banded]		0 - 3	26	226
Hammer, 1-Handed		{20'}	10	40	240
Dagger (12")		{20'}	10	40	240
Staff			0 - 5	30	230
Arrow	[Tipped]	.5	.5 (ea.)	5 (ea.)	20 (ea.)
Sheaf Arrow	[Tipped]	.5	5 (ea.)	50 (ea.)	200 (ea.)
Mace		2	12	64	328
Axe, 1-Handed		2 {20'}	12	64	328
Javelin	[Tipped]	{40'}	5	20	220
Sword, Short		2	20	80	480
Spear	[Tipped]	{35'}	10	40	240
Battle Hammer		4	30	140	940
Sword, Long		3	30	120	720
Trident		3	30	120	720
Battle Axe		4	35	150	950
Sword, Hand-and-a-half		4	40	160	960
Pole Arm,		3	50	160	760
Battle Sword		5	70	240	1240 Silver
Lance or Long Spear [Tipped]		2	30	100	500
Bow, Short		{50'}	25	---	---
Bow, Short, Compound [Reinforced]		2 {100'}	--	130	430
Bow, Long		{100'}	40	---	---
Bow, Long, Compound [Reinforced]		2 {150'}	--	175	475
Crossbow +1, +2/+3/+4, +5		2 {75'}	60	160 /300 /500	840
Star, ea.		.5 {40'}	5	25	75
Nunchuck (12"-5"-12") [Banded]			10	60	360
Tonfa, per pair [Banded]			15	75	375
Kama, per pair		2	20	120	720
Sai, per pair		2	30	150	750
Ninja-to		4	50	270	1470
Ninja Shogee		3	40	110	800
Manriki Gusari		3 {30'}	30	90	700
Kusari-Gama		3	35	100	750
Ninja Hand Claws, per pair		2	25	80	400
Garrote	[Weaved]	.5	0	15	165
Blackjack		.5	0	15	165
Blowgun & Needles(5)		.5 {25'}	25	90	240
Knife		.5	5	20	220
Throwing Dagger		{30'}	10	40	240
Molintof Cocktail (Oil)		{30'}	5	--	---
WristBow & Quarrels(10) +1, +2/+3, +4	{40'}		80	270 / 425	570
Scimitar		3	25	110	310
Rapier (+10% SPT/but can't Parry)		2	35	210 **	810 **
Bardiche		4	50	270	1470 Silver
Construction Materials			Regular	Ransium	Langor

**   Anyone using Rapier that is made of Ransium or Langor gains a +10% to their SPT roll but may not
      Parry, unless his opponent is also using a Rapier.

ARMOR PRICES (Silver Pieces)

Armor		PTE	1,2 HUMAN	3,2 HEMAR	1,3 KRILL
Half Suit Plated Leather		+25 %	75 Silver	150 Silver	125 Silver
Ransium	1	+28 %	170	360	305
Langor	1	+30 %	370	560	705
Full Suit Plated Leather		+30 %	100	200	150
Ransium	2	+33 %	240	520	480
Langor	2	+35 %	640	1720	1110
Mail Shirt		+35 %	125	250	200
Ransium	5	+38 %	350	800	700
Langor	5	+40 %	1350	3800	3900
Half Suit Iron		+45 %	150	300	----
Ransium	8	+48 %	460	1080	----
Langor	8	+50 %	2060	5880	----
Full Suit Iron		+55 %	300	500	----
Ransium	10	+58 %	750	1500	----
Langor	10	+60 %	3000	8000	----

SHIELD PRICES (Silver Pieces)

			PTE	Cost in Silver Pieces	
Large Shield (Iron Plated)			+10 %	25 Silver	
Ransium Plated	1	.5	+13 %	30	
Langor Plated	1	.5	+15 %	80	
Large Shield, Spiked (Iron Plated)			+ 8 %	50	Add +1d10 EP Damage to your Shield Bash total.
Ransium Plated	2	1	+11 %	120	(Ditto) (Please see the Shield Use Survival
Langor Plated	2	1	+13 %	320	(Ditto) Skill's 2nd Specialization)
Knight's Shield			+12 %	30	
Ransium	1	1	+15 %	40	
Langor	1	1	+17 %	140	
Small Helm (Plated Leather)			!	10 Silver	
Ransium	1	.5	+3%	15	
Langor	1	.5	+5%	65	
Large Helm (All Metal)			!!	30	
Ransium	1	1	+13%	40	
Langor	1	1	+15%	140	
Large Helm with Visor (All Metal)			!!!	60	
Ransium	2	2	+13%	160	
Langor	2	2	+15%	560	
Dog Barding			+35 %	200 Silver	
(1,3)	Ransium		+38 %	800	
	Langor	7	+40 %	920	
Horse Barding			+40 %	400	
(3,2)	Ransium	11	+43 %	1300	
	Langor	11	+45 %	7500	

! A Small Helm gives your head the same PTE as your body.

!! A Large Helm gives your head a +10% bonus to your PTE total.

!!! A Large Helm with Visor gives your head, face, eyes and neck a +10% bonus to your PTE total.

→ Note: These bonuses are gained for all types of helmets regardless of what material they are made from.

CURRENCY

Gold - Heavy golden colored metal with a low melting point which is used in the making of very expensive decorations, jewelry, very small statues, etc.
It is also the most valuable metal.

Americanium - Glowing lava colored metal that may "transmit" and "hold" **all** Classes of enchantment.
[Class (A), (B), (C), (D), and (E) Spells]
This metal is used with Iron and Mithral to make Langor, an enchantable metal.

Mithral - A light grayish metal that may "transmit" and "hold" **some** Classes of enchantment.
[Class (A), (B), and (C) Spells]
This metal seems to "suck" in light and never causes a reflection.
This metal is used with Iron to make Ransium, an enchantable metal.

Silver - Very lustrous shinny metal.
This metal is the basic currency.

Iron - Hard, strong metal used for money and the construction of many weapons, armor and items.

	COIN Value	=	EQUIVALENCE	
1	Gold	=	10 Amer.	[AP]
1	Americanium	=	10 Mithral	[MP]
1	Mithral	=	10 Sliver	[Silver]
1	Silver	=	10 Iron	[IP]

Physical appearance of the coins

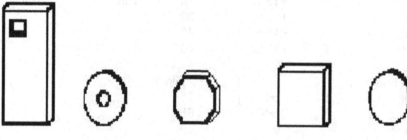

Currency Exchange Rate	10,000 Iron	= 1,000 Silver	= 100 Mithral	=	10 Amer.	=	1 Gold
Weight of Coins	1 oz.	= ½ oz.	= ½ oz.	=	½ oz.	=	½ oz.

NOTE: The holes in the iron and silver pieces are there so you can keep them on a leather strap forming a ring. Usually 10 silver or 100 Iron pieces are kept on a leather ring.

EQUIPMENT LIST and PRICES (Silver Pieces)

Item	Cost	Item	Cost
Boots, Ankle, Soft	5	Paper, 10 sheets	5
Boots, Ankle, Hard	10	Quill and Ink for 50 sheets	5
Boots, Knee, Soft	15	Mirror, small, 6" x 6"	20
Boots, Knee Hard	20	Mirror, Large, 3' x 6'	100
Pants, White (+5-10 Silver for Color)	5	Watch (Accurate & Hand Held)	100
Belt with Buckle	3	Astrolabe	150
Sash, White (+5-10 Silver for Color)	1	Telescope	75
Shirt, White (+5-10 Silver for Color)	4	Compass, Hand Held	40
Blouse, White (+5-10 Silver for Color)	5	Small Box, 6"L x 3"W x 3"T [with Hasp = +5]	15
Vest, White (+5-10 Silver for Color)	5	Medium Box, 3'L x 2'W x 2'T [w/Hasp = +5]	40
Dress, White (+5-10 Silver for Color)	8	Medium Chest with Metal Bands, 3'x2'x2'	70
Cloak, White (+5-10 Silver for Color)	5	Large Chest w/ Metal Bands, 4'x3'x3'	120
Robe, White (+5-10 Silver for Color)	10	Pill Box, holds (1024) 1/4" or (2) 2" pills	10
Coat, Summer, White (+5-10 Silver for Color)	15	Alchemist Set, Beginners & 10 Potion Vials	20
Coat, Spring/Fall, White (+5-10 for Color)	20	Alchemist Set, Advanced & 25 Potion Vials	50
Coat, Winter, White (+5-10 Silver for Color)	30	Alchemist Set, Professional & 50 Potion Vials	100
Gloves, Riding, Brown Leather (+10 Color)	10	Alchemist Potion Vial, 1 ea.	1
Gloves, Fencing, Brown Leather (+10 Color)	15	Elementalist Set, Beginners & 1 lb of wax	20
Gloves, Winter, Brown Leather (+10 Color)	20	Elementalist Set, Advanced & 2 lbs of wax	50
Hat, Straw, Brown (+5-10 Silver for Color)	5	Elementalist Set, Professional & 3 lbs of wax	100
Hat with bill, Brown (+5-10 Silver for Color)	7	Wax, 1lb (Used to make Rings/Disks &Badges)	5
Hat, Winter, Brown (+5-10 Silver for Color)	10	Scabbard, Axe	1
Pouch, Leather, Brown, (+10-15 for Color)	2	Scabbard, Dagger	2
Small Cloth Sack, White, (+5-10 for Color)	2	Scabbard, Sword	4
Large Cloth Sack, White (+5-10 for Color)	5	Quiver, Arrows (1 Score = 20)	8
Small Leather Sack, Brown, (+10-15 for Color)	10	Quiver, Bolts (1 Score = 20)	8
Large Leather Sack, Brown, (+10-15 for Color)	15	Sharpening Stone & Oil bottle, (50 blades)	5
Back Pack, Brown (+15-20 for Color)	30	Axe, Woodmen's [1d12+2]	20
Potion Bandolier (Holds 10 Potion Vials)	15	Pick - Axe [1d12]	25
Dust Armband (Holds 5 measures of Al. Dust)	20	Shovel or Crowbar [1d10]	25
Sleeping Bag, Brown (+20-30 for Color)	15	Saw, Hand Held	25
Tent, 2 man	25	Hammer, Hand Held [1d6+1]	10
Tent, 4 man	40	Hammer, Sludge [1d10+1]	30
Sanitary Kit, Male, 1 month	3	Nails, bunch = 40	5
Sanitary Kit, Female, 1 month	7	Spike, bunch = 5	5
First Aid Kit	10	File, Course	10
Cooking Set (Travel)	10	File, Fine	15
Reg. Rations, 1 week, (Stays good for 3 wks)	5	Bar Stools	10
Hard Rations, 1 week, (Good for 3 months)	10	Bar Chairs	20
Water, Flask, 2 weeks	4	Bar Tables	40
Whiskey, Flask (20 shots)	18	Bar Doors	30
Whiskey, 1 Shot	1	Bar Stages	100
Ale, Flask (10 glasses)	4	Glasses	5
Ale, 1 glass	0.5	Plates	4
Cigarettes, 1 pack = 20	10	2-wheel Cart with 1 extra wheel	50
Cigars, 1 pack = 5	10	4-wheel Wagon with 1 extra wheel	100
Flint, Steel and Tinder box	5	Raft	20
Torch, lasts 3 hours	2	Boat, 2 man (10', with 2 ores)	100
Candle, box = 10, lasts 1 hour each	5	Boat, 8 man (30', with 6 ores & sail)	500
Lantern	25	Ship, Small (60' with sail, 20 man)	1000
Oil, Flask, lasts 6 hours	10	Ship, Cargo (80' with 2 sails, 25 man)	3000
Rope, 50'	3	Ship, Battle (100' with 3 sails, 50 man)	6000
Grappling Hook	25	Ship, War (200' with 4 sails, 80 man)	10000

Trained Horses & Dogs (cost in Silver)

Horse, Riding = Mustang *	40	War Dog (Trained=Guard,attack,+1extra)	35
Horse, Riding (w/Everything) **	50	Dog collar with name plate	2
Horse, War = Clydesdale *	60	Horse Saddle Bag, Small	10
Horse, War (w/Everything) **	75	Horse Saddle Bag, Large	30

* Please see the Creature Section for more details.
** w/Everything = all equipment needed to ride the horse (Saddle, blanket, bridal, ect) plus 2 small saddle bags.

Services (cost in Silver)

Lodging, 1 night	1	Repair any Mundane Object	½ Cost
Breakfast or Lunch	1	Repair a Wagon Wheel	7
Dinner	2	Shoe a Horse	5
Lodging, 1 week	7	Stable and Feed a Horse, 1 night	1
Bed & Breakfast, 1 night	1.5	Stable and Feed a Horse, 1 week	7
Bed & Breakfast, 1 week	12	Wash, Dry & Fold one set of Clothes	2
Bath	1	Iron one set of Clothes	1
Shave & Hair Cut	1		
Nails & simple Hairdo	2	Note: There are 10 days in a week.	

Locks & Picks (costs in Silver)

LOCK	Cost	% - to Pick	Damage Taken	PICK	Cost	% PLUS to Lock Picking Skill
Poor	5	-0	10 EP	Poor	3	+0
Fair	15	-5 %	25 EP	Fair	7	+3 %
Good	25	-10 %	40 EP	Good	15	+5 %
Great	50	-15 %	65 EP	Great	25	+7 %
Awesome	75	-20 %	90 EP	Awesome	40	+10 %

% - to Pick: is a negative added to your Lock Pick percentage when you try to pick this type of lock.
Damage Taken: is the amount of physical or magical damage the lock will take before breaking.
% PLUS to Lock Picking Skill: is the bonus you get to add to the percentage you must roll in order to open any lock when you use these lock picks.

Enchanted Gem Prices (cost in Silver)

Gem Perfection Ratings (GPR)

Spell Classifications: ENCHANTED GEM TYPE	A I2 & I1	B SI2 & SI1	C VSI2 & VSI1	D VVSI2 & VVSI1	E
Colored Quartz	5 & 10	15 & 20	30 & 40	----	
True Gems (Ruby, Sapphire)	15 & 20	25 & 30	50 & 60	80 & 100	
Opaque Quartz	25 & 30	35 & 40	70 & 80	----	
Diamonds & Onyx	35 & 40	45 & 50	90 & 100	125 & 150	

Enchanted and Special Item Prices (cost in Silver)

Scrolls	Gem Price + (Spell Points / 4) + 2
Potions	Gem Price + (Spell Points / 4) + 5
Dusts	Gem Price + (Spell Points / 4) + 10
Pills	Gem Price + (Spell Points / 4) + 20
Enchanted Items	Cost of Item + (Gem Price if included) + (Spell Points / 4) + 5
Elementalist Ring / Disk	Gem Price + {Mithral =+10 or Americanium=+100} + (Spell Points / 4) + 25
Mentalist Badge	{Mithral =+10 or Mithral=+50 or Americanium=+100} + (Mental Points/4) + 10

112

RESIST ENCHANTMENT ROLL   (RER)

All characters and creatures when struck by a spell or an Enchanted / Mental attack rate a Resist Enchantment Roll (RER). This is a percentage roll made by the character (or creature) at the time the spell first makes contact with them. As with all percentage rolls, you must roll **below** (or equal to) the stated number. A Character's RER is based on his level, but certain spells and/or abilities may add to this total percentage - please remember to add these bonuses to your normal RER percentage total before making your roll.

If you roll a percentage lower than the RER total (with any bonuses added), you only take 1/2 the **base** EP Damage which is normally caused by the spell or mental ability. In some cases, a successful RER will negate certain effects caused by a particular spell.

Here are the Resist Enchantment Roll percentages you rate depending on your Level:

LEVEL	RER PERCENTAGE	General Bonuses added to your RER total
1	10 %	add ½ Wisdom Score vs. Illusions
2 – 4	15 %	add ½ Agility Score vs. Nets, Rocks, Waves
5 – 9	20 %	
10 – 14	25 %	
15th and up	30 %	

NOTE: All Regular and Mutated Creatures normally have a RER percentage of 20%.

: *Rules for experienced players* :

+3%   Added to the base percentage for every column TO THE LEFT of the zero position which correspond to your level.

-2%   Subtracted from the base percentage for every column TO THE RIGHT of the zero position which correspond to your level.

The totals for the adjusted RER used for experienced players appear on the right hand side of the table below.

Spell Classification of spell effecting Victim

Level	A	B	C	D	E	A	B	C	D	E
1	0	1	1	1	1	10%	8%	6%	4%	2%
2 - 5	1	0	1	1	1	18	15	13	11	9
5 - 9	1	1	0	1	1	26%	23	20	18	16%
10 - 14	1	1	1	0	1	34	31	28	25	23
15 - 19	1	1	1	1	0	43%	39%	36%	33%	30%

RER PERCENTAGE TOTAL

MORALITY RATING

Morality is sometimes defined as the "rightness" or "wrongness" of an action or deed. This description is adequate for our purposes, but because your Ref. is directing your adventures, his or her interpretation of the morality of a specific action is what you must abide by. A specific number called your Morality Rating (MR) classifies your character's morals at any given time. The range goes from 1 to 20. Low numbers represent low morals and high numbers represent High morals. All characters when they start out have a MR of 10; this is adjusted either up or down depending on your actions throughout the game. I could have included a long list of actions and deeds which reflect positive or negative modifiers to your MR, but I prefer to let your Ref. use his or her own judgment.

Certain Occupations require you to maintain a certain MR. These restrictions are listed under each Occupation's description.

NOTE: New players may wish to skip these rules and all related rules in the Occupation's description.

Here is a table that compares Morality Ratings with common Terms:

MR	Description
1	Black Hearted
2 - 4	Low down dirty Morals
5 - 8	Shady
9	Beginning of Low Morals
10	Beginning of High Morals
11 -14	Wholesome Morals
15 -18	Exceptional Morals
19	Enlightened
20	Pure

Some acts should automatically change your MR to a specified value, for consistency during the game.

Automatic Morality Adjustments

Attack a Stunned / Defenseless or Opponent	= 10
Successful use of Non-Lethal Poison	= 10
Attacking while invisible	= 9
Killing a Stunned / Defenseless Opponent	= 7
Violating a Tradition of Penicia	= 5
Your trap becomes deadly for any reason	= 5
Successful use of Lethal Poison (Opp. Dies)	= 5
Killing while invisible	= 3

NOTE2: These 'Automatics' can NEVER bring you 'up', they can only force you 'down' the MR scale.

TIME SCALE

In order for any mortal to judge or classify his or her life, they need to have a means of expressing their accomplishments in a specific order. This need requires all peoples to impose a scale to list and synchronize their actions. This conceptual scale is commonly known as Time.

The races of Penicia surprisingly use the same scale to measure the passage of Time. Every revolution of Penicia around the Column Sun, is known as a Year. The Time it takes for Penicia to revolve one full cycle on it's axis is known as a Day and lasts twenty-four Hours. You get the picture – so listed here after is the Time Scale:

5 Seconds	=	1 Attack		
60 Seconds	=	1 Minute	=	12 Attacks
60 Minutes	=	1 Hour		
24 Hours	=	1 Day		
10 Days	=	1 Week		
5 Weeks	=	1 Month		
10 Months	=	1 Year		

NOTE3: As you can see there are 50 days in a month and 500 days in a year.

SURVIVAL SKILL TABLE

Ability used for Check	Skill	Occupation
None	Attack Unseen Enemy	Any
Agility	Blind Shot and Accurate Pass	Any
Intellect	Boat, Construction (Small)	Any
Intellect	Boat, Pilot (Small)	Any
Intellect	Bower / Fletcher	Any
Will	Detect Ambush	Any
Will	Fishing	Any
Wisdom	Fire Starting	Any
Intellect	First Aid	Any
Wisdom	Gambling	Any
Will	Hunting	Any
Intellect	Horsemanship	Any
Intellect	Identify Plants (or Identify any one type of thing)	Any
Wisdom	Judge Quality of Weapon or Armor	Any
Agility	Juggling	Any
Intellect	Locate Traps	Any
Intellect	Measure Distance by Sight	Any
Intellect	Measure Distance by Sound	Any
Will	Mountain Climbing	Any
Intellect	Navigate on Land	Any
Intellect	Navigate on Open Seas or Star Navigation	Any
None	Paired Weapons	Warrior, Ninja or Spy/Ass.
Will	Singing or Playing an Instrument	Any
None	Shield Use	Any
None	Swimming	Any
Intellect	Tell Time Using the Sky	Any
Will	Train and Maintain Animals	Any
Wisdom	Tracking	Any
Wisdom	Ventriloquism	Any
None	Wrestling / Boxing	Any
None	Color / Element / Discipline Master	Enchanter, Alchemist, Elementalist or Mentalist
Will	Leather working	Any
Will	Ring / Disk Construction	Any
Will	Rope Making	Any
Will	Sewing	Any
Will	Woodworking	Any
Will	Badge / Pin Construction	Any
None	Endurance	Any
None	Agility	Any
None	Strength	Any
None	Intellect	Any
None	Wisdom	Any
None	Improve Charging Rate	Any

NOTE: Most Survival Skills use Ability Checks to test for success.
This is a percentage your character must roll <u>below or equal to</u> in order to accomplish the Skill in question.

Ability Check Percentage = Named Ability * 3

Example: You want to use the Survival Skill: Boat, Construction (small) and your character has an Intellect Score of 15. You simply multiply (15 * 3) which equals 45 %.
Your character has a 45% chance to correctly construct a small seaworthy boat.
Ie: Any roll lower or equal to 45% reflects a successful attempt and this means your boat will float.

NOTE2: If anyone attempts to duplicate any skill listed here and doesn't have the Survival Skill in question then they must roll a percentage less than their natural ABILITY SCORE stated in the description to successfully use the skill.
Ref note: That would be a percentage less than a maximum of 20% to correctly use the skill.

NOTE3: You can initially learn most Skills <u>once</u> and specialize in them <u>twice</u>. If you want to specialize in a skill, you must use another one of your Survival Skill Slots and "pump" it back into that same Skill. This gives you a bonus to your existing percentage and may enhance the aspects of that Skill. The bonuses given by Specializing in a Skill are in parentheses at the end of the skill's description denoted by the abbreviation : Sp.

NOTE4: You may substitute 2 Survival Skill Slots to learn 1 weapon or visa versa.

NOTE5: These next tables are for your reference. Please note that your character gains his or her Initial Weapon and Survival Skills in additional to these:

Gaining New Weapon Sill Slots

Level	Additional Weapon		Level	Additional Weapon
3	+ 1		6	+ 1
9	+ 1		12	+ 1
15	+ 1		18	+ 1

Gaining New Survival Skill Slots

Level	Additional Skill Slots		Level	Additional Skill Slots
2	+ 1		4	+ 2
6	+ 1		8	+ 2
10	+ 1		12	+ 2
14	+ 1		16	+ 2
18	+ 1			

SURVIVAL SKILLS

As you travel through life, you may find it convenient to possess skills in addition to those provided by your Occupation. As a matter of fact, in some cases you'll find it necessary to learn certain skills in order for you to perform your Occupation correctly. This section describes these extra skills which I call Survival Skills. Please, be sure you know which Survival skills are required by your Occupation, and also be mindful of what you want your character to be able to **do**, because you only have a finite number of "Survival Skill Slots". The specific number of Survival Skill Slots your character rates depends on your Occupation and your level – please see Note5 on page 116.

Attack Unseen Enemy:

Normally, while if you are in total darkness or are blinded, your Opponent receives a +40% on his or her PTE total. While concealed in deep shadows, your Opponents normally gains a +30% to their PTE total. If you take this Survival Skill, your Opponent will only receive a +30% (40-10%) in total darkness and a +20% (30-10%) in deep shadows.
(Sp : -10% to your Opponents PTE bonus while they are concealed within total darkness or shadow, each time you specialize.)   Ref note: Maximum= +10% in Total Darkness and +0% in Deep Shadows.

Blind Shot and Accurate Pass:

This skill allows your character to play the IronBall game well. You must roll a successful Ability Check with Agility to make an accurate Pass with your catcher to a teammate. If you didn't learn this Survival Skill then you must roll a percentage less then your Agility score to make an accurate pass to one of your teammates. Anyone can catch the Iron Ball with their catcher by making a successful Ability Check with Agility. If the person passing the IronBall to you made an Accurate Pass, then you - the receiver - gains a +25% added to your total Ability Check Percentage with Agility to catch that Pass with your catcher. Ie. If your Agility Score is a 20, you have a maximum of 85% to catch an Accurate Pass, if not specialized.

In order to score, one of the Runners has to enter the Canopy alone and try to shoot the IronBall into the diamond shaped hole at it's back. Listed below are negatives to your Ability Check percentage total. They are separated into different circumstances :

Learned Survival Skill: 'Blind Shoot and Accurate Pass'		Negative to your Ability Check with Agility
To Sink the Ball from inside a lighted Canopy:		-10%
To Sink the Ball from inside a Dark Canopy:		-20%
Shoot from OUTSIDE Canopy:	Lit Canopy	-40%
	Dark Canopy	-50%

Did **NOT** Learn Survival Skill: 'Blind Shoot and Accurate Pass'		
To Sink the Ball from inside a lighted Canopy:		Percentage lower then your Agility Score!
To Sink the Ball from inside a Dark Canopy:		-10% lower than your Agility Score.
Shoot from OUTSIDE Canopy:	Lit Canopy	-15% lower than your Agility Score.
	Dark Canopy	Only a roll of **00** on your Percentage roll.

(Sp : +1/2 Agility score added to your Survival Skill percentage each specialization. Add this to ALL rolls.)

Boat, Construction (Small):

With this Survival Skill, you may construct a small boat (with or without sail.) You must buy or "find" the tools (axe, hammer, saw, etc.) and materials (wood, rope, nails, etc.) necessary to make the boat. Roll an Ability Check with Intellect and the lower the roll the better you've constructed the boat. If you roll higher than your percentage, the boat is so poorly made it will sink very quickly. You may also fix a small boat correctly with a successful Ability Check. Construction times for 1 person: Raft = 4 hours, 1 man boat = 8 hours, 2 man boat = 16 hours. If you want to add a sail to your craft it will take an additional 3 hours.
(Sp : +1/2 Intellect score added to your Survival Skill percentage each specialization and -1 hour off production time per Specialization.)

HUMAN SHIPS   HEMAR SHIPS

117

Boat, Pilot (Small):

This skill will allow you to correctly pilot any small boat (with or without a sail) on any river, inland lake, or along a coast (it won't help you much if you want to sail on the open seas.) If you can't see land, make an Ability Check with Intellect every mile to stay on course. You also will be required to make an Ability Check to keep the boat from capsizing in adverse conditions or in fast rapids.
(Sp : +1/2 Intellect score added to your Survival Skill percentage each specialization.)

Bower / Fletcher:

This skill is known as "Bower/Fletcher", but you learn "Fletching" first. When learning this skill, you are taught how to properly make and fletch arrows and quarrels. You must choose the correct wood for the shaft, the material for the tip and right type of feathers. The lower the Ability Check with Intellect the better the arrows or quarrels are made. I allow someone to make 10 arrows or quarrels with one successful Ability Check. You are taught to make quarrels for both crossbows and wristbows.
(Sp : +1/2 Intellect score added to your Survival Skill percentage each specialization.
        1st: Learn to construct regular Short Bows (Bower) and Sheaf Arrows.
        2nd: Learn to construct regular Long Bows and Crossbows.)

Detect Ambush:

This skill will give you a bonus of +20% to your Detect Ambush total (remember you must roll lower than your total percentage to detect an ambush.) Your character gains this percentage bonus verse both Hasty and Set Ambushes.

I also use this roll in another capacity: any time there is a chance that one of the party will see something that will help them, I let them roll their Detect Ambush percentage. The lower they roll the more details I give them about the situation or surroundings.
(Sp : +1/2 Will score added to your Detect Ambush total each specialization.)

Fire Starting:

A fire can be started by just about anyone under normal conditions. Unfortunately, the weather doesn't always cooperate. Rain, snow, or even heavy due can cause you problems and cold nights. Anyone with this skill may start a fire under adverse conditions by successfully making an Ability Check with Wisdom. Remember, if someone tries to start a fire without this skill in anything but favorable conditions, they may try but they must roll a percentage under their unmodified Wisdom score.
(Sp : +1/2 Wisdom score added to your Survival Skill percentage each specialization.)

First Aid:

This skill will allow you to correctly perform many treatments: dress an open wound, stop the bleeding, set a broken bone, restart someone's breathing, treat for shock, diagnose a fever or a cold and even diagnose a major disease. You may do any one of the above listed activities by simply making a successful Ability Check with Intellect. If you miss your Ability Check, you will not set the bone correctly, not stop the bleeding, or miss diagnose the problem. If you succeed with your Ability Check, your patient immediately receives 1d6 EP and will receive an additional 1d4 EP if she receives a "good nights sleep" (That's an overnight total of 1d10 for sleep + 1d4 EP for being bandaged).
(Sp : +1/2 Intellect score added to your Survival Skill percentage, each specialization.
        You receive other bonuses from your 1st and 2nd specializations as follows:
1st: 1) If you have Identify Plants, you are trained to know which types of plants and herbs will reduce pain, extract poisons, etc. by making a successful Ability Check with Intellect.
      2) With a successful Ability Check, you may stitch up major cuts and gashes correctly.
      3) A successful check gains your patient 1d8 right away & an extra 1d6 overnight for the total of 1d10+1d6.
2nd: A) You learn to do minor surgery to remove foreign objects from someone. You must make your Ability Check at a -20% to do this successfully.
      B) A successful check gains your patient 1d10 right away & an extra 1d8 overnight for the total of 1d10+1d8.)

Gambling:

This skill will help you in more ways than just winning at cards. If you make a successful Ability Check with Wisdom, you can tell if the "game is rigged" or if someone is cheating - here is at little hint: Most games start off straight and then lapse to a "rigged" nature. This skill will also automatically increase your odds at any gambling game by 10%, if you make a successful Ability Check with Wisdom.

(Sp : +1/2 Wisdom score added to your Survival Skill and increases your odds of winning by 5% each time you specialize. Other bonuses received:

1st: Teaches you to "stack" your hand when dealing cards, or to switch the dice you are holding, etc if you make a successful Ability Check. You also gain the ability to make a Marked Card, Loaded Die, or any other single instrument of gambling. The time and materials of course varies for each different item and you must successfully make an Ability Check at a -25% to correctly make each single item.

2nd: Teaches you to stack anyone's hand when dealing or switch dice that are "sitting" at the table. Your penalty to make a marked card or loaded die is now only a -20% to make a single item.

NOTE: If you're a 'strait shooter', which most of us good people are, you can force the entire game to be fair, if you have a higher specialization rating than the person who is dealing or running the game. If your specialization is at the same level as the dealer/game boss, he can't cheat you, but may be able to cheat someone else at the table.)

Hunting:

A successful Ability Check with Will reveals the most probable areas where the prey you are hunting will pass. There is no chance that an experienced hunter will scare off any game. If and when your prey appears, just make another successful Ability Check with Will to deduct -20% from the animals PTE total and this roll also gives you a -10% on your SPT roll – this cannot be used in Combat, only when you are hunting a particular beast or bird.

(Sp : You may specialize in Hunting only 1 type of animal or bird (deer, rabbit, moose, pheasant, etc.) each time you specialize with this skill. You gain +1/2 your Will score when stalking that type of prey and an additional -5% on the prey's PTE total and -5% on your SPT rolls against that animal type, each time you specialize.)

Fishing: Follow same rules as stated in Hunting, but you just stalk your prey in a river or lake with a rod and line.

Horsemanship:

As with many skills, most people can ride under favorable circumstances without taking this skill. If you want to ride your mount and keep your Agility bonus to your PTE, mount while the horse is moving, or shift in the saddle placing more of the horse's body between you and your Opponent, you must study this Skill. You learn how to care for the horse, check it's hooves for damage, and even learn to tell the animal's general age and general health. A successful Ability Check with Intellect will let you accomplish any of the above listed activities, although while riding you <u>automatically receive</u> your normal Agility bonus to your PTE <u>without</u> an Ability Check when you learn this skill. When you shift your body in the saddle to shield yourself from an Opponent's strike, you gain another +1/2 of your Agility score bonus added to your PTE total on your next three PTE rolls, if you make a successful Ability Check with Agility.

(Sp : +1/2 Intellect score added to your percentage each time you specialize. Other bonuses from your first and second specialization are listed below:

1st: With a successful Ability Check you may :
1) Jump you mount over low fences, bushes or logs.
2) Bring your mount to a dead stop and put it on it's side for protection or so you can get "low" and out of sight - you may do this all by using only 2 Actions.
3) Shoe any horse correctly.

2nd: With a successful Ability Check you may :
A) Mount your horse from above. (a fall over 40 feet will damage the mount.)
B) If you make a successful Ability Check at a -20%, you may "break" a wild horse to a saddle and bit.
C) You are now able to train the horse to run faster. i.e. - Improve it's CRM by ONE, one ping only please.)

NOTE: Knights gain all 1st and 2nd specialization bonuses by Specializing only <u>once</u> in this skill!

Identify Plants:

This skill gives you the ability to recognize plants that can be helpful or harmful to you. A successful Ability Check with Intellect will tell you if there is a plant in the immediate area which will have the affects you are looking for. This skill will also give you information on where (what terrain and season) is the best place to look for a specific plant. If you know the name or type of plant (ie. First Aid with 1 Specialization) that will reduce the sting of a burn, draw out some poison or help you sleep, you roll your Ability Check with Intellect to find the best place to search for it. When you get close you may roll again to see if you can find that plant with out searching. Unfortunately there isn't enough room here to list all the plants and their affects on the body, so your Ref. will handle that.

(Sp : +1/2 Intellect score added to your Survival Skill percentage each specialization.)

NOTE2: There are actually many other Identify skills, you only need to change the information the character receives depending on the type of skill. A favorite is **Identify Enchanted Gems**. This skill allows you to recognize an Enchanted Gem just by studying it. You will automatically know if a gem is enchanted just by holding it and if you roll a successful Ability Check with Intellect, you will even know the Enchanted Gem's GPR, if there are any spells held within the Gem and what their Trigger Words are. You may use many other Identify skills in <u>your</u> game, just use these as guidelines.

Judge Quality of Weapon or Armor:

This skill's name is very self-explanatory. If you succeed with an Ability Check with Wisdom you can tell if the weapon, shield, or suit of armor in question was constructed correctly to stand the test of time and battle. You will also know if the specific item is Enchanted in any way! This Survival Skill will reveal the Trigger Word to activate the item, but it will not tell you what the Enchantment will do, so have fun and good luck, you may need it!

(Sp : +1/2 Wisdom score added to your Survival Skill percentage each specialization.)

Juggling:

This entertaining skill is not really necessary for your survival, but it could help to round out your Occupation. By making a successful Ability Check with Agility, you may juggle up to 4 small items. If you wish to try to catch ONE small "slow" moving object flying at you, such as a thrown dagger; you have a chance equal to 1/2 of your normal Ability Check percentage. (You can't attempt to catch fast moving objects such as speeding arrows, quarrels, etc.) This requires 1 Action per projectile you wish to catch.

(Sp : +1/2 Agility score added to your Survival Skill percentage each specialization.
Catching an object is still 1/2 of your percentage. You may also juggle an additional +1 item each time you specialize. The object may be flaming after you specialize once.)

Locate Traps:

This ability may be very necessary for your survival. In order to locate a trap, you must be looking - you just don't notice one. While actively searching, you must pass within 5 feet of the trap's trigger mechanism and make a successful Ability Check with Intellect to spot the trap. If you are successful, you won't set off the trap and may be able to devise a way around it – Only a Spy / Assassin may disarm a trap. If you come within 1/2 foot of the trap, while looking, and miss your Ability Check there is a 20% chance of setting it off. It takes 1 Attack (5 seconds) to check a 2' x 2' area.
(Sp: +1/2 Intellect score added to your Survival Skill percentage each specialization.
Other bonuses received:
1st: 1) You may now check a 5'x5' area in 1 Attack.
       2) You have only a 15% chance of setting off a trap while actively searching for it.
2nd: A) You also may check a 10'x10' area in 1 Attack.
       B) You have only a 10% chance of setting off the trap while actively searching for it.)

Measure Distance by Sight:

This skill is especially useful to Warriors and Enchanters, who need to know how far an Opponent is from them, so at the right time they can unleash their arrows and spells. Roll an Ability Check with Intellect and the lower the percentage rolled the more accurate your estimate is. If you fail your roll, your guess is completely wrong. Another way to use this skill is to say "Tell me when he is __ft away" and the lower your roll the closer he is to your stated distance.
NOTE: You can do this in <u>addition</u> to your regular Actions; it does not cost you an Action to estimate a
         distance.
(Sp : +1/2 Intellect score added to your Survival Skill percentage each specialization.)

Measure Distance by Sound: (Follow same rules listed in Measure Distance by Sight.)

Mountain Climbing:

This skill gives you the knowledge to use ropes, pitons, carabineers, and a harness to ascend or descend any vertical surface. You must place a Piton and carabineer every 20ft and use at least 1 rope. An Ability Check with Will must be rolled to set up the equipment and every time you place a Piton (you must make a "blind roll" so you'll have no idea which Pitons will hold and which ones will give way if you fall.) You can only carry the amount of weight reflected by your Strength score listed under the Bench Press column as you climb.
(Sp : +1/2 Will score added to your Survival Skill percentage each specialization.)

Navigate on Land:

This skill will allow you to find your way through unfamiliar territory to your intended destination. You may judge the distance and the time it will take to make the journey by making an Ability Check with Intellect. When you actually begin your journey, you will need an accurate map and a way to find North (this skill also teaches you to find North by using the sun or stars.) With the map's North facing True (Actual) North, make an Ability Check with Intellect. You may make your checks as often as you like, but it does slow you down. If your Ability Check is successful, you are on course and doing fine. If unsuccessful, you will travel 100 yards off course for every 1000 yards you've traveled since your last check.

[example: Roge has an Intellect of 15, a map, has found North, and rolled a 55% for his last check
(which fails). It was 10 clicks (10,000 yards) since his last check so he ends up
1 click (1000 yards) off course.]

The roll should be "blind" so the person doesn't know he is off course. If you fail to make your roll on a check and successfully make it the next time, you will discover your error and be able to get back on course. If you don't have a map, you will incur a -20% on your roll. A grossly inaccurate or false map will give you a -25% or -50% respectively! If you can't find North for some reason, you will incur a -20% on your percentage.

(Sp : +1/2 Intellect score added to your Survival Skill percentage each specialization.)

Navigate on Open Seas:

(Follows same rules as above, except that you need an astrolabe and an accurate time piece. This skill teaches you to use the astrolabe and time piece to find your position on open seas at night or during the day.)

Paired Weapons:

When you learn this Survival Skill, it allows you to use 2 weapons at once in melee combat. You may parry with one weapon [see Note2] and strike with your second weapon, strike with both weapons [if you have 2 available Strike slots] or parry with both of your weapons [this gives you a Double Parry bonus, see Note]. You must make one of these selections before you use any of your Actions. You gain your Strength Damage Bonus on both weapons you attack with. (Sp : can't)

NOTE: When using a Double Parry, you gain your full (Agl Score) added to your PTE total verses
1 Opponent for _that_ Attack.

NOTE2: You can only parry with the Paired Weapon skill, if you have learned the Parry Skill or if you have
learned how to use a Shield. Ie. Survival Skill "Shield Use".

NOTE3: The example uses Warrior / Ninja Strikes per Attack, but a S/A may learn this skill as well.

War/Nin Lvl	Strikes	Parries	Example
1st - 4th	1	1	Strike with 1st melee weapon and use other weapon to Parry 1 strike from 1 Opponent
5th - 9th	1	2	Strike with Sword and use your dagger to Parry 1 strike from two different Opp.
10th - 14th	2	2	Strike with both of your Swords and Double Parry 1 Strike from 1 Opponent.
15th - 19th	3	2	Strike 3 times with your Sais and Parry 2 strikes from 1 Opponent or Unleash 3 Strikes from your two Sais and Parry 1 Strike from 2 different Opps.

Singing or Playing an Instrument:

You may only choose to learn to sing or to play one instrument every time you take this skill. When you learn this skill, you become proficient to perform in public. If you make a successful Ability Check with Will you preformed well, ie. you won't get booed off the stage but will receive applause instead.

(Sp : <u>Full</u> Will score added to your Survival Skill percentage each specialization, but a 99% roll always fails!

1st: You become a master performer; if your Ability Check is successful, you awarded lots of applause and invitations to return at a latter date.

2nd: You become a virtuoso; A successful Ability Check gets you standing ovations, set performance dates and perks, like free rooms, meals and drinks)

Shield Use:

You are taught how to defensively employ a shield verses either Projectiles or Melee weapons. You may add the percentage bonus from the <u>particular</u> shield you are using to your PTE total. You must use a Parry Action to employ a shield and gain <u>its</u> bonus to your PTE from any ONE specific attack from an Opponent.

(Sp: 1st: Gain +5% PTE to the Shield bonus and Use your Shield as a Weapon. Using your Shield as a weapon costs you 1 Strike Action and does 1d8 Damage + your Strength Damage bonus, if your opponent fails his PTE roll.

2nd: Gain +10% PTE to the Shield bonus and Employ a 'Shield Bash' – This costs you 1 Strike Action; it does 1d8 Damage + your (Str. Dam Bonus)x2 & knocks back your Opponent a total of 1 foot per point of damage you've inflected with the Bash, if he fails his PTE roll. Also your Opponent must make a successful Ability Check with Agility to stay on his or her feet.)

Swimming:

Almost anyone can swim to some extent under favorable conditions (CRM: 1), but to swim for long periods of time, against currents, or in adverse conditions, you will need this skill. Swimming will enable you to tread water for an amount of time in minutes equal to your Endurance score, to swim up stream, or in stormy weather without penalties. Your swimming speed in calm water will increase to a Charging Rate of 15 feet/sec (CRM: 3). Unlike most Survival Skills where anyone of any Race may be your teacher, you can only learn Swimming from someone of your own Race.

(Sp : +5 minutes treading water and increase swimming speed by ONE Charging Rate multiple

[or 5 feet/second] every time you Specialize.)

Ref. note: 2 specializations = Tread water for 30 min and swim CRM: 5.

Tell Time Using the Sky:

The name explains this Survival Skill well. It will allow you to pinpoint the time either day or night by simply inspecting the sky above you. It will also let you estimate the coming of Dawn or Dusk in hours or minutes. Roll an Ability Check with Intellect and the lower the percentage rolled the more accurate your estimation is. If you roll above your percentage you estimation will be off by 3d10 minutes.

(Sp : +1/2 Intellect score added to your Survival Skill percentage each specialization.

1st: If you roll above your percentage, you will only be off by 2d10 minutes.

2nd: If you roll above your percentage, you will only be off by 1d10 minutes.)

Train and Maintain Animals:

When you start learning this skill, you must pick 1 type of small animal - falcon, dog, mongoose, etc – to train. You may train an animal of this type to do simple, specific tasks by teaching it a command (your commands may be <u>either</u> words, hand signals, whistles, etc.) You may teach the animal to respond to 5 commands. The "pup" can start learning immediately and it will take 1 week to learn each command. Make an Ability Check with Will at the end of each week of training; if this is successful the animal has learned the task. If it is not successful the animal does not learn the trick, but you can try and retrain it in a following week. You can also tell the approximate age and health of <u>ANY TYPE</u> of animal by simply successfully making an Ability Check with Will.

(Sp : +1/2 Will score added to your Survival Skill percentage each specialization.

1st: Pick 1 more animal type and you may add horses to the list. You may teach up to 7 commands.

2nd: 1) Pick any animal type (within reason) to teach and you may teach a total of 10 commands.

2) You are now able to train one animal type to run or fly faster. i.e. - Improve it's CRM by ONE.)

Tracking:

This skill will let you follow and hopefully find whatever creature is trying to elude you. Your base percentage to track something or someone is an Ability Check with Wisdom. You must check the trail and roll your Ability Check at least every 30 yards in dense foliage or rough terrain and every 100 yards in open terrain or field. Tracking slows you to no faster than a jog (CRM: 3). Your base percentage may be modified either positively or negatively by the circumstances listed below. If you "loss the trail", you may backtrack and roll your Ability Check to pick it up again. If you fail on 3 consecutive rolls, you can't find the trail and will have to rely on someone else with this skill to find it again.

This skill also allows you to attempt to cover your tracks so someone else may not track you. If you roll **your** Ability Check with Wisdom successfully then whoever is following you will suffer a -30% on **their** Ability Check roll to track **you**.

Listed below are conditions and circumstances which will affect your base percentage for tracking. All negatives and bonuses are cumulative and adjust your **total** percentage:

Negatives			Bonuses	
1) Weather :	Mild Rain	= - 5%	1) If quarry is bleeding :	+10-30% depending on
	Heavy Rain	= -10%		how bad the bleeding is.
	Storm	= -25%		
2) Darkness :	Shadowy	= -30%	2) Quarry is running :	Hemar size = +30%
	Complete	= -40%	(CRM => 4)	Human size = +15%
3) Terrain :	Rocky	= -20%		
	Through River	= losses but	3) Terrain :	Sandy = +15%
		may pick up on other side.		Snowy = +30%
4) Opponent Covering Tracks = -30%			4) If you check trail frequently (Once per 15 or 50 yds)	
			+20% if you check twice as often.	

(Sp : +1/2 Wisdom score added to your Survival Skill percentage each specialization.
   1st: 1) Only receive -25% when Opponent is covering her tracks, unless she is Specialized.
      2) You may track while sitting on the back of a horse OR a Hemar may track while cantering
         (CRM: 4).
   2nd: A) Receive -20% if Opponent is covering her tracks, unless she is Double Specialized.
      B) A Krill may track while flying in the air (Height depends on the conditions of the tracks).)

Ventriloquism:

By making a successful Ability Check with Wisdom, you may "throw your voice" anywhere within 30 ft. Your voice will sound clear and will sound as if you are actually speaking from that location. You may do this for any length of time. If you miss the Ability Check, your voice won't be thrown to the correct location. If you miss your percentage by 25% or more, your position will be given away.

(Sp : +1/2 Wisdom score added to your Survival Skill percentage each specialization.
   1st: 1) You may throw your voice 45 feet.
      2) You are discovered only if you roll a 90% - 99% for your Survival Skill percentage.
   2nd: A) You may throw your voice 60 feet.
      B) You are discovered only if you roll a 99% for your Survival Skill percentage.)

Wrestling / Boxing:

See the Combat Section for complete details on how to use the Wrestling and Boxing Survival Skills.

This next skill may only be learned by any Spell Caster or Mentalist:

Color / Element / Discipline Master:

This survival skill allows you to change the damage rolled when you use an attack spell or skill. You may move ½ of the total die damage normally rolled into the base damage of the spell or skill.
Example 1: for Enchanter, Alchemist or Elementalist: Flame bolt 2 damage = 12+1d20, a Master may do 22+1d10.
Example 2: for Mentalists at 10 level: Searing Ray damage = 10+1d20, a Master may do 20+1d10.

The stipulation is you may only Master ONE Color, Plane or Discipline for each time you take the skill. The victim still gets a RER and if she succeeds, she will take ½ of the new base damage. The user of this skill will do more damage over time, but when a victim does succeed in a RER, he will actually take less damage on average.
(In Ex1, a victim making a successful RER would take 11+1d10 (max=21), instead of 6+1d20 (max=26)).

124

All of these next skills can be learned by anyone, but are required by some Occupations. All making or working skills that an Enchanter, Elementalist or Mentalist must learn are all basically the same, just the mediums are different. I've listed these next Skills with the Occupation that must learn it, but again – anyone may choose to acquire these Skills. For all of the skills listed below, if you roll higher than your percentage, you've constructed an item so poorly that it can't be used or enchanted. The lower the roll the higher quality it is, but any successful roll makes a usable item.

Also these skills may be used to repair damaged items. A Leather worker could repair damage to the leather part of a ½ suit of plated leather or a seamstress could repair a ripped cloak. As always, the lower the roll the better the repair job is but if your roll exceeds your percentage in the skill, you have botched the repair job.

When you specialize in these skills, you may add your full Will score to your Ability Check percentage, but a roll of 99% is always a complete failure of the job and the item can not be used or enchanted.

Leather working:

This skill teaches the Enchanter how to make leather items and it also teaches her to cure leather. The Enchanter must make or buy cured leather and construct the item completely. The larger and fancier the item the longer it will take to make. To construct a usable item, you must make a successful Ability Check with Will, and the lower the roll the better the quality of the item.
(Sp : Full Will score added to your Survival Skill percentage each specialization.)

Rope Making:

After learning this skill, the Enchanter must buy dried hemp or harvest it and then prepare the hemp. The character may then weave the rope himself. The Enchanter must roll an Ability Check with Will and the lower the roll the better the final product is. You may weave up to 50 foot of rope per day with only one successful Survival Skill check.
(Sp : Full Will score added to your Survival Skill percentage each specialization.)

Sewing:

The Enchanter must buy cloth and sew the item completely - if the item is a cloak then you must sew the collar, neck strap, back, and hem. The larger and fancier the item the more time it will take, but here are some basic sewing rates: a regular cloak in 1 day and a pair of gloves in 2 days. You must make an Ability Check with Will and the lower the roll the higher the quality.
(Sp : Full Will score added to your Survival Skill percentage each specialization.)

Woodworking:

An Enchanter may whittle 1 cubic foot per day with little detail and 6 cubic inches per day with a great amount of detail. (You don't have to do much whittling at all to make a club or staff). Make an Ability Check with Will and the lower the roll the higher the quality of the workmanship.
(Sp : Full Will score added to your Survival Skill percentage each specialization.)

Ring / Disk Construction:

The Elementalist must acquire the metal and the enchanted gem, then he can start making the Ring or Disk. You will need to carve the Ring or Disk from wax, melt the metal and pour it into a mold. Spin the apparatus, allow the metal to melt the wax and then harden, extract the rough form, clean the excess off the Ring or Disk, polish the gem setting and set the enchanted gem into it. This process takes at least 1 week and a vast amount of concentration, so no interruptions. Roll an Ability Check with Will to see if the Ring or Disk was made well, remember the lower the roll the better the quality of the Ring or Disk. A weeks worth of work decided in one roll so be lucky or specialize twice.
(Sp : Full Will score added to your Survival Skill percentage each specialization.)

Badge / Pin Construction:

A Mentalist must obtain the metal for the badge or pin. Then she must find a way to melt the metal and pour it into a relief mold made of oiled sand. You will also need to make the needle and hook of the same metal. Now solder the needle and hook onto the badge / pin and then clean it up by filling and polishing it. You may then use the badge / pin for the Embedding Skill. This entire process will take a full week to accomplish. A weeks worth of work decided in one roll so be lucky or specialize twice.
(Sp : Full Will score added to your Survival Skill percentage each specialization.)

Ability Increase:

If you don't wish to learn a Survival Skill, you can improve yourself physically or mentally by raising one of your Ability Scores! You may enhance one of the following attributes, if you spend one of your Survival Skill Slots.

ABILITY
1) **Endurance**
2) **Agility**
3) **Strength**
4) **Intellect**
5) **Wisdom**

You may not raise any one ability score by more than 3 points (one with the 1st Ability Increase and two more if you Specialize twice).

NOTE: If you raise your Endurance, Intellect or Wisdom, your Will may increase.

Improve Charging Rate:

If you use 1 Survival Skill slot you will increase your Charging Rate by 1 CRM each time you take this skill. A Human goes from a CRM of 3 (15 ft/sec) to a CRM of 4 (20 ft/sec) by using one Skill Slot. A Hemar's galloping or a Krill's flying rate increases from a CRM of 4 (20 ft/sec) to a CRM of 5 (25 ft/sec) by using one Skill Slot.

(Sp : Each time you specialize, you increase your Charging Rate multiple by 1.

The fastest a Human can "run" is a CRM of 6 or 30 ft/sec with 2 specializations.

The fastest a Hemar or Krill can gallop or fly is a CRM of 7 or 35 ft/sec with 2 Specializations.)

NOTE2: When a Krill learns this skill, she is taught how to **FLY** faster, not run. A Krill can only ever run at a maximum CRM of 3 or a charging rate of 15 ft/sec.

ADDITIONAL OCCUPATIONS & SKILLS

There are many Occupations and Skills that are not listed in the previous section. The reason is: these other jobs and areas of expertise fall into one of three categories:

1) They are too mundane or boring to be used by your Character   : Bartender or Housekeeper.
2) They are too specialized or time consuming to be used by a character   : Weaver or Blacksmith.
3) They are too powerful for one character to use   : King or Council Member.

Here I will give a brief description of some of the Occupations and Skills that are not usable by players. This is primarily for the Ref.'s use.

Smithy (Blacksmith)   : This is a common enough job, but he gains some very specialized skills. After 5 years of experience he is able to make Ransium Items and after 10 years he can make Langor items.

Sailor or Pirate   : Professional Sailors are very dedicated and set out on voyages for long periods of time. The Pirate on the other hand is just as dedicated to acquiring your treasures (those scoundrels), besides they make great challenges for higher level characters.

Weaver   : A Weaver is a specialized type of Enchanter. They gain the ability to fashion all items listed in the Enchanter section at 2 spots better than a regular Enchanter. Ie: They are able to Enchant everything up to leather, silver and iron after 1 year in their field and they are able to Enchant items they create with Langor in them after 5 years of experience! (We all need someone to look up to.)

Cost of Items made by a Weaver in Silver Pieces
1) Items with a single spell or with Spell Points pumped into them =
Item cost + (Spell Points / 4) + 5.
2) Items with Mithral or Americanium Strands woven into them =
Item cost + (Mithral=+10 or Americanium=+100) + (Spell Points / 4) + 5
3) Items with a Gem set into them (NOTE: these items must already have Mithral of Amer. Strands woven into it). Woven item cost (#2 above) + Gem Cost

Seer   : A Seer is also another specialized type of Enchanter. They gain all vision type spells plus additional spells that reveal the past and present. They have the ability the employ spells that grant them the powers of psychometry, which is the ability to analyze the history of objects and substances.
a) 'See' general location of a friend in the present or get a vague description of your future.
b) 'See' past of friend, use psychometry on an object or get a general description of your future.
c) 'See' general location of an enemy in the present (if he is not shielded) or get a broad description of your future.
Cost of Seer's time: a) 50 Silver   b) 100 Silver   c) 250 Silver

Apothecary   : An Apothecary is someone who obtains mundane herbs and brews elixirs which have many effects. They can concoct elixirs to speed healing, draw out poisons, cure headaches and kill pain to name just a few.
Cost of remedy: Speed Healing = 10 Silver (+2d10 for nights rest, not 1d10)   Cure Poison = 50 Silver
Headache Cure = 5 Silver (Plus cures a hangover!)   Pain Cure (12 hrs) = 25 Silver
NOTE2: The Cure Poison elixir is for a specific type of poison. If used on another type of poison, the elixir will only slow the poisons progress to 20% of normal.

Gem Cutter   : A Gem Cutter works with gems BEFORE they are enchanted. If you find, dig up or acquire a gem before it has been enchanted, you can take it to a Gem Cutter to be reduced in size. The Gem Cutter can cut a gem from any size down to ¼ Karat, but they charge per cut. Each cut will reduce the size of the gem by ½. So you could cut a 1 Karat gem down to 4 ¼ Karat gems but it would take 3 cuts or cutting a 2 Karat gem to 4 ½ Karat gems would also take 3 cuts. The costs are priced in silver pieces per cut:
Colored Quartz = 2;   True Gems = 4;   Opaque Quartz = 6;   Diamond/Onyx Gems= 8
Most bankers are also Gem Cutters.
Banks: The five functions of banks are:
(1) Money Exchange = Free.   (2) Cutting Gems = Prices Above.
(3) Safely holding your money = Free.   (4) Transfer of Funds = cost of travel.
(2) Buying / Selling Non-Enchanted Gems.   NOTE3: See page 324 for Details.

BIRTH GIFTS

: Rules for Experienced Players :

Everyone has a chance to be born with a Birth Gift. The enchantment of the land is so intense that the miracle of birth may focus itself into a "gift". A Birth Gift is purely magical and may work to your character's advantage or disadvantage. Everyone may roll on the Gift Percentage Table <u>ONCE</u> when they <u>initially create</u> a character. I allow everyone to make their own decision about rolling on the table, because there is a definite chance of receiving a magical gift that is not helpful. I suggest that inexperienced players skip this stage of their "character's development.".

First roll a percentage on the Gift Percentage Table. This will tell you **if** you gain a Gift and **if** it is Beneficial, Neutral, or Harmful. Then you roll 2d12 ("Two D Twelve" - or two 12-sided dice) and add the results together. Use this number on the particular Birth Gift Table – Beneficial, Neutral, or Harmful – to find out which gift your character will have for the rest of his or her life.

Gift Percentage Table		Gift Uses / Day Table	
01 - 20%	Beneficial Gift	(A) = 1/day	(B) = 2/day
21 - 39%	None	(C) = 3/day	(D) = 4/day
40 - 60%	Neutral Gift	(E) = 5/day	
61 - 79%	None	(F) = 1/day per level of character	
80 - 99%	Harmful Gift		
100%	Pick which table to roll on.	constant = some Gifts are "ON" all the time.	

Beneficial Birth Gift	roll	2d12	
Neutral	Birth Gift	roll	2d12
Harmful	Birth Gift	roll	2d12

NOTE: Some Gifts provide Resistance to certain forms of attack or certain phenomenon.
  All gifts that Bestow resistances grant you a:
  1) +25% to your Resist Enchantment Roll (RER) percentage total.
  2) Successful RER = ½ Base Damage.
  3) Unsuccessful RER = Full damage.

NOTE2: Most damage producing Birth Gifts have their Base Damage based on the Character's level.
  If your character is 5th level, (+2/Lvl)+1d6 would mean the damage done is equal to 10+1d6 EP.

NOTE3: All damage producing Gifts have a Use / Day of (B) = twice per day, but they all may be used in "one shot" for double damage and twice the Range stated (of course this may only be done ONCE Per Day).

NOTE4: All Gifts require NO Concentration Time to activate them!
  They may be used "at a drop of a Silver Piece" in just 1 Action!

NOTE5: All Victims are entitled to a Resist Enchantment Roll from any and all magical effects or damage caused by a gift.

NOTE6: The Ref. may implement the Gift at any time during the "life" of the Character.
  As a character playing the game, you may know of your Gift from birth or the Ref. may elect to postpone the discovery of your Gift until a critical or stressful moment in your life.

NOTE7: Some Gifts are only usable a certain number of times each day. This is specified by a LETTER in parenthesis in the Gift's description and these are listed on the Gift Uses / Day table directly above.

KEY:	EP	=	Endurance Points
	Dam	=	Damage done to your Opponent.
	R:	=	Range - How far the Gift can be cast.
	D:	=	Duration the Gift lasts after it is activated. (Note: some Gifts are instantaneous)
	AOE:	=	Area of Effect - Area, Individual, or what the Gift affects.
	+1/L	=	Read as : "Plus One per Level"

BENEFICIAL BIRTH GIFTS

Die Roll	Gift	Uses / Day
2	Increased Stat	Constant
3	Magically Healthy	Constant
4	Extraordinary Sense	Constant
5	Healing	(B) OR (A) – depending on how used.
6	Speak with and Command	(C) / (A) or (F) – depending on what picked.
7	Summon Animals	(B)
8	Polymorph	(B)
9	Fancy Footwork	(B) & (B)
10	Vision	(C)
11	See and Do	Constant
12	Commander	(B) = Order Spell
13	Lucky	Constant
14	Chameleon Ability	(E)
15	Empathy	(E) & Constant
16	Telekinesis	(D)
17	Psychic Link to an Element	(B) & (B) (roll a 1d8 for a specific Element)
18	Blast of Breath	(B)
19	Bubble of Force	(C)
20	Thunder Clap	(B)
21	Invisible Extra Arm	Constant
22	Shrink or Grow	Shrink = (C) Grow = (B)
23	Shield Yourself: Pick one.	(B)
24	Pick Your own	WITHIN REASON & REFEREE WILL SET LIMITS COMPARABLE TO THOSE LISTED IN THIS SECTION!

Increased Stat: Pick any one ability and add +3 points. (All abilities have a Max of 20)
You have a 25% chance to increase 2 abilities by +2 points EACH.

Magically Healthy: You initially gain a +1 to your Endurance Score and a +10 to your EP!
You may go 4 days without food or water and you Age at ½ normal rate.

Extraordinary Sense: You may pick any ONE sense (you rate a 25% chance of 2 senses being heightened).   The benefits are listed below.

Sight = -20% SPT roll	Smell = Track by Scent
Hearing= +20% Detect Ambush	Taste = Detect Poison
Touch = Information of an object's past – psychometry.	

Healing: This Gift can be used either 2/day [(B)] OR 1/day [(A)].
2/day: Heal 40 EP+1/Level, Heal Paralysis, or Heal Blindness
OR   1/day: Heal Disease or Heal Poison
i.e.   If you heal someone's Blindness, you can't Heal Poison that day.

Speak w/Command: You are able to Speak With ONE of the below listed things. (Pick ONE)
If you pick either an Animal or a Plant, you may Command it 1/day.

Animal:	Speak With = (C)	Command = (A)
Plant:	Speak With = (C)	Command = (A)
Inanimate Object:	Speak With = (F)	

Summon Animal: Your are able to summon to your side one type of common animal.
The Summoned animals will be magically transported to your side and will be magically returned to it's original location at the end of the Duration.
You are able to converse with the Animals summoned and they will obey you.
Summon EITHER: 4 creatures with less then 30 EP   D: 30 mins.
OR   2 creatures with less then 60 EP   Uses: 2/day (B)

Polymorph: Pick one small Animal, Plant, or Inanimate Object to polymorph into.
You may only Polymorph into that particular thing.
You may stay in this form for up to 2 hours.   [Uses: (B)]

Fancy Footwork: You gain a +2 to your initial Agility score.
You may also add a +1 to your CRM for a D: 30 min., [Uses: (B)]   and
You are able to Jump=30'+2'/ Level forward or 20'+1'/Level up or backward [Uses: (B)]
If you are able to make a running start, you can add 20' to your forward jump.

129

Vision: You are able to choose between Telescopic, Magnification, or X-ray.
You are able to use the chosen type of vision 3 times per day for 10 minutes each.
[Uses: (C)].

See and Do: You gain DOUBLE your Initial number of Weapons and Survival Skills.
All "Action Type" Survival Skill Ability Check rolls: you subtract a -25% from your roll!

Commander: You have an Enchanted "Commanding Aura!"
You initially gain a +2 to your Wisdom & a +4 to your Charm Score (if applicable).
You are able to cast an Order Spell twice per day.   [Uses: (B)].

Lucky: Never roll a 90-99 (Automatic Miss) on Strike Placement Table (SPT).
You never Slip, drop a weapon or item, or say the wrong thing.
You also gain a +25% to your PTE total.   (All stated limits still apply – can't exceed 85%.)

Chameleon Ability: While you are not moving, you are able to magically blend into your surroundings, so as
to become virtually invisible. While moving at a CRM: 1, you Opponents must subtract
-30% from their Detect Ambush rolls to see or hear you.   [Uses: (E)]
A S/A gets +30% to his Conceal Self and this happens automatically when you sleep.

Empathy: Same as spell and uses = (E)   D: 30 min/L   R: 20' + 2'/L
You gain +25% added to your Detect Ambush total (Constant).

Telekinesis: Same as spell. Uses per day are (D).   R: 10'/L   D: 15 min   AOE: 50lbs/L

Psychic Link to an Roll a 1d8 to ascertain which Elemental Plane you are linked to:
 Elemental Plane: 1)Air 2)Water 3)Earth 4)Fire 5)Fog 6)Smoke 7)Lava 8)Mud

Air	= I) Wind Blot	Dam=(+2/Lvl)+1d10 (***)	II) Levitate	
Water	= I) Water Bolt	Dam=(+2/Lvl)+1d12 (~~~)	II) Water Adaptation	
Earth	= I) Stone Storm	Dam=(+2/Lvl)+1d8	II) Earth Armor +20%	
Fire	= I) Flame Bolt	Dam=(+2/Lvl)+1d20	II) Flaming Hand or Weapon	
Fog	= I) Fog Jet	Dam=(+1/Lvl)+1d6 (^^^)	II) Fog Wall	
Smoke	= I) Smoke Jet	Dam=(+1/Lvl)+1d6 (""")	II) Smoke Adaptation	
Lava	= I) Lava Pool	Dam=(+2/Lvl)+2d12	II) Lava Walk	
Mud	= I) Mud Pool	Touch = (as Spell)	II) Resist Poisons	

Both (I) & (II) may be used twice per day.   [Uses: (B) & (B)]

Blast of Breath: You are able to cause a Blast of Cold or Hot Breath. Pick only one.
Dam=(+2/Lvl)+1d12 damage   R: 20'+1'/L   AOE: 1'-10'cone.
Opponent falls 20% of time.   Uses / Day = (B).

Bubble of Force: As Spell, Except: May cast on yourself, but Duration is 3 Attacks (15 sec).
R: 20'+1'/L   D: 2 min (when cast on someone else)
AOE: 15' diameter bubble   [Uses: (C)]

Thunder Clap: AOE:10' semi-circle to front. Victims stunned 5-12 Actions (roll 4+1d8).   Uses / Day = (B).

Invisible Extra Arm: Located under Regular Arm.   Do Anything a Regular arm may do.
If caught in a Detect Enchantment spell, you must make a Ability Check with Will or
your invisible arm will glow.

Shrink or Grow: You must Pick one only.   The change occurs in 1 Action.
Shrink = 1-inch tall w/ 1" mass   (C) D: 20 min.   EP: Same.
Grow = x2 size   w/ x2 mass   (B) D: 5 min.   EP bonus: (End Score x 2).

Shield Yourself: You may pick any one of the three listed below: D: 60 min
1) 30% Melee shield   (B)
2) 30% Projectile shield   (B)
3) Shield Magic   (B)   (Only pick **1** classification of spell)

Pick Your own: WITHIN REASON!   Referee will set Limits!   Don't allow a Gift to get away from you.

All spells are the same as stated in their description, except where noted in Gift's Description.
(***)   10% Fall and Possible "Dust Bolt".
(~~~)   15% Fall and Pure Water.
(^^^)   D: 2 min.   4 cubic feet per Attack.
(""")   D: 2 min.   2 cubic feet per Attack. Victim may be Asphyxiated.

NEUTRAL BIRTH GIFT

Die Roll	Gift	Uses / Day
2	Partially Immune to Enchantment	Constant
3	Cast Sound	(E)
4	Light	(E)
5	Slide	(B)
6	Natural Runner	(B)
7	Fast Hands	Constant
8	Insomniac	Constant
9	Can't be Killed by Magic	Constant
10	Can't be Killed by Physical Attack	Constant
11	Can't Make any Sounds	Constant
12	Never Gets Drunk	Constant
13	Boomerang	Constant
14	Musical	Constant
15	Fall	Constant
16	See Enchantment	(E)
17	See Life	(E)
18	Initiate Breeze	(E)
19	Can't be Killed by Male or Female	Constant
20	Temp Ability Burst	(B) & (B)
21	Resist Illusion	(B)
22	Invisibility or Visibility	(B) or Constant - depends on characters MR.
23	Choose ONE Neutral Gift	Please choose any one Neutral Gift listed above.
24	Pick Your own	WITHIN REASON & REFEREE WILL SET LIMITS. A Neutral Gift should be relatively non-powerful (Cast Sound) or have a downside (Boomerang).

Partially Immune to Enchantment: +25% Bonus added to your RER total, but you can't Cast any Class (C), (D), or (E) spells.

Cast Sound: Sound picked at casting time (Footfall, laugh, etc.) (E=5/day)
R: 20'+2'/L   D: 10 min.

Light: Ball of light may be of any color, chosen at casting time.   (E)
R: 5'+1'/L   D: 3 hr.   AOE: 10 'rad

Slide: Character able to Slide over any type of surface. (B)**
R: 20' + 2'/L,   Rate = Your CRM or Your CRM+1 on Downward Slope.

Natural Runner: +1 CRM (B) & Run for twice as long, but you jog everywhere.

Fast Hands: Initially add +1 to your Agility Score.
Able to **throw** <u>twice</u> as many projectiles as normal per Attack.
Able to make "Secret Pockets" and +10% to physical S/A abilities totals.
You are always very jittery and Automatically Miss on a SPT roll of 85-99%.

Insomniac: Can't sleep for 10 days, then must sleep for 10 hrs.
Nothing can wake you up except Pain, but then you are groggy (+10% on ALL Rolls) until you receive a full 10 hours sleep.

Can't be Killed by Magic: You cannot drop below 10 EP do to Magical damage, but you may only cast Class (A) spells.

Can't be Killed by any Physical Attack: You cannot drop below 10 EP do to any physical attack, but you can't Specialize in any Weapon.

Can't Make any Sounds: Can't speak, moan, laugh, yell, etc. Even riding and swordplay are completely silent.

Never Gets Drunk: Immune to and automatically recognizes all orally taken Poisons or drugs, but you can't Taste anything else.

Boomerang: Any Item you Throw Comes Back to you if it misses: If you have a free hand and 1 Action, you may make an Ability Check with Agility to catch the item.
NOTE: If you don't have a Free hand or extra Action, then roll your PTE!

Musical: Either Sing or Play an Instrument as a virtuoso (see Survival Skills), but if you attempt the other, even your friends tell you they would rather listen to a steal nail scrapped across a chalk board.

Fall: You may fall any distance less than 1000 ft and take no Damage.
If you hit the ground from over 1000', your character automatically Dies. (Period)

See Enchantment: You are able to "See" the colored glow surrounding Enchanted Objects, Gems, Creatures, ect.
Please remember, the color perceived depends on the Enchantment encountered.
R: 30'+1'/L   D: 20 min   AOE: Everyone within Range   (E)

See Life: You are able to "See" a yellowish glow around any living Persons, Creatures, or Plants even if they are concealed or invisible.
R: 30'+1'/L   D: 20 min   AOE: Everyone within Range   (E)

Initiate Breeze: Initiate a breeze in any direction you wish, even canceling out the 'prevailing' winds.
The breeze you initiate moves at 25 mph.
R : 50' + 1'/Level   D: 1 hr.   (E)
You may only hold your breath for: {(End Score + Will Score + 1d10) * 2} seconds.   Ref Note: Max = 100 sec.

Can't be Killed by Male or Female: You cannot drop below 10 EP do to any damage inflicted by either a Male or a Female.
You may pick which gender your Gift effects.
Can't experience True Love or enter into Marriage.

Temp Ability Burst: Pick ONLY ONE ability (except Endurance) and add a +4 to your score for the Duration. (B)
You may burst the chosen Ability for 5 minutes twice per day. (B)
You must initially subtract two (2) points from the converse ability.
Converse abilities: Strength vs. Agility; Intellect vs. Wisdom; Charm vs. Beauty.

Resist Illusion: This Gift is automatic and is activated twice per day. (C)
This is different from the other Gifts in that it provides a bonus to your RER verses the FIRST three Illusions you encounter during the day.
You gain a +25% bonus to your RER.
May never cast a "See Enchantment" Spell.

Invisibility/Visibility: The Enchantment that this Gift purveys depends on your Morality Rating.
If your MR >= 10; you may become Invisible twice per day (B).
If your MR <= 9; you are magically Visible. If there is any way to see you, you will be seen. You always stand out in a crowd.

** You may not Slide uphill, but you may slide over any surface (this is a controlled slide).
i.e.:   slide over ice, mud, water, lava, a wooden beam, a rope, ect.
You incur no penalty to your SPT or PTE rolls while sliding.

HARMFUL BIRTH GIFTS

Die Roll	Gift	Uses / Day	
2	Reduced Stat	Constant	
3	Poor Sense	Constant	- roll a 1d6 to choose.
4	Prejudiced vs. some Race	Constant	
5	Clumsy	Constant	
6	Phobia of Darkness	Constant	
7	Phobia of Heights	Constant	
8	Claustrophobia	Constant	
9	Phobia of Open Areas	Constant	
10	Alcoholic	Constant	
11	Asthma	Constant	
12	Facial Problem	Constant	
13	Body Odor	Constant	
14	Loses 1 Item/Day	Constant	
15	Follower	Constant	
16	Born without a Hand	Constant	
17	Born without a Big Toe	Constant	
18	Born with only One Eye	Constant	
19	Magical Pain	Constant	
20	Intense Fear to one Creature type	Constant	- roll a 1d6 to choose.
21	Unlucky	Constant	
22	Unlucky Vs. Projectiles	Constant	
23	Smoker	Constant	
24	Extra Vulnerable to One particular Effect	Constant	- roll a 1d12 to choose.

Reduced Stat: Pick any One Ability and reduce it by a -3.
>You have a 25% chance that 2 ability scores are decreased by a -2.

Poor Sense: You must roll a 1d6 and you gain the sense rolled, re-roll a 6.
>(1) Sight = While using Projectile Weapons, your Opponent gains a +25% to his PTE total.
>(2) Hearing = +25% to be Ambushed, can't hear well in crowded room or on a battle field.
>(3) Smell = Can't smell anything!
>(4) Taste = Can't taste anything!
>(5) Touch= You have a low tolerance for pain, so you take 10% more EP damage from all attacks.

Prejudiced against: 1) Human   2) Hemar   3) Krill   ---   Pick ONE.
>Won't associate with that race and may pick fights with anyone of that Race.
>Initial score penalties: -4 to Wisdom, -4 to Intellect & -5 to Charm.

Clumsy: -2 on your initial Agility Score.
>(1) + 10% to all Opponent's PTE totals.
>(2) + 20% to all Climbing percentages.
>(3) Auto miss on any SPT roll of 85% - 99%.

Phobia of Darkness: While you are in Darkness, your Opponent gains a +25% to all PTE totals and
>you have a -10% to all your character's RER percentages totals.
>You won't stand watch at night.

Phobia of Heights: While you are on High (above 20'), your Opponent gains a +25% to all PTE totals and
>you have a -10% to all your character's RER percentages totals.
>You won't fly and hate to climb.

Claustrophobia: While you are underground or in a tunnel (less than 20' wide), your Opponent gains a
>+25% to all PTE totals you have a -10% to all your character's RER
>percentages totals.
>You won't put items in a box, trunk or safe.

Phobia Of Open Areas: While you are outside (more than 50' wide), your Opponent gains a +25% to all
>PTE totals you have a -10% to all your character's RER percentages totals.
>Will not sleep or stand watch in an open field, ect.

Alcoholic: -1 to your initial Intellect Score. Your character must consume at least 1 pint per day OR
>Withdrawal = +25% to any Opponent's PTE totals and
>- 1% to your character's RER percentage total **per day** you are dry.
>-1 point from your Endurance score **per 2 days,** you are 'dry'.
>[Remember to adjust your EP accordingly]

Asthma:	-2 on your initial Endurance Score.
	Any prolonged Physical Activity = 10% chance of Coughing Fit for 1d10 Actions.
Facial Problem:	You have permanently recurring Acne = -5 Beauty **or**
	a permanent Wart on Nose or Face = -3 Beauty.
	(This is evident in any and all forms. Ie. polymorph, disguise, ect)
Body Odor:	Your character has this constant problem: -2 initial Charm Score. All Animals and
	Savages in the Blood Frenzy, gain a +25% to Ambush and track you.
Loses 1 Item/Day:	You loose a Random object from your inventory once per day. The only objects you
	can't loose are ones that have been given to you by someone.
Follower:	-2 to your initial Wisdom score.
	You character is very Indecisive and will Follow strong willed people.
Born w/o a Hand:	You may not use any 2-Handed Weapons and may only use a shield if it is strapped to
	your arm.
Born w/o Big Toe:	-1 on your initial Agility Score and you have a -10% to all your PTE total verse any Strike.
Born w/ One Eye:	-2 on your initial Beauty Score (this eye is completely White) and you cannot judge
	distances.
	Also loose a -10% on your Detect Ambush total & on all Detect Trap rolls.
Magical Pain:	You roll on the SPT to determine the Area affected.
	-1 on your character's initial Endurance Score.
	Extra Penalties from Ref. Examples: -1d6 EP, -1 Str, -1 Agl, -1 CRM, etc.

Intense Fear to one Creature type: **roll 1d6**

1) Undead   2) Snakes   3) Spiders   4) Cats   5) Rats and Mice   6) Goblins & Ghouls

Fear – roll a percentage to find out what happens when you come in contact with the stated creature.

Percentage	Reaction	
01 - 25%	Your fear causes you to viciously attack attempting to eradicate the creatures.	
	D: Until all creatures that you are fearful of are eradicated.	
26 - 50%	Stand still – unable to take any action or evade any attack.	D: 1d10 Actions.
51 - 75%	Scream and/or cry while slowly backing away as you Beg for Mercy.	D: 1d8 Actions.
76 - 99%	RUN AWAY, RUN AWAY!	D: 1d20 Actions
	Percentage of dropping what you are holding = 50% - (2% per level of experience)	
100%	React Normally.	

Unlucky:	You totally miss your Target on all rolls between 80-99% on the SPT.
	-1 to your initial Charm Score.
	Add +5% to all RER's.
	25% likely to make a sound at a bad time or say the wrong thing to the wrong person.

Unlucky Vs. Projectiles:	-10% to your PTE total verse any Projectile.
	Any Opponent who uses a Projectile weapon against anyone in your party and
	rolls a 99% for their SPT roll, that Projectile will automatically hit you!
	(Bummer!)

Smoker:	-2 to your initial Endurance Score. You're always Edgy - can't sit still.
	Your character must smoke at least 1 pack per day OR
	Withdrawal = +25% to any Opponent's PTE totals.
	+10% to all of your SPT rolls.
	- 1% to your RER percentage total **per day** you don't light up.

Extra Vulnerable to One particular Effect: **roll 1d12**

1) Fire	2) Cold	3) Lightning	4) Paralysis
5) Acid	6) Harmful Gases and Mists	7) Poisons	8) Mind Attacks
9) Any natural Ench. Ability	10) All Enchanted Creatures	11) Illusions	12) one Enchantment type**

**: an Enchantment type is by color. Roll a 1d10 to decide the Enchantment's color.

Any Vulnerability =   -25% on **all** your character's RER percentages totals verses the Vulnerability.

You receive an extra 1d10 points of Damage **and**

you are affected for an extra 1d4 Actions. (where applicable)

NOT TO BE PUBLISHED - "it's a Gift" - Gifts are the purest and strongest types of Enchantment.

TRAVELING RATE

All people and creatures walk at about the same rate, but this isn't what we're concerned with. What we are concerned with is the maximum speed something can move. We call this maximum speed, the Charging Rate (CR) of the person or creature. The CR is based on the universal walking rate of all creatures which is 5 feet per second or about 7.33 miles per hour.

All creatures and people have Basic Charging Rates. The Basic Rates for creatures are stated under their descriptions. The Basic Rates for people are listed below :

1) A Human's basic CR is 3 times the walking rate or 15 ft/sec.
2) A Hemar's basic CR is 4 times the walking rate or 20 ft/sec.
3) A Krill's basic CR, like all flying things, is figured when he flies, but is still based off the walking rate. The Krill's normal "flying" rate is 4 times the walking rate or 20 ft/sec.
(The fastest a Krill may ever RUN is 15 ft/sec).

These Basic Rates can be improved with practice and time. A wild creature increases their CR with age and a domestic creature (like a dog or horse) can improve it's CR if it receives the proper training from a Trainer. The only way a person can improve his or her CR is also to receive training. To receive training you must take the 'Improve Charging Rate' Survival Skill. When you learn this Survival Skill, you will improve your CR by 5 ft/sec, either your running rate - in the case of Humans and Hemars - or your flying rate - in the case of a Krill. You may learn this survival skill a total of three times, just like any other. This would be learning it once and specializing in it twice. If you specialize in this Survival Skill Twice or put 3 points into it, you may move at these maximum rates:

1) Human's maximum CR (running)   = 30 ft/sec.
2) Hemar's maximum CR (galloping)   = 35 ft/sec.
3) Krill's maximum CR (flying)   = 35 ft/sec.

Now that you know all about Charging Rates, I'd like to discuss a simpler way to handle these rates.

This simplification deals with the use of what I call Charging Rate Multiples (CRM). You'll notice that your character moves at rates that are multiples of 5. We'll make a CRM of 1 equal 5 ft/sec and a CRM of 2 equal to (2*5) ft/sec or 10 ft/sec. You just need to multiply a CRM by 5 to convert it back to ft/sec. This means that a CRM of 10 reflects 50 ft/sec (10*5 ft/sec) - this also is the CRM of a cheetah running at top speed (47 ft/sec = 70 miles/hour). A complete list of CR, CRM, and how they relate to rates in miles/hour is at the end of this section. The CRM's for every creature is listed under its individual description, located in the Creatures section, and the CRM's for people are recorded next :

		Feet / Second	CRM	Feet / Attack or Feet / 5 Seconds
1) Human Basic CR	(running)	= 15	3	75
Human Maximum CR	(running)	= 30	6	150
2) Hemar Basic CR	(galloping)	= 20	4	100
Hemar Maximum CR	(galloping)	= 35	7	175
3) Krill Basic CR	(flying)	= 20	4	100
Krill Maximum CR	(flying)	= 35	7	175

If you are using CRM's to keep track of movement in battle (and other situations), you can simplify things even more if you mark off your maps in "squares" of 5 ft. Now if you are using a Human with a CR of 15 ft/sec (CRM = 3), and you are swiftly retreating from a Bear with a CR of 20 ft/sec (CRM = 4). The Human can move 3 spaces for every Attack that he retreats and the Bear moves 4 spaces for every Attack that it follows. You can see the Human is in trouble. If he survives he may wish to learn the Survival Skill Improved Charging Rate which increases his CRM to 4. If taken three times - "spend" a total of 3 Survival Skill slots, 1 to learn the skill and 2 to specialize in it - he may increase his CRM to a maximum of 6 and out run the bear every time.

Conversions:

CRM	feet / sec.	feet / Attack	miles / hour	CRM	feet / sec.	feet / Attack	miles / hour
1	5	25	7.3	2	10	50	14.7
3	15	75	22.0	4	20	100	29.3
5	25	125	36.7	6	30	150	44.0
7	35	175	51.3	8	40	200	58.7
9	45	225	66.0	10	50	250	73.3
11	55	275	80.7	12	60	300	88.0
13	65	325	95.3	14	70	350	102.7
15	75	375	110.0	16	80	400	117.4
17	85	425	124.7	18	90	450	132.0
19	95	475	139.3	20	100	500	146.7

A Bonus and a Penalty for Charging:

When you charge with a weapon, you get extra damage. The damage is an extra 1d6 per CRM above **2** that you are moving. You must be moving **faster** than a CR of 10 ft/sec or a CRM of 2 to get any bonus at all. When you charge you loose your Agility Bonus on your PTE total.

Example - If a Hemar is Double Specialized in Improve Charging Rate (he has taken the Survival Skill 3 times), he can charge 35 ft/sec and has a maximum CRM of 7. When he charges into battle at his full CRM, he can do an extra (7-2=5 or) 5d6 EP Damage (added to regular weapon damage and his STR. Dam. Bonus). As he charges at his intended victim, his looses his Agility Bonus on his PTE until he has completed his charge. This penalty is applied to all PTE rolls regardless of the attacker's relative position to the Charging Hemar. Ie. The Hemar's victim or one of the victim's companions.

COMBAT

All smart adventurers know that most misunderstandings can by remedied through conversation and compromise. But, unfortunately, sometimes the other guy - who is wrong of course - won't admit it so you must take action, or maybe you must defend a beautiful damsel, or you must protect your village from marauders, etc. Whatever the reason, there comes a time when you are compelled to take up arms.

There are several types of combat: Projectile, Melee or Hand-to-Hand, and Spell Casting.

Projectile combat occurs when something is thrown, hurled, or shot. The distance that separates you from your enemies varies with the type of projectile weapon that is being used.

Melee or Hand-to-hand combat refers to combat using hand held weapons, Mother Nature's gifts (fists, claws, teeth, etc.), or wrestling. Wrestling can be used to cause pain or to incapacitate your opponent. A person's fist does 1d6 Endurance Points damage plus any Strength bonuses you have due to your STR score.   **NOTE:** All weapons have a minimum Strength requirement to wield them.

The casting of spells can be done at anytime, either during an adventure, downtime, or combat. The Caster must follow all of the rules for casting a spell, which are listed in the Spell Section. If the Caster is disturbed during the Concentration Time of the spell, i.e. he looses his concentration, the spell is not cast. "Disturbed" means taking harsh damage (more than 50% of his EP total), being dazed or stunned, ect. Remember it is possible for Warriors, Spies / Assassins and Mentalists to cast Class (A) spells from the Enchanter / Alchemist spell list - if they meet the Intellect requirements.

Projectiles and hand held weapons affect only a specific area of the body. When you use one of these forms of attack, you must roll on the Strike Placement Table (SPT) - Located later in this section. A spell affects *EVERYTHING* within it's Area of Effect (AOE), so you don't roll on the SPT. Anyone affected by a spell does get to roll a Resist Enchantment Roll (RER) to resist part or all of the effects of the spell and also a successful RER allows the victim to take ½ the base damage done by the spell.

FACTS ABOUT ACTIONS:

All characters have a TOTAL number of ACTIONS that they may use in **one 5 second period or Attack**.

Every character receives a specified number of Actions per Attack. The total number of Actions per Attack depends on the character's Occupation and Level. These total number of Actions are separated into Strikes and Parries - which are different for every Occupation. Anyone may elect to use an Action to do something other than Strike or Parry - such as say a Trigger Word, start concentrating on a spell, or move during battle, etc. - but you may never exceed your total number of actions.

Example: A 5th level Warrior rates 1 Strike and 2 Parries (or a total of 3 Actions). He may use these to strike with a sword and parry with that same sword - this uses 2 Actions, he has 1 Action left for movement.

   OR   He may elect to use 1 Strike Action and swing the sword, 1 Parry Action to employ his Shield and use his last action to say a Trigger Word and activate one of his Enchanted Items.

   OR   His companion a 5th level Enchanter (3 Attacks = 1 Strike and 2 Parry Actions) may elect to use 1 Parry Action for movement, 1 Parry Action to concentrate on a Class (A) spell and his Strike Action to say the Trigger Word and cast the spell.

When you are successfully struck by a weapon, or affected by most spells, you lose Endurance Points (EP). If your character falls to ZERO Endurance Points (EPs), he must make an Ability Check with Will score, to remain Conscious. If you remain Conscious and your wounds permit, you may still use Trigger Words, Potions, Pills, etc; but you can't concentrate well enough to cast a spell or strike with a weapon. Your character expires when he falls to a negative number of Endurance Points equal to his Endurance Score through loss of blood caused by wounds.

NOTE2: Ability Check = Ability score x 3.   Success = any percentage roll that is less then or equal to the calculated number.

NOTE3: You <u>always</u> rate a PTE or a RER verses <u>every</u> Strike or spell - even if you have used all your Actions for <u>that</u> Attack (5 second period).

STEPS FOR COMBAT

Combat can be between individuals or by opposing forces, either way there are certain steps to follow.

1) The first step of combat is to determine which side seizes the initial action - the 'Initiative' - or which side goes first. This is done by "rolling for the Initiative". The players elect 1 person to roll a 12-sided dice and the Ref. rolls one for the opposing force. The side with the highest roll becomes the "Attackers" for **this** 5-second period (or this "Attack"). The loser / lu-who-who-whoo-serss of the Initiative Roll become the "Defenders" for **this** Attack.

NOTE: Because only one person needs to make the Initiative Roll for the entire party (or group of Companions) prior to each Attack, players take turns making this roll. If you win, you keep on rolling Initiative every Attack until you lose, then you pass the honor onto one your teammates.

2) The "Attackers" may use any or all of their *Actions* that they rate according to their Level and Occupation.
   a) If your character strikes with a weapon, you must roll on the Strike Placement Table (SPT) to ascertain if and where you hit your opponent.
   b) If your character wishes to cast a spell, you must first concentrate for the specified number of Actions, then you say the Trigger Word or Phrase which costs 1 additional Action, and finally spend the Spell Points & Endurance Points required. These specifications are listed under the spell's description. You may use both Strike and/or Parry slots to do this, but you may only cast ONE Offensive spell per Attack.
   c) If your character wishes to move, it takes him the entire 5 seconds, or Attack, to move the entire distance stated by your CRM. (distance covered per Action = CRM / total number of Actions you rate.)

The "Defenders" must make either Percentage To Evade (PTE) rolls or Resist Enchantment Rolls (RER), depending on how they are attacked.

→ You always receive your Agility Bonus to your PTE total, unless you are adversely effected by some means. Max = 10%, if your Agility score is 19 or 20.

→ You may employ a Shield by using a Parry Action. Doing this allows you to add the Shield's PTE bonus to your total Percentage To Evade roll verses that SINGLE Strike from an Opponent.

→ **Dodge = +5% + your entire Agility Score, instead of +1/2 Agility Score, added to your PTE total. A Dodge takes 2 Actions - You may use either Strike and/or Parry slots to do this. Max = 25%**

NOTE2: Regardless if you have any Actions left, you always rate a PTE roll or RER from all opponents that strike at you during this Attack. If 100 arrows fly at you, start rolling your 100 PTE rolls.

NOTE3: You may use any of your Strike Actions for Parry Actions, but <u>NOT</u> the other way around. The one exception is if your character is specialized in a weapon.

NOTE4: If a "Defender" is successful with his PTE roll, the "Attacker" must disregard his SPT roll and the defender takes no damage.
If a "Defender" makes his RER roll, the "Attacker's" spell will do less damage or have a lesser effect.

3) Now the "Attackers" must defend and the "Defenders" may use their remaining Actions to move or attack.

4) When all combatants have used up their total number of ACTIONS (that they wish to), Go to Step (1) and continue these steps until one side is defeated, retreats or is granted a truce.

NOTE5: All Actions actually occur **simultaneously**, so even if a defender incurs damage greater than his EP total, he still may use all of his Actions for that Attack. At the end of the Attack, he must make his Ability check with Will to stay conscious.

NOTE6: An exception to these rules is if one of the opposing sides are in hiding and plan to ambush the other. If this is the case than follow the Ambush rules. The side that is doing the ambushing, the "Attackers", may get additional Actions, if they surprise the "Defenders".

STRIKE PLACEMENT TABLE (SPT)

	Human	Hemar	Krill	Animal	Snake	Bird
Head	1 - 5	1 - 5	1 - 5	1 - 5	1 - 5	1 - 5
Body	6 - 20	6 - 20	6 - 20	6 -20	6 -20	6 -20
Left Arm	21 - 38	21 - 32	21 - 30			
Right Arm	39 - 54	33 - 44	31 - 40			
Left Wing			41 - 55			21-45
Right Wing			56 - 70			46-70
Left Front Leg		45 - 57		21-38		
Right Front Leg		58 - 70		39-56		
Left Rear Leg	55 - 73	71 - 80	71 - 80	57-73		71-80
Right Rear Leg	74 - 89	81 - 88	81 - 89	74-88		81-88
Tail		89		89	21-89	89
Near Miss	90 - 99	90 - 99	90 - 99	90-99	90-99	90-99

Any Roll of "00" with percentage dice on the SPT table is an Automatic HIT – The attacker may pick any **General** area and do <u>double normal damage</u> – this includes your Str. Damage bonus.

NOTE: If you roll a low SPT percentage, and for any reason you want to hit an area listed in a "higher" percentage spot, you may do this - a General area only, please. (So if you roll a head shot and want to hit the body, left arm, right wing, tail, etc, you may do this).

NOTE2: Depending on the situation, the Ref. may have to amend the SPT roll.
I.e. You are attacking a Giant with a Long Sword and your SPT roll says you hit the Right ARM, but from the ground you could only hit a Leg, so the Ref. commutes the roll to a Right Leg hit.

NOTE3: Beginning Players may find this next set of rules to be too complicated - if so, don't use them.

Some specific rolls rate additional damage or deficiencies to your Opponent. This next section lists these. In some cases it matters what you stuck your Opponent with; a sword or claw (blade), club (blunt), fist or foot. There may be additional rolls necessary to find out if you did extra damage to your Opponent.

CRITICAL DAMAGE
KEY: 1) TOEP = Total Original Endurance Points.
2) There are healing spells and first aid skills listed in *italics* after the body part descriptions below.
This healing numbers indicate the minimum amount of EP required to magically heal the wound.
HW=30 means a Heal Wounds spell with a minimum of 30 EP is required.
The first aid listings represent the number of points or specializations needed to cure the wound:
FA = 1 point; FA+1 = 2 points (1 Specialization); FA+2 = 3 points (2 Specializations).
3) When the wound is cured, either by a spell or natural means, the negatives listed are also cured.
4) A character heals, through natural means, at 1d10 EP per night they rest.
This requires at least 8 hours of uninterrupted sleep.

ARM : If your character, during the coarse of one battle, sustains Wounds (EP damage) on one Arm, that are greater than ½ of your TOEP – than that Arm will become useless until healed.
(Drop whatever you are holding with that arm/hand. I.e. your weapon, shield, etc.)
HW=30; FA

LEG : If the Total Wounds on one Leg are greater than ¼ of your TOEP, your Charging Rate (CR) is lowered to one-half of normal. *HW=30; FA*
If the Total Wounds on one Leg are greater than ½ of your TOEP, you may only limp at a CRM of 1 and you can't add your Agility bonus to your PTE total. *HW=40; FA+1*

WING : If the Total Wounds on Either Wing are greater than ½ your TOEP, than the Creature can't fly!
HW=30; FA

CRITICAL STRIKES

BODY :   SPT ROLL OF **06-16**   STRIKES STOMACH OR KIDNEY

Fist / Foot / Blunt   = 10% chance to Stun Opponent for 1 Attack.

SPT ROLL OF **17** STIRKES A LUNG

Fist / Foot / Blunt   = There is a 10% chance to break a rib and puncture the lung.   *HW=50; FA+1*
Blade   = 1% chance per damage point inflicted, to puncture a lung.   *HW=60; FA+2*

SPT ROLL OF **18**   STRIKES MID CHEST

Blade   = 10% chance to hit Opponent's HEART.   If you hit the Heart there is a 1% chance per point
of damage done to cause DEATH in 1-4 Attacks.   *HW=60; FA+2*
(i.e.: If you've rolled the correct percentages and have done a total of 22 points damage, you
have a 22% chance that your Opponent's heart will be slashed and he will die in
1-4 Attacks unless healed.)

SPT ROLL OF **19-20**   STRIKES SPINE

Blade / Blunt   = 1% chance per point of damage done to cause immediate Paralysis.   *Heal Paralysis*

HEAD & THROAT :   SPT ROLL OF **01** HITS EYES

Blade   = 15% chance to Blind Opponent.   *Heal Blindness*
Acid, Fire, etc. = 30% chance to Blind Opponent.   *Heal Blindness*

SPT ROLL OF **05** HITS THROAT

Blade   = 20% to cut artery and cause Death from bleeding in 2 Attacks.   *HW=50; FA+1*

SPT ROLL OF **02-04**   HITS HEAD

Blunt weapon = Force Opp. to make an Ability Check with Will or be Stunned for 2 Attacks.
If you Opp. is wearing a helmet, he does not have to make the Ability Check.
Fist   = Force Opp. to make an Ability Check with Will or be Stunned for 1 Attack.
If you Opp. is wearing a helmet, he does not have to make the Ability Check,
and you just probably hurt your hand.

TAIL : If the Total Wounds are greater than ½ TOEP then the Tail is cut off.   *Restore*

NOTE4: You must ALWAYS roll a <u>natural</u> **01** or **05** to Strike the Specific Area of Eyes or Throat and you
must <u>naturally</u> roll a **18** or **19-20** to have any chance to Strike your Opponent's Heart or Spine! If you have
any Negatives to you SPT roll, your Strike is only brought to a <u>General Area</u> not a Specific Area!
     i.e. If you have a SPT Negative of -10%, due to using your Specialized Weapon for example, and
you roll an 11% when you subtract you get a 01% - BUT you DON'T hit your Opponents eyes. You only hit
the General Area of you Opponent's head!

COMMON COMBAT RELATED AFLICTIONS

STUNNED: If your Opponent is stunned, he will suffer these penalties :
(1) Loss Agility Bonus to his PTE while stunned.   (2) Can't make any loud warning sounds.
(3) He may not Strike with a weapon or begin the Concentration Time for any spell.

BLINDED: If a victim is Blinded he looses his Agility bonus to his PTE roll. Also, if the blinded victim
attacks anyone, his opponents receive a +40% bonus to their PTE totals, while the victim is blinded.

DAZED: The victim becomes disoriented. This disorientation will cause:
(1) The victim's Opponents gain a +25% to their PTE totals. (2) Stop Charging Hemar / Krill must Land.
(3) Victim can't use any Occ. Skills or start Concentrating.   (4) Victim looses Agility bonus to his PTE.

PERSON CONCEALED or INVISIBLE: Gains a +40% to PTE; Concealed in Deep Shadow gains +30% PTE.

CHARACTER FALLS BELOW EP TOTAL: Ability Check with Will score, to remain Conscious.

If any Character falls below their EP total and accumulates negative EP > then his End score = Death.
NOTE5: A Stunned or Dazed victim may always use Potions, Pills, or any Enchanted Item activated by a
Trigger Word.

AMBUSH

An Ambush is simply a concealed person or group, waiting to make a surprise attack. There are 2 kinds of Ambushes, Set and Hasty. A Set Ambush is one that is carefully thought out and planned. The people setting it up know of their victim's intentions and arrive well in advance and all wait, out of sight and in total silence, for the intended victims. A Hasty Ambush is one that is made possible through circumstance - like you are in a room and hear someone coming down the corridor or your companions and you are journeying through the wilderness and glimpse a group of goblins coming toward you. That sounded like the introduction to a History class ---- Oh No - Lets hit it!

Now, down to the nitty-gritty, figuring out if the Ambush is successful. First we need to know the terms:

Attackers – those who set up the ambush. They can either set up a Set or Hasty Ambush.

Defenders – those who move into the ambush area. They can be either be Wary or Un-Wary.

We next need to know if the defenders are surprised: First, you must know if the intended victims are Wary, or "looking", for an Ambush. Next, you must add up the percentage bonuses from the table below and **any other Detect Ambush bonuses the Defender's rate.** This total percentage is what the intended victims need to roll lower than in order to discover the ambush. This percentage is known as their Detect Ambush total.

If more than 50% of the party of Defenders have Detect Ambush percentage rolls equal to or lower than their personal Detect Ambush totals, then ALL of the Defenders (the entire Party of Companions) discover the Ambush and notice the Attackers.

If the Ambush is <u>detected</u> then the Defenders are not surprised. Now you should roll the initiative in the regular way and then begin combat.

When an Ambush is <u>successful,</u> the Attackers get 2 "free" Attacks to move or strike. (Remember that an Attack is 5 seconds long.) During this "free" time the Defenders may scramble for cover, shout, cry or weep, etc but may not strike, cast spells, or use enchantments until the Attacker's 2 "free" Attacks (ie. 10 seconds) have passed.

These are the columns of the table below:

(A) Wary Victims - those people who are actively looking for or are expecting an Ambush.

NOTE: All the companions in a group can NOT be Wary; some must navigate, check for traps, etc.

(B) Unwary Victims - those people who are navigating, speaking with a companion, counting their treasure or are just to busy to worry about who may be behind that bush or around the next corner.

(C) Wisdom Bonus - If you have a high enough (or low enough) Wisdom score, you get a modifier to your Detect Ambush total.

Wisdom	Modifier	Wisdom	Modifier
1 - 2	- 5%	3 - 5	- 3%
6 - 14	+ 0%	15 - 18	+ 3%
19 - 20	+ 5%		

(D) Total Occupation Bonus - When a Spy / Assassin learns a Skill called Find Concealed Areas or when a Mentalist learns the ESP Discipline, they get a percentage bonus to this total whether they are Wary or Unwary.

(E) Detect Ambush bonus - If you take this Survival Skill, you receive a +20% bonus to notice an Ambush. You receive the bonus whether you are Wary or Unwary.

(F) Weather, Light Conditions or a Creature's Ambush modifier may give the characters negatives to their Detect Ambush roll.
Low Light or bad weather could give a -5% or greater. This is left up to your Ref.

(G) Totals for Wary (G1) and Unwary (G2) parties Vs. Set and Hasty ambushes.

Ambush Type	Victims (A)	(B)	(C)	(D)	(E)	(F)	Wary (G1)	Unwary (G2)
SET	+20%	+0%	+3%	+5%	+20%	(Poss. Neg.)	20-48%	0-28%
			or	to				
HASTY	+40%	+0%	+5%	+35%	+20%	(Poss. Neg.)	40-100%	0-60%
	Wary	UnW	Wis	Occ	Detect	Weather/Light	Wary	UnWary

WRESTLING

Wrestling is a skill that has been around as long as anyone can remember. It is fairly barbaric, but very effective for causing pain or incapacitating your Opponent. Although Wrestling usually only causes pain, it is very possible to dislocate an Opponents shoulder, elbow, knee, or hip. The Combat Steps for a Wrestling "match" are about the same as for other combat, but the modifications are listed below.

Steps for a Wrestling Match

The steps are basically the same as for regular Combat. You still roll on the SPT, but you affect your Opponent in different ways.

1) The first step of combat is to determine which side seizes the initial action. Unlike usual combat, the person with the highest Agility score strikes first. (If Agility scores are equal then roll).

2) The Attacker may use any / all ACTIONS he rates according to his or her Level and Occupation.

When you wrestle, you must still roll on the Strike Placement Table to ascertain if and where you grabbed your opponent. After you know where you grabbed your Opponent, check the table below to see if you have a percentage to knock your Opponent off his feet.

When your Opponent is on the ground, you roll a percentage to see if you actually do damage to your Opponent. You may only make one roll for each Action you rate. You may of course simply attempt to hold your Opponent in a position until he cries 'uncle'.

NOTE: The "Defender" rates a Percentage To Evade (PTE) roll. If a "Defender" makes his PTE roll, the "Attacker" must disregard his SPT roll.

3) Now the "Attacker" must defend and the "Defender" may use his remaining Actions to move or attack.

If you are being 'held', you may use your Actions and get a chance to 'break' the hold.

If you are standing: you must make a successful Ability Check with Strength to break the hold.

If you are not standing: you must make a successful (Ability Check with Strength) / 2 to break the hold.

4) When all Combatants have used up their total number of ACTIONS (that they wish to), go to Step (1) and continue these steps until one side is defeated, retreats or cries 'UNCLE'.

SPT Area	: Opp Standing - Percentage		Opponent Not Standing -	Penalty
Head	: Headlock	- 20% Take Down	Headlock	- (a)
Body or Wing	: Bear hug	- 30% Take Down	Bear hug	- (b)
Either Arm	: Arm bar	- (c)	Arm bar	- (d)
Either Leg	: Leg Sweep	- 50% single-leg Take Down	Leg bar	- (e)

Take Down = Opponent hits the ground and you have a 1% chance per Strength point to Stun him for 1-2 Actions. (if you have a Strength of 15, then you have a 15% chance to Stun your Opponent for 1-2 Actions.)

(a) Opponent is on the ground and if he wants to break the hold, he must use 1 of his Actions for the attempt and make a successful (Ability Check with Strength) / 2.

(b) Opponent is on the ground and must use 1 Action to attempt to break the hold. Your Opponent's attempt is successful if he makes an (Ability Check with Strength) / 2.

(c) If you hold onto your Opponent's arm for 6 consecutive Attacks (30 sec), you will automatically dislocate either the shoulder or elbow, the Ref will decide.

(d) Opponent makes an (Ability Check with Strength) / 2 to break your hold. If he can't accomplish this within six consecutive Attacks (30 sec), see (c).

(e) Your Opponent makes an (Ability Check with Strength) / 2 to break your hold but if you hold your Opponent for 6 consecutive Attacks, you will automatically dislocate either your Opponents hip or knee.

NOTE2: If a person tries to Wrestle (or is forced to) and he doesn't have the Wrestling Skill, all percentages are cut in **HALF!,** bummer for those non-wrestling dudes.

NOTE3: If someone has a dislocated arm, leg, ect. It will only require a Heal Wounds spell = 30 EP or someone who has First Aid (1 point) to set the appendage back in place and reduce the swelling.

BOXING

Boxing is almost as old as wrestling. It has always been an acceptable means for 2 people to "discuss" their differences in a "civilized" way. When you learn this skill, you learn how to correctly jab and punch. Certain punches cause unique affects. The punches you learn are the jab, the right/left cross, the hook, the uppercut, and the knockout punch. The jab is used to annoy your Opponent, the right/left cross, the hook and the upper cut are used to hurt, stun, or thrown your Opponent off balance, and I bet you can guess what the knockout punch is used for.

0 – 10% = Jaw	11 – 25% = an Eye	26 – 50% = an Ear
51 – 75% = Cheeks or Nose	76 – 99% = Glancing Blow – only 1d6 EP Damage (no Str.)	
00 (100%) = Anywhere in the head you want		

The first two punches have modified SPT rolls (the Jab & the Hook). If your Opponent fails to make his PTE roll, you automatically strike him somewhere in the head area.

1) **Jab:** This can be used **twice** with one Action, but you must make 2 special SPT rolls. If your Opponent makes either of his PTE rolls, you miss with that Jab. If your Opponent fails either of his PTE rolls, you hit him in the area of the head you rolled with your special SPT roll.
   The Damage done with each Jab is a 1d6 [No Str. Dam. Bonus]   [Use twice per Attack]

2) **Hook:** This is either thrown by the Left or Right hand.   [Use every Attack]
   This punch is used by the greatest Boxers to show an Opponent what true boxing skill is – there is nothing more annoying then to be continuously pummeled 'about the head and shoulders'. The damage done by this punch is 1d6 + your regular Strength Damage Bonus. If your opponent makes his PTE roll, you miss.

3) **Right / Left Cross:** Use a 1d6 + Strength Damage Bonus to determine this Damage.   [Use every Attack]

4) **Upper Cut:** If hit Opponent in the unprotected Stomach, Kidney or the Head, you can stun him for 1-2 Actions if he fails an Ability Check with Will.   [Use Every Other Att.]
   (**NOTE:** Disregard the extra effects stated in the SPT when you use this punch.)

5) **Knock-out:** Damage = 1d6 + DOUBLE your regular Str Dam Bonus,   [Use Every Other Att.]
   If you hit your Opponent in the Head, you get DOUBLE the percentage (or 2% per Strength Point) to stun him. If you do succeed in stunning your Opponent, he must successfully make another Ability Check with Will or be Knocked Out for 1d4 Attacks.

The steps for Boxing combat, like the ones for wrestling, are modified a bit.

1) The first step of combat is to determine which combatant seizes the initial action. Unlike usual combat, the person with the highest Agility score strikes first. (If Agility scores are equal then roll).

2) The Attacker may use any or all ACTIONS he rates according to his or her Level and Occupation. When you Box, you must first state which punch you will use and then you must roll on the Strike Placement Table or make a special SPT roll to assertion if and where you hit your opponent. After you have checked where you have struck your Opponent, do the correct damage and determine if you stunned him.

The "Defender" must make his Percentage To Evade (PTE) roll.
NOTE2: If a "Defender" makes his PTE roll, the "Attacker" must disregard his SPT roll.

3) Now the "Attacker" must defend and the "Defender" may use his or her remaining Actions to move or attack. If someone is Stunned of Knocked Out you will rate some additional Actions, but remember we of High Morals would never attack a compromised opponent.

4) When all combatants have used up their total number of ACTIONS (that they wish to), go to Step (1) and continue these steps until one side is defeated, retreats or is knocked out.

NOTE3: If one of the combatants is in full or a half suit of metal armor, boxing can only be used if the other Combatant is also wearing metal gauntlets (Damage = 1d6+Strength Damage Bonus).

NOTE4: Remember to add any Bonuses to your PTE total that you rate.
   i.e. Warrior ability: Fancy Footwork, Bob and Weave, etc.

A SIMPLE COMBAT EXAMPLE: 2 Friends vs. a Black Bear

Kloak and Castlin just turned 5th level and traveled back to Kloak's Ninja camp. This journey was necessary so Kloak could become Castlin's Guardian. The ceremony went well and the next day they start traveling to Huntsville in order to meet three of their friends. While traveling they have to take shelter from an intense storm in a cave. As they venture into the darkness to escape the lightning and hail, they stumble into worse peril.

As they take one to many steps into the cave, the Black Bear awakens to the noises of two intruders bumbling into his home. Having just woke from his daily nap, the Bear has not eaten yet and there is nothing better than prey bringing themselves to lunch. The Bear is slightly concerned that there are two of them, but as long as he can kill one of them quickly, he will be set for many days.

The Ref calls for an initiative roll because there is no chance for either side to Ambush the other. The Ref rolls a 10 on a 12-sided die for the Bear and the players pick one person who rolls a 7 out of 12. The companions lose the initiative so the Bear will get to act first. Let's take a quick break to meet our combatants:

Black Bear	= EP: 90	PTE: 40%	Strikes: 2 paws or 1 bite / Attack	Damage: 1d10+3 ea or 2d8+3	
Kloak (Level 5)	= EP: 54	PTE: 25%	Attacks: 1 Strike / 2 Parry	Sword Damage: 1d20+3	KP: 50
Castlin (Level 5)	= EP: 38	PTE: 23%	Attacks: 1 Strike / 2 Parry	Sword Damage: 2d6	SP: 60

The EP, SP, KP and PTE totals for each combatant are broken down by Attack at the end of this example.

The Bear takes an instant to determine which of the foes is the weaker and then charges. He has just enough room to build up enough speed to and get the Charging bonus. He charges and strikes at Castlin with his bite and the Ref rolls a 25% for the Bear's SPT roll.

Castlin makes a PTE roll to evade the strike. He rolls a 67% which fails. The Ref rolls 2d8 for the Bear's bite damage, he will add +3 for the Bear's Strength bonus and a 1d6 for the Charging Damage. By moving at a rate of CRM=3, the Bear gets a Charging bonus of +1d6, please see the Traveling Rate Section for more details. The Ref rolls the dice and gets a 10 from the 2d8 and adds +3 to get 13, he also gets a 4 on the 1d6 for a total of 17 EP Damage that is done to Castlin.   This ends the Bear's actions.

Castlin regains his composure, steps nimbly back and casts a 3rd level spell: Mind Blast - One. As he pronounces the last syllable of the spell's Trigger Word, he hopes the vicious Black Bear succumbs to the magical force the spell. Castlin spends 34 SP and 4 EP to cast the spell and the Bear must make a RER. The Ref rolls a 35% for the Bear's RER and because all creatures only have a 20% RER, this fails and the massive bear is Dazed for 5 Actions. He also takes 8+1d12 damage from the spell so Castlin rolls a 4 and adds +8 to do 12 EP Damage to the Bear.

Kloak recognizes the Dazed expression on the Bear's face and strikes with his Ninja-to. He rolls a 12% for his SPT roll and the Dazed Bear rolls a 34% for his PTE. This roll would normally succeed but because the Bear is Dazed it loses its Agility Bonus to its PTE total, which is a +10% PTE bonus for all creatures. The Bear also charged this Attack so its total PTE for this Attack is (40-10-0) or 30% so it fails (The bear can only loose its Agility Bonus to its PTE once). Kloak has successfully stuck the Bear's body leaving a nice gash. He rolls damage and gets 17+3 for Str Dam bonus. This ends the 1st Attack.

They Ref calls for the next Initiative and rolls a 5 out of 12. The companion's roll is a measly 2, so the Bear wins again.

The Bear will be Dazed this entire round and part of the next (Duration of the Daze effect from the Mind Blast 1 spell was rolled at 5 Actions). While the bear is Dazed, his prey will gain a +25% to their PTE totals making their percentages 50% for Kloak and 48% for Castlin. The Ref rolls for the Bear's 2 paws on the SPT and gets a 43% and an 11% which will strike Castlin's Right Arm and Body if he doesn't make his PTE rolls. Castlin rolls a 75% and a 90% so he is hit both times. The Bear's damage is 1d10+3 for each paw, the Ref rolls an 6+3 and a 4+3 for a total of 16 EP damage.

Through the newly acquired link of Guardianship, Kloak knows that Castlin is in great danger of dying during the next Attack. He decides to move and use his Dust of Heal Wounds on Castlin. He reaches out and sprinkles the Dust over Castlin and says the Trigger Word 'Heal'. Castlin instantly receives +55 EPs, but because you can never have more EP than your original total, Castlin now has his maximum EP which equals 38.

Castlin takes another few steps back and casts his Flame Bolt 1 spell at the Bear. This costs Castlin 18 Spell Points and 2 EP to cast. The Ref rolls a RER for the Bear and gets a 68% which fails so the Bear receives spell damage of 4+1d20 points from Castlin's Flame Bolt 1 spell. Castlin rolls an 18, so the total damage is 4+18 = 22 EP. This ends the 2nd Attack.

The Ref rolls for the 3rd Initiative and gets an 8 but the companion's roll is an 11, so they finally win.

Kloak strikes at the Bear with his Ninja-to and rolls a 46% for his SPT roll. The Bear is still Dazed for 2 Actions and rolls a 65% for its PTE, so it fails again. Kloak rolls a 12 on a 1d20 and adds +3 for his Strength Damage Bonus, so the total damage is 15. Now the Bear has a newly bleeding, good sized slash on his Right Front Leg.

Castlin hopes he can put the Bear out of their misery and slashes with his short sword. Castlin rolls a 34% on the SPT which hits the Bear's Left Front Leg. The Bear makes a PTE roll of 55% which fails. Castlin then rolls 10 on his 2d6 for the Bear's Damage. Please note that Castlin doesn't get a Strength Damage Bonus to his sword damage.

The Bear fiercely battles though the flames and makes 2 lunging strikes at Castlin rolling SPT rolls of 19% and 88%. Castlin must make 2 PTE rolls, they are: 12% and 79%. This means he is only hit by the 2nd strike on the Right Leg for 1d10+3 EP Damage. The Bear rolls a 5 and adds +3 for a total of 8 EP Damage to Castlin. This ends the 3rd Attack.

Castlin's player grabs a 12-sided die and spins the die to win Initiative and put an end to this combat. He rolls a 7 and the Ref rolls a 6, so as the companions celebrate, Kloak strikes at the Bear with his sword.

Kloak rolls a SPT of 7% and the Bear rolls a PTE of 58% which fails and Kloak rolls a 5 on a 1d20 and adds +3 giving a measly damage total of 8 EP.

Castlin swipes with his sword and rolls a SPT of 13%, the Bear's PTE roll is 49% and it takes 9 EP Damage.

The Bear is at -6 EP so he will fall unconscious at the end of this Attack, but because all attacks are simultaneous, the bear gets to strike at Castlin. It strikes with its dying rage, not understanding why this puny prey has not died yet, with all the damage he has done to it. The Bear rolls SPT rolls of 82% and 63%, Castlin makes opposing PTE rolls of 27% and 72% so he gets struck both times. The Ref rolls Damage for the Bear of 5+3 and 9+3 for a total of 20 EP Damage. This ends the 4th Attack and the combat.

Totals at the END of each Attack

NAME	1st Attack EP - PTE - *P	2nd Attack EP - PTE - *P	3rd Attack EP - PTE - *P	4th Attack EP - PTE - *P
Black Bear	58 - 30% - 0	36 - 30% - 0	11 - 40% - 0	-6 - 40% - 0
Kloak	54 - 25% - 50	54 - 50% - 50	54 - 25% - 50	54 - 25% - 50
Castlin	17 - 23% - 26	36 - 48% - 8	28 - 23% - 8	8 - 23% - 8

*P = KP for Kloak or SP for Castlin.

The Ref tells the players that the Bear will die from excessive bleeding in 2 Attacks. The companions decide to search the Bear's cave for treasure. Kloak activates his Sense Enemy's Skill and they venture further into the cave.

Please see the Random Treasure section for details of this next sequence.

Using the equation listed in the Random Treasure section: [(EP + PTE + # Att) / 10] + 1 / M or E .
So the Bear is [(90 + 40 + 3) / 10] + 0   or   [(133)/10] + 0   or   13.3 and rounding the number gives us a 13.

The Ref generously gives them 1 roll on the Enchanted Items table and 2 rolls on the Regular Equipment table (this actually adds up to 14 points, but our Ref is in a good mood, just having received a bribe of pretzel rods and mild cheese dip - sooooo cheesy and crunchy!). The players decide to give the extra roll to Castlin, because his player delivered the best insult during this battle sequence. Kloak rolls a 4 on the Regular Equipment table which is a Great treasure. Castlin rolls a 10 on the Regular Equipment table which is a Fair treasure and rolls a 1 on the Enchanted Items table which is an Awesome treasure. The Ref awards a Wand with (2) Uncontrollable Fires held in it, a Flask of Oil and a Lantern.

Next time Kloak will make sure he uses his new Sense Enemy's Skill before adventuring into a cave in order to escape from a dark and stormy night!

Ref Note: I skipped XPO in this example. I deal with an accounting of XPO after the next example.

A GLIMPSE OF THE BATTLE TO COME!

AN IN-DEPTH COMBAT EXAMPLE: A Group of Companions vs. a Pack of Wolves

Here after is documented a combat encounter between a pack of wolves and a party of companions. Before we break into combat, let's list some abbreviations and terms so we are speaking the same language, then we will get to know our combatants and finally we'll get into combat.

Abbreviations are listed here for convenience; for a complete description please see the Glossary.

PTE : Percentage to Evade — This percentage tells you what you need to roll below to evade a strike. You roll this percentage whenever anyone strikes at you with a Projectile or Melee weapon.

SPT : Strike Placement Table — Every time you strike at an Opponent with a Projectile or Melee Weapon, you must roll on this table to find out what part of his body your strike hits. The [SPT] is located on page 139.

EP : Endurance Points — A number representing your total health.

Dam : Damage — The amount of Damage you do with a single strike or spell.

RER : Resist Enchantment Roll — A percentage roll that indicates if you are able to resist some of the effects of the enchantment that has been directed at you.

SP : Spell Points — These are what you must spend in order to Cast a Spell.

KP : Ki Points — These are what a Ninja must spend in order to use any Ninja Ki Power.

MP : Mental Points — A Mentalist must spend these points to use any Mental Skill.

Att : Attack — A measure of Time.   1 Attack = 5 seconds.   12 Attacks = 1 Minute.

I will be referring to tables and sections in this book by a certain manner for convenience:
Tables and sections are both referred to in square brackets: [Table Name] or [Section Name] or [Appendix X].

The short hand I will use to sum-up stats and effects distressing the combatants of our little scuffle will be in brackets. Ie. {info}
I will refer to the wolves as: W_1, W_2, W_3, W_4 and W_5. We will call the leader by his name – Vladistock or Vlad.

I will refer to the companions by the first letter of their names: R=Roge; V=Violet; J=Jake; C=Castlin and K=Kloak.
The information in the brackets will be laid out like this:
{Name=EP; PTE total at that instance in time; Description of effect}

{R=34 EP; 45 PTE} means Roge has 34 EP and a PTE roll of 45% at the moment.
{W_5=60 EP; but stunned} means Wolf #5 has 60 EP but is stunned at the moment.   Get it? Got it? GOOD!
Lets go!!

147

The Wolf Pack's Stats

This small pack of wolves is led by a mutated male wolf named Vladistock. Vlad has two mutations: Wings and a Non-Deadly Poison accompanying his bite which causes some additional damage and intense pain. He leads 5 regular wolves and I will refer to them as W_1, W_2, W_3, W_4 and W_5. The stats of our wolf pack are as follows:

Vlad's Stats:	EP:75;	Strikes:1;	Bite Dam: 1d12 +2 Str Dam plus +1d6 & Pain;	PTE: 55 / Flying=80%
Wolves Stats:	EP:60;	Strikes:1;	Bite Dam: 1d12 +2 for their Str Dam bonus;	PTE: 55

The wolves also have a Special Strike: if a wolf successfully strikes its prey during an Attack, it will hold on to its victim and do automatic damage on the next Attack without needing to make a new SPT roll. Also, the held prey looses its Agility Bonus to its PTE for as long as the wolf holds on. NOTE: Because Vlad flies, he wont use this Strike.

> Note1: All Creatures gain a bonus to setting up ambushes. This negative percentage is -20% for wolves.
> Note2: All Creatures (Mutated and Regular) have a Resist Enchantment Roll (RER) equal to 20%.
> Note3: The Will Score of any Regular or Mutated Creature is : 15

The Companion's Stats

The companions are led by Roge, a 5th level Warrior. Some of their stats are here, a complete list is in [Appendix C].

Name	5th Level	EP	PTE**	Agl Bonus	# Actions	S/K/M Points	Detect Ambush
Roge	Warrior	62	45%	+9%	1 Strike / 2 Parry	21 SP	40% for Wary
Violet	Alchemist	39	45%	+8%	1 Strike / 2 Parry	60 SP	
Jake	Mentalist	45	40%	+6%	1 Strike / 2 Parry	40 MP	45% for Wary
Castlin	Enchanter	38	15%	+8%	1 Strike / 2 Parry	60 SP	
Kloak	Ninja	54	15%	+10%	1 Strike / 2 Parry	50 KP	45% for Wary

** All PTE numbers listed are NOT including the character's Agility Bonus. I've done this because of the Wolf's special ability. The PTE number above does include Armor and Shield bonuses.
Also, you'll notice that I'm not adding in Roge's or Kloak's Parry bonus. You can only Parry someone wielding a melee weapon – not a creature wielding it's teeth or claws.

The companions are traveling along a forested path during dusk. The column sun has already set, but the full moon of the 4th month hasn't yet risen. The companions haven't made camp yet because they are hurrying to meet two other members of their party in the next town. Vlad's pack is hunting, this dim dusky light is excellent for ambushing prey. While walking with his pack, he instantly knows when the lead wolf catches the scent of humans. Vlad has hunted humans before and thinks this will be good training for the younger wolves. The pack quickly disperses along the trail the lazy humans are most certainly using and set up their HASTY Ambush. As the companions round the bend, Roge is on point, followed by Violet, Jake, Castlin and Kloak. Roge has used this short cut before, so there is no need to navigate. But looking for ambushes, on the other hand, is another matter indeed. Roge knows that during this time of dusk, with out a full moon overhead, it's harder for him, Jake and Kloak to spot an ambush.

The Ref. decides he will only allow Detect Ambush rolls from those characters who are Wary. He then informs the players that all Detect Ambush totals will be given a -5% penalty because of the dimly lighted surroundings. That means that the companions have a total of -25% to their Detect Ambush totals – a -20% from the wolves [See the Wolf Pact Stats above] and -5% from the dim light penalty.

The Ref then adds up all the percentage bonuses for the companions verses a Hasty Ambush:

	Wary	Wisdom	Detect Ambush Bonus	Wolves Negatives	Low Light Penalty	TOTALS
Roge's =	+40%	---	+20%	-20%	-5%	= 35%
Jake's =	+40%	+5%	+20%	-20%	-5%	= 40%
Kloak's =	+40%	+5%	+20%	-20%	-5%	= 40%

The Detect Ambush rules state that 50% of the total companions in the party have to successfully roll below their Detect Ambush totals in order for PARTY not to be surprised by an Ambush. In this case, this means that all three of the companions that are actively looking for an ambush must successfully make their rolls. Ie. 3 out of 5 > 50%.

The Ref asks for Detect Ambush rolls from Roge, Jake and Kloak. Their percentage rolls are: 15%, 72% and 35% respectively. Due to the penalties, only 2 out of the 3 companions are successful. Therefore, according to the [Ambush Section], the companions are surprised for a total of 10 seconds or 2 Attacks. The wolves will get to harass the companions for 2 Attacks and then we will roll for the 1st initiative of the combat.

Vlad waits for the perfect moment to spring his trap. As the humans move into the correct area of the trail, Vlad lets out one quick howl and the pack of wolves attack the companions. All five wolves leap out to strike at the companions: the first three on Roge who is at the front of the column and the last two on Kloak at the end of the party's column. Vlad leaps into the air, spreading his grayish wings and quickly rises into the night sky. He will identify the strongest human and attack him to demoralize his prey.

The 3 wolves on Roge strike so the Ref makes 3 SPT rolls. W_1 rolls 62%, W_2 rolls 88% & W_3 rolls a 25%. Before Roge rolls, he chooses to spend his Strike Action to gain his shield's bonus on his last PTE roll. Roge makes 3 opposing PTE rolls of 35%, 92% and 12% respectively. Roge uses all of his Actions to gain his shield's bonus to his PTE rolls making them 54%. One of the percentages rolled is higher than Roge's total PTE so he was struck once and missed twice. According to the SPT roll of the 2nd wolf (W_2=88%), Roge is hit on the right leg. The Ref rolls a 1d12 and adds 2 for W_2 total damage. The Ref gets a 6+2=8 for damage which comes directly off Roge's EP total.

The Ref makes two SPT rolls for the 2 wolves that attacked Kloak. W_4 rolls 2% and W_5 rolls 57%. The 4th wolf's (W_4) SPT roll actually strikes the head and this is very unlikely, because the wolf did not jump up, so the Ref. commutes that roll to a body hit instead – please see Note2 under the [SPT] for details. Kloak's opposing PTE rolls are 74% & 16%. Kloak's current PTE total is 25%, so W_4 strikes him on the body. W_4's damage roll was 8+2=10 which is taken off of Kloak's total EP score. As Vlad continues to rise into the air and begins circling the party, the first ambush Attack is over.

Roge and Kloak are both held by wolves, so they have both taken damage and both lose their Agility Bonus to their PTE rolls – see [The Wolves Stats] table above and read about the wolves Special Strikes. This is how Roge and Kloak are looking:

Roge's EP = 62 – 8 from W_2 = 54   &   His PTE = 54 – 9 for his Agility Bonus = 45.

Kloak's EP = 54 – 10 from W_4 = 44   &   His PTE = 25 – 10 for his Agility Bonus = 15.

These are their updated stats: {R=54 EP; 45 PTE}   {K=44 EP; 15 PTE}.

At the beginning of the second Attack, Roge and Kloak receive automatic damage from the wolves holding onto them. Roge takes 9+2 & Kloak takes 3+2 points of EP damage. The two other wolves at the head of the column strike at Roge with STP rolls of 92% & 81%. The 1st wolf (W$_1$) misses with a [SPT] roll over 90%, so Roge only needs to make one PTE roll which is a miraculous 00 (a 100% is always a success) and completely avoids the strike from W$_3$. The remaining wolf (W$_5$) attacking Kloak makes a SPT roll of 28% and Kloak's opposing PTE roll is 62%. W$_5$ latches onto Kloak's left arm and does 5+2 EP Damage. Vlad sees his prey becoming overwhelmed by his scouts and swoops out of the night sky striking at Roge with a SPT roll of 15%. Roge elects to employ his shield again but still fails his PTE roll with a 96% and takes 6+2 points of physical damage from Vlad's bite and an additional 4 points from the pain poison. Roge screams and the echo fads as the second and final ambush Attack comes to an end.

Roge is held by one wolf (W$_2$) and Kloak is held by two wolves (W$_4$ & W$_5$).
Let's do the math one more time:
Roge's EP = 54 – (11 from W$_2$) – (12 from Vlad) = 31 & His PTE is still 54% – 9% = 45%.
Kloak's EP = 44 – (5 from W$_4$) – (7 from W$_5$) = 32 & His PTE is still 15%
        (You can only lose your Agility bonus once.)
The companions' current stats are: {R=31 EP; 45 PTE}   {V=39 EP; 53 PTE}   {J=45 EP; 46 PTE}
                                        {C=38 EP; 23 PTE}   {K=32 EP; 15 PTE}

After the 2 Ambush Attacks, the companions get to roll their first initiative roll. The players pick one person to roll initiative on a 12-sided die and she rolls an 11 out of 12! The Ref. also rolls a 12-sided die for the vicious wolves and gets a 3. The companions win and are finally able to spring into action.

Roge uses his sword to strike at W$_2$ and makes a SPT roll of a natural 5%! (Please, remember this astounding roll). W$_2$ has a PTE of 55%, the Ref rolls a PTE for W$_2$ and gets a 77% which is a failure. Therefore, Roge successfully makes a Critical Strike on W$_2$'s throat for 18 EP damage. According to the [SPT], Roge gets to make a 20% roll to cut the wolf's artery because he is using a blade – please refer the Critical Strikes section of to the [SPT] for details. Roge's roll is 14%, so W$_2$ will die from massive bleeding in 2 Attacks from the Critical Strike.

Violet surveys the battle, and decides to cast her Wound 1 spell at W$_4$, the wolf clinging to Kloak's body. The Wound 1 spell is fully explained in the Green section of the [Ench/Al Spell] List. This spell is one of Violet's most powerful and costs 53 SP to cast (Violet must also spend 6 EP – see spell section). Violet rolls for damage and does 12+11 EP damage. W$_4$ is forced to make a RER. The Ref rolls and it is a 58% which fails, so W$_4$ takes the full amount of damage (23), releases Kloak and proceeds to spew it's last meal along the trailside. Please note that the spell's effects will last for a total of 3 Actions.

Jake nimbly moves past Violet, which uses one of his Parry Actions for movement, reaches out his hand and uses his Bio-Electric Shock Skill on W$_1$. Jake's Bio-Electric Shock is explained in the [Mentalist] section. W$_1$ makes a RER roll of 72% which fails. Jake rolls 2d10, adds his Level and does a total of 20 EP damage to W$_1$.

Castlin was aware of Vlad when he attacked Roge last Attack, so he decides to pull out his new wand. He points it at Vlad, who is circling the party, yells the wand's Trigger Word 'Boom' and shoots an Uncontrolled Fire spell at him. The Uncontrolled Fire spell is explained in the Red Section of the [Ench/Al Spells]. The burst of flame strikes Vlad square in the chest and forces Vlad to make a RER. Vlad rolls a 12%, which is a success. Castlin rolls 10+16 EP damage. Vlad only needs to take ½ the base damage produced by the spell because of his successful RER and receives 21 EP damage (5+16).

Kloak uses his Stun Strike ability, which is explained in the [Ninja] section, on the wolf W$_5$ clinging to his left arm. Kloak's SPT roll is 3%, a head strike. W$_5$ makes a PTE roll of 87% which fails, so it must make a Special Ability Check with Will – it must roll less than it's (Will score – Kloak's Level) which equals 10 and multiply it by 3 or 30%. It rolls an 87%, fails and falls unconscious for a total of 9 of it's Actions. With one of his remaining Parry Actions, Kloak yells the Trigger Word 'Knife' and actives the Shield, Melee, +30% spell stored in his cloak which increases his PTE total by +30% verses any melee attack.

The pack's stats are: {W$_1$=40 EP} {W$_2$=42 EP; but bleeding to death from a Critical Strike} {W$_3$=60 EP} {W$_4$=37 EP; but Puking for 3 Actions} {W$_5$=60 EP; but Stunned for 9 Actions} {Vlad=54 EP}. This is important: All attacks are simultaneous, so even though W$_2$ & W$_5$ will be incapacitated during the next Attack, they still cling to their prey and do their damage during this Attack. W$_4$ was affected by a Wound 1 spell and that spell's effects are immediate, so it must use it's strikes during this Attack to release Kloak and unload it's lunch.

At this the beginning of the Attack, W$_2$ & W$_5$ are still clinging to Roge & Kloak. W$_2$ does 8+2 EP Damage to Roge and Kloak receives 8 total EP damage from W$_5$. W$_1$ turns and strikes at Jake with a SPT roll of 64%. Jake chooses to employ his shield by using his remaining Parry Action but his PTE roll is 76% which still fails so he takes a total of 11 EP damage and is now held by that wolf. W$_3$ strikes at Roge with a SPT roll of 25%, Roge makes a PTE roll of 52% which fails and he receives 9 more EP damage. W$_4$ vomits violently by the trailside and Vlad swoops down towards Roge with a SPT roll of 49%, Roge rolls a 64% for his PTE which fails so he receives 8 total physical and 3 poison EP damage. Roge again screams from the intense pain but the coming night seems to pay no attention.

At this point, the companions stats are: {Roge=31-10-9-11=1 EP; 35 PTE*}   {V=39-6=33 EP}
{J=45-11=34 EP; 46-6=40 PTE}   {C=38 EP; 23 PTE}
{K=32-8=24 EP; 25+30=55 PTE vs. melee}.

Note: Roge's PTE is 35% because he is being held by the left arm which means he gets no Agility or Shield bonus to his PTE total.

At this point Kloak doesn't have any wolves clinging to him and he also gains the magical bonus of his activated cloak which gives him the higher PTE total of 55% verses melee attacks. This bonus lasts 30 minutes.

For the next initiative roll, the companions roll a 7 and the Ref rolls a 6 for the wolves, so it is again the companions honor.

Roge tries frantically to pull his left arm out of W_3's jaws. He realizes he is very close to death and if W_3 is allowed to inflect any more damage, Roge knows he's done for. The Ref. tells him he may pull his arm out of the wolf's jaws by making a successful Ability check with Strength. He rolls an 82%, which fails.

Violet moves toward Roge, swings her hand in an arc over his head, sprinkling a dust in the air directly over him and yells 'Heal'. She is using one of her Heal Wound Alchemist's Dusts to heal Roge and he instantly gains +36 EP to his meager total – please note that Violet has just saved Roge's life.

Jakes points the Elementalist ring he wears at W_1, yells 'Avalanche' which activates the Stone Storm 1 spell stored within it. The rain of stones leaps from the ring pummeling W_1 doing 4+11 EP damage. W_1 rolls a RER of 38% which fails so he receives the full 15 EP damage.

Castlin uses his Sting Ray 2 spell. He concentrates for the Concentration Time listed under the spell, spends 54 SP and 3 EP (He has his staff in the "Open" position, so the normal 6 EP cost for a SP use of 56 SP is cut in half), says the Trigger Word and then releases 5 Sting Rays. He chooses not to hit W_5 because it's stunned, but the other wolves must make one RER each. W_1 through W_4 roll, 35%, 28%, 94% and 3% respectively and Vlad rolls a 17% for his RER. Castlin rolls the Sting Ray 2 Damage, it equals 12+8. W_1 through W_3 take 20 EP damage but W_4 & Vlad only receive 14 EP Damage (14 EP Damage = 6+8 or ½ base damage + Castlin's roll).

Kloak instantly contemplates a Moral Dilemma. His charge is in mortal danger, he is certain of this because of two facts: (1) Roge, the strongest warrior in the party, nearly just died. (2) Castlin has used one of his precious higher level spells, and that is never a good sign. The tide of battle does seem to be turning, but if W_5 & Vlad can rally their troops, the consequences will be deadly. Kloak decides to insure his charges continued existence: he moves, swings his Ninja-to and strikes W_4. He rolls a 16% on the SPT and W_4 fails it's PTE roll with an 86%. Kloak rolls Max damage, doing 23 EP to W_4, which brings the wolf to Zero EP. The wolf rolls its Ability Check with Will to stay conscious, it rolls a 73% which fails. Anyone or thing that falls to Zero EP and misses its Ability Check with Will goes unconscious and is unable to attack, please see the [Endurance] table Note2 for details.

REF NOTE: If W_4 bleeds to death of these wounds, Kloak will have killed a Stunned or Defenseless opponent so his Morality Rating score would instantly drop to a 7 – please see the [Morality section] for details. Also, Kloak has just attacked a Stunned or Defenseless opponent so according to the [Morality Rating] table his MR would fall to 10, but because it is 10 already, there is no change.

Here is a look at our combatant's totals as of this moment:
{W_1=5 EP}   {W_2=22 EP & will die next Attack from bleeding}   {W_3=40 EP}   {W_4=0 EP}
{W_5=60}   {Vlad=40 EP}

{R=37 EP; 35 PTE}   {V=33 EP; 7 SP}   {J=34 EP; 40 PTE}   {C=35 EP; 6 SP}
{K=24 EP; 55 PTE}.

Vlad servers the battle field from his elevated location. Two of his pack are dying or dead and at least one of the remaining three is gravely injured. He howls the retreat, realizing that this group of humans are more skilled than he expected. No matter; the humans would still have to travel within the dense forest for at least several hours, more than enough time for Vlad to gather a truly formidable force and crush these puny beings. Vlad flaps his wings, gliding off toward his lair, contemplating the human's demise. The surviving wolves, immediately disperse into the foliage, leaving the companions and moving back toward their lair.

The companions gather themselves together and try to decide what to do: Do they camp and try to regain some of their precious Endurance Points (EP) or do they try to continue on and hope not to encounter another vicious band of creatures? As Roge speaks with the group, Kloak feels a moral obligation to ask Violet to bandage W_4 so it will not die of its wounds. Violet does this and Kloak's Morality Rating remains at 10 and does not fall to 7.

Ref.'s Notes for this In-Depth Combat Sequence:

(A) Experience Points (XPO): The companions were victorious during this battle and they also gain Experience.

Situation – please see the [XPO section]		XPO received
(1) Common = Surviving REAL Combat with 11 combatants	:	45 XPO
(2) One-Timer = ONLY Violet (Saved Roge's Life)	:	+58 XPO **
(3) Odds = The companions overcame a larger more powerful force so I would award them: Overcoming 5-1 (Steep) Odds	:	16 XPO

XPO totals for: Roge, Jake, Castlin, and Kloak   =   +61 XPO
XPO total for: Violet   =   +119 XPO

** Violet has never truly saved someone else's life, until now.
> This is the FIRST time so she gains the One-Timer bonus or +58 XPO.
> Let's break this down: The One-Timers bonus for saving HER 1st life is 25 XPO + 55% of the difference between 5th & 6th level or 55% of 60 XPO so   that is 25+ (60*.55)= 25+33 this is equal to 58 XPO. The next time she saves a life, she will gain NO additional XPO – please see the [XPO section] for details.

(B) At this point, all five companions have gone up to 6th level: they all have more than 200 XPO points.
> Roge, Jake, Castlin & Kloak have 203 XPO and Violet has 212 total XPO – please see the [Experience table] for a full description. Violet may not receive more than 20% of the difference between 5th & 6th levels or (60*.20) = 12 XPO for a total of 212 XPO.
> All characters gain additional Endurance Points and may gain additional abilities if they can complete training. Kloak will receive a new Ninja Ability, if he has a chance to meditate.
> Roge, Violet, Castlin, Jake & Kloak will all gain a new maximum number of either Spell, Mental or Ki points, if they survive to experience the next sunrise.

(XX) Author's Note: All of these characters are now 6th level. Their Character Sheets show them as 5th level. You may update their character sheets to 6th level now or you may use them in your game at 5th level of experience. This discussion is left up to the Ref.

THE IRONBALL GAME

The IronBall game was created to literally save the Races from war. It is true that members of the human race spotted a member of each of the other races on the same day hundreds of years ago (on different coasts, of course). It is also true that the Krill King was the first to hear this news. Sometime after this, the races came together in peace and made "loose" trade agreements with each other - but much Prejudice and Hate blossomed from the ignorance of each race's different appearances and cultures.

Fortunately the leaders of their races were wise and close to their peoples. They saw this rank creature known as Hate creep and charge across each of their realms. They came together with the determination to forge their peoples together with the bonds of peace. After many failures, the wise rulers came to the realization that simple but friendly competition is the best way to hold men's Hearts on the steady path of racial tranquility. They finally decided upon a game in which all three races could excel. They then, all with one voice, strongly recommended and funded this new Game - sponsoring it among their peoples. Luckily for us they succeeded and as they planned, a team made up of 2 Hemars playing the Runner Guards, 2 Krill playing the Runners, and 1 Human playing the Goalie is virtually unbeatable when faced by a team made up of all one Race. The Game has been adapted so a 10th level Enchanter or Alchemist can make the enchanted playing field for **TWO** 3 player teams. An Enchanter or Alchemist of 15th level must cast the official version and the enchanted playing field is large enough for **TWO** 5 player teams.

Practically every town has a resident IronBall team. Towns usually have teams with 3 players and Cities have teams made up of 5 players. In either case the town or city makes sure it has the allowed number of team replacements. When your team arrives at a new settlement, you may want to challenge the resident team. To make the challenge simply tell any of the guards of your intent and where you are staying. You will be informed within one day if your challenge was accepted.

If you are turned down don't make a fuss; the resident team may already have a game scheduled or may have just played a match recently.

If your challenge is accepted, you will be asked to report to a designated area at noon the next day – this is usually a field just outside of town or within the courtyard of the city. When you reach the area you will be asked to present your entire team, including any replacements that you have with you. All the members of the resident team will be presented there as well, including any of their replacements. The town will always provide the playing field – it will be cast by someone or be read from a scroll, etc. Once the spell has been cast, you will take your places on the field and the game will begin.

One of the challenging runners always starts the game with the IronBall in his catcher. When a point is scored by a team, the IronBall will reappear in the opposing Goalie's catcher 1 minute after the point was scored. The Goalie may then shoot the IronBall to one of his players and the game can proceed.

If a player has specialized in the Survival Skill: Blind Shot and Accurate Pass, he may add those bonuses to ALL ability check percentages rolled during the IronBall match.

Team Make-Up					**IronBall Field Spell**
5 Player teams =	2 Runners +	2 Runner Guards +	1 Goalie	& 2 Replacements	= 150 SP
3 Player teams =	1 Runner +	1 Runner Guard +	1 Goalie	& 1 Replacement	= 100 SP

Size of IronBall Field — see Pictures at end of this section

	At 10th Level	At 15th Level
Canopy:	20 yds wide x 10 yds high diamond	30 yds x 10 yds high diamond
General Playing Field:	50 yds long x 20 yds wide	100 yds long x 30 yds wide
Height of Playing Field:	Left Goal: 10 -> Center: 20 -> Right G: 10	Left Goal: 10 -> Center: 30 -> Right G: 10

The IronBall Field spell creates the field, the canopy (where the goal is located), the IronBall, standard
     catchers (enough for both teams), and "bleachers" for the spectators. These spells have been redone
     and revamped over the years many, many times to reduce the spell points required to cast them.

The IronBall — used while playing the game

The IronBall is an Enchanted multicolored glowing ball 8" in diameter. It is composed of 2 inches of a semi-hard magical covering over an Iron Core of 4 inches in diameter. If anyone is struck with the ball during the game, they will take 1d8 EP Damage.

Catchers – wielded by each of the players

Goalies' = wooden ring with a 1' handle, meant for one handed use. Connected to the ring is a rubbery net which may be used to catch the ball and then the Goalie may pull back on the net and "shoot" the IronBall back into play. The maximum distance the Goalie may shoot the IronBall is 40 yds.

Runner's = 2' long Single handed "Catcher" that has a small net used to catch, pass and shoot the ball.

Runner Guard's = 5' long "Catcher" with a small net for catching and passing the ball. This is used with 2 hands.

The other end is selectable by the particular player. Any non edged and non pointed weapon is legal. The standard 2 handed catchers supplied by the spell have a club at their opposite ends. The club end will do a total of 1d8 EP damage to anyone struck by it.

Because the Catchers provided by the spell are magical, they are unbreakable but only until the game is over and then they vanish with everything else.

Canopy – where the goal is located

All players on the playing field see this as a Dark, Opaque Area. This is where the goalie stays and protects the goal.

Only the team's Goalie can see inside his Canopy without magical assistance.

All spectators see the Canopy as a slightly shaded area so they can definitely see all the action.

NOTE: The only way the Canopy can be tampered with is a Light or any Midnight spell – please see below.

The Pass and the Catch

If you have learned the Survival Skill "Blind Shot and Accurate Pass", you must roll a successful Ability Check with Agility to make an Accurate Pass to one of your teammate's. If you didn't learn the Survival Skill then you must roll a percentage less then your Agility score to make an Accurate Pass.

Anyone can catch the IronBall with their catcher by making a successful Ability Check with Agility. If the person passing it to you made an Accurate Pass, you - the receiver - gains a +25% added to your total Ability Check with Agility percentage to catch that Pass with your catcher. Ref note: That is a maximum of 85% to catch an Accurate Pass, if the player is not specialized in the Survival Skill "Blind Shot and Accurate Pass".

The Point

In order to score, one of the Runners has to enter the Canopy alone and try to shoot the IronBall into the diamond shaped hole, which is 14' off the ground located at the Canopy's rear. The largest factor when someone shoots for the point is if he or she has learned the IronBall game's Survival Skill: 'Blind Shoot and Accurate Pass'. Listed below are negatives to your Ability Check with Agility percentage total. They are separated into different circumstances:

Learned the Survival Skill: 'Blind Shoot and Accurate Pass'		Negative to your Ability Check with Agility
To Sink the Ball from inside a Lighted Canopy:		-10%
To Sink the Ball from inside a Dark Canopy:		-20%
Shoot from OUTSIDE the Canopy:	Lit Canopy	-40%
	Dark Canopy	-50%

Did **NOT** Learn the Survival Skill: 'Blind Shoot and Accurate Pass'		
To Sink the Ball from inside a Lighted Canopy:		Percentage lower then your Agility Score!
To Sink the Ball from inside a Dark Canopy:		-10% lower than your Agility Score.
Shoot from OUTSIDE the Canopy:	Lit Canopy	-15% lower than your Agility Score.
	Dark Canopy	Only a roll of **00** on your Percentage.

NOTE2: A successful Ability Check with Agility = any percentage roll less then your personal Agility Score * 3.

IronBall Game General Rules

1) The Goalie must stay within the Canopy. He may intercept any missed shot at the goal by making an Ability Check with Agility. He may then pass the IronBall to one of his fellow teammates, shot the IronBall directly at an opponent or anywhere into the playing field. The maximum distance he can shoot the IronBall is 40 yds.

2) Only the Goalie and ONE Hostile Runner are allowed within a Canopy at any one time!

3) **No one** may ever change or trap either Canopy in any way. The only exceptions are that an opposing Runner may cast a Light 1 spell while inside the Canopy and the Goalie may cast any Midnight spell in opposition.

4) When a Runner successfully shoots the IronBall into the goal, which is a diamond shaped hole at back of the opposing Canopy, her team receives 1 point.

5) The most points scored within a 20 minute game wins.

6) If a player becomes unconscious or severely injured during the game, he may be replaced.

> 5 players / team = maximum of 2 replacements - shown before game.
> 3 players / team = maximum of 1 replacement - shown before game.

The replacement must play his fallen team member's position.

7) Only game catchers, either provided by the spell or by each individual player, AND only game armor, always provided by each individual player, may be used by the players during an IronBall game.

8) A maximum of 40 SP may used per person per Game and no more than 150 SP per Team per Game.

9) No one may ever use any Ki or Mental powers during an IronBall Game. Ki Points or Mental Points may NEVER be used during the game.

NOTE: Inside the Canopy a Light 1 spell only lasts 5 seconds / Level (1 Attack / Level) instead 1 hour / Level. [any Midnight spell cast within the Canopy cancels the Light 1 spell].

NOTE2: If any player falls to zero EP, he is unconscious. He is instantly teleported off of the field and a replacement player may enter the field. The replacement MUST play his fallen comrades position.

IRONBALL CATCHERS AND THE IRONBALL
FROM LEFT TO RIGHT: RUNNER'S CATCHER, IRONBALL, GOALIE'S CATCHER, AND RUNNER GUARD'S CATCHER

A SPECTATOR'S LOOK AT AN IRONBALL GAME

3 Player Iron Ball Field

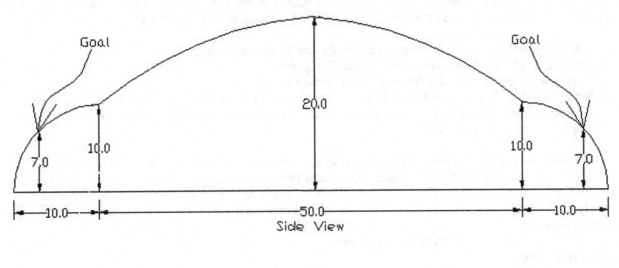

Goal

Goal

20.0

10.0

10.0

7.0

7.0

10.0

50.0

10.0

Side View

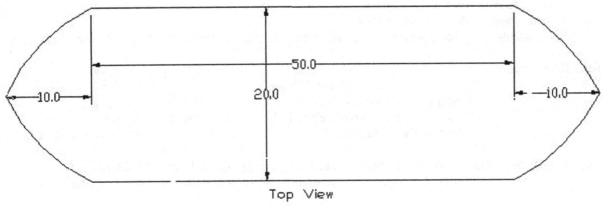

10.0

50.0

20.0

10.0

Top View

5 Player Iron Ball Field

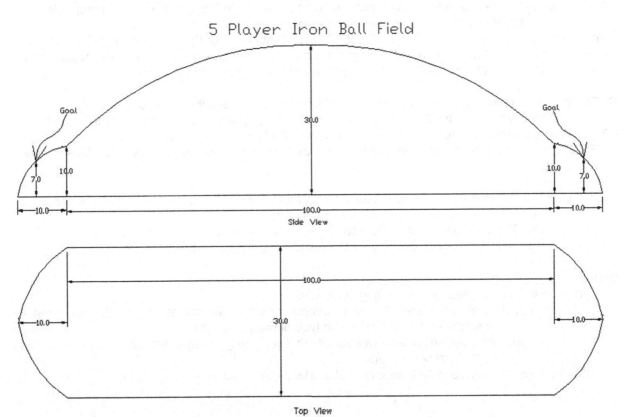

Goal

Goal

30.0

10.0

10.0

7.0

7.0

10.0

100.0

10.0

Side View

10.0

100.0

30.0

10.0

Top View

156

SPECIALIZATION WITH WEAPONS

Warriors, Spies / Assassins, and Ninja may Specialize in certain weapons at certain levels. When you Specialize in a weapon, you learn to use that weapon to it's fullest extent in combat.

In order to Specialize in a weapon you must meet 2 requirements :
(1) First, you must reach the stated level in your Occupation.
   (These levels are stated at the end of this section.)
(2) Next, you must already have formal training in the weapon you want to Specialize in. ie. You must already have learned how to use a Long Sword before you may specialization in that weapon at the level stated in your Occupation.

There are different bonuses depending on whether you Specialize in a Melee weapon or a Projectile weapon. There are also 2 sets of bonuses listed under Projectile weapons. The difference between these are the firing or throwing rates: 'Fast' or 'Slow'. 'Fast' means putting as many Projectiles down range as quickly as possible in one Attack. 'Slow' involves taking careful aim and firing only <u>one</u> well aimed shot during a single Attack.
              The bonuses are listed here :

Melee Weapons:
   (1) Opponent receives a -20% on his PTE total.
   (2) You receive a -10% on your SPT roll.
   (3) Substitute <u>ONE</u> Parry Action for a Strike Action during an Attack with your Specialized Weapon.

Projectile Weapons:

	:	FAST	:	SLOW
(1) Negative to Opponents PTE total:	:	- 0%	:	- 20%
(2) Negatives to your SPT rolls:	:	- 5%	:	- 15%
(3) Gain Strength Damage Bonus: *	:	Str. Bonus	:	Str. Bonus
(4) Fire or Throw Faster: **	:	+ 1	:	(Only **1** projectile / Attack)

* Spy / Assassins, Ninja and Warriors now may use a <u>Composite</u> type of Bow and receive their
      Strength Damage Bonus when they hit someone with an arrow from that Bow.

** When you Specialize in a Projectile Weapon, you gain the ability to fire or throw an extra projectile each
      Attack, if you choose to use the 'Fast' firing option.
Maximum for a Warrior = (Total Actions) + (1 for 3rd Level ability) + (1 for Specialize in Projectile Weapon).
Maximum for a S/A = (Total Actions) + (1 for Specialization in a Projectile Weapon) (or see Dagger=Melee).
Maximum for a Ninja = (Total Actions) + (1 for Specialization in a Projectile Weapon).

NOTE: To Use a Composite Bow you need formal Training in a Bow and then use your weapon
         Specialization for that Bow. No one can use a <u>Composite Bow</u> unless they Specialize in the Bow.
NOTE2: Warriors, remember to add your 4th level Warrior Skills to these bonuses!!
NOTE3: If you shot or throw an accurate projectile, ie. fire SLOW, you use up ALL of your Actions for that
         Attack.

Next, Let us move on to take a closer look at each Occupation that can Specialize. We shall discuss :
      (1)   What level your Occupation may Specialize at.
      (2)   The weapon type your Occupation may Specialize in.
      (3)   Which specific weapons your Occupation may learn to Specialize with.

Warrior:
   (1)   A Warrior may Specialize at 5th <u>and</u> 7th levels.
   (2)   You may Specialize in either a Projectile weapon **or** Melee weapon at 5th level, but you must
            Specialize in the other weapon type of weapon at 7th.
         i.e. - If you Specialize in a melee weapon at 5th level, you <u>must</u> Specialize in a Projectile weapon
               at 7th level or visa versa.
   (3)   You may Specialize in ANY weapon that you've already had formal training in.

Spy / Assassin:
    (1) You may only Specialize at 7th level.
    (2) You may only Specialize in ONE Projectile weapon, unless you
           Specialize in the Dagger (see below).
    (3) The only projectile weapons a Spy / Assassin may Specialize in are:
           (A) Dagger **   (B) Bolo   (C) Javelin   (D) Spear   (E) Short or Long Bow
           (F) Blowgun   (G) Lasso   (H) Net   (I) Crossbow
    Note: A Krill may also Specialize in the WristBow.
    ** **Note2:** Dagger – If the S/A Specializes in the Dagger, she or he may gain <u>BOTH</u> the Melee and
                 Projectile benefits.

Ninja:
    (1) Ninja may only Specialize at 7th **OR** 9th level - depending on which type of weapon they want to
           Specialize in.
    (2) If you want to Specialize in a Projectile weapon, you may Specialize at 7th level.
           If you want to Specialize in a Melee weapon, you must wait until 9th level.
    (3) The only weapons you may Specialize in are:
           (A) Ninja-to (Melee) (B) Star (Proj) (C) Sai (Melee) (D) Kama (Melee) (E) Nunchuck (Melee)
           (F) Short or Long Bow (Proj)   (G) Blowgun (Proj)   (H) Dagger (Proj)
                  (or **any** Other Ninja weapon; such as any chain or claw weapon.)

Extra: If the Ninja Specializes in the Ninja-to, he may use the backside of the blade causing 1d10 EP of Blunt
          type Damage and the butt end of the handle for 1d8 EP of Blunt type Damage and not harm
          the sword in anyway.
      If the Ninja Specializes in a Bow, they may do 1d10 Endurance Points Damage by using a Bow in
          Melee combat as a blunt weapon and not harm the bow in anyway.

Information about using a CrossBow or a WristBow:
1) It always takes 1 Action to Fire the CrossBow or WristBow and 1 Action to load it.
    You must pull back on the string to cock the weapon and then load the quarrel into it, this takes time.
2) If you Specialize in the operation of a CrossBow or a WristBow:
    a) You learn how to load it quicker, so you can gain the ability to load and fire an
          extra shot per attack. – **NOTE3:** Firing 'Slow' still means firing only 1 quarrel per Attack.
    b) You never gain your Strength Damage bonus, but ALL Cross / Wrist Bows have a 'built in' Damage
          bonus due to their construction. Please see the Weapons section for the bonus damage.

Break Down of Information for Melee & Projectile Weapon Specialization per Occupation

Level	Total # of Actions/Att.	Melee Strikes War / Ninja / S/A	Arrows/Attack War / Ninja / S/A	Quarrels/Attack War / Ninja / S/A
1st – 4th	2	1 / 1 / 1	2 / 2 / 2	1 / 1 / 1
3rd			3	{A}
5th – 9th	3	1 (2) / 1 (2) / 1 (2*)	4 (5) / 3 (4) / 3 (4)	2 {B} / {A} 2 / {A} 2
10th – 14th	4	2 (3) / 2 (3) / 1 (2*)	5 (6) / 4 (5) / 4 (5)	5/2 {3} / 2 {B} / 2 {B}
15th – 19th	5	3 (4) / 3 (4) / 2 (3*)	6 (7) / 5 (6) / 5 (6)	3 {C} / 5/2 {3} / 5/2 {3}

NOTE4: (1) The number in parentheses is the bonus for Weapon Specialization with a certain weapon type.
        (2) The numbers in brackets only pertain to someone who Specializes with a Crossbow or WristBow.
           These are the number of Quarrels a Specialized person may fire per Attack:
           {A} = 3 Quarrels / 2 Att.   {B} = 5 Quarrels / 2 Att.   {C} = 7 Quarrels / 2 Att.
        (*) The S/A only gains this Melee bonus if they have been trained in: Specialization with the Dagger.

SWITCHING OCCUPATIONS

When you learn an Occupation and start to rise in level, there is a time at which you may want to learn another Occupation; to make your character more well rounded. When you switch, it must be at the "crux" between 2 levels; right after you've gone up a level in your current Occupation and before you start gaining Experience Points again.

You then must be accepted by a school or a private teacher to learn the new Occupation. After you have completed your new training, you may start gaining experience in your new Occupation. You must continue in your new Occupation for at least 2 levels. At that time you can change back to your original Occupation or start another.

NOTE: You won't be able to learn some Occupations, once you've already gotten experience in others - like you can't be a Ninja, Alchemist, or an Elementalist if you have already trained as an Enchanter.

You can use all abilities from any previous Occupations as soon as you complete your training in your new Occupation and you start adventuring again.

NOTE2: You can't learn more than **3** Occupations.

NOTE3: You can not ascend **passed** 15th level in the second Occupation you've learned.
You can not ascend **passed** 10th level in the third and last Occupation you've learned.

Combinations of Occupations that Can NOT be used together

1) Ninja - Can't become an Enchanter, Alchemist, Elementalist or Mentalist.
Reason: Ninja can't generate Spell or Mental Points once they have learned to consolidate Ki points.

2) Enchanter, Alchemist, or Elementalist - Can't become a Ninja.
Reason: Enchanter, Alchemist, or Elementalist can not ever generate Ki Points.

3) Enchanter - Can't become an Alchemist, Elementalist or Ninja.
Reason: You may only use Spell Points for 1 discipline. Besides an Alchemist must be 'changed' at adolescence & an Elementalist WILL NEVER teach anyone who already knows another Occupation.

4) Alchemist - Can't become an Enchanter, Elementalist or Ninja.
Reason: Can only use Spell Points for 1 discipline during your life and never consolidate Ki Points.

5) Elementalist - Can't become an Enchanter, Alchemist or Ninja.
Reason: Can only use Spell Points for 1 discipline during your life and never consolidate Ki Points.

6) Mentalist - Can't become a Ninja.
Reason: Can't generate Ki Points.

Endurance Points (EP):

After you "graduate" from your new Occupational school, **you DON'T gain any EP.** Remember when you began adventuring with your character, you received your basic (Endurance score) * 2 + 1 die per level. Also, right before you started training for your new occupation, you just attained a level in your pervious Occupation and you gained EP for that. When you reach **2nd level** in you new Occupation, you may roll the EP die listed for that **new** Occupation. Remember, when you rise in Level, always roll the die listed for the Occupation you are currently studying and putting XPO into.

Number of Actions Per Attack:

To ascertain the total number of Actions per Attack you rate, add up your total number of levels from all of your Occupations and compare that total to your **1st** Occupation's Total Actions table. You MUST always use the Strike and Parry Actions listed on the table of the FIRST Occupation you learned.

Ie. If you are an Enchanter and then learn to be a Warrior, you will never rate 3 Strikes and 2 Parries per Attack. You always will only rate 1 Strike and 4 Parries per Attack if your total levels add up to 15 or above.

Resist Enchantment Rolls and Number of Enchanted or Mentalist Items:

To figure what your RER total is and how many Enchanted or Mentalist items you may carry, you simply add all your total levels together and that is the level you use.

Example - You became a Spy until 5th level, then a Warrior until 4th level and now you are studying the Enchanter's trade and are 3rd level. Your total levels are 12 so your RER is 25% and the number of Enchanted or Mentalist items you can hold is 13.

Number of Weapons and Survival Skills:

To figure out these totals you add all your levels together. This means that you only <u>start</u> once and when you switch Occupation's, you <u>don't</u> rate the number of Weapons or Survival Skills listed under the "Starting Weapons and Survival skills" Table!

Example - If you're a 4th level Enchanter and you decide to learn the Warrior's Occupation, you DON'T learn any additional weapons when your "at school"! When you become a 2nd level Warrior, your total levels will be 6 and you can learn an extra weapon and an extra Survival Skill, or Specialize in a Survival Skill you already know, etc.

Will: To figure this, you add all your levels together and take that level's bonus listed on the Will table.

Number of times per day you may Regenerate Spell, Ki or Mental Points:

To figure out how many times per day you can regenerate your points, add up your levels and take that total. If you are a 5th level Warrior and a 4th level Enchanter, you may Regenerate your Spell Points 5 times per day, ie. At 9th level ability.

NOTE: You can never count any total levels over 19. So, if you are a 15th level Warrior and a 10th level Enchanter, your total is 25 but you can't count any past 19, so your RER total is 30%, the maximum number of slots of Enchanted or Mentalist Items you can hold are 18, and you gain the Will Bonus for level 15+.

A few more things to keep in mind :

1) You can only put Experience Points into ONE Occupation at a time. You must complete **2** levels in your secondary Occupation, before you can start putting XPO back into your primary Occupation or start to learn another.

2) You may only use Weapon Specialization in **1 Occupation!** The Occupation you 1st take a Weapon Specialization in is the one you must stay with.
   Examples: If you Start off as a Spy, reach 7th level, Specialize in a Dagger, and then learn to be a Warrior, you CAN'T Specialize when you reach 5th or 7th level as a Warrior.
   But if you are a Spy, reach 7th level, don't Specialize, and then learn the Warrior Occupation, you may Specialize as a Warrior and gain all of the Warrior Specialization benefits, like Specialization in a melee AND a projectile weapon – when you reach 5th and 7th Levels in the Warrior Occupation.

3) A One-Timer on the XPO table can only be used ONCE during a character's <u>life journey</u>, **NOT** once per Occupation.

4) Every time you switch Occupations, you must start over on the XPO table. You will have an XPO total for EACH Occupation you have studied. If you are a 16th level Enchanter, a 12th level Mentalist and a 8th level Spy, your XPO totals may be:
   Enchanter = 3,118 XPO   Mentalist = 952 XPO   Spy = 335 XPO.

5) If you are relatively high level in an Occupation and you start to learn a new one, you may receive a large amount of XPO for doing a task. Please remember, you must still go through the low levels (1-4) of your new Occupation. You only gain 20% additional XPO added to your total experience towards your next level in your new Occupation when you receive experience.

Learning New Survival Skills, Weapons, Spells and Occupational Skills

When your character gains a new level, she or he is usually able to learn some new type of skill. There are two situations in which you may find yourself when it comes time to learn a new skill: You may be somewhere which has training facilities with specialized instructors trained to teach the subject in question or you could be in the middle of nowhere or just in a small village traveling with your companions.

I usually prefer to hear the bad news first, so here it goes. If you need new training and you can't find someone to teach you who is a close and personal friend, you must go to a regular school and they will ask that you spend some of your hard earned coin to cover their expenses. When you pay for your training, you will be taught by a 'Designated Instructor' [D.I.]. This is someone who has been taught to teach the skill in question. Because you are learning this skill directly from a D.I., it will take less time for you to learn the skill then it does for the next situation.

The good news is if you can get one of your friends, acquaintances, or someone who owes you a favor to teach you; you wont have to pay anything! The only down side to this situation is that it will take longer for you to completely learn the new skill because 'your friend' has probably not been taught to teach that skill.

There are four distinct areas your character may wish to gain training in, so I have separated this discussion into those possibilities: Learn a new Survival Skill, Learn how to correctly use a new Weapon, Learn a new Spell or Mental skill, or learn a new Occupational ability. Each particular situation is described by the times and costs your character will have to pay when you learn from a D.I. or when you learn from a friend. All time requirements and costs have been summarized on the tables at the end of this section.
NOTE: Ninja acquire their next Ki ability by just meditating.

When it's time for you to learn a new **Survival Skill** and if you go to a D.I., it will take you 1 week of intensive study to fully learn the skill and it will cost you 25 silver pieces.

If you learn the skill from a friend, you must spend 3 weeks with at least 3 hours per day in study and practice. During the first week of study, your percentage to correctly perform the skill is the same as it is for anyone else attempting any skill without training, ie. a percentage equal to your Ability Score. During the second week, your percentage increases to your Ability Score x 2. During the last week of training you percentage slowly increases to your Ability Score x 3.

When it's time for your character to learn to correctly use a **New Weapon** and is trained by a D.I., you are required to purchase the weapon you want to learn and spend 1 week in intensive training. You will be charged a total of 2 Silver pieces per Strength point required to wield the weapon. I.e. To learn a long sword you will be charged 28 Silver pieces and 18 Silver pieces to learn a mace.

If you can learn the weapon from a friend it requires 3 weeks of training by working out 3 hours per day with the weapon you picked.

Naturally, there are some restrictions on who can teach you to correctly use certain weapons: only a Ninja is qualified to instruct another Ninja to wield a pair of Nunchucks and only a Krill could teach another Krill to use a WristBow.

If you want to learn a **New Spell** and are able to attend a school or be taught by a D.I., it will require 1 full day to completely copy one Class (C) spell – a spell between 5th and 9th levels. You will be required to pay a specific fee depending on the Class of the spell learned.

If you learn the spell from a friend it will take twice as long to copy the spell. Please, see the table at the end of this section for complete details.

If you want to learn a new **Mental Skill** and you receive formal training from a D.I., it will require 1 hour of study per MP needed and cost you 1 silver piece per MP to learn the new ability.

If you learn the Mental Skill from a friend or acquaintance it will require 2 hours of study per MP needed. **NOTE2:** You may only learn a Mental Discipline from a Master and it will require 1 month of study to attain the new Mental Discipline. It is expected of you to reimburse your mentor for his time, this costs 50 Silver.

If your character is a Warrior, Spy / Assassin, or Ninja and want to master an new **Occupational Skill,** you will have to endure intensive training for 2 weeks. The payment varies depending on your occupation and your level.

If you get a friend to teach you, you must spend at least 3 hours per day for 4 weeks.

The next set of tables summarize the rules stated above.

Learning a new Survival Skill

Time Required	Cost	Source of Training
3 weeks	0	Friend or for a favor - No cost.
1 week	25 Silver	School or Designated Instructor [D.I.].

Learning a new Weapon

Time Required	Cost	Source of Training
3 weeks	0	Friend or for a favor - No cost.
1 week	2 Silver / Str. Pt.	School or Designated Instructor [D.I.].
		(Cost is per Weapon Learned.)

Learning a new Spell

Class	(A)	(B)	(C)	(D)	(E)		Source of Training
Time	6 hr.	12hrs.	2days	3days	4days		Friend or for a favor - No cost.
Time	3 hrs.	6 hrs.	1 day	1.5 d	2 days		School or Designated Instructor [D.I.].
Cost	2	4	8	16	32	Silver	(Cost is per spell Learned.)

Learning a new Mental Skill

Time Required	Cost	Source of Training
2 hours per MP	0	Friend or for a favor - No cost.
1 hour per MP	1 Silver / MP	School or Designated Instructor [D.I.].
		(Cost is per skill Learned.)

Learning a new Occupational Skill
Warrior

Level	2 - 4	5th **	6 - 9	7th **	10 - 14	15		Source of Training
Time	<------------------ 4 weeks ------------------>							Friend or for a favor - No cost.
Time	<------------------ 2 weeks ------------------>							School or Designated Instructor [D.I.].
Cost	10	50	20	50	40	50	Silver	

Spy / Assassian

Level	Individual Skills	7th **	Source of Training
Time	<----- 4 weeks ----->		Friend or for a favor - No cost.
Time	<----- 2 weeks ----->		School or Designated Instructor [D.I.].
Cost	25 Silver	50 Silver	NOTE: S/A gain percentage bonuses each
			level on their General Skills without training.

Ninja

Level	2 - 3	4th	5th	6 - 8	7th **	9th **	10th	15th		Source of Training
Time	<---------------------- 4 weeks ---------------------->									Friend or for a favor - No cost.
Time	<---------------------- 2 weeks ---------------------->									School or Designated Instructor [D.I.].
Cost	10	--	20	20	50	50	40	60	Silver	NOTE2: Ninjas Automatically gain new
										Ki Abilities through Meditation.

** The cost to Specialize in a weapon is 50 Silver Pieces.

NOTE3: If you want to Specialize in a any skill you already know, it will cost you ½ of the time to learn and ½ of the Listed price.

ENCHANTER / ALCHEMIST SPELLS

This section contains a full description of Enchanter and Alchemist spells – Elementalists use a different set of spells. The first thing we'll discuses is what exactly a spell is and what is magic. The next thing described is how the information about each spell is laid out. Then there is a description of a Bolt, Jet, Barrier and Globe which are forms some spells can take. Then finally the list of the individual spells and their descriptions.

A Spell is a means by which Magic may be focused and cast. Magic is a force that has the ability to manipulate and control matter, energy and living creatures or inanimate objects in many different ways. The procedure required to actually cast a spell is stated in the steps listed below:

1) Concentrate for the time listed under the Concentration Time of the spell. While you concentrate, you review the entire spell's description and gather your inner self.
2) Say the Trigger Word or Phrase which takes 1 additional Action and then spend the Spell Points (and Endurance Points) called for by the spell at the end of the Concentration Time.
NOTE: The Endurance Points (EP) needed to be spent to cast any spell are equal to its Spell Point Cost Divided by TEN (rounded up).
I.e. The Glowing Hand spell requires 5 Spell Points to cast; this means that 1 EP **must** be spent by the caster to cast this spell and an Uncontrolled Fire spell means a cost of 43 SP so you must spend 5 EP.
NOTE2: The caster may end the Duration of any spell, any time she chooses.
NOTE3: The caster is NOT immune to the effects of his own spells, ie. If Castlin casts the Uncontrollable Fire spell on the chair he is sitting on, he must make a RER and take damage.

Each spell is laid out in a specific way. The Name is first, then the Range the spell may be cast, the Area which it affects, the Spell Point Cost needed to cast the spell, the Duration the spell lasts, and finally the number of Actions required for Concentrating to cast the spell. The letter in parentheses after the name of the spell is the Classification of the spell – this increases from (A) to (E) – and tells us the spell's relative strength. Directly after the Spell Point Cost of the spell is a M, D or A. This letter indicates if the spell is of the Miscellaneous, Defensive, or Attack type.

All of the spells listed here are divided into colors: Red, Orange, Yellow, Green, Blue, Indigo, Violet, Brown, White/Clear, Black, and Opaque. Each color, and the specific gems that are associated with each spell color, are listed at the top of each section. All gem color categories have two extra spells that are associated with that color but are not of it. These spells are listed under the Secondary Section at the end of each color section.

Spells can come in many forms. Some of these forms are used to attack or defend against an opponent. The most common of these are the Bolt, the Jet, the Barrier, and the Globe.

Bolt -   Every "Bolt" is 2 foot long and all "Bolts" conform to the diameter stated in the AOE. The AOE increases as the Bolt shoots outwards, this means that the "Bolt" actually gets larger as it gets closer to it's target. The "Bolt" is shot from the caster's palm and is limited to the stated Range, although they cross that distance with extraordinary speed. All "Bolt" spells are numbered because there are more powerful versions that may be learned at higher levels. All Bolts may only be used against one Opponent per spell. The caster must be able to see the intended victim and the victim always rates an RER vs. the bolt's damage. A successful RER roll always cuts the base damage done by the spell in half, ie. The victim makes an RER vs. Firebolt 2. Firebolt 2 does 10+1d20 damage. A successful RER roll cuts the base damage of 10 in half, so the total damage would now be 5+1d20.

Jet -   All "Jet" spells blast forth from the casters' palm, reaching to the stated Range, and form a cone encompassing to the AOE. All "Jets" continuously blast outward until the Duration ends! Some "Jets" inflict Damage every Attack the Victim is engulfed within it and some only inflict initial Damage, but these Jets give other penalties to your Opponent. Anyone within the AOE takes damage. The intended victim of a Jet spell rates a RER roll to receive half base damage.

Barrier - Any "Barrier" spell that an Enchanter or Alchemist may cast is Stationary and the caster must be in the exact center when it's cast (Elementalists Barriers are different). These defensive spells, encircle the caster in a cylinder of a particular enchantment with a 10 foot radius and walls that are 15 feet tall. The walls are 1 foot thick and inflict damage on anyone trying to pass through them. Because this is a defensive spell, it can only be cast defensively around the caster.

Globe - All "Globes" can only be used for Defensive purposes. When cast, the walls are 1 foot thick and they encircle the caster in a sphere of enchantment with a 15 foot radius. They encompass the entire AOE and the air inside is breathable and plentiful. An Enchanter / Alchemist must be in the exact center of their Globe when it is cast and all are stationary and do not move. If anyone tries to pass through the Globe they receive Damage - even the caster will incur damage if he flies through it! Any Globe cast while standing on the ground will become a Dome over the caster and any Globe that is cast while the caster is in mid the air will become a sphere and be suspended there for the Duration and then vanish.

Abbreviations :

RER	=	Resist Enchantment Roll		EP	=	Endurance Points
CRM	=	Charging Rate Multiple		SPC	=	Spell Point Cost
T	=	Touch		Person	=	Any Human, Hemar or Krill
Act.	=	Actions		Att.	=	Attack (5 Second time period)
1 hr/L	=	"One Hour per Level"		inst.	=	Instantaneous
15'+1'/L	=	"Fifteen feet Plus One foot per Level"		1 victim	=	One of *THEM*.

Damage: 4+1d20 EP = "Four Plus One D Twenty" – roll 1d20 and add 4 to the total.

NOTE: All victims of any spell rate a Resist Enchantment Roll (RER). A successful RER roll always cuts the base damage done by the spell in half and may protect the victim from the full affects of the spell.
ie. A victim makes a RER vs. the Wound 2 spell. Wound 2 does 18+2d8 damage. A successful RER roll cuts the base of 18 in half, so the damage would now be 9+2d8 <u>and</u> the victim also isn't forced to vomit all over his shinny new boots.

NOTE2: The caster may mold the area a spell effects into any size as long as the AOE stated in the spell's description is not exceeded. If the spell's AOE is 5 cubic feet, the caster may mold the spell into a size of 1'x1'x5' or 1'x2'x2.5' or .5'x1'x10', ect.

NOT TO BE PUBLISHED: Ongoing Duration Equations =	*Actions / Attack*	*vs.*	*Level*
I) (Level-1 + Total Actions) + 1d (Total Actionsx2)	2		1
II) (Level-5 + Total Actions) + 1d (Total Actionsx2)	3		5
III) (Level-10 + Total Actions) + 1d (Total Actionsx2)	4		10
IV) (Level-15 + Total Actions) + 1d (Total Actionsx2)	5		15

SPELL CLASSIFICATIONS	CT	SPELL POINT RANGE
(A)	1	1 - 19
(B)	1	20 - 49
(C)	2	50 - 99
(D)	3	100 - 149
(E)	4	150 - 199

Glowing Hand (A)   R: --   AOE: 15' Radius
SPC: 5 - M   D: 1 hr/L   CT: 1 Act

      This simple spell produces light that illuminates everything within the AOE. The source is your hand, but you may use your hand normally and the light remains steady because the light produced is magical and does not flicker.

Sparking Fingers (A)   R: 1'   AOE: 1" - 6 inches
SPC: 10 - A   D: 1 Act   CT: 1 Act

      This spell causes sparks to shoot from your fingertips up to 1ft. away. It may be used to start oil, straw, etc. on fire and may even blind your Opponent if you hit him in the eyes! It causes no Damage otherwise.

Flame Bolt 1 (A)   R: 15'+1'/L   AOE: 6" - 1'
SPC: 18 - A   D: --   CT: 1 Act

      As with all Attack spells, a Flame Bolt speeds from the palm of your hand to your target. When this Bolt hits, it will ignite any flammable materials 50% of the time and the Victim takes 4+1d20 EP Damage. (He is, of course, entitled to a RER for 1/2 base damage or 2+1d20).

Uncontrolled Fire (B)   R: 20'+1'/L   AOE: 2' Radius +
SPC: 43 - A   D: 1 Attack   CT: 1 Action

      This spell can be cast anywhere within the Range and causes a small explosion that ignites all flammable materials within the AOE. Everyone within the AOE takes 10+1d20 Endurance Points (EP) of Damage from the blast. This spell is commonly cast into arrows, quarrels, spears, etc. After the Projectile is launched and the Trigger Word is spoken, the spell will explode when the projectile hits anything. Remember, Regular Fire causes 1d10 EP Damage per Attack while your victim is caught in the flames.

Flame Jet (B)   R: 10'+1'/L   AOE: 6"-1' cone +
SPC: 44 - A   D: 5 seconds/L   (1 Attack / L)   CT: 1

      The Flame Jet is very destructive because there is a 50% chance per Attack that any ignitable material within the AOE will catch fire. Anyone within the AOE takes 10+1d6 EP Damage on the first Attack and will take an additional 1d6 EP Damage per Attack they are engulfed in the Jet of Flames.

Flame Barrier (C)   R: Self   AOE: 10' radius x 15' tall
SPC: 52 - D   D: 5 min +   CT: 2

      This defensive spell encircles the caster in a cylinder of flames with a 20' diameter and walls that are 15' tall. The walls are 1' thick and inflict 12+1d20 EP Damage to anyone trying to pass through them and all flammable materials will ignite 50% of the time.   (Remember that you can't cast a Defensive spell ON someone.)

Flame Bolt 2 (C)   R: 25'+1'/L   AOE: 6" - 2'
SPC: 53 - A   D: --   CT: 2

      This spell is much like Flame Bolt 1, except it speeds to a Range of 25'+1'/L, causes all flammable materials to ignite 70% of the time, and inflicts 12+1d20 EP Damage to the Victim.

Flame Bolt 3 (D)   R: 35'+1'/L   AOE: 6" - 3'
SPC: 108 - A   D: --   CT: 3

      This spell is much like Flame Bolt 1&2, except it reaches out to a Range of 35'+1'/L, causes all flammable materials to ignite 90% of the time, and inflicts 22+1d20 EP Damage to the Victim.

Fire Globe (E)   R: Self   AOE: 15' radius.
SPC: 157 - D   D: 15 min +   CT: 4

      If anyone tries to pass through a Fire Globe, regardless of CR, they will receive 30+2d20 EP Damage and there is a 90% chance any flammable materials on them will catch fire, even the caster will incur damage if he flies through it!

FireBall (E)   R: 45'+2'/L   AOE: Blast Area = 45' dia. (22.5' rad.)
SPC: 159 - A   D: --   CT: 4

This is one of the most destructive spells anyone can cast. It may travel to the full distance stated in the Range or the Enchanter may "blast" it at any distance along the way. It travels in the form of a small ball of fire, until either of the two above conditions are met, and then it explodes, affecting everyone within the AOE. It will also explode on its own if it runs into something first, so make sure you're out of the AOE or you'll be affected also. The explosion causes much destruction, ignites flammable materials 90% of the time and does 34+2d20 EP Damage to all within the AOE.

Secondary Spells for Red Enchanted Gems:

Fly 1 (C)   R: T   AOE: 1 Object
SPC: 52 - M   D: 30 min/L   CT: 2

(This spell is exactly the same as the one described under the Blue Gem Spells.)

Light 3 (B)   R: 10'+1'/L   AOE: 60' radius
SPC: 40 - M   D: 2 hr/L   CT: 1

(Follows all rules stated in the spells described in the Yellow Gem section.)

Shield, Melee (*)   R: T   AOE: Recipient
SPC: ^ - D   D: 30 min. +   CT: **

This spell may be cast on any one person. It provides a Percentage Bonus to the recipient's PTE total on every Attack that is received from any Melee combat weapon; this includes spears, clubs, fists, claws, jaws, feet and much more. The number of Attacks or Opponents doesn't matter. It provides "all-round" protection, until the Duration ends. Everyone may only gain benefits of ONE shield spell at a time. If you try to use Shield, Melee, 10% and Shield, Projectile, 10% at the same time, both will be canceled. This spell is unique because the it has different Spell Point Costs to gain different bonuses to your PTE total.

SPC^	Percentage Plus	Casting Time **	Classification*
12	+10%	1 Action	(A)
32	+20%	1	(B)
52	+30%	2	(C)
72	+40%	2	(C)
102	+50%	3	(D)

Shield, Projectile (*)   R: T   AOE: Recipient
SPC: ^ - D   D: 60 min. +   CT: **

This spell provides a percentage bonus to the recipient's PTE total on all Attacks vs. any type of Projectile. The number of Opponents, Projectiles or the direction of the attacks doesn't matter.   This spell also has different Spell Point costs to gain different bonuses to your PTE total.

SPC^	Percentage Plus	Casting Time **	Classification*
10	+10%	1 Action	(A)
22	+20%	1	(B)
42	+30%	1	(B)
62	+40%	2	(C)
92	+50%	2	(C)

Shield, Magic: Class (A) [B]   R: T   AOE: Recipient
SPC: 25 - D   D: 15 min +   CT: 1

These spells provide the recipient with complete protection against any spell with the classification stated in the spell's name. These spells are only useful against that spell classification - the Shield, Magic: Class (A) will only protect you from Class (A) spells NOT Class (B) or (C) spells! This spell protects you from the minor enchantments of Class (A) spells for the Duration. This protects you from ALL effects of any Class (A) spell, including knowing if you are being assaulted by or looking at a Class (A) illusion.

Force Bolt (B)   R: 25'+1/L   AOE: 1' bolt
SPC: 33 - A   D: --   CT: 1

This is a translucent Bolt that stops all forward movement of the victim it strikes. It also causes 8+2d8 EP Damage + 1d8 per Charging Rate Multiple (CRM) that victim is moving toward the caster. There may also be extra Damage from falling off a charging horse, etc.

Shield, Magic: Class (B) [C]   R: T   AOE: Recipient
SPC: 55 - D   D: 15 min +   CT: 2

This Shield spell will protect you from Class (B) spells only. Please see Shield, Magic: Class (A) spell above. Anyone may only benefit from ONE type of Shield spell at any one time.

Force Net (C)   R: 30'+1'/L   AOE: 1 victim
SPC: 56 - A   D: 5 min.   CT: 2

When this spell is cast a plethora of force strands shaped as a net will spring from your palm. When the Net hits your victim, it will tangle and wrap them up. This will drop a Krill out of the sky and will even stop a charging Hemar. Your victim may not break these enchanted bonds. If your victim misses his adjusted RER, the only way out is to use a Cancel Enchantment spell on it - otherwise your victim is stuck until the Duration ends. Your victim gets a RER plus 1/2 of his Agility score to totally evade the Net. If your victim does not evade the Net, he is wrapped within the Net. Any Victim caught within the Force Net will lose their Agility Bonus to their PTE total while trapped in the net.

Repulsion Beam (C)
R: 35'+1'/L
AOE: 50 lbs / Level
SPC: 80 - A
D: inst.
CT: 2

    This pencil thin translucent Beam will repel a victim weighing less than the AOE to the extent of the Range. If the target is charging at the caster, the Repulsion Beam will cause 1d12 EP Damage per Charging Rate multiple the victim is moving at the caster and repel the victim to the extent of the Range. (A Warrior charging toward an Enchanter of 8th level at 20 ft/sec [CRM: 4] will be receive 4d12 EP Damage and will be repelled to 43 ft.) If the victim weighs more than the AOE, he will take full damage and be stopped in his tracks.

    If the victim is not charging at the caster, he will take 18+2d8 damage and be pushed to the maximum of the Range if he weighs less than the AOE. The victim only rates a RER if his is NOT charging.

Bubble of Force (C)
R: 25'+1'/L
AOE: 1 Victim
SPC: 95 - A
D: 1 min +
CT: 2

    This spell encompasses the victim in an giant bubble which is invulnerable to anyone and anything, nothing may pass in either direction (including any type of enchantment.) The caster may mentally move the bubble in any direction at a CR=5 ft per second (CRM: 1) to the extent of the Range, even upwards. The caster may also cause the bubble to "pop" at any time - this could put a Human in some difficulty and stop a Krill in flight. The bubble must be cast around a living thing. The weight of the victim doesn't matter, but she or he cannot have a height greater then 10 ft. This has also been known to be cast around a companion to protect him, but you may never cast it around yourself.

Shield, Magic: Class (C) [D]
R: T
AOE: Recipient
SPC: 105 - D
D: 15 min +
CT: 3

    This spell is the same as the Shield, Magic spells above, except that is protects you from the enchantments of Class (C) spells <u>only</u> and if you are being assaulted by or looking at a Class (C) illusion. Anyone may only benefit from ONE type of Shield spell at any one time.

Shield, Magic: Class (D) [E]
R: T
AOE: Recipient
SPC: 155 - D
D: 15 min +
CT: 4

    This spell is the same as the Shield, Magic spells above, except that is protects you from the enchantments of Class (D) spells <u>only</u> and if you are being assaulted by or looking at a Class (D) illusion. Anyone may only benefit from ONE type of Shield spell at any one time.

Force Globe (E)
R: Self
AOE: 15' Radius
SPC: 157 - D
D: 15 min +
CT: 4

    This is a Translucent Globe that conforms to the AOE and must be cast around the caster. Anyone accidentally crashing into this Globe will receive 2d8 EP Damage per Charging Rate multiple. Remember all Globe spells may only be cast Defensively. Nothing can pass through this Globe – physical or enchanted. The only ways to cancel this Globe before the Duration ends is if the caster wants it gone or if a Cancel Enchantment spell is used against it.

Secondary Spells for Orange Enchanted Gems:
All Resists (B) or (C)
R: T
AOE: Recipient
SPC: 44 or 54 - D
D: (see below)
CT: 1

    See the Opaque spell section for a complete description of these spells. All Resist spells last from the time of casting to the next sunrise or until they contact the enchantment they are to protect you from, for <u>first</u> time. They all give you a +25% bonus on your first RER when you come in contact with the enchantment type the spell is to protect you from. The Resist spells that you may learn at 4th level give you protection from one particular spell. The Resist spells you may learn at 5th level gives you protection from any spell that may be held by a particular Gem. The source of the enchantment does not matter.

Weight (B)
R: 15+1'/L
AOE: 1 Victim
SPC: 34 - A
D: 10 min/L
CT: 1

    (Follow same rules that are listed in the Opaque Spell Section.)

Light 1 (A)   R: T   AOE: 20' radius. +
SPC: 8 - M   D: 1 hr/L   CT: 1 Act

    This is one of the most commonly known spells, because of its obvious uses. You may cast this spell on any inanimate object you are able to touch. The light is a soft yellow that is superb for reading, writing and searching dark catacombs. It does not flicker, completely lights up the AOE and because of the enchantment it casts no shadows within the AOE.

Note: If this Light spell is used during the IronBall game, the Duration changes. All Light spells cast during the IronBall game only overcome the darkness of the Canopy for 5 seconds / level or 1 Attack / level of the caster.

Sting Ray 1 (A)   R: 25+1'/L   AOE: 1 victim
SPC: 10 - A   D: --   CT: 1 Act

    This small yellowish ray shoots from the caster's palm and does 4+1d10 EP Damage to your Opponent. This spell has the lowest Spell Point Cost of any Attack spell and almost anyone may learn it and cast it, because it is a Class (A) spell. A RER will allow your victim to take ½ base damage or 2+1d10.

Blind-One (A)   R: 15+1'/L   AOE: 1 victim
SPC: 15 - A   D: 2+1d4 Actions *   CT: 1 Act

    This spell is very useful and dangerous because there is no downside. It will cause one victim to become blind for the duration rolled plus one Action recovering time. The Opponents of the victim (your friends) immediately receive all bonuses as if they were in complete darkness (+40% to their PTE totals) and the victim receives NO Agility bonus to his PTE roll. The victim does get a RER and if he is successful then he will only be blinded for 1 Action.

Light 2 (B)   R: 5'+1'/L   AOE: 40' radius +
SPC: 22 - M   D: 1 hr/L   CT: 1

    This spell is identical to Light 1, except that it can be cast within a greater Range and lights up a 40 ft. radius. (One question always asked is, "Can this spell be cast in someone's eyes and blind them?"; Answer = NO.)

Light 3 (B)   R: 10'+1'/L   AOE: 60' radius +
SPC: 40 - M   D: 2 hr/L   CT: 1

    Since this spell is the same as the above spells, except for AOE, Duration, SPC, and Range – I don't need to say anything about it.

Sun Light (B)   R: 5'+1'/L   AOE: 20' radius +
SPC: 43 - A   D: 1 hr +   CT: 1

    This spell is much like the other Light spells with regard to Range, Duration, and AOE, but this is where the similarities end. The light produced by this spell is a 2' Long x 1" Wide horizontal column of pure sunlight, but it DOES NOT have the power to renew initial spell points. It does, on the other hand, have the power to keep Enchanted Creatures at bay that are "Purely Evil" or that shun the light of day. This horizontal column may be mentally moved anywhere within Range and then it will move with the caster. Any creature that is affected by sunlight and "falls" into the AOE will receive 1d10 EP Damage for each Attack it stays there. If a Purely Evil creature comes in direct contact with this column of Sun Light, it will take 2d10 EP Damage every Attack.

Invisibility (one) (C)   R: T   AOE: 1 recipient
SPC: 52 - M   D: 10 min/L   CT: 2

This very powerful spell will encase you within an enchantment so no one can see you. Unfortunately, you still leave tracks and make sounds. The spell lasts until the Duration ends. If you wish to make someone else disappear you have to touch them, while casting the spell. Anyone who kills someone while invisible immediately falls to a MR of 3 and even by merely attacking someone while invisible will drop you to a MR of 9. If you are invisible and someone attempts to attack you, you receive a +40% bonus to your PTE total. The only exception is if your attacker has the Survival Skill: Attack Unseen Enemy. If they do have this survival skill, you will only receive a +30% bonus. With one specialization, your attacker knocks your bonus down to +20%, with two specialization's, you receive only a +10% bonus on your PTE total. Someone may detect you and attack you normally if they are using a See Enchantment or See Life spell.

Lightning Bolt 1 (C)   R: 35'+1'/L   AOE: 1 victim
SPC: 54 - A   D: --   CT: 2

This produces a 2 ft. bolt of lightning (3" in diameter) that flashes from the casters open palm to the victim. When the bolt strikes someone it does 12+2d10 EP Damage to him, unless they are wearing a full suit of metal armor, then it does 24+2d10 EP Damage (double the base damage.) In either case, a successful RER will allow the victim to take ½ base damage (6+2d10 or 12+2d10, respectively). When this lightning bolt strikes flammable materials, there is a 20% chance that they will catch fire.

Sting Ray 2 (area) (C)   R: 30'+1'/L   AOE: 20' radius
SPC: 54 - A   D: --   CT: 2

This spell is much like Sting Ray 1, but it can affect anyone within the AOE out to the Range. The Enchanter may release as many Sting Rays as he or she has levels, but anyone within the AOE may not be hit by more than **ONE** Sting Ray. (If the Enchanter is 5th level, she may release up to 5 Sting Rays. Charging the Enchanter this time are 3 Opponents, so when the Enchanter casts the spell only 3 Sting Rays are released - one at each Opponent.) Each Sting Ray does 12+1d10 EP Damage to anyone it strikes that doesn't make their RER.

Blind - Many (C)   R: 30'+1'/L   AOE: 20' radius +
SPC: 73 - A   D: 5+1d6 Actions   CT: 2

This spell causes no damage, never-the-less, it is very powerful. Everyone within the AOE is automatically blinded for 3 Actions, but everyone affected does receive a RER. If the victim's RER is successful, his vision clears during his next or 4th Action. If any victim fails their RER, that victim is blinded for a total of 5+1d6 Actions and then their vision clears on the following Action.

Sun Light Beam (C)   R: 40'+2'/L   AOE: 6"-2'+
SPC: 88 - A   D: --   CT: 2

This is a Beam of pure Column Sunlight that shoots from the palm of the caster and it expands to fill the AOE as it speeds toward the extent of the Range. This will cause all creatures, except "Purely Evil" ones, to take 18+2d10 EP Damage. If this spell is used against a "Purely Evil" Enchanted creature the damage is 36+2d10 EP. Even these creatures are entitled to a RER for ½ of the doubled base damage.

Lightning Bolt 2 (D)   R: 45'+1'/L   AOE: 1 victim
SPC: 108 - A   D: --   CT: 3

This awesome spell will create a Lightning Bolt that is 4' long and 6" in diameter. This spell will only affect one person and it will cause 22+2d10 EP Damage, unless he or she is wearing a full-suit of metal armor, then you may double the base and roll 44+2d10 EP Dam. When this lightning bolt strikes any flammable materials, it will ignite them 40% of the time. The victim is allowed a RER to receive ½ base damage.

Ability Bonus: Intellect (E)   R: T   AOE: Recipient
SPC: 155 - M   D: 1 day/L   CT: 4

This spell will increase your Intellect score. You gain enough points to increase your score so that you gain the next ability increase. I.e. If your score is 7, it increases to 10; if it's 14 it becomes 15. You will receive all bonuses of the higher Intellect score until the Duration ends. You don't lose anything you've learned during the time the Attribute was raised, except any spells that you learned and now don't have enough slots or Spell Points to keep. NOTE: When your Intellect increases, your Will score may increase.

Lightning Bolt 3 (E)　　　　　R: 65'+2'/L　　　　　AOE: 1 victim
SPC: 159 - A　　　　　　　　　　D: --　　　　　　　　　CT: 4

This awesome spell will create a Lightning Bolt that is 8' long and 1' in diameter. This spell will only affect one person and it will cause 34+4d10 EP Damage, unless you Opponent is wearing a full-suit of metal armor, then you may double the base and roll 68+4d10 EP Dam. When this lightning bolt strikes any flammable materials, it will ignite them 50% of the time. The victim is allowed a RER to receive ½ base damage.

Secondary Spells for Yellow Enchanted Gems:

Heal Wounds 1 (B)　　　　　R: T　　　　　　　　　AOE: 1 person
SPC: 30+ - D　　　　　　　　　D: --　　　　　　　　　CT: 1

(Follow same rules that are listed in the Green Spell Section.)

In Sight Teleport (C)　　　　R: 5'+1'/L　　　　　AOE: 1 recipient per 3 levels of the Caster
SPC: 95　　　　　　　　　　　D: --　　　　　　　　　CT: 2

(Follow same rules that are listed in the Black Spell Section.)

These next spells all give you some type of Enchanted sight. These spells all can be held within a Yellow gem, but are listed here at the end of this section for conveyance.

See Enchantment 1 (A)   R: 10'+1'/L   AOE: Everything within Range
SPC: 8 - M   D: 1 hour / Level   CT: 1

    All Enchanters are able to learn this spell, in addition to the spells they rate from their Intellect score at 1st level. This simple spell will show the recipient any Enchanted Items, Creatures, invisible objects or illusions within the AOE, by making them glow a distinct color. The color and brightness of the glow depends on the spell that is being viewed and is more intense for stronger Enchantments. This spell reveals all Enchanted objects, illusions and invisible creatures within Range. An invisible or otherwise unseen Enchanted Creature will glow a dull yellow.

Type of Enchanted Item	Glow under 'See Enchantment' spell	Example
1) Spell cast into a item.	Main Part of item or weapon will Glow.	Dagger's Blade glows.
2) Enchanted Gem set into item.	The Enchanted Gem will Glow.	Gem as clasp of a cloak.
3) Raw Spell Points pumped into item.	Whole Item Glows with same Intensity.	Whole Door Glows.
4) Potion, Alchemist Dust or Pill.	The Potion, Dust or Pill will Glow.	The potion glows, not bottle.
5) Elementalist Ring / Disk.	The Enchanted Gem will Glow.	Ring's Gem glows brightly.

See Truth / Lie (B)   R: T   AOE: 1 Victim
SPC: 20 - M   D: 1 hour or Question / Level   CT: 1

    You must be touching you victim as you say the last syllable of the Trigger Word. If the victim fails their RER the spell will take effect, if they succeed their RER, you will know that the spell is not affecting them. While speaking to a victim that failed their RER, you will instantly know if his or her answers are truthful or not. The Duration of the spell is either the limit of questions, which is one question per level, or one hour per level of caster, which ever event comes first.

Magnification Sight (B)   R: 10+1'/L   AOE: Everything within Range
SPC: 20 - M   D: 1 hour / Level   CT: 1

    This spell enhances your natural sight. It will increase your near sighted vision by 2 times per 20 Spell Points. Also, you receive an additional +5% on your Survival Skill percentage to Locate Traps or on a Spy / Assassin's percentage to Find Concealed Areas per 20 Spell Points spent. 40 Spell Points cast will result in x4 Magnification and +10% to Locate Traps or to Find Concealed Areas.

Telescopic Sight (B)   R: 100'+10'/L   AOE: Everything within Range
SPC: 20 - M   D: 1 hour / Level   CT: 1

    This spell enhances your natural sight. It will increase your far sighted vision by 2 times per 20 Spell Points. Also, you receive an additional +5% on your Detect Ambush total and -5% to your SPT roll when using a Projectile weapon per 20 Spell Points spent. 40 Spell Points cast will result in x4 power to your Telescopic Sight and a +10% to Detect Ambush roll and -10% to your SPT roll when using a Projectile weapon.

See Morality Rating (B)   R: 10+1'/L   AOE: Everyone within Range
SPC: 20 - M   D: 1 hour / Level   CT: 1

    This spell will allow you to ascertain the MR of anyone who is within the AOE out to the spell's Range. You can scan as many people as you like as long as the Duration lasts.

See Life (B)   R: 10'+1'/L   AOE: Everything within Range
SPC: 20 - M   D: 1 hour / Level   CT: 1

    The more Life Force there is the greater the glow, ie. the higher the Level of the person who you are looking at the greater the glow. This spell will even illuminate a Ninja using Shadow Step, but is _ineffective_ if he is using the 8th level Pass ability. This spell will also reveal the location of an invisible opponent.

See Enchantment - area (B)   R: 25+2'/L   AOE: 10' radius
SPC: 40 - M   D: 1 hour / Level   CT: 1

    This spell is the same as See Enchantment 1, except that it does not conform to a cone, but is a circle with a Radius of 10 ft. The caster may mentally move the AOE at a CRM of 2 anywhere within the Range, until the Duration ends. Like See Enchantment 1, this spell will reveal any and all invisible creatures, illusions or Enchanted Items in the area.

Heal Wounds 1 (A)   R: T   AOE: 1 person
SPC: 15 - M   D: inst.   CT: 1 Action

This spell may be confusing because it has two different sets of rules. The first set deals with everyone, <u>except Alchemists</u>, and the second set is <u>for Alchemists only</u>.

These rules are for everyone except Alchemists: When you cast this spell, you must spend 15 Spell Points and you <u>transfer</u> some of your own Endurance Points to the recipient, so you **can't** heal yourself! The most EP you may TRANSFER is equal to three times your Endurance Score, but you can transfer any amount you wish, with out exceeding that number. The transfer of EP from you to your companion (at least I hope the transferee is your friend) is very quick, so quick that there is a Backlash to you. The Backlash causes you to lose your next 2 Actions on the next Attack. The recipient is immediately cured of the wounds equal to your Endurance Points transfer. The extent the wounds are healed depends on their severity; bleeding stopped, cut closed, swelling reduced. There is no Backlash to your companion, so he or she can "make a move" that same Attack. Now, the caster must be very careful, because you could Actually kill yourself by unknowingly sacrificing too many EP. Remember, you must spend 2 EP in order to cast 15 SP.

The second set of rules is for <u>Alchemists only</u>. The Alchemist has to spend Spell Points to heal someone so he or she can heal themselves (1 SP = 1 EP Healed.) You still must spend at least 15 SP, but you may spend Spell Points up to x3 of your Endurance Score (so you may heal someone from 15 EP to a max of 60 EP - if your Endurance Score is 20.) Alchemists do not transfer EP, so there is NO Backlash!

In either case you may never heal someone past their Total Original Endurance Points (TOEP).

Shrink Animal or Bird (B)   R: 15'+1'/L   AOE: 1 Animal or Bird
SPC: 23 - M   D: 10 min/L   CT: 1

This spell will decrease the size of an animal or bird to 4 inches in height. This will also decrease the weight and the damage proportionally. The creature must be in Range and will stay small until the Duration ends, unless the creature makes its RER, in which case it is not affected by the spell.

Converse with Plants (B)   R: 10'+1'/L   AOE: 1 plant type
SPC: 31 - M   D: 5 min +   CT: 1

All of the Converse spells are very similar. This one will enable you to converse with one type of plant of your choice within the Range for the Duration. Yes, you may move about and the Range moves with you. Plants can tell you if someone has passed within 3 days, because of the short "memories". They have no concept of numbers but have vivid "memories" of colors and animals. They can also name the kinds of animals that frequent their immediate area and other plant types which are common to the same area and climate.

Vine Net (B)   R: 25'+1'/L   AOE: 1 victim
SPC: 32 - A   D: 5 min   CT: 1

When this spell is cast, a Net of strong vines will spring from your palm. When the Net hits your victim it will wrap and tangle them within the vines. This will drop a Krill out of the sky and will stop a charging Hemar. Your victim may break out in 8 Actions if they make an Ability Check with Strength. A friend can cut the victim out in 5 Actions or burn the vines off in 3 Actions - the victim may take fire damage though. Your intended victim gets a <u>RER plus 1/2 of his Agility score</u> to evade the Net. If the victim does not evade the Net, he's entangled. Victims lose their Agility Bonus to their PTE totals while trapped in the net.

Vine Arms (B)   R: T   AOE: 1 or 2 arms
SPC: 35 - M   D: 30 min   CT: 1

This unique spell transforms your arm (1 or both) into strong heavy vines! Your hands will also be transformed into a 3 "fingered" vine hand. The vines are 10' long +1'/level. These "arms" have your personal Strength and because the "hands" are close to your own, you may manipulate many objects. The "arms" last until the Duration ends or until they take 40 EP Damage at which time they transform back into your regular arms. You feel no pain and take no personal damage from injures to your transformed appendages, so you could reach into a fire, swing through the trees, etc. You can transform both arms if you spend 52 Spell Points. The caster may cancel the spell with a thought before the Duration ends.

Plant Wall (B)
SPC: 41 - D

R: 1'/L
D: 15 min

AOE: 15' tall x 15' wide
CT: 1

The caster may cause a Plant Wall to spring up from any stretch of open earth, stone or wooden floor. The wall is 2' thick and is composed of thick vines and branches. It is possible to Break through it in 5 min if you successfully make an Ability Check with Strength. You may cut through it in approximately 3 min and you can burn through it in about 1 min. (You may always use the Cancel Enchantment spell to dispel it.)

Plant Growth (B)
SPC: 42 - M

R: T
D: 15 min

AOE: 1 plant
CT: 1

This spell will mature any non-intelligent plant to "middle-aged" in an instant. If the plant is already "middle-aged" or older, the spell will not age it. If it is cast on a plant with any Intellect Score, it will only mature it 5 years. This may be done until the plant reaches "middle-aged". All ages are permanent and the normal aging process will take over as usually after the spell's Duration ends.

As the plant grows and for a time after it reaches "middle-aged", ie. until the Duration ends, the caster has control of it. Once you tell the plant to do something it will do that until you tell it to do something else - you use mental commands to control the plant. This means that you could issue it an Attack order, cast a few spells, give it another target, and quietly retreat into the forest.

Enlarge Animal or Bird (C)
SPC: 51 - M

R: 5'+1'/L
D: 10 min/L

AOE: 1 Animal or Bird
CT: 2

This spell will enlarge one animal or bird per spell. It will double the size of the animal or bird, double its Endurance Points and it's capacity to do damage, including to its Str. Dam. Bonus. It is possible for you to increase the size to any amount by sacrificing an extra 26 Spell Points for each multiple (76 SP = x3 size, 102 SP = x4, etc.) The damage it causes goes up with the increase in size and EP bonus. Note, this will not automatically compel the creature to obey you, so you had better be on "good terms" with it before you enlarge it! Of course, the creature must be within Range to cast the spell.

Plant Control (C)
SPC: 51 - M

R: 20'+1'/L
D: 10 min +

AOE: 30' x 30' square
CT: 2

This spell will let you control all plants within the AOE and you can cause the center of the AOE to be anywhere within the Range. Once you tell the plants to do something they will do it until you tell them to do something else - you use mental commands to control the plants. The strength of the plants depends on the vegetation in question - a full grown oak tree can cause 1d10 EP Damage with a good sized limb and can easily restrain someone. On the other hand, knee deep grass would only slow a Human or Krill on the ground and a Hemar at full charge would hardly even notice it.

Wound 1 (C)
SPC: 53 - A

R: 30'+1'/L
D: 3 Actions

AOE: 1 victim
CT: 2

This spell shoots out toward the victim as an emerald green ray. When it strikes your Opponent, it will cause 12+2d8 EP Damage and will cause him to immediately vomit, if his RER fails. A successful RER = ½ base Damage and no spewing of his last meal. All victims are considered Defenseless while puking (-MR if Stuck/Killed) and loose their Agility Bonus on their PTE rolls for the Duration.

Enlarge Person (C)
SPC: 71 - M

R: 5'+1'/L
D: 10 min/L

AOE: 1 person
CT: 2

This will increase someone's size by x2 for the Duration, double their Strength Damage Bonus, and add 5 EP per level of the caster to their EP total for the Duration. It will double their weight and also increase the size of all their possessions for the Duration. It is possible to increase the Physical Size and Strength Damage Bonus to any multiple by sacrificing an extra 36 Spell Points per increase, but the EP gained are always added at 5 EP per the caster's Level. Ref note: 107 SP = x3, etc.

Shrink Person (C)
SPC: 71 - M

R: 10'+1'/L
D: 10 min/L

AOE: 1 person
CT: 2

This spell will decrease the size of any one person to 1 inch. It will also decrease the size of any possessions, weight, and the damage they do proportionally. If the person doesn't want to be shrunk, he or she is entitled to a RER.

Plant Decay 1 (C)   R: 10'+1'/L   AOE: 1 plant
SPC: 71 - A   D: (see below)   CT: 2

    This destructive spell will completely decay any one non-intelligent plant. The plant's size has no bearing on this enchantment and the affect is permanent. If the plant has any Intellect at all, this spell will cause 16+2d8 EP Damage.   NOTE: Only intelligent plants receive a RER.

Wound 2 (C)   R: 40'+1'/L   AOE: 1 victim
SPC: 85 - A   D: 3 Actions   CT: 2

    Like Wound 1, this shoots out as an emerald green ray. It will inflict your victim with 18+2d8 EP Damage and will cause her to immediately vomit on her next Action, if she fails her RER. A successful RER = ½ base Damage and no spewing of her last meal. All victims are considered Defenseless while retching (-MR if Stuck/Killed) and loose their Agility Bonus on their PTE rolls for the Duration.

Polymorph, Plant (D)   R: 1'/L   AOE: Recipient
SPC: 107 - M   D: **   CT: 3

    With this spell, you may turn yourself or someone else into any type of non-intelligent plant for the Duration of the spell. Anyone who is polymorphed into a plant may still hear regularly, see to the front and smell. You can still feel pain but will not die if someone "chops you down" – the spell's Duration would just automatically end. The caster may end the spell at any time. If the recipient doesn't wish to be turned into a tulip, he or she is entitled to a RER.

    ** The Duration is special. This spell has two different Durations: the first is if the recipient is willing and the second is if you are casting it on an Opponent. If the recipient is willing the Duration is 30 min / L; If you are casting the spell on an Opponent the Duration is 4+1d8 Actions.

Plant Decay 2 (D)   R: 20'+1'/L   AOE: 10' radius +
SPC: 136 - A   D: (see below)   CT: 3

    This devastating spell will kill every non-intelligent plant within the AOE! The size or number of plants has no bearing on this enchantment and the effects are permanent. If this spell is used against plants with an Intellect score it will do 28+3d8 EP Damage to them.   NOTE: Only intelligent plants receive a RER.

Secondary Spells for Green Enchanted Gems:
Polymorph 1 (C)   R: 5'+1'/L   AOE: Recipient or victim
SPC: 58 - M   D: 30 min/L   CT: 2

    (Follow same rules that are listed in the Violet Spell Section.)

Mesmerize Animal or Bird (B)   R: 10'+1'/L   AOE: 1 Animal or Bird
SPC: 24 - A   D: 1 day/L   CT: 1

    (Follow same rules that are listed in the Indigo Spell Section.)

Float (A)   R: 1' / Level   AOE: One Person
SPC: 2 - D   D: varies   CT: 1 second

This potentially life saving spell will magically decrease your weight so that you slowly float to the ground, regardless of height. You don't have any control over the direction or the rate at which you make your way to the ground; you're at the mercy of the wind (If you're a Krill, you can't fly if under the affects of the Float Spell.) Notice that the Casting Time for this spell is only 1 second, so if you cut the corners, I'd say you could concentrate and cast it in only 1 Action. The Duration ends when you first touch the ground, body of water or solid surface, but not until then.

Cloud Part (A)   R: **   AOE: 50' radius
SPC: 6 - M   D: 15 min   CT: 1 Act

This seemingly worthless spell is highly prized by ship captains and those who use the sky to correct their direction. Cloud Part will part the clouds directly between you and the Column Sun to allow you to take a Sun-Sight with an Astrolabe, or so you can tell your general direction or the time. If you cast this at night, the "hole" will appear directly between you and that month's full moon.

Breeze (A)   R: 20'   AOE: 6"-10'
SPC: 8 - M   D: 5 min.   CT: 1 Act

This simple spell will create an enchanted breeze in one direction anywhere within the Range. The breeze can fan a fire, hold back a poisonous mist, or even disturb a steady fog. The breeze moves at 20 mph.

Glide (A)   R: T   AOE: Recipient
SPC: 10 - M   D: 20 min +   CT: 1 Act

This spell will let you glide a maximum lateral distance of twice your elevation when it's cast, Ie. If you cast the spell and jump off a 50 ft high wall, you may glide a maximum of 100 ft. You may control your direction, even making slow turns, and your descent is silent. If you are still airborne at the end of the spell, you will gently Float down until you reach the ground.

Wind Bolt 1 (A)   R: 25'+1'/L   AOE: 1' - 2'
SPC: 12 - A   D: --   CT: 1 Act

This spell will cause a short blast of wind beginning at the Enchanter's out-stretched palm and will speed out to the Range stated. It will grow and conform to the AOE as it gusts toward your Opponent. If the victim misses his RER, the Blast will do 4+1d12 EP Damage and knock him off his feet 15% of the time. If the victim makes his RER, he will only have to take ½ of the base damage or 2+1d12, but will still be blown off his feet 15% of the time. The blast travels approximately 45 mph and will definitely cause a "dust bolt" if the conditions are right.

Bridge 15' (A)   R: 5'+1'/L   AOE: 15' long x 5' wide
SPC: 15 - M   D: 10 min.   CT: 1 Act

This spell will bring into existence a bridge conforming to the AOE which may be cast within the Range. The bridge must be anchored on two sides, but will support any weight. It will glow a light blue so that you can tell exactly where the edges are. The caster may cancel the spell at any time before the Duration ends. The caster may double the AOE, if she spends 30 SP. (Triple = 45 SP & 45' long x 15' wide bridge).

Levitate (A)   R: 5'+1'/L   AOE: Recipient
SPC: 15 - M   D: 1 min +   CT: 1

This spell will let you levitate yourself, straight up and down, for the Duration. You do not have to concentrate for the Duration, just select your direction of movement. Your rate of movement will be 5 feet / Attack (CRM: 1) in either direction, up or down. You may double the movement rate (CRM: 2), if you spend 30 SP. (Triple = 45 SP and a CRM: 3).

Bridge 35'+ (B)   R: 10'+1'/L   AOE: 35' long x 10' wide
SPC: 35 - M   D: 30 min +   CT: 1

This spell is much like Bridge 15', but there are some unique differences. The bridge conforms to the AOE and may be cast anywhere within Range. It glows a light blue, will support any weight, but only has to be anchored on one side. The caster may cancel the spell at any time or may double the AOE, if she spends 70 SP. (Triple = 105 SP & 105' long x 30' wide bridge).

Converse with Clouds (B)   R: **   AOE: 1 cloud
SPC: 31 - M   D: 5 min +   CT: 1

This spell will allow you to converse with any one cloud passing overhead. The cloud can tell you everything it has "seen" in it's short "life" (a cloud will "live" from the time it forms to the next rainfall, this could be a couple of weeks or just a few hours.) A cloud pays a great deal of attention to what it passes over but has a short memory and can't remember things for more than 3 days. It may be able to give you a vast amount of information of a town, farmstead, or even a castle it has passed over. The cloud will even be able to tell you if any **flying** Elementals passed it recently (Air, Fog, Fire, or Smoke). You may converse with the cloud, in a normal voice - regardless of distance (within reason) - until the Duration expires.

Cloud Summon, Rain (B)   R: **   AOE: 50' Radius
SPC: 32 - A   D: form within 3 minutes   CT: 1

This spell will create one rain cloud that covers the AOE. This cloud will form within the time stated in the Duration and last until it dissipates as rain. The amount of rain is equal to a small shower and will start to fall immediately after it forms.

Wind Jet (B)   R: 15'+1'/L   AOE: 6"-1' + cone
SPC: 44 - A   D: 1 Attack / L   CT: 1

This jet will reach to the stated Range and conforms to the AOE, continuously blasting outward for the Duration. The Wind Jet will only do initial damage, but will cause anyone caught in it to lose his or her concentration, shield their eyes, and even slip if the conditions are right. This can also "kick up a lot of dust" to conceal yourself and your companions, if the conditions are right. The damage done when the Jet initially strikes your Opponent is 10+1d6 EP Damage, but it does not do ongoing damage. All victims rate a RER for ½ base damage.

Fly 1 (C)   R: 5'+1'/L   AOE: 1 object
SPC: 52 - M   D: 30 min/L   CT: 2

This wondrous spell will let anyone fly in any direction they wish. If cast on an inanimate object, the object will fly in any direction you tell it to and carry you with it. The maximum speed you may fly is a CRM of 6. You may touch ground and lift off again as many times as you wish during the Duration. When the Duration ends, you will fall straight down unless you have some other means of flight. This spell may easily be cast on a scepter, a carpet, or cape. If the spell is used on anything that has enough surface area to carry more than one person, the "carpet" will magically lift one **person** per the caster's level - but **not** the equivalent weight.
NOTE: The total surface area the caster may affect is a maximum of: 4 foot wide by 8 foot long and 1 inch thick.

Wind Bolt 2 (C)   R: 35'+1'/L   AOE: 1' - 4'
SPC: 53 - A   D: --   CT: 2

Follow same rule as described above. This Wind Blast does 12+1d12 and has a 20% chance to knock your Opponent off his feet (even if he makes her RER, which will only lesson the base damage.) The wind speed is 60 mph.

Fly 2 (D)   R: 10'+1'/L   AOE: any one thing
SPC: 107 - M   D: 30 min/L   CT: 3

This spell is exactly like Fly 1, except that you may fly at a CRM of 8 for the Duration. You may increase the speed to a CRM of 10 if you spend 159 Spell Points.
NOTE2: The total surface area the caster may affect is a maximum of: 6 foot wide by 10 foot long and 2 inches thick.

Wind Bolt 3 (D)   R: 50'+2'/L   AOE: 2' - 8'
SPC: 108 - A   D: --   CT: 3

    This is much like Wind Blast 1 & 2. The Range and AOE are greater and the victim will take 22+1d12 EP Damage. The speed of the Blast is approximately 75 mph and will knock the victim off his feet 25% of the time (even if he makes his RER, which will only lesson the base damage).

Wind Globe (D)   R: Self   AOE: 15' radius
SPC: 121 - D   D: 15 min +   CT: 3

    As with all Enchanter Globes, this one is 1' thick, can only be cast defensively, and fills the AOE. This spell will cause a Globe of Wind to surround the caster. Anyone within the Globe receives a +50% PTE bonus verses all projectiles. If someone or something runs through the Globe, they will receive 24+1d10 EP Damage.

Cloud Summon, Storm (D)   R: **   AOE: 100' Radius
SPC: 137 - A   D: forms within 5 minutes   CT: 3

    This spell will create a storm cloud overhead covering the AOE and will form in 5 minutes, lasting until it rains itself out. The storm will probably produce lightning and darken the area it covers. The rains will be heavy and will start to fall immediately after it forms.

Ability Bonus: Agility (E)   R: T   AOE: Recipient
SPC: 155 - M   D: 1 day/L   CT: 4

    This spell will increase your personal Agility score. You gain enough points to increase your score so that you gain the next ability increase, ie. If your score is 10, it will increases to 12; if it's 14, it becomes 16. You are entitled to all bonuses of the higher Agility, including any increase to the Agility bonus added to your PTE for the duration.

Storm Summon (E)   R: **   AOE: 1/2 mile radius
SPC: 158 - A   D: form within 10 minutes   CT: 4

    This spell will create a whole storm directly overhead covering the AOE. It will form within 10 minutes and last at least 5 hrs. It will have all the characteristics of a regular storm, including lightning, thunder, and strong wind. It will reduce visibility by at least half and reduce Traveling Rates by the same amount. It will be raining "cats and dogs" until it disperses and the deluge will start as soon as the storm forms. This storm may cause landslides or floods if the conditions are right.

Secondary Spells for Blue Enchanted Gems:

Lightning Bolt 2 (D)   R: 45'+1'/L   AOE: 2' radius
SPC: 108 - A   D: --   CT: 3

    (Follow same rules that are listed in the Yellow Spell Section.)

Speed (C)   R: 5'+1'/L   AOE: Recipient
SPC: 71 - M   D: 10 min/L   CT: 2

    (Follow same rules that are listed in the Opaque Spell Section.)

Converse with Animal or Bird (A)   R: 10'+1'/L   AOE: 1 Animal or Bird
SPC: 8 - M   D: 15 min./level   CT: 1 Act

    This spell will allow you to converse with any one type of animal or bird per spell. The animals must be within the stated Range and you may talk to any number of that type of animal until the Duration ends. Animals or birds have no concept of numbers (a lot or a few is the closest they can come). The creature will only remember something for a long period of time if it interests them (an eagle will remember for many years if someone tried to take her eaglets.) They can tell you a great deal of where enemies of their species are, including people if they are cruel to them.   **NOTE:** Just because you can talk with an animal or bird doesn't mean that they'll be friendly.

Daze - one (A)   R: 15'+1'/L   AOE: 1 victim
SPC: 13 - A   D: 2+1d4 Actions *   CT: 1 Act

    This spell will cause the victim to become disoriented. This disorientation will cause:

    (1)   Your victim's vision will become blurred.
    (2)   The victim's Opponents (you and your friends) gain a +25% to their PTE totals.
    (3)   The victim looses much of his natural equilibrium.
    (4)   The victim looses his Agility bonus to his PTE roll.

    Because of your victim's blurred vision, anyone they Strike at gets to add +25% to their PTE total; this means you and your friends. The lose of much of his natural equilibrium forces the victim to stumble to a halt if charging or forces him to immediately land if flying. If in the process of casting a spell, your victim will lose his concentration and he cannot begin casting another - but anyone affected can still say and use Enchanted Items that are initiated by a Trigger Word. Also, no one can use any Occupational skill - including Warrior abilities such as Parry, or Ninja Ki abilities or Spy / Assassins General or Individual skills, etc. You roll a 2+1d4 to find out how many Actions your victim will be affected. There is a star next to the Duration because even after the affects of the spell "wear off", it will take one Action for the victim to totally recover. If the victim makes his RER, he will not be affected.

Converse w/Reptile, Fish, or Insect (B)   R: 10'+1'/L   AOE: 1 Reptile, Fish or Insect
SPC: 21 - M   D: 15 min/level   CT: 1

    This spell is much like Converse with Animal or Bird, except it will work on any reptile, fish, or insect. These creatures remember much the same information and for the same reasons that animals and birds do.

Mesmerize Animal or Bird (B)   R: 10'+1'/L   AOE: 1 Animal or Bird
SPC: 24 - A   D: 1 day/L   CT: 1

    This spell will allow you to mesmerize one animal or bird which has Endurance Points less than or equal to yours. The creature must be within the Range and the affects will last until the Duration ends. A mesmerized creature will follow any commands that you issue to it to the best of its ability. These commands are issued mentally to the subject. The Animal or Bird cannot communicate or relate it's thoughts back to you by means of this spell alone. It takes only a few moments to give the mental commands. The subject won't try to twist anything you say and because the commands are given mentally, they **can't** be misunderstood by the creature.

Sleep - One (B)   R: 15'+1'/L   AOE: 1 victim
SPC: 24 - A   D: 3+1d4 Actions   CT: 1

    This spell will cause a person to fall immediately into a deep sleep that she or he won't wake up from for the entire Duration or until they are forcefully shaken or any Damage is done to them. Any initial fall caused by speed or the altitude of the victim effected by the spell will **not** awaken him. The spell causes no direct damage but falling out of the sky will. It will take 1 Action for the victim to fully awaken if someone tries to wake him up or if _any_ Damage is done to them. If the victim makes his RER, he will not be affected.
Ref. Note: I do NOT allow someone to kill a victim effected by this spell.

Order Spell (B)   R: 20"+1'/L   AOE: 1 victim
SPC: 30 - M   D: 10 min / Level   CT: 1 Act.

You may only successfully cast this spell if your Will Score or your Level is above that of your intended victim. The Order must be a short phrase and must coincide with the Morality of the victim. The victim must clearly hear and understand the Order given, ie. He must speak the same language. If the victim fails his RER, he will do his best to accomplish the Order. If the victim is harmed in any way the enchantment is immediately broken.

Mesmerize Reptile / Fish / Insect (B)   R: 10'+1'/L   AOE: 1 Reptile, Fish or Insect
SPC: 31- A   D: 1 day/L   CT: 1

This spell is exactly like the one listed above, except that it will mesmerize any one reptile, fish or insect and the Spell Point Cost is different.

Empathy (B)   R: 15'+1'/L   AOE: 1 person
SPC: 32 - M   D: 5 min / Level   CT: 1 Act.

This spell will allow you to sense someone's basic emotions (fear, love, hate, jealously, etc.). The person must be within Range, but does not have to be in sight (may be behind a door, ect.). You may only "scan" one person at a time, but you may change subjects until the Duration ends.

Mind Blast - One (B)   R: 20'+1'/L   AOE: 1 victim
SPC: 34 - A   D: Daze = 4+1d4 *   CT: 1

This interesting spell is a favorite of many Enchanters, because it has no "down side". Any one person within the Range may be affected. This spell will inflict 8+1d12 EP Damage and magically Daze the victim for 4+1d4 Actions (see the Daze-One spell for more details.) If the victim makes his RER, he will only take 4+1d12 damage, but will still be Dazed for TWO Actions - this is not cumulative.

Sleep Wall (B)   R: 1'/L   AOE: 15' tall x 15' wide
SPC: 43 - D   D: 10 min   CT: 1

This wall will glow a dull indigo and anyone or anything trying to pass through, must make a RER, or immediately fall into a deep sleep that is exactly like the one described in the Sleep-One spell, but the Duration is 5+1d4 Actions. The Wall will last for 10 min and doesn't need to be "anchored" to anything, it may be cast in mid-air, but must be cast Defensively – NOT directly on someone! The victim could be awakened by a friend shaking them or by any Damage done to them.
Ref. Note: I do NOT allow someone to kill a victim effected by this spell.

Summon Animal or Bird (B)   R: 1 mile   AOE: 1 type
SPC: 43 - A   D: 30 min / Level   CT: 1

This spell will Summon any 1 type of Animal or Bird that the caster calls as long as all the stipulations listed below are met. The type of animal or bird you call must be within the Range. The number of creatures that respond to the call can not exceed your level. The type of animal or bird that you call must have less Endurance Points than you do. The creatures that answer will follow any simple mental commands that you give them. They will even protect and fight for you, if you command them to. These creatures will do as you command until the Duration ends then they will immediately leave the area. The creatures will arrive within 1d20 minutes, depending on the type of creature and their distance away.

Summon Reptile / Fish / Insect (B) R: 1 mile   AOE: 1 type
SPC: 44 - A   D: 30 min +   CT: 1

This spell is essentially the same as the one listed above. The only difference is that the creatures affected are Reptiles, Fish, or Insects. You also can not summon a fish out of water, ect.

Return Item Spell (B)   R: T   AOE: 1 item
SPC: 47 - M   D: until used once   CT: 1

This spell will cause the item it is cast on to return to your hand when the Activation word is uttered. Once the spell is cast, it will be temporarily dormant until the Activation word is said and then the item will instantly fly to your open hand. You must be touching the item to cast it and mentally "say" the Activation word at the end of the casting. The item must be within normal hearing range so it may "hear" the Activation word; you may have to yell if the distance is great, but that is the only factor on how far the item may be from you. It will return to your hand on the next Attack, and if you don't have an open hand and Action, you must make a PTE roll.

ESP (C)   R: 20'+1'/L   AOE: 1 person
SPC: 51 - M   D: 5 min / Level   CT: 2

This stands for Extra Sensory Perception and this means you may actually read someone's mind. The person must be within Range. The victim rates a RER, if he is successful the spell does not effect him. You may read only surface thoughts of a person. There is no limit to what you can find out about what the person is currently thinking, but you must concentrate on that person to detect his subject's surface thoughts. You may scan more than one person if you wish and you even get a +10% on your Detect Ambush total while the Duration lasts. You CANNOT do this to any sleeping victim.

Telekinesis (C)   R: 25'+2'/L   AOE: 200 lbs
SPC: 52 - M   D: 15 min +   CT: 2

This spell will allow you to mentally manipulate any object that weighs less than the AOE and is within Range for the Duration. You may move the object in any direction at a rate of 5 feet/second (CRM: 1). This may also be used to stop a charging Opponent. You may move about but may not strike or attack and you must concentrate to do all of the above. You may manipulate these weights by spending these amounts of Spell Points:

200 lbs	52 SP	
300 lbs	78 SP	
400 lbs	104 SP	etc. (+26 SP each 100 lbs.)

Send Message (C)   R: -----   AOE: 1 person
SPC: 61 - M   D: Instantaneous   CT: 2

Casting this spell will allow your character to send a complete message to someone you know. The caster must know the recipient of the message well or he must be in her employ. (The recipient can not just be an acquaintance.) The distance separating the caster and the recipient does not matter. The message must be less than 100 words and is mentally composed and instantaneously sent and received.

Mesmerize Person (C)   R: 5'+1'/L   AOE: 1 person
SPC: 63 - A   D: 1 hr/L   CT: 2

This spell will allow you to mesmerize any one person for the Duration (he does have to be within the Range.) To cast the spell the Enchanter must only concentrate for the time stated and say the Trigger Phrase which is: "Hello, Good fellow", so the victim doesn't necessarily know a spell is being cast. This is very powerful because like the other mesmerize spells, the Enchanter may send the commands mentally (but can speak them if she wishes.) The person will do anything within his ability that the caster commands that is not contrary to his beliefs. If he is told to physically harm himself, one of his close friends or if he is asked to perform a task contrary to his MR, the spell is immediately broken. The victim is allowed an initial RER when the spell is cast and if this is successful, he will not be affected by the spell and will also have a chance equal to his regular Ability Check with Will to know that someone has just tried to mesmerize him. All Mesmerized victims will tend to be slightly slow in their reactions and answers, (never get initiative) but will otherwise seem normal.

Item Dance (C)   R: 20'+1'/L   AOE: 1 item
SPC: 75 - A   D: 3 min +   CT: 2

This spell will cause any item to dance in the air in the general vicinity the caster points to. The caster must touch the item to enchant it. If cast on a weapon, the weapon will "fight" on its own, making one strike per Attack. Your Opponent has no way to stop the item except to destroy the weapon, kill the caster or to use a Cancel Enchantment spell.

Daze - Many (C)   R: 20'+1'/L   AOE: 10' radius +
SPC: 78 - A   D: 5+1d6 Actions   CT: 2

This spell follows all the rules of Daze-One, it differs because it affects all persons in the AOE. The Duration is longer and so is the Range. The disorientation will cause the same affects as stated above. It will have the same affects on a flying Krill or someone that is charging. No one may start or continue to concentrate on a spell while being affected by Daze = Many. Because of your victim's blurred vision, anyone she or he Strikes gets to add +25% to their PTE totals and the victims loose there Agility Bonus to their PTE. Also, no use of Warrior, S/A or Ninja skills.

Project Thought (+ ESP) (D)   R: 40'+2'/L   AOE: 1 person
SPC: 106 - M   D: 10 min+   CT: 3
        You get all the bonuses listed under the ESP Spell and the ability to project your thoughts to the person you are in "contact" with. If the person you are in contact with has an Intellect Score of less than 11, there is a 30% chance you may "plant" a suggestion in the subjects mind that he or she will follow (See Order Spell for details).

Sleep - Area (D)   R: 30'+1'/L   AOE: 20' radius +
SPC: 108 - A   D: 4+1d8 Actions   CT: 3
        This will cause all persons within the AOE to instantly fall into a deep sleep, (the same as explained in the Sleep – One spell.) If anyone makes their RER, they are not affected by this spell. The victim could be awakened by a friend shaking them or by any Damage done to them.
Ref. Note: I do NOT allow someone to kill a victim effected by this spell.

Mind Blast - Many (D)   R: 10'+2'/L   AOE: 10' radius +
SPC: 138 - A   D: 7+1d8 Action **   CT: 3
        This devastating spell will cause all persons within the AOE to take 28+2d12 EP Damage and will magically Daze them for 7+1d8 Actions plus 1 Action to fully recover. If anyone makes their RER, they will only take 14+2d12 but still will be Dazed for FOUR Actions.

Mesmerize Enchanted Creature (D) R: 15'+1'/L   AOE: 1 Enchanted Creature
SPC: 148 - A   D: 1 hr/L   CT: 3
        This spell is exactly like Mesmerize Person except it can be used on most enchanted creatures. The Enchanted Creature must have less EP than you do.
You are not able to affect these Enchanted Creatures with this spell :
      1) Unicorns   2) Goblin Queens   3) Dragons   4) Elementals 5) Vampires
      6) Zonith Wood Trees 7) Life Trees

Ability Bonus: Wisdom (E)   R: T   AOE: recipient
SPC: 155 - M   D: 1 day/L   CT: 4
        This spell will increase your personal Wisdom Score. You gain enough points to increase your score so that you gain the next ability increase. I.e. If your score is 6, it will increases to 15; if it's 15 it becomes 19. You are entitled to all bonuses of the higher score. If you learn something through experience or insight while "under" this spell, you will remember it even after the spell duration has ceased.
NOTE: When your Wisdom increases, your Will score may increase.

Secondary Spells for Indigo Enchanted Gems:
Fly 1 (C)   R: 5'+1'/L   AOE: 1 object
SPC: 52 - M   D: 30 min/L   CT: 2
        (Follow same rules that are listed in the Blue Spell Section.)

Uncontrolled Fire (B)   R: 20'+1'/L   AOE: 5' Radius +
SPC: 43 - A   D: (burn out)   CT: 1 Action
        (Follow same rules that are listed in the Red Spell Section.)

NOTE2: Some Enchanted creatures are not affected by the primary spells held in an Indigo Gem.
      1) Unicorns   2) Goblin Queens   3) Dragons 4) Elementals 5) Vampires
      6) Zonith Wood Trees 7) Life Trees

Illusion 1 (A)   R: 20'   AOE: < Human size
SPC: 11 - M   D: 5 min.   CT: 1 Act

     Illusions are "phantoms of reality." They look and in some cases sound real, but are not actually there. A misunderstanding that most people have is: "If it is not real, it can't hurt me." This is very wrong. If you are confronted by an illusion and you believe it is harming you in some way, the enchantment of the spell will cause you to feel pain and you will actually see blood running from your wounds. The enchantment of illusions is very strong if you *believe* what you see, because the illusion uses the magic within all of us to "heighten the experience." If you die at the hands of an illusion, you actually go into a coma for 1 hour (an Alchemist's Heal Disease or Restore spell will bring you out of it.)

     This spell will allow you to create an illusion of anything that is less then human size. No sound will accompany this illusion, but if used in the correct circumstances you may not need sound. You must form a detailed picture of the object or thing you wish to create while you are concentrating (if you have not seen the creature you are making an illusion of, and your Opponent has, then your Opponent will get a bonus of his FULL Wisdom Score added to his RER.) If you wish to make the illusion move, you must concentrate on it and "tell" it what to do every step of the way. If your victim sees your "wild wolf" and doesn't take time to disbelieve it, then he will take actual damage when he gets bitten. This damage will last until he is convinced that his bleeding wounds are an illusion, which won't be easy. The victim's RER verses an illusion is the victim's regular <u>RER percentage plus ½ of his Wisdom Score</u>, but he must state "I think this is an Illusion and want to disbelieve" (or something to that effect) and take 2 full Actions to confirm. [You may make 1 Strike and 1 Parry per Attack with the Illusion.]

Smoke Bomb (A)   R: 10'+1'/L   AOE: 20'+1'/L
SPC: 15 - M   D: 2 min.   CT: 1

     This spell will allow the caster to fill any area conforming to the AOE within Range with Smoke. If the caster is an Enchanter or Alchemist, she may cause the Smoke to be any color she chooses, but if the caster is anyone else the Smoke is always Dark Violet in color. If anyone can't see their opponent, that opponent gains +40% on their PTE total.

Disappear 1 (B)   R: 1'/Level   AOE: 1' x 1' x 1'
SPC: 22 - M   D: 5 min +   CT: 1

     This spell will allow you to make one object that is smaller than the AOE disappear. You can even make the first object you've chosen reappear, point to another within Range and make it disappear as long as the Duration lasts. The object must be inanimate and not in someone else's possession.

Disguise (B)   R: Recipient   AOE: Recipient
SPC: 31 - M   D: 30 min/L   CT: 1

     This spell will let you change your appearance or even let you appear as another race. You must form a detailed picture of how you wish to disguise yourself while you are concentrating. If you are a human and disguise yourself as a Krill, you won't be able to fly, but if you have an Enchanted Item that will permit you to fly, you can make it seem as if your wings are doing the work. An Opponent is not entitled to a RER, unless he is very suspicious of you, (you seem to be a Hemar and can't speak the language or can't speak to a mustang, ect.) OR if he touches you. If the Opponent does make his RER, then he will see your disguised outline, glowing a dull violet. A See Enchantment spell will also show the disguised outline.

Duplicates (B)   R: T   AOE: 3' radius
SPC: 32 - D   D: 3 min +   CT: 1

     This illusion is a warrior's nightmare. It produces two exact copies of yourself which duplicate your every move and are randomly stationed within the AOE. A fighter can't parry, feign strike, or use any fighting skills if he can't tell where the correct weapon or Opponent is. Any Strike that is directed at the caster has an equal chance to hit the duplicates or the caster himself. If one of the copies is hit by a weapon, the weapon will pass through that Duplicate and the attacker has a percentage chance equal to his Ability Check with Intellect to keep track of that Duplicate. If a Duplicate is struck by a spell or an enchanted weapon, it will automatically disappear. Remember that if the caster is hit and starts to bleed, so will the Duplicates. The Enchanter may add additional copies when casting the spell by adding 15 additional Spell Points for each copy required: SPC: 47 = 3 duplicates, SPC: 62 = 4 duplicates, ect.

Cause Fear-One (B)   R: 15'+1'/L   AOE: 1 victim
SPC: 34 - A   D: 4+1d4 Actions   CT: 1

This spell will cause your victim to see a personal horror right before her eyes. If she misses her RER, she will believe that the horror is quite real and she must roll a percentage to find out what her reaction is:

01% - 50%	Shaken with Fear: The Victim looses 1 Action/Attack and looses her Agility Bonus to her PTE.
51% - 89%	Slowly backs away from the caster: The Victim looses 1 Action/Att. and looses -10% on RERs.
90% - 99%	Victim runs away from the caster at full CRM. The victim drops what they are carrying 25% of the time.
100%	Victim attacks furiously, trying to eradicate her Opponents.

The victim gets a <u>RER + ½ of her Wisdom Score</u> added to the percentage. The effects may be canceled by the Cancel Enchantment spell or by an Alchemist's Heal Blindness spell.

NOTE: The Duration is counted from the victims Total Actions / Attack, ie. the lose of 1 Action/Att. is not counted against the victim when ascertaining the number of Actions the victim is effected by the spell.

Illusion 2 (B)   R: 20'+1'/L   AOE: < Hemar size
SPC: 44 - M   D: 10 min   CT: 1

This illusion may be cast and move anywhere within the stated Range. The Illusion must be less than the size of a Hemar. If you wish it to be larger than then that, you must add 5 Spell Points to the cost for every cubic foot you wish to enlarge it. This illusion will not be accompanied by sound. When your Opponent rolls his RER, he <u>gains ½ his Wisdom Score</u> added to his regular RER total to disbelieve this illusion.

Disappear 2 (C)   R: 5'+1'/L   AOE: 5' x 5' x 5' +
SPC: 52 - M   D: 5 min +   CT: 2

This spell will allow you to make anything that is smaller than the AOE to disappear from sight. You may affect a number of objects equal to your level. The objects must stay within Range and you may make an object reappear and then another disappear as long as you have time left on the Duration. The objects must be inanimate and not in someone else's possession.

Polymorph 1 (C)   R: 5'+1'/L   AOE: Recipient or victim
SPC: 58 - M   D: **   CT: 2

This powerful spell will actually let you change your form. This form change is limited in size to any creature that is no smaller than a squirrel and no larger than a horse or Hemar. The limits on weight are similar. When you polymorph into another creature, you retain your Intellect, Wisdom and Endurance Points. You gain all physical attributes of the form you take, including it's PTE, strikes, and damage capability. Depending upon the shape you've chosen, you may not be able to speak or cast spells, but you gain the ability to converse with the type of creature you polymorph into. You may change back to your original form at any time. If you still have time left on your Duration you may assume another form, but <u>this decreases the time left on your Duration by HALF</u>. You must ALWAYS return to your natural form before assuming another, i.e. you can never change from one polymorphed form to another.

Ie. Castlin is a 6th level Enchanter and after casting this spell assumes the form of a hawk - now he is able to fly and converse with hawks, but not any other type of bird. One hour later he finds that the form of a hawk doesn't suit his purposes - he has 2 hours left on his Duration - so he changes to his natural form and then to the form of a tiger and has a total of **1** hour left on his Duration.

All form changes take 1 Action of concentration and 2 Actions for the change to take place. When changing back to your original form you don't have to concentrate. If your victim doesn't wish to become a frog, he is entitled to a RER. If he is successful, there is no affect.

** The Duration is special. This spell has two different Durations: the first is if the recipient is willing and the second is if you are casting it on an Opponent. If the recipient is willing the Duration is 30 min / L; If you are casting the spell on an Opponent the Duration is 3+1d6 Actions.

Illusion 3 (C)   R: 20'+2'/L   AOE: < Human size
SPC: 65 - M   D: 15 min+   CT: 2

This illusion must be smaller than human size, but will make whatever sound you want. It must stay within the Range and the sounds it makes can NOT be heard outside of the Range. The victim gains <u>½ his Wisdom Score</u> added to his RER total to disbelieve this illusion.

Illusion 4 (C)　　　　　　　R: 30'+2'/L　　　　　　AOE: > Human size
SPC: 81 - M　　　　　　　　　D: 15 min +　　　　　　　CT: 2

This illusion may be greater then human size and will be accompanied by any sound you wish. It must be less than to the size of a Hemar. If you wish it to be larger than then that, you must add 10 Spell Points to the cost for every cubic foot you wish to enlarge it. The sounds it makes can NOT be heard outside of the Range. The victim gains ½ his Wisdom Score added to his RER total to disbelieve this illusion.

Polymorph 2 (D)　　　　　　R: 10'+1'/L　　　　　　AOE: Recipient or victim
SPC: 118 - M　　　　　　　　D: **　　　　　　　　　CT: 3

This spell follows the rules of Polymorph 1, except you may assume a form no smaller then that of a mouse and no larger than that of an Elephant. You still gain all of the same abilities stated in Polymorph 1. (Note: If you change into a form of an Enchanted Creature like a Unicorn, you will gain its form only, **not** any of it's Enchanted abilities, but you may converse with Unicorns.) You may still change into different forms, but you must make a transitional "stop" in your original form and it still uses up ½ the duration left on the spell. It still takes 1 Action for concentration and 2 Actions to make the actual change, regardless of the size of the creature. If your Opponent still does not wish to be turned into an even smaller frog, he does rate a RER, and if successful, there is no affect.

** The Duration is special. This spell has two different Durations: the first is if the recipient is willing and the second is if you are casting it on an Opponent. If the recipient is willing the Duration is 30 min / L; If you are casting the spell on an Opponent the Duration is 5+1d8 Actions.

Cause Fear - Many (D)　　　　R: 40'+1'/L　　　　　　AOE: 15' radius +
SPC: 129 - A　　　　　　　　D: 6+1d8 Actions　　　　CT: 3

This spell follows the same rules as Cause Fear-One, except for what is listed above and the spell affects all persons within the AOE. Each person in the AOE must make a percentage roll and compare to the reactions below:

01% - 50%　　Shaken with Fear: The Victim looses 2 Actions/Attack and looses their Agility Bonus to their PTE.
51% - 89%　　Slowly backs away from the caster: The Victim looses 2 Actions/Att and looses -10% on RERs.
90% - 99%　　Victim runs away from the caster at full CRM. The victim drops what they are carrying 25% of the time.
100%　　Victim attacks furiously, trying to eradicate her Opponents.

If any person manages to make their RER plus ½ their Wisdom Score they are not affected by the spell. This illusionary Fear may be countered by a Cancel Enchantment or a Heal Blindness spell.
NOTE2: The Duration is counted from the victims Total Actions / Attack, ie. the lose of 2 Actions/Att. is not counted against the victim when ascertaining the number of Actions the victim is effected by the spell.

Ability Bonus: Charm or Beauty (E)　　R: T　　　　　　AOE: Recipient
SPC: 155 - M　　　　　　　　　　　　　D: 1 day/L　　　CT: 4

This spell will improve your Charm Score **or** Beauty Score. You gain enough points to increase your score so that you gain the next ability increase. I.e. If your score is 12, it will increases to 14; if it's 16 it becomes 18. You will receive all bonuses of the higher score for the Duration. This will even help you phrase sentences more eloquently **or** straiten your crooked teeth for the Duration.

Secondary Spells for Violet Enchanted Gems:
Invisibility (C)　　　　　　　R: T　　　　　　　　AOE: 1 recipient
SPC: 52 - M　　　　　　　　　D: 10 min/L　　　　　CT: 2

(Follow same rules that are listed in the Yellow Spell Section.)

Silence - One (B)　　　　　　R: 5'+1'/L　　　　　　AOE: Recipient
SPC: 31 - M　　　　　　　　　D: 10 min/L　　　　　CT: 1

(Follow same rules that are listed in the Black Spell Section.)

Stone Move 1 (A)   R: 15'+1'/L   AOE: 1 stone <= 25 lbs
SPC: 10 - M   D: 2 min.   CT: 1 Action
    This spell will allow you to move a stone weighing 25 lbs or less anywhere within the stated Range.
If used as a weapon, the stone will always strike an Opponent below the waist unless it is falling from above.
A 12 pound stone will cause 1d4 EP Damage and a 25 pound stone will cause 1d8 EP Damage when moving
at full speed. You may cause the stone to move at a rate of 10 feet/second (CRM: 2), just by concentrating
on it. The victim does not get a regular RER for reduced damage, but is allowed a chance to completely
avoid the "bouncing" stone. The victim will avoid the stone and take no damage if he rolls a percentage lower
than his RER plus 1/2 his Agility score. If the victim does not successfully avoid the stone, he will take full
damage. This spell will also allow you to sense large stones within the range.

Paralyze Animal or Bird (A)   R: 25'+1'/L   AOE: 1 Animal or Bird
SPC: 17 - A   D: 1d4 minutes   CT: 1 Act
    This spell will fire a pencil thin brownish ray at the creature. It will only affect animals or birds, but they
will become paralyzed and surrounded by a dull brownish glow when they are struck by this beam. A
paralyzed creature can't move, call out a warning, or even bleed to death because the victim is encased
within a solid brownish casing - this casing is invulnerable, so the encased creature cannot be harmed. The
affects will last for 1d4 minutes and then the creature will be released. The brownish casing will slowly
diminish as the Duration comes to an end. A successful RER will allow the creature to not be paralyzed and
encased.

Paralyze Reptile / Fish / Insect (B)   R: 25'+1'/L   AOE: 1 Reptile, Fish or Insect
SPC: 23 - A   D: 1d4 minutes   CT: 1
    This spell follows all rules of Paralyze Animal or Bird including the invulnerable casing.

Earth Barrier (B)   R: Self   AOE: 20' diameter x 15' tall
SPC: 48 - D   D: 15 min   CT: 1
    This circle has 15 foot tall walls of hard, packed earth. The walls are 20' in radius and 1 foot thick.
The Barrier's wall is very solid so no-one can pass though it, but it is possible to climb over it. If anyone
crashes into it, they will take 1d8 EP Damage per Charging Rate multiple they are traveling.

Stone Move 2 (C)   R: 20'/L   AOE: 1 stone <= 50lbs +
SPC: 52 - M   D: 5 min +   CT: 2
    This spell follows the rules of Stone Move 1, except you may move stones of greater weight. It will
allow you to move a stone weighing 50 pounds or less. A 50 pound stone will cause 2d8 EP Damage to the
victim. If you wish to move a stone greater than 50 pounds, you must spend an additional 15 Spell Points for
each additional 25 pounds. Larger stones will do an extra 1d8 EP Damage for every 25 pounds they weigh
over 50 lbs. A one-hundred pound bolder will do 4d8 EP damage and cost 82 SP. This spell will cause the
stone to move at a rate of 20 feet/second (CRM: 4) while you concentrate. Your Opponent does get a
chance to avoid the stone for no damage, which is his RER plus 1/2 his Agility Score. This spell will also
allow you to sense large stones within the range.

Paralyze Person (C)   R: 35'+1'/L   AOE: 1 person
SPC: 53 - A   D: 3+1d6 Actions   CT: 2
    This spell is essentially the same as the above listed paralyze spells. The victim is aware of all that is
going on around him, but cannot move, feel pain or even bleed. The brownish casing is invulnerable and will
diminish as the duration comes to an end. The victim is allowed a RER and he will suffer no ill effects if
successful. NOTE: A "Person" is any Human, Hemar, or Krill.

Stone Mold (C)   R: T   AOE: 10' high x 4' wide x 2' thick
SPC: 62 - M   D: 30 min +   CT: 2

This spell will make it possible for you to mentally mold any regular stone, which you touch, as if it were clay. This spell will allow you to construct anything from stone statues to doors in solid rock. All changes in the stone's shape are permanent, but you must complete your work within the stated Duration or recast the spell. You shape the stone with your mind, not with your hands, so anything you can imagine you can construct.

Quicksand (C)   R: 30'+1'/L   AOE: 10' radius +
SPC: 73 - A   D: 10 min +   CT: 2

This spell will turn any piece of horizontal ground, rock, sand or stone, ect. into a pool of quicksand conforming to the AOE. This pool will be 15' deep but will appear to be composed of the original material. If anyone steps into it, they will start to sink at a rate of 5 foot per Attack or 1 foot per second. This rate will triple if the victim struggles within the Quicksand pit. If you go beneath the surface you will start to suffocate. When the Duration ends the pool will revert to it's original form, "spitting" out all victims that are still alive and "keeping" all those who have died in it's clutches. The victim could of course be pulled out by his friends, fly out or get out by other means.

Earth Globe (D)   R: Self   AOE: 15' Radius
SPC: 136 - D   D: 15 min +   CT: 3

This Globe is made out of hard earth and conforms to the AOE. Anyone who smashes into this Globe will receive 1d8 EP Damage per Charging Rate multiple. If you are charging at a rate of 20 ft/second, which is a multiple of 4, you'll suffer 4d8 EP Damage. This will disappear at the end of the Duration.

Ability Bonus: Strength (E)   R: T   AOE: Recipient
SPC: 155 - M   D: 1 day/L   CT: 4

This spell will increase your personal Strength Score for the Duration stated. You gain enough points to increase your score so that you gain the next ability increase. I.e. If your score is 13, it will increases to 15; if it's 16 it becomes 17. You will gain all abilities of the higher strength including damage bonus, lifting and bench pressing.

Stone Pass (E)   R: 5'+1'/L   AOE: Recipient
SPC: 156 - M   D: 15 min +   CT: 4

This awesome spell will permit you to walk through solid rock. You may cast it on anyone within the Range or on yourself. The amount of stone you may pass through is unlimited, but you must complete your "journey" before the Duration ends. Your Traveling rate through stone is 10 feet/second (CRM: 2). You may never charge or fly through stone. You may even pass through consecutive walls if time permits, but if you don't pass completely out of the wall before the end of the Duration you will surely die.

Paralyze Enchanted Creature (E)   R: 10'+2'/L   AOE: 1 Victim
SPC: 157 - A   D: 5+1d10 Actions   CT: 4

This follows all rules of the Paralyze Person spell, except that this spell may affect any one Enchanted Creature. If the creature is successful on it's RER, the spell will have no affect. This is an awesome spell, but it does not affect seven types of Enchanted Creatures :

1) Unicorns	2) Goblin Queens	3) Dragons	4) Elementals
5) Vampires	6) Zonith Wood Trees	7) Life Trees	

Stone Globe (E)   R: Self   AOE: 15' Radius
SPC: 157 - D   D: 15 min +   CT: 4

This Globe follows all rules of the Earth Globe spell except for the composition and anyone smashing into this Globe will receive 2d8 EP Damage per Charging rate multiple.

Secondary Spells for Brown Enchanted Gems:
Polymorph 1 (C)   R: 5'+1'/L   AOE: Recipient or victim
SPC: 58 - M   D: 30 min/L   CT: 2

    (Follow same rules that are listed in the Violet Spell Section.)
Plant Control (C)   R: 20'+1'/L   AOE: 30'x30'+
SPC: 51 - M   D: 10 min +   CT: 2

    (Follow same rules that are listed in the Green Spell Section.)

Purify Water (A)   R: 10'   AOE: 1 cubic foot / Level
SPC: 5 - M   D: inst.   CT: 1 Act
    This spell will purify any amount of water less than or equal to the AOE. The water affected will become crystal clear, free of diseases and poisons and even become cool, perfect for drinking.

Ice Walk (A)   R: 10'   AOE: Recipient
SPC: 8 - M   D: 15 min.   CT: 1 Act
    When you cast this spell, it allows you to transverse any ice covered or slippery surface as if it were summer turf. You may walk, fight and even charge with no penalties. You may only cast this spell on one person per spell.

Water Bolt 1 (A)   R: 20'+1'/L   AOE: 6"-1'
SPC: 14 - A   D: inst.   CT: 1 Act
    Like all other Bolts, the Water Bolt speeds from the palm of the caster's hand out to the stated Range. When it strikes the intended victim it will inflict 4+2d8 EP Damage and cause the victim to fall 15% of the time. The type of water produced by this spell is a replication of the closest large body of water. If you are near the ocean, you will unleash a "Salt Water Bolt" or if you are next to a swamp, you'll be able to soak your Opponent in a "splash" of nasty swamp water. If your Opponent manages to make his RER, he will take half base Damage (2+2d8), but will still be soaked and knocked over 15% of the time.

Slide (B)   R: 10'/L   AOE: Recipient
SPC: 22 - M   D: Until you reach the R: CT: 1
    This spell will let you slide across any horizontal surface to the extent of the Range. You may slide at a rate equal to one multiple higher than your personal Charging Rate. You may slide down a surface that is sloping at a rate of two multiples higher than your Charging Rate. You may even slide across a tightrope with no chance of falling.

Water Walk, Calm (B)   R: 5'+1'/L   AOE: Recipient
SPC: 23 - M   D: 5 min +   CT: 1
    This spell will let you walk over calm water as if it were regular ground. You may run or even do handsprings over the surface. If you trip or fall, you will not sink. You may only cast this spell on people.

Water Adaptation (B)   R: 5'+1'/L   AOE: Recipient
SPC: 31 - M   D: 30 min/L   CT: 1
    This spell will allow you to breathe water as if it were air for the Duration. While under the enchantment of the spell you will be able to see, talk and cast spells normally (although some spells won't work well underwater, such as Flame Bolt 1.) Also this spell will let you control your buoyancy, which means you may cause yourself to float at any depth or even to walk along the bottom, as if you were on dry land. You may even see and hear normally for the Duration. NOTE: The great pressures that are proportional to your depth don't affect you at all, while the spell lasts.

Converse with Water (B)   R: 100'   AOE: 1 'patch' of water is 2' x 2' x 2'
SPC: 31 - M   D: 5 min +   CT: 1
    This spell will allow you to converse with any small 'patch' of water. The 'patch' of water may be flowing down a stream or on the waves of the sea. The water patch can tell you everything that has past by it in the last 3 days. It can describe fish, wild life and even vessels it has encountered. You may stop speaking to one patch of water and start up with another for as long as the Duration lasts. The water patch will even be able to tell you if any **Swimming** Elementals passed it recently (Water, Ice or Fog). You may converse with the water patch, in a normal voice - regardless of distance within Range, until the Duration expires.

Water Control 1 (B)   R: 5'/L   AOE: 5 cubic feet
SPC: 33 - M   D: 5 min +   CT: 1 Action

       All of the Water Control spells are essentially the same. They differ in the total amount of water each spell can control. With this spell you may control an amount of water equal to the AOE. As long as you concentrate, you may quickly mentally "mold" the water into any shape you wish and make it move anywhere within the Range as long as it is still attached to the surface of the water. This means you may mentally mold the water into a Hand or Wall on the surface of the water. The strength of a water 'hand' is equal to your strength. The damage the water may cause is always 1d8 EP Damage for every 1 cubic foot of water that strikes your Opponent. The rate at which the water object may move is 20 ft/second (CRM: 4) while you concentrate. Your Opponent may Attempt to avoid your "watery hand" by rolling lower than her RER plus 1/2 her Agility score. If successfully, she completely evades the "hand" and will take no damage; if not, she will take full damage. It is also very possible to tip a small boat over with this spell. The small boat has a simulated RER of 50% and if the driver has either 'Boat Construction, Small' or 'Navigate on Open Seas', then the boat gains a RER bonus equal to the driver's Intellect Score.

Frost Jet (B)   R: 10'+1'/L   AOE: 6"-1'+
SPC: 44 - A   D: 5 seconds/L (1 Attack/Level) CT: 1

       This jet will continuously blast out from the caster's palm, reaching the stated Range and conforming to the AOE. It will also coat everything within the AOE with a thin layer of frost automatically putting out any regular flames. Anyone within the AOE takes 10+1d6 EP Damage on the first Attack and they will take an additional 1d6 EP Damage per Attack they are engulfed in the Jet of Frost.

Water Jet (B)   R: 15'+1'/L   AOE: 6"-1'+
SPC: 44 - A   D: 5 seconds/L (1 Attack/Level)   CT: 1

       This jet will also continuously blast from the caster's palm, encompassing the Range and AOE. The Water Jet will only cause initial damage, but will cause your Opponent to shield his eyes, lose his concentration, and even slip if the conditions are right. The jet will do 10+1d6 EP Damage on its initial strike. Like the water produced in the Water Bolt spells, the water put forth is a replica of the nearest body of water.

Frost Barrier (C)   R: Self   AOE: 10' radius x 15' walls
SPC: 52 - D   D: 5 min +   CT: 2

       This Barrier is 1' thick, encircles the caster in a Barrier of frost with walls 20' in diameter and 15' tall. This Barrier must be cast defensively and will stay stationary for the Duration. Anyone trying to pass through the wall will receive 10+2d8 EP Damage.

Water Control 2 (C)   R: 10'/L   AOE: 10 cubic feet
SPC: 52 - M   D: 5 min +   CT: 2

       This follows all rules stated above, except you may control 10 cubic feet of water with this spell. The damage and strength is still the same. The rate which the "wave" may move is 25 feet/second (CRM:5). [Damage = 1d8 / cubic foot of water that strikes your Opponent]. For small boats follow rules above, but it has a simulated RER of 40%.

Water Bolt 2 (C)   R: 30'+1'/L   AOE: 6"-2'
SPC: 53 - A   D: --   CT: 2

       This spell is the same as Water Bolt 1, except that this spell will cause 12+2d8 EP Damage to an Opponent and causes her to fall 30% of the time. The type of water is a replica of the nearest body of water.

Snow Balls (C)   R: 30'+1'/L   AOE: 6" Balls
SPC: 57 - A   D: --   CT: 2

       When you cast this spell, you will cause 2 Snow Balls per spell to fly at either one or two Opponents. Each Snow Ball will cause 12+1d8 EP Damage to the victim. If you cast both Snow Balls at one Opponent, he gets two RERs. If you cast the Snow Balls at two different Opponents, they each get one RER. If either RER is successful the victim will take ½ base damage (6+1d8).

Water Spout (C)　　　　R: 5'/L　　　　　　　AOE: 10' radius +
SPC: 71 - A　　　　　　　　D: 5 min +　　　　　　CT: 2

　　This spell will cause a spout of water to explode from the surface of the water to a height of 3'/L of the Enchanter. The spout will have enough force to impede large ships and even capsize small ones. It will not cause damage, but will clear the way of just about anything in your path that lives in the sea. The caster is able to direct where the water from the Spout falls. This will cause no direct damage either, but Opponents won't be able to concentrate, may slip and fall, get washed over board, etc. The spout is stationary but continuous so you only need to concentrate to move where the water lands.

Water Control 3 (C)　　　R: 10'/L　　　　　　AOE: 20 cubic feet
SPC: 72 - M　　　　　　　　D: 5 min +　　　　　　CT: 2

　　Follows all rules stated in Water Control 2, except that the water "hand" has a strength that is 1 more than your personal strength score. For small boats follow the rules above, but it has a simulated RER of 30%. [Damage = 1d8 / cubic foot of water that strikes your Opponent].

Ice Elevator (C)　　　　R: 20'+1'/L　　　　　AOE: 10' radius +
SPC: 78 - M　　　　　　　　D: 15 min +　　　　　CT: 2

　　This spell will let you create a platform of ice that is 20' wide and that will quickly elevate you to a height of 25'+1'/L. You may cast this under your companions or your Opponents. The elevated platform will last until the Duration ends and then slowly "sink" to the ground.

Part Water 1 (C)　　　　R: **　　　　　　　AOE: 300' long x 10' wide
SPC: 90 - M　　　　　　　　D: 10 min/L　　　　　CT: 2

　　This spell will allow you to part a stretch of water equal to the AOE. The 300 feet length starts directly in front of you and must end at the other shore of a river, etc. The depth of the river makes no difference and the water will rush back in when the Duration ends or when you want it to.

Water Globe (D)　　　　R: Self　　　　　　　AOE: 15' Radius
SPC: 106 - D　　　　　　　　D: 15 min +　　　　　CT: 3

　　As with all Enchanter Globes, this one is 1' thick, can only be cast defensively and encompasses the AOE. This spell will cause a Globe of water to spring up from the surface, which will impede all but the largest ships. If something runs into the Globe, it will receive 1d8 EP Damage per Charging Rate multiple. It may only be cast when <u>you</u> are on a body of water.

Ice Spikes (D)　　　　　R: 40'+1'/L　　　　　AOE: 1' long
SPC: 108 - A　　　　　　　　D: inst.　　　　　　　CT: 3

　　This spell is similar to the Snow Ball spell because you fire 2 Ice Spikes at one or two Opponents. Each Ice Spike will cause 22+1d8 EP Damage. If you cast this spell at one Opponent, he will get two RERs and if you split the spikes up between two Opponents, they each get one RER. If either RER is successful the victim will take ½ base damage (11+1d8).

Water Bolt 3 (D)　　　　R: 40'+1'/L　　　　　AOE: 6"-4'
SPC: 108 - A　　　　　　　　D: --　　　　　　　　CT: 3

　　Water Bolt 3 follows all rules stated in the other Water Bolt spells. This bolt will cause 22+2d8 EP Damage and cause your Opponent to slip and fall 60% of the time. The type of water is a replica of the nearest body of water.

Water Control 4 (D)　　　R: 10`/L　　　　　　AOE: 40 cubic feet
SPC: 127 - M　　　　　　　　D: 10 min +　　　　　CT: 3

　　Follows all rules stated above, except the strength of the water "hand" has 3 more than your personal strength score. For small boats follow rules above, but it has a simulated RER of 20%. [Damage = 1d8 / cubic foot of water that strikes your Opponent].

Ability Bonus: Endurance (E)　　R: T　　　　　　AOE: recipient
SPC: 155 - M　　　　　　　　D: 1 day/L　　　　　CT: 4

　　This spell will increase your personal Endurance Score. You gain enough points to increase your score so that you gain the next ability bonus. I.e. If your score is 15, it will increases to 16; if it's 18 it becomes 19. You are entitled to all bonuses of the higher score, including an extra 2 Endurance Points per point gained. NOTE: When your Endurance increases, your Will score may increase.

Ice Globe (E)   R: Self   AOE: 15' Radius
SPC: 157 - D   D: 15 min +   CT: 4

Like all Enchanter Globes, this one is 1' thick, can only be cast defensively, and fills the AOE. If a victim crashes into the Globe, he will take 2d8 EP Damage per Charging Rate multiple. Any Globe cast while the caster is standing on the ground, will become a Dome. Yes, any Globe that is cast in the air will be suspended there for the Duration and then disappear. This Globe may be cast in the air, on land and sea. (OO-Ra!!).

Water Control 5 (E)   R: 10'/L   AOE: 80 cubic ft.
SPC: 189 - M   D: 10 min +   CT: 4

Same as stated in Water Control 1. With this much water you can probably impede even a large cargo ship. The strength of any water shape is 6 more than your personal strength score. The rate is 30 ft/second (CRM : 6). For small boats follow rules above, but it has a simulated RER of 10%. [Damage = 1d8 / cubic foot of water that strikes your Opponent].

Part Water 2 (E)   R: **   AOE: 1 mile long x 50' wide
SPC: 195 - M   D: 1 hr/Level   CT: 4

This spell follows the rules of Part Water 1, but this spell will allow you to part the water in any river as long as the other bank is within 1 mile of your location. The width will be 50' across and the depth does not matter.

Secondary Spells for Clear Enchanted Gems:

Cancel Enchantment (C)   R: 10'+1'/L   AOE: 1 enchantment (see below)
SPC: 51+ - D   D: inst.   CT: 2

This unique spell has the potential to cancel any continuing enchantment from a Fire Globe to a Mesmerized Person spell, regardless of the source. You must cast this spell on one particular enchantment - this infers that you know about it. When the Cancel Enchantment spell is cast, it sets up a temporary link between you and the enchantment you want canceled. This link pulls Spell Points from you until the total number that was spent by the original caster of the spell is matched. When the Spell Points are matched the affects of the other enchantment will be canceled. The link pulls Spell Points from you very fast and if for some reason you don't have enough, you may be "pulled" below Zero Spell Points. If this happens you will suffer the same effects as if you had cast any other spell and didn't have enough Spell Points (refer to the OVERCAST TABLE.) If you cancel ALL Spell Points in question, the effects the Cancel Enchantment spell has on the enchanted object or lasting effect are listed below :

1) All Enchantments that still have a Duration left, regardless of the source: Cancel all effects of the spell. (i.e. Any spell that is still 'working' when the Cancel Enchantment is cast against it.)
2) An Enchanter made Enchanted Item without a gem: Cancel any enchantment either working or "dormant".
3) An Enchanter made Enchanted Item with a gem: Has no effect on "held" or "dormant" spells.
4) Potions: This spell will "separate" the base components and cancel the particular enchantment.
5) Alchemist's Dusts or Pills: This spell will NOT effect enchantments that are "held" in them, but if one is in your possession, you may convert a Pill to a Dust and a Dust to a Potion by casting this spell multiple times.
6) Elementalist's Rings or Disks: This spell will not effect spells that are "held" within them, ie. castable 1/day.
7) Spinning Rings or Disks: This spell will stop it from spinning, cause it to fall to the ground, and send the summoned Elemental back to it's plane.

(Special)   R: AOE:
SPC: D: CT:

You may cast any spell with a classification of (A), (B) or (C), that can be held by a Yellow, Indigo, or Brown Gem, into an enchanted diamond or a clear quartz! This is true for all Enchanters and all Alchemists (the potion will change hue depending on which spell is cast into it.)

Midnight Wall (A)   R: 10'   AOE: 15' tall x 15' wide
SPC: 8 - D   D: 15 min.   CT: 1 Action
    This Wall will create a vertical plane of complete darkness that is 2' thick and fills the AOE. You can see nothing through it and it will conceal all light from either side. The Wall may be cast in the air, it doesn't need to be anchored to a surface. The caster may not see through it, but may cancel at it anytime.

Cube of Midnight 1 (A)   R: 5'+1'/L   AOE: 20'x20'x20'
SPC: 15 - D   D: 5 min   CT: 1 Act
    This spell will cause everything within the AOE to become as black as midnight. No one, including the caster, can see while he is inside the Cube of Midnight and from the outside it appears to be a box of blackness. All persons within the cube gain +40% to their PTE totals while inside the box. This spell also stops all See Enchantment Spells, but if a Light Spell is cast within the box, it will cancel the magical darkness. This Cube is rooted to the spot it is cast on.

Acid Pool, mild (A)   R: 15'+1'/L   AOE: 10' radius.
SPC: 15 - A   D: 5 min.   CT: 1 Action
    All "Pools" can be cast anywhere on a flat horizontal surface within the Range and will cover the AOE. The Mild Acid Pool will destroy rope and cloth in 1 Attack (5 seconds) and destroy leather in 5 Attacks. Any victim touching the acid pool will receive 4+3d6 EP Damage per Attack. If cast on water, it will float and stay in the form of a pool. The acid pool is 4 inches deep for the Duration and when it expires, it will disappear, "spitting" out any surviving victims, like the Quicksand Spell.

Acid Spray, mild (B)   R: 15'+1'/L   AOE: 1" - 6"
SPC: 24 - A   D: inst.   CT: 1 Action
    All "Sprays" are thin gusts of acid that closely resemble a jet, except that they are instantaneous, NOT constant. These sprays will extend to the stated Range and encompass the AOE for an instant. All acids will eat through certain materials and harm people by "burning" into their skin. These acids are black and will leave nasty scars even if healed by a Heal Wounds spell. These scars will reduce the victim's Beauty Score by a variable amount depending on how bad the acid burn is (a Heal Disease or Beauty Spell will restore 2 points to the recipients Beauty Score.) The Mild Acid Spray is fired from the caster's palm, will destroy rope and cloth and cause 6+3d6 EP Damage if it falls on skin, hide, fur etc. If the acid strikes an Opponent's head from the front, it will blind them for 3+1d4 Actions. The victim rates a RER for ½ base damage from the spell.

Silence - One (B)   R: 5'+1'/L   AOE: Recipient
SPC: 31 - M   D: **   CT: 1
    This spell will totally Silence one person. The recipient may not talk or make any noise, even if he tries. Stairs will not creak under his feet, armor will make no sound and even when engaging in sword play there will be no sound made from the ringing of steal on steal. You can't cast spells or use Trigger Words if you can make no sound. If the recipient does not wish to be silenced, he is entitled to a RER and will suffer no affects if successful.
    ** The Duration is special. This spell has two different Durations: the first is if the recipient is willing and the second is if you are casting it on an Opponent. If the recipient is willing the Duration is 10 min / L; If you are casting the spell on an Opponent the Duration is 4+1d4 Actions.

Silence - Area (B)   R: 20'+1'/L   AOE: 10' radius +
SPC: 41 - M   D: **   CT: 1
    This spell follows all rules that are stated above, but it encompasses a 10 foot radius. No sound will pass in, out or through of the Dome of silence. If cast on a moveable object or person the spell will move with that object or person for the Duration. If cast directly on your Opponent, he rates a RER. If successful, the circle will not move when your Opponent moves, but will still silence the area and the center of the AOE will be based where the intended victim was standing. You can't cast spells or use Trigger Words if you can make no sound.
    ** The Duration is special. This spell has two different Durations: the first is if the recipient is willing and the second is if you are casting it on an Opponent. If the recipient is willing the Duration is 5 min / L; If you are casting the spell on an Opponent the Duration is 5+1d4 Actions on the entire area.

Cube of Midnight 2 (B) R: 5'+1'/L AOE: 40'x40'x40'
SPC: 42 - D D: ** CT: 1

This follows all rules of Cube of Midnight 1. The affected area is larger and the Duration is longer. The major advantage of this Cube is it can be mobile. If cast directly on your Opponent, he rates a RER. If successful, the Cube will not move when your Opponent moves, but will be centered where the intended victim was standing. If cast on a willing person, object or your Opponent fails her RER, it will move with her for the Duration.
Note: No one can see in or out of the cube, including the caster.
** The Duration is special. This spell has two different Durations: the first is if the recipient is willing and the second is if you are casting it on an Opponent. If the recipient is willing the Duration is 5 minute / L; If you are casting the spell on an Opponent the Duration is 5+1d4 Actions on the entire area.

Acid Pool, medium (B) R: 25'+1'/L AOE: 10' radius +
SPC: 43 - A D: 10 min + CT: 1

A Medium Acid Pool will destroy rope, cloth, and leather in 1 Attack (5 seconds) and destroy wood in 5 Attacks. If someone touches the acid, they will receive 10+4d6 EP Damage per Attack they are in contact with the pool. This pool follows all rules stated above, is 6 inches deep and will disappear, "spitting" out any surviving victims, when the Duration ends.

Acid Spray, medium (C) R: 25'+1'/L AOE: 6"-1'
SPC: 54 - A D: inst. CT: 2

A Medium Acid Spray will destroy rope, cloth and leather and cause 12+4d6 EP Damage to your victim. If you strike your Opponent in the face, he will be blinded for 3+1d6 Actions and disfigured (a Heal Blindness will correct the former.)

In Sight Teleport (C) R: 5'+1'/L AOE: 1 friend / 3 levels of the Caster
SPC: 95 - M D: inst. CT: 2

This spell will transfer you and your friends instantly to any place you choose within your sight. You will appear to "blip" from where you are and you will arrive at your sighted position unharmed and ready to take action. You may teleport a maximum of 1000 feet per Level or to the edge of your Sight whichever comes first. The teleportation makes no sound. If you cast it on an Opponent, she or he rates a RER that will negate any affects. You may NEVER teleport someone INTO any solid object because this will cause a Backfire and kill the caster. A caster may use this spell to Teleport to the SEEN location when using the Observation spell.

This spell may also be used in a special way. If TWO Black or Yellow gems are cut from the same stone, Enchanted to the same Gem Perfection Rating (GPR) and then BOTH have an In Sight Teleport spell cast into them, they will be linked in a special way. These TWO gems will be given unique "names" and then can be moved to distant locations. When an In Sight Teleport spell is cast on one of the gems and the other gem's name is spoken, the speaker and recipients will be relocated from the position of the first gem to the location of the second gem. (Of course, this special circumstance will even work if the gems are not within sight of one another.)

Acid Pool, potent (D) R: 40'+1'/L AOE: 20' radius +
SPC: 108 - A D: 15 min + CT: 3

A Potent Acid Pool will destroy rope, cloth, leather, and wood in 1 Attack (5 seconds). This deadly acid will even pit iron in 5 Attacks (but Silver, Mithral, Americanium, Ransium, and Langor will be unharmed). Any victim will receive 22+4d6 EP Damage per Attack they are in contact with the pool. This pool is 8 inches deep and follows all rules stated in the Pool spells above.

Acid Spray, Potent (D) R: 40'+1'/L AOE: 6"-2'
SPC: 139 - A D: inst. CT: 3

A Potent Acid Spray is so dangerous that it will completely destroy rope, cloth, leather, and wood as well as cause 28+4d6 EP Damage to anyone it touches. If your victim gets sprayed in the face, this potent acid will blind him for 7+1d8 Actions and horribly disfigure him.

Attribute Drain, temporary (E)   R: 1'/L   AOE: 1 Attribute / Victim
SPC: 158 - A   D: 1 day/L   CT: 4

This spell will lower any one of your Opponent's Attributes by one bonus [an 18 Strength would become a 16 and a 16 Intellect would become a 15 for the Duration]. You may choose the Attribute to be lowered, but the victim must be within Range. The victim will receive and have to live with all negatives imposed by the lower score until the Duration ends. This can only be canceled by the caster, a successfully cast Cancel Enchantment, or by a spell to enhance the affected Attribute. A successful RER will negate any affects.

Teleport, Out of Sight (E)   R: 10'+1'/L   AOE: 1 friend / 3 levels of the Caster
SPC: 158 - M   D: inst.   CT: 4

This spell will allow you and your friends to teleport to an unseen location. This unseen location must be well known to the caster, if it is not the spell will "backfire" and kill the caster and his friends. The location change is instantaneous, totally quiet, and causes no disorientation. If you try to teleport someone else, the location must still be well known and if not it will still Backfire and kill the caster. Your Opponent rates a RER and if successful will not be relocated. The distance you may Teleport is 1000 miles per Level. A caster may use this spell to Teleport to a the SEEN location when using the Observation spell.

This spell may also be used in a special way. If TWO Black gems are cut from the same stone, Enchanted to the same Gem Perfection Rating (GPR) and then BOTH have a Teleport spell cast into them they will be linked in a special way. These TWO gems will be given unique "names" and then can be moved to distant locations. When a Teleport spell is cast on one of the gems and the other's name is spoken, the speaker and recipients will be relocated to the position of the other linked gem.

Attribute Drain, Permanent (E)   R: T   AOE: 1 Attribute / Victim
SPC: 198 - A   D: Permanent   CT: 4

This spell will Drain an Attribute permanently to the next lower bonus, until the caster cancels it, or a Cancel Enchantment spell is successfully cast. You must touch the victim and you may choose the Attribute to be drained. If the victim successfully makes his RER there will be no affects.

Secondary Spells for Black Enchanted Gems:
Cancel Enchantment (C)   R: 10'+1'/L   AOE: 1 enchantment
SPC: 51+ - D   D: inst.   CT: 2

(Follow same rules that are listed in the White/Clear Spell Section.)

Special   R: AOE:
SPC: D: CT:

You may cast any spell with an (A), (B) or (C) Classification that can be held by a Red, Blue, or Violet gem into an enchanted Black Quartz or Onyx gem.

A FROST JET VERSES A FLAME JET

Find North (A)   R: **   AOE: Recipient
SPC: 6 - M   D: 5 min   CT: 1
    This simple but useful spell will allow the caster to Find North at any time of the day or night. This spell can also be used under ground, on the sea or under it, etc.

Weapon Quality spell (A)   R: T   AOE: 2 weapons
SPC: 10 - M   D: 2 min   CT: 1
    By casting this spell you will be able to tell exactly how well constructed any 2 weapons are. This spell can be used on different types of weapons during each casting, but it is used more often after you have determined which 2 weapons seem to be the best and you use the spell to make the choice.

Gem See (B)   R: T   AOE: 1 gem
SPC: 23 - M   D: 1 min   CT: 1
    This spell will allow you to "see" the spells that are held in an enchanted gem or item. It will also tell you if any spell is permanent, and each spell's Range, Duration, AOE, SPC and the Trigger Word / Phrase to activate each spell.
    This spell also works on any Potion, Dust, Pill, Scroll, Ring, Disk, Wand or Enchanted Item the caster holds. It will reveal all the pertinent information listed above about any Enchanted Items the caster holds within the 1 minute Duration.

Nourishment (B)   R: 10'   AOE: 1 person / Level
SPC: 23 - M   D: perm   CT: 1
    This simple but life saving spell will create enough food and water for 1 days survival for 1 person per level of the caster. The food created is simple bread, cheese, and fruit. The water created is cool and pure.

Wall Walk (B)   R: 5'+1'/L   AOE: Recipient
SPC: 24 - M   D: 10 min/L   CT: 1
    This spell will enable the caster to walk on any non-slippery surface as if it were flat ground. This includes walls, cliffs, ceilings, etc. You may travel at a CRM: 1.

Language Spell (B)   R: Touch   AOE: 1 Recipient
SPC: 25 - M   D: 1 hour/L   CT: 1
    This useful spell will allow you to speak and understand any language for the duration of the spell.

Death Trance (B)   R: 5'+1'L   AOE: Recipient
SPC: 31 - D   D: 30 min/L   CT: 1
    This spell will cause all of the life signs of the recipient to totally stop. The recipient will stay alive through the power of the spell's enchantment. You can't die from suffocation, drowning, ect while the Duration lasts and you won't even bleed while under the spells influence. You may hear and see your surroundings, if your eyes and ears are open.

Reveal Gem Quality (B)   R: T   AOE: 2 gems
SPC: 31 - M   D: 1 min   CT: 1
    This useful spell will reveal the Gem Perfection Rating (GPR) of any 2 **Enchanted** gems.

Use Weapons Spell (B)   R: 5'+1'/L   AOE: Recipient
SPC: 31 - M   D: 30 min/L   CT: 1
    This spell will allow the recipient to wield the first weapon she touches. You may use the weapon as if you have had formal training in it, ie. your opponent won't receive his normal PTE bonus. The type of weapon does not matter. It could be anything from a sword, to a bow, to a lasso, to a club. This spell also negates the strength requirement to use the weapon.

Fuse (B) R: T AOE: 1" long / L & up to 6" thick
SPC: 32 - M D: perm CT: 1

This useful spell will completely Fuse two like substances together. This means that you would be able to mend a broken sword, a spear's shaft, a bow's arm, or even fix a tear in your expensive cloak. You may even Fuse a stone door to the stone floor, etc. You must run your finger or thumb over the area to be Fused. The Fused area will be as good as new and will be undetectable. You can only Fuse like substances and this spell doesn't work on any type of living matter.

Leaper Spell (B) R: T AOE: Recipient
SPC: 33 - M D: 15 min CT: 1

This spell will allow you to leap up to 20'+1'/L forward or 5'+1'/L up or backward for the Duration. After casting the spell you may make up to 5 Leaps + 1/Level as long as you use them before the Duration ends and you don't go into combat. If you enter combat, you only receive 2 more leaps.

Touch of Pain (B) R: T AOE: 1 victim
SPC: 34 - A D: 4+1d4 Actions CT: 1

All of the Touch spells listed hereafter are very unique. These spells all are cast normally and cause the affect listed in the spell name. You must touch the victim to be affected and once the spell starts the affect will last until the end of the Duration. The unique aspect of the spell is that the caster may have the spell's Duration start anytime within 1 hour per level after the caster's initial touch. The Touch of Pain spell will cause a strong pain to be produced in the area of the victim that was touched. If an appendage is touched the pain will reduce all Strength, Endurance, Agility, etc. of the limb by half. If the mid-section is touched the pain will cause the victim to double over 25% of the time. If the head is touched the severe headache caused will make the victim unable to concentrate and force him to go unconscious 10% of the time. The victim is allowed a RER, but NOT when he's touched. The victim can make the RER when the caster wants the spell's Duration to begin. If the RER is successful the victim is unaffected - this is true for all of the Touch spells. A Cancel Enchantment spell will release a victim from the clutches of these dastardly spells.

Weight (B) R: 10'+1'/L AOE: 1 victim
SPC: 34 - A D: 1d4 minutes CT: 1

This Attack spell will cause the victim's weight to double. A Krill can't fly and if she is in the air when affected she will be forced to land unless her new weight is less than her Strength Bench Press Bonus. All victims will be slowed by 1/2 and can only fight, run, etc. for 1/2 the usual time. The caster can spend 70 Spell Points and triple the victim's weight (All penalties will be increased by that amount.) If the victim makes her RER then she is unaffected.

Slippery Surface (B) R: 15'+1'/L AOE: 15' radius
SPC: 41 - A D: 5 min CT: 1

This spell produces a thin layer of clear liquid that is very slippery. Anyone initially caught within the AOE will AUTOMATICALLY slip and fall forward, if attempting to move. Once you are on the ground, you may try to get up by making a successful RER + 1/2 your Agility score. If you are not successful you will fall again. Once standing you need to make one more RER + 1/2 your Agility score to get out of the AOE. NOTE: All Enchanter / Alchemist and Elementalist walk spells cancel the effects of this spell on the recipient.
Also all Ninja Walk Over Un-solid Surfaces (WOUS) Ki abilities cancel the effects of the spell.

Howard's Cave (B) R: Touch AOE: 2 foot radius / Level
SPC: 41 - M D: 2 hours / Level CT: 1

This spell has been refined and remade many times, but it's nickname still prevails: "Howard the Coward's Cave". Originally an Enchanter who had more cowardice than sense created this spell to protect himself during combat, but now the spell is used to provide a safe resting place for a party during the night. It will create a Hemisphere (or Dome) of solid rock 6" thick that will surround the AOE. It makes a perfect haven for resting while in a hostile zone – as long as your opponents don't have a Cancel Enchantment spell!

Noise - static (B) R: 10'+1'/L AOE: 1 victim
SPC: 42 - A D: 5+1d4 Actions CT: 1

This unique spell will cause the victim to hear nothing but "static" or "white noise." This will make it impossible for the victim to concentrate and cast spells, hear speech or anything else for that matter. It will make it very difficult for the victim to even talk. A RER will spare the victim of the results of the spell.

Touch of Retching (B)   R: T   AOE: 1 victim
SPC: 43 - A   D: 5+1d4 Actions   CT: 1

This Touch spell will cause the victim to start violently throwing-up for the entire Duration. The Duration may start whenever the caster wants, as long as it is within 1 hour per level of the initial touch. The retching victim can't concentrate or run, but is able to initially double-over, fall to the ground and spew chunks. Remember the victims RER is rolled at the start of the Duration. The victim can't swallow Potions or Pills but may use Alchemists Dusts or any Enchanted Item initiated by a Trigger Word. A Cancel Enchantment spell will release a victim from the clutches of these dastardly spells.

Sticky Surface (B)   R: 15'+1'/L   AOE: 10' radius
SPC: 43 - A   D: 5 min   CT: 1

This powerful "show-stopper" spell will cause a thin layer of clear liquid to materialize anywhere the caster wants within Range and will cover the AOE. Anyone caught within or trying to run through the AOE will have to make a RER. If the RER is successful, they are not stuck. If you become stuck, a successful Ability Check with Strength for every 5' you want to travel will eventually release you from the spell. If the caster spends 63 SP the Ability Check with Strength is at -10% for every 5' moved. Stuck victims lose their Agility Bonus on their PTE rolls.
NOTE: All Enchanter / Alchemist and Elementalist walk spells cancel the effects of this spell on the recipient.
          Also all Ninja Walk Over Un-solid Surfaces (WOUS) Ki abilities cancel the effects of the spell.

Resists Enchantments (B) / (C)   R: T   AOE: Recipient
SPC: 44 or 54 - D   D: **   CT: 1 / 2

There are 2 different spells discussed here. A 4th level version (SPC=44) and a 5th level version (SPC=54). All Resist Spells will grant the recipient a +25% bonus on their <u>first</u> RER verses the Enchantment type the spell is to protect you from.

The Duration of all Resist spells are special. All Resist spells last from the time they are cast to sunrise the next morning **OR** until you come in contact with the enchantment type the spell is meant to protect you from for the <u>first</u> time. Once you come in contact with the enchantment type in question, you will receive the +25% bonus on your RER and then the spell's Duration will end. It doesn't matter if you are affected 5 minutes after you receive the Resist spell or 5 minutes before the Column Sun rises.

A common question asked is: What happens if I cast 2 resists on my person.
                (1) Same Resist Spells
                (2) Different Resist Spells
(1) If the Resist Spells are the same, then you get a +25% bonus on consecutive RER's verse consecutive Attack Enchantments. I.e. If you had 2 Resist Flame Bolt spells cast on you and 3 Flame Bolts are fired at you, you receive a +25% bonus on your RERs verses the first 2 Flame Bolts and you must make an ordinary RER verse the last one.
(2) If the Resist Spells are different, when either of the enchantments to be resisted affects you, you get the +25% bonus verses that enchantment. They do not need to be consecutive and may be spaced out over a length of time.
Each 4<u>th</u> level Resist spell is different. This means that Resist Fire, Resist Acid, Resist Charm, etc. are all different and all take up different spell "slots" when you pick your spells each level.
At 5th level, you may learn a new type of Resist Spell which costs you a SPC of 54 SP to cast.
     This new spell gives +25% bonus on all spells related to a specific COLOR : Resist Yellow, Resist Black, Resist Opaque, etc.

NOTE2: If you have a Resist: Red spell cast on you, you will gain the RER bonus verses any spell causing flame or fire damage regardless of the source.
          This could be damage from a Mentalist's Pyrokinetics skill, Goblin Warrior's Birth Gift, ect.
          This is the same for any Resist spell with a Spell Point Cost of 54 SP.
      i.e. If you have a Resist: Clear spell cast on you, you get the RER bonus for any cold or ice spell regardless of the source. Resist: Brown will give you a RER bonus verses all types of paralyzation – including from a goblins bite. Resist: Green will give you a RER bonus verses all poisons, ect.

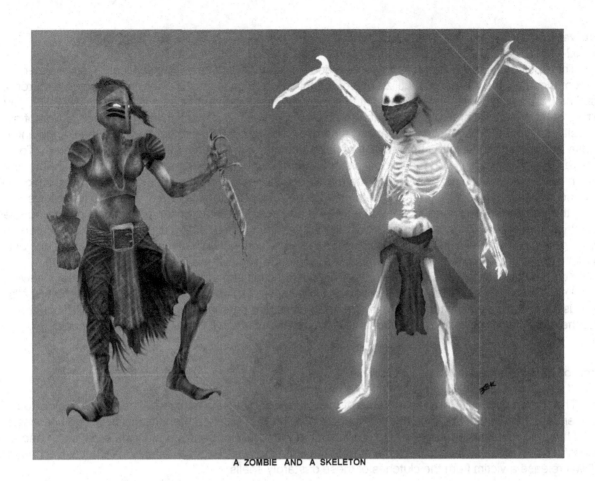

A ZOMBIE AND A SKELETON

Enchant Skeletons (B) R: 10'/L AOE: 10' radius / Level
SPC: 44 - A D: 30 min/L CT: 2

This spell will allow the caster to magically enchant a number of skeletons equal to his level that are lying within the AOE of the spell. These Enchanted skeletons become animated and will follow any simple commands such as defend, attack, etc. The skeletons must stay within the stated Range from the caster and will "last" until the Duration ends or they are destroyed. Naturally if the caster moves, so must the Skeletons (remember the Skeleton's CRM). A Skeleton to be enchanted must have most of its bones intact. If the subjects of the spell have any flesh or muscle tissue left on their bones, these will turn to dust and fall away. The bones of all Skeletons are so clean they gleam, almost glowing in the dark. This spell will only work on skeletons of Bi-pedal creatures or people (Humans, Hemars or Krills - an Enchanted Krill Skeleton can't fly.)

The statistics for an Enchanted Skeleton are:

EP: 25 each	Ambush: -5%	PTE: 25% + Armor/Shield
Strikes: 1 Strike & 1 Parry	CRM: 2 = 10 ft/sec	Damage: 1d6+ Strength Damage Bonus= +1
Pack: 1 per Level of caster	Str. Bonus: +1	RER: Same as Caster

All Skeletons and Zombies have the ability to cause terror in Regular and Mutated Creatures. These Regular Creatures must make a successful RER (= +20%) or flee. Skeletons may use their fists as weapons: 1d6 + 1 EP Damage (the +1 is for their Strength of 14). If they use a Melee weapon, the damage they do is the particular weapon damage + 1 EP Damage for their Strength Damage Bonus.

Gem Cleanse 1 (C) R: 5'+1'/L AOE: 1 Enchantment
SPC: 51+ - M D: perm CT: 3

This unique spell has the potential to Cleanse any dormant enchantment Held within an Enchanted Gem which is not Permanent. When cast, it sets up a temporary link between you and the enchantment you want Cleansed. This link pulls Spell Points from you until the total number that was originally used is matched. When the Spell Points are matched the enchantment will be "erased". The link pulls Spell Points very fast and if for some reason you don't have enough, you may be "pulled" below zero Spell Points. If this happens you will suffer the same effects as if you had cast any other spell and didn't have enough Spell Points (refer to the OVERCAST TABLE.) Now the gem is 'clean' or empty and is ready to receive new spells.

Observation (C)
R: 1 mile/L
AOE: Anything within R:
SPC: 52 - M
D: 10 min/L
CT: 2

This spell enables the caster to Observe a general location or a specific individual. To use either aspect of the spell, the caster must utilize one of the following to gaze into: a clear pool of water, a mirror, a crystal ball, a burning flame, etc. If you want to survey a general location or area it must be OUTSIDE, you can't survey any general areas that are enclosed by walls - even city or castle walls. To "look" inside of a room, city, castle, etc. you must be Observing a person. The general area must be within the Range and it will take approximately 1 min to survey 100 ft of flat plains or 1 min to survey 25 ft of a wooded area. To Observe a particular person you must know his or her birth name - a nickname jest don't cut it! If that person is within range and missed his or her RER, the mirror, etc. will instantly focus on that person. The image will follow the subject anywhere he goes within the Range and will provide a picture of about 10 feet radius around the person. If you spend 72 SP you may hear and speak with the observed subjects and if you spend 102 SP you can cause your image to appear in the area of the subject. If this is cast on a particular person, then he gets a RER if he wants. If he is successful then the "connection" will not be made and the subject can make an Ability Check with Will to realizing that someone somewhere is trying to Observe them.

You may cast certain spells through the Observation spell and affect something that is being viewed.
1) All Class (A) spells !!!!   2) Any Vision or Sight spell   3) The Language spell   4) Teleport Spells
If you use any of the spells listed to do damage to an Observed person, they rate an normal RER. If they make their RER they only take ½ base damage from the spell but the Observation spell is canceled either way.

Touch of Partial Paralysis (C)
R: T
AOE: 1 victim
SPC: 54 - A
D: 3+1d6 Actions
CT: 2

This Touch spell will Paralyze the area of the victim's body that is touched. The affects are obvious if an appendage is touched, but if the mid-section, back, or head is touched then the victim will go unconscious 25% of the time. The caster may start the spell anytime within 1 hour per level after the initial touch and a successful RER, rolled by the victim at the start of the Duration, will cancel all affects. A Cancel Enchantment spell will release a victim from the clutches of these dastardly spells.

Enchant Zombie (C)
R: 15'/L
AOE: 15' radius / Level
SPC: 64 - A
D: 30 min/L
CT: 2

This spell is much like Enchant Skeleton, except that the subjects of this spell must not have been dead for more than 5 weeks. Because the subjects are "fresher" they are stronger and more durable. The spell will enchant a number of bodies within the AOE equal to the level of the caster. The Zombies must stay within the stated Range from the caster and will "last" until the Duration ends or they are destroyed. Naturally if the caster moves, so must the Zombies (remember their CRM). An Enchanted Krill Zombie can fly and an Enchanted Hemar Zombie retains it's +1 Damage Bonus.

The statistics for an Enchanted Zombie are:

EP: 35 each	Ambush: -10%	PTE: 20% + Armor/Shield
Strikes: 1 Strike & 1 Parry	CRM: 4 = 20 ft/sec	Damage: 1d6+2 or Weapon
Pack: 1 per Level of caster	Str. Bonus: +2 (+3 for a Hemar)	RER: Same as Caster

All Skeletons and Zombies have the ability to cause terror in Regular and Mutated Creatures. These creatures must make a successful RER (= +20%) or flee. Zombies may use either their fists or a Melee weapon to attack with. Their fists do 1d6 + 2 EP Damage (+2 is for their Strength of 16). If they use a Melee weapon, the damage they do is the particular weapon damage + 2 EP Damage for their Strength Damage Bonus.

Pass Area (C)
R: T
AOE: 1 person
SPC: 61 - M
D: 1 hour/L
CT: 2

This spell will enchant your footsteps so you leave no trail and make no sound. While the Duration lasts you won't even leave footprints in the sand or snow and you also can't break twigs, etc. In addition, you can't be tracked by scent. You do NOT cancel the Ninja's 5th level Ki Ability: Sense "Enemies" with this spell.

Slow (C)
SPC: 62 - A

R: 10'+1'/L
D: 1d4 minutes

AOE: 1 victim
CT: 2

The offensive spell will Slow the Opponent you cast it on by one-half. His Charging Rate will be reduced by one-half. He requires 2 Actions to perform tasks that previously took him 1 Action. Because the spell affects Time in NO way (not even magic can affect a concept), if it is cast on a Krill in flight that Krill will start to crash (or may glide) to the ground because he can't flap his wings fast enough (of course a Krill under this spell can't take-off either.) Anyone who successfully makes their RER will be unaffected by the spell.

Age (C)
SPC: 63 - A

R: T
D: **

AOE: 1 victim
CT: 2

This dastardly spell will magically Age your victim! To cast the spell you must have a PERSONAL item that recently belonged to your victim. Once you have "acquired" the personal item, you must than confront your victim and cast the spell showing him his formally possessed item. The spell will instantly Age your victim by 1 year/Level of your experience. The next day all you have to do is recast the spell onto your victims personal item and where ever your victim is he will again Age the stated amount - you only have to be in the victim's presence the first time you cast the spell. The victim is allowed a RER when you first cast the spell. If he is successful then there is no affect, but if he misses his first RER he instantly ages and doesn't get any additional RER's if you recast the spell on the object on successive days. For the victim to end this "hold" you have on him, he must either kill you, make you voluntarily end the enchantment, destroy the personnel item, or recover it and get a Cancel Enchantment spell cast on the item!

Mist of Choking (C)
SPC: 63 - A

R: 15'+1'/L
D: 3 min

AOE: 20' radius
CT: 2

This spell will cause a smoky colored mist to appear anywhere the caster wishes within Range. This mist will fill the AOE and anyone caught within it must make a RER or fall to the ground choking and coughing for the 4+1d6 Actions. At the end of this time, the victim may move or act for 1 Attack and then if they are still in the AOE they must make another RER. If any of the RERs are successful then the victims will suffer no continuing ill affects. A wind of 30 mph will break up the mist. NOTE : All Mists are stationary.

Speed (C)
SPC: 79 - M

R: T
D: 5 minutes

AOE: Recipient
CT: 2

No spell has ever been able to affect Time in any way! [Even Magic cannot effect a concept]. So this spell only enchants the recipient in such a way as to Speed up their movements, Actions, etc. The spell will give you 2 additional physical Actions per Attack (1 Strike & 1 Parry) or double your Charging Rate. After the spell wears off, you require a rest period. If you are still in combat and can't rest, you lose 1 Action / Attack until you can rest. If you have another Speed spell cast on you during this period, you gain +2 Actions / Attack added to obtain your NEW total Actions = (Regular Actions – 1 + 2). When this second Speed spell runs out, you will require 2 rest periods or lose 2 Actions / Attack. The rest period is 20 minutes per Speed Spell and you may not engage in Any Strenuous activates until you rest for the entire period. Strenuous activities include: Running, Fighting, Casting Spells, ect. No one can receive benefits of more than one Speed spell cast on them at one time.

Poisonous Mist (C)
SPC: 85 - A

R: 15'+1'/L
D: 5 min

AOE: 20' radius
CT: 2

This greenish Mist is much like the one discussed above, except that anyone who misses their RER will fall to the ground and go unconscious for 6+1d6 Actions. At the end of this time, the victim may move or act for 1 Attack and then if they are still in the AOE they must make another RER. Anyone who lies unconscious within the mist for more than 3 minutes will be affected by a deadly poison. The victim will die within 1 min per each point of their Endurance score point unless a Heal Poison spell is cast on them. The sample of poison an Alchemist needs to totally heal the victim is a measure of any common rattlesnake venom or she may use ¼ Karat of Enchanted Emerald Dust. Anyone who makes their RER must loose 2 Actions to coughing, but will still remain conscious and then may move out of the AOE. A wind of 50 mph will break up this Mist.
NOTE: All Mists are stationary.

Gem Cleanse 2 (D) R: 1'/L AOE: 1 permanent enchantment
SPC: 100+ - M D: perm CT: 3

This unique spell has the potential to Cleanse any permanent enchantment Held within an Enchanted Gem. When cast, it sets up a temporary link between you and the enchantment you want Cleansed. This link pulls Spell Points from you until the total number that was originally spent is matched. When the Spell Points are matched the enchantment will be "erased". The link pulls Spell Points very fast and if for some reason you don't have enough, you may be "pulled" below Zero Spell Points. If this happens you will suffer the same effects as if you had cast any other spell and didn't have enough Spell Points (refer to the OVERCAST TABLE.) Now the gem is 'clean' or empty and is ready for to receive new spells.

Deadly Mist (D) R: 20'+1'/L AOE: 20' radius
SPC: 129 - A D: 10 min CT: 3

This Mist is so thick and is such a sickly, opaque emerald green in color that it is very hard not to recognize. Anyone within the cloud who misses their RER, will immediately fall to the ground and go unconscious for 7+1d8 Actions. At the end of this time, the victim may move or act for 1 Attack and then if they are still in the AOE they must make another RER. Anyone who lies unconscious, within the cloud, for more than 2 minutes will be affected by a deadly poison. The victim will die within ½ minute per Endurance score point unless a Heal Poison spell is cast on them. An Alchemist will need a measure of Cobra or Asp venom or ½ Karat of Enchanted Emerald Dust to completely Heal the victim. Anyone who makes their RER must loose 2 Actions to coughing, but will still remain conscious and then may move out of the AOE. A wind of 75 mph will break up this Mist.
NOTE: All Mists are stationary.

ELEMENTALIST SPELLS

This section contains a full description of Elementalist spells – Enchanters and Alchemists use the previous set of spells. The first thing we'll discuses is what exactly a spell is and what is magic. The next thing described is how the information about each spell is laid out. Then there is a description of a Bolt, Jet, Barrier, Globe and Robe which are all forms a spell may take. Then finally the list of spell descriptions.

A Spell is a means by which Magic may be focused and cast. Magic is a force that has the ability to manipulate and control matter, energy and living creatures or inanimate objects in many different ways. The procedure required to actually cast a spell is stated in the steps listed below:

1) Concentrate for the time listed under the Concentration Time of the spell. While you concentrate, you review the entire spell's description and gather your inner self.
2) Say the Trigger Word/Phrase which takes 1 additional Action and spend the Spell Points (and Endurance Points) called for by the spell at the end of the Concentration Time.
NOTE: The Endurance Points (EP) needed to cast any spell are equal to its Spell Point Cost Divided by TEN (rounded up). I.e. The Blue Flame spell's cost equals 6 SP; this means that 1 EP **must** be spent by the caster to cast the spell. Also the Burn spell has a Spell Point Cost of 54 SP so 6 EP are spent.
NOTE2: The caster may end the Duration of any spell, any time she chooses.
NOTE3: The caster is NOT immune to the effects of their own spells, ie. If Jewels casts the Uncontrollable Fire spell on the chair she is sitting on, she must take damage.

Each spell is laid out in a specific way. The Name is first, then the Range the spell may be cast, the Area which it affects, the Spell Point Cost needed to cast the spell, the Duration the spell lasts, and finally the number of Actions needed to Concentrate on the spell. The letter in parenthesis after the name of the spell is the Classification of the spell – this increases from (A) to (E) – and tells us the spell's relative strength. Directly after the Spell Point Cost of the spell is an M or D or A. This letter indicates if the spell is of the Miscellaneous, Defensive, or Attack type.

Spells can come in many forms. Some of these forms are used to attack or defend against an opponent. The most common are the Bolt, the Jet, a Barrier, and a Globe, which are fully described in the Enchanter / Alchemist Spell Section – only the differences are described here. There are some other forms that are very common for Elementalists. These are the Robe and the Converse with Elemental spell.

Bolt - If the Elementalist uses a Ring to "bridge the gap" between Planes, the "Bolt" – and any Attack spell – is shot from his Ring. If the Elementalist uses a Disk or just extra Spell Points to "bridge the gap" between Planes, the "Bolt" is shot from his palm.

Jet - "Jets" cast by Elementalists last for 2 Attacks per the caster's Level.

Barrier - Wind, Smoke, and Fog Barriers may move with the caster. Elementalists are not required to be it the exact center of the "Barrier" when it is cast and their "Barriers" have from 20 foot to 30 foot walls. They can only be used for Defensive purposes.

Globe - Wind, Smoke, and Fog Globes may move with the caster and Elementalists don't have to be in the exact center of the Globe when it is cast. All Elementalist's Globes have a 20 foot radius.

Robe - These spells encase the Elementalist in an actual piece of an Elemental Plane. This piece envelops the Elementalist in a "Robe" type armor - covering his whole body. It protects you from all forms of attack from anything related to the enchantment matching the Robe's Plane. You also gain a bonus to your PTE total. This bonus depends on the Elemental Plane the Robe is associated with.
You gain certain special abilities that an Elemental from that plane naturally has. Your hands even take on the same shape as an Elemental of that plane and the damage you do with a fist strike is also the same – you can't use weapons while "Robed".
Also, no spell or ability that requires a touch can be used against you while you are encased in an Elementalists' Robe.

Converse - All "Converse with Elemental" spells are very unique because they require <u>no Spell Point Cost</u>, if you are <u>an Elementalist wearing an Enchanted Ring or Disk</u>, linked with the appropriate plane. While wearing an Enchanted Ring or Disk you may converse with all elementals within Range that are from the plane the Ring or Disk is linked to. If you don't have a Ring or Disk then you only need to spend 1 SP for every 5 minutes you want to speak with any Elementals from any Plane.

You only need to learn this spell once and to cast it you simple say the name of the Plane that is related to the Elementals you want to speak with. This is a Class (A) spell.

In order for the Elementalist to "bridge the gap" into a Secondary Elemental Plane, he must construct a Ring or Disk with TWO Enchanted Gems set into it – see information below. While wearing one of these Rings or Disks, you may converse with all Elementals from either of the Primary Elemental Planes or the Secondary Elemental Plane the dual gem Ring or Disk is related to.

Special Notes :

Elementalists use the enchantments associated with the Elemental Planes. They use Rings, Disks or simply more Spell Points to "bridge the gap" between our Plane and the Elemental Plane they wish to draw a spell or enchantment from.

In order for the Elementalist to "bridge the gap" into a Secondary Elemental Plane, he must construct a Ring or Disk with TWO Enchanted Gems set into it. A Ring or Disk with TWO Enchanted Gems will bridge the gap between all 3 of the Planes represented by the gems held in the Ring or Disk, which will enable you to cast any spell from any of the represented Planes without doubling the Spell Point Cost.

"Bridging the Gap": An Elementalist may cast <u>any</u> Class (A) Spell without needing to "Bridge the Gap".
Rings and Disks automatically "Bridge the Gap" to the particular Plane.
If Spell Points are used, then the spell's Spell Point Cost is doubled and you may only contact the Primary planes NOT the Secondary ones.

Metal with Gems: If you want your Ring or Disk to hold only Class (A), (B), and (C) spells, you can use Mithral and / or Quartz Gems to construct the Ring or Disk.
If you want your Ring or Disk to hold Class (A), (B), (C), (D), and (E) spells you must use Americanium <u>and</u> True Gems to construct the Ring or Disk.

Abbreviations:

RER	= Resist Enchantment Roll	EP	= Endurance Points
CRM	= Charging Rate Multiple	SPC	= Spell Point Cost
T	= Touch	unlim.	= Unlimited
Act.	= Actions	Att.	= Attack (Time period equaling 5 Seconds)
1 hr/L	= "One Hour per Level"	inst.	= Instantaneous
Person	= Any Human, Hemar or Krill	1 victim	= One of Them (Ha!)
15'+1'/L	= "Fifteen feet Plus One foot per Level"		

Damage: 4+1d20 EP = "Four Plus One D Twenty" – roll 1d20 and add 4 to the total.

Elemental Plane = Fire   Gem = Ruby or Red Quartz

Converse with Fire Elementals R: 15'/L   AOE: all within R:
SPC: None or 1   D: unlimited or 5min   CT: none

When wearing this Enchanted Ring or Disk type, you may converse with all Fire Elementals within Range for an unlimited amount of time and cast. You may also cast any spell from any spell from the Elemental Plane of Fire without doubling the Spell Point Cost.

Blue Flame (cold) (A)   R: 5'   AOE: 20' radius
SPC: 6 - M   D: 1 hr/L   CT: 1 Action

This simple spell will cause a cold bright blue flame that is 1 foot tall to come into being for the Duration. The Flame will light up the entire AOE. It must be cast on an object within Range. The flame does not burn, so it can even be cast on your hand or your cap.

Sparking Fingers (A)   R: 2' long   AOE: 2 inches – 8 inches
SPC: 8 - A   D: 1 Attack   CT: 1 Action

Follows same rules as listed under Red Gem spells, except for what is stated above and the Length of the Spark is 2 feet long.

Extinguish Fire, Regular (A)   R: 15'+1'/L   AOE: 10' radius
SPC: 10 - D   D: inst.   CT: 1 Act

This spell will extinguish all non-enchanted flames within the AOE. The spell may be centered anywhere within the Range. When cast, it will even lessen the smoke in the AOE by half.

Flaming Hand (A)   R: **   AOE: 1 hand
SPC: 12 - M   D: 5 min/L   CT: 1 Act

This spell will cause flames to burn from the recipient's hand. This is a hot flame but does not burn the recipient. You may cause the flames to burn 2 foot in any direction from your hand. It may be used as a "torch" and will light a 20 foot radius. You may use it to cook, burn away webs or vines, light fires or even use it as a weapon. Your Opponent will suffer 4+1d10 EP Damage every Attack they are exposed to the flames. All victims are entitled to a regular RER. You may cause both hands to flame by sacrificing 18 Spell Points. This spell may also be cast on a weapon, but the Spell Point Cost increases to 38.

Flame Bolt 1 (A)   R: 20'+1'/L   AOE: 6"-2'
SPC: 16 - A   D: --   CT: 1 Act

Follows same rules as listed under Red Gem spells, except for what is stated above.
Any Victim takes 4+1d20 EP Damage.

Control Fire (B)   R: 5'+1'/L   AOE: 6' long x 6' wide x 10' tall area
SPC: 23 - M   D: 5 min +   CT: 1 Action

This spell will allow you to control any unenchanted fire or flames that are smaller than the AOE. You may cause these flames to lean or burn in one direction, part for you or to stay at bay. Regular flames cause 1d10 EP Damage per Attack if they burn someone. You may move the AOE while the Duration lasts.

Resist Cold (B)   R: T   AOE: one person
SPC: 33 - D   D: Until Next Sunrise or Ench.   CT: 1

All resist spells last from the time of casting to the next sunrise or until the recipient comes in contact with the enchantment the spell is to protect her from for the first time. They all give you a +25% bonus on your first RER. When you come in contact with any type of enchanted cold, frost, etc. this spell activates and you gain the +25% RER bonus.

Flame Jet (B)   R: 15'+1'/L   AOE: 6"-2'cone
SPC: 35 - A   D: 2 Attacks/L   CT: 1

Follows same rules as listed under Red Gem spells, except for what is stated above.
Anyone within the AOE initially takes 10+1d6 EP Damage on the first Attack and will take an additional 1d6 EP Damage per Attack they are engulfed in the Jet of Flames.

Flame Walk (B)
SPC: 41 - M

R: 5'+1'/L
D: 10 min/L

AOE: any recipient
CT: 1

    This spell will let you walk over regular or enchanted flames, hot coals, etc. No burning structure will collapse under your feet while the Duration lasts, although it may as soon as you pass. The Elementalist may cast the spell on any person, animal or even a wagon.

Flame Barrier (B)
SPC: 42 - D

R: Self
D: 5 min +

AOE: 15' radius x 20' walls
CT: 1

    These "Barriers" are much like the ones cast by an Enchanter, but when cast by an Elementalist, he doesn't have to be in the exact center of the Barrier. The cylinder of flames is 30 feet in diameter, has 20 foot walls and is 1 foot thick. Anyone trying to pass through it will take 10+1d20 EP damage, and all flammable materials will ignite 50% of the time. If the caster wishes, he may cause the barrier to become a wall (15' High x 20' Long). (Remember that you can't cast a Defensive spell on someone!)

Flame Bolt 2 (B)
SPC: 43 - A

R: 30'+1'/L
D: --

AOE: 6"-3'
CT: 1

    Follows same rules as listed under Red Gem spells, except for what is stated above.
Inflicts 12+1d20 EP Damage to one victim.

Uncontrolled Fire (B)
SPC: 48 - A

R: 20'+1'/L
D: (burn out)

AOE: 4 foot radius
CT: 1 Action

    This spell can be cast anywhere within the Range and causes a small explosion that ignites all flammable materials 50% of the time within the AOE. Everyone within the AOE takes 12+1d20 Endurance Points (EP) of Damage from the blast. Remember, Regular Fire causes 1d10 EP Damage / Attack while you're caught in the flames.

Burn (C)
SPC: 54 - A

R: 10'+1'/L
D: *

AOE: 20' wide x 20' long x 1' high
CT: 2

    This powerful spell will cause any uncovered natural surface to burst into flame that the Elementalist points at. The surface may be any uncovered patch of stone, field, wooden floor or wall, ect. An Enchanted Item is no longer 'natural' so they are not susceptible to this spell. The spell will keep the area burning for at least 2 Attacks. During the Attacks anyone or thing with in the AOE will take 14+1d20 per Attack. (Victims get regular RERs.) After the 2 Attacks the materials will keep burning unless flame wouldn't usually burn easily. (Example: A dry patch of wooded floor would keep burning but a patch of due soaked field would probably go out.) After the spell ends only regular flames persist (1d10 EP Dam per Attack.) The AOE is meant to be a total volume. The caster may change it to be a 1ft wide x 20 ft tall x 20 ft long wall of flames or into any other shape fitting the volume described in the AOE.
NOTE: This spell can obviously <u>NOT</u> be cast on skin, feathers, hide, fur, hair, scales, etc.

Fire Bolt 3 (C)
SPC: 80 - A

R: 40'+1'/L
D: --

AOE: 6"-4'
CT: 2

    Follows same rules as listed under Red Gem spells, except for what is stated above.
Inflicts 22+1d20 EP Damage to one victim.

Fire Ball (D)
SPC: 139 - A

R: 50'+2'/L
D: --

AOE: Blast = 40' radius
CT: 3

    Follows same rules as listed under Red Gem spells, except for what is stated above.
The explosion causes much destruction and 34+2d20 EP Damage to all within the AOE.

Fire Globe (D)
SPC: 138 - D

R: 5'+1'/L
D: 20 min +

AOE: 20' radius
CT: 3

    Follows same rules as listed under Red Gem spells, except for what is stated above.
Damage = 30+2d20 EP.

Towering Inferno (D)
SPC: 148 - A

R: T
D: 2-5 min +

AOE: Body x 10' High x 1' Thick
CT: 3

    This awesome spell will closely encircle your body with 1 foot thick flames that have 10 foot walls. These walls will burn up most projectiles and anyone touching or trying to pass through them will take 30+1d20 EP Damage. The Elementalist may see out, move and attack normally.

Fiery Robe (E)   R: T   AOE: self
SPC: 157 - M   D: 5 min.   CT: 4

     This spell encases the recipient in an actual piece of the Elemental Plane of Fire. If anyone touches you they take 1d20 EP damage for every Attack they are in contact with you. They receive NO RER.

Protection: Regular or Enchanted Fire and Red Gem based enchantments.
                       PTE Bonus: +20%

Special Abilities: Fly as Fire Elemental   CRM = 8
                       Flaming Form -   If anyone touches you they take 1d20 EP.
                       Fist = Ball   Damage :   1d20+1 EP / Level per strike

Extinguish Enchanted Fire (E)   R: 25'+1'/L   AOE: 20' radius
SPC: 169 - D   D: inst.   CT: 4

     This spell will extinguish all flames, even enchanted ones, within the AOE. This means that you may even reduce the <u>size</u> of a Fire Globe. If the Fire Barrier is 20'x20', you may cancel it, but if it is 25'x25', you reduce it to 5'x5'. This spell only does damage to Fire Elementals and you may only affect one per spell. The Fire Elemental will take 34+1d20 EP Damage if it doesn't make its RER, if it does succeed its RER it will take 17+1d20.

Converse with Air Elementals   R: 15'/L   AOE: all within R:
SPC: None or 1   D: unlimited or 5min   CT: none
    When wearing this Enchanted Ring or Disk type, you may converse with all Air Elementals within Range for an unlimited amount of time. You may also cast any spell from any spell from the Elemental Plane of Air without doubling the Spell Point Cost.

Cloud Part (A)   R: **   AOE: 20' long x 20' wide
SPC: 5 - M   D: 30 min   CT: 1 Action
    Follows same rules as listed under Blue Gem spells, except for what is stated above.

Air Bubble 1 (A)   R: 5'+1'/L   AOE: recipient's head
SPC: 10 - M   D: 30 min/L   CT: 1 Action
    When the Elementalist casts this life saving spell, an Air Bubble forms around his head. This Air Bubble will supply clean, clear air to the Elementalist for the Duration. The bubble cannot be popped, but provides no additional head protection to the Elementalist. The spell is very effective in any type of a harmful mist or fog or under water, where it acts as a "skin-divers mask".

Wind Bolt 1 (A)   R: 30'+1'/L   AOE: 6"-2'
SPC: 10 - A   D: inst.   CT: 1 Action
    Follows same rules as listed under Blue Gem spells, except for what is stated above.
Inflicts 4+1d12 EP Damage plus it travels at 45 mph.

Levitate (A)   R: 5'+1'/L   AOE: Recipient
SPC: 12 - M   D: 2 min +   CT: 1 Action
    Follows same rules as listed under Blue Gem spells, except for what is stated above and the rate of levitation is 15 foot per Attack (CRM: 3) in either direction. You may double the movement rate (CRM: 6), if you spend 24 SP. (Triple = 36 SP and a CRM: 9).

Glide (A)   R: 5'+1'/L   AOE: Recipient
SPC: 14 - M   D: 15 min +   CT: 1 Action
    Follows same rules as listed under Blue Gem spells, except for what is stated above.

Whirl Wind 1 (A)   R: 35'+1'/L   AOE: 3' radius
SPC: 15 - A   D: 2 min +   CT: 1 Action
    This spell will form a small Whirl Wind that can be mentally moved anywhere within the Range, including, over your head. The Elementalist must concentrate to move the Whirl Wind and its rate of travel is 20 ft/sec (CRM: 4). The Whirl Wind is 10 foot tall and 6 foot in diameter at the top, but comes down to almost a point at the bottom. The Whirl Wind will kick up any dust, and anyone caught in it will lose all concentration and take 4+1d4 initial EP Damage and 1d4 EP Damage for every additional Attack they are caught in it.

Converse with Clouds (B)   R: **   AOE: 1 cloud
SPC: 21 - M   D: 10 min +   CT: 1
    Follows same rules as listed under Blue Gem spells, except for what is stated above.

Wind Wall (B)   R: 10'+1'/L   AOE: 15' tall x 20' wide
SPC: 22 - D   D: 20 min +   CT: 1
    It will give anyone standing behind it a +30% on their PTE total verses any projectile. Anyone tying to charge through it will suffer 6+1d10 EP Damage.

Wind Jet (B)   R: 20'+1'/L   AOE: 6"-2'
SPC: 33 - A   D: 2 Act/L   CT: 1
    Follows same rules as listed under Blue Gem spells, except for what is stated above.
The damage done when the jet initially strikes your Opponent is 10+1d6 EP.

Wind Barrier (B) R: Self AOE: 15' radius x 30' walls
SPC: 34 - D D: 5 min + CT: 1

This Barrier is a 1 foot thick swirling mass of winds that are 30 feet in diameter and 30 feet tall. The Elementalist doesn't have to be in the exact center when forming the circle and this Barrier will move with the caster for the Duration. The circle will provide a +50% PTE bonus verses all projectiles to anyone inside it. Anyone trying to enter the circle will receive 8+1d10 EP Damage. If the caster wishes, he may cause the barrier to become a wall (15' High x 30' Long).

Wind Bolt 2 (B) R: 40'+1'/L AOE: 6"-3'
SPC: 43 - A D: inst. CT: 1

Follows same rules as listed under Blue Gem spells, except for what is stated above. Inflicts 12+1d12 EP damage and flies at 60 mph.

Fly (B) R: 5'+1'/L AOE: Recipient
SPC: 45 - M D: 30 min/L CT: 1

Follows same rules as listed under Blue Gem spells, except for what is stated above.

Control Wind 1 (C) R: 30'+3'/L AOE: **
SPC: 52 - A D: 1 hr. CT: 2

This spell will allow the Elementalist to control any non-enchanted wind within the Range. The Elementalist must concentrate to do this but the speed of the natural wind doesn't matter and will actually increase by 50%. While concentrating, the Elementalist may cause the wind to blow in any direction and accomplish anything the wind could naturally do.

Whirl Wind 2 (C) R: 45'+1'/L AOE: 5' radius
SPC: 53 - A D: 3 min + CT: 2

This Whirl Wind is much like Whirl Wind 1. As long as the Elementalist concentrates, she may move the Whirl Wind anywhere within the AOE at a rate of 30 ft/sec (CRM: 6). This Whirl Wind is 15 feet high and 10 feet in diameter at the top. Anyone caught in the spell's AOE will suffer a total loss of concentration and take 12+1d6 plus 1d6 Damage for every additional Attack they are caught in it. Krill will find it very difficult to fly while in it.

Air Bubble 2 (C) R: 5'+1'/L AOE: 15' radius
SPC: 55 - M D: 30 min/L CT: 2 Actions

When the Elementalist casts this life saving spell, an Air Bubble forms around the entire AOE. This Air Bubble will supply clean, clear air to everyone inside the AOE for the Duration. The bubble cannot be popped, but provides no additional protection. It may move with the caster. The spell is very effective in any type of a harmful mist or fog or under water where it acts as a "diving bell".

Cloud Cover (C) R: 25'+1'/L AOE: 30' radius
SPC: 61 - D D: 5 min/L CT: 2

Immediately after the Elementalist casts this spell, a dense cloud will form over the complete AOE and touch the ground. This Cloud Cover will cause regular vision to become so impaired that everything more than 10 feet away from the victims will appear blurred and shadowy. This cloud is 30 feet in height and 60 feet in Diameter and the Elementalist may cancel it at any time. If your Opponent can't totally see you, you gain a +30% to your PTE total.

Also, if the caster wants, he can make it begin to rain within 6 Attacks (30 seconds) and the rain will continue until the Duration ends.

Whirl Wind 3 (C) R: 55'+1'/L AOE: 10' radius
SPC: 83 - A D: 5 min + CT: 2

This spell is the same as Whirl Wind 1 and 2, except it is 30 feet tall and 20 feet in diameter, at the top. You may move this Whirl Wind at a rate of 40 ft/sec (CRM = 8). Anyone caught in it will lose all concentration, suffer 18+1d8 plus 1d8 EP Damage for every Attack they are caught in it. No Krill can fly in this Whirl Wind and will probably get sucked in and bashed to the ground if flying near it. This will even stop a charging Hemar or horse.

Fly 2 (C) R: 10'+1'/L AOE: Recipient
SPC: 85- M D: 1 hr/L CT: 2

Follows same rules as listed under Blue Gem spells, except for what is stated above.

Wind Globe (C) R: 5'+1'/L AOE: 30' radius
SPC: 91 - D D: 20 min + CT: 2

Follows same rules as listed under Blue Gem spells, except for what is stated above and this Globe will move with the caster for the Duration. (+50% verses all projectiles. If anyone runs into the Globe, they will receive 24+1d10 EP Damage.)

Wind Bolt 3 (C) R: 45'+1'/L AOE: 6" - 4'
SPC: 94 - A D: inst. CT: 2

This spell is much like Wind Bolt 1 and 2 listed in the Blue Gem section. It will speed (100 mph) to the stated Range constantly growing and conforming to the AOE. The Blast will do 22+1d12 EP Damage to anyone it strikes and will throw the victim to the ground 40% of the time. The victim is entitled to a RER for half the base damage, but they will still be blown off their feet 40% to the time.

Control Winds 2 (D) R: 50'+3'/L AOE: **
SPC: 118 - A D: 4 hrs. CT: 3

This spell is exactly like Control Winds 1, except for what is stated above, and the winds will increase by 100%.

Summon Storm (D) R: ** AOE: 1 mile radius
SPC: 138 - A D: form within 10 mins CT: 3

Follows same rules as listed under Blue Gem spells, except for what is stated above.

Air Robe (E) R: T AOE: self
SPC: 157 - M D: 5 min. CT: 4

This spell encases the recipient in a piece of the Elemental Plane of Air.

Protection: Regular and Enchanted Air and Blue Gem based enchantments.
  PTE Bonus: +20%
Special Abilities: Fly CRM : 12
  Invisibility @ will.
  Fist = Club Damage : 2d8+ 1 EP per Level

Air Absence (E) R: 10'+2'/L AOE: 10'x10'x10'
SPC: 169 - A D: 3 min + CT: 4

This greatly respected spell will force all air out of the AOE and may be cast anywhere within the Range. When the spell is cast, all air instantly leaves the AOE and all unenchanted fires instantly go out. This spell will even put out enchanted fires in 2 Attacks. All persons will start to suffocate, but can't make a sound. Air Elementals caught in the spell will take 34+1d20 EP Damage. When the spell ends, it will cause a loud thunder type sound as the air rushes back into the AOE.

Converse with Water & Ice Elementals   R: 15'/L   AOE: all within R:
SPC: None or 1   D: unlimited or 5min   CT: none
    When wearing this Enchanted Ring or Disk type, you may converse with all Water and Ice Elementals within Range for an unlimited amount of time. You may also cast any spell from any spell from the Elemental Plane of Water without doubling the Spell Point Cost.

Ice Walk (A)   R: 10'+1'/L   AOE: Recipient
SPC: 8 - M   D: 15 min/L+   CT: 1 Action
    Follows same rules as listed under Clear Gem spells, except for what is stated above and the Elementalist may cast the spell on any person, animal or even a wagon.

Slide (A)   R: 10'/L   AOE: Recipient
SPC: 12 - M   D: 2 Act/L+   CT: 1 Action
    Follows same rules as listed under Clear Gem spells, except for what is stated above.

Water Bolt 1 (A)   R: 25'+1'/L   AOE: 6"-3'
SPC: 12 - A   D: inst.   CT: 1 Action
    Follows same rules as listed under Clear Gem spells, but all water produced by this spell comes directly from the Elemental Plane of Water and Ice. Water from this plane is always cold and crystal clear. The Damage is 4+2d8 + pure water.

Water Adaptation (B)   R: 10'+1'/L   AOE: Recipient
SPC: 22 - M   D: 30 min/L+   CT: 1 Action
    Follows same rules as listed under Clear Gem spells, except for what is stated above.

Water Control 1 (B)   R: 15'/L   AOE: 5 cubic feet
SPC: 23 - M   D: 5 min +   CT: 1
    Follows same rules as listed under Clear Gem spells, except for what is stated above.

Water Walk, calm (B)   R: 5'+1'/L   AOE: Recipient
SPC: 23 - M   D: 5 min/L+   CT: 1
    Follows same rules as listed under Clear Gem spells, except for what is stated above and the Elementalist may cast the spell on any person, animal or even a wagon.

Dispel Water or Ice 1 (B)   R: 5'+1'/L   AOE: 20 cubic feet
SPC: 24 - D   D: inst   CT: 1
    This spell will change any non-enchanted water or ice that has less volume than the AOE into air. This can't be cast on someone, but can dispel water in any nonliving thing, including any moisture in the soil. Elementalists use this spell in a special way, they dry fruits and vegetables for use while on the road.

Water Jet (B)   R: 20'+1'/L   AOE: 6"-2'
SPC: 33 - A   D: 2 Act/L   CT: 1
    Follows same rules as listed under Clear Gem spells, except for what is stated above. Remember, the water produced is always cool and clear. The Damage is 10+1d6 & pure water.

Frost Jet (B)   R: 15'+1'/L   AOE: 6"-2'
SPC: 35 - A   D: 2 Act/L   CT: 1
    Follows same rules as listed under Clear Gem spells, except for what is stated above.
Damage is 10+1d6 + 1d6/Attack.

Frost Barrier (B)   R: T   AOE: 15' radius x 20' tall
SPC: 42 - D   D: 5 min+   CT: 1
    This Barrier's walls are 30' in diameter and 20' tall. No one can see through the 1 foot thick walls and anyone trying to pass through them will suffer 10+2d8 EP Damage. If the caster wishes, he may cause the barrier to become a wall (15' High x 20' Long).

Resist Fire (B)
SPC: 42 - D

R: T
D: **

AOE: Recipient
CT: 1

    See the section of Opaque Enchanter spells for a complete description of resist spells.

Water Control 2 (B)
SPC: 42 - M

R: 15'/L
D: 5 min +

AOE: 10 cubic feet
CT: 1

    Follows same rules as listed under Clear Gem spells, except for what is stated above.

Snow Balls (B)
SPC: 43 - A

R: 25'+2'/L
D: inst.

AOE: 6" Balls +
CT: 1

    Follows same rules as listed under Clear Gem spells, except for what is stated above.
Damage = 12+1d8 ea.

Water Bolt 2 (B)
SPC: 43 - A

R: 35'+1'/L
D: inst.

AOE: 6"-3'
CT: 1

    Follows same rules as listed under Clear Gem spells, except for what is stated above and the water is always pure, crisp and clear. The Damage is 12+2d8 + pure water.

Ice Sheet (B)
SPC: 44 - A

R: 25'+1'/L
D: 20 min +

AOE: 15' long x 15' wide
CT: 1

    This spell produces a sheet of smooth ice that conforms to the AOE. You may cast the sheet on any flat surface. Your Opponent will fall 30% of the time if he is standing in one place. If he attempts to move, his percentage increases 30% for every 5 feet/sec he tries to move.

Water Walk, Wavy (C)
SPC: 52 - M

R: 1'/L
D: 5 min/L

AOE: Recipient
CT: 2

    This spell follows all rules of the Water Walk, Calm spell, except that you may travel on wavy bodies of water. The Elementalist may cast the spell on any person, animal or even a wagon.

Ice Elevator (C)
SPC: 61 - M

R: 20'+1'/L
D: 20 min +

AOE: 15' radius
CT: 2

    Follows same rules as listed under Clear Gem spells, except for what is stated above and the height the elevator will rise to is 40'+1'/L.

Water Spout (C)
SPC: 61 - A

R: 10'L
D: 10 min +

AOE: 15' radius
CT: 2

    Follows same rules as listed under Clear Gem spells, except for what is stated above.

Part Water 1 (C)
SPC: 71 - M

R: 5'+1'/L
D: 15 min/L

AOE: 350' long x 15' wide
CT: 2

    Follows same rules as listed under Clear Gem spells, except for what is stated above.

Snow Storm (C)
SPC: 72 - A

R: 25'+1/L
D: 3 min+

AOE: 20x20x20 ft
CT: 2

    This spell will instantly cause a Snow Storm to fill the AOE. All persons within the storm will initially take 16+3d8 EP Damage, slip 30% of the time, and will lose their concentration as the snow and winds hit them. While the storm lasts, it will continue to blow and snow, making snow drifts up to 3 feet in height. The wind and snow will slow everything to a walk and everyone will take 1d8 EP Damage for every Attack they are in the AOE. Enchanted Creatures that are sensitive to cold will continue to take 2d8 EP Damage for every Attack they in the AOE as well as initial double base damage.

Water Bolt 3 (C)
SPC: 94 - A

R: 45'+1'/L
D: inst.

AOE: 6"-5'
CT: 2

    Follows same rules as listed under Clear Gem spells, except for what is stated above and the water is always pure, crisp and clear. The Damage is 22+2d8 + pure water.

Ice Spikes (C)
SPC: 95 - A

R: 45'+1'/L
D: inst.

AOE: 1' long
CT: 2

    Follows same rules as listed under Clear Gem spells, except for what is stated above.
The Damage is equal to 22+1d8 for each Ice Spike.

Water Control 3 (D)   R: 20'/L   AOE: 20 cubic feet
SPC: 106 - M   D: 10 min +   CT: 3
   Follows same rules as listed under Clear Gem spells, except for what is stated above.

Water Globe (D)   R: 5'+1'/L   AOE: 20' radius
SPC: 107 - D   D: 20 min +   CT: 3
   Follows same rules as listed under Clear Gem spells, except for what is stated above.

Water Control 4 (D)   R: 20'/L   AOE: 40 cubic feet
SPC: 125 - M   D: 10 min +   CT: 3'
   Follows same rules as listed under Clear Gem spells, except for what is stated above.

Ice Blizzard (D)   R: 45'+1'/L   AOE: 30x30x30 ft
SPC: 139 - A   D: 5 min+   CT: 3
   This powerful spell will immediately cause an Ice Blizzard to accost the AOE. Everyone within the AOE
will suffer 30+4d8 EP Damage, slip 50% of the time, and lose their concentration as the blizzard hits them.
The blizzard will throw ice, snow and high gusts of wind at your Opponents, slowing them to a crawl, and
continue to cause everyone to loss their concentration. The ice will coat every non-moving thing and keep
building up to 3 inches thick by the end of the Duration. Everyone will take 2d8 EP Damage for every Attack
they are in the AOE. Enchanted Creatures that are sensitive to cold will continue to take 4d8 EP Damage for
every Attack they in the AOE as well as initial double base damage.

Ice Globe (D)   R: 5'+1'/L   AOE: 20' radius
SPC: 147 - D   D: 20 min +   CT: 3
   Follows same rules as listed under Clear Gem spells, except for what is stated above.

Water or Ice Robe (E)   R: T   AOE: Recipient
SPC: 157 - M   D: 5 minutes   CT: 4
   This spell encases the recipient in a piece of the Elemental Plane of Water and Ice. Your CRM
increases by 2 when you move through water. You must pick either Water or Ice at the onset of the spell.
Protection: Regular or Enchanted Water based and White/Clear Gem enchantments.
                       PTE Bonus for Water Robe: +20%
                       PTE Bonus for Frost Robe: +25%
Special Abilities: Water Adaptation.
                       Water Form -   may flow into many areas.
          or   Ice Form -   Chilly   Touch :   1d10
                       Fist =   Club (Water)   Damage :   2d8+ 1 EP / Level
          or   Ball (Ice)   1d20+ 1 EP / Level

Dispel Water or Ice 2 (E)   R: 10'+1'/L   AOE: 10x10x10 ft
SPC: 169 - M   D: inst.   CT: 4
   This spell will turn any water or ice within the AOE into air, including enchanted types. It will even work
on controlled amounts of water and Ice (Water 'hands', 'walls' or 'waves', ect). If it is cast on a Water or Ice
Elemental, it will take 34+1d20 EP Damage.

Part Water 2 (E)   R: 10'+2'/L   AOE: 1 mile x 50'
SPC: 189 - M   D: 10 min +   CT: 4
   Follows same rules as listed under Clear Gem spells, except for what is stated above.

Converse with Earth Elementals   R: 15'/L   AOE: all within R:
SPC: None or 1   D: unlimited or 5min   CT: none
     When wearing this Enchanted Ring or Disk type, you may converse with all Earth Elementals within Range for an unlimited amount of time. You may also cast any spell from any spell from the Elemental Plane of Earth without doubling the Spell Point Cost.

Stone Move 1 (A)   R: 10'/L   AOE: Stone <= 25lbs
SPC: 8 - M   D: 3 min+   CT: 1 Action
     Follow same rules as listed under Brown Gem spells, except for what is stated above, including the damage a "bouncing" stone does and the victim may add ½ Agility score to his RER. The rate at which the stone is able to move is 15 feet/sec (CRM: 3). Note: 25 lb stone = 1d8 Damage.

Earth Armor 10% (**)   R: T   AOE: Recipient
SPC: varies - D   D: 60 min.   CT: *
     This spell gives a bonus to your PTE verses all non-projectile strikes. The number of your Opponents or their attacks doesn't matter, as long as their weapons are all Melee or hand-held. The Earth Armor spell will not protect you from projectiles, because when they are flying through the air they are "closer" to the Elemental Plane of Air then to the Elemental Plane of Earth.

SPC	Percentage Plus	Casting Time *	Classification **
12	+10%	1 Action	(A)
32	+20%	2	(B)
52	+30%	2	(C)
72	+40%	2	(C)
102	+50%	3	(D)

Paralyze Animal or Bird (A)   R: 30'+1'/L   AOE: 1 Animal or Bird
SPC: 15 - A   D: 3-6 min (1d4+2 minutes) CT: 1 Action
     Follows same rules as listed under Brown Gem spells (including Glow), except for what is stated above.

Stone Storm 1 (A)   R: 15'+1'/L   AOE: 10' Radius
SPC: 17 - A   D: Inst.   CT: 1 Action
     This spell will cause a "storm" of stones to fly from the caster's ring. The stones will arc in such a way as to rain down upon the AOE and strike the victims from above. This pelting storm will cause 4+1d12 EP Damage to everyone within the AOE! The caster may choose to only effect one victim at the time the spell is cast.

Converse with Stones (B)   R: 5'+1'/L   AOE: 5' Radius
SPC: 21 - M   D: 5 min +   CT: 1
     This spell will allow you to converse with any stone within the AOE. If you decide to move about, the AOE will move with you, so you may get information from many stones along your way. A stone may give you information of any one passing within 3 days. Stones, like plants have vivid "memories" of colors and animals. Stones also can tell you if any walking Elemental passed by.

Paralyze Reptile, Fish, or Insect (B) R: 30'+1'/L   AOE: 1 Reptile, Fish, Insect
SPC: 24 - A   D: 3-6 min (1d4+2 minutes) CT: 1
     Follows same rules as listed under Brown Gem spells (including glow), except for what is stated above.

Stone Move 2 (B)   R: 20'/L   AOE: stone <= 50lbs
SPC: 33 - M   D: 5 min +   CT: 1
     Follows same rules as listed under Brown Gem spells, except for what is stated above and the rate is 20 ft/sec (CRM: 4). The Elementalist may spend an additional 10 SP / 25 lbs of stone.
Note2: 50 lbs stone = 2d8 Damage.

Earth Barrier (B)   R: T   AOE: 15' radius x 20' walls
SPC: 40 - D   D: 5 min +   CT: 1

     This Barrier has 20' tall walls of hard, packed earth. The walls are 30' in diameter and 1' thick. The walls are very solid so no-one can pass though it, but it is possible to climb over it. If anyone crashes into it, they will take 1d8 EP Damage per Charging Rate multiple they are traveling at the time of impact. If the caster wishes, he may cause the barrier to become a wall 15' High x 20' Long.

Paralyze Person (B)   R: 40'+2'/L   AOE: 1 person
SPC: 44 - A   D: 3-6 min (1d4+2 minutes)   CT: 1

     Follows same rules as listed under Brown Gem spells (including the Glow), except for what is stated above.

Stone Crumble 1 (C)   R: 5'+1'/L   AOE: 6' tall x 6' wide x 2' thick
SPC: 52 - M   D: Perm   CT: 2

     When the Elementalist casts this spell he will cause a portion of regular stone equaling the AOE to crumble into dust and small pebbles. The spell will only affect non-enchanted walls, tables, floors, ceilings, boulders, doors etc. The transfer is from stone to dust and small pebbles, so it makes very little noise.

Quicksand (C)   R: 25'+1'/L   AOE: 15' radius
SPC: 53 - A   D: 15 min +   CT: 2

     Follows same rules as listed under Brown Gem spells, except for what is stated above and the pool is 30' deep.

Stone Storm 2 (C)   R: 25'+2'/L   AOE: Rain = 25' radius
SPC: 53 - A   D: inst.   CT: 2

     This spell is exactly like Stone Storm 1, except for what is stated above and this spell will cause 14+1d12 EP Damage to everyone within the AOE. The caster may choose to only effect one victim or a lesser AOE at the time the spell is cast.

Landslide (C)   R: 35'+1'/L   AOE: 15' long x 15' wide
SPC: 62 - A   D: inst.   CT: 2

     This spell will cause seemingly stable ground that conforms to the AOE to start tumbling down the side of the hill in question. It's hard to approximate the damage this spell may cause, except that any 100 pounds of stone will do 4d8 EP Damage to anyone it strikes.   A Landslide may even be used to start an avalanche.

Hole (C)   R: 30'+1'/L   AOE: 10' radius x 25' deep
SPC: 63 - A   D: Perm.   CT: 2

     This spell will cause a Hole to form on any horizontal surface. The Hole will be 20 feet in diameter and 25 feet in depth. Anyone falling into the hole will suffer regular falling damage (1 EP/foot>10' or 15 EP Damage). If the Hole is cast on the 2nd, 3rd, etc. floor of a building, it will make a hole in that floor only (not any ones below it, even if they are less than 25' apart.)

Paralysis Wall (C)   R: 5'+1'/L   AOE: 15' tall x 20' long
SPC: 71 - D   D: 20 min +   CT: 2

     This spell produces a Wall conforming to the AOE that glows a dull brown. Anyone or anything passing through this wall must successfully make their RER or become paralyzed (the affects are the same as listed under the Paralyze Person spell on the Brown Gem spell list.) The wall does not need to be anchored to anything; it may be cast in mid air, but must be cast defensively.

Earth Globe (D)   R: 5'+1'/L   AOE: 20' radius
SPC: 107 - D   D: 20 min +   CT: 3

     Follows same rules as listed under Brown Gem spells, except for what is stated above.

Stone Pass (D)   R: 5'+1'/L   AOE: Recipient
SPC: 118 - M   D: 3 min +   CT: 3

     Follows same rules as listed under Brown Gem spells, except for what is stated above.

Stone Globe (D)   R: 5'+1'/L   AOE: 20' radius
SPC: 147 - D   D: 20 min +   CT: 3

     Follows same rules as listed under Brown Gem spells, except for what is stated above.

Paralyze Enchanted Creature (E)   R: 20'+1'/L   AOE: 1 Enchanted Creature
SPC: 158 - A   D: 3-6 min +   CT: 4
    Follows same rules as listed under Brown Gem spells, except for what is stated above.

Statue, Person (E)   R: 10'+1'/L   AOE: 1 victim
SPC: 159 - A   D: Prem.   CT: 4
    This is one of the most powerful spells anyone may cast at an opponent and the effects are permanent (unless a Cancel Enchantment or "Melt Statue" is successfully cast on the victim.) When this spell is cast, a pencil thin, sparkling brown ray will shoot from the Elementalist's Ring. When the ray strikes a person, that victim will rate a RER. If the victim is successful, he will suffer no ill affects. However, if he misses the RER, he will be turned into an actual stone statue. The victim does not age, is not aware of the passage of time and nothing can destroy it. The victim will stay this way until the spell is canceled, but the caster may cancel it at anytime. Also, the victim must be lower in level or have a lower Will score than the caster for the spell to work.

Earth Robe (E)   R: T   AOE: self
SPC: 157 - M   D: 5 min.   CT: 4
    This spell encases the recipient in a piece of the Elemental Plane of Earth.

Protection:	Earth based and Brown Gem enchantments.	
	PTE Bonus: +30%	
Special Abilities:	Pass Earth @ Will.	
	Polymorph into a Large Rock.	
	Gain +20% to your PTE vs. Melee attacks.	
	Fist = Hammer	Damage : 2d12+ 1 EP per Level

Stone Crumble 2 (E)   R: 10'+1'/L   AOE: 10' tall x 10' wide x 2' thick
SPC: 169 - M   D: Perm.   CT: 4
    This spell will allow the Elementalist to Crumble any "slab" of stone within the AOE. The spell will work if the stone is enchanted or non-enchanted. It may put a hole in an enchanted Stone Wall, convert enchanted Quicksand back to normal and even cause 34 +1d20 to an Earth Elemental.

Chasm (E)   R: 50'+2'/L   AOE: 100' Long x 50' wide x 50' deep
SPC: 185 - A   D: 30 min/L   CT: 4
    This spell will cause a Chasm to appear anywhere within the Range. The size of the Chasm is 100 feet long, 50 feet wide and 50 feet deep. Anyone falling into the Chasm will receive appropriate falling damage. As with the Quicksand spell, the Chasm will "disappear" at the end of its Duration, "spitting" out anyone that is still alive. This spell will demolish most buildings it is cast against.

Elemental Plane = Fog: Gems = Diamond & Sapphire or Clear & Blue Quartz

Converse w/ Fog, Water & Air Elementals   R: 15'/L   AOE: all within R:
SPC: None or 1   D: unlimited or 5min   CT: none
    When wearing an enchanted Ring or Disk with 1 gem linked to the Elemental Plane of Water and 1 linked with the Elemental Plane of Air, you may "bridge the gap" into the Elemental Plane of Fog. You may converse with all Elementals from the planes of Air, Water, and Fog within Range for an unlimited Duration. You may also cast any spell from any one of the above listed Elemental Planes without doubling the Spell Point Cost.

Rain Clouds (B)   R: **   AOE: 75' radius
SPC: 33 - M   D: form within 1 min   CT: 1
    This spell is much like the Cloud Summon, Rain spell (Blue Gem spell). The differences are listed above and this spell will create 2+1d4 Rain clouds directly overhead. The amount of rain is equal to a Medium shower.

Dispel Fog 1 (B)   R: 5'+1'/L   AOE: 40 cubic feet
SPC: 37 - D   D: inst   CT: 1
    This spell will change any non-enchanted Fog, Cloud or Haze that has less volume than the AOE into clear air.

Soothe Burns (B)   R: T   AOE: 1 person
SPC: 40 - M   D: Perm.   CT: 1
    This unique spell will allow an Elementalist to actually heal any type of burn, including those caused by heat, flames, oils, and even acids. The Elementalist is able to heal only those EPs that were caused by burns. The Elementalist spends Spell Points to heal the victim, like an Alchemist would. For every 1 Spell Point you spend, you may heal 1 Endurance Point of burn type damage. You may only spend four times your End Score in spell points, but the spell automatically heals 40 EP of burn Damage.

Fog Walk (B)   R: 5'+1'/L   AOE: Recipient
SPC: 41 - M   D: 30 min/L   CT: 1
    This spell will allow the caster to walk on any amount or type (regular or enchanted) of fog or cloud as if it where solid ground. Your Charging Rate will not be diminished and you may take part in melee, magical or even projectile combat with no penalties. If the Elementalist "runs" out of fog or clouds, she will float to the ground or down to the next "patch" of fog. The Elementalist may cast the spell on any person, animal or even a wagon.

Fog Wall (B   R: 5'+1'/L   AOE: 15' tall x 20' wide
SPC: 41 - D   D: 20 min +   CT: 1
    This spell will create a wall of solid looking fog that will stop all vision. If anyone tries to pass through this swirling mass of fog they will receive 10+2d10 EP Damage. This wall doesn't need to be "anchored" to anything, but must be cast defensively.

See Through Fog (B)   R: 40'+1'/L   AOE: 1 person
SPC: 41 - M   D: 15 min/L+   CT: 1
    This spell will allow the caster to see through any amount or type of fog, cloud or haze - including enchanted types. You may see perfectly to the end of the Range.

Fog Bank 1 (C)   R: 30'+1'/L   AOE: 35' radius
SPC: 51 - D   D: 10 min/L   CT: 2
    This spell will instantly cause a Fog Bank to occupy the AOE. No one can see more than 5 foot in front of them and the bank will put out all regular flames. The Fog Bank is 35 feet high and 70 feet in diameter.

Resist Fire & Heat (C)   R: T   AOE: Recipient
SPC: 51 - D   D: **   CT: 2
    All Resist spells last from the time of casting until the next sunrise or until you come in contact with what the resist spell is to protect you from. This resist spell gives you protection from enchanted AND non-enchanted types of fire and heat. This spell will protect you from non-enchanted heat and flames as long as the spell lasts. It will also give you a +25% bonus to your first RER verses enchanted fire or flames.

Fog Jet (C) R: 20'+1'/L AOE: 1'-5'
SPC: 52 - A D: 2 Act/L CT: 2

    This jet will blast forth a stream of fog continuously. It will fill the AOE and reach to the stated Range. The fog will stop all vision beyond 5 feet and will put out all regular flames instantly. This jet will initially cause 12+1d6 EP Damage and will cause everyone within the AOE to loss their concentration. It will shoot out an equivalent of 2 cubic feet of fog per Attack.

Fog Barrier (C) R: T AOE: 15' radius x 30' tall
SPC: 61 - D D: 5 min + CT: 2

    This Barrier is 30 feet in diameter, 30 feet tall and 1 foot thick. Like the other Elementalist Barriers, the caster doesn't have to be in the exact center when cast but unlike them this barrier will move with the Elementalist. No one can see through the 1' thick walls and anyone trying to pass through the wall will receive 16+1d10 EP Damage. Anyone inside the barrier will gain a +40% to their PTE total verses any attacks that originate outside the barrier. If the caster wishes, he may cause the barrier to become a wall (15' High x 30' Long).

Fog Bank 2 (C) R: 65'+1'/L AOE: 70' radius
SPC: 71 - D D: 15 min/L CT: 2

    This follows all rules of Fog Bank 1 except for what is stated above and this Fog Bank is 70' high and 140' in diameter.

Part Fog (C) R: 10'+1'/L AOE: 60' long x 10' wide
SPC: 71 - M D: 5 min/L CT: 2

    This spell will part any amount of fog within the AOE regardless if it is enchanted or not. The starting point can be anywhere within the Range. Once cast the spell will clear a path 60 feet long and 10 feet wide or the equivalent, i.e. 30' long and 20' wide.

Fog Globe (C) R: 5'+1'/L AOE: 30' Radius
SPC: 81 - D D: 20 min + CT: 2

    This Globe is 60 feet in diameter and 1 foot thick. It will move with the caster for the Duration of the spell. It will give anyone inside of it a +40% PTE bonus verses projectiles. If anyone attempts to pass through the swirling mass of fog, they will take 20+1d10 EP Damage.

Polymorph into Fog (D) R: T AOE: Recipient
SPC: 108 - M D: 10 min/L CT: 3

    This spell will allow you to Polymorph into Fog for the entire Duration. As fog you may travel at a rate of 15 ft/sec (CRM: 3) and may travel through cracks or anywhere else fog may go. You may change from fog to your original form at will as many times as you wish as long as the Duration lasts. If someone casts the See Enchantment or See Life spell and looks in your direction, you will glow while in fog form. While you are in fog form no weapon will harm you, only magic will. If you try to cast this spell on someone else, they are entitled to a RER, if they don't want to become a mass of fog.

Dispel Fog 2 (E) R: 10'+1'/L AOE: 100' long x 100' tall x 10 ft wide
SPC: 159 - M D: inst. CT: 4

    This spell will turn any Fog, Cloud or Haze within the AOE into air, including enchanted types. If it is cast on a Fog Elemental, it will take 34+1d20 EP Damage.

"Melt" Statue (E) R: 5'+1'/L AOE: 1 person
SPC: 169 - M D: Perm. CT: 4

    This is the only Elementalist spell that will free someone from a Statue spell. The effect is instantaneous and permanent.

Fog Robe (E) R: T AOE: self
SPC: 177 - M D: 5 minute CT: 4

    This spell encases the recipient in a piece of the Elemental Plane of Fog.

Protection: Regular Fog and Fog based enchantment.
                  PTE Bonus: +20%

Special Abilities: Polymorph into Fog.
                  See through Fog, Clouds or Haze.
                  Fly   CRM: 11
                  Fist = Club   Damage :   2d8 +1/Level

Converse with Smoke, Fire and Air El.   R: 15'/L   AOE: all within R:
SPC: None or 1   D: unlimited or 5min   CT: none

       While wearing an enchanted Ring or Disk linked with the Elemental Plane of Fire and the Plane of Air, you may converse with any Smoke, Fire, or Air Elemental within Range for an unlimited span of time and cast any spell from any one of the above listed Elemental Planes without doubling the Spell Point Cost.

Dispel Smoke 1 (B)   R: 5'+1'/L   AOE: 40 cubic feet
SPC: 37 - D   D: inst   CT: 1

       This spell will change any non-enchanted smoke that has less volume than the AOE into clear fresh air.

Smoke Adaptation (B)   R: 20'+1'/L   AOE: see to R:
SPC: 41 - M   D: 30 min/L+   CT: 1

       This useful spell will allow you to see through any type of smoke to the stated Range. Also, you will be able to breathe within any type of smoke, enchanted mist or cloud normally for the Duration.

Smoke Walk (B)   R: 5'+1'/L   AOE: Recipient
SPC: 43 - M   D: 30 min/L   CT: 1

       This spell will allow you to transverse any patch of smoke or cloud as if it where regular ground. You will rise with the smoke and if you step off, you will gently float down to the ground or the next patch of rising smoke or cloud. The Elementalist may cast the spell on any person, animal or even a wagon.

Smoke Wall (B)   R: 5'+1'/L   AOE: 15' tall x 20' wide
SPC: 45 - D   D: 20 min +   CT: 1

       This Opaque wall may be cast anywhere within the Range and will conform to the AOE. It must be cast defensively, but does not have to be anchored to any surfaces. Anyone charging through this wall will receive 10+2d8 EP Damage and must make a successful RER or become Asphyxiated for 5+1d4 Actions. (See Below).

Smoke Balls (C)   R: 25'+2'/L   AOE: 2' radius
SPC: 52 - A   D: 1 min   CT: 2

       This spell will cause 2 Smoke Balls to be launched from your Ring or Disk. Each ball is 4 foot in diameter and is composed of thick black smoke. The Smoke Balls will fly out to any distance within Range you wish and "hang" there. When you cast the smoke ball at an Opponent, she or he will suffer 14+2d8 EP Damage and rates a RER. If the RER is successful then the victim will only suffer ½ base damage and does not become asphyxiated. If the RER is unsuccessful then the victim takes full damage and becomes asphyxiated.

       <u>Asphyxiation</u> caused by any Smoke spell means watering eyes, loss of concentration and you must make an Ability check with Will each Attack you are in the smoke. If you fail any of the Ability Checks before you get out of the smoke you will fall to the ground coughing. The asphyxiation caused by the Smoke Balls spell will last for 3+1d6 Actions. An Asphyxiated victim only rates 1 Action / Attack but may use Potions, Pills, Dusts or Enchanted / Mentalist objects. At the end of this time, the victim may move or act normally for 1 Attack and then if they are still in the AOE they must make another Ability Check with Will or become Asphyxiated again. A Cancel Enchantment or a Heal Wounds spell = 50 EP will cure the victim of the Asphyxiation.

       (Roge has an Will Score of 16 and missed his RER. His regular Ability check with Will percentage is 48%, so the chances of him resisting coughing and falling to the ground while he is engulfed within the smoke is 48%.)

Smoke Jet (C)   R: 15'+1'/L   AOE: 1'-4' cone
SPC: 53 - A   D: 2 Act/L   CT: 2

       This jet will produce 2 cubic feet of thick black smoke per Attack continuously until the Duration ends. The jet will cause only an initial 12+1d6 EP Damage to anyone it strikes. Every victim must make a RER to see if they become Asphyxiated per Attack they are encompassed within the smoke created by the Jet. (See above for details.) The asphyxiation from the Smoke Jet spell will last 3+1d6 Actions.

Smoke Barrier (C)
SPC: 61 - D

R: T
D: 5 min

AOE: 15' radius x 30' walls
CT: 2

    This Barrier will ring the caster in 30 foot tall walls of thick black smoke that have a 30 foot diameter. The Elementalist doesn't have to be in the exact center when the spell is cast and the circle will move with the caster for the Duration. Anyone trying to pass through the wall will take 16+2d8 EP Damage and must make a RER to see if they become Asphyxiated for 4+1d6 Actions. At the end of this time, the victim may move or act for 1 Attack and then if they are still in the AOE they must make another RER. If the caster wishes, he may cause the barrier to become a wall (15' High x 30' Long).

Part Smoke (C)
SPC: 71 - M

R: 10'+1'/L
D: 5 min/L

AOE: 60' long x 10' wide = Lane
CT: 2

    This spell follows all rules stated in Part Fog above, excepts it works on all types of enchanted or non-enchanted smoke or clouds. Note: No one can become Asphyxiated while they are within the "Lane."

Smoke Bank 1 (C)
SPC: 71 - D

R: 30'+1'/L
D: 10 min/L

AOE: 35' Radius
CT: 2

    This spell will cause a Smoke Bank to instantly occupy the AOE. The bank will be 35 feet high and composed of thick black smoke which no one can see though. All persons within the AOE must successfully make a RER or become Asphyxiated for 5+1d6 Actions. At the end of this time, the victim may move or act normally for 1 Attack and then if they are still in the AOE they must make another RER.

Smoke Screen (C)
SPC: 81 - M

R: 5'+1'/L
D: 20 min +

AOE: 30' tall x 30' wide
CT: 2

    This very unique spell will create a "screen" out of smoke which is comparable to chicken wire. This Smoke Screen is immobile, must be anchored to at least one surface, and cannot be broken, bent, or ripped (it may only be Canceled.) Do to the "chicken wire" construction it may be climbed and will support any weight (within reason). Note: it will not cause Asphyxiation and can be any shape as long as it does not exceed the AOE. The AOE may be increased by 5'x5' for every additional 10 SP you spend.

Smoke Globe (C)
SPC: 88 - D

R: 5'+1'/L
D: 20 min +

AOE: 30' Radius
CT: 2

    This Globe is 60 foot in diameter and will move with the caster for the Duration of the spell. It will give anyone inside of it a +40% PTE bonus to all attacks that originate outside the Globe because no one can see in or out of it. If anyone attempts to pass through the swirling mass of Smoke, they will take 22+1d10 EP Damage and must make a RER or become Asphyxiated for 6+1d6 Actions. At the end of this time, the victim may move or act normally for 1 Attack and if they are still in the AOE they must make another RER.

Polymorph into Smoke (D)
SPC: 108 - M

R: T
D: 30 min/L

AOE: Recipient
CT: 3

    This spell follows all rules stated in Polymorph into Fog, except that you may only travel at rate of 10 ft/sec (CRM: 2) horizontally but may rise or descend at 20 ft/sec. It is NOT possible for you to Asphyxiate someone while in smoke form and you cannot cause any other physical damage.

Smoke Bank 2 (D)
SPC: 137 - D

R: 65'+1'/L
D: 15 min/L

AOE: 70' Radius
CT: 3

    This spell follows all rules of Smoke Bank 1, except for what is stated above and the bank is 70' high. The asphyxiation will last 7+1d8 Actions. At the end of this time, the victim may move or act normally for 1 Attack and if they are still in the AOE they must make another RER.

Dispel Smoke 2 (E)
SPC: 159 - M

R: 10'+1'/L
D: inst.

AOE: 30 cubic feet
CT: 4

    This spell will turn any type of smoke within the AOE into clear air, including enchanted types of Smoke. If it is cast on a Smoke Elemental, it will take 34+1d20 EP Damage.

Smoke Robe (E)
SPC: 177 - M

R: T
D: 5 min.

AOE: self
CT: 4

    This spell encases the recipient in a piece of the Elemental Plane of Smoke.

Protection:	Regular Smoke and Smoke based enchantments.	
	PTE Bonus: +20%	
Special Abilities:	Polymorph into Smoke.	Fly == CRM: 9
	Fist = Club	Damage : 2d8 +1/Level

Converse with Mud, Earth & Water El.   R: 15'/L   AOE: all within R:
SPC: None or 1   D: unlimited or 5min   CT: none

       While wearing an enchanted Ring or Disk linked with the Elemental Plane of Earth and the Elemental Plane of Water, you may converse with any Earth, Water, Ice or Mud Elemental within Range for an unlimited amount of time. The Ring or Disk will bridge the gap between all 3 of the above listed planes, which will enable you to cast any spell from any of the represented planes without doubling the Spell Point Cost.

Mud Walk (B)   R: 5'+1'/L   AOE: Recipient
SPC: 41 - M   D: 10 min/L   CT: 1

       This spell will allow the recipient to transverse across any amount of non-enchanted or enchanted mud as if it were solid ground. The Elementalist may cast this spell on any person, animal, or even on a wagon.

Mud Pool (B)   R: 20'+1'/L   AOE: 12.5' radius x 5' deep +
SPC: 43 - A   D: 15 min+   CT: 1

       This spell will cause an enchanted pool of mud to instantly form anywhere within the Range. The pool will be 25 feet in diameter and 5 feet deep. The mud will effect any person, horse, wagon, etc. passing through it. All within the Mud Pool must successfully make a RER or become stuck for the Duration. A successful Ability Check with Strength will release one stuck appendage.

Mold Mud & Harden (C)   R: T   AOE: 10'x10'x10'+
SPC: 50 - M   D: Perm.   CT: 2 + mind mold

       This spell will let you mold an amount of mud equal to the AOE into any shape and then harden it to stone. The molding of the mud is done totally with the Elementalist's mind! The Elementalist casts the spell, completely forms a detailed picture in his mind and then the mud he is touching will take on that form and harden to stone.

Resist Poisons (C)   R: T   AOE: Recipient
SPC: 51   D: **   CT: 2

       When this spell is cast it will last until the next sunrise or until the recipient comes in contact with the substance it is meant to protect her from. The Resist Poisons spell will give you a +25% bonus to your RER if you come in contact with a enchanted poison. It will completely protect you from "bites" from all non-enchanted poisonous creatures. This spell also grants an additional RER to someone who is already "bitten" or "poisoned" to cure them of the poison.

Mud to Dust 1, regular (C)   R: 5'+1'/L   AOE: 50' long x 50' wide
SPC: 52 - M   D: Perm.   CT: 2

       This spell will instantly transform any non-enchanted mud within the AOE to dust. If the Elementalist wants, he can convert the mud to solid ground instead of dust. The affects are permanent.

Stone to Mud 1 (C)   R: 10'+1'/L   AOE: 10' long x 10' wide
SPC: 60 - M   D: Perm.   CT: 2

       This spell will change any stone, rock, etc. within the AOE into a small mound of mud. The wall, etc. must be within Range and may not be enchanted.

Mud Barrier (C)   R: T   AOE: 15' radius x 20' wall
SPC: 62 - D   D: 5 min +   CT: 2

       This Barrier is composed of sticky, enchanted mud. The walls that encircle you and are 30 foot in diameter, 20 feet tall, 1 foot thick, and are rooted to the ground. The Elementalist doesn't have to be in the exact center when casting the spell. Anyone charging into the wall will receive 1d8 EP Damage per Charging Rate multiple. This wall is impossible to climb and if anyone even touches it they must make a RER or be stuck - an Ability check with Strength will get one appendage unstuck.
NOTE: The insides of the walls are always hard and smooth, not sticky. If the caster wishes, he may cause
         the barrier to become a wall (15' High x 20' Long). Only one side of the wall will be sticky,
         enchanted mud.

Mud Elevator (C)
SPC: 71 - M

R: 5'+1'/L
D: 1d6 minutes

AOE: 15' Radius
CT: 2

This spell is much like the Ice Elevator spell listed in the Water and Ice Elemental section. It may be cast anywhere within Range, will create a platform of mud 30 feet in diameter, will rise to a height of 30'+1'/L, and will sink slowly to the ground when the Duration ends. This does have a difference though, if the Elementalist desires, the people on the Mud Elevator must successfully make their RER or be stuck there until they can make a successful Ability Check with Strength per stuck appendage and find a way off the platform, like flying. If the Elementalist is on top, etc. then he will usually not force anyone to make a RER, because if he does he will also have to make his RER.

Mud Globe (C)
SPC: 93 - D

R: 5'+1'/L
D: 20 min +

AOE: 20' Radius
CT: 2

Like all other Globe spells, this spell will create a globe of mud that conforms to the AOE anywhere within Range. Anyone charging into the Globe's wall will receive 2d8 EP Damage per Charging Rate Multiple they are moving and they must make a RER or be stuck. If the Globe is cast while standing on the ground it will become a Dome and the inside is not sticky but smooth earth. If cast in the air, it will be a hanging but stationary Globe until the Duration ends.

Mud Balls (C)
SPC: 95 - A

R: 20'+1'/L
D: Perm

AOE: Balls = 8" diameter
CT: 2

This spell will cause 2 Mud Balls to fly from your enchanted Ring or Disk to the Range stated. The balls may be cast at 1 or 2 Opponents, but if both balls are cast at one Opponent and he fails both his RERs, he will be slowed to 1/2 his CR. The RER lessens the total damage and the victim must fail both rolls to be slowed. The damage caused by each ball is 22+2d8 EP Damage.

Mud to Dust 2 (D)
SPC: 105 - M

R: 10'+1'/L
D: Perm.

AOE: 10' long x 10' wide
CT: 3

This spell follows all rules of Mud to Dust 1, except that you may turn enchanted mud to dust and even reduce the size of an enchanted Mud Wall, Pool, etc by the AOE. If used against a Mud Elemental, this spell will cause it 22+1d20 EP Damage.

Polymorph into Mud (D)
SPC: 108 - M

R: T
D: 30 min/L

AOE: Recipient
CT: 3

This spell follows all rules of Polymorph into Fog. You may change back and forth, and no weapon may harm you while in Mud form, only magic can. You travel at a maximum rate of 5 feet/sec (CRM: 1). Anyone stepping in your mud form will become stuck. A successful Ability Check with Strength will release one stuck appendage. Your mud form will glow, if someone looks at you with a See Enchantment or See Life spell.

Part Mud (D)
SPC: 116 - M

R: 5'+1'/L
D: 10 min +

AOE: 100' long x 15' wide = Lane
CT: 3

This spell will part an expanse of enchanted or non-enchanted mud in your path starting anywhere within Range. The "lane" will be 100 feet long and 15 feet wide. The mud will pile up on either side to a height of 10 feet each. The mud will rush back at the end of the Duration or whenever the Elementalist wants.

Stone to Mud 2 (E)
SPC: 155 - M

R: 10'+1/L
D: perm.

AOE: 10' long x 10' wide
CT: 4

This spell follows all rules of Stone to Mud 1, except that it will reduce even enchanted stone, earth, or rock to mud. It will also inflict 34+1d20 EP Dam to Earth Elementals.

Mud Robe (E)
SPC: 177 - M

R: T
D: 5 min.

AOE: self
CT: 4

This spell encases the recipient in a piece of the Elemental Plane of Mud.

Protection: Regular Mud and Mud based enchantments.
               PTE Bonus: +25%
               Anyone touching your mud form will become stuck.
Special Abilities: Polymorph into Mud Pool – You may go wherever mud could travel at a CRM of 1.
               Pass Mud at will.
               Fist = Ball   Damage :   1d20 +1/Level

Converse with Lava, Earth & Fire El.   R: 15'/L   AOE: all within R:
SPC: None or 1   D: unlimited or 5min   CT: none

While wearing an enchanted Ring or Disk linked to both the Elemental Plane of Earth and the Plane of Fire, you may converse with any Fire, Earth, or Lava Elemental within Range for an unlimited amount of time and cast any spell from the above stated Planes with out any additional Spell Point Cost.

Lava Walk (C)   R: 5'+1'/L   AOE: Recipient
SPC: 51 - M   D: 10 min/L+   CT: 2

This spell will allow the recipient to transverse any amount of non-enchanted or enchanted lava, flame, hot coals, etc. as if it were regular stone. The Elementalist may cast the spell on any person, animal or even a wagon.

Cool Lava 1 (C)   R: 5'+1'/L   AOE: 50' long x 50' wide
SPC: 55 - M   D: 10 min/L   CT: 2

This spell will cool any amount of non-enchanted lava within the AOE for the Duration. The "cooled" lava will become normal stone and will cause you no damage. It will take some time after the Duration ends for the cooled lava to melt back into its original form.

Lava Pool (C)   R: 15'+1'/L   AOE: 10' radius x 6" deep
SPC: 63 - A   D: 10 min+   CT: 2

This spell will create a pool of lava conforming to the AOE anywhere within the Range. The pool measures 20 feet in diameter and is 6 inches deep. Anyone touching the pool will receive 16+2d20 EP Damage per Attack they are in contact with it. When the Duration ends, the pool will disappear, returning the ground to normal, "spitting" out anything still alive and keeping any non-living substances.

Lava Barrier (C)   R: T   AOE: 15' radius x 20' walls
SPC: 73 - D   D: 5 min +   CT: 2

This Barrier is composed of scalding hot lava. Its walls are 30 feet in diameter, 20 feet tall, 1 foot thick and rooted to the ground. The walls are only hot on the outside and anyone touching the outside will suffer 18+2d20 EP Damage per Attack they are in contact with them. If the caster wishes, he may cause the barrier to become a wall (15' High x 20' Long). Only one side of the wall will be scalding hot.

Polymorph into Lava (D)   R: T   AOE: Recipient
SPC: 108 - M   D: 30 min/L   CT: 3

This spell is the same as Polymorph into Mud, except for what is stated above. The other differences are the maximum traveling rate is 2.5 feet/sec (CRM: .5) and anyone touching you will suffer 14+2d20 EP damage. Your lava form will glow, if someone looks at you with a See Enchantment or See Life spell.

Lava Balls (D)   R: 15'+1'/L   AOE: Ball = 6" diameter
SPC: 109 - A   D: **   CT: 3

These Balls will catapult out of the enchanted Ring or Disk towards your Opponent. They may be cast at either 1 or 2 Opponents. Anyone struck by one of these burning balls of molten stone will suffer 24+1d20 Damage. If both are cast at one Opponent, that victim rates 2 RERs. The Lava Balls will stay hot for 2 min and anyone touching them during this time will receive 1d20 EP damage. If a Lava Ball falls on a wooden floor or flammable surface, the surface will catch fire.

Part Lava (D)   R: 5'+1'/L   AOE: 50' long x 10' wide
SPC: 127 - M   D: 10 min +   CT: 3

This spell is the same as the Part Mud spell, except for what is stated above.

Lava Globe (D)   R: 5'+1'/L   AOE: 20' Radius
SPC: 147 - D   D: 20 min +   CT: 3

This is probably the most powerful globe castable by anyone. It will totally fill the AOE for the Duration. Anyone touching the outside will suffer 34+2d20 EP Damage, plus if they charge into it they will suffer an extra 1d8 EP Damage per Charging Rate Multiple. Like all globes, this one must be cast defensively! If the Globe is cast while standing on the ground it will be a Dome. If cast in the air, it will be a suspended stationary Globe until the Duration ends. The inside of the walls are always cool stone.

Cool Lava 2 (E)   R: 10'+1'/L   AOE: 10' long x 10' wide
SPC: 155 - M   D: perm.   CT: 4
      This spell will cool any amount of enchanted or non-Enchanted lava within the AOE. If cast against a Lava Wall, etc. it will cool it and turn it into a slab of normal, non-enchanted stone. If cast against a Lava Elemental it will cause 34+1d20 EP Damage.

Lava Robe (E)   R: T   AOE: self
SPC: 177 - M   D: 5 min.   CT: 4
      This spell encases the recipient in a piece of the Elemental Plane of Lava.
Protection: Regular Lava and Lava based enchantments.
                         PTE Bonus: +25%
                         Anyone touching your lava form will receive 1d20 EP Damage.
Special Abilities: Polymorph into Lava Pool.   Movement = CRM of .5
                         Pass Lava at will.
                         Fist = Hammer   Damage :   2d12 +1/Level

ENCHANTED GEMS

Gems are highly valuable because they are able to be Enchanted. After a Gem has been Enchanted it is able to store and discharge Spells. The types of spells a particular Enchanted Gem can manipulate depends on its color and its Gem Perfection Rating (GPR). First we'll discuss what the gem's color means and then how the GPR of the gem reflects how powerful the Enchanted Gem is.

The **color** of the Gem is the factor that determines what **type** of spells can be manipulated by that Gem after it is Enchanted. Notice that all Fire type spells are manipulated by Rubies and Rose Quartz which are Red Gems. Shields and Force type spells are manipulated by Orange Gems, and spells related to Light by Yellow Gems and so on. [Opaque Quartz may manipulate <u>any</u> type of spell including those of a Miscellaneous type, but may only hold spells with a Spell Classification of (A), (B), or (C).]

The Gems that may manipulate spells **after they are Enchanted** are:

Color of GEM		I	II	III
Red	##	Ruby	Rose Quartz	Fire and Heat
Orange		Topaz	Orange "	Shields and Force
Yellow		Helidor	Yellow "	Light and Sight
Green		Emerald	Green Quartz	Healing and Nature
Blue	##	Sapphire	Blue "	Wind and Weather
Indigo		Indiglow	Indigo "	the Mind and Language
Violet		Amethyst	Violet Quartz	Illusions and Polymorph
Brown	##	Andalusite	Brown "	Earth and Stone
Clear	##	Diamond	Clear "	Water and Ice
Black		Onyx	Obsidian Quartz	Acid and Darkness
Opaque	##	----------	Opaque Quartz	All Spells, including Miscellaneous.

Headings :
I) These True Gems may hold and manipulate those spells associated with its **color** or **type** and with ANY Spell Classification of Enchantment, ie. (A), (B), (C), (D) or (E).
II) When Quartz gems are Enchanted they may hold and manipulate those spells with the less powerful Spell Classifications of (A), (B), or (C).
III) This is a brief description of the **types** of spells the Enchanted Gems may manipulate.

These True and Quartz Gems may be used by Elementalists.

NOTE: All Enchanted Gems used by an Enchanter or Alchemist are able to hold TWO additional spells that they are associated with it but not of its color - these spells are called **Secondary Spells** and are expressly listed at the end of each color in the Enchanter / Alchemist Spell Section.
Ex.) A Fly spell is listed under the Sapphire or Blue Section, but this certain spell can be held by a Ruby or a Rose Quartz, ie. the Fly spell is listed at the end of the RED spell section under the heading of Secondary Spells.

There are 5 categories of spells that an Enchanted Gem may manipulate. These categories are called **'Spell Classifications'**. The classifications are: (A), (B), (C), (D) and (E). All Gems that have been Enchanted gain a Gem Perfection Rating (GPR). The Gem Perfection Rating (GPR) determines how many spells of each Spell Classification may be held within the Gem. Enchanted Gems with the lowest GPR: I2, pronounced as "Included 2", may only hold 1 Class (A) spell – those spells that require less than 20 Spell Points to cast them. Higher GPRs allow the owner to put either more spells with low classifications into the Enchanted Gem or a fewer number of spells with higher classifications. An Enchanted Gem with a GPR of SI2, pronounced as "Slightly Included 2", may hold either 3 Class (A) spells <u>or</u> 1 Class (B) spell – please see the Gem Perfection Rating Table for a complete list.

NOTES ON QUARTZ GEMS :
1) Quartz Gems may only have GPRs between: I2 - VSI1. Ie. They can never hold Class (D) or (E) spells.
2) A Quartz Gem will <u>NEVER shatter</u> when it's being Enchanted, regardless of the percentage rolled.
Please see below for details.

GEM PERFECTION RATING (GPR) TABLE

GPR	Spell Classifications Stored according to GPR					GPR Pronunciation
I2	1(A)					"Included Two"
I1	2(A)					"Included One"
SI2	3(A) or	1(B)				"Slightly Included Two"
SI1	6(A) or	2(B)				"Slightly Included One"
VSI2	9(A) or	3(B) or	1(C)			"Very Slightly Included Two"
VSI1	10(A) or	6(B) or	2(C)			"Very Slightly Included One"
VVSI2	10(A) or	9(B) or	3(C) or	1(D)		"Very Very Slightly Included Two"
VVSI1	10(A) or	10(B) or	6(C) or	2(D) or	1(E)	"Very Very Slightly Included One"

IMPORTANT FACTS:

When there are **different** Classes stored in the same Gem,

You can never put more than 5 spells of any one Class into that Gem. I.e. If you have a gem with a GPR of VSI2 and you are holding one Class (B) spell in it, you could only put in FIVE Class (A) spells, even through there are six slots left available.

If you only put **ONE** Class into your Enchanted Gem, you may hold up to 10 of that Class, depending on the GPR of that Enchanted Gem.

Possible Combinations:

SI1	3(A) & 1(B)		VSI2	3(A) & 2(B)
VVSI1	5(A) & 5(B) & 1(C) & 1(D)		VSI1	5(A) & 1(B) & 1(C)
VVSI2	3(B) & 2(C) <u>or</u> 5(A) & 5(B) & 1(C) <u>or</u> 10(A) <u>or</u> 9(B) **			

** These are possible combinations, but sometimes you must sacrifice some slots to get the configuration of your choice.

In order to prepare a raw gem to manipulate spells, it must first be Enchanted. All spell casting Occupations have their own way to Enchant a Gem, but once enchanted the gem may be used by **anyone** that has the knowledge. Enchanting a Gem can only be done by a Caster of at least 10th level. Regardless of how the Caster attempts to Enchant the Gem, he or she must spend some Spell Points and roll a percentage which will determine <u>Success or Failure.</u> If you look at the next table, you'll notice that the percentage to Enchant a Gem with a high GPR is slim. You'll also notice that it is possible for any True Gem to **shatter** during the process.

(Note: The size of the Gem has nothing to do with its GPR: a huge Gem could have a GPR of I2 - which is the lowest rating - but a Gem weighing less then 1/4 karat could have a GPR of VSI1!)

Each Occupation that uses spells as their primary form of offense and defense can use Gems, but each uses them in a different way. Each Occupation also uses different means to Enchant a Gem:

1) Enchanters: Simply "pumps" Spell Points into the Gem to be Enchanted.
2) Alchemists: Submerges the Gem in 2 ounces of the Liquid of Life [found in the coconut type fruit of the Life Tree] and then spends the stated number of Spell Points.
3) Elementalist: Immerses Gem in a **PURE** element and then spends the stated Spell Points.

Color	Element	Location
a) Blue	Air	Found only at the peak of the Highest mountains.
b) Red	Fire	Lava from an active source or placed in the center of a forest fire.
c) Brown	Earth	Bowl made of Mithral or Americanium.
d) Clear	Water	Rain that falls from a single <u>natural</u> cloud or water directly from a glacier.

STEPS: 1) Caster must prepare a Quite area where he will not be disturbed; unless an Elementalist is enchanting the gem and then he probably must go on a walk-about to find the special area.
2) Alchemists and Elementalists will have to prepare the gem for enchantment.
3) Caster must state the GPR he wants to <u>attempt</u> to "give" the Gem.
4) Caster must spend the stated number of Spell Points.
5) Caster must roll a Percentage on the table listed below (the lower the better – Good Luck).

The possible Gem Perfection Ratings (GPRs) of the Enchanted Gem, the amount of Spell Points that need to be spent and the **maximum** Spell Classifications the Gem may manipulate are listed below:

GPR	Spell Points needed to ATTEMPT to Enchant a Gem	Chance TO Enchant THE GEM	Highest Classification Held or Manipulated
I2	105	90 %	(A)
I1	115	85 %	(A)
SI2	125	80 %	(B)
SI1	135	75 %	(B)
VSI2	145	60 %	(C)
VSI1	155	55 %	(C)
VVSI2	165	40 %	(D)
VVSI1	175	35 %	(E)

NOTE: If your roll exceeds the stated percentage by **25%**, the Gem **SHATTERS** causing 1 Endurance Point Damage per 5 Spell Points spent. The AOE is everything within 20 feet of the Gem.
-- Quartz gems won't Shatter, but you still have to roll the Percentage to <u>Attempt</u> to Enchant them.

NOTE2: The person must be holding or touching the gem he is attempting to Enchant. An Alchemist touches the submerged Gem and an Elementalist may have to protect himself from the element the gem is engulfed in, like Fire or Water!

NOTE3: If a " 00 " {or 100%} is rolled for the Enchanting Percentage, the gem is <u>Enchanted</u> **and** the GPR of the Enchanted Gem is bumped up to the next higher GPR!!

ENCHANTED GEM PRICES

	Gem Perfection Ratings (GPR) & Cost in Silver Pieces			
Spell Classifications:	A	B	C	D E
Enchanted Gem Type	I2 & I1	SI2 & SI1	VSI2 & VSI1	VVSI2 & VVSI1
Colored Quartz	5 & 10	15 & 20	30 & 40	----
True Gems (Ruby, Sapphire)	15 & 20	25 & 30	50 & 60	80 & 100
Opaque Quartz	25 & 30	35 & 40	70 & 80	----
Diamonds & Onyx	35 & 40	45 & 50	90 & 100	125 & 150

NOTE4: Usually, an Alchemist will cast the Gem to Dust spell for a customer for 25 Silver (SP / 4), but a Master won't usually charge her students.

Miscellaneous Information about Gems:
(1) For any gem to operate (either it's attached to an item or not) it must be exposed. This means an Enchanted Gem attached to the inside of a cloak will <u>not</u> work, etc.
(2) Enchanted gems are not affected by heat, fire, acid, lighting, cold, etc. in any way - this includes ALL Enchanted and natural affects!
(3) Enchanted Gems are sometimes set into weapons, objects, or clasps. Clasps can be made by a Weaver, but weapons must be constructed by both a Smithy and a Weaver, Enchanter or an Elementalist.

NOTE5: Info on an Object's Metal -
Mithral: May Manipulate certain Spell Classifications: (A), (B) or (C).
Americanium: May Manipulate ANY Spell Classification: (A), (B), (C), (D) or (E).

NUMBER OF ENCHANTED OR MENTALIST ITEMS

: Rules for Experienced Players :

A person is only able to carry a certain number of Enchanted or Mentalist Items with him at any one time. This number increases as you rise in level, but if you ever exceed it for any reason, you will immediately become aware of a very annoying buzzing sound. The buzzing increases as you acquire more Enchanted or Mentalist Items. The reason for this is: every Enchanted and Mentalist Item sets up its own magical vibrations which radiate from it in all directions for about 1'. As different Enchanted Items come into proximity with one another, the vibrations harmonize and gain audible strength. When your character is low in level (Low EP and therefore low in the amount of magical points), a few Enchanted or Mentalist Items can quickly 'over power' the field produced by your life-force. As you rise in level, your life-force becomes stronger and able to contain more enchantment.

The measurement of the amount of enchantment you may hold is described as 'slots'. Relatively minor Enchanted and Mentalist Items only require one slot, but the more powerful the Enchanted or Mentalist Item is the more slots it requires. Also, if you make an Item yourself, it is given to you by your Master, one of your teammates (you must have been adventuring together for 3 months) or Charge (Ninja Only), the Enchanted or Mentalist Item becomes more in tune with your personnel life-force and therefore takes up less slots.

Level	MAX # of Enchanted or Mentalist Items Slots	Level	MAX # of Enchanted or Mentalist Items Slots
1 - 2	5	11 - 12	13
3 - 4	6	13 - 14	14
5	8	15	16
6 - 7	9	16 - 17	17
8 - 9	10	18 - 19	18
10	12		

Number of Slots Required per Enchanted or Mentalist Item

ITEM TYPE	Spell Classification	Made By or Given Too*	Found or Bought
Alchemist Potion:	Any	0	1
Alchemist Dust or Pills:	A	0	1
	B	1	2
	C	2	3
	D	3	4
	E	4	5
Spells cast directly into an Item	A	0	1
or Scrolls:	B	1	2
(or By Spell Classification)	C	2	3
	D	3	4
	E	4	5
Spell Points 'pumped' Directly into an	1 – 50 SP	0	1
Enchanted item:	51 – 100 SP	1	2
	101 – 150 SP	2	4
An Enchanted Gem attached or	GPR= I2 – I1	1	2
set into an Item:	GPR= SI2 – SI1	2	4
	GPR= VSI2 – VSI1	3	6
	GPR= VVSI2 – VVSI1	4	8
Enchanted Ring or Disk:	1 Enchanted Gem	1 + GPR cost	(1 + GPR cost) x 2
	2 Enchanted Gems	2 + GPR cost	(2 + GPR cost) x 2
Wand:		2 or (Spell Classification cast into and) x 2	
Enchanter's Staff:		1	
Mentalist's Item:	1 – 20 MP	1	3
	20 – 29 MP	2	4
	30 – 39 MP	3	5
	40 – 49 MP	4	6
	50 – 59 MP	5	7
	=> 60 MP	MP/10	(MP/10) + 2

* You only rate this "Slot" expense if the item was given to you by your personal Master,
   your Charge (Ninja Only), your teammate (adventuring together for at least 3 months) or
   if you personally constructed the Enchanted or Mentalist Item in question.

Enchanted Item Examples

The Isles of Penicia are an enchanted realm and this enchantment shows up in many different forms. There are several types of enchanted items and several ways in which an item can be enchanted. This section lists and explains the different methods to enchant an item.

First let us start by looking at the 1st column of the table below which is a basic list of enchanted items and who enchants them. As you can see in the table below, Elementalists and Alchemists have only a few ways to enchant items so they are easy to deal with. Enchanters, on the other hand, have many ways to enchant an item; plus the type listed last spans practically any item you can think of, so it would be impossible to list all the possibilities.

Occupation and Type	Lasts	Description of How Item was Enchanted
Elementalists		
1) Rings	Permanent	Pulled Spells through an enchanted gem from an Elemental.
2) Disks	Permanent	Pulled Spells through an enchanted gem from an Elemental.
Alchemists		
1) Potions	50+2days/L	Prepared the Ingredients and cast a spell into the mixture.
2) Dusts	Permanent	Converted the Dust from a Potion.
3) Pills	Permanent	Converted the Pill from a Dust.
Enchanters		
1) Spells cast directly into items	Until Used	Enchanter has Made the item and cast a spell into it.
2) Spells cast directly into gems	Until Used	Obtained an Enchanted Gem and cast a spell or spells into it.
3) Wands	Until Used	Prepared or found the wand and cast spells into it.
4) Staffs	Until Used	Won the Staff and cast your spell or spells into it.
5) Spell Points "pumped" directly into Items.	Permanent	"Pumped" spell points directly into the item which improves how the item functions. Ie. makes it work better.

The second column lists how long the enchantment in the item lasts and the third column gives a brief description of what was done to enchant the item. The complete descriptions and rules for making enchanted items are located under the Occupation's descriptions, all except one. That one is number five under the Enchanter's list above. The rest of this section is dedicated to examples and rules for these specially enchanted Items.   NOTE: Scrolls may be made by either Enchanters or Alchemists and are permanent until used.

Below is a list of common items and the bonuses the items gain when spell points are pumped directly into them. When you Enchant an object in this way, the item becomes better at whatever it is supposed do. A craftsman could make something with a specific purpose, have it enchanted and it would "do its job better."

You'll notice that the more spell points that are used, the 'better' the item becomes and the more it can do. One IMPORTANT thing to remember, spell points can only be 'pumped' into an object but ONCE. You CANNOT put 25 SP into a door today and do the same tomorrow. This ensures that only high level Enchanters may make items that are highly enchanted.

Because there are so many possibilities, please follow the examples below and use your best judgment. You could apply the table labeled "Cloak" for robes or capes.

An Item with any Spell Points "pumped" into it, gains ALL enchanted bonuses listed for all lesser Spell Point costs.   I.e. A wooden chair with 100 SP "pumped" into it would: Recline and rock, swivel and lock in place, adjust in height and would feel soft as if it had cushions on it – good lumbar support, oh yah.

In order to Enchant an Item, the spell caster must use the 1st set of spell points he rates from the dawning of the Column Sun, not any regenerated sets of Spell Points.

NOTE2: It is possible to negate the effects on one of these enchanted items, if someone uses a Cancel Enchantment spell and 'erases' all of the spell points previously 'pumped" into the item.

NOTE3: Any one item may only have ONE type of enchantment on it at any one time. If a Cloak has spell points "pumped" into it, then an Enchanter can't cast a defensive spell into it.

NOTE4: Once an object is enchanted, it is totally resistant to Fire, Acid, ect. The object only, not the person wearing or using the item.

Ref. note: Some 'insightful' players might try to wrap themselves in an enchanted cloak and say that they are immune to Fire. Don't let them scam you like that, brother.

Slashing Weapon (Sword / Dagger)

25 Never rusts, pits, breaks, or chips. (within reason)
50 Lighter (-1 Strength to wield) & Sharper +1 Dam.
75 Wielder can't be disarmed and Weapon can't be stolen.
100 Razor Sharp, +4 damage done.
125 Much Lighter, -3 Strength & will Never Critical Miss!
150 Recognizes Wielder, no one else may use the weapon.

Bludging Weapon (Club / Staff)

25 Never breaks or chips. (within reason)
50 Lighter (-1 Strength to wield) & Denser +1 Dam.
75 Wielder can't be disarmed and Weapon can't be stolen.
100 Very Hard, +4 damage done.
125 Much Lighter, -3 Strength & will Never Critical Miss!
150 Recognizes Wielder, no one else may use the weapon.

Scabbard

25 Weapon won't rust while in Scabbard.
50 Weapon is completely silent when drawn.
75 Chameleon like, scabbard/weapon are easily overlooked.
100 Weapon is sharpened as it is drawn.
125 Weapon cannot be harmed while sheathed.
150 Recognizes Wielder, no one else may draw sword.

Armor

25 Never dents or get dirty (within reason).
50 +3% PTE bonus.
75 +3% RER bonus.
100 +7% PTE bonus.
125 The Armor and Strikes against it are Totally Silent.
150 +7% RER bonus.

Mask

25 Conceals face from recognition and can't be Scarred.
50 Wearer may Breath in Smoke, Poisonous Clouds, ect.
75 +5% PTE bonus.
100 +5% RER bonus.
125 Only will come off if wearer wishes.
150 Wearer may Breath under water.

Belt

25 +50 lbs. bonus to Bench / Leg Press.
50 +10% bonus on all Ability Checks with Strength.
75 +100 lbs. bonus to Bench / Leg Press.
100 +20% bonus on all Ability Checks with Strength.
125 Strength of the Hemar = +1 Damage to Melee.
150 Fight for Extended Amount of Time: +30 sec/End Pt.

Cloak

25 Warmth, wearer will never freeze.
50 Changes color on command. & Always Clean.
75 Waterproof, nothing it covers will get wet.
100 Chameleon like: -10% on Opp. Detect Ambush.
125 Adjusts length and size on command.
150 Take off, Fold & becomes a Sleeping bag.

Piecering Weapon (Spear / Arrow)

25 Never rusts, pits, breaks, or chips. (w/in reas.)
50 Lighter (-1 Strength to wield) & +1 Dam.
75 Wielder can't be disarmed and can't be stolen.
100 Razor Sharp Point, +4 damage done.
125 -3 Strength & will Never Critical Miss!
150 Recognizes Wielder, no one else may use.

Bow, CrossBow or WristBow

25 Never rusts, pits, breaks, or chips. (w/in reas.)
50 Bow is Silent & Accurate. (Miss only: 95-99)
75 Weapon can't be stolen or lost.
100 Use Xbow as Club (1d8) or Bow as Staff (1d10)
125 -3 Strength & will Never Critical Miss!
150 Recognizes Wielder, no one else may use.

Quiver

25 Protects all contents from breakage, ect.
50 Holds 2 times amount of Arrows.
75 Delivers whatever Ammo wielder wants.
100 Holds 3 times ammo up to Javelin length.
125 Holds 4 times ammo up to Spear length.
150 Only Wielder can draw ammo.

Shield

25 Never Breaks or Chips (within reason).
50 +3% PTE bonus.
75 Will never glisten in Moonlight, Torchlight, ect.
100 +5% PTE bonus.
125 All blocks of the Shield are Totally Silent.
150 Shield blocks 1 Strike/Att without Parry used.

Hat / Helm

25 Protects eyes from blinding, acid, ect.
50 Enchantment conceals face from recognition.
75 +5% PTE bonus.
100 +5% RER bonus.
125 Only will come off if wearer wishes.
150 Telescopic or Magnification sight.

Loin Cloth / Bikini Top (Can't be Covered)

25 Warmth, wearer will never freeze.
50 Wearer only gives off 50% the normal scent.
75 Only requires 50% normal Food, Water, Rest.
100 +10% PTE bonus.
125 Only will come off it wearer wishes.
150 Chameleon like: -25% on Opp. Detect Amb.

Gloves

25 Hands will never sweat while wearing them.
50 Lets you wield a heavier weapon (-1 Strength).
75 Lets you wield a heavier weapon (-2 Strength).
100 Lets you wield a heavier weapon (-3 Strength).
125 Lets you wield a heavier weapon (-4 Strength).
150 Wield a 2-handed weapon with 1 hand.

Boots

25 Feet are always warm, won't freeze.
50 You travel 20% quieter than normal.
75 Waterproof, feet are always dry.
100 Leaves no tracks.
125 You travel 50% quieter than normal.
150 Walk Over Un-solid Surfaces: Ice,Snow,Mud,Quicksand.

Candle / Torch / Lantern

25 Lights on command and consumes nothing.
50 Gives off double the normal amount of light.
75 Levitates on it's own and burns without heat.
100 Gives off three times the normal amount of light.
125 Only Wielder can see illumination.
150 Floats at specified height and stays 1' from wielder.

Glass Potion Vial / Jar

25 Air Tight & Vial/Jar is hard as Oak.
50 Automatic Open/Close & Vial/Jar hard as Granite.
75 Vial/Jar may hold 4 potions of the same type.
100 Vial/Jar may hold 8 potions of the same type.
125 Vial/Jar may hold 16 potions of different types.
150 Vial/Jar may hold 32 potions of different types.

Tools (Hammer, Saw, ect.)

25 Never Rusts, Pits or Dulls, ect. (within reason)
50 Sure held, never slip out of user's hand.
75 Accurate: Never Miss a Nail or Cut off of the Line, ect.
100 Does twice the work with 1/2 of the effort.
125 Locamotion: once started, tool works by itself.
150 Recognize owner, only he can use & can't be stolen.

Chair

25 Feels like there are cushions on it.
50 Adjusts in height.
75 Swivels and locks in any position.
100 Reclines and rocks.
125 Glides across floor on command.
150 Recognizes owner, only he can sit in it.

Boat / Raft / Cart / Wagon

25 The craft is 25% Faster.
50 50% Stronger wheels, hull, mast, ect.
75 The craft Holds Twice the normal cargo.
100 The craft is 50% Faster.
125 The craft is Totally Silent as it moves.
150 Moves at top speed without external force.

Horse Shoes

25 Hoves are always warm, won't freeze.
50 You travel 20% quieter than normal.
75 Sure Footed = +50% chance not to break leg.
100 Leaves no tracks.
125 You travel 50% quieter than normal.
150 W.O.U.S.: Ice,Snow,Mud,Quicksand.

Pouch / Sack / Backpack

25 Full bag holds twice and weighs 1/2 normal.
50 Keeps contents warm or cold (not age).
75 Never rips or tares and is waterproff.
100 Holds 3 times normal and weighs 1/3 normal.
125 Holds 4 times normal and weighs 1/4 normal.
150 Recognizes wielder, opens only for her.

Plates / Trays / Cups

25 Doubles the aroma of the food / liquid.
50 Keeps food / liquid Hot or Cold.
75 Keeps animals / insects 6" away.
100 Neutralizes Poision / Diease.
125 Doubles the protion of the food / liquid.
150 Recognizes owner, only she can use the item.

Rope

25 Never Tangles. (within reason)
50 Twice as Strong as normal.
75 Can't be Cut & no one will get rope burns.
100 Three Times as Strong as normal.
125 Can't be Burnt.
150 Moves on wielder's command (CRM: 2).

Door

25 Won't squeak.   -5 % to Break Open
50 Can't hear through.   -10%
75 Air & Water Tight.   -15%
100 Opens / closes on command.   -20%
125 Recognizes Enchanter only.   -25%
150 Recognizes anyone designated.   -30%

Glass Window

25 Air Titght & Make Transparent or Frosted.
50 Hard as Granite.
75 Able to see only one way = out of building.
100 Hard as Iron.
125 May be camoflaged as adjacent material.
150 Will desinigrate when Trigger Word spoken.

25	
50	
75	
100	
125	
150	

25	
50	
75	
100	
125	
150	

CREATURES

There are many different types of Creatures that you will encounter and interact with while traveling about Penicia. First, let us discuss what I refer to as a Creature. A Creature is any free willed, intelligent living thing that is not either Human, Hemar or Krill. This encompasses a great variety of species. Just for the record – and everyone's understanding – wild animals have some intelligence and are defiantly free willed, also there are some plants that have a type of intelligence. I include all these and so much more when I speak of Creatures.

There are so many different types of Creatures, that it is convenient to put them into well defined groups. All Creatures will fall into three basic groups: Regular, Mutated, and Enchanted. Regular Creatures are the common types we all know about: wolves, panthers, hawks, mustangs, grizzlies, Venus fly traps, jellyfish, etc. Mutated creatures are regular creatures enhanced in some way. Enchanted Creatures were never mundane in any way, they are the creatures out of Fairy Tails and our nightmares: Unicorns, Vampires, Trolls, Dragons, etc.

Each Creature has unique Stats that are listed under its name. These Stats are explained below:

EP:	(1)	Ambush:	(6)
PTE:	(2)	Strikes:	(7)
CRM:	(3)	Damage:	(8)
Pack:	(4)	Strength Bonus:	(9)
React:	(5)		

(1)   EP - Average Endurance Points of a healthy creature in it's prime.

(2)   PTE - Percentage to Evade of an uninjured creature. PARENTHESES = FLYING PTE.
                (for Creatures, while they are flying, this is always a bonus of +50% to their regular PTE total).

(3)   CRM - Charging Rate Multiple of the creature.   Charging Rate in feet / sec = CRM x 5.

(4)   Pack, etc. - Social habitat of creature: some live with large families and some are solitary.

(5)   Reaction - A number that is added to a 12-sided die roll. This roll will determine how the Creature or
                Creatures will react to your presents in its area.

Result of MODIFIED 12-sided die roll

1	Trusting	2 - 3	'Don't care' attitude
4 - 5	Unsure	6 - 7	Wary
8 - 9	Hostile	10 - 11	Antagonistic
12	Violent		

(6)   Ambush - A Negative percentage that is added to your Detect Ambush total; and you thought that
                percentage was low to begin with! Creatures have this bonus because of their acute senses
                and instincts.

(7)   Strikes - The number of Strikes the creature may use in 1 Attack. The number in brackets is the total
                number of Actions / Attack the creature rates.

(8)   Damage - The Damage the creature can do with each Strike.

(9)   Strength Bonus - The equations is: Creature's Str. Damage Bonus = EP / 30, but drop the decimals.

NOTE: The **Resist Enchantment Roll (RER)** for a Regular or a Mutated Creature is: **20%**
                - unless stated otherwise in the Creature's description.

NOTE2: The **Will Score** of any Regular or Mutated Creature is: **15**

NOTE3: All Creatures have an Agility Bonus of +10% that is included in its PTE total.

NOTE4: If anyone happens across a parent protecting its young, that parent will assuredly protect its young
                from any threat WITHOUT venturing far from its young. An immediate retreat of the intruders
                is usually sufficient to avoid a confrontation.

NOTE5: If a regular creature is not listed, use these as references and your good judgment.

NOTE6: Flying Creatures only receive their +50% PTE flying bonus after they are in the air for 1 Attack,
                not on take off or landing. [This Includes Krill (+25%), Dragons, Ravens, ect.]

NOTE7: Regular and Mutated Creatures always rate 1 Parry Action that they may use for movement. This
                also is added if the creature is adversely effected by a spell/skill. Ie: A Wolf has 1 Strike Action
                per Attack, but if it is affected by a Blind Spell, it rates 2 Actions / Attack when you figure out the
                Duration it is blinded by the spell.

REGULAR CREATURES

BATS

Fruit

EP:	15		Ambush:	- 20%	PTE:	25% (75%)
Strikes:	1	{2}	CRM:	Fly = 3	Cave:	20 - 200
Damage:	1d2		Str. Bonus:	----	React:	4

Vampire

EP:	30		Ambush:	- 20%	PTE:	25% (75%)
Strikes:	1	{2}	CRM:	Fly = 4	Cave:	20 - 200
Damage:	1d8 + Drain 2 HP / Att.		Str. Bonus:	+1	React:	4

A Vampire Bat must consume 4 EP of Blood per night or they will begin to starve.

BEARS

Black

EP:	90		Ambush:	- 10%	PTE:	40%
Strikes:	2 paws or 1 bite	{3}	CRM:	5	Den:	1 family
Damage:	Paw = 1d10 ea. / Bite = 2d8		Str. Bonus:	+3	React:	5

Brown

EP:	120		Ambush:	- 15%	PTE:	40%
Strikes:	2 paws or 1 bite	{3}	CRM:	4	Den:	1 family
Damage:	Paw = 1d12 ea. / Bite = 2d10		Str. Bonus:	+4	React:	5

Grisly / Polar

EP:	150		Ambush:	- 15%	PTE:	40%
Strikes:	2 paws or 1 bite	{3}	CRM:	4	Den:	1 family
Damage:	Paw = 2d8 ea. / Bite = 2d12		Str. Bonus:	+5	React:	6

BIRDS

Crow / Raven

EP:	20		Ambush:	- 10%	PTE:	25% (75%)
Strikes:	2 Talons and Beak	{3}	CRM:	Fly = 4 ; Dive = 8	Flock:	5 - 50
Damage:	Talons = 1d2 * / Beak = 1d4		Str. Bonus:	----	React:	2

Hawk / Falcon

EP:	25		Ambush:	- 10%	PTE:	25% (75%)
Strikes:	2 Talons and Beak	{3}	CRM:	Fly = 6 ; Dive = 10	Flock:	1 family
Damage:	Talons = 1d4 * / Beak = 1d6		Str. Bonus:	----	React:	3

Owl

EP:	30		Ambush:	- 25%	PTE:	25% (75%)
Strikes:	2 Talons and Beak	{3}	CRM:	Fly = 6 ; Dive = 8	Flock:	1 family
Damage:	Talons = 1d4 * / Beak = 1d6		Str. Bonus:	+1	React:	1

Geese

EP:	35		Ambush:	- 20%	PTE:	25% (75%)
Strikes:	1 Beak	{2}	CRM:	Fly = 4	Gaggle:	10-100
Damage:	Beak = 1d4		Str. Bonus:	+1	React:	5

Eagle / Vulture

EP:	40		Ambush:	- 15 %	PTE:	20% (75%)
Strikes:	2 Talons and Beak	{3}	CRM:	Fly = 6 ; Dive = 9	Flock:	1 family
Damage:	Talons = 1d6 * / Beak = 1d8		Str. Bonus:	+1	React:	4

* If a bird attacks a victim while it is in a full Dive, it will do an extra 2 EP damage per CRM added to its normal damage with its Talons.

CANINE

Dogs

EP:	40		Ambush:	0%	PTE:	45%
Strikes:	1	{2}	CRM:	4	Pack:	5 - 10
Damage:	1d10 **		Str. Bonus:	+1	React:	0

(If a player Bards a Dog or Horse the maximum PTE is 85%, just like everything and everyone else).

Wolves

EP:	60		Ambush:	- 20%	PTE:	55%
Strikes:	1	{2}	CRM:	5	Pack:	10 - 60
Damage:	1d12 **		Str. Bonus:	+2	React:	4

** Special Strike for ALL Canine's: If a Canine's bite is successful, it will hold on and cause automatic bite damage every Attack. Also, the prey will loose its Agility Bonus to its PTE total while the Canine is holding on.

BIG CATS

Cheetah

EP:	60		Ambush:	- 25%	PTE:	50%
Strikes:	2 Paws & 1 Bite ^^	{3}	CRM:	10 / 8	Pride:	10 - 20
Damage:	Paw = 1d6 / Bite = 1d10		Str. Bonus:	+2	React:	4 to 6

Panther / Leopard

EP:	75		Ambush:	- 30%	PTE:	50%
Strikes:	(same) ^^	{3}	CRM:	7	Pride:	(Solitary)
Damage:	Paw = 1d8 / Bite = 1d10		Str. Bonus:	+2	React:	4 to 6

Cougar / Tiger

EP:	90		Ambush:	- 25%	PTE:	45%
Strikes:	(same) ^^	{3}	CRM:	6	Pride:	5 - 20
Damage:	Paw = 1d8 / Bite =1d12		Str. Bonus:	+3	React:	5 to 6

Lion

EP:	100		Ambush:	- 25%	PTE:	45%
Strikes:	(same) ^^	{3}	CRM:	6	Pride:	10 - 20
Damage:	Paw = 1d10 / Bite = 2d8		Str. Bonus:	+3	React:	6 to 7

^^ All Cats: If both the paws and its bite successfully strike a target in the same Attack, the Cat will hold on with its bite for automatic damage every Attack and will 'rake' the target with all of it's claws during the next attack: Strike = 4 paws + bite damage. Also, the prey will loose its Agility Bonus to its PTE total while the Cat is holding on.

HORSES

Mustang / Andalusian

EP:	70		Ambush:	- 10%	PTE:	40%
Strikes:	1 Bite or 1 Buck	{2}	CRM:	5	Herd:	5 - 50
Damage:	Bit = 1d4 / Buck = 1d20		Str. Bonus:	+2	React:	3

Clydesdale

EP:	85		Ambush:	- 10%	PTE:	40%
Strikes:	1 Bite or 1 Buck	{2}	CRM:	4	Herd:	5 - 50
Damage:	Bit = 1d6 / Buck = 1d20		Str. Bonus:	+2	React:	4

(If a player Bards a Dog or Horse the maximum PTE is 85%, just like everything and everyone else).

SNAKES

Boa

EP:	40		Ambush:	- 20%	PTE:	15%
Strikes:	Strangulation	{2}	CRM:	1	Pit:	1
Damage:	1d8 / Attack		Str. Bonus:	+1	React:	5

Rattler

EP:	15		Ambush:	0	PTE:	25%
Strikes:	1 bite	{2}	CRM:	1	Pit:	1 - 10
Damage:	1d8 + poison		Str. Bonus:	----	React:	5

Rattle Snake poison will do 1d10 EP damage per 5 minutes and must be cured or the victim will eventually die.

Cobra

EP:	25		Ambush:	0	PTE:	25%
Strikes:	1 bite / spitting	{2}	CRM:	1	Pit:	1 - 10
Damage:	1d10 + poison or blindness		Str. Bonus:	----	React:	6

Cobra Poison will do 1d10 EP damage per minute and must be cured or the victim will quickly die. Also a Cobra may spit its venom into someone's eyes. If hit in the face, the victim rates a RER or becomes blind for 1d20 Actions.

SPIDERS

Garden type / Jumper type / Wolf type

EP:	3		Ambush:	- 15%	PTE:	30%
Strikes:	(None unless Mutated)	{2}	CRM:	2	Niche:	1 - 100
Damage:	(same)		Str. Bonus:	----	React:	0

Black Widow

EP:	5		Ambush:	- 20%	PTE:	30%
Strikes:	1	{2}	CRM:	3	Niche:	1 - 100
Damage:	1-2 + poison = 1d6		Str. Bonus:	----	React:	4

Tarantula

EP:	10		Ambush:	- 10%	PTE:	35%
Strikes:	1	{2}	CRM:	4	Niche:	1 – 100
Damage:	1d4 + poison = 1d4		Str. Bonus:	----	React:	0

MONKEYS

Spider

EP:	20		Ambush:	-15 %	PTE:	35%
Strikes:	2 Hands	{3}	CRM:	4	Family:	1 – 100
Damage:	1d4 ea.		Str. Bonus:	----	React:	-2

Chimpanzee

EP:	35		Ambush:	-10%	PTE:	35%
Strikes:	2 Hands	{3}	CRM:	4	Family:	10
Damage:	1d6 ea.		Str. Bonus:	+1	React:	-1

Orangutan

EP:	75		Ambush:	-10%	PTE:	35%
Strikes:	2 Hands	{3}	CRM:	4	Family:	10
Damage:	1d12 ea.		Str. Bonus:	+2	React:	0

Gorilla

EP:	125		Ambush:	- 10%	PTE:	40%
Strikes:	2 Hands	{3}	CRM:	4	Family:	10
Damage:	2d8 ea.		Str. Bonus:	+4	React:	3

SHARKS

Nurse

EP:	90		Ambush:	-25 %	PTE:	50%
Strikes:	1 Bite ** ^^	{2}	CRM:	6	School:	1 - 10
Damage:	2d10		Str. Bonus:	+3	React:	5

Tiger / Hammerhead

EP:	140		Ambush:	-25 %	PTE:	50%
Strikes:	1 Bite ** ^^	{2}	CRM:	7	School:	1 - 10
Damage:	4d6		Str. Bonus:	+4	React:	5

Great White

EP:	200		Ambush:	-35 %	PTE:	45%
Strikes:	1 Bite ** ^^	{2}	CRM:	6	School:	1 - 5
Damage:	4d8		Str. Bonus:	+6	React:	6

** If a Shark's bite is successful, it will hold on and cause automatic bite damage every Attack. Also, the prey will loose its Agility Bonus to its PTE total while the Shark is holding on.

^^ Also, If any Shark does a total amount of damage to a limb that is greater than 1/3 the character's Total Original Endurance Points (TOEP), the Shark will bite off that limb.

FISH

Jellyfish

EP:	25		Ambush:	-10 %	PTE:	25%
Strikes:	2 stings	{3}	CRM:	2	School:	1 – 50
Damage:	1d8 ea.		Str. Bonus:	+0	React:	5

Each sting delivers a venom which causes 1 EP per minute which lasts for 10 minutes. This damage is cumulative.

Piranha

EP:	15		Ambush:	-50 %	PTE:	35%
Strikes:	1 Bite	{2}	CRM:	4	School:	10 – 100
Damage:	1d10		Str. Bonus:	+0	React:	10

Barracuda

EP:	40		Ambush:	-35 %	PTE:	35%
Strikes:	1 Bite	{2}	CRM:	5	School:	1 – 10
Damage:	2d8		Str. Bonus:	+1	React:	4

Octopus / Squid

EP:	60		Ambush:	-5 %	PTE:	35%
Strikes:	8-10 Arms / 1 Bite	{4}	CRM:	6	School:	Solitary
Damage:	Arms = 4 EP / Bite = 1d10		Str. Bonus:	+2	React:	2

WHALE

Hump Backed

EP:	800		Ambush:	-5 %	PTE:	30%
Strikes:	Swallow @@	{2}	CRM:	4	School:	Solitary
Damage:	Digestion or Smash		Str. Bonus:	+26	React:	-3

@@ If swallowed by a Hump Backed whale, the victim suffers 1d10 EP damage per hour until he is digested. A smash can only be used against a boat, ship or large structure and causes 3d20+26 damage.

Blue

EP:	1200		Ambush:	-5 %	PTE:	30%
Strikes:	Swallow &&	{2}	CRM:	4	School:	Solitary
Damage:	Digestion or Smash		Str. Bonus:	+40	React:	-3

&& If swallowed by a Blue whale, the victim suffers 1d12 EP damage per hour until he is digested. A smash can only be used against a boat, ship or large structure and causes 4d20+40 damage.

MUTATED CREATURES

Mutated Creatures are adaptations of Regular creatures. In some cases, a group of regular creatures are lead by a mutated one of their type, but some times an entire pack of creatures will show various types of mutations.

A Creature may exhibit one or many mutations and some or all of these are usually passed onto its young.

MUTATION	BENEFITS
1) Giant	- Mammal or Bird = 2 - 10 times larger **
	- Insect, Reptile or Arachnid = 5-20 times larger **
2) Additional Heads	- 1d6 additional heads. Grows 50% larger per head **
3) Fangs & Claws	- or x2 size and damage of existing ones & grows 30% **
4) Wings	- or x2 size, strength and speed of existing ones & grows 30% **
5) Deadly Poison	- Death within 10+1d20 minutes unless cured (+1d10 damage each Strike)
6) Thicker Skin or Scales	- +30% PTE and +15% RER & grows 50% **
7) Agility	- +1d10; maximum is 20. (includes PTE) & grows 20% **
8) Strength	- +1d10; maximum is 20. (includes Strength Damage Bonus) & grows 30% **
9) Endurance	- +1d10; maximum is 20. (includes EP) & grows 50% **
10) Intellect or Wisdom	- +1d10; maximum is 20. Gain +10% RER & +5 Will & gains Speech & grows 20% **
11) Extraordinary Sense	- Pick 1 or 2 Senses to Heighten - grows 10% each sense **
12) Extra Legs or Arms	- Extra Strikes or greater CRM - grows 30% per appendage **
13) Extra Eyes	- +1d12 Eyes & Heighten / Multidirectional Vision & grows 5% per Eye **
14) Strange Color	- +10% PTE & RER & gains Speech & grows 30% **
15) Horns	- or x3 size and damage of existing ones: Horns can be Projectiles & grows +30% **
16) Tail Spikes	- or x3 size and damage of existing ones: Spikes can be Projectiles & grows +30% **
17) Enchanted Resistance	- a) +25% RER verses ALL types of Enchantments & grows 20% **
	b) +25% RER verses a certain color of Enchantment & grows 30% **
	c) +25% RER verses a specific Enchantment & grows 50% **
18) Immunity	- A) specific Class of spell (A,B,C,D, or E) B) Poison
	C) Acid D) Fire & grows 20% **
	E) Cold F) Lightning
19) Non-Deadly Poison	- a) Paralysis if fail RER, +1d6 EP Damage either way.
	b) Extreme Pain if fail RER, +1d6 EP Damage either way. & grows 30% **
	c) Additional Damage: 10+1d8, victim gets a RER for ½ base damage.
20) Additional Actions	- The creature Gains addition Actions (Usually Strikes) to use during combat.
21) Additional Tails	- +1d10 additional tails = +1 Str & Agl & Int & Wis & Will & +5% PTE & RER per Tail & gains Speech & grows 20% larger ** per Tail, but may control size.
22) Enchantment	- Creature acquires an Enchantment, Ref's Choice. Grows 20%.

** If the creature grows larger, its EPs are increased by the same percentage:

   i.e. 3 times larger = 3 times original EP.

   +30% larger = +30% increase to original EP.

   Optional: If the creature 'grows', it may normally be regular size and can spontaneously grow 5 times/day.

NOTE: A Mutated Creature is affected the same as Regular Creatures with regards to Enchantments.
(I.e. Converse with Animal or Bird lets you speak with Mutated animals and birds and the Paralyze Animal or Bird works on them as well.)

NOTE2: If the Mutated Creature gains Speech, the Ref. may pick any or one to three languages.
The possibilities are: Human, Hemar, Krill, Travelers or a particular Creature's Type.

NOTE3: It is also possible that a Creature has a Cross Species Mutation. A Cross Species Mutation is a common physical attribute from one creature bestowed on another. Next is a list of some common Cross Mutations. These Creatures also gain size and EP increases of between 50% – 100%.

CROSS SPECIES MUTATIONS

a) Wolf-Octopi – Wolves with internal gills and two tentacles protruding from their shoulders.
b) Shark-Snakes – Sharks with extendable necks and possible fangs.
c) Wolf-Sharks – Amphibian wolves with a shark's jaws and tail.
d) Shark-Hawks – Shark with the lungs and wings of a giant hawk.
e) Tiger-Bear – Head, shoulders and front claws of a Tiger but the body and hind legs of a bear.
f) Owl-Bull – Head, talons and wings of an Owl but the body of a Brahma bull.
g) Fox-Eagle – A large fox with the wings and front talons of an Eagle.

h) Sky Panther – A giant panther (x3 Size) with large Falcon Wings.

EP:	150		Ambush:	-30 %	PTE:	50% (Fly: 85%)
Strikes/Parry:	2 / 1	{3}	CRM:	6 (Fly: 8)	Pride:	3 - 10
Damage:	Paw= 1d10+5 / Bite= 1d12+5		Str. Bonus:	+5	React:	8
Special:	2/day: Lightning Bolt 2		R:55'	Dam: 22+2d10.		

These are normally Mutated Creatures, but when bonded to a True Knight they become an Enchanted Creature.

i) Fire Steed – A Large Clydesdale (x2 Size) with a mutated enchantment of Fiery Flight.

EP:	150		Ambush:	-30 %	PTE:	50% (Fly: 85%)
Strikes/Parry:	1 / 1	{2}	CRM:	6 (Fly: 8)	Herd:	10 - 30
Damage:	Bite= 1d10+5 / Buck= 1d20+5		Str. Bonus:	+5	React:	8
Special:	2/day: Fire Bolt 3		R:45'	Dam: 22+1d20.		

These are normally Mutated Creatures, but when bonded to a Black Knight they become an Enchanted Creature.

These are examples, but are by no means the only Cross Mutations within Penicia's Isles.

There are several types of creatures that seem to be a mutation of a lower creature and that of a person. These Mutated Creatures have the mutation of Intellect, Strength and a partial human form. (There are rumors of Mutated Creatures having the attributes of a Krill and Hemar also.) The most well known of this type of Mutated Creature is the "race" of Lizard-men. All Lizard-men form communities and share a single Language. Lizard-men have been known to attack established villages and sweep over farm lands for no apparent reason. Lizard-men always look partially human, walking in a bi-pedal manor and employing certain types of race specific weapons and armor.

LIZARDMEN

Collard Lizard-man

EP:	30	Ambush:	-10 %	PTE:	15%+Armor &/or Shield
Strikes/Parry:	1 / 1	CRM:	3	Tribe:	10 – 100
Damage:	Claw = 1d4+1 or by Weapon	Str. Bonus:	+1	React:	8

These small Lizard-men stand only 3' tall, but are very savage and attack their prey with overwhelming numbers. They have compact bodies with thick skin, strong legs, sharp claws, and long prehensile tails that can be used for hanging onto a branch or cliff. They use an unusual weapon: A one handed mace with a nasty hook protruding off the front side. The back side of this weapon has an indentation which allows them to throw small javelins with great accuracy. The Javelin inflicts 1d6 damage and the Mace/Hook deals 1d8 damage plus 1 Strength Damage Bonus per successful strike. Some employ small wooden shields or even ½ suits of leather armor (+5% & +15% bonus to PTE, respectively).
Ability Scores: End=10 Agl=17 Str=13 Int=4 Wis=8 Will=15.

Iguana Lizard-man

EP:	50	Ambush:	-10 %	PTE:	20%+Armor &/or Shield
Strikes/Parry:	1 / 2	CRM:	4	Tribe:	5 – 50
Damage:	Claw=1d10+2, Weapon + Tail	Str. Bonus:	+1	React:	6

These medium-sized Lizard-men stand 5' tall and are separated into 3 types: Common, Rhinoceros, and Marine. They have large bodies with thick skin, strong legs, sharp claws, and powerful tails that can be used as a weapon. They usually employ tridents (2d8+1+2) and crossbows (1d8+2) in battle. Every type of Iguana-man may attack with his tail instead of a claw or weapon. The tail does 1d6+2 EP damage and knocks the victim down if struck 'below the belt' unless he makes an Ability Check with Agility.

Common Iguana-men are brown or grayish in color and have a unique defensive ability: They may spray blood from their eye lids at their opponents once per day [R:15' AOE:1"-4' cone]. This spray will blind every-one within the AOE for 1 Attack. Victims must make a RER or be blinded for an additional 1d4 Actions.

Rhinoceros Iguana-men are tan to black in color and are distinguished by three large horns jutting from the front of their head and are known for their charging attack. While in a charge, they inflict with their horns 1d20+2 + CRM bonus damage (+1d6 EP Damage per CRM > 2.)

Marine Iguana-men are blue to green in color and are always found close to a water source. They are at home in the water and swim at a CRM of 6, but they make their homes upon the Land. They are amphibian and may breath both water and air.

All three types sometimes employ large wooden shields or full suits of leather armor (+8% & +20% bonus to PTE respectively).

Some say that Iguana-men have been known to speak the Traders Language.
Ability Scores: End=16 Agl=14 Str=15 Int=8 Wis=8 Will=15.

Komodo Lizard-man

EP:	125	Ambush:	-10 %	PTE:	30%+Armor &/or Shield
Strikes/Parry:	2 / 2	CRM:	5	Tribe:	2 – 40
Damage:	Claw = 2d8+4, Weapon + Tail	Str. Bonus:	+4	React:	10

These large-sized Lizard-men stand 7' tall and always show brutality to other races. They have huge bodies with very thick skin, strong legs and arms, piercing claws, and powerful tails that can be used as a weapon. The Komodo-man's tail strike does 1d8+4 EP Damage plus knocks the victim back 20' unless he makes an Ability Check with Strength. They employ a very deadly weapon known as a 'Chopper' and are marksmen with their unique Composite Short Bow (1d10 EP damage + Str. Dam. Bonus = +4). The Chopper is a off-shoot of the Battle-Axe. The difference is that the Chopper has four blades not only two. The Chopper inflects 1d20 EP Damage + Str. Dam. Bonus = +4 {i.e.. 1d20 + 4}. Komodo-men usually employ large wooden shields or full suits of leather armor (+8% & +20% bonus to PTE respectively).
Ability Scores: End=18 Agl=14 Str=19 Int=4 Wis=8 Will=15.

Chameleon Lizard-man

EP:	40	Ambush:	-10 %	PTE:	20%+Armor &/or Shield
Strikes/Parry:	1 / 2	CRM:	4	Tribe:	2 – 10**
Damage:	Claw = 1d6+1 or by Weapon	Str. Bonus:	+1	React:	2

These small-sized Lizard-men stand 4' tall and have several unique abilities. The most well known is their chameleon ability. This allows them to completely blend into any background while they are not moving. Their Chameleon ability gives them a +40% PTE and -50% to anyone's Detect Ambush roll while it is active. They also possess specially developed eyes which allow them to watch different targets on opposite sides of their head or they may precisely determine the distance between themselves and any one target. Their most amazing ability is their use of spells and simple Enchanted items.

Chameleon-men receive 50 SP per day that they may use to cast spells or create Enchanted Items. They may only cast Green, Orange or Class (A) spells. Each Chameleon-men knows 10 Class (A) spells and 10 other spells of their choice as well as these: Revitalize Nature, Heal Wounds 2, Converse with Plants, Shield-Magic (Class A). The spells they may choose to learn are any Class (A) spells and those Green / Orange spells between 1st - 4th Levels. They may regenerate their Spell Points 2 times per day. They regenerate their Spell Points at 1 SP per 1 Attack (5 second period).

They prepare a small wand to Enchant by whittling down a Rainbow Eucalyptus tree branch. They may cast only one type of spell into a wand at any one time. Also, they may only store up to 2 spells of the same type into a single wand. They have to make up a Trigger Word or Phase to initiate the spell. They may never carry more than 3 wands at any one time.

The weapons they normally employ are Blow Darts (1d4 EP Damage) and Short Curved Blades (2d6 +1 EP Damage.) Chameleon-men may employ small shields (+5% PTE) or ½ suits of Leather Armor (+15% PTE).

Chameleon-men all Speak / Read & Write both the Lizard-man and the Trader Languages.
Ability Scores: End=16 Agl=15 Str=14 Int=14 Wis=15 Will=15.
NOTE: Chameleon-men usually make their homes within the tribes of all other Lizard-men; they are rarely found living on their own. They prefer the company of Iguana-men and are normally found among tribes.

LIZARD MEN: IGUANA, COLLARD, CHAMELEON AND KOMODO

GIANT MUTANT BATS

EP:	80	Ambush:	-20%	PTE:	40% (65% flying)
Strikes/Parry: 2 / 2		CRM:	2 / 4 = Flying	Cave:	10 – 100
Damage:	Claw & Bite = 1d8+2 & 1d12+2	Str. Bonus:	+2	React:	7

These bi-pedal mutant bats stand between 5 - 6 feet tall. They have leathery wings that attach from below their knees and flow up under their arms all the way to their writs. There are 4 types of Giant Mutant Bats (GMB) but only members of the species can tell each other apart. The four types of GMB are: Scouts, DeathStrikers, Soldiers and Leaders. All GMB clans are structured in a tribal format. All elders of any type are allowed to speak during a tribal counsel, but the eldest GMB of the Leader type will always make the final decision. There may be several Leader types within the same tribe, but all will follow the directions of the eldest Leader.

All types are able to see well in normal conditions but also may use their echolocation ability. They use their echolocation ability to locate prey in any situation that they can not see in, ie. too dark for normal sight. This ability works very well inside the large caves where they make their homes.

Giant Mutant Bats (GMB) may use either melee, spells or their Screech ability in combat. Each type of GMB has its own unique spells, but all types have the same melee offensive abilities. They attack with their claws and their bite in melee. They all gain a +2 to their damage because of their Strength Damage Bonus.

GMB all have a Screech that they use to cast spells and attack at range. Their regular Screech ability has a range of 30' and when they cast a spell using their Screech ability, the spell's Range is doubled. The table below summarizes their Spell and Screech abilities:

Type	Screech Spells (Use: 1 / 6 hrs; R: x2 listed under spell)	Regular Screech (Use: 1 / Att; R: 30')
Scout	Cause Fear-One; Send Message; Paralyze Person	Damage: 1d12
DeathStriker	Blind-One; Daze-Many; Statue (affects up to 16th Level Characters)	Damage: 1d12
Soldier	Cause Fear-Many; Fire Bolt 2; Acid Spray, Potent	Damage: 1d20
Leader	Blind-Many; Deadly Mist *; Cancel Enchantment @ 160SP	Damage: 1d20

* The Deadly Mist Screeched out by a Leader is very special. All GMB are unaffected by the Mist and they utilize their echolocation ability very well while within the opaque Mist to find and attack their prey. Their prey cannot see while inside the Mist.

Giant Mutant Bats all Speak / Read & Write their own language and all Leaders and DeathStrikers are taught to Speak / Read & Write the Krill language as well.

ENCHANTED CREATURES

There are a multitude of Enchanted Creatures inhabiting the Isles of Penicia. The most common type of enchanted creature is one that is related to a color. These enchanted creatures are always a hew of a specific color and has certain abilities related to that color. There are stories of Fairies, Pixies, Unicorns and Dragons all possessing enchantments related to colors. Listed here are the most well known Enchanted Creatures.

GOBLINS

All Goblins utterly hate all other living things because if not for the goblin's affliction for the light of the Column Sun, they would surely rule the Isles of Penicia. These Purely Evil creatures are committed to the glorious day when they will be able to RULE the isles.

Different types of Goblins possess many diverse powers, but all Goblins have some abilities and liabilities in common.
1) <u>Harmed by sunlight:</u> They all suffer 1d10 EP damage per Attack when exposed to Sunlight.
    The light of the sun also <u>negates</u> the paralyzing effect of a Goblin's bite.
2) <u>Paralyzing Bite:</u> When a goblin bites a victim, the victim suffers 1d10 EP damage from a special poison and must make an Ability Check with Will or become paralyzed. A victim who fails his Ability Check will literally be 'Scared Stiff' [HEHE HEHE he said 'Stiff']. The victim will be paralyzed for 4+1d8 Actions. Anyone who actually dies while they are paralyzed becomes a Ghoul – see end of this section for a description of Ghouls.
3) <u>Language:</u> Goblins have their own language and they can all Speak, Read and Write it.

The different kinds of Goblins are: a) Assassin   b) Warrior   c) Wizard   d) Queen

<u>Goblin Assassins:</u> These goblins are 3' – 4' tall with wasp type wings on their back. They can fly in either goblin (CRM=5) or wasp (CRM=2) form.
a) Their main ability is being able to Polymorph into a Wasp and back again at will.
b) While in Wasp form they may travel in sunlight without suffering damage.
c) While in Wasp form they do not radiate any type of enchantment.
d) While in Wasp form their sting is treated the same as their bite, unless they are in direct Sunlight and then it is only a regular wasp sting. While in Sunlight, the sting only does 1 EP Dam and has no Paralyzing effect.
e) They may converse with wasps at will and command 2d20 of them 2 times per day.
f) They know how to use Short Swords, Garrotes, Daggers, Clubs, Bolos and Short Bows.
g) Ability Scores: End=17 Agl=18 Str=14 Int=14 Wis=16 Will=14   (Str. Bonus for creatures = EP/30)
h) Number of Actions / Attack : 3

Goblin Assassin EP:	75	Ambush:	- 40 %	PTE:	50% (75%)
Strikes/Parries:	1 / 2	CRM:	2 / Fly = 5 (2)	Horde:	varies
Damage:	Bite=1d10 / Fist=1d4	Str. Bonus:	+2	React:	12
RER:	30%				

Goblin Warriors: These goblins are 10' tall and relentlessly train to defeat all 'Sun Dwellers'. All Goblin Warriors have a Psychic Link to one of the Elements – the specifics are listed below. For large battles Warrior Goblins are usually divided into common squads related to their Psychic links.

Elemental Planes: 1) Air   2) Water   3) Earth   4) Fire   5) Fog   6) Smoke   7) Lava   8) Mud

Air	= I) Wind Blot	Dam = 10+1d10 (***)	II) Levitate
Water	= I) Water Bolt	Dam = 10+1d12 (~~~)	II) Water Adaptation
Earth	= I) Stone Storm	Dam = 10+2d8	II) Earth Armor +20%
Fire	= I) Flame Bolt	Dam = 10+1d20	II) Flaming Weapon
Fog	= I) Fog Jet	Dam = 10+1d6 (^^^)	II) Fog Wall
Smoke	= I) Smoke Jet	Dam = 10+1d6 (""")	II) Smoke Adaptation
Lava	= I) Lava Pool	Dam = 10+2d12	II) Lava Walk
Mud	= I) Mud Pool		II) Resist Poisons

NOTE: All abilities listed as (I) may be used twice per hour and all listed as (II) may be used once per hour.

All spells are the same as stated in their description, except where noted in the table above or below:
- (***)   10% Fall and Possible "Dust Bolt".
- (~~~)   15% Fall and Pure Water.
- (^^^)   Only Initial damage, but D: 2 min.   4 cubic feet per Attack.
- (""")   Only Initial damage, but D: 2 min.   2 cubic feet per Attack.   Victim may be Asphyxiated.

a) They are taught the Warrior Skills: Parry, Shield Use, Feign Strike, Improved Firing Rate and Accuracy Training with the Crossbow, Power Strike, Disarm and Thrust.
b) They know how to use a long sword, battle sword, the trident, the spear, the bardiche, the battle hammer, and the crossbow.
c) Ability Scores: End=19 Agl=17 Str=18 Int=10 Wis=15 Will=13   (Str. Bonus for creatures = EP/30)
d) Number of Actions / Attack : 4

Goblin Warrior EP:	125	Ambush:	-20 %	PTE:	65%
Strikes/Parries:	2 / 2	CRM:	4	Horde:	varies
Damage:	Bite=1d10 / Fist=1d8	Str. Bonus:	+4	React:	12
RER:	35%				

Goblin Wizard: These goblins are 5' tall and wear long black robes.
a) The total number of Spell Points (SP) they rate per day is 110. They prepare the brew vats in which the Queen's eggs are soaked. These vats designate the type of goblin the egg will hatch into. They may learn any spell associated with these colors: Black, Blue, Red and Violet. They may learn a maximum of 10 Class (A) spells and 10 additional spells of each listed color. In addition, they are also taught all the spells necessary to prepare the brew vats for the Queen's eggs. Goblin Wizards may regenerate their Spell Points 4 times per day. They regenerate their Spell Points at a rate of 1 SP per 1 Attack (5 second period).
b) Goblin Cloud – All Goblin Wizards may cause a midnight black cloud to appear around them. The AOE that the cloud encompasses is a globe of 50' diameter. The wizard may do this 2 / day and the cloud will last for 30 minutes. Sunlight may not pass through the cloud and it may move with the wizard who casts it. Any Enchantment dealing with sunlight will cancel a portion of the Goblin cloud equal to the spell's AOE. All goblins may see through the Goblin Cloud normally, but all others see only blackness.
c) They are able to Enchant Gems with these colors: Black, Blue, Red and Violet. They may Enchant the gem by holding the gem and sacrificing 100 SP. The gem will never shatter but can only be enchanted to a GPR of VSI2. A Goblin Wizard may only enchant and wield 3 Enchanted Gems at a time. These Gems are usually attached to the end of a piece of bone and is known as a Goblin Wand. They may cast any spell they know into the gem that matches its color and is within the gem's GPR. The held spells are cast when the Trigger Word is spoken which takes one Action.
d) They know how to use the staff, the spear, the bolo, and the mace.
e) Ability Scores: End=17 Agl=17 Str=16 Int=18 Wis=16 Will=15   (Str. Bonus for creatures = EP/30)

Goblin Wizard EP:	85	Ambush:	- 20 %	PTE:	50%
Strikes/Parries:	2 / 2	CRM:	3	Horde:	varies
Damage:	Bite=1d10 / Fist=1d6	Str. Bonus:	+2	React:	12
RER:	40%				

Goblin Queens: These goblins are 6' tall and appear to be a female human but have dark complexions and giant black leathery wings on their backs.

a) The Queen holds complete control over her horde by being able to telepathically speak to and cause pain to any goblin she has given birth to. This "family" is know as her Horde.

b) The Queen is the driving force behind her Horde and she can cause the entire Horde to set forth to accomplish any task she wishes. Also, a Goblin Queen may employ any Enchanted Item they may wield. Slots = 16.

c) They have SP totaling 150, and may cast spells of the colors Black, Blue, Red and Violet.
    They may learn up to 15 Class (A) spells and 15 additional spells per color listed above.
    They may regenerate their Spell Points 7 times per day. The SP are regenerated at a rate of 1 SP per 1 Attack.

d) They know how to use every type of sword, the whip, the mace, the trident and all Bows.

e) Ability Scores: End=18 Agl=18 Str=20 Int=18 Wis=18 Will=17   (Str. Bonus for creatures = EP/30)

f) Number of Actions / Attack : 5

g) Goblin Queens are unaffected by indigo colored spells.

Goblin Queen EP:	175	Ambush:	- 30 %	PTE:	70% (Fly: 85%)
Strikes/Parries:	3 / 2	CRM:	5 (Fly = 7)	Horde:	50-500 per 1 Queen
Damage:	Bite=1d10 / Fist=1d6	Str. Bonus:	+5	React:	varies
RER:	70%			Enchanted Slots:	16

Ghouls

EP:	(-20% of Original)	Ambush:	-10%	PTE:	40%
Strikes:	2	CRM:	4	Horde:	varies
Damage:	1d8	Str. Bonus:	+1	React:	12
RER:	25%				

When someone dies while they are 'Scared Stiff', they become a Ghoul. All Ghouls eat the flesh of both living and dead creatures. Ghouls consider the flesh of people to be a delicacy. They will obey the commands of any Goblin and will protect one with its life. A person who has become a ghoul can only be changed back if they receive a HEAL DISEASE or RESTORE spell BEFORE they consume dead flesh. Their EP total is equal to 20% less than their EP total before they were turned into a Ghoul.

A QUEEN OF GOBLINS WITH A WARROIR, A WZARD AND AN ASSASSIAN

VAMPIRE

EP:	200	Ambush:	- 50 %	PTE:	70% (Fly: 85%)
Strikes / Parry:	3 / 2	CRM:	6 (Fly = 8)	Niche:	varies
Damage:	Bite=1d10 / Fist=1d8+4	Str. Bonus:	+6	React:	varies
RER:	50%	Will Score:	17	Enchanted Slots:	16

Vampires are probably the most powerful and dangerous Purely Evil creatures known. They may appear to be human but are very pale and have unusually long fingers.

There are different types of Vampire and each type can transform into 2 different animals. This can be done at will as many times per day as necessary. Each type of vampire also lives in specific areas related to the animals the vampire may transform into. A Vampire may also speak with those animal types at will and command 2d20 of each type twice per day.

Animal Types	Location	Related Powers – All spells at 15th level ability.
Bat & Rat	Planes and Lt. Woods	Fly 2 (1/hour) & Disease (Infect 1 victim/hour)
Bat & Cloud *	Mountains and Hills	Fly 2 (1/hour) & Lightning Bolt 2 (1/hour)
Bat & Wolf	Wooded and Mountains	Fly 2 (1/hour) & Command Lycanthropes
Bat & Spider	Towns and Villages	Fly 2 (1/hour) & Webbing
Bat & Snake	Deep Forests and Jungles	Fly 2 (1/hour) & Poison (1/hour)
Wolf & Rat !!	Wooded and Fields	Command Lycanthropes & Disease (Infect 1 victim/hour)
Wolf & Cloud *	Colder Climates	Command Lycanthropes & Lightning Bolt 2 (1/hour)
Wolf & Spider	Lake areas and Fields	Command Lycanthropes & Webbing
Wolf & Snake	Fields and Streams	Command Lycanthropes & Poison (1/hour)
Rat & Cloud *	Forests and Fields	Disease (Infect 1 victim/hour) & Lightning Bolt 2 (1/hour)
Rat & Snake	Fields and Swamps	Disease (Infect 1 victim/hour) & Poison (1/hour)
Spider & Rat	Cities and Towns	Webbing & Disease (Infect 1 victim/hour)
Spider & Cloud *	Jungles and Swamps	Webbing & Lightning Bolt 2 (1/hour)
Spider & Snake	Deserts and Planes	Webbing & Poison (1/hour)
Snake & Cloud *	Swamps and Lowlands	Poison & Lightning Bolt 2 (1/hour)

ANIMAL TYPES AND RELATED POWERS

Bat: Any Vampire that can transform into a Bat may cast a Fly 2 Spell 1/hour. Also, the Vampire may cause Wings to appear on its back while it is in any form and fly at a CRM: 7.

Cloud*: I know a Cloud is not an animal, but gimme a break. The Cloud type Vampire may converse with clouds at will and may cast a Summon Storm 1/hour in addition to using a Lightning Bolt 2 spell once per hour. Of course, he may change into a cloud at will and may fly at a CRM: 5, while in Cloud form.

Rat: Any Vampire that can transform into a Rat may infect 1 victim per hour with any Disease it chooses. The Vampire only needs to touch the victim, but a bite does just as well. The victim is allowed a blind RER. If he fails, he contracts the Disease, but if he succeeds, he will be spared the Disease's effects. If this type of Vampire infects a regular animal, it has a 25% chance to attain a mutation instead of the Disease.

Wolf: Any Vampire that can transform into a Wolf may command Lycanthropes (see end of section). Someone infected with Lycanthropy is forced to transform into a horrible creature when its moon rises. This type of Vampire may NOT command a master Lycanthrope, but may command a regular Lycanthrope when it is transformed during its full moon. They also gain a special Bite for 3d10 dam.

Snake: Any Vampire that can transform into a Snake may poison a victim just by touching them. The victim is allowed a RER, but if he fails he is poisoned and will fall under the Vampire's spell. The Poison clouds the mind and for the next 1 hour the victim will follow all commands given to him by the Vampire. After the 1 hour, the victim gets another RER. Success = you have regained your free will, but Failure = Coma. An Alchemist needs ½ ounce of Enchanted Emerald Dust to cure this poison with their Heal Poison spell or he may use a Heal Disease or Restore spell.

Spider: Any Vampire that can transform into a Spider may cast an amount of webbing sizable enough to entrap a horse. It may do this 4 times per hour or it may use 2 at once to cause a giant web anchored to four surfaces. This Vampire may also climb or walk on any vertical or inverted surface at will.

!!*Wolf & Rat:* Any Vampire that can transform into both a Wolf and a Rat may infect a victim with a ghastly disease know as Lycanthropy. This disease changes the victim into a Master Lycanthrope. See end of section for details. This is also the only type of Vampire that may command a Master Lycanthrope.

NOTE: If the Vampire is killed all effects are instantly canceled. All victims will immediately return to normal state.

All Vampires stay alive by draining the blood (or Endurance Points) of living creatures. The Vampire must Bite its victim to drain his blood (the blood is measured in Endurance Points.) A Vampire must drain a total of 20 Endurance Points per day to survive. If a Vampire steals more EP then it needs to survive in one day, it converts the excess EP to Spell Points. The Vampire gains 10 SP for every extra 1 EP it consumes. A Vampire may never gain more than 150 SP regardless how many EP it drains in one day. The Vampire may spend Spell Points to cast the spells it has learned. Vampires may learn and cast any spell related to the following colors: Black, Blue, Red, Violet or Opaque. The Vampire may learn no more than 20 Class (A) spells and 20 spells per each color listed above.

Harmed By:
1) Sunlight – Vampires can be mortally injured by sunlight. They take 1d10 EP damage from mere Sunlight and because the are Purely Evil they suffer double base damage from Sunlight based spells – see the Yellow Spells section for details.
2) Life Tree Liquid – 1 oz. will do 1d20 points of damage to any Vampire.
     (Note2: 1 Nut = 4 oz of liquid = 4d20).
3) Any weapon made of Ransium or Langor will do normal damage to the Vampire.
     Mundane Iron weapons do **NO** damage to the Vampire.

Slain By:
Unlike most creatures, the Vampire must be brought down to ZERO EP and then have one of the listed events occur before it ceases to exist. If the body is not "treated" in a manner listed below, the vampire will start to regenerate its EP at a rate of 1 EP per Attack. It may regenerate to a maximum of 50 EP and then it must feed to regain the rest of its EPs.
   1) Expose body to actual sun light from the Column Sun for 5 minutes.
   2) 8 ounces of Life Tree Liquid poured over its body and 4 ounces poured over its head.
   3) A Unicorn's horn thrust through the Heart or the Head.

NOTE3: Vampires are unaffected by Indigo colored spells.

Master Lycanthrope

EP:	Wolf form=100; @ night= 300	Ambush:	- 40 %	PTE:	75%
Strikes / Parry:	2 / 2	CRM:	7	Niche:	varies
Damage:	Bite = 2d12 or 6d12	Str. Bonus	+3 / +10 @ night	React:	varies
RER:	45%	Number of Actions / Attack: 4		Will Score:	16

When a Wolf/Rat Vampire inflects someone with this unique disease, that <u>person</u> becomes a carrier of the Lycanthropy disease and permanently changes into the form of a wolf. This is a Master Lycanthrope and is always the leader of its pack. By day the Master Lycanthrope is a regular sized wolf but at night it grows to 3 times normal size. In either form it's bite does enormous damage. During the day the damage from its bite is 2d12+3 for Strength and at night in Huge form the damage is 6d12+10 for Strength, which is one of the most devastating attacks known.

The Master Lycanthrope may inflect anyone with the 2nd and most common form of Lycanthropy. Its bite will transform the victim into a monster that is ½ wolf and ½ regular person, a Were Wolf. While the victim is in the form of a Were Wolf, his endurance, agility and strength are increased by +5 (maximum of 20) and the Were Wolf gains the Blood Frenzy ability. While in Were Wolf form, they don't recognize anyone, they would gleefully tear apart their brother or best friend if given the chance.

A Were Wolf monster can only be cured if the original Master Lycanthrope is killed. A Master Lycanthrope may only be cured if the Vampire that infected it is slain. Master Lycanthropes may telepathically communicate to Vampires, Were Wolves, regular wolves and dogs at will. It holds complete control over any Were Wolf it has made while the person is in Were Wolf form.

Were Wolf: Transformed Person

EP:	Normal Persons EP + 50 + 1d12	Ambush:	- 40 %	PTE:	60%
Strikes / Parry:	4 / 0	CRM:	6	Niche:	varies
Damage:	Bite=2d12 / Claw=1d10+Str	Str. Bonus:	varies	React:	varies
RER:	35%	Number of Actions / Attack: 4		Will Score:	14

A person infected with the most common form of Lycanthropy is forced to change form into a murderous creature any time the full moon which he was infected under shines full across the land (There are 10 moons which circle Penicia, See Appendix F). At this time the creature transforms into a blood thirsty beast that will hunt and attack any misfortunate person it senses. The Blood Frenzy ability is the same as described in the Savage section and the Were Wolf gains the skill at 10th level ability, except they will automatically plunge into the Blood Frenzy when their transformation is complete.

A Hemar Were Wolf gains a +1 CRM and a +1 Strength Damage Bonus.

A Krill Were Wolf retains her wings and the ability to fly at a CRM: 7. While the victim is in the form of a Were Wolf, his endurance, agility and strength are increased by +5 to a maximum of 20 each.

TROLLS

EP:	120	Ambush:	- 25 %	PTE:	40% + Substance bonus
Strikes/Parries:	2 / 1	CRM:	4	Niche:	Solitary or Tribe
Damage:	Claw=1d10 + 3	Str. Bonus:	+3	React:	0
RER:	25%	Number of Actions / Attack: 3		Will Score:	15

These malevolent creatures are closely linked to the material they are composed from. The types of Trolls that are known may be composed of plants, earth, mud, stone or water. It has been found that a Troll may never be composed of any type of metal or gem material.

The veil troll is made when the liquid from a full Life Tree's nut falls on a natural substance which is tainted in some manner. The liquid would have to fall on a group of plants that have some type of disease or would have to spill into some stagnant or contaminated water, etc.

All trolls have low intelligence but can fashion clubs, shields and other simple equipment as well as small cages to hold or trap their prey.

All Trolls stay alive by draining the Endurance Points of living creatures. The troll must firmly grasp its victim with both hands and concentrate for 1 Action to drain EP. A surviving troll's victim will always look older and have a complexion relating to that of the troll. A troll must drain a total of 15 Endurance Points per day to survive. In an emergency, a troll may gain ½ of the required amount of EP from 1 cubic foot of the material it is composed of – they may only do this once per day. If a troll steals more EP then it needs to survive, it converts the access EP to Spell Points. The troll gains 10 SP for every extra 1 EP it consumes. A troll may never gain more than 50 SP regardless of how many EP it steals. It may spend these SP to use its innate enchanted abilities.

1) The troll may cause 6 cubic feet of the material it is composed of to encase its body in what looks to be armor. The PTE bonus that the troll adds to its PTE total depends on the substance it is related to, but the cost is always the same.   SPC: 10 SP

Material Type	PTE Bonus
Water	+10%
Plant	+15%
Mud	+20%
Earth	+25%
Stone	+30%

2) If the troll spends 15 SP it can gain control over an area of the substance it is made of. For simplicity the troll uses the actual spell that is listed below. The only differences are the Spell Point Cost, Range and Duration and the Casting Time is always zero, or at will.

Type	Spell	Range	Duration	AOE	Damage / 4 cubic feet
Water	Water Control 2	100'	30 min.	8 Cubic Ft	4d8 per 4 ft³ that strikes
Plant	Plant Control 2*	75'	30 min.	8 Cubic Ft	(Large Tree Limb= 1d10)
Mud	Mud Control 2*	60'	30 min.	8 Cubic Ft	4d8 per 4 ft³ that strikes
Earth	Earth Control 2*	50'	30 min.	8 Cubic Ft	4d8 per 100 lb rock
Stone	Stone Control 2*	40'	30 min.	8 Cubic Ft	4d8 per 100 lb stone

* Use the rules for Water Control 2, just substitute the different material: Mud, Earth, Stone or Plant.

3) The last ability of a troll is to be able to polymorph into a 'patch' of the substance it is composed of. The troll must spend 25 SP to use its polymorph ability. The troll may change back and forth at will but the Duration ends after 6 hours. Each transformation takes 1 Attack to complete. The substance appears to be normal and is undetectable to the eye, but the area will glow, if someone uses a See Enchantment or See Life spell.

UNICORNS

EP:	150	Ambush:	- 40 %	PTE:	60 %
Strikes:	2 / 2	CRM:	6	Herd:	2 - 20
Damage: Horn=2d8+charge / Buck=1d30+5		Str. Bonus:	+5	React:	1
RER:	50%	Number of Actions / Attack: 4		Will Score:	18

These creatures all have the highest Morality Rating (19-20) of any other known enchanted creature. They have made a commitment to oppose evil in all of its forms. Luckily they have been friends and allies to all the races of the three Isles. They are intelligent and social creatures which are about the size of a mustang and their coloring is always pure white. The leader of a unicorn herd (herd leader) is always of the Yellow type. This type refers to the color of the Iridescent Spiral along the length of the Unicorn's Horn.

Their single horn is the source of their power. Each unicorn's horn is always pure white with an iridescent swirl that spirals the length of the horn. The color of the swirl reflects the type of the unicorn. There is a different Unicorn type for ever major color (same as the gem colors). All unicorns have some common abilities that they may employ, but they also have enchantments that they can employ which are unique to their color.

Common Abilities: All abilities listed here are the same as the spell that matches its name, but a unicorn employs its abilities at 15th level strength and there is no Casting Time involved (all abilities require 1 Action to use).

1) In Sight Teleport – All unicorns may use this ability once per hour.

2) Project Thought (ESP) – All may telepathically speak with all animals, people, birds and Enchanted Creatures at will.

3) Sun Light spell – the 2 foot column appears as a Lance off the tip of the Unicorn's horn. Usable 2/hour.

4) Sunlight Beam – usable 1/hour but with double the stated Range so R:140'; Dam: 18+2d20 or 36+2d20 verse Purely Evil creatures.

5) <u>Barrier of Sun Light</u> – may only be done if 5 or more unicorns stand in a circle with their horns facing outwards. This powerful circular barrier has 20' tall walls and creates a wall that is connected to each of the participating Unicorn's horns.   Usable 1/hour.
R: Tips of Horns.   AOE: depends on the number of unicorns evolved, 5 unicorns = 40' Radius.
D: unlimited but the Unicorns must not break formation.
Damage: Purely Evil creatures are unable to cross the barrier and receive 2d10 EP damage per Attack while in contact with the barrier.
The formation need not be stationary, but the Unicorns must move together and not break the formation.

6) <u>Globe of Sun Light</u> – may only be done if a herd leader participates with 9 or more unicorns standing in a circle with their horns facing outwards. This globe's AOE encompasses and is connected to each of the participating Unicorn's horns. Any Purely Evil Creature looking at this incredible sight when the Globe is invoked will be blinded for 5+1d10 Actions unless it makes a RER. Usable 1/hour.
R: Tips of Horns.   AOE: depends on the number of unicorns evolved, 10 unicorns = 80' radius.
D: unlimited but the Unicorns must not break formation.
Damage: Purely Evil creatures are unable to cross into the globe and receive 2d10 EP damage per Attack while in contact with the globe.
The formation need not be stationary, but the Unicorns must move together and not break the formation.

Individual Unicorn powers based on color: (same rules as above: 15th level strength and CT=1 Action)

Color	1st ability (usable 3/hour)	2nd ability (usable 2/hour)
Red	Fire Bolt 3 & Flame Barrier	Flame Jet
Orange	Force Shield** & Force Net	Shield Magic (Any Classification or Color: Pick One per use)
Yellow	Lightning Bolt 3 & See MR, Enchantment & Life	Invisibility
Green	Wound 2 & Heal Wounds (+150 EP)	Restore (+200 EP or any one effect listed)
Blue	Wind Bolt 3 & Bridge (100' long x 25' wide)	Fly 2
Indigo	Mind Blast - Many & Sleep, Area	Mesmerize Enchanted Creature
Violet	Create Illusion 4 & Cause Fear, Many	Polymorph 2
Brown	Paralyze (All Regular & People) & Earth Barrier	Paralyze Enchanted Creature
Clear	Water Bolt 3 & Water Adaptation	Frost Jet
Black	Acid Spray, Potent & Silence, Area	Teleport, Out of Sight

** Force Shield will prevent 100 EP damage from Melee or Projectile strikes. May be cast on self or someone else.

251

GIANTS

EP:	1000 + (100 * 1d10)	Ambush:	- 10%	PTE:	50% / 25%
Strikes/Parries:	2 / 1 or 3 / 1	CRM:	7	Home:	1
Damage:	Club = 1d8 * 50	Str. Bonus:	+33 - +66	React:	7
RER:	20%	Actions/Attack:	3 or 4	Will Score:	17
Height:	300' tall = Average	Weight:	A WHOLE BUNCH		

Description – Huge Bi-pedal creatures with generally low intelligence. They are vegetarians with intelligence enough to grow crops and use simple tools, weapons and armor. Like people, giants may have High or Low morals.

Lifestyle – They only live on the Krill Isle within the vast mountain ranges found there. Many plants grow to enormous size on this Isle and the Giants use and cultivate them for food, clothes and shelter. Their shelter usually consists of large caves, lean-toos, or even crude cabins. The Krill hierarchy has unsuccessfully attempted to gain treaties with them for many years.

Combat Skills – Giants are natural hunters and woodsmen. Their 100' clubs and humongous staves do tremendous damage. All Giants are allowed 3 Actions / Attack and use heavy leathers and wooden plates for armor.
NOTE: Their PTE has two numbers. The first one if verses other Giants and the second is verses people.

Ruled By – Giant King [400' tall]. Every Giant king has been born with the BirthGift of Intellect and Wisdom. The King Speaks, Reads and Writes Giant plus Speaks the Trader and Krill languages. The Giant King lives in a great castle on top of the northeastern plateau of the Krill Isle. The Giant King gets 4 Actions/Attack and wields an immense Langor Sword and Shield. He is dressed in a Mail Shirt, helmet, gauntlets, and boots all made from Langor as well. The King's EP=4000, his PTE=85%/70% and his Str. Bonus is +133. His blade does 2d8 * 50 dam.

Ref Note: All ordinary Giants have the same Birth Gift. This beneficial Birth Gift enables all regular plants within 100 miles of the Giant's home to grow to enormous size. This allows a Giant to survive wherever he makes his home.

A HEMAR CATCHING SIGHT OF A COLLOSAL DRAGON AND RUNNING AWAY!   A KRILL FLYING PAST A GIANT

DRAGONS

EP:	5000 + (1000 * 1d4)	Ambush:	- 50%	PTE:	85%
Strikes/Parries:	4 / 2	CRM:	Fly = ?	Home:	?
Damage:	********	Str. Bonus:	+200 - +300	React:	?
RER:	80%	Actions/Attack: 6		Will Score:	20
Height:	500' tall & 1000' long	Weight: YOU GOTTA BE KIDDING.			

Description – Dragons are majestic beats full of intelligence, cunning and strength. The Dragon is the most powerful and feared Enchanted creature on Penicia. They are of lizard lineage having sharp teeth, long necks, four appendages, two humongous wings and a gigantic tail. Their back two appendages are legs and the front two are arms that end in 3 fingered hands. Their great wings can darken the sky, but you can always see a gleam from their huge single eye. This eye is actually a humongous enchanted gem, the source of the Dragon's incredible power.

Lifestyle – It is sung and told that the Race of Dragons are the true protectors of Penicia. The role that they will play in the War of the Isles vs. the Goblins (which was predicted by Horis the Seer) is unsure, but all the stories hint that the Dragons will pay no heed. They do not tend to interact with the other intelligent races of Penicia. It is said that their true task is to protect the whole world of Penicia from Outsiders – whatever that means.

It has been confirmed that there is a different type of Dragon for every color of enchanted gem, but little else is know of this colossal race of beings.

Combat Skills – Their great size alone must be listed as a Combat Skill. Think of this monster flying low over your tiny village or worse landing on it. In spite of their size they are not only quick, but in most sonnets concerning Dragons it's sung, that their grace equals their immense size. They may cast spells from their single eye. All Dragons rate certain spells per hour because of their race, but they also rate unique spells reflecting the color of their Enchanted Eye.

A Dragon may cast any spell related to its color 5 / hour. All Dragons may cast any Yellow, Green, Orange, Blue or Opaque Defensive or Miscellaneous spells 5 / hour. All Dragons may also cast the Cancel Enchantment spell with 200 SP capacity 5 / hour (but they absorb the Spell Points instead of wasting them.) Also, every Dragon learns 3 favorite spells which it may cast 5 times per hour each. Lastly, a Dragon may polymorph into any other intelligent creature 3 times a day. The Level at which these spells are cast is left up to the Ref. but are usually at 15 level ability.

NOTES: A Dragon is unaffected by spells held by an Indigo gem and can see through any Illusion.
A Dragon may employ any Enchanted Item that it may wield.

********	Claw	=	1d10 * 25	250
	Tail	=	1d12 * 42	504
	Bite	=	1d20 * 50	1000

ZONITH WOOD TREES

Zonith Wood is one of the most magical types of trees in all of Penicia. It resembles a weeping willow except its leaves are Golden or Deep Red in color, depending on the species. The leaves stay this color year around and never fall off. Immediately within the folds of the branches are what appear to be poles that protrude up from the ground and entirely encircle the tree. These are actually the tree's roots, they stick up from the ground to "catch" magical energy. Zonith wood trees use magical energy as food to survive. The distance between the roots is between 2-4 feet and they completely encircle the tree about 10 feet from the trunk. The tree may "part" them to accommodate the creatures that it provides a home for.

All mature Zonith Wood Trees have Intellect and Wisdom scores between 11 - 20. Each tree is telepathically linked to every other tree of its type (either Golden or Red.) Each type of tree remembers every place and person any tree of that type has ever come in contact with. They live for great amounts of time, usually 500 years or more. Do to their collective memory and their life span they may telepathically communicate with any creature and they know how to speak every language. Yes! They actually speak with a mouth which is located on one side of it's trunk about 14 feet up from the ground. They have very low hollow voices which tend to frighten common folk.

The only way for these trees to move is to teleport. They may teleport to any location that any of their type has ever stood. When they teleport, they can take anything within their circle of roots as well as leave whoever they want behind. When they die, their roots launch into the air, speeding to far off random areas. Although most roots die because they land on bad ground, solid rock, or in deep water, one is sure to take up root somewhere. Once a root does find good ground, it will sprout into a fledgling tree and then immediately teleport to a protected location. Now a fully-grown Zonith Tree can teleport in to check out this new local.

These trees inspired the IronBall game, which brought the races together in peaceful coexistence. Also, the roots of the Zonith Wood Tree are what an Enchanter must acquire in order to construct and enchant an Enchanter's staff or an Enchanter's wand.

254

Every Zonith Wood tree has certain Defensive and Offensive capabilities, these are listed here. Also the common stats for the trees are also listed.

Defense Capabilities

1) <u>Detect Intellect, Enchantment and Morals</u> – This works like Radar and it is how the tree "sees". The tree can Detect the Intellect Score of anyone or thing that comes within the AOE. The tree can also may detect the number of Enchanted Items, the color they are related to and the general strength of each item. Lastly, the tree may detect the Morality Rating of anyone within the AOE.
Uses: at will   AOE: 100 yards radius centered on the tree. This forms a globe of "sight" around the tree.

2) <u>Shield vs. Enchanted Creatures</u> – When the Zonith Wood invokes this ability, NO Enchanted Creature may pass into the AOE.   Uses= 1/day   D: 6 hrs.   AOE: Leaf Barrier + 10 feet

3) <u>Enchantment Barrier</u> – No spell may pass from one side of the Willowy Branches to the other. Spells cast at the leaf barrier will be absorbed by the tree. Zonith Trees may use these absorbed SP to cast its Spells, but the tree may never absorb more than its maximum available SP. Only spells that are cast at the tree's trunk, from within the leafy barrier, will affect or damage the tree in anyway.

4) <u>Immune to Fire</u> – All Zonith Wood trees are completely immune to Regular and Enchanted Fire.

5) <u>Teleport</u> – They may teleport to any location any of its type has ever stood. This may be done at will.

6) <u>Stats</u> for an average healthy Zonith Wood Tree:

EP = 200		PTE = 35% - 1/2 damage from blunt objects.	
RER = 75%		MR = Golden Zonith = 17 - 19	Red Zonith = 2 - 4
Strikes = 4		Parries = 0	
Number of Actions/Attack = 4	Intellect & Wisdom = 10 + 1 / year ea.		Max = 20 ea.

NOTE: If you do more than 10 EP Damage to any of the tree's Willowy Branches with an edged weapon, you will cut it off at that spot, but this will not do any damage to the Tree itself. You must actually strike the trunk of the tree for it to take any EP Damage – this includes weapons and spells.

NOTE2: Blunt weapons only do 1/2 normal damage to a tree's trunk and NO damage to its branches.

Offensive Capabilities

<u>Intellect Blast</u> – Victim temporarily loss 5 Intellect points for the Duration and is <u>Dazed</u> for 4+1d8 Actions.
R: 50'   AOE: 1 victim   CT: Zero; The tree may do this at will but only once per Attack. The intended victim rates a RER and if successful they don't loss any Intellect points but are still Dazed for 4 Actions.
NOTE3: This ability does not affect those creatures listed in the Indigo spell section.

<u>Willowy Branches</u> – The tree may manipulate objects with its Branches with a dexterity equal to that of a person. Usually however, the Branches simply hang down forming a barrier that no enchantment may pass through. This barrier also obscures the tree's roots from vision, which grow just inside them up toward the sky. Each Branch only has a Strength Score of 1, but if the tree uses many of them together, the Branches can be a formidable force (total Strength = 1 per branch used.)

<u>Spell Use</u> – This falls into three sections:

(A) All mature Zonith Wood trees automatically know and can cast <u>these</u> spells at 10th level ability Once per Day with No SPC. If the tree needs to cast any of these spells a second time in the same day, it can spend the specified number of Spell Points. (Range, Duration and AOE of the spell are the same as listed in the spell's description but the Concentration Time is Zero) :

(a) Item Dance	SPC: 75	(b) Project Thought	SPC: 106
(c) Mind Blast - One	SPC: 34	(d) Mind Blast - Many	SPC: 138
(e) Order Spell	SPC: 30	(f) "See" Truth	SPC: 25

Any Zonith Wood may "learn" spells through participation in the Challenge of the Staff. The tree actually absorbs the pattern of the Spell held within the item that is exchanged for one of the tree's roots. The tree may cast any spell it has learned or any it automatically knows from the end of any one of its Willowy Branches.

(B) <u>Spell Points</u>: All Zonith Wood trees rate a total of 10 SP per day per point of Intellect they have. [Minimum = 110 SP   Max = 200 SP]. They gain their total number of Spell Points back each day at sunrise – just like everyone else – but remember they can also absorb any spell that is cast at their Willowy barrier and convert these to Spell Points that it may use. They can use these Spell Points to cast any of the spells it knows. (They may never absorb more SP than their Max).

(C) <u>Number of Spells</u>: The total number of spells a Zonith Wood may learn is FIVE times the number listed on the Intellect Table under the Spell "II" heading.   (Min=5, Max = 50 spells) (These are in addition to those which all mature Zonith Wood trees know: See Spell Use section (A) above).

CHALLENGE OF THE STAFF

An Enchanter must complete this challenge in order to obtain his staff. Here are rules and regulations:

Overview

1) Seek out and speak with a Zonith Wood Tree with the same Morals as yours. If your MR is 10 or greater than a Golden Zonith is what you seek and if your MR is 9 or below then you must find a Red Zonith. When you address a Zonith Wood tree remember to show respect – they are very old and powerful, beside if you anger one, you may anger ALL of their type. If you approach a tree and don't have the same Morals, you will probably be attacked.
2) The Enchanter must recite the age old Challenge: "I Challenge thee o' Wise Tree for the Root and I offer this in trade. (You show the object) Do you accept or deny."
3) The Tree will inspect "the prize" you show so you must hold out the item that contains <u>the spell</u> you are offering in exchange for one of the tree's roots. NOTE: the Tree may Accept, Decline or Make a Counter offer.
4) If the Tree accepts: You (and your companions) attempt to outmaneuver the tree and its inhabitants in order to put the Enchanter into position so he can win the challenge.
5) To win the Challenge, the Enchanter must "shoot" the agreed upon Enchanted Item into the tree's mouth. If you accomplish this the Zonith Wood tree will reward you by presenting you with one of its roots. The root given to you will be exactly 25 inches taller than you are.

Why the Zonith Wood tree might Decline the Enchanter's offer:
1) Spell not high enough level.   2) Your companions and you are too enchanted.
3) Tree has given up a root within the last month.

Why make Counter offer:
1) Ask you for a different spell.
2) Ask you to challenge another tree of its type – Teleporting takes no time at all.

NOTE: If the Companions try to take the root by force, the kid gloves come off; the tree will defend itself.

Guidelines of the Challenge :

1) You (and your companions) are allowed to prepare yourselves, but must start 200 feet away from the tree. Your companions help you by distracting the defenders, getting a defender away from you or by helping you over or through the circle of roots. Once inside the circle, you and <u>you alone</u> must try to position yourself so you can shoot the Enchanted Item into the tree's mouth.
2) If you miss the shoot or become pinned or trapped by one of the defenders, such that you can no longer move forward, combat will stop. You will be allowed to recover the item and your composure, then you (and your companions) must return to the starting point. You must immediately restart – no prep time. You may only restart twice; three strikes and your out. (You must not damage the tree or the defenders permanently in any way !! - Don't use Acid, Fire, etc.)
3) The Inhabitants of the tree will become the tree's Defenders. They will work against you and your companion's to try to stop you from winning the Challenge. These creatures will try not to mortally harm you, unless you're competing against a Red Zonith Tree, of course.
4) The Zonith Wood tree also has rules it must follow :
   1st: The tree will simply let its Willowy Branches hang down, forming the Enchanted Barrier. It won't use them in a hostile manner.
   2nd: The tree will hold open its mouth giving you a good target. The only reason it would close it is if you tried to stick your hand or anything else but the enchanted item in it.
   NOTE2: The Enchanted Item must be <u>shot</u> into the tree's mouth.
   3rd: The tree won't Teleport to another location during the Challenge.
5) The tree will attack you with any spells it knows which are 5th - 9th level, but can't use more than 100 SP (+ any Spell Points it Absorbs) during the Challenge.
6) The tree may NOT employ its Intellect Blast against you or your companions.
7) You can loose the Challenge of the Staff in three ways:
   1st: Enchanter misses the shot or becomes pinned and/or trapped 3 times in a row.
   2nd: Enchanter takes enough damage to falls below ZERO Endurance Points.
   3rd: Enchanter or anyone in Enchanter's party does not follow these Guidelines or deliberately kills one of the Zonith Tree's defenders.

The Survival Skill 'Blind Shot and Accurate Pass' is used slightly differently when you use it for the Challenge of the Staff:

Blind Shot and Accurate Pass: This skill is modified when used in the Challenge. The 'Canopy' is used to describe the area within the tree's roots. The Canopy will be dark on the inside because of the Willowy Barrier, but all light spells work normally. When you want to make a shot, you receive a negative to your percentage roll depending on the circumstances you are in. These negatives are listed below:

Learned the Survival Skill: 'Blind Shoot and Accurate Pass'		Adjustments to your Ability Check for shooting
Shot taken while inside a Lighted Canopy:		Roll a successful Ability Check with Agility.
Shot taken while inside a Dark Canopy:		-10% lower than your Ability Check w/ Agility.
Shoot from OUTSIDE the Canopy:	Lit Canopy	Can't – Willowy Branches are in way.
	Dark Canopy	Can't – Willowy Branches are in way.

Did **NOT** Learn the Survival Skill: 'Blind Shoot and Accurate Pass'		
Shot Taken while inside a Lighted Canopy:		Roll a Percentage lower then your **Agility Score**.
Shot Taken while inside a Dark Canopy:		Roll a Percentage -10% lower than your Agility Score.
Shoot from OUTSIDE the Canopy:	Lit Canopy	Can't – Willowy Branches are in way.
	Dark Canopy	Can't – Willowy Branches are in way.

NOTE: A successful **Ability Check with Agility** is a percentage roll that is less than your **Agility Score x 3.** (ex: Agility Score = 14, then roll a percentage below or equal to 42%.)

NOTE2: If you go to the exact spot where a Zonith Wood tree has stood, you may call to a tree of that type by using an ESP or Project Thought spell or by thrusting your Enchanted Staff into the spot. A tree may or may not respond to the call.

NOTE3: If you do loose the Challenge, find another tree then rinse and repeat.

NOTE4: The defenders may be any wood land animal. Most are Regular or Mutated, but some are Enchanted.

NOTE5: If you have taken the Survival Skill 'Blind shot and Accurate Pass' and have specialized in that skill, you gain all percentage bonuses from your specializations added to your percentage totals for use in the Challenge of the Staff.

LIFE TREE

Description – The Life Tree looks like a regular oak tree at first glance. On closer inspection you'll notice that this tree has thick vines (tentacles) coiled about its limbs and trunk. The Life Tree also bears a large nut that holds the Liquid of Life. This Liquid is one of the main ingredients for all potions made by Alchemists. The tree may Telepathically Communicate with all Plants, Alchemists, Regular, Mutated, and Enchanted Creatures at will. These trees are not carnivorous, they feed just like regular plants: through photosynthesis.

Abilities – As a Life Tree grows it gains the ability to naturally heal itself, other creatures and plants. It can also cast each of the spells listed below **1/day** - as long as the tree meets the age requirements.

Revitalize Nature	= 1 year old	AOE: 10' x 10' area / year of tree is revitalized.
Heal Wounds **1**	= 3 years old	30+1/Yr EP healed with no Spell Point Cost from Life Tree.
Heal Paralyzation	= 5 years old	Any type of natural or Enchanted Paralyzation.
Heal Disease	= 7 years old	Any Disease natural or Enchanted.
Heal Poison	= 9 years old	Any Type (No Venom or Enchanted Emerald Dust needed).
Heal Wounds **3**	= 10 years old	100 +1/Yr EP healed with no Spell Point Cost from Life Tree.

Intellect Score – To figure out a Life Tree's Intellect Score use this equation:

1 point / year of the tree + 1d6. The maximum Intellect Score possible for a Life Tree is 18, regardless of age.

Once a Life Tree has an Intellect Score of 11 or more, it may learn these types of spells:
1) Any spell held by Green Gems - These spells are listed in the Enchanter / Alchemist spell list.
2) Any spell held by Orange Gems - These spells are listed in the Enchanter / Alchemist spell list.
3) Any Class (A) spells - These spells require less than 20 Spell Points in order to cast them.

Total Spell Points: 6 Spell Points for every 1 Intellect point (Maximum = 108 SP).
   The Life Tree may use its Spell Points to cast any spell it knows.
   The Life Tree regains all of its Spell Points at the rising of the Column Sun every morning.

Learning a Spell: The Life Tree must have enough Spell Points to cast the spell it wants to learn.
   To learn a spell the tree touches the caster's brow with a Tentacle as he casts the spell.
   The tree now learned the patterns of the new spell and has the ability to cast it by sacrificing some of its Spell Points!

Total Number of Spells the tree may Learn: THREE times the number listed on the Intellect Table under the Spell "II" heading.

Example: The Life Tree is 10 years old, so start with a Intellect Score base of 10. I rolled a 4 on a 1d6, so its Intellect Score = 10 + 4 = an Intellect Score of 14.
   Now this Life Tree may learn up to 12 spells (4 on Intellect table x 3) and may cast any of them in any combination as long as it doesn't exceed 84 SP (14 Intellect Score x 6) in one day.

Fruit – The Fruit produced by a Life Tree resembles a coconut and it is filled with the Liquid of Life. There is always **4 Ounces** of the Liquid in every nut. Only a Plant may take a full 2 ounces of the pure Liquid of Life without dying. These are the effects of the Liquid of Life on creatures:

2 ounces for a Plant	= Speeds up growth – automatically becomes "Mature".
1 ounce for an animal	= roll on Mutated Creature table.
1 ounce for an Alchemist	= a special spell will curb the effects and 'make' an Alchemist.
1 ounce for any person	= Insanity.

NOTE: 1 ounce of the Liquid of Life is enough for an Alchemist to make ONE Potion.
NOTE2: Every 1 Life Tree Nut = 4 ounces of the Liquid of Life = 4 Potions.

Tentacles – Damage = 1d10 ea. – Each tentacle looks like a thick vine and extends from the top or bottom of the tree's trunk. The tentacles are between 20 - 30 feet long. They are capable of picking up objects, but can't manipulate small things. Each Tentacle has a Strength Score of 9 and the Life Tree can use them in tandem to hold a strong victim. During Combat the Tentacles can be used as clubs, to cast spells or to grasp an opponent and employ their most feared attack: their ability to drain Endurance Points from their victim directly to themselves.

Numbers of Tentacles

Age of Tree	Top of Trunk	Bottom of Trunk	Nuts / Season
1 - 3 yrs.	1	1	1d4
4 - 6	2	3	2+1d4
7 - 9	4	6	4+1d6
10+ yrs.	8	12	8+1d8

Endurance Points Drain – The Life Tree is able to Drain 2 EP for every ONE Spell Point it spends. The tree must grasp the victim with one of its tentacles and the Endurance Points are transferred from the victim directly to the tree. The tree can never exceed its regular EP total but may continue to Drain a victim even after it reaches its maximum EP total. If the tree chooses to do this it will begin to glow an intense green. The victim does NOT rate a RER and the only way to stop the EP Drain is to cut off the Tentacle or to kill the tree.

Attacking – The tree may use any of the methods discussed below to protect itself. They are intelligent and will use offensive spell types to attack first. The Tree may:

1) Use any spell it has learned.   2) Use any spell it is able to cast 1/day.
3) Use its Endurance Point Drain.   4) Use its Tentacles to do damage.

Self Defense – "Domestic" trees will attack anyone its Planter tells it to (such as trespassers) or anyone who tries to harm it or take it's fruit. "Wild Ones" will attack anyone or anything that tries to harm it, take its fruit or anyone who may be unlucky enough to trespass to close to it. All Stats are by AGE: 1-3 / 4-6 / 7-9 / 10+ years.

EP	= 100/150/200/250	PTE = 20/30/40/50%	RER = 40/50/60/70%
MR	= 11 / 12 / 13 / 14	Strikes = 2 / 3 / 4 / 5	Parries = 0 / 0 / 0 / 0

NOTE: If you do more than 15/25/35/50 EP Damage to any of the tree's tentacles with a bladed weapon, a pointed weapon or with a spell, you will sever the tentacle off at that spot, but this will not do any damage to the Tree. You must actually strike the trunk of the tree for it to take any EP Damage – this includes weapons and spells. PTE for the tentacles: 10/20/30/40%

NOTE2: Blunt weapons only do 1/2 damage to a tree's trunk and 1/2 damage to its tentacles.

Movement – Yes! These trees can move. They "Float through the ground" not disturbing a stone.
They are able to move at 5 feet/Attack. (CRM: 1).
They may "charge" at 10 ft/Attack (CRM: 2) for 1 minute per hour. (120 feet burst in 60 sec.)

Immunities – Life Trees are Immune to all forms of Regular and Enchanted Poisons, Diseases and Venoms.

Home Life – All Life Trees hate - yes, they do have emotions disturbingly close to ours - Red Zonith Wood Trees because a Red Zonith often uses fire to "burn out" all other vegetation in the area. You will often find a "Wild" Life Tree living close to where Golden Zonith Wood Trees are known to appear.

Random Treasure Table

There will be many times when your Ref. must determine if a defeated person, party or creature has any valuables in its possession. I have provided a Random Treasure table for you to use if your Ref. does not generate these in advance. I've separated the tables into five categories: Poor, Fair, Good, Great and Awesome. I used this type of separation so your Ref. could utilize the tables regardless of your Party's level. The Ref. can determine what a 'Good' roll entails so he has the ability to keep control of your adventure. I.e. If the party members are all around 5th level, the category of 'Good' on the Money table represents quite a different amount than if the party is 15th level.

To ascertain what your defeated enemy is 'worth' with regard to the tables below, use this equation:
[(EP + PTE + # of Actions) / 10] + 1 point per Mutation + Enchantment Spell Class castable = Total 'worth'

Points awarded for each Spell Classification the creature may cast: (A)= +1; (B)= +2; (C)= +3; (D)= +4; (E)= +5.

Examples: (1) Defeated Opponent = Black Bear with wings (1 mutation):
EP:90; PTE:45; # of Actions: 2; Mutations: +1; Total 'worth' = [(137/10)+1] = 14.7 or 15 points.

(2) Defeated Opponent = Mud Troll:
EP:100; PTE:50; # of Actions:3; Enchantments: +8; Total 'worth' = [(153/10)+8] = 23.3 or 23 points.
Enchantment Summary: PTE@+20%= (B), Mud Control 2= (C), Polymorph= (C).

(3) Defeated Opponent = Psycho Savage Marauder:
EP:70; PTE:40; # of Actions:2; Enchantments: +5; Total 'worth' = [(112/10)+5 = 16.2 or 16 points.
Enchantment Summary: Potion of Healing @ 45= (B), Cloak with a Shield, Projectile 40%= (C).

The total 'worth' you attained from the equation above is converted to a number of rolls on the tables below. A single roll on the Regular Equipment table costs 2 points. A single roll on the Money table costs 5 points and a single roll on the Enchanted table costs 10 points. Your Ref. will decide how to split up the total points and will tell you which tables to roll on.

To continue with the example, if you defeated the mutated black bear above you would rate 15 points. Your Ref. may tell you to roll 5 times on the Regular Equipment table and once on the Money table **or** he may tell you to roll once on the Money table and once on the Enchanted table. You'll notice that both examples add up to 15 total points.

The die used to roll on all of the tables listed below is a 1d12. Notice that the lower the number the better the result. In my games we go by this rule: "Low is better for the Party."

RANDOM TREASURE TABLE

Regular Equipment (cost = 2)		Money (cost = 5)		Enchanted Items (cost = 10)	
1	Awesome	1	Awesome	1	Awesome
2 - 4	Great	2 - 4	Great	2 - 4	Great
5 - 8	Good	5 - 8	Good	5 - 8	Good
9 - 11	Fair	9 - 11	Fair	9 - 11	Fair
12	Poor	12	Poor	12	Poor

After you ascertain how many Poor, Fair, Good, Great or Awesome Treasures you rate, go to the next table for some examples of what you may find on your fallen victims.

NOTE: If you roll "Poor" on the Enchanted Items portion of the Random Treasure Table, you're Party receives nothing! I call that: "The cost of doing biness, baby!"
BUT, If you choose to roll on the Money portion of the table, Everyone in the party receives that amount of money.

Examples for Payoffs (Treasure)

Level	Rating	Regular Equipment	Money (Silver)	Enchanted Items
1st	Awesome	Mace	10	Arrow: Water Bolt (1)
	Great	Small Helm	7	Small Wooden Shield: Shield, Proj., 10%
	Good	100' Rope	5	Potion: Healing @ 40EP
	Fair	Torch	3	Armband: Float
	Poor	Leather Pouch	1	Nothing Found

Level	Rating	Regular Equipment	Money (Silver)	Enchanted Items
5th	Awesome	Short Bow	20	Leather BlackJack: Paralyze Person
	Great	Human, 1/2 Suit Armor	15	Large Wooden Shield: Plant Wall
	Good	1 wk. Hard Rations	10	Enchanted Cloak**: 75 SP (Waterproof, ect.)
	Fair	Tinder Box & (1) Torch	7	Alchemist's Dust: Healing @ 60EP
	Poor	Sharpening Stone & Oil	5	Nothing Found

Level	Rating	Regular Equipment	Money (Silver)	Enchanted Items
10th	Awesome	Ransium Banded Nunchucks	40	Red Zonith Wood Wand: Wind Bolt 3 (4 spells)
	Great	Ransium Knights Shield	30	Small Helm w/ Opaque Quartz (VSI2=1(C), ect.)
	Good	Scimitar & Scabbard	20	Enchanted Pouch**: 100 SP (Holds x3, ect.)
	Fair	Flask of Whiskey	15	Enchanted Boots**: 75 SP (Waterproof, ect.)
	Poor	Cold Weather Gloves	10	Nothing Found

Level	Rating	Regular Equipment	Money (Silver)	Enchanted Items
15th	Awesome	(5) Langor Tipped Arrows	80	Reg. Spear: Lightning Bolt 3 spell (Damage: 34+4d10)
	Great	Langor Large Shield	60	Full Suit Leather w/ Opaque Quartz (VVSI2=1(D), ect.)
	Good	Med. Chest with Metal Bands	40	Enchanted Gloves**: 150 SP (Wield 2-Handed, ect.)
	Fair	Saw, Hand Hammer, 40 nails	30	Alchemist's Pill: Healing @ 100EP
	Poor	Tent, 4 Man	20	Nothing Found

** These Items were enchanted by an Enchanter who "pumped" Spell Points into the item.

NOTE: The first column (1st, 5th, 10th & 15th) is the average level of the Companion's Party.
    – Your group of adventures, "for those at home."

NOTE2: If the Money Column is chosen, everyone in your Party will receive the listed amount of money.

NOTE3: If you roll an amount of money with a high enough value, your Ref. may elect to exchange it for some other equal monetary amount. I.e.:
    20 Silver is equal to 2 MP.
    40 Silver is equal to 4 MP.
    10 Silver would equate to an Enchanted Red or Yellow Quartz with a GPR of I1.
    60 Silver would equate to an Enchanted Amethyst Gem with a GPR of VSI1.

GLOSSARY

NAME	ABBREVIATION	DESCRIPTION

Abilities — Aspects that define your character in many ways.
These are : Endurance, Agility, Strength, Intellect, Wisdom, and Will.
All Abilities have a numeric Score between 1 and 20.

Ability Check — This is a percentage rolled to determine Success or Failure when using certain abilities or certain Survival Skills.
Any roll less than or equal to the percentage is a Success.
Ability Check percentage = (Named Ability Score) x 3.

Action — *Act* — Enough time for you to do 1 quick thing.
A 1st level character rates 1 Striking Action and 1 Parry Action per Attack.
As your Character increases in level the number of Actions she rates per Attack increases depending on her Occupation.

Attack — *Att.* — A measure of Time. 1 Attack = 5 seconds; 12 Attacks = 1 Minute.

Character — What you as a person creates to interact with the Isles of Penicia.

Charging Rate — *CR* — This number is always a multiple of 5 and is in the units: feet / sec.

Charging Rate Multiple — *CRM* — A number used to directly relate Charging Rate (CR) in game terms.
Multiply your CRM by 5 to attain your CR.
(ie. A CRM of 3 = a Charging Rate (CR) of 15 ft per second).

Concentration Time — *CT* — The number of ACTIONS a spell caster must spend to review a spell's description and focus his energies before he may cast a spell.

Experience Points — *XPO* — As you accomplish tasks you gain Experience.
Certain completed tasks or situations are worth a certain number of Experience Points.
Check the Experience Point Table to find out how many Experience Points you need to gain in order for your character to attain the next Level.

Endurance Points — *EP* — Maximum Score = (End. Score * 2) + Level bonuses.
As you are injured this number decreases.
As you rest or are healed this number increases.
If you Cast a Spell, you will also have to spend some EP –
spend 1 EP / 10 Spell Points cast.

Gem Perfection Rating — *GPR* — This is a designation that describes how perfect an Enchanted gem is.
The lowest usable rating is: I2 or 'Included 2'
The highest usable rating is: VVSI1 or 'Very Very Slightly Included 1'

Ki Points — *KP* — These are what a Ninja must spend in order to use any Ninja Ki Power. See the table in Appendix M for totals or:
Total KP = Wisdom + { (Wisdom / 4) * (Level - 1) }.
Maximum at 1st Level: 20 KP   &   Maximum at 5th Level: 40 KP
You gain this total back at the rising of the Column Sun each morning.
Regeneration of Ki Points: This can be done ONCE per day per every 2 levels of the character.
(i.e.: 1st-2nd Level = 1/day; 3rd-4th Level = 2/day)
When activated: The Ninja gains back 1 KP per 1 Attack (5 seconds).

Level	L	A number representing the amount of expertise you have in your Occupation.
		The possible ranges of Levels are between 1 and 20.
		You character must gain a certain number of Experience Points in order to advance in level.
		NOTE: Please see the Experience Points Table (XPO Table) to see the Experience Points necessary for your character to rise from one Level to the next.

Mental Points   MP   A Mentalist must spend these points to use any Mentalist Skill – See table in Appendix M for totals or:

Total Mental Points = { (Will score / 2) * Your Level }.

Maximum at 1st Level: 7 MP   &   Maximum at 5th Level: 40 MP

You gain this total back at the rising of the Column Sun each morning.

Regeneration of Mental Points: This can be done ONCE per day per every 2 levels of the character.

(i.e.: 5th-6th Level = 3/day; 7th-8th Level = 4/day)

When activated: Mentalists gain back 1 MP per 1 Attack (5 seconds).

Morality Rating   MR   The range is a number between 1 - 20.

High numbers indicate high morals.

Those vile, untrustworthy men with low morality would have low numbers.

Occupation   Occ.   This is your profession. Your Occupation includes your primary means of offense and defense, among other things.

Opponent   Opp.   One of them.

Percentage To Evade   PTE   This percentage tells you what you need to roll to evade a strike.

You must roll equal to or under this percentage to Evade a strike.

You roll this percentage whenever anyone strikes at you with a melee (hand-held) or projectile weapon.

PTE = (Agility Score / 2) + Armor + Shield + Spell or other bonuses.

Race   There are 3 divisions of peoples that you may choose your character to be: Human, Hemar, or Krill.

Each Race originated on one of the 3 Isles of Penicia, but anyone of any Race may freely travel, trade or live on any Isle.

Resist Enchantment Roll   RER   A percentage roll that indicates if you are able to resist some of the effects of the enchantment that has just been directed at you.

This is Only rolled when you are adversely affected by a spell and this percentage increases as you rise in level.

You must always roll lower than or equal to your RER percentage to resist the effects of the spell.

Spell   Means by which Magic may be shaped and cast.

It has been stated: "Magic is a force that you can learn to direct which has the ability to manipulate and control matter, energy and living creatures or inanimate objects in many different ways."

Spell Point Cost   SPC   The total amount of Spell Points your character must spend in order to cast a spell.

| Spell Points | SP | These are what you must spend in order to Cast a Spell. |
| | | You rate a certain total number per day, which you gain back at the rising of the Column Sun each morning. |

Spell Points   <u>SP</u>

These are what you must spend in order to Cast a Spell.

You rate a certain total number per day, which you gain back at the rising of the Column Sun each morning.

See table in Appendix M for totals or:

Use this Equation if you are an <u>Alchemist</u>, <u>Elementalist</u>, or an <u>Enchanter</u>:

Total SP per day = Intellect Score + { (Intellect Score /2) * (Level -1)}.

If your Int Score= 20 at 1st Level; total Spell Points= 20 SP.

If your Int Score= 20 at 5th Level; total Spell Points = 60 SP.

Use this equation if you are a <u>Warrior</u>, <u>Spy / Assassin</u> or <u>Mentalist</u>:

Total SP per day = Intellect Score + 1 SP per Level.

NOTE: For every 10 SP anyone uses, they must also spend 1 EP.

Regeneration of Spell Points: This can be done ONCE per day per every 2 levels of the character.

(i.e.: 9th-10th Level = 5/day; 11th-12th Level = 6/day)

When activated: Everyone gains back 1 SP per 1 Attack (5 seconds).

Strike Placement Table   <u>SPT</u>

Every time you strike at an Opponent with a melee or projectile weapon, you must roll on this table to find out what part of you victim's body your strike hits.

NOTE2: Your Opp. always rates a PTE roll. If he succeeds with his PTE roll, you must disregard your SPT roll.

Survival Skill

You may learn certain skills to supplement your Occupation.

To perform some skills you must roll a successful Ability Check.

Ability Check percentage = (Named Ability Score) x 3

You are also able to increase any Ability Score or your CRM by using a Survival Skill slot.

TOEP

Total Original Endurance Points.

You can never be healed passed your TOEP.

This total is usually used during combat to determine if your character severely wounded your opponent.

Trigger Word / Phrase   <u>Trigger</u>

Enchanted Items activate their stored spell / skill when their "Trigger" is Forcefully spoken.

Also it begins the Spell you are Casting OR Activating :

1) After you have spent the Spell and Endurance Points necessary and then you spend the required Actions listed under the Spell's Casting Time.

2) Activates the spell / skill that is stored in the Enchanted Item or Gem.

NOTE3:   Radius = The distance from the center point of a circle to its outer edge.

Radius = Diameter / 2.

Diameter = The distance from the outer edge of a circle to the opposite edge measured through the circle's center.

Diameter = Radius x 2.

NOTE4:   Area Of Effect (AOE) Example – 8 Cubic Feet = 1'x1'x8' or 2'x2'x2' or 1'x2'x4' or .5'x1'x16'

NOTE5:

Spy / Assassin	<u>S/A</u>
Enchanter	<u>Ench.</u>
Alchemist	<u>Al.</u>
Elementalist	<u>El.</u>

STRENGTH TABLE

Total	Damage Bonus	Bench Press (LBS)	Leg Press (LBS)
1	-4	-50	-10*
2-4	-3	-25	BW
5-7	-2	-10	+10
8-9	-1	BW	+25
10-12	0	+25	+50
13-14	+1	+50	+100
15-16	+2	+100	+200
17-18	+3	+150	+300
19-20	+4	+200	+400

NOTE: Hemars gain a +1 to all Damage Bonuses.   BW=Body Weight   *=Can't Walk

INTELLECT

Score	Language	Spells		Spy / Assassin Formal training	Informal training
1	Can't learn to speak				
2					
3	Speak National (Nat'l)				
4	Language			1/L	1/L
5					
6	Speak / Read & Write				
7	Nat'l Lang. and				
8	Speak the				
9	Traders Language	I	II		
10					
11	Speak / Read & Write	A	1		
12	1) National Language	B	2		
13	2) Traders Lang.		3	2/L	2/L
14		C	4		
15	Speak / Read & Write		5		
16	1) National Language	D	6		
17	2) Traders Lang. and		7		
18	3) ONE extra Lang.	E	8	3/L	2/L
19			9		
20	Speak / Read & Write 1) National Language 2)Traders Lang. 3)TWO extra. Lang.		10		
Score	Language	Spells		Spy / Assassin	

Number of "Slots" rated per level

WISDOM TABLE

Score	Ambush Bonus	Wisdom Bonus vs. Illusions
1 - 2	- 5%	1%
3 - 5	- 3%	2 - 3%
6 - 14	0	3 - 7%
15 - 18	+3%	8 - 9%
19 - 20	+5%	10%

WILL TABLE

Level	Bonus	Ability Score	Intellect Bonus	Wisdom Bonus	Endurance Bonus
1st - 4th	+ 4	1 – 6	+ 0	+ 0	+ 0
5th - 9th	+ 6	7 – 11	+ 1	+ 1	+ 0
10th - 14th	+ 8	12 – 15	+ 2	+ 2	+ 1
15th on up	+ 10	16 – 18	+ 3	+ 3	+ 1
		19 – 20	+ 4	+ 4	+ 2

Will Score = (Level Bonus) + (Intellect Bonus + Wisdom Bonus + Endurance Bonus)

AGILITY

Agility Bonus to PTE total = Agility Score / 2 (rounded up).

STRIKE PLACEMENT TABLE (SPT)

	Human	Hemar	Krill	Animal	Snake	Bird
Head	1 - 5	1 - 5	1 - 5	1 - 5	1 - 5	1 - 5
Body	6 - 20	6 - 20	6 - 20	6 -20	6 - 20	6 -20
Left Arm	21 - 38	21 - 32	21 - 30			
Right Arm	39 - 54	33 - 44	31 - 40			
Left Wing			41 - 55			21-45
Right Wing			56 - 70			46-70
Left Front Leg		45 - 57		21-38		
Right Front Leg		58 - 70		39-56		
Left Rear Leg	55 - 73	71 - 80	71 - 80	57-73		71-80
Right Rear Leg	74 - 89	81 - 88	81 - 89	74-88		81-88
Tail		89		89	21-89	89
Near Miss	90 - 99	90 - 99	90 - 99	90-99	90-99	90-99

Any Roll of "00" with percentage dice on the SPT table is an Automatic HIT – The attacker may pick any **General** area and do <u>double normal damage</u> – this includes your Str. Damage bonus.

COMMON COMBAT RELATED AFLICTIONS

STUNNED: If your Opponent is stunned, he will suffer these penalties :
(1) Loss Agility Bonus to his PTE while stunned.   (2) Can't make any loud warning sounds.
(3) He may not Strike with a weapon or begin the Concentration Time for any spell.

BLINDED: If a victim is Blinded he looses his Agility bonus to his PTE roll. Also, if the blinded victim attacks anyone, his opponents receive a +40% bonus to their PTE totals, while the victim is blinded.

DAZED: The victim becomes disoriented. This disorientation will cause:
(1) The victim's Opponents gain a +25% to their PTE totals. (2) Stop Charging Hemar / Krill must Land.
(3) Victim can't use any Occ. Skills or start Concentrating.   (4) Victim looses Agility bonus to his PTE roll.

PERSON CONCEALED or INVISIBLE: Gains a +40% to PTE; Concealed in Deep Shadow gains +30% PTE.

CHARACTER FALLS BELOW EP TOTAL: Ability Check with Will score, to remain Conscious.

If any Character falls below their EP total and accumulates negative EP > then his End score = Death.

NOTE: A Stunned or Dazed victim may always use Potions, Pills, or any Enchanted Item activated by a Trigger Word.

HUMAN

Bonuses : All Humans gain a +1 to their initial Intellect Ability Score.
Speak +1 additional Racial Language.

Age : Morning = 1 - 20 yrs.   Noon = 21 - 130 yrs.   Night = 130 - 150 yrs.

Height : Female = 5.0 - 6.5 ft.   Male = 6.0 - 8.0 ft.

Weight : Female = 120 - 180 lbs.   Male = 150 - 350 lbs.

Standing Leap : 15 ft.   **Running Leap :** 30 ft.

Charging Rates : Minimum = 15 ft/sec; Maximum = 30 ft/sec   CRM: Min = 3; Max = 6.

Types : Skin colors are Red, Yellow, Brown, Blue, Green and White.

HEMAR

Bonuses : +1 on initial Strength Ability Score.   (Shetlands = +1 Wisdom, not Strength)
+1 to all melee Damage rolls.
Speak with particular Horse type at will.

Age : Morning = 1 - 40 yrs.   Noon = 41 - 160 yrs.   Night = 160 - 200 yrs.

Height : Female = 6.0 - 8.0 ft.   Male = 7.5 - 9.0 ft.

Weight : Female = 800 - 1200 lbs.   Male = 1100 - 1400 lbs.

Standing Leap : 25 ft.   **Running Leap :** 45 ft.

Charging Rates : Minimum = 20 ft/sec; Maximum = 35 ft/sec   CRM: Min = 4; Max = 7.

Types : Clydesdale, Mustang, Appaloosa and Shetland.

KRILL

Bonuses : +1 on initial Agility Ability Score.
+25% on PTE total while flying - not hovering.
Speak with particular Bird type at will.

Age : Morning = 1-10 yrs.   Noon = 11-110 yrs.   Night = 111 - 130 yrs.

Height : Female = 4.5 - 6.0 ft.   Male = 5.5 - 7.0 ft.

Weight : Female = 100 - 180 lbs.   Male = 140 - 200 lbs.

Standing Leap : 10 ft.   **Running Leap :** 15 ft.

Charging Rates : Minimum = 20 ft/sec; Maximum = 35 ft/sec   CRM: Min = 4; Max = 7.

Types : Eagle, Vulture, Owl, and Hawk.

STARTING WEAPONS AND SURVIVAL SKILLS

Occupation	Number of **Starting** Weapons	Opp. Bonus to PTE	Number of **Starting** Skills	Endurance Points Per Level
Warrior	3 or 4	+15 %	3 + Shield + Wr/B	1d8
Spy / Assassin	3	+25 %	3	1d6
Ninja	1 + Staff	+20 %	2 + Imp CR	1d6
Enchanter	1	+35 %	2 + Rope M.	1d4
Alchemist	2	+30 %	3 + Plant ID	1d4
Elementalist	1	+40 %	2 + Ring M.	1d4
Mentalist	2	+40 %	2 + (+2 to 1 Abl.)	1d4

Level	Additional Weapon		Level	Additional Weapon
3	+ 1		6	+ 1
9	+ 1		12	+ 1
15	+ 1		18	+ 1

Level	Additional Skill Slots		Level	Additional Skill Slots
2	+ 1		4	+ 2
6	+ 1		8	+ 2
10	+ 1		12	+ 2
14	+ 1		16	+ 2
18	+ 1			

NOTE: You may exchange 2 Survival Skill slots for 1 Weapon slot OR 1 Weapon slot for 2 Survival Skill slots.

ELEMENTALISTS, ENCHANTERS, ALCHEMISTS AND MENTALIST: ACTIONS / ATTACK

Level	Strikes	Parries	Total Actions
1st - 4th	1	1	2
5th - 9th	1	2	3
10th - 14th	1	3	4
15th - 19th	1	4	5

SPY / ASSASSIAN: ACTIONS / ATTACK

Level	Strikes	Parries	Total Actions
1st - 4th	1	1	2
5th - 9th	1	2	3
10th - 14th	1	3	4
15th - 19th	2	3	5

WARRIORS AND NINJA: ACTIONS / ATTACK

Level	Strikes	Parries	Total Actions
1st - 4th	1	1	2
5th - 9th	1	2	3
10th - 14th	2	2	4
15th - 19th	3	2	5

NOTE: Anyone may substitute a Strike Action for a Parry Action; NOT the other way around, unless you are Specialized in the weapon you are using.

RESIST ENCHANTMENT ROLL

LEVEL	RER PERCENTAGE	General Bonuses added to your RER total
1	10 %	add ½ Wisdom Score vs. Illusions
2 – 4	15 %	add ½ Agility Score vs. Nets, Rocks, Waves
5 – 9	20 %	
10 – 14	25 %	
15th and up	30 %	

NOTE2: All Regular and Mutated Creatures normally have a RER percentage of 20%.

The **Spy / Assassin** gains percentage increases on his or her **General skills** at every level.
You receive additional **Skill Slots** at these levels: **1st, 3rd, 5th, 7th, 10th, 13th, 16th and 19th.**

Ability Check Percentage   =   Named Ability * 3.
Example: If you want to use the Survival Skill: Boat, Construction (small) and your character
has an Intellect Score of 15, you simply multiply it by 3 (15 * 3) which equals 45 %.
Your character has a 45% chance to correctly construct a seaworthy small boat, this means
that any percentage roll of 45% or less is a success.

Mentalist's Disciplines: Learn 1 every three levels. The 1st at 1st level, the 2nd Discipline at 4th level, the 3rd at 7th level. You learn the 4th Discipline at 10th level, the 5th at 13th level and you learn your 6th and final Discipline at 16th level.
Your Disciplines are supplemented by many different Skills. You learn to use a total of 2 skills each level.

NUMBER OF ENCHANTED OR MENTALIST ITEMS

Level	MAX # of Enchanted or Mentalist Items Slots	Level	Max # of Enchanted or Mentalist Items Slots
1 - 2	5	11 - 12	13
3 - 4	6	13 - 14	14
5	8	15	16
6 - 7	9	16 - 17	17
8 - 9	10	18 - 19	18
10	12		

GEM PERFECTIONS RATING

GPR	Spell Classifications Held according to GPR	Name
I2	1(A)	"Included Two"
I1	2(A)	"Included One"
SI2	3(A) or 1(B)	"Slightly Included Two"
SI1	6(A) or 2(B)	"Slightly Included One"
VSI2	9(A) or 3(B) or 1(C)	"Very Slightly Included Two"
VSI1	10(A) or 6(B) or 2(C)	"Very Slightly Included One"
VVSI2	10(A) or 9(B) or 3(C) or 1(D)	"Very Very Slightly Included Two"
VVSI1	10(A) or 10(B) or 6(C) or 2(D) or 1(E)	"Very Very Slightly Included One"

When there are **different** Classes stored in the same Gem,

You can never put more than 5 spells of any one Class into that Gem. I.e. If you have a gem with a GPR of VSI2 and you are holding one Class (B) spell in it, you could only put in FIVE Class (A) spells, even through there are six slots left available.

If you only put **ONE** Class into your Enchanted Gem, you may hold up to 10 of that Class, depending on the GPR of that Enchanted Gem.

EXPERIENCE POINT TABLE

Level	XPO Total	Diff. between current and next level	20% of Diff.**
1	0	20	4
2	20	30	6
3	50	40	8
4	90	50	10
5	140	60	12
6	200	65	13
7	265	70	14
8	335	75	15
9	410	90	18
10	500	150	30
11	650	200	40
12	850	250	50
13	1,100	300	60
14	1,400	600	120
15	2,000	1,000	200
16	3,000	2,000	400
17	5,000	4,000	800
18	9,000	6,000	1,200
19	15,000	10,000	2,000
20	25,000		

If you ever gain more experience then is necessary to bring you to the next level, you may add up to 20% of what is needed to take you to your next level. This 20% amount is listed in the 4th column above.

Appendix B   **BEGINNING CHARACTER SHEETS**

NAME :   AGE   :

ENDURANCE :   OCC   : **WARRIOR** (_____)

AGILITY   :   LEVEL :

STRENGTH   :   RACE :

INTELLECT :   MR   :

WISDOM   :   RER   :

WILL   :   PTE :

Spell Points :   Regen=___/day

                                EP :

Strikes/Parries:
Total Actions :

SEX:	HANDED:	
EYES:	HAIR:	

HT: WT:

CRM:
BIRTHGIFT:

WEAPONS

Short Sword   2d6

_____

_____

ARMOR

Agility Bonus : ____%

½ Suit of Leather : +15%

ENCHANTED ITEMS

SPECIAL ABILITIES
SPELLS:

WARRIOR ABILITIES: Combat Skills

1st)   PARRY   _____% to PTE

2nd)   FEIGN STRIKE   Opponent receives no Agility bonus on their PTE roll.

3rd)   DOUBLE PROJ. RATE w/ _____ Bow   A) Shoot +1 _____ / Attack.

4th)   ACCURACY   w/ _____ Bow   A) -10% Opponent's PTE   B) -5% on your SPT roll.

5th)   SPECIALIZE   _____   A) -20% Opponent's PTE   B) -10% / -5% on SPT.

EXPERIENCE POINTS

SURVIVAL SKILLS
Boxing or Wrestling (Circle One)
Shield Use
(1)
(2)
(3)

KNOWN WEAPONS
(A)
(B)
(C)
(D)   (If Trained)

REGULAR EQUIPMENT
Standard Adventurer's Pack (SAP)

1	Back Pack
1	Large Brown Leather Sack
1	Pouch, Leather
2 wk.	Food & Water
50'	Rope
3	Torches
1	Box: Flint, Steel and Tinder
1	Skinning Knife (1d6)
1	Bedroll
1	Cooking Set (travel)
1	Sanitary Set (M or F)
1	First Aid Kit

MISC. EQUIP.

SPECIAL EQUIPMENT

WAR DOG   -

TREASURE

SILVER	MITHERAL	GEMS & JEWERLY	POCKET CHANGE
25			

NAME :

ENDURANCE :

AGILITY :

STRENGTH :

INTELLECT :

WISDOM :

WILL :

Spell Points :   Regen=___/day

Strikes/Parries:
Total Actions :

AGE :

OCC :   **SPY (_____)**

LEVEL :

RACE :

MR :

RER :

PTE :

EP :

SEX:	HANDED:
EYES:	HAIR:

HT: WT:

CRM:
BIRTHGIFT:

WEAPONS

Black Jack

Short Bow   1d10   [1/Act]

_____

ARMOR

Agility Bonus : ___%

ENCHANTED ITEMS

SPECIAL ABILITIES
SPELLS:

SPY ABILITIES   Specialized Once = √

GENERAL :   1) Conceal Object   5) Item Appropriation
               2) Conceal Self   6) Pick Locks
               3) Fall   7) Scale Walls
               4) Running Jump   8) Soundless Travel

INDIVIDUAL :

EXPERIENCE POINTS	SURVIVAL SKILLS	KNOWN WEAPONS
	(1)	(A)
	(2)	(B)
	(3)	(C)

REGULAR EQUIPMENT
Standard Adventurer's Pack (SAP)

1	Back Pack
1	Large Brown Leather Sack
1	Pouch, Leather
2 wk.	Food & Water
50'	Rope
3	Torches
1	Box: Flint, Steel and Tinder
1	Skinning Knife (1d6)
1	Bedroll
1	Cooking Set (travel)
1	Sanitary Set (M or F)
1	First Aid Kit

MISC. EQUIP.

20	Arrows
1	Quiver (1 score arrows)

SPECIAL EQUIPMENT

1   'Poor' Lock Picking Set = +0% to Lock Picking skills.

TREASURE

SILVER	MITHERAL	GEMS & JEWERLY	POCKET CHANGE
25			

NAME :

ENDURANCE :

AGILITY   :

STRENGTH   :

INTELLECT   :

WISDOM   :

WILL   :

Ki Points   :   Regen=___/day

Strikes/Parries:
Total Actions :

AGE   :

OCC   :   *NINJA*

LEVEL :

RACE :

MR   :

RER   :

PTE :

EP   :

SEX:	HANDED:
EYES:	HAIR:

HT: WT :

CRM :

BIRTHGIFT:

WEAPONS

Staff   1d10

_____

ARMOR

Agility Bonus : ____%

Gee :   15%

ENCHANTED ITEMS

A) Dust of Smoke Bomb
      (Violet)   TW = Bye!

B) Potion : _____

SPECIAL ABILITIES

BELT = _____

NINJA ABILITIES

			SPC	KI ABILITIES
1st)	Front or Circle Kick _____ Block Projectile	2d6 + Strength Bonus	12	Consolidate Ki Death Trance Heal x2 normal
2nd)	Parry _____	+_____% PTE	14 7	Go without Food & Drink WOUS : Ice
3rd)	Back Kick _____	3d6 + Strength Bonus	16	Minds Eye _____ ft.
4th)	Vow Level Tip turned:	_____ _____	18 9	Stun Strike WOUS : Mud
5th)	Flying Kick Fist Damage Bonus	4d6 + Strength Bonus 1d6 + (Strength Bonus * 2)	25	Sense Enemies R:_____ D:_____ Consolidate Ki on the Move Guardian = _____

EXPERIENCE POINTS

SURVIVAL SKILLS

Improved Charging Rate
(1)
(2)

KNOWN WEAPONS

Staff [1d10]
(A)

REGULAR EQUIPMENT
Standard Adventurer's Pack (SAP)

1	Back Pack
1	Large Brown Leather Sack
1	Pouch, Leather
2 wk.	Food & Water
50'	Rope
3	Torches
1	Box: Flint, Steel and Tinder
1	Skinning Knife (1d6)
1	Bedroll
1	Cooking Set (travel)
1	Sanitary Set (M or F)
1	First Aid Kit

MISC. EQUIP.

1	Gee (+15% PTE) - Extra
1	Map of Area (Detailed)

SPECIAL EQUIPMENT

TREASURE

SILVER	MITHERAL	GEMS & JEWERLY	POCKET CHANGE
10			

NAME :

ENDURANCE :

AGILITY   :

STRENGTH :

INTELLECT :

WISDOM   :

WILL   :

Spell Points   :   Regen=___/day

Strikes/Parries:
Total Actions :

AGE   :

OCC   :   *ENCHANTER*

LEVEL :

RACE :

MR   :

RER   :

PTE :

EP   :

SEX:	HANDED:
EYES:	HAIR:

HT: **WT:**

CRM:

BIRTHGIFT:

WEAPONS

Staff   1d10

ARMOR

Agility Bonus : ___%

SPECIAL ABILITIES

Construct Enchanted Items:
1st) Rope,String,Cloth:DM&A
2nd) Wood & Glass: DM&A
5th) Leather,Silver,Iron: D

ENCHANTED ITEMS

[Trigger Word / Phrase]

EXPERIENCE POINTS

SURVIVAL SKILLS

Rope – Making
(1)
(2)

KNOWN WEAPONS

(A)

REGULAR EQUIPMENT

Standard Adventurer's Pack (SAP)

1	Back Pack
1	Large Brown Leather Sack
1	Pouch, Leather
2 wk.	Food & Water
50'	Rope
3	Torches
1	Box: Flint, Steel and Tinder
1	Skinning Knife (1d6)
1	Bedroll
1	Cooking Set (travel)
1	Sanitary Set (M or F)
1	First Aid Kit

MISC. EQUIP.

1	Large Cloth Sack
50'	Rope
2	Quills & Bottle of Ink
1	Scroll Case
10	Paper Sheets
10	Candles
1 set	Sewing

SPECIAL EQUIPMENT

COMPANION

TREASURE

SILVER	MITHERAL	GEMS & JEWERLY	POCKET CHANGE
30			

ENCHANTER SPELLS   (Example)   [___ Slots Available]

1st		2nd		3rd	
Heal Wounds 1	15	Light 2	22	Vine Net	32
Flame Bolt 1	18	Mesmerize Animal / Bird	24	Force Bolt	33
Cube of Midnight	10	Sleep – One	24	(Shield, Melee 20%	32)
Paralysis Animal / Bird	17	Acid Spray, Mild	24	Mind Blast - One	34
Shield, Melee 10-40%	12 - 72	Gem See	23	Silence - One person	31
Daze - One	13	Nourishment	23	Duplicates	32
See Enchantment 1	9	Wall Walk	24	Weight	34
Water Bolt 1	14	See Truth	25	Cause Fear - One	34
Wind Bolt 1	12	Shield, Magic Class(A)	25	Fuse	32
Converse w/ Animal/Bird	9	Shrink Animal / Bird	23	Revel Gem Quality	31
Illusion 1	11	Slide	22	Water Adaptation	31
Shield, Projectile 10-50%	10 - 92	Language Spell	25		
Levitate	11	Disappear 1	22		
Smoke Bomb	15	(Shield, Projectile 20%	22)		
Light 1	8				
Find North	6				

4th		5th		6th	
Plant Wall	41	Lightning Bolt 1	54	Send Message	61
Flame Jet	44	(Shield, Melee 30%	52)	Slow	62
Enchant Skeletons	44	Invisibility	52	Mist of Choking	63
Sticky Surface	43	StingRay 2 (Area)	54	Age	63
Sun Light	43	Acid Spray, Medium	54	Mesmerize Person	63
Frost Jet	44	Flame Circle	52	Enchant Zombie	64
Uncontrolled Fire	43	Fly 1	52	(Shield, Projectile 40%	62)
Sleep Wall	43	Cancel Enchantment	51		
Summon Rep / F / In.	44	Shield, Magic Class (B)	55		
Return Item Spell	47	Snow Balls	57		
Summon Animal / Bird	43	Observation	52		
Cube of Midnight 2	42	Sticky Surface	53		
(Shield, Projectile 30%	42)	Paralyze Person	53		
		Resist Enchantment, Color	54		

7th		8th		9th	
Quicksand	73	Repulsion Beam	80	Part Water 1	90
Blind, Many	73	Illusion 4	81	Bubble of Force	95
Item Dance	75	Poisonous Mist	85	In Sight Teleport	95
Ice Elevator	78	Wound 2	85	(Shield, Projectile 50%	92)
Daze, Many	78	Sun Light Beam	88		
Speed	79				
Enlarge Person	71				
(Shield, Melee 40%	72)				

Note : The spells in Parenthesis are not New Spells, they are just place holders for spells learned at previous levels.   The Shield Projectile & Melee spells only need to be learned at 1st level, but to cast the better forms of the spell at later levels, you must spend more spell points.

NAME :

ENDURANCE :

AGILITY   :

STRENGTH   :

INTELLECT   :

WISDOM   :

WILL   :

Spell Points   :   Regen=___/day

Strikes/Parries:
Total Actions :

AGE   :

OCC   :   *ALCHEMIST*

LEVEL :

RACE :

MR   :

RER   :

PTE :

EP   :

SEX:	HANDED:
EYES:	HAIR:

HT: WT:

CRM:

BIRTHGIFT:

WEAPONS

Mace   1d10+1

Woodman's Axe   1d12+2

ARMOR

Agility Bonus : ___%

½ Suit of Leather : +15%

SPECIAL ABILITIES
1st Level
1) Enchant Potions
2) Converse w/Plants: 3/d
3) Converse w/LifeT:@Will
5th Level
1) Plant Growth: 1/day
2) +25% vs. Ench. Poison
3) Immune Non-Ench.P/V

ENCHANTED ITEMS

POTIONS	DUSTS	PILLS
	5'+ R:	1'/L + R:

EXPERIENCE POINTS

SURVIVAL SKILLS

Plant Identification :
(1)
(2)
(3)

KNOWN WEAPONS

(A)
(B)

REGULAR EQUIPMENT

Standard Adventurer's Pack (SAP)

1	Back Pack
1	Large Brown Leather Sack
1	Pouch, Leather
2 wk.	Food & Water
50'	Rope
3	Torches
1	Box: Flint, Steel and Tinder
1	Skinning Knife (1d6)
1	Bedroll
1	Cooking Set (travel)
1	Sanitary Set (M or F)
1	First Aid Kit

MISC. EQUIP.

SPECIAL EQUIPMENT

COMPANION

TREASURE

SILVER
15

MITHERAL

GEMS & JEWERLY

POCKET CHANGE

** 1st **		2nd		3rd	
Revitalize Nature	10 - 50	** Shield, Class A	25	** Heal Wounds2	30
Heal Wounds 1	15	** Shrink Animal / Bird	23	** Vine Net	32
Light 1	8	Acid Spray, Mild	24	** Vine Arms	35
Water Bolt 1	14	Sleep, ONE	24	** Plant Wall	31
Cube of Midnight	15	See Truth or Lie	20	** Force Bolt	33
Daze, ONE	13	See Morality Rate	20	** Weight	34
Converse w/ An & Bird	9	See Life	20	Mind Blast, ONE	34
Shield, Projectile 10-50%	10 - 92	Magnification Sight	20	Reveal Gem Quality	31
Float	2	Telescopic Sight	20	Water Adaptation	31
Wind Bolt 1	12	Converse w/ Rep,F&I	21	Duplicates	31
Illusion 1	11			Cloud Summon, Rain	32
Fire Bolt 1	18			Revel Gem Quality	31
See Enchantment	8			Use Weapon Spell	31
Shield, Melee 10-40%	12 - 72				
Glowing Hand	5				
Find North	6				
Purify Water	5				
Breeze	8				
Converse w/ Animal/Bird	9				

4th		5th		6th	
** Plant Growth	42	** Heal Poison	50	** Heal Disease	60
** Heal Blindness	40	** Heal Paralyzation	55 / 75	Enchant Zombie	64
** Plant Wall	41	** Potion to Dust	20	Slow	62
Sunlight	46	** Dust to Pill	20	Stone Mold	62
Sleep Wall	43	** Force Net	56	Send Message	61
Summon An &B	43	** Shield, Magic, Class B	55		
Return Item Spell	47	** Enlarge Animal/Bird	51		
Wind Jet	44	** Wound 1	53		
Frost Jet	44	Fly	52		
See Enchantment, Area	40	Cancel Enchantment	51		
Summon Animal / Bird	43	Frost Barrier	52		
Summon Rep/F/I	44	Resist Enchantment, Color	54		
Howard's Cave	41	Acid Spray, Medium	54		
Cube of Midnight 2	42	Sting Ray, Area	54		

7th		8th		9th	
** Plant Decay	71	** Wound 2	85	** Bubble of Force	95
** Shrink Person	71	** Repulsion Beam	80	Part Water 1	90
** Enlarge Person	71	Poisonous Mist	85	In Sight Teleport	95
Speed	79	Illusion 4	81		
Item Dance	75				
Daze, Many	77				

**   MAY ONLY CAST THESE SPELLS INTO THE ENVIROMENT.
ALL OTHERS MUST BE CAST INTO POTIONS AND THEN THEY MAY BE CONVERTED TO
ALCHMIST DUSTS AND PILLS

NAME :

ENDURANCE :

AGILITY :

STRENGTH :

INTELLECT :

WISDOM :

WILL :

SPELL POINTS :   Regen=___/day

Strikes/Parries:
Total Actions :

AGE :

OCC : *ELEMENTALIST*

LEVEL :

RACE :

MR :

RER :

PTE :

EP :

SEX:	HANDED:
EYES:	HAIR:

HT: **WT:**

CRM:

BIRTHGIFT:

WEAPONS

2 Javelins   1d12   [1/Act]

ARMOR

Agility Bonus : ____%

½ Suit of Leather : +15%

SPECIAL ABILITIES

1) Enchant Rings
   A) One Stone @ 1st Lvl.
   B) Two Stones @ 5th

ENCHANTED ITEMS

[Trigger Word / Phrase]

EXPERIENCE POINTS	SURVIVAL SKILLS	KNOWN WEAPONS
	Ring Making	(A)
	(1)	
	(2)	

REGULAR EQUIPMENT
Standard Adventurer's Pack (SAP)

1	Back Pack
1	Large Brown Leather Sack
1	Pouch, Leather
2 wk.	Food & Water
50'	Rope
3	Torches
1	Box: Flint, Steel and Tinder
1	Skinning Knife (1d6)
1	Bedroll
1	Cooking Set (travel)
1	Sanitary Set (M or F)
1	First Aid Kit

MISC. EQUIP.

SPECIAL EQUIPMENT

TREASURE

SILVER	MITHERAL	GEMS & JEWERLY	POCKET CHANGE
30			

ELEMENTALIST SPELLS   (Example) [__ Slots Available]

1st		2nd		3rd	
Converse w/ Elementals	0/1	Converse w/ Clouds	21	Flame Jet	35
Flame Bolt 1	16	Water Walk, calm	23	Wind Jet	35
Whirl Wind 1	15	Wind Wall	22	Earth Armor 20%	32
Earth Armor 10%	12	Water Adaptation	21	Wind Circle	34
Stone Storm 1	17	Control Flames	23	Frost Jet	35
Levitate	12	Water Control 1	23	Wind Barrier	34
Paralysis Animal / Bird	15				
Water Bolt 1	14				
Wind Bolt 1	10				
Blue Flame	6				
Flaming Hand	12				
Air Bubble	10				
Extinguish Reg. Flames	10				
Levitate	12				
Stone Move 1	8				
Sparking Fingers	8				
Ice Walk	8				
Slide	12				
Cloud Part	5				
Glide	14				

4th		5th		6th	
Flame Barrier	42	Invisibility	55	Cloud Cover	61
Flame Bolt 2	43	Burn	55	Ice Elevator	61
Fly 1	43	Stone Storm 2	53	Water Spout	61
Paralysis Person	44	Stone Crumble 1	52	Land Slide	62
Ice Sheet	44	Earth Armor 30%	52	Hole	63
Snow Balls	43	Mold Mud	50		
Wind Blast 2	43	Ring Spin	50		
Mud Walk	41	Resist Poisons	51		
Mud Pool	43	Mud to Dust 1	52		
Water Control 2	42				
Uncontrolled Fire	48				

7th		8th		9th	
Paralysis Wall	71	Fire Bolt 3	80	Water Bolt 3	94
Part Water	71	Whirl Wind 3	83	Wind Bolt 3	94
Snow Storm	72	Fly 2	85	Ice Spikes	95
				Wind Globe	91

NOTE: Many Slots are left available so you can pick spells depending on what Elements are represented by your Rings / Disks.

NAME :

ENDURANCE :

AGILITY :

STRENGTH :

INTELLECT :

WISDOM :

WILL :

Mental Points :   Regen=___/day

Strikes/Parries:
Total Actions :

AGE :

OCC : *MENTALIST*

LEVEL :

RACE :

MR :

RER :

PTE :

EP :

SEX:	HANDED:
EYES:	HAIR:

HT: WT:

CRM:

BIRTHGIFT:

WEAPONS

2	Th. Daggers	1d8	[1/Act]
1	Club	1d8	

ARMOR

Agility Bonus : ___%

½ Suit of Leather : +15%

ENCHANTED ITEMS

SPECIAL ABILITIES
SPELLS:

MENTALIST ABILITIES

EXPERIENCE POINTS

SURVIVAL SKILLS

_____ Ability: +2
(1)
(2)

KNOWN WEAPONS

(A)
(B)

REGULAR EQUIPMENT

Standard Adventurer's Pack (SAP)

1	Back Pack
1	Large Brown Leather Sack
1	Pouch, Leather
2 wk.	Food & Water
50'	Rope
3	Torches
1	Box: Flint, Steel and Tinder
1	Skinning Knife (1d6)
1	Bedroll
1	Cooking Set (travel)
1	Sanitary Set (M or F)
1	First Aid Kit

MISC. EQUIP.

SPECIAL EQUIPMENT

TREASURE

SILVER	MITHERAL	GEMS & JEWERLY	POCKET CHANGE
25			

NAME :   AGE   :

ENDURANCE :   OCC   :

AGILITY   :   LEVEL :

STRENGTH   :   RACE :

INTELLECT   :   MR   :

WISDOM   :   RER   :

WILL   :   ## PTE :

_____ Points :   Regen=___/day

                          ## EP :

Strikes/Parries:
Total Actions :

SEX:	HANDED:
EYES:	HAIR:

HT: WT:

CRM:

BIRTHGIFT:

WEAPONS   ## ARMOR   ## ENCHANTED ITEMS

Agility Bonus : ____%

ABILITIES :

EXPERIENCE POINTS   **SURVIVAL SKILLS**   **KNOWN WEAPONS**

REGULAR EQUIPMENT   **MISC. EQUIP.**

Standard Adventurer's Pack (SAP)

1	Back Pack
1	Large Brown Leather Sack
1	Pouch, Leather
2 wk.	Food & Water
50'	Rope
3	Torches
1	Box: Flint, Steel and Tinder
1	Skinning Knife (1d6)
1	Bedroll
1	Cooking Set (travel)
1	Sanitary Set (M or F)
1	First Aid Kit

SPECIAL EQUIPMENT   **ANIMAL / COMPAINION**

TREASURE

SILVER   **MITHERAL**   **GEMS & JEWERLY**   **POCKET CHANGE**

Appendix C 5th *LEVEL CHARACTER SHEETS*

NAME : **ROGE WITHERSTREAM**   AGE : 24

ENDURANCE :	19		OCC :	**WARRIOR** (Schooled)

SEX: Male	HANDED: R
EYES: Dull Yellow	HAIR: Red

AGILITY   :   17   9% PTE   LEVEL :   5th

STRENGTH   :   20   +4 Dam.   RACE :   HUMAN

INTELLECT :   16   MR :   9

WISDOM   :   10   RER :   20 %

WILL   :   12

PTE : 54% [63%]

Spell Points :   21   Regen=3/day

HT: 7.0'   WT: 300 lbs.

EP :   62

CRM: 3

BIRTHGIFT:

Strikes/Parries: 1 / 2
Total Actions :   3

WEAPONS

Hand+1/2 Sword	1d20 +4	[2/Att]
Long Bow	1d10	[4/Att]
Axe, 1 handed	1d12 +4	
Hammer, Battle	2d8 +4	

ARMOR

Agility Bonus (9%)

Mail Shirt (+35%)

Large Metal Shield (+10%)

Large Helm

Parry (Melee) (+9%)

ENCHANTED ITEMS
(Used/Total: 8/8)

1) Potion:(1) of Heal Wounds (B)
   EP = 60

2) Armband:(6)
   ONYX = VSI2

A) Cancel Enchantment (C)
   TW= Cancel (58 SP)

3) Potion:(1) Prot. Vs Proj. (C)
   (+30% PTE vs. Proj.)

SPECIAL ABILITIES

Total Spell Points: 16+1/level = 21

SPELLS:		SPC	R	D	
	1) Converse w/An. or Bird	SPC = 9	R: 10'	D: 5 min.	(Jed)
	2) See Enchantment	SPC = 9	R: 10'	D: 5 min.	
	3) Shield, Projectile, 10%	SPC = 10	R: T	D: 60 min.	
	4) Shield, Melee, 10%	SPC = 12	R: T	D: 30 min	
	5) Heal Wounds 1	SPC = 15			
	6) Cube of Midnight	SPC = 16	R:5'+1'/L	AOE: 20' x 20' x 20'	

WARRIOR ABILITIES: Combat Skills

1st) PARRY   +9% to PTE

2nd) FEIGN STRIKE   Opponent receives no Agility bonus on their PTE roll.

3rd) DOUBLE PROJ. RATE w/ Long Bow   A) Shoot +1 arrow / Attack.

4th) ACCURACY   w/ Long Bow   A) -10% Opponent's PTE   B) -5% on your SPT roll.

5th) SPECIALIZE   HAND+1/2 Sword   A) -20% Opponent's PTE   B) -10% / -5% on SPT.

EXPERIENCE POINTS	SURVIVAL SKILLS	KNOWN WEAPONS
142	Boxing	(Learned to Cast Spells)
	Shield Use	Long Bow
	Fire Starting: 30%	Axe, 1 handed
	Horsemanship: 48% (But, Auto Agl)	Hammer, Battle
	Detect Ambush: +20%	Hand+1/2 Sword – Specialized.
	Attack Unseen Enemy	
	Locate Traps: 45%	
	Tracking: 30%	

REGULAR EQUIPMENT
Standard Adventurer's Pack (SAP)

1	Back Pack
1	Large Brown Leather Sack
1	Pouch, Leather
2 wk.	Food & Water
50'	Rope
3	Torches
1	Box: Flint, Steel and Tinder
1	Skinning Knife (1d6)
1	Bedroll
1	Cooking Set (travel)
1	Sanitary Set (M)
1	First Aid Kit

MISC. EQUIP.

20	Arrows
1	Quiver (20 Arrows)

SPECIAL EQUIPMENT

WAR DOG   - JED

EP	: 40	PTE	: 45%
Strikes	: 1	Dam	: 1d10+1

Lock Jaw = Successful Hit equals Automatic
Damage on successive Att.

Trained Commands	Whistles
Guard	Low
Attack	High
Track	Wolf
Come to Me	Double
Retrieve	Long

TREASURE

SILVER	MITHERAL	GEMS & JEWERLY	POCKET CHANGE
100			400 Iron Pieces on
			4 Leather Rings

NAME : WILLAMINA (SASHA NIGHTSHADE)   AGE : 16

			SEX: Female	HANDED: L
			EYES: Green	HAIR: Blonde

ENDURANCE : 17   OCC : **SPY** (Formal Training)

AGILITY : 20   +10% PTE   LEVEL : 5th

STRENGTH : 16   +2 Dam.   RACE : Human

INTELLECT : 17   (3 Spy Skills/Adv)   MR : 12

WISDOM : 13   RER : 20 %

WILL : 12

PTE : 30% [35%]

Spell Points : 22   Regen=3/day

EP : 50

HT: 5.0'   WT: 120 lbs.

CRM: 3

Strikes/Parries: 1 / 2   BIRTHGIFT:
Total Actions : 3

WEAPONS

Long Sword   2d8 + 2

Short Bow   1d10   [3/Att]

Black Jack   ***

ARMOR

Agility Bonus (+10%)

Full Suit Leather (20%)

Small Shield (5%)

ENCHANTED ITEMS
(Used/Total: 8/8)

1) <u>BLACKJACK</u>(4)Indi= SI2
   A) Sleep - One
      TW = Sleep

2) <u>POTION</u>(1): Heal Poison

3) <u>DUST</u>(2): Heal Wounds
      Healing = 50 EP

4) <u>POTION</u>(1): of Invisibility

SPECIAL ABILITIES

Total Spell Points: 17 + 1/L = 22

SPELLS:

1) Light	SPC = 8	R: T	D: 1 hr./L	AOE: 20' rad.
2) See Enchantment	SPC = 8	R: 10'	D: 1 hr./L	
3) Shield, Projectile, 10%	SPC = 10	R: T	D: 60 min.	
4) Bridge, 15'	SPC = 11	R: 5'	D: 5 min.	
5) Shield Melee, 10%	SPC = 12	R: T	D: 30 min.	
6) Blind – One	SPC = 15	R: 15'	D: 2+1d4 Actions	
7) Smoke Bomb	SPC = 16	R: 10'+1'/L	D: 2 min.	AOE: 20'+1/L (25')

SPY ABILITIES

Specialized Once = √

GENERAL :

1) Item Appropriation	40% outside / 20% inside	√	5) Pick Locks	41% (+3% = Picks)
2) Conceal Object	35% for 2 Obj.@ 6 in. ea.		6) Running Jump	40'
√ 3) Conceal Self	50%		7) Scale Walls	1 foot / Att.
4) Fall	70 ft. for NO dam.		8) Soundless Travel	CRM = 1

INDIVIDUAL :

1) Unseen Attack ***		4) Roll & Evade*	Regular PTE + 25%
√ 2) Remove Trap	60% @ 2 sq.ft. or 65% for Locks	5) Spy Fingers	Ardric Agency
3) Find Concealed Areas	51% @ 2x2 area	6) Disguise Self: 51%	current = 20%
			[Old Beggar]

*   = Fall an Extra 10' and receive NO damage.   ***   = -20% on SPT roll.
Stun Victim for 1d10 Attacks & 5% chance per Strength Point (80%) to knock victim out for 2d10 Attacks.
Add Additional +1 EP / Level (+5) to Damage.

EXPERIENCE POINTS	SURVIVAL SKILLS	KNOWN WEAPONS

EXPERIENCE POINTS

142

SURVIVAL SKILLS

Locate Traps: 51% @ 2x2
Shield Use
Horsemanship: 51% (But, Auto Agl)
Measure Distance by Sound: 51%
Agility: 19+1
Endurance: 16+1

KNOWN WEAPONS

(Learned to Cast Spells)
Black Jack
Short Bow
Long Sword

REGULAR EQUIPMENT

Standard Adventurer's Pack (SAP)

1	Back Pack
1	Large Brown Leather Sack
1	Pouch, Leather
2 wk.	Food & Water
50'	Rope
3	Torches
1	Box: Flint, Steel and Tinder
1	Skinning Knife (1d6)
1	Bedroll
1	Cooking Set (travel)
1	Sanitary Set (F)
1	First Aid Kit

MISC. EQUIP.

1	Grappling Hook
50'	Rope
20	Arrows
1	Quiver (20 arrows)

SPECIAL EQUIPMENT

1	'Fair' Lock Picking Set = +3% to Lock Picking Skills
1	Ardric Agency Iron Piece Badge
	– disguised within a Leather Ring.

TREASURE

SILVER	MITHERAL	GEMS & JEWERLY	POCKET CHANGE
100	8	1 Topaz (Non-Enchanted) ½ Karat	500 Iron Pieces on 5 Leather Rings

NAME : KLOAK(Cloak) **WHITEFLAME**   AGE : 26

ENDURANCE :	19		OCC :	**NINJA**	
AGILITY :	19	+10% PTE	LEVEL :	5th	
STRENGTH :	17	+3 Dam.	RACE :	Human	
INTELLECT :	17		MR :	10	
WISDOM :	20	+5% D.Amb.	RER :	20 %	
WILL :	15				

SEX: Male   HANDED: R
EYES: Light Brown   HAIR: Black

Ki Points : 50   Regen=3/day

PTE : **25% [35%]**

EP : **54**

Strikes/Parries: 1 / 2
Total Actions : 3

HT: 6.0'   WT: 200lbs.
CRM: 4
BIRTHGIFT:

WEAPONS

Ninja - To	1d20 +3	
Staff	1d10 +3	
Long Bow	1d10	[3/Att]

ARMOR

Agility Bonus	(10%)
Gee	(15%)
Parry (Melee)	(10%)

ENCHANTED ITEMS
(Used/Total: 8/8)

A) Dust(2) of Heal Wounds 2 (B)
    TW = Heal   EP = 55

B) ARMBAND(2)
    Invisibility (Given) TW=Bye

C) Alchemist Pill(2)
    Heal Wounds (B) EP: 50

D) CLOAK(2=Given)
    Shield, Melee(30%)
    TW=Knife

SPECIAL ABILITIES
NINJA ABILITIES

BELT = GREEN

		SPC	KI ABILITIES

1st)	Front or Circle Kick	2d6 + Strength Bonus			Consolidate Ki - Using a KI Position
	Conceal Self	39%		12	Death Trance
	Block Projectile	57% / 24%	3 Projectiles		Heal x2 normal = 2d10 EP
2nd)	Parry	+10% PTE		14	Go without Food & Drink
	Scale Walls	1 ft / Att.		7	WOUS : Ice
3rd)	Back Kick	3d6 + Strength Bonus		16	Minds Eye 5 ft. / Level = 25'
	Soundless Travel	Rate = CRM: 1			
4th)	Vow Level	Absence of Ki (+10 KP)		18	Stun Strike Stunned= Level + 1d4 Act.
		Tip turned : Silver		9	WOUS : Mud
5th)	Flying Kick	4d6 + Strength Bonus + % to Stun		25	Sense Enemies R: 250' D:50 min.
	Fist/Foot Dam Bonus	1d6 + (Strength Bonus* 2)			Consolidate Ki on the Move
					Guardian = Castlin

EXPERIENCE POINTS	SURVIVAL SKILLS	KNOWN WEAPONS

EXPERIENCE POINTS

142

SURVIVAL SKILLS

Improved Charging Rate
Bower / Fletcher: 51%
Locate Traps: 51%   2x2 area
Tracking: 60%
Horsemanship: 51% (But, Auto Agl Bonus)
Detect Ambush: +20%

KNOWN WEAPONS

Ninja - To
Staff
Long Bow

REGULAR EQUIPMENT

Standard Adventurer's Pack (SAP)

1		Back Pack
1		Large Brown Leather Sack
1		Pouch, Leather
2 wk.		Food & Water
50'		Rope
3		Torches
1		Box: Flint, Steel and Tinder
1		Skinning Knife (1d6)
1		Bedroll
1		Cooking Set (travel)
1		Sanitary Set (M)
1		First Aid Kit

1   Flask of Oil
1   Lantern

MISC. EQUIP.

1	Gee (+15% PTE) - Extra
1	Map of Area (Detailed)
20	Arrows
1	Quiver (20 Arrows)

SPECIAL EQUIPMENT

10   Shafts for Arrows
10   Arrow Tips
30   Feathers

TREASURE

SILVER	MITHERAL	GEMS & JEWERLY	POCKET CHANGE
100			300 Iron Pieces on 3 Leather Rings

NAME : CASTLIN (Cast-lin) **LONGSTAR**   AGE :   28

ENDURANCE :   17   OCC : **ENCHANTER**

AGILITY   :   16   +8% PTE   LEVEL :   5th

STRENGTH   :   12   RACE :   HUMAN

INTELLECT :   20   10 Sp / L   MR :   12

WISDOM   :   18   +3% D.Amb. RER : 20 % (30% vs. Fire)

WILL   :   15   PTE :   23%

Spell Points :   60   Regen=3/day

EP : 38 [43-5]

HT: 6'   WT: 200 lbs.

CRM: 3

BIRTHGIFT:

Strikes/Parries: 1 / 2
Total Actions :   3

WEAPONS

Short Sword 2d6

Staff - His 1d10

Crossbow   1d8 + 1   [2 Act/1 Quarrel]

ARMOR

Agility Bonus (8%)

1/2 Suit Leather (15%)

SPECIAL ABILITIES

Construct Enchanted Items:
1st) Rope,Cloth,String:DM&A
2nd) Wood & Glass: DM&A
5th) Leather, Silver, Iron: D

ENCHANTED ITEMS (Used/Total: 8/8)   [Trigger Word / Phrase]

STAFF(1)(A) Spells   1: Frost Jet   10+1d6 +1d6/Att R:30' D:10 Act TW: Chill'in
           2: Cancel Enchantment (60 SP) R:30'   TW: Not Today
    (B) Telekinesis: 40'   (C) +10% RER vs. Fire
    (D) 1/2 EPs spent for Spells   (E) May Shrink Staff to 1' Long
    (F) May use as weapon.

WAND – Red Zonith(2) (A) Uncontrolled Fire R:50' Dam: 10 + 2d10   TW: Boom
            (B) Uncontrolled Fire R:50' Dam: 10 + 2d10

L. ARMBAND(1) (Rope) (A) Shield, Melee 30%   TW: Shield

HEADBAND(4)   (A) See Enchantment (1)   TW: Sight beyond Sight
Helidor = SI2   (B) Heal Wounds (34 EP)   TW: Feel the Power of Comedy

EXPERIENCE POINTS	SURVIVAL SKILLS	KNOWN WEAPONS

EXPERIENCE POINTS

142

SURVIVAL SKILLS

Rope Making: 45%
Measure Dist by Sight: 60%
Blind Shot & Accurate Pass: 48%
Wood Working: 45%
Sewing: 45%
Identify Precious Gems: 60%

KNOWN WEAPONS

Short Sword
Cross Bow
Castlin's Zonith Staff - only

REGULAR EQUIPMENT

Standard Adventurer's Pack (SAP)

1	Back Pack
1	Large Brown Leather Sack
1	Pouch, Leather
2 wk.	Food & Water
50'	Rope
3	Torches
1	Box: Flint, Steel and Tinder
1	Skinning Knife (1d6)
1	Bedroll
1	Cooking Set (travel)
1	Sanitary Set (M)
1	First Aid Kit

MISC. EQUIP.

1	Large Cloth Sack
100'	Rope
2	Quills & Bottle of Ink
1	Scroll Case
10	Paper Sheets
10	Candles
1 set	Sewing
20	Quarrels
1	Quiver (20 Quarrels)

SPECIAL EQUIPMENT

COMPANION: Humming Bird

Speedy: Original =Wooden hummingbird
EP = 10 & 40 = Once per day
PTE = 15 (65) & 40 (85*) Once per day
Dam = 1d4 & 1d10+3 Once per day
Size = 6" & 6 feet tall Once per day
Gem = Helidor @ VSI2 [1 (C) or 3 (B), ect.]
          Location = Center of Breast
   1) Sting Ray – Area:
       # of Victims: 5
       R: 35'   AOE: 20' rad.
       Damage: 12+1d10

*Note: Nothing may exceed 85% PTE.

TREASURE

SILVER	MITHERAL	GEMS & JEWERLY	POCKET CHANGE
100			100 Iron Pieces on 1 Leather Ring

CASTLIN'S SPELLS　　　　(5 Open Spell Slots)

1st		2nd		3rd	
Heal Wounds 1	15	(Shield, Projectile 20%	22)	Vine Net	32
Flame Bolt 1	18	Mesmerize Animal / Bird	24	Force Bolt	33
Cube of Midnight	10	Sleep - One	24	(Shield, Melee 20%	32)
Paralyze Animal / Bird	17	Acid Spray, Mild	24	Mind Blast - One person	34
Shield, Melee 10%	12	Gem See	23	Silence - One person	31
Daze - One	13	Nourishment	23	Duplicates	32
See Enchantment 1	9	Wall Walk	24	Weight	34
Water Bolt 1	14	See Truth	25		
Wind Bolt 1	12	Shield, Magic Class(A)	25		
Converse w/ Animal/Bird	9				
Illusion 1	11				
Shield, Projectile 10%	10				
Levitate	11				
Smoke Bomb	15				
Float	2				

4th		5th		6th
Plant Wall	41	Lightning Bolt 1	54	
Flame Jet	44	(Shield, Melee 30%	52)	
(Shield, Projectile 30%	42)	Invisibility	52	
Sticky Surface	43	StingRay - Area	54	
Sun Light	43	Acid Spray, Medium	54	
Frost Jet	44	Flame Barrier	52	
Uncontrolled Fire	43	Fly 1	52	
Sleep Wall	43	Cancel Enchantment	51	
		Shield, Magic Class (B)	55	
		Snow Balls	57	

Note : The spells in Parenthesis are not New Spells, they are just place holders for spells learned at previous levels. The Shield Projectile & Melee spells only need to be learned at 1st level, but to cast the better forms of the spell at later levels, you must spend more spell points.

NAME : **VIOLET AUTUMLEAF**   AGE :   19

ENDURANCE :   18   OCC   : **ALCHEMIST**

AGILITY   :   16   +8% PTE   LEVEL :   5

STRENGTH :   17   +3 Dam.   RACE :   HUMAN

INTELLECT :   20   10 Sp/L   MR   :   12

WISDOM   :   13   RER   :   20 (25%)

WILL   :   13   **PTE :   53%**

Spell Points :   60   Regen=3/day

                                           EP : 39 [44-5]

Strikes/Parries: 1 / 2
Total Actions :   3

HT: 6'   WT: 175 lbs.

CRM: 5

BIRTHGIFT:

WEAPONS

Mace	1d10+1	+3
Woodman's Axe	1d12+2	+3
Short Bow	1d10	[3/Att]

ARMOR

Agility Bonus (+8%)

Mail Shirt (+35%)

Small Shield (+5%)

Enchanted Beret,
    Raspberry(2)
    (+5% PTE & RER)
(Protects Eyes & Conceals Face)

SPECIAL ABILITIES
1st Level
1) Enchant Potions
2) Converse w/Plants: 3/d
3) Converse w/LifeT:@Will
5th Level
1) Plant Growth: 1/day
2) +25% vs. Ench. Poison
3) Immune Non-Ench.P/V

ENCHANTED ITEMS (Used/Total: 8/8)

| Elementalist Disk(6) | (A) Water Bolt 1 | R: 27' | Dam: 4+2d8 + water | TW: Sink |
| Blue Quartz = I1 | (B) Water Bolt 1 | R: 27' | Dam: 4+2d8 + water | TW: Swim |

POTIONS(0)

2	Healing @ 54 EP
2	Healing @ 60 EP
3	See Enchantment
2	Shield, Melee = +30% PTE
2	Shield, Proj. = +30% PTE
1	Heal Blindness
1	Invisibility
3	Light 1

DUSTS(0-Unless stated after spell)
5'+ R:

2	Heal Wounds @ 36 EP
1	Sting Ray – One
1	Flame Bolt 1
1	Water Bolt 1
2	Acid Spray, Mild

PILLS(0-Unless stated after spell)
1'/L + R:

2	Float
1	Con w/ An/Bird
1	Cube of Midnight

EXPERIENCE POINTS

142

SURVIVAL SKILLS

Identify Plants: 60%
Shield Use
Improved Charging Rate (1st Sp.)
First Aid: 1st Sp. = 70%
Tracking: 39%

KNOWN WEAPONS

Mace
Axe
Short Bow

REGULAR EQUIPMENT

Standard Adventurer's Pack (SAP)

1	Back Pack
1	Large Brown Leather Sack
1	Pouch, Leather
2 wk.	Food & Water
50'	Rope
3	Torches
1	Box: Flint, Steel and Tinder
1	Skinning Knife (1d6)
1	Bedroll
1	Cooking Set (travel)
1	Sanitary Set (F)
1	First Aid Kit

MISC. EQUIP.

20	Arrows
1	Quiver (20 arrows)

SPECIAL EQUIPMENT

1	**Alchemist Set, Advanced**
2	Potion Bandoliers
2	Dust Armbands
1	Pill Box
7	Empty Potion Vials

Enchanted Dusts
1 Karat = Emerald

COMPANION: Bear

**Teddy: Original form=Metal Belt Buckle
             with a Small Bear Engraving**
EP = 10 & 40 Once per day
PTE = 15 & 40 Once per day*
Dam = 1d4 & 1d10+3 Once per day
Size = 1 foot & 6 feet tall Once per day
        1) Lightning Bolt 1 = R: 40'
              Dam: 12+2d10

*Note: Nothing may exceed 85% PTE.

TREASURE

SILVER	MITHERAL	GEMS & JEWERLY	POCKET CHANGE
50			300 Iron Pieces on 3 Leather Rings

** 1st **

Revitalize Nature - 10,   25, 50=Small Field
Heal Wounds 1   -   15
Light 1   -   8;   20' rad;   1hr/L
Water Bolt 1   -   14;   20+1/L;   4+1d12
Cube of Midnight - 15;   5+1/L; $10'^3$ 5 min
Daze, ONE   -   13;   15'+1'/L;   2+1d4Att
Con. with An &B -   9;   10'/L;   5 min.
Shield, Projectile -10=10%, 22=20%, 42=30 60 min.
Float   -   2;   10';   5 min.
Wind Bolt 1   -   12;   25+1/L;   4+1d12
Illusion 1   -   11;   20+1/L;   5 min.
Fire Bolt 1   -   18;   15+1/L;   4+1d20
See Enchantment -   9;   6"-2';   5 min.
Shield, Melee   -12=10%, 32=20%,52=30 30 min.
Weap. Quality   -   10
Sting Ray 1   -   10

2nd

** Shield, Class A -   25;   15 min.
Con. with Rep,F&I - 21;   10'/L;   5 min.
Acid Spray, Mild   - 24;   15+1/L6+3d6;
Sleep, ONE   - 24;   15+1/L

3rd

** Heal Wounds2- 30;
** Force Bolt   - 33;   25'+1'/L;   8+2d8 + 1d8/CRM
** Vine Net   - 32;   25'+1'/L;   5 min.
** Plant Wall   - 31;   AOE:15'x15';   15 min
Water Adaptation- 31;   5'+1'/L;   30 min/L
Duplicates   - 31;   Dups=2;   3 min.
Mind Blast, ONE - 34;   20'+1'/L;   8+1d12+Daze
Reveal Gem Qual- 31;   GPR=2 Gems   1 min.

4th

** Plant Growth   - 42;
** Heal Blindness- 40;
Sunlight   - 46;
Sleep Wall   - 43;
Summon An &B   - 43;
Return Item Spell- 47;
Wind Jet   - 44;
Frost Jet   - 44;

5th

** Potion to Dust - 20
** Dust to Pill   - 20
** Force Net   - 56
** Heal Para.   - 55
** Heal Wound 2 - 50
** Wound 1   - 53
** Enlarge An/B - 51
** Plant Control - 51
Acid Spray, Med.- 54
Lightning Bolt 1 - 54
Snow Balls   - 57
Resist Enchant   - 54
Fly 1   - 52

6th

**   MAY ONLY CAST THESE SPELLS INTO THE ENVIROMENT
 - ALL OTHER SPELLS MUST BE CAST INTO POTIONS AND THEN MAY BE CONVERTED TO DUSTS OR
      PILLS!

NAME : JEWELS FOXYTAIL

ENDURANCE :	20	
AGILITY :	16	+8% PTE
STRENGTH :	13	+1 Dam.
INTELLECT :	20	10 Spells/L
WISDOM :	15	+3% D.Amb.
WILL :	14	

AGE :		27
OCC :	*ELEMENTALIST*	
LEVEL :		5th
RACE :		HUMAN
MR :		8
RER :		20 %

Spell Points : 60   Regen=3/day

PTE : 23% [36%]

EP : 48

Strikes/Parries: 1 / 1
Total Actions : 3

HT: 5.5'   WT: 135 lbs.
CRM: 3
BIRTHGIFT:

WEAPONS

Mace	1d10 +1	
Cross Bow	1d8 +2	[2 Act/1 Quarrel]

ARMOR

Agility Bonus (+8%)

1/2 Suit Leather (+15%)

Large Ransium Shield (+13%)

Small Helm

SPECIAL ABILITIES

1) Enchant Rings
   A) One Stone: 1st Lvl
   B) Two Stones: 5th

ENCHANTED ITEMS (Used/Total: 8/8)

[Trigger Word / Phrase]

EL. RING(3)					
SI2	(1) Blue Flame (A)	D: 1 hr/L	AOE: 20' rad.		TW: Stellar
Red.Q. + Mith	(2) Flaming Hand (A)		4+1d10		TW: Steam
	(3) Flame Bolt 1 (A)	R: 30'	4+1d20		TW: Spark

EL. RING(4)					
SI2 & SI2	(1) Earth Barrier (B)	20'tallx30'dia.x1'thick Barrier or Wall			TW: Circle (Krill)
Br.Q&Cl.Q.	(2) Con. w/ Elemental (A)	R: 75'			TW: Tower of Bable (K)
+ Mithral	(3) Water Bolt 1 (A)	4+2d8+water	A: 1 victim		TW: Shower (Krill)
	(4) Slide (A)				TW: Glide (Krill)

POTION(1)   Heal Wounds @ 50 EP

310

EXPERIENCE POINTS

142

SURVIVAL SKILLS

Ring Making: 42%
Shield Use
Horsemanship: 60% (But, Auto Agl)
Endurance: 19+1
Identify Precious Gems: 60%
First Aid: 60%

KNOWN WEAPONS

Mace
Cross Bow

REGULAR EQUIPMENT

Standard Adventurer's Pack (SAP)

1	Back Pack
1	Large Brown Leather Sack
1	Pouch, Leather
2 wk.	Food & Water
50'	Rope
3	Torches
1	Box: Flint, Steel and Tinder
1	Skinning Knife (1d6)
1	Bedroll
1	Cooking Set (travel)
1	Sanitary Set (F)
1	First Aid Kit

MISC. EQUIP.

20	Quarrels
1	Quiver (20 Quarrels)

SPECIAL EQUIPMENT

Elementalist Equipment, Advanced

TREASURE

SILVER	MITHERAL	GEMS & JEWERLY	POCKET CHANGE
100			100 Iron Pieces on 1 Leather Ring

JEWEL'S SPELLS (2 Open Spell Slots)

1st		2nd		3rd	
Converse w/ Elementals	0/1	Converse with Clouds	21	Flame Jet	35
Flame Bolt 1	16	Water Walk, calm	23	Wind Jet	35
Whirl Wind 1	15	Wind Wall	22	(Earth Armor 20%	32)
Earth Armor 10%	12	Water Adaptation	21	Wind Barrier	34
Stone Storm 1	17	Control Flames	23	Frost Jet	35
Levitate	12	Water Control 1	23		
Paralyze Animal / Bird	15				
Water Bolt 1	14				
Wind Bolt 1	10				
Blue Flame	6				
Flaming Hand	12				
Air Bubble	10				
Extinguish Reg. Flames	10				
Levitate	12				
Stone Move 1	8				
Sparking Fingers	8				
Ice Walk	8				
Slide	12				

4th		5th		6th
Flame Barrier	42	Invisibility	55	
Flame Bolt 2	43	Burn	55	
Fly 1	43	Stone Storm 2	53	
Paralyze Person	44	Stone Crumble 1	52	
Ice Sheet	44	(Earth Armor 30%	52)	
Snow Balls	43	Mold Mud	50	
Wind Blast 2	43	Ring Spin	50	
Mud Walk	41	Resist Poisons	51	
Mud Pool	43	Mud to Dust 1	52	

Note : The spells in Parenthesis are not New Spells, they are just place holders for spells learned at previous levels.

312

NAME : JAKE RAPIDS AGE : 29

ENDURANCE :	19		OCC :	**MENTALIST**	
AGILITY :	12	+6%	LEVEL :	5th	
STRENGTH :	14	+1 Dam.	RACE :	HUMAN	
INTELLECT :	20	10 Spells	MR :	10	
WISDOM :	19	+5% D.Amb.	RER :	20%	
WILL :	16				

SEX: Male   HANDED: R

EYES: Brown   HAIR: Gray/Brown

Mental Points : 40 = 28 / 12

Regen=3/day

PTE : 46%

EP : 45

Strikes/Parries: 1 / 2
Total Actions : 3

HT: 5' 10"   WT:180lbs.

CRM: 3 (Mentalist= 4/5)
BIRTHGIFT:

WEAPONS

3 Th. Daggers   1d8 [1/Act]

1 Long Sword   2d8 +1

ARMOR

Agility Bonus (+6%)

Mail Shirt (+35%)

Small Wooden Shield (+5%)

MENTAL DISIPLINES

1) BODY CONTROL: 1st Aid
    Know if Poisoned,
    Diseased, ect.

2) EMBEDDING: +2 Intell.

SPECIAL ABILITIES

Total Spell Points: 20 + 1/Level = 25

SPELLS:

1)	See Enchantment	SPC = 9	R: 10'	D: 1 hr./L	
2)	Shield, Proj (+10%)	SPC = 10	R: T	D: 1 hr.	
3)	Bridge, 15'	SPC = 11	R: 5'	D: 5 min.	
4)	Shield, Melee (+10%)	SPC = 12	R: T	D: 30 min.	
5)	Daze – One	SPC = 13	R: 15'+1'/L	D: 2+1d4 Actions	
6)	Acid Pool, Mild	SPC = 15	R: 15'+1'/L	D: 5 min.	AOE: 10' rad.
7)	Blind – One	SPC = 15	R: 15'	D: 2+1d4 Actions	
8)	Cube of Midnight	SPC = 15	R: 5'+1'/L	D: 5 min.	AOE: 20' box
9)	Smoke Bomb	SPC = 16	R: 10'+1'/L	D: 2 min.	AOE: 20'+1'/L
10)	Flame Blot 1	SPC = 18	R: 15'+1'/L	Dam: 4 + 1d10	

ENCHANTED ITEMS (Used/Total: 8/8)

ELEMENTALIST RING(6)   (A) Earth Armor (10%) D: 60 min.   TW: Rock
Andalusite = I1   (B) Stone Storm 1   R: 25'   AOE: 10'rad   Dam: 4+1d12 TW: Avalanche

POTION(1)   Heal Wounds @ 50 EP

POTION(1)   Shield, Projectile = 30%

EXPERIENCE POINTS

142

SURVIVAL SKILLS

Endurance: 17+2
Shield Use
Gambling: (1st Sp. = 67%)
Detect Ambush: +20%
1st Aid (Mentalist)
Badge / Pin Construction: 48%

KNOWN WEAPONS

(Learned to cast Spells)
Throwing Daggers
Long Sword

REGULAR EQUIPMENT

Standard Adventurer's Pack (SAP)

1	Back Pack
1	Large Brown Leather Sack
1	Pouch, Leather
2 wk.	Food & Water
50'	Rope
3	Torches
1	Box: Flint, Steel and Tinder
1	Skinning Knife (1d6)
1	Bedroll
1	Cooking Set (travel)
1	Sanitary Set (M)
1	First Aid Kit

MISC. EQUIP.

SPECIAL EQUIPMENT

3 lbs Wax for Badge Construction

TREASURE

SILVER	MITHERAL	GEMS & JEWERLY	POCKET CHANGE
100			200 Iron Pieces on 2 Leather Rings

DISIPLINE = BODY CONTOL   Body Control MP = 28

Psychic Healing	1+ (Automatic)	Heal = 1 EP / 1 MP	
Bio – Electric Shock	5	R: 20'	Dam: Level + 2d10
Harden Body	5 / 1	Fist = +1d4 Dam. or	Body = +1% to PTE / 1 MP
Adrenaline Control	3+	CRM = +1	23 MP : CRM = +2
Ability Boost	20	Strength or Agility Score = +2	D: 1 min. / L
Vascular Control	7	Fight Longer (x2 End. Score)	Hold Breath = 4 times longer
Chameleon Skin	10	D: 30 min. / L	
Body Stretch	4+	+2' Appendage length / 4 MP	D: 5 min. / L

DISIPLINE = EMBEDDING   Embedding MP = 12

Detect Embedded	2 (Automatic)	R: 30'	D: 10 minutes / Level
Embed Discipline	12	R: T	D: Permanent.

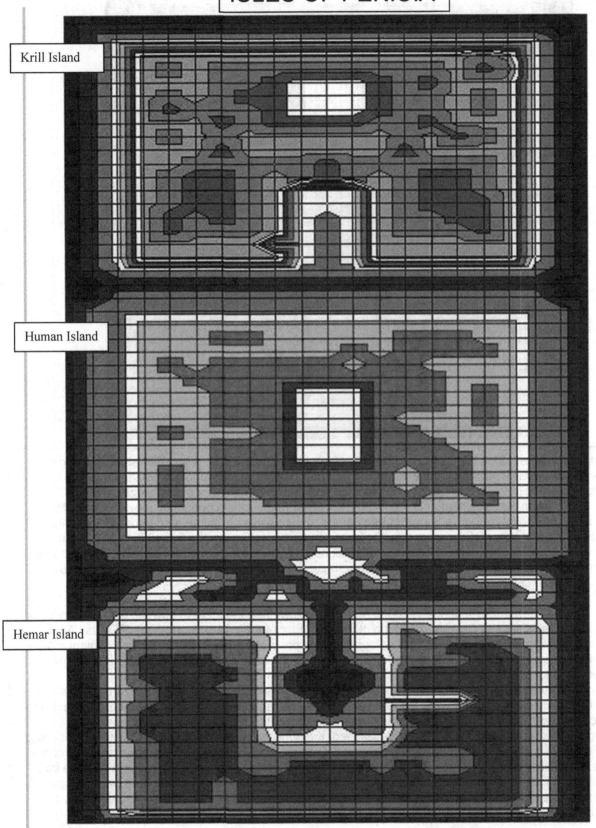

KRILL ISLE

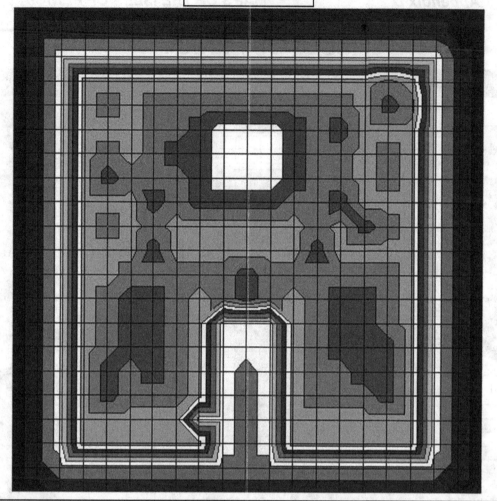

Continent Description: This continent is comprised of enormous mountains. The Krill historically made their homes on the upper regions of these mountains but have recently needed to protect the coves and trails to promote trade. Most of the plants when located on the Krill Isle are of a gigantic size, which is strange because when these same plants are located on either of the other continents, they only grow to "normal" size. The Krill have always known of and defended themselves from the gargantuan Giants that inhabit their continent. When of a mature age, these horrendous creatures range from 300 to 350 feet in height. The Giants have always been hostile to all other races even when peace, trade or negotiating parties have been dispatched to speak with them. Thankfully these great foes are not very intelligent, numerous or located on any other continent.

Legends: The Krill have many legends but none are more known then the story of how the giant mutant bats became their mortal enemies. One afternoon the eldest daughter of King Apex StormWing, Princess Arial, was exploring some mountain caves with her entourage. The party was ambushed by a horde of giant mutant bats. The bats overwhelmed the princess's guards and caused the cave entrance to collapse. That night a ransom note arrived with proof of the capture: the princess's signet ring and her severed finger. These mysteriously appeared in the King's chambers. Everyone was amazed by this cruelty and that the mutant bats had acquired the ability to read and write the Krill Language. The ransom demands where meet and delivered to the specified place, but the princess was never returned. The entire Krill race went to war at this insult. Although many bat caves were discovered and cleansed, the princess was never found. The closest a raiding party ever came was after long months of searching and combat. This raiding party had gone deeper into the cavernous mountains then any before. They caught a glimpse of some retreating bats carrying a statue that resembled their princess. Unfortunately these warriors were ambushed and the encumbered bats escaped. At the end of that terrible year, King Apex declared the mutant bats to be the mortal enemy of the Krill race. This ghastly event occurred over 300 years ago.

HUMAN ISLE

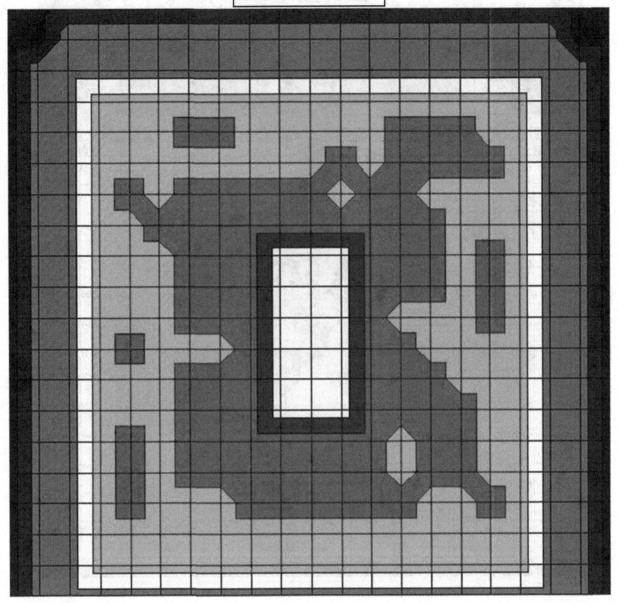

Continent Description: Most of the continent is comprised of planes and wooded areas, but also has the largest known desert. This Great Desert is located in the center of the continent on a plateau. There is also a large undersea ridge that surrounds the entire continent. This undersea ridge holds a very diverse array of sea life and is probably the best fishing in the world.

Legends: The oldest Human Legend is that of the formation of the Great Desert. The story tellers say that the Dragons, which are fabled to guard and protect the world of Penicia, knocked invaders from the sky and the tremendous impact and resulting explosion desolated the plateau located in the center of the continent. It is also told that the Dragons created the undersea ridge that surrounds the central continent as compensation. But no one, thus far, has ever spoken to one of these colossal beasts and lived to tell the tale.

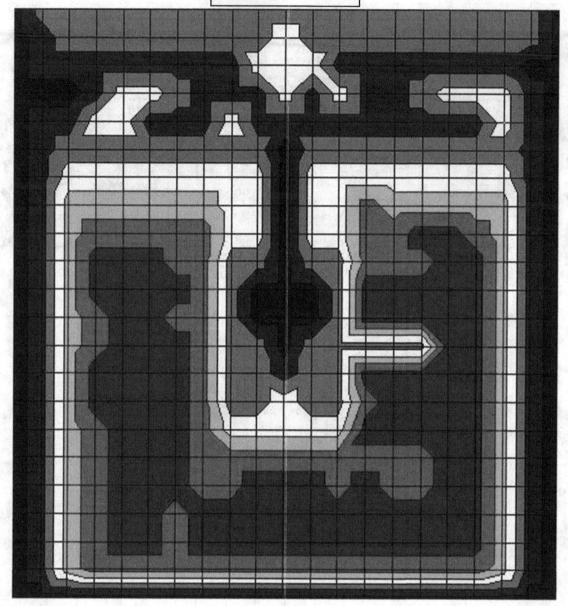

Continent Description: The southern continent has two major terrain features. The vast bay, which is located in the northern center of the Isle, is known as EverDeep Bay. The other notable feature is a deep jungle that covers most of the rest of the continent. Hemars use the great trees that grow in their jungle to fashion ships. There are numerous shipyards located along the shores of EverDeep Bay.

Legends: The most mysterious legend among Hemars is the tale of Horis the Seer who was a renowned Seer and Sailor. His predictions always came true from warnings of the Great Tsunami of 320 to the time when then Chief of Strength: Mantle's hair turned purple. Horis had a recurring dream of a humongous continent so far away that it could not be reached by any Hemar ship. The dream went on to show a terrible menace allying themselves with the Goblins and planning an invasion that will attack all three of the races.

Another legend is considered to be fact by at least 25% of all Hemars. Many peoples Grandfathers or Aunts claim to have actually spied the Beast of EverDeep. This Beast is said to be 700 feet long from it's lizard type snout to the tip of it's tail. It is a grayish color, has a long neck, a huge body with four feet shaped like flippers and an immense tail. The last time it was reported was 10 years ago in almost the exact center of EverDeep Bay.

1) <u>Sharing of Water</u> – This shows good will to strangers. You may use this anytime you meet someone you don't know on the road. You must sheath your weapons and produce a flask of water. You then move up to the people you are passing and offer them a drink. If the stranger or strangers accept the flask and drink, both groups are guaranteed safe passage and amnesty for a short period of time, usually 20 minutes or so. This is a good time to share information.

2) <u>Taunt of the Foolhardy</u> – This is used when you are insurmountably outnumbered. As the waves and waves of enemy swarm at you, you pool all of your courage and yell nasty insults at the horde and challenge them to a fight of equal numbers. If the enemy horde accepts, they will only send an equal number of combatants at your party at one time until either your party dies or you wipe out the entire multitude.

3) <u>Returning a Family Treasure or an Organization's Mascot</u> – If you have the opportunity to return a Family Heirloom / Treasure or an Organization's specific Mascot / Item, you can participate in this Tradition of Penicia. The Family / Organization will appoint a personal representative to receive the mascot/object and you will be thanked accordingly.

4) <u>Returning a loved one to their family</u> – Given the unique opportunity to return a loved one to their family is a prestigious occasion indeed. You must be specifically charged or volunteer for the honor of returning the loved one in question. Regardless of the time incurred or the peril encountered, once you return the loved one in question, you will be appropriately thanked by the person who initiated the request.

5) <u>Waving the White Flag</u> – No one has EVER violated a truce begun with a White Flag. There is a practical reason for this: there are times when it is imperative for enemies to communicate with each other on the battle field. A common situation is after a large battle and the wounded need to be evacuated from the field. Also, sometimes right before hostilities break out, one side will offer the other a chance to surrender.

NOTE: Anyone who violates any Tradition of Penicia automatically falls to a Morality Rating of 5.

6) _____   –

1) <u>Column Sun</u> – There are myths that somewhere in the wide universe there exist suns that are round; this is certainly not so within the solar system that Penicia is located in. The world of Penicia revolves around the long axis of the Column Sun. As you watch the Column Sun rise over Penicia, you behold an enormous horizontal column of fire. This miraculous sight is not only beautiful, but it also brings with it the gift of Spell, Mental and Ki point renewal. The immense Column Sun is not only a source of light and heat, but also of enchanted energy.

If you were standing on a little planet called earth, then you would measure the distance between Penicia and its Column Sun as the distance between Jupiter and Sol, the earth's round sun. Penicia is so close to the Column Sun that while you stand upon Penicia, you cannot see the ends of the sun. During the night, you can see other Column Stars. These stars are of course very far away and appear as lines or curves in the sky. They are not nearly as numerous as the stars seen from Sol's planets; these Column Stars number in the thousands not the billions. On the other hand, the Column Stars are brighter and some can even be seen through the clouds on a stormy night.

The size of Penicia is half again as large as Jupiter and all three Isles are located on one hemisphere of the planet. There are ten moons that circle Penicia, a different one is full for every month of the year. The moons and the Column Stars insure that every night on Penicia is quite bright. The names of the moons are: Lunar, Lunaor, Lunay, Lunag, Lunab, Lunain, Lunav, Lunabro, Lunac, Lunabla.

2) <u>Endura Bush</u> – The most legionary and nourishing plant on all of Penicia is the Endura Bush. This plant is a small bush which produces tiny orange flowers and 1 inch sized purple berries. These berries are about the size and consistence of 'cherry tomatoes'. A single Endura Berry can sustain you all day without food, quenches your thirst <u>and</u> miraculously heals 10 EP Damage. The small plant only produces 1d6 berries at any one time and if the last berry is plucked, the plant shrivels and dies. These plants seem to grow in any environment: jungle, desert, tundra, along seashores, ect., but always very sparsely. These plants cannot be artificially grown or transplanted, they are even unaffected by the Alchemist's Revitalize Nature or Plant Growth spells. A traveler that is lucky enough to find this bush may harvest some of the berries (but never pick the last one!). Once picked, the berries stay fresh for 10 days.

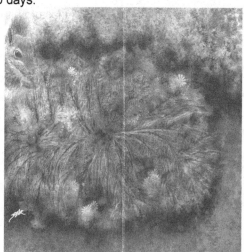

3) <u>Weekly Pay</u> – Most people work 8 days / week and take Saturday & Sunday off, so:
   (A) Minimum wage is 6 Silver / Day = 6*8 = 48 Silver / week, thus:
      If you stay at a bed & breakfast, pay by the week, eat Lunch & Dinner it will cost:
         (12+10+20) 42 Silver / week for Food & Lodging.
      SO: you could pay for Food & Lodging, have 2 beers on Friday night & save 5 Silver/week,
         This means you could work, eat, relax & Save enough for a
            Horse w/ Everything (50 Silver) in 2 months. (10 days/week & 5 weeks/month).
   (B) Better than Minimum wage is 7 Silver / Day = 7*8 = 56 Silver / week, thus:
      If you stay at a bed & breakfast, pay by the week, eat Lunch & Dinner it will cost:
         (12+10+20) 42 Silver / week for Food & Lodging.
      SO: you could pay for Food & Lodging, have a good time and 8 beers on Friday night &
         save 10 Silver/week,
         This means you could work, eat, relax & Save enough for a
            Horse w/ Everything (50 Silver) in 1 month. (10 days/week & 5 weeks/month).

4) There is **NO prejudice** toward ANY Race on the Isles. This was the reason for Instituting the IronBall game in the first place. [The only person who still harbors the evil emotion of prejudice is someone stricken with the Harmful Birthgift of that name.]

5) No one, including Krill, may fly into or through <u>any</u> city, town or village. They must land well outside the city limits and walk into town. This is true even on the Krill Isle when a Krill enters one of their own cities or towns. If you see a Krill flying in town, it's a bad sign. Ie. Trouble somewhere and the guards have been dispatched to that area. If a civilian flies through town: a Krill under their own power or someone using magical means; they will be arrested.

6) <u>Knight's Corp</u> – The guards of any city/town patrol it and keep order. The Knight's Corp is charged with the safety of the Isles themselves. If any criminals or organizations operate over great distances or between the Isles or threaten the tranquility of the Isles, the Knights take charge of the situation. The Knights are marshals who's authority is second only to Kings and high Court Rulers. There are manned Knight's Offices in most major towns and some Knights are tasked to roam the Isles keeping the Peace and hunting down criminals.

7) <u>Wed-lets</u> – When a couple gets married they usually exchange thin silver bracelets. These thin silver bands are referred to as Wed-lets. When the couple has children the mother will usually have a gem embedded in her Wed-let. The father will usually add an additional band representing each child. These extra bands are sometimes woven together to form a larger bracelet. Both the mother and father will usually have a spell embedded into their Wed-lets to help their family in an emergency. A mother may have an Enchanted diamond gem imbedded into her Wed-let and then hold a few Heal spells within it. A father may have each of his bands enchanted with the Light 2 spell to cast on each member of his family during an earthquake or flood.

8) Regular people's Endurance Point total is equal to: (their Endurance Score x2) + (their Age/5).

9) <u>Banks</u> – The Five areas that a bank does business in are:
  (A) Money Exchange – Free – Exchange one currency into another, ie IP into Silver, Silver into MP.
  (B) Buy & Sell Non-Enchanted Gems – The Costs are listed below:

Gem	Buy	Sell
Colored Quartz	2 Silver / Karat	4 Silver / Karat
True Gems (Ruby, Sapphire, ect)	3 Silver / Karat	6 Silver / Karat
Opaque Quartz	4 Silver / Karat	8 Silver / Karat
Diamond & Onyx	5 Silver / Karat	10 Silver / Karat

  (C) Cut Gems – Most Bankers are trained Gem Cutters. They can cut gems at a certain price <u>per cut</u>.
      Colored Quartz= 2 True Gems= 4; Opaque Quartz= 6; Diamond/Onyx Gems= 8.
      Gems may only be cut if they are NOT enchanted.
  (D) Hold your money – Free – A bank will hold any amount of money for you for an unlimited time.
  (E) Transfer of Funds – The cost is 1 Silver Piece per 20 miles traveled to deliver the funds to you.

10) <u>Guest Rooms</u> – Most residential homes are built with small Rooms for Guests located on one side of the house. Poor or lower class homes usually have a single guest room furnished very simply with a small bed, chair and small table. Moderate or Middle class homes usually have two to four guest rooms furnished with a bed, chair, desk and a night stand. Rich or upper class homes usually have many guest rooms sometimes quite luxuriously furnished.

Color	Spell Name	SPC
Red	Glowing Hand	5
Red	Sparking Fingers	10
Red	Flame Bolt 1	18
Red	Uncontrolled Fire	43
Red	Flame Jet	44
Red	Flame Barrier	52
Red	Flame Bolt 2	53
Red	Flame Bolt 3	108
Red	Fire Globe	157
Red	Fire Ball	159

Color	Spell Name	SPC
Yellow	Light 1	8
Yellow	See Enchantment 1	8
Yellow	Sting Ray 1	10
Yellow	Blind-One	15
Yellow	See Truth / Lie	20
Yellow	Magnification Sight	20
Yellow	Telescopic Sight	20
Yellow	See Morality Rating (MR)	20
Yellow	See Life	20
Yellow	Light 2	22
Yellow	See Enchantment 2 (Area)	40
Yellow	Light 3	40
Yellow	Sun Light	43
Yellow	Invisibility	52
Yellow	Sting Ray 2 (Area)	54
Yellow	Lightning Bolt 1	54
Yellow	Blind - Many	73
Yellow	Sun Light Beam	88
Yellow	Lightning Bolt 2	108
Yellow	Ability Bonus: Intellect	155
Yellow	Lightning Bolt 3	159

Color	Spell Name	SPC
Orange	Shield, Projectile, 10%	10
Orange	Shield, Melee, 10%	12
Orange	Shield, Projectile, 20%	22
Orange	Shield, Magic, Class (A)	25
Orange	Shield, Melee, 20%	32
Orange	Force Bolt	33
Orange	Shield, Projectile, 30%	42
Orange	Shield, Melee, 30%	52
Orange	Shield, Magic, Class (B)	55
Orange	Force Net	56
Orange	Shield, Projectile, 40%	62
Orange	Shield, Melee, 40%	72
Orange	Repulsion Beam	80
Orange	Shield, Projectile, 50%	92
Orange	Bubble of Force	95
Orange	Shield, Melee, 50%	102
Orange	Shield, Magic, Class (C)	105
Orange	Shield, Magic, Class (D)	155
Orange	Force Globe	157

Color	Spell Name	SPC
Green	Revitalize Nature	10
Green	Heal Wounds 1	15
Green	Dust to Pill	20
Green	Potion to Dust	20
Green	Shrink Animal / Bird	23
Green	Heal Wounds 2	30
Green	Converse with Plants	31
Green	Vine Net	32
Green	Vine Arms	35
Green	Heal Blindness	40
Green	Plant Wall	41
Green	Plant Growth	42
Green	Heal Poison	50
Green	Plant Control	51
Green	Enlarge Animal / Bird	51
Green	Wound 1	53
Green	Heal Paralyzation	55
Green	Heal Disease	60
Green	Enlarge Person	71
Green	Shrink Person	71
Green	Plant Decay 1	71
Green	Wound 2	85
Green	Heal Wounds 3	100
Green	Gem to Dust	100
Green	Polymorph, Plant	107
Green	Plant Decay 2	136
Green	Restore	155

Color	Spell Name	SPC
Blue	Float	2
Blue	Cloud Part	6
Blue	Breeze	8
Blue	Glide	10
Blue	Wind Bolt 1	12
Blue	Bridge: 15'	15
Blue	Levitate	15
Blue	Converse with Clouds	31
Blue	Cloud Summon, Rain	32
Blue	Bridge: 35'	35
Blue	Wind Jet	44
Blue	Fly 1	52
Blue	Wind Bolt 2	53
Blue	Fly 2	107
Blue	Wind Bolt 3	108
Blue	Water Globe	121
Blue	Cloud Summon, Storm	137
Blue	Ability Bonus: Agility	155
Blue	Storm Summon	158

Color	Spell Name	SPC
Violet	Illusion 1 [< Human, no Sound]	11
Violet	Smoke Bomb	15
Violet	Disappear 1	22
Violet	Disguise	31
Violet	Duplicates	32
Violet	Cause Fear - One	34
Violet	Illusion 2 [< Hemar, no Sound]	44
Violet	Disappear 2	52
Violet	Polymorph 1	58
Violet	Illusion 3 [< Human, with Sound]	65
Violet	Illusion 4 [< Hemar, with Sound]	81
Violet	Polymorph 2	118
Violet	Cause Fear - Many	129
Violet	Ability Bonus: Beauty & Charm	155

Indigo	Converse with Animal / Bird	8
Indigo	Daze - One	13
Indigo	Converse with Reptile, Fish, or	21
Indigo	Sleep - One	24
Indigo	Mesmerize Animal / Bird	24
Indigo	Order Spell	30
Indigo	Mesmerize Reptile, Fish, or	31
Indigo	Empathy	32
Indigo	Mind Blast - One	34
Indigo	Sleep Wall	43
Indigo	Summon Animal / Bird	43
Indigo	Summon Reptile, Fish, or Insect	44
Indigo	Return Item Spell	47
Indigo	ESP	51
Indigo	Telekinesis	52
Indigo	Send Message	61
Indigo	Mesmerize Person	63
Indigo	Item Dance	75
Indigo	Daze - Many	78
Indigo	Project Thought	106
Indigo	Sleep - Area	108
Indigo	Mind Blast - Many	138
Indigo	Mesmerize Enchanted Creature	148
Indigo	Ability Bonus: Wisdom	155

Brown	Stone Move 1	10
Brown	Paralyze Animal / Bird	17
Brown	Paralyze Reptile, Fish or Insect	23
Brown	Earth Barrier	48
Brown	Stone Move 2	52
Brown	Paralyze Person	53
Brown	Stone Mold	62
Brown	Quicksand	73
Brown	Earth Globe	136
Brown	Ability Bonus: Strength	155
Brown	Stone Pass	156
Brown	Paralyze Enchanted Creatures	157
Brown	Stone Globe	157

Color	Spell Name	SPC
White	Purify Water	5
White	Ice Walk	8
White	Water Bolt 1	14
White	Slide	22
White	Water Walk, Calm	23
White	Converse with Water	31
White	Water Adaptation	31
White	Water Control 1	33
White	Frost Jet	44
White	Water Jet	44
White	Cancel Enchantment	51
White	Water Control 2	52
White	Frost Barrier	52
White	Water Bolt 2	53
White	Snow Balls	57
White	Water Spout	71
White	Water Control 3	72
White	Ice Elevator	78
White	Part Water 1	90
White	Water Globe	106
White	Water Bolt 3	108
White	Ice Spikes	108
White	Water Control 4	127
White	Ability Bonus: Endurance	155
White	Ice Globe	157
White	Water Control 5	189
White	Part Water 2	195

Color	Spell Name	SPC
Opaque	Find North	6
Opaque	Weapon Quality Spell	10
Opaque	Nourishment	23
Opaque	Gem "See"	23
Opaque	Wall Walk	24
Opaque	Language Spell	25
Opaque	Death Trance	31
Opaque	Revel Gem Quality	31
Opaque	Use Weapon Spell	31
Opaque	Fuse	32
Opaque	Leaper Spell	33
Opaque	Weight	34
Opaque	Touch of Pain	34
Opaque	Slippery Surface	41
Opaque	Howard's Cave	41
Opaque	Noise - Static	42
Opaque	Sticky Surface	43
Opaque	Touch of Retching	43
Opaque	Resist Enchantment, Particular	44
Opaque	Enchant Skeletons	44
Opaque	Scroll Spell	50
Opaque	Wand Preparation Spell	50
Opaque	Gem Cleanse 1	51
Opaque	Observation	52
Opaque	Resist Enchantment, Color	54
Opaque	Touch of Partial Paralyzation	54
Opaque	Pass Area	61
Opaque	Slow	62
Opaque	Mist of Choking	63
Opaque	Age	63
Opaque	Enchant Zombie	64
Opaque	Speed	79
Opaque	Poisonous Mist	85
Opaque	Gem Cleanse 2	100
Opaque	Iron Ball Field Spell (3-Player)	100
Opaque	Staff Link Spell	100
Opaque	Companion Spell	100
Opaque	Deadly Mist	129
Opaque	Oath Spell	150
Opaque	Iron Ball Field Spell (5-Player)	150
Opaque	Marriage Spell	150

Color	Spell Name	SPC
Black	Midnight Wall	8
Black	Cube of Midnight 1	15
Black	Acid Pool, Mild	15
Black	Acid Spray, Mild	24
Black	Silence - One	31
Black	Silence - Area	41
Black	Cube of Midnight 2	42
Black	Acid Pool, Medium	43
Black	Cancel Enchantment	51
Black	Acid Spray, Medium	54
Black	In Sight Teleport	95
Black	Acid Pool, Potent	108
Black	Acid Spray, Potent	139
Black	Teleport, Out of Sight	158
Black	Attribute Drain, Temporary	158
Black	Attribute Drain, Permanent	198

SPC	Spell Name	Color	SPC	Spell Name	Color
2	Float	Blue	24	Mesmerize Animal / Bird	Indigo
5	Purify Water	White	24	Wall Walk	Opaque
5	Glowing Hand	Red	25	Shield, Magic, Class (A)	Orange
6	Find North	Opaque	25	Language Spell	Opaque
6	Cloud Part	Blue	30	Heal Wounds 2	Green
8	Midnight Wall	Black	30	Order Spell	Indigo
8	Breeze	Blue	31	Converse with Clouds	Blue
8	Converse with Animal / Bird	Indigo	31	Mesmerize Reptile, Fish, or	Indigo
8	Ice Walk	White	31	Disguise	Violet
8	See Enchantment 1	Yellow	31	Water Adaptation	White
8	Light 1	Yellow	31	Death Trance	Opaque
10	Stone Move 1	Brown	31	Use Weapon Spell	Opaque
10	Weapon Quality Spell	Opaque	31	Revel Gem Quality	Opaque
10	Glide	Blue	31	Converse with Plants	Green
10	Sting Ray 1	Yellow	31	Silence - One	Black
10	Shield, Projectile, 10%	Orange	31	Converse with Water	White
10	Sparking Fingers	Red	32	Duplicates	Violet
10	Revitalize Nature	Green	32	Vine Net	Green
11	Illusion 1 [< Human, no Sound]	Violet	32	Cloud Summon, Rain	Blue
12	Shield, Melee, 10%	Orange	32	Shield, Melee, 20%	Orange
12	Wind Bolt 1	Blue	32	Fuse	Opaque
13	Daze - One	Indigo	32	Empathy	Indigo
14	Water Bolt 1	White	33	Force Bolt	Orange
15	Blind-One	Yellow	33	Water Control 1	White
15	Acid Pool, Mild	Black	33	Leaper Spell	Opaque
15	Cube of Midnight 1	Black	34	Mind Blast - One	Indigo
15	Heal Wounds 1	Green	34	Cause Fear - One	Violet
15	Bridge: 15'	Blue	34	Weight	Opaque
15	Smoke Bomb	Violet	34	Touch of Pain	Opaque
15	Levitate	Blue	35	Bridge: 35'	Blue
17	Paralyze Animal / Bird	Brown	35	Vine Arms	Green
18	Flame Bolt 1	Red	40	Heal Blindness	Green
20	See Morality Rating (MR)	Yellow	40	Light 3	Yellow
20	Magnification Sight	Yellow	40	See Enchantment 2 (Area)	Yellow
20	Telescopic Sight	Yellow	41	Howard's Cave	Opaque
20	See Truth / Lie	Yellow	41	Slippery Surface	Opaque
20	Potion to Dust	Green	41	Plant Wall	Green
20	Dust to Pill	Green	41	Silence - Area	Black
20	See Life	Yellow	42	Plant Growth	Green
21	Converse with Reptile, Fish, or	Indigo	42	Noise - Static	Opaque
22	Shield, Projectile, 20%	Orange	42	Shield, Projectile, 30%	Orange
22	Disappear 1	Violet	42	Cube of Midnight 2	Black
22	Light 2	Yellow	43	Uncontrolled Fire	Red
22	Slide	White	43	Sun Light	Yellow
23	Shrink Animal / Bird	Green	43	Sticky Surface	Opaque
23	Water Walk, Calm	White	43	Sleep Wall	Indigo
23	Paralyze Reptile, Fish or Insect	Brown	43	Summon Animal / Bird	Indigo
23	Nourishment	Opaque	43	Touch of Retching	Opaque
23	Gem "See"	Opaque	43	Acid Pool, Medium	Black
24	Acid Spray, Mild	Black	44	Flame Jet	Red
24	Sleep - One	Indigo	44	Illusion 2 [< Hemar, no Sound]	Violet

SPC	Spell Name	Color	SPC	Spell Name	Color
44	Summon Reptile, Fish, or Insect	Indigo	64	Enchant Zombie	Opaque
44	Wind Jet	Blue	65	Illusion 3 [< Human, with Sound]	Violet
44	Water Jet	White	71	Plant Decay 1	Green
44	Resist Enchantment, Particular	Opaque	71	Water Spout	White
44	Frost Jet	White	71	Enlarge Person	Green
44	Enchant Skeletons	Opaque	71	Shrink Person	Green
47	Return Item Spell	Indigo	72	Shield, Melee, 40%	Orange
48	Earth Barrier	Brown	72	Water Control 3	White
50	Wand Preparation Spell	Opaque	73	Blind - Many	Yellow
50	Heal Poison	Green	73	Quicksand	Brown
50	Scroll Spell	Opaque	75	Item Dance	Indigo
51	ESP	Indigo	78	Ice Elevator	White
51	Cancel Enchantment	White	78	Daze - Many	Indigo
51	Plant Control	Green	79	Speed	Opaque
51	Enlarge Animal / Bird	Green	80	Repulsion Beam	Orange
51	Gem Cleanse 1	Opaque	81	Illusion 4 [< Hemar, with Sound]	Violet
51	Cancel Enchantment	Black	85	Poisonous Mist	Opaque
52	Fly 1	Blue	85	Wound 2	Green
52	Observation	Opaque	88	Sun Light Beam	Yellow
52	Telekinesis	Indigo	90	Part Water 1	White
52	Stone Move 2	Brown	92	Shield, Projectile, 50%	Orange
52	Frost Barrier	White	95	In Sight Teleport	Black
52	Disappear 2	Violet	95	Bubble of Force	Orange
52	Flame Barrier	Red	100	Iron Ball Field Spell (3-Player)	Opaque
52	Shield, Melee, 30%	Orange	100	Gem to Dust	Green
52	Invisibility	Yellow	100	Gem Cleanse 2	Opaque
52	Water Control 2	White	100	Companion Spell	Opaque
53	Water Bolt 2	White	100	Staff Link Spell	Opaque
53	Wind Bolt 2	Blue	100	Heal Wounds 3	Green
53	Paralyze Person	Brown	102	Shield, Melee, 50%	Orange
53	Wound 1	Green	105	Shield, Magic, Class (C)	Orange
53	Flame Bolt 2	Red	106	Project Thought	Indigo
54	Acid Spray, Medium	Black	106	Water Globe	White
54	Touch of Partial Paralyzation	Opaque	107	Polymorph, Plant	Green
54	Lightning Bolt 1	Yellow	107	Fly 2	Blue
54	Sting Ray 2 (Area)	Yellow	108	Flame Bolt 3	Red
54	Resist Enchantment, Color	Opaque	108	Water Bolt 3	White
55	Heal Paralyzation	Green	108	Lightning Bolt 2	Yellow
55	Shield, Magic, Class (B)	Orange	108	Sleep - Area	Indigo
56	Force Net	Orange	108	Wind Bolt 3	Blue
57	Snow Balls	White	108	Ice Spikes	White
58	Polymorph 1	Violet	108	Acid Pool, Potent	Black
60	Heal Disease	Green	118	Polymorph 2	Violet
61	Pass Area	Opaque	121	Water Globe	Blue
61	Send Message	Indigo	127	Water Control 4	White
62	Shield, Projectile, 40%	Orange	129	Deadly Mist	Opaque
62	Stone Mold	Brown	129	Cause Fear - Many	Violet
62	Slow	Opaque	136	Plant Decay 2	Green
63	Age	Opaque	136	Earth Globe	Brown
63	Mist of Choking	Opaque	137	Cloud Summon, Storm	Blue
63	Mesmerize Person	Indigo	138	Mind Blast - Many	Indigo

SPC	Spell Name	Color	SPC	Spell Name	Color
139	Acid Spray, Potent	Black			
148	Mesmerize Enchanted Creature	Indigo			
150	Oath Spell	Opaque			
150	Iron Ball Field Spell (5-Player)	Opaque			
150	Marriage Spell	Opaque			
155	Ability Bonus: Beauty & Charm	Violet			
155	Ability Bonus: Strength	Brown			
155	Ability Bonus: Endurance	White			
155	Restore	Green			
155	Ability Bonus: Agility	Blue			
155	Shield, Magic, Class (D)	Orange			
155	Ability Bonus: Intellect	Yellow			
155	Ability Bonus: Wisdom	Indigo			
156	Stone Pass	Brown			
157	Ice Globe	White			
157	Fire Globe	Red			
157	Force Globe	Orange			
157	Paralyze Enchanted Creatures	Brown			
157	Stone Globe	Brown			
158	Storm Summon	Blue			
158	Attribute Drain, Temporary	Black			
158	Teleport, Out of Sight	Black			
159	Lightning Bolt 3	Yellow			
159	Fire Ball	Red			
189	Water Control 5	White			
195	Part Water 2	White			
198	Attribute Drain, Permanent	Black			

Spell Name	SPC	Color	Spell Name	SPC	Color
Ability Bonus: Agility	155	Blue	Enlarge Person	71	Green
Ability Bonus: Beauty & Charm	155	Violet	ESP	51	Indigo
Ability Bonus: Endurance	155	White	Find North	6	Opaque
Ability Bonus: Intellect	155	Yellow	Fire Ball	159	Red
Ability Bonus: Strength	155	Brown	Fire Globe	157	Red
Ability Bonus: Wisdom	155	Indigo	Flame Barrier	52	Red
Acid Pool, Medium	43	Black	Flame Bolt 1	18	Red
Acid Pool, Mild	15	Black	Flame Bolt 2	53	Red
Acid Pool, Potent	108	Black	Flame Bolt 3	108	Red
Acid Spray, Medium	54	Black	Flame Jet	44	Red
Acid Spray, Mild	24	Black	Float	2	Blue
Acid Spray, Potent	139	Black	Fly 1	52	Blue
Age	63	Opaque	Fly 2	107	Blue
Attribute Drain, Permanent	198	Black	Force Bolt	33	Orange
Attribute Drain, Temporary	158	Black	Force Globe	157	Orange
Blind - Many	73	Yellow	Force Net	56	Orange
Blind-One	15	Yellow	Frost Barrier	52	White
Breeze	8	Blue	Frost Jet	44	White
Bridge: 15'	15	Blue	Fuse	32	Opaque
Bridge: 35'	35	Blue	Gem "See"	23	Opaque
Bubble of Force	95	Orange	Gem Cleanse 1	51	Opaque
Cancel Enchantment	51	Black	Gem Cleanse 2	100	Opaque
Cancel Enchantment	51	White	Gem to Dust	100	Green
Cause Fear - Many	129	Violet	Glide	10	Blue
Cause Fear - One	34	Violet	Glowing Hand	5	Red
Cloud Part	6	Blue	Heal Blindness	40	Green
Cloud Summon, Rain	32	Blue	Heal Disease	60	Green
Cloud Summon, Storm	137	Blue	Heal Paralyzation	55	Green
Companion Spell	100	Opaque	Heal Poison	50	Green
Converse with Animal / Bird	8	Indigo	Heal Wounds 1	15	Green
Converse with Clouds	31	Blue	Heal Wounds 2	30	Green
Converse with Plants	31	Green	Heal Wounds 3	100	Green
Converse with Reptile, Fish, or	21	Indigo	Howard's Cave	41	Opaque
Converse with Water	31	White	Ice Elevator	78	White
Cube of Midnight 1	15	Black	Ice Globe	157	White
Cube of Midnight 2	42	Black	Ice Spikes	108	White
Daze - Many	78	Indigo	Ice Walk	8	White
Daze - One	13	Indigo	Illusion 1 [< Human, no Sound]	11	Violet
Deadly Mist	129	Opaque	Illusion 2 [< Hemar, no Sound]	44	Violet
Death Trance	31	Opaque	Illusion 3 [< Human, with Sound]	65	Violet
Disappear 1	22	Violet	Illusion 4 [< Hemar, with Sound]	81	Violet
Disappear 2	52	Violet	In Sight Teleport	95	Black
Disguise	31	Violet	Invisibility	52	Yellow
Duplicates	32	Violet	Iron Ball Field Spell (3-Player)	100	Opaque
Dust to Pill	20	Green	Iron Ball Field Spell (5-Player)	150	Opaque
Earth Barrier	48	Brown	Item Dance	75	Indigo
Earth Globe	136	Brown	Language Spell	25	Opaque
Empathy	32	Indigo	Leaper Spell	33	Opaque
Enchant Skeletons	44	Opaque	Levitate	15	Blue
Enchant Zombie	64	Opaque	Light 1	8	Yellow
Enlarge Animal / Bird	51	Green	Light 2	22	Yellow

Spell Name	SPC	Color	Spell Name	SPC	Color
Light 3	40	Yellow	See Truth / Lie	20	Yellow
Lightning Bolt 1	54	Yellow	Send Message	61	Indigo
Lightning Bolt 2	108	Yellow	Shield, Magic, Class (A)	25	Orange
Lightning Bolt 3	159	Yellow	Shield, Magic, Class (B)	55	Orange
Magnification Sight	20	Yellow	Shield, Magic, Class (C)	105	Orange
Marriage Spell	150	Opaque	Shield, Magic, Class (D)	155	Orange
Mesmerize Animal / Bird	24	Indigo	Shield, Melee, 10%	12	Orange
Mesmerize Enchanted Creature	148	Indigo	Shield, Melee, 20%	32	Orange
Mesmerize Person	63	Indigo	Shield, Melee, 30%	52	Orange
Mesmerize Reptile, Fish, or	31	Indigo	Shield, Melee, 40%	72	Orange
Midnight Wall	8	Black	Shield, Melee, 50%	102	Orange
Mind Blast - Many	138	Indigo	Shield, Projectile, 10%	10	Orange
Mind Blast - One	34	Indigo	Shield, Projectile, 20%	22	Orange
Mist of Choking	63	Opaque	Shield, Projectile, 30%	42	Orange
Noise - Static	42	Opaque	Shield, Projectile, 40%	62	Orange
Nourishment	23	Opaque	Shield, Projectile, 50%	92	Orange
Oath Spell	150	Opaque	Shrink Animal / Bird	23	Green
Observation	52	Opaque	Shrink Person	71	Green
Order Spell	30	Indigo	Silence - Area	41	Black
Paralyze Animal / Bird	17	Brown	Silence - One	31	Black
Paralyze Enchanted Creatures	157	Brown	Sleep - Area	108	Indigo
Paralyze Person	53	Brown	Sleep - One	24	Indigo
Paralyze Reptile, Fish or Insect	23	Brown	Sleep Wall	43	Indigo
Part Water 1	90	White	Slide	22	White
Part Water 2	195	White	Slippery Surface	41	Opaque
Pass Area	61	Opaque	Slow	62	Opaque
Plant Control	51	Green	Smoke Bomb	15	Violet
Plant Decay 1	71	Green	Snow Balls	57	White
Plant Decay 2	136	Green	Sparking Fingers	10	Red
Plant Growth	42	Green	Speed	79	Opaque
Plant Wall	41	Green	Staff Link Spell	100	Opaque
Poisonous Mist	85	Opaque	Sticky Surface	43	Opaque
Polymorph 1	58	Violet	Sting Ray 1	10	Yellow
Polymorph 2	118	Violet	Sting Ray 2 (Area)	54	Yellow
Polymorph, Plant	107	Green	Stone Globe	157	Brown
Potion to Dust	20	Green	Stone Mold	62	Brown
Project Thought	106	Indigo	Stone Move 1	10	Brown
Purify Water	5	White	Stone Move 2	52	Brown
Quicksand	73	Brown	Stone Pass	156	Brown
Repulsion Beam	80	Orange	Storm Summon	158	Blue
Resist Enchantment, Color	54	Opaque	Summon Animal / Bird	43	Indigo
Resist Enchantment, Particular	44	Opaque	Summon Reptile, Fish, or Insect	44	Indigo
Restore	155	Green	Sun Light	43	Yellow
Return Item Spell	47	Indigo	Sun Light Beam	88	Yellow
Revel Gem Quality	31	Opaque	Telekinesis	52	Indigo
Revitalize Nature	10	Green	Teleport, Out of Sight	158	Black
Scroll Spell	50	Opaque	Telescopic Sight	20	Yellow
See Enchantment 1	8	Yellow	Touch of Pain	34	Opaque
See Enchantment 2 (Area)	40	Yellow	Touch of Partial Paralyzation	54	Opaque
See Life	20	Yellow	Touch of Retching	43	Opaque
See Morality Rating (MR)	20	Yellow	Uncontrolled Fire	43	Red

Spell Name	SPC	Color		Spell Name	SPC	Color
Use Weapon Spell	31	Opaque				
Vine Arms	35	Green				
Vine Net	32	Green				
Wall Walk	24	Opaque				
Wand Preparation Spell	50	Opaque				
Water Adaptation	31	White				
Water Bolt 1	14	White				
Water Bolt 2	53	White				
Water Bolt 3	108	White				
Water Control 1	33	White				
Water Control 2	52	White				
Water Control 3	72	White				
Water Control 4	127	White				
Water Control 5	189	White				
Water Globe	121	Blue				
Water Globe	106	White				
Water Jet	44	White				
Water Spout	71	White				
Water Walk, Calm	23	White				
Weapon Quality Spell	10	Opaque				
Weight	34	Opaque				
Wind Bolt 1	12	Blue				
Wind Bolt 2	53	Blue				
Wind Bolt 3	108	Blue				
Wind Jet	44	Blue				
Wound 1	53	Green				
Wound 2	85	Green				

Element	Spell Name	SPC		Element	Spell Name	SPC
Air	Converse with Air Elemental	1		Earth	Converse with Earth Elementals	1
Air	Cloud Part	5		Earth	Stone Move 1	8
Air	Air Bubble 1	10		Earth	Earth Armor 10%	12
Air	Wind Bolt 1	10		Earth	Paralyze Animal/Bird	15
Air	Levitate	12		Earth	Stone Storm 1	17
Air	Glide	14		Earth	Converse with Stones	21
Air	Whirl Wind	15		Earth	Paralyze Reptile,Fish,or Insect	24
Air	Converse with Clouds	21		Earth	Earth Armor 20%	32
Air	Wind Wall	22		Earth	Stone Move 2	33
Air	Wind Jet	33		Earth	Earth barrier	40
Air	Wind Barrier	34		Earth	Paralyze Person	44
Air	Wind Bolt 2	43		Earth	Stone Crumble 1	52
Air	Fly 1	45		Earth	Earth Armor 30%	52
Air	Control Wind 1	52		Earth	Quicksand	53
Air	Whirl Wind 2	53		Earth	Stone Storm 2	53
Air	Air Bubble 2	55		Earth	Landslide	62
Air	Cloud Cover	61		Earth	Hole	63
Air	Whirl Wind 3	83		Earth	Paralysis Wall	71
Air	Fly 2	85		Earth	Earth Armor 40%	72
Air	Wind Globe	91		Earth	Earth Armor 50%	102
Air	Wind Bolt 3	94		Earth	Earth Globe	107
Air	Control Winds 2	118		Earth	Stone Pass	118
Air	Summon Storm	138		Earth	Stone Globe	147
Air	Air Robe	157		Earth	Earth Robe	157
Air	Air Absence	169		Earth	Paralyze Enchanted Creature	158
				Earth	Statue, person	159
				Earth	Stone Crumble 2	169
				Earth	Chasm	185

Element	Spell Name	SPC		Element	Spell Name	SPC
Fire	Converse with Fire Elementals	1		Fog	Converse w/ Fog,Water&Air El.	1
Fire	Blue Flame (cold)	6		Fog	Rain Clouds	33
Fire	Sparking Fingers	8		Fog	Dispel Fog 1	37
Fire	Extinguish Fire, Regular	10		Fog	Soothe Burns	40
Fire	Flaming Hand	12		Fog	Fog Wall	41
Fire	Flame Bolt 1	16		Fog	See Through Fog	41
Fire	Control Fire	23		Fog	Fog Walk	41
Fire	Resist Cold	33		Fog	Fog Bank 1	51
Fire	Flame Jet	35		Fog	Resist Fire and Heat	51
Fire	Flame Walk	41		Fog	Fog Jet	52
Fire	Flame Barrier	42		Fog	Fog Barrier	61
Fire	Flame Bolt 2	43		Fog	Fog Bank 2	71
Fire	Uncontrolled Fire	48		Fog	Part Fog	71
Fire	Burn	54		Fog	Fog Globe	81
Fire	Fire Bolt 3	80		Fog	Polymorph into Fog	108
Fire	Fire Globe	138		Fog	Dispel Fog 2	159
Fire	Fire Ball	139		Fog	Melt Statue	169
Fire	Towering Inferno	148		Fog	Fog Robe	177
Fire	Fiery Robe	157				
Fire	Extinguish Enchanted Fire	169				

Element	Spell Name	SPC
Mud	Converse w/ Mud,Earth&Water	1
Mud	Mud Walk	41
Mud	Mud Pool	43
Mud	Mold Mud and Harden	50
Mud	Resist Poisons	51
Mud	Mud to Dust 1, Regular	52
Mud	Stone to Mud 1	60
Mud	Mud Barrier	62
Mud	Mud Elevator	71
Mud	Mud Globe	93
Mud	Mud Balls	95
Mud	Mud to dust 2	105
Mud	Polymorph into Mud	108
Mud	Part Mud	116
Mud	Stone to Mud 2	155
Mud	Mud Robe	177

Element	Spell Name	SPC
Smoke	Converse w/ Smoke, Fire&Air El.	1
Smoke	Dispel Smoke 1	37
Smoke	Smoke Adaptation	41
Smoke	Smoke Walk	43
Smoke	Smoke Wall	45
Smoke	Smoke Balls	52
Smoke	Smoke Jet	53
Smoke	Smoke Barrier	61
Smoke	Part Smoke	71
Smoke	Smoke Bank 1	71
Smoke	Smoke Screen	81
Smoke	Smoke Globe	88
Smoke	Polymorph into Smoke	108
Smoke	Smoke Bank 2	137
Smoke	Dispel Smoke 2	159
Smoke	Smoke Robe	177

Element	Spell Name	SPC
Water	Converse with Water & Ice El.	1
Water	Ice Walk	8
Water	Slide	12
Water	Water Bolt1	12
Water	Water Adaptation	22
Water	Water Control 1	23
Water	Water Walk, Calm	23
Water	Dispel Water or Ice 1	24
Water	Water Jet	33
Water	Frost Jet	35
Water	Frost Barrier	42
Water	Water Control 2	42
Water	Resist Fire	42
Water	Water Bolt 2	43
Water	Snow Balls	43
Water	Ice Sheet	44
Water	Water Walk, Wavy	52
Water	Ice Elevator	61
Water	Water Spout	61
Water	Part Water 1	71
Water	Snow Storm	72
Water	Water Bolt 3	94
Water	Ice Spikes	95
Water	Water Control 3	106
Water	Water Globe	107
Water	Water Control 4	125
Water	Ice Blizzard	139
Water	Ice Globe	147
Water	Water or Ice Robe	157
Water	Dispel Water or Ice 2	169
Water	Part Water 2	189

Element	Spell Name	SPC
Lava	Converse w/ Lava,Earth&Fire El.	1
Lava	Lava Walk	51
Lava	Cool Lava 1	55
Lava	Lava Pool	63
Lava	Lava Barrier	73
Lava	Polymorph into Lava	108
Lava	Lava Balls	109
Lava	Part Lava	127
Lava	Lava Globe	147
Lava	Cool Lava 2	155
Lava	Lava Robe	177

SPC	Spell Name	Element	SPC	Spell Name	Element
1	Converse w/ Fog,Water&Air El.	Fog	41	Mud Walk	Mud
1	Converse w/ Lava,Earth&Fire El.	Lava	41	See Through Fog	Fog
1	Converse w/ Mud,Earth&Water	Mud	41	Smoke Adaptation	Smoke
1	Converse w/ Smoke, Fire&Air El.	Smoke	42	Flame Barrier	Fire
1	Converse with Air Elemental	Air	42	Frost Barrier	Water
1	Converse with Earth Elementals	Earth	42	Resist Fire	Water
1	Converse with Fire Elementals	Fire	42	Water Control 2	Water
1	Converse with Water & Ice El.	Water	43	Flame Bolt 2	Fire
5	Cloud Part	Air	43	Mud Pool	Mud
6	Blue Flame (cold)	Fire	43	Smoke Walk	Smoke
8	Ice Walk	Water	43	Snow Balls	Water
8	Sparking Fingers	Fire	43	Water Bolt 2	Water
8	Stone Move 1	Earth	43	Wind Bolt 2	Air
10	Air Bubble 1	Air	44	Ice Sheet	Water
10	Extinguish Fire, Regular	Fire	44	Paralyze Person	Earth
10	Wind Bolt 1	Air	45	Fly 1	Air
12	Earth Armor 10%	Earth	45	Smoke Wall	Smoke
12	Flaming Hand	Fire	48	Uncontrolled Fire	Fire
12	Levitate	Air	50	Mold Mud and Harden	Mud
12	Slide	Water	51	Fog Bank 1	Fog
12	Water Bolt1	Water	51	Lava Walk	Lava
14	Glide	Air	51	Resist Fire and Heat	Fog
15	Paralyze Animal/Bird	Earth	51	Resist Poisons	Mud
15	Whirl Wind	Air	52	Control Wind 1	Air
16	Flame Bolt 1	Fire	52	Earth Armor 30%	Earth
17	Stone Storm 1	Earth	52	Fog Jet	Fog
21	Converse with Clouds	Air	52	Mud to Dust 1, Regular	Mud
21	Converse with Stones	Earth	52	Smoke Balls	Smoke
22	Water Adaptation	Water	52	Stone Crumble 1	Earth
22	Wind Wall	Air	52	Water Walk, Wavy	Water
23	Control Fire	Fire	53	Quicksand	Earth
23	Water Control 1	Water	53	Smoke Jet	Smoke
23	Water Walk, Calm	Water	53	Stone Storm 2	Earth
24	Dispel Water or Ice 1	Water	53	Whirl Wind 2	Air
24	Paralyze Reptile,Fish,or Insect	Earth	54	Burn	Fire
32	Earth Armor 20%	Earth	55	Air Bubble 2	Air
33	Rain Clouds	Fog	55	Cool Lava 1	Lava
33	Resist Cold	Fire	60	Stone to Mud 1	Mud
33	Stone Move 2	Earth	61	Cloud Cover	Air
33	Water Jet	Water	61	Fog Barrier	Fog
33	Wind Jet	Air	61	Ice Elevator	Water
34	Wind Barrier	Air	61	Smoke Barrier	Smoke
35	Flame Jet	Fire	61	Water Spout	Water
35	Frost Jet	Water	62	Landslide	Earth
37	Dispel Fog 1	Fog	62	Mud Barrier	Mud
37	Dispel Smoke 1	Smoke	63	Hole	Earth
40	Earth barrier	Earth	63	Lava Pool	Lava
40	Soothe Burns	Fog	71	Fog Bank 2	Fog
41	Flame Walk	Fire	71	Mud Elevator	Mud
41	Fog Walk	Fog	71	Paralysis Wall	Earth
41	Fog Wall	Fog	71	Part Fog	Fog

SPC	Spell Name	Element	SPC	Spell Name	Element
71	Part Smoke	Smoke	159	Statue, person	Earth
71	Part Water 1	Water	169	Air Absence	Air
71	Smoke Bank 1	Smoke	169	Dispel Water or Ice 2	Water
72	Earth Armor 40%	Earth	169	Extinguish Enchanted Fire	Fire
72	Snow Storm	Water	169	Melt Statue	Fog
73	Lava Barrier	Lava	169	Stone Crumble 2	Earth
80	Fire Bolt 3	Fire	177	Fog Robe	Fog
81	Fog Globe	Fog	177	Lava Robe	Lava
81	Smoke Screen	Smoke	177	Mud Robe	Mud
83	Whirl Wind 3	Air	177	Smoke Robe	Smoke
85	Fly 2	Air	185	Chasm	Earth
88	Smoke Globe	Smoke	189	Part Water 2	Water
91	Wind Globe	Air			
93	Mud Globe	Mud			
94	Water Bolt 3	Water			
94	Wind Bolt 3	Air			
95	Ice Spikes	Water			
95	Mud Balls	Mud			
102	Earth Armor 50%	Earth			
105	Mud to dust 2	Mud			
106	Water Control 3	Water			
107	Earth Globe	Earth			
107	Water Globe	Water			
108	Polymorph into Fog	Fog			
108	Polymorph into Lava	Lava			
108	Polymorph into Mud	Mud			
108	Polymorph into Smoke	Smoke			
109	Lava Balls	Lava			
116	Part Mud	Mud			
118	Control Winds 2	Air			
118	Stone Pass	Earth			
125	Water Control 4	Water			
127	Part Lava	Lava			
137	Smoke Bank 2	Smoke			
138	Fire Globe	Fire			
138	Summon Storm	Air			
139	Fire Ball	Fire			
139	Ice Blizzard	Water			
147	Ice Globe	Water			
147	Lava Globe	Lava			
147	Stone Globe	Earth			
148	Towering Inferno	Fire			
155	Cool Lava 2	Lava			
155	Stone to Mud 2	Mud			
157	Air Robe	Air			
157	Earth Robe	Earth			
157	Fiery Robe	Fire			
157	Water or Ice Robe	Water			
158	Paralyze Enchanted Creature	Earth			
159	Dispel Fog 2	Fog			
159	Dispel Smoke 2	Smoke			

Spell Name	SPC	Element	Spell Name	SPC	Element
Air Absence	169	Air	Fly 2	85	Air
Air Bubble 1	10	Air	Fog Bank 1	51	Fog
Air Bubble 2	55	Air	Fog Bank 2	71	Fog
Air Robe	157	Air	Fog Barrier	61	Fog
Blue Flame (cold)	6	Fire	Fog Globe	81	Fog
Burn	54	Fire	Fog Jet	52	Fog
Chasm	185	Earth	Fog Robe	177	Fog
Cloud Cover	61	Air	Fog Walk	41	Fog
Cloud Part	5	Air	Fog Wall	41	Fog
Control Fire	23	Fire	Frost Barrier	42	Water
Control Wind 1	52	Air	Frost Jet	35	Water
Control Winds 2	118	Air	Glide	14	Air
Converse w/ Fog,Water&Air El.	1	Fog	Hole	63	Earth
Converse w/ Lava,Earth&Fire El.	1	Lava	Ice Blizzard	139	Water
Converse w/ Mud,Earth&Water	1	Mud	Ice Elevator	61	Water
Converse w/ Smoke, Fire&Air El.	1	Smoke	Ice Globe	147	Water
Converse with Air Elemental	1	Air	Ice Sheet	44	Water
Converse with Clouds	21	Air	Ice Spikes	95	Water
Converse with Earth Elementals	1	Earth	Ice Walk	8	Water
Converse with Fire Elementals	1	Fire	Landslide	62	Earth
Converse with Stones	21	Earth	Lava Balls	109	Lava
Converse with Water & Ice El.	1	Water	Lava Barrier	73	Lava
Cool Lava 1	55	Lava	Lava Globe	147	Lava
Cool Lava 2	155	Lava	Lava Pool	63	Lava
Dispel Fog 1	37	Fog	Lava Robe	177	Lava
Dispel Fog 2	159	Fog	Lava Walk	51	Lava
Dispel Smoke 1	37	Smoke	Levitate	12	Air
Dispel Smoke 2	159	Smoke	Melt Statue	169	Fog
Dispel Water or Ice 1	24	Water	Mold Mud and Harden	50	Mud
Dispel Water or Ice 2	169	Water	Mud Balls	95	Mud
Earth Armor 10%	12	Earth	Mud Barrier	62	Mud
Earth Armor 20%	32	Earth	Mud Elevator	71	Mud
Earth Armor 30%	52	Earth	Mud Globe	93	Mud
Earth Armor 40%	72	Earth	Mud Pool	43	Mud
Earth Armor 50%	102	Earth	Mud Robe	177	Mud
Earth barrier	40	Earth	Mud to Dust 1, Regular	52	Mud
Earth Globe	107	Earth	Mud to dust 2	105	Mud
Earth Robe	157	Earth	Mud Walk	41	Mud
Extinguish Enchanted Fire	169	Fire	Paralysis Wall	71	Earth
Extinguish Fire, Regular	10	Fire	Paralyze Animal/Bird	15	Earth
Fiery Robe	157	Fire	Paralyze Enchanted Creature	158	Earth
Fire Ball	139	Fire	Paralyze Person	44	Earth
Fire Bolt 3	80	Fire	Paralyze Reptile,Fish,or Insect	24	Earth
Fire Globe	138	Fire	Part Fog	71	Fog
Flame Barrier	42	Fire	Part Lava	127	Lava
Flame Bolt 1	16	Fire	Part Mud	116	Mud
Flame Bolt 2	43	Fire	Part Smoke	71	Smoke
Flame Jet	35	Fire	Part Water 1	71	Water
Flame Walk	41	Fire	Part Water 2	189	Water
Flaming Hand	12	Fire	Polymorph into Fog	108	Fog
Fly 1	45	Air	Polymorph into Lava	108	Lava

Spell Name	SPC	Element
Polymorph into Mud	108	Mud
Polymorph into Smoke	108	Smoke
Quicksand	53	Earth
Rain Clouds	33	Fog
Resist Cold	33	Fire
Resist Fire	42	Water
Resist Fire and Heat	51	Fog
Resist Poisons	51	Mud
See Through Fog	41	Fog
Slide	12	Water
Smoke Adaptation	41	Smoke
Smoke Balls	52	Smoke
Smoke Bank 1	71	Smoke
Smoke Bank 2	137	Smoke
Smoke Barrier	61	Smoke
Smoke Globe	88	Smoke
Smoke Jet	53	Smoke
Smoke Robe	177	Smoke
Smoke Screen	81	Smoke
Smoke Walk	43	Smoke
Smoke Wall	45	Smoke
Snow Balls	43	Water
Snow Storm	72	Water
Soothe Burns	40	Fog
Sparking Fingers	8	Fire
Statue, person	159	Earth
Stone Crumble 1	52	Earth
Stone Crumble 2	169	Earth
Stone Globe	147	Earth
Stone Move 1	8	Earth
Stone Move 2	33	Earth
Stone Pass	118	Earth
Stone Storm 1	17	Earth
Stone Storm 2	53	Earth
Stone to Mud 1	60	Mud
Stone to Mud 2	155	Mud
Summon Storm	138	Air
Towering Inferno	148	Fire
Uncontrolled Fire	48	Fire
Water Adaptation	22	Water
Water Bolt 2	43	Water
Water Bolt 3	94	Water
Water Bolt1	12	Water
Water Control 1	23	Water
Water Control 2	42	Water
Water Control 3	106	Water
Water Control 4	125	Water
Water Globe	107	Water
Water Jet	33	Water
Water or Ice Robe	157	Water
Water Spout	61	Water

Spell Name	SPC	Element
Water Walk, Calm	23	Water
Water Walk, Wavy	52	Water
Whirl Wind	15	Air
Whirl Wind 2	53	Air
Whirl Wind 3	83	Air
Wind Barrier	34	Air
Wind Bolt 1	10	Air
Wind Bolt 2	43	Air
Wind Bolt 3	94	Air
Wind Globe	91	Air
Wind Jet	33	Air
Wind Wall	22	Air

SPELL POINTS

Level	Intellect Score 11	12	13	14	15	16	17	18	19	20
1	11	12	13	14	15	16	17	18	19	20
2	17	18	20	21	23	24	26	27	29	30
3	22	24	26	28	30	32	34	36	38	40
4	28	30	33	35	38	40	43	45	48	50
5	33	36	39	42	45	48	51	54	57	60
6	39	42	46	49	53	56	60	63	67	70
7	44	48	52	56	60	64	68	72	76	80
8	50	54	59	63	68	72	77	81	86	90
9	55	60	65	70	75	80	85	90	95	100
10	61	66	72	77	83	88	94	99	105	110
11	66	72	78	84	90	96	102	108	114	120
12	72	78	85	91	98	104	111	117	124	130
13	77	84	91	98	105	112	119	126	133	140
14	83	90	98	105	113	120	128	135	143	150
15	88	96	104	112	120	128	136	144	152	160
16	94	102	111	119	128	136	145	153	162	170
17	99	108	117	126	135	144	153	162	171	180
18	105	114	124	133	143	152	162	171	181	190
19	110	120	130	140	150	160	170	180	190	200
20	116	126	137	147	158	168	179	189	200	210

	Spell Point Information		1 SP / 5 seconds (1 Attack)		
			720 SP/Hr or 12 SP/Minute		
			Total Hours and Minutes to Regenerate a SINGLE Use		Total HOURS necessary to Regenerate ALL Uses / Day
Level	Max. SP	Regenerations per Day **			
1	20	1	0.03	2	0.01
2	30	1	0.04	3	0.04
3	40	2	0.06	3	0.08
4	50	2	0.07	4	0.14
5	60	3	0.08	5	0.21
6	70	3	0.10	6	0.29
7	80	4	0.11	7	0.39
8	90	4	0.13	8	0.50
9	100	5	0.14	8	0.63
10	110	5	0.15	9	0.76
11	120	6	0.17	10	0.92
12	130	6	0.18	11	1.08
13	140	7	0.19	12	1.26
14	150	7	0.21	13	1.46
15	160	8	0.22	13	1.67
16	170	8	0.24	14	1.89
17	180	9	0.25	15	2.13
18	190	9	0.26	16	2.38
19	200	10	0.28	17	2.64
20	210	10	0.29	18	2.92

** All Characters get their Original Points PLUS the number of Regenerations / Day.

Your Character's Original Points come from the Column Sun and are what MUST be used to Enchant Items / Potions or make Badges, ect.

KI POINTS	Wisdom Score									
Level	11	12	13	14	15	16	17	18	19	20
1	11	12	13	14	15	16	17	18	19	20
2	14	15	16	18	19	20	21	23	24	25
3	17	18	20	21	23	24	26	27	29	30
4	19	21	23	25	26	28	30	32	33	35
5	22	24	26	28	30	32	34	36	38	40
6	25	27	29	32	34	36	38	41	43	45
7	28	30	33	35	38	40	43	45	48	50
8	30	33	36	39	41	44	47	50	52	55
9	33	36	39	42	45	48	51	54	57	60
10	36	39	42	46	49	52	55	59	62	65
11	39	42	46	49	53	56	60	63	67	70
12	41	45	49	53	56	60	64	68	71	75
13	44	48	52	56	60	64	68	72	76	80
14	47	51	55	60	64	68	72	77	81	85
15	50	54	59	63	68	72	77	81	86	90
16	52	57	62	67	71	76	81	86	90	95
17	55	60	65	70	75	80	85	90	95	100
18	58	63	68	74	79	84	89	95	100	105
19	61	66	72	77	83	88	94	99	105	110
20	63	69	75	81	86	92	98	104	109	115

Ninja Information			1 KP / 5 seconds (1 Attack)		
			720 KP/Hr or 12 KP/Minute		
			Total Hours and Minutes to Regenerate a SINGLE Use		Total HOURS necessary to Regenerate ALL Uses / Day
Level	Max. KP	Regenerations per Day **			
1	20	1	0.03	2	0.01
2	25	1	0.03	2	0.03
3	30	2	0.04	3	0.06
4	35	2	0.05	3	0.10
5	40	3	0.06	3	0.14
6	45	3	0.06	4	0.19
7	50	4	0.07	4	0.24
8	55	4	0.08	5	0.31
9	60	5	0.08	5	0.38
10	65	5	0.09	5	0.45
11	70	6	0.10	6	0.53
12	75	6	0.10	6	0.63
13	80	7	0.11	7	0.72
14	85	7	0.12	7	0.83
15	90	8	0.13	8	0.94
16	95	8	0.13	8	1.06
17	100	9	0.14	8	1.18
18	105	9	0.15	9	1.31
19	110	10	0.15	9	1.45
20	115	10	0.16	10	1.60

MENTAL POINTS

Level	11	12	13	14	15	16	17	18	19	20
1	6	6	7	7	--	--	--	--	--	--
2	11	12	13	14	--	--	--	--	--	--
3	17	18	20	21	--	--	--	--	--	--
4	22	24	26	28	--	--	--	--	--	--
5	28	30	33	35	38	40	--	--	--	--
6	33	36	39	42	45	48	--	--	--	--
7	39	42	46	49	53	56	--	--	--	--
8	44	48	52	56	60	64	--	--	--	--
9	50	54	59	63	68	72	--	--	--	--
10	55	60	65	70	75	80	85	90	--	--
11	61	66	72	77	83	88	94	99	--	--
12	66	72	78	84	90	96	102	108	--	--
13	72	78	85	91	98	104	111	117	--	--
14	77	84	91	98	105	112	119	126	--	--
15	83	90	98	105	113	120	128	135	143	150
16	88	96	104	112	120	128	136	144	152	160
17	94	102	111	119	128	136	145	153	162	170
18	99	108	117	126	135	144	153	162	171	180
19	105	114	124	133	143	152	162	171	181	190
20	110	120	130	140	150	160	170	180	190	200

Mentalist Information

1 MP / 5 seconds (1 Attack)
720 MP/Hr or 12 MP/Minute

Level	Max. MP	Regenerations per Day **	Total Hours and Minutes to Regenerate a SINGLE Use		Total HOURS necessary to Regenerate ALL Uses / Day
1	7	1	0.01	1	0.00
2	14	1	0.02	1	0.02
3	21	2	0.03	2	0.04
4	28	2	0.04	2	0.08
5	40	3	0.06	3	0.14
6	48	3	0.07	4	0.20
7	56	4	0.08	5	0.27
8	64	4	0.09	5	0.36
9	72	5	0.10	6	0.45
10	90	5	0.13	8	0.63
11	99	6	0.14	8	0.76
12	108	6	0.15	9	0.90
13	117	7	0.16	10	1.06
14	126	7	0.18	11	1.23
15	150	8	0.21	13	1.56
16	160	8	0.22	13	1.78
17	170	9	0.24	14	2.01
18	180	9	0.25	15	2.25
19	190	10	0.26	16	2.51
20	200	10	0.28	17	2.78

NOTES